PENGUIN

Judy Nunn's career has been long, illustrious and multifaceted. After combining her internationally successful acting career with scriptwriting for television and radio, Judy decided in the '90s to turn her hand to prose.

Her first three novels, *The Glitter Game*, *Centre Stage* and *Araluen*, set respectively in the worlds of television, theatre and film, became instant bestsellers, and the rest is history, quite literally, in fact. She has since developed a love of writing Australian historically based fiction and her fame as a novelist has spread rapidly throughout Europe, where she has been published in English, German, French, Dutch, Czech and Spanish.

Her subsequent bestsellers, *Kal*, *Beneath the Southern Cross*, *Territory*, *Pacific*, *Heritage*, *Floodtide*, *Maralinga*, *Tiger Men*, *Elianne*, *Spirits of the Ghan*, *Sanctuary* and *Khaki Town*, have confirmed Judy's position as one of Australia's leading fiction writers. She has now sold over one million books in Australia alone.

In 2015 Judy was made a Member of the Order of Australia for her 'significant service to the performing arts as a scriptwriter and actor of stage and screen, and to literature as an author'.

Visit Judy at judynunn.com.au or on
facebook.com/JudyNunnAuthor

Books by Judy Nunn

The Glitter Game
Centre Stage
Araluen
Kal
Beneath the Southern Cross
Territory
Pacific
Heritage
Floodtide
Maralinga
Tiger Men
Elianne
Spirits of the Ghan
Sanctuary
Khaki Town

Children's fiction
Eye in the Storm
Eye in the City

Short stories (available in ebook)
The House on Hill Street
The Wardrobe
Just South of Rome
The Otto Bin Empire: Clive's Story
Oskar the Pole
Adam's Mum and Dad

May 2021

Kal

JUDY NUNN

PENGUIN BOOKS

PENGUIN BOOKS

UK | USA | Canada | Ireland | Australia
India | New Zealand | South Africa | China

Penguin Books is part of the Penguin Random House group of companies whose addresses can be found at global.penguinrandomhouse.com.

First published by Random House Australia, 1996
Published by Arrow, 2006, 2007, 2011
This edition published by Penguin Books, 2020

Cover photograph © Wildlight
Cover design by Blue Cork
Typeset by Midland Typesetters, Australia

Printed and bound in Australia by Griffin Press, part of Ovato, an accredited ISO AS/NZS 14001 Environmental Management Systems printer

A catalogue record for this book is available from the National Library of Australia

ISBN 978 1 76104 123 5

penguin.com.au

To my mother, Margaret Anne Nunn, whose childhood years were spent in Kal. Thanks, 'Nancy', you're an inspiration.

ACKNOWLEDGEMENTS

I would like to especially thank my husband Bruce Venables and Jane Palfreyman for their invaluable assistance in the creation of this book.

A special thanks to Marg Mason of the Kalgoorlie-Boulder Tourist Centre and the many helpful people in Kalgoorlie to whom I spoke, particularly Pud and Vera Mann, Lorna Mitchell and the late, and sadly missed, Keith Quartermaine.

Thanks also to Maddalena Sanders, Caterina Panuccio and Dr Robert Muller.

Last but not least, my thanks to my friend and researcher, Robyn Gurney, for her tireless and inspirational struggle through the military history of World War I.

I am indebted to Walter C. Belford and his fascinating account of the 11th Battalion, *Legs Eleven*.

BOOK ONE

THE MIGRANTS
1892

Chapter One

'Vide 'o mare quant'e bello,
Spira tantu sentimento,
Comme tu a chi tiene mente,
Ca scetato 'o faie sunna.'

A light snowfall started to blanket the earth as the men's voices rang out across the mountainside. The men ignored the snow as they squatted around the open fire, clutching their mugs of red wine, their coat collars raised, their woollen caps pulled down over their ears.

'Guarda, gua', chistu ciardino;
Siente, sie' sti sciure arance . . .'

Giovanni's voice was raised above the others'. Although the youngest worker at the camp, he was the only one who could play the concertina and he always led the evening song. Besides, he had by far the finest voice. At least that's what Rico thought as he glanced fondly at his younger brother as they sang the haunting 'Torna a Surriento'. Several of the dozen or so men sang well, and all were of robust voice, but Giovanni, with his fine natural tenor, was a joy to the ear.

Half an hour later the men acknowledged defeat—the snowfall had all but extinguished the fire—and, with mugs freshly refilled, they retreated to their tents. But, from Giovanni and Rico's tent, the concertina played on.

''Vide 'o mare quant'e bello . . .'

Gradually, the men joined in and, from tent to tent, their voices once more rang out until the wine was finished and it was time to sleep.

THE FOLLOWING MORNING it was Rico who first saw the four figures trudging up the mountain track, their bulky wool-clad bodies black against the snow.

They looked tiny in the distance. Four dark dots. But then everything looked tiny in the Alps. Even the fir trees, thirty, forty feet high and shaggy with snow, were dwarfed by the landscape. And in the summer months, free of their white disguise, the massive grey boulders, some of which were as large as the village church, looked like pebbles on the side of the mountain.

But amongst the magnitude of nature's architecture it was the village itself that looked tiniest of all. Nestled in the valley far below and built of rock quarried from the very mountains which dwarfed it, the village looked defiant. Its church bell rang importantly on Sundays, its stone chimneypots puffed busy smoke into the Alpine air, and its people lived their lives ignoring nature's surrounding statement that human existence might not be of vast importance in the ultimate scheme of things. Against the backdrop of the mountain splendour, the village and its people were a testament to the wonderful audacity of man.

That it was Rico who first saw the girls was no accident—he'd been watching for Teresa since the dawn light first cut the icy air. While the men scraped clear the small stone fireplace and fetched dry wood from their tents to boil their mugs of thick, black coffee, Rico stood stamping his heavy work boots in the snow, his black eyes searching the track to the village for the first sign of the girls.

'She is coming,' he said to Giovanni as his brother handed him a tin mug of scalding coffee, so hot he could feel the warmth of the metal through his thick leather working gloves. 'See? There.' He pointed. 'She is coming.'

It wasn't long before the other men noticed the girls and gathered to whistle and heckle as they passed by.

There were always girls climbing the mountain at this time of the year, peasant girls from nearby villages and farms, crossing the Alps to work in the chalets during the heavy tourist season when extra chamber-maids and serving girls were required. The workers always whistled and heckled—but nothing more. They themselves were peasants, employed by the government to work in the stone quarries, or to chop the timber for railway sleepers, or to dig the railroad tunnels and service the tracks through and over the Alps. They came from similar farms and villages and they knew the girls to be good Italian virgins, just like their sisters. They would never dream of accosting them.

For the most part the girls enjoyed the flirtation. Some pretended they didn't and marched past with their noses in the air but, more often than not, they smiled saucily at the men and called out their own cheeky responses as they walked on.

This morning, though, was different. This morning the girls stopped.

'Teresa!' Rico ran to the tallest of the group. He took her in his arms, lifted her into the air and kissed her passionately. She returned his kiss with equal ardour and the heckling died away as the men watched in envy. The couple's lips finally parted and, arm in arm, they walked several paces away where, oblivious to their onlookers, they again fell into each other's embrace.

Giovanni was the first to initiate a conversation with one of the other girls. She had been standing closest to Teresa as the couple kissed and had stared with open-mouthed fascination at their passion.

Teresa and the other two girls wore heavy skirts hitched up at the waist with twine to prevent the hems from dragging in the snow. However, the raised hem-lines revealed no tempting display of ankle, just heavy walking shoes and thick woven leggings. They wore bulky overcoats and large woollen shawls draped over their heads and shoulders.

The girl who attracted Giovanni's attention was different. She wore men's trousers, far too big for her, tied at the waist with a length of rope. Through the open front of her coat the swell of her breasts was visible beneath the coarse fabric of her shirt. A long woollen scarf was woven around her head and neck in the style that many men adopted when they worked in the bitter cold.

Giovanni walked over to her. 'You look like a boy.'

She glanced down at the trousers. 'They are my brother's,' she answered. 'I did not want my skirt to be ruined.'

Each of the girls was carrying a knapsack, on which was tied a pair of snowshoes. As several of the men drifted over, they put their bundles down and prepared to stop for a chat. Giovanni was determined to keep his girl to himself and as she eased her knapsack from her back, he took it from her.

'Let me help you,' he said, managing to edge her to one side. 'My name is Giovanni.' The girl gave him a friendly smile and her blue eyes danced, but she did not offer her own name in reply. Her skin was milky white and Giovanni noticed that a wayward auburn curl had escaped the confines of her scarf.

'Where have you come from?' he asked, fascinated. She was beautiful.

'My family has a farm near Ridanna.'

'Ah,' he nodded. 'So how do you know Teresa and the other girls? They come from Santa Lena.'

'I do not know them,' she answered. 'My father made enquiries. There were no girls from Ridanna climbing the mountain and he did not want me to walk on my own, so he took me to Santa Lena.' She gave him a cheeky smile. 'I do not know why Papa did not want me to walk alone—perhaps he worried about the railroad workers.' Again the blue eyes danced. Laughter bubbled beneath the surface of her beauty.

Giovanni knew she was joking but he was defensive nevertheless. 'Oh we mean no harm, we are no danger—'

'I know,' she laughed. The young man was so serious, she should not make fun of him. 'I know you are not.' She cast a glance in Teresa's direction. The lovers were still in a deep embrace. Rico had taken off his gloves and Teresa's shawl lay unheeded on the snow as he raked his fingers through her dishevelled hair. A handsome woman with a strong-boned face and wild black tresses, Teresa clung fiercely to Rico's body as his mouth left her lips and started to travel down her neck. She appeared transported, her mouth open, her eyes closed.

The girl watched, shocked but fascinated. They were so blatant they might as well have been naked, she thought. They were making love, fully clothed, out here on the snowy mountainside for all to see.

She was suddenly aware that Giovanni was watching her with as much interest as she was watching Teresa and she averted her eyes, embarrassed.

Giovanni himself was a little embarrassed by his brother's behaviour and felt he owed some explanation. 'Rico is my brother,' he said. 'We also come from Santa Lena. He and Teresa have known each other for a long time, they are bound to marry some day.'

The girl's momentary confusion was over and her

smile was warm. Genuine. 'They love each other very much. That is good.'

Then as quickly as Teresa had fallen into Rico's arms, she thrust him away from her. 'Enough, Rico, leave me alone,' she cried laughingly. 'It is a full day's walk to Steinach and we must get there before dark.' He tried to embrace her again but she pushed him away. 'I will see you in four months,' she said, picking up her knapsack. She started up the track, turning to wave every few steps, and the other girls followed.

'Goodbye,' the girl said to Giovanni.

'Goodbye.' He watched the four of them as they trudged on up the track but he was really only looking at the girl.

THE FIRST HOUR wasn't heavy going. The track wound gently around the base of the mountain and there was not much climbing. The girls chattered and breathed puffs of white steam as they walked. It was cold but there was little breeze and the sun's rays would soon warm the air. It was going to be a fine day.

The girls were excited, undaunted by the eight-hour trek to Steinach, the little Austrian village on the other side of the mountain where a sleigh would be waiting to take them to the ski resort.

Teresa and her two friends had worked in chalets for the past two seasons. As they compared notes and giggled at stories about the incompetence of tourist skiers, the girl studied Teresa. Tall, handsome, strong, she wore her woman's sexuality like a badge of honour. The image of the lovers and their unashamed passion was still fresh in the girl's mind.

Caterina had never seen people kiss like that. She had just turned eighteen and she had kissed several boys over the past two years, one of them a number of times. She had even parted her lips for Roberto and once his hand had brushed her breast as if by accident. Her heart had pumped wildly at the time but she had suffered terrible pangs of guilt until confession the following Sunday. After that, she avoided Roberto, but she could not keep at bay the memory of his moist lips and the tantalising touch of his hand on her breast.

And now there was the image of Teresa and Rico. Rico had been strong, virile. He had lifted Teresa from her feet when he had embraced her. Caterina wondered momentarily what it might be like to kiss Rico's brother, the serious young man, the one who'd said his name was Giovanni. He was certainly very handsome. But she breathed a sigh of frustration and forced the images from her mind. It was not only sinful, it was foolish to torment herself like this. Determined to concentrate instead on the exciting new world that lay ahead, she tuned into the girls' chatter.

They were agreeing that it was wise to be especially nice to the Americans—they invariably tipped. The Italians, Austrians, Swiss and Germans rarely did, the English only sparingly and the French never. No, definitely the Americans, they said, and Caterina thought they were very sophisticated.

They were not. Of course, the girls liked to think they were. Each year they came back over the mountain with fresh tales of what was happening in the outside world. 'An Italian opera called *La Tosca* is famous throughout Europe,' they would boast. Or 'There is a famine in Russia and hundreds are dying.' But they did not really understand what they were saying. The farms and villages nestled in the Alpine valleys were rarely affected by the dramas of their far distant neighbours.

Next the girls gave Caterina an English lesson. It was the most useful language by far, they told her. Americans did not speak anything else.

All four of them were panting by now as the walk

grew more strenuous, but still they talked. Caterina learned 'good morning', 'good afternoon', 'good evening' and 'thank you'. One of the girls had a favourite phrase, 'I do beg your pardon', which she had learned from a very nice English woman the previous season, and they all agreed it seemed a very complicated way of saying *'scusi'*.

Gradually the track became steeper and the girls' conversation finally dwindled as they conserved their energy for the climb ahead.

AS THE MEN gathered their tools and prepared for the day's digging, Giovanni nudged Rico and signalled him to wait until the two workers who shared their tent had gone.

The workers' camp was comprised of four tents, the larger one a communal mess and the other three sleeping accommodation for between four to six men. Supplied by the company and constructed of strong canvas with solid wood supports, the tents were designed to withstand the harsh winter. A new tunnel was being built through the Alps and the men were contracted to dig and remove debris after the blastings.

'You are a fool, Rico,' Giovanni said when they were alone. 'Being so open with Teresa. If her father finds out he will kill you.'

But Rico only laughed. 'You worry too much.'

He looked like their father, Salvatore, when he laughed, Giovanni thought. Strong and confident, his sturdy body constantly poised as if to charge, Rico seemed afraid of nothing and Giovanni often envied him.

'There is no one here at the camp who comes from Santa Lena,' Rico continued. 'There is no one who knows Teresa or her father, so who is going to tell him?'

'What about her friends?'

'Girls never tell, Gio. They band together and keep

their secrets to themselves. You think Teresa is the only girl in Santa Lena who is no longer a virgin?'

Giovanni felt irritated. It was always annoying when Rico patronised him. At twenty-two, his brother was only two years older than he was, so what right did he have to act as though he knew so much more of the world? 'You are so clever,' Giovanni said, 'but what happens if you get her with child, eh? What happens then?'

Rico shrugged dismissively. 'So what?' he scoffed. 'We love each other. We will marry one day. Who cares whether it is sooner or later?'

Picks and shovels over their shoulders, they joined the rest of the men for the ten-minute walk from the camp to the tunnel face.

Glancing sideways at Giovanni as they walked, Rico chastised himself. He should not have been so condescending; Giovanni was offended, he could tell. Gentle Gio, with his man's body and his boy's face. Framed in soft brown curls, it was the face of their mother before time and hardship had greyed her hair and weathered her skin. And he had her eyes too, the same intense hazel which turned brown in anger. They were brown now.

There were depths to Giovanni which Rico could not understand. Why complicate life? he thought. One should simply grab it, devour it. Giovanni thought too much, that was his problem. He was too serious, too earnest. It made him vulnerable. The only time he seemed able to give himself up to the simple joy of living was when he had his concertina in his hands and his voice was raised in song.

Rico felt protective of his younger brother. Overprotective, he chided himself. He must stop treating Giovanni like a child, he was a man now. Indeed, when they wrestled it was all Rico could do to best him. Besides, how could Giovanni possibly be a child when he was seducing the most desirable woman in Santa Lena?

'You are one to talk,' he jested, trying to tease him out of his ill-humour. 'I am to worry about Teresa and her father? What about the widow?' He had Giovanni's attention now and he ignored the fact that his brother's eyes still flashed a warning. 'I risk the wrath of a village blacksmith,' he continued, 'and you risk the vengeance of the De Cretico family.' He shook his head in mock admiration. 'And you call me the fool. Ah, Gio, you are a brave man.'

Giovanni knew his brother was teasing him and usually he allowed himself to be humoured, but not this time. He wished he had not told Rico about Sarina.

But Rico continued regardless. 'Come, do not look so serious. If it were not for the De Cretico brothers I would boast to my friends of your conquest. The widow is the most desirable woman in the village—you should be proud.'

Still Giovanni did not rise to the bait. But there was no longer annoyance in his eyes. He was troubled; Rico could sense it. 'What is it, Gio? Something worries you. Is it the De Cretico brothers?' He slowed his pace a little. 'Tell me, I can help.'

But Giovanni did not slow his pace and Rico was forced to keep up. 'If there is any danger of discovery then you should be worried.' His tone was no longer flippant. 'The De Creticos are far more of a threat than Teresa's father.'

Rico was right. Giovanni knew that only too well. The widow was no longer an adventure—she was dangerous, and Giovanni would do anything to be free of her. But he did not want to admit his fear to his brother. With their father and two older brothers away on contract work for most of the year, it was Rico who was the head of the Gianni family. When any Gianni was threatened,

Rico became fiercely protective and that worried Giovanni. If, in defending him, his headstrong brother were to take on the widow and the De Cretico family, God only knew what might happen.

'I can look after myself,' he muttered.

'Oh yes, I know you are discreet, I know you meet in secret. But I tell you, Gio, you make sure you leave her alone when the De Creticos come to the village.'

Giovanni finally slowed his pace and looked squarely at his brother. 'I said I can look after myself.'

'Oh you can, can you?' Rico smiled to himself. He was indeed proud that his younger brother was the secret lover of the proud wealthy widow who lived in the big house on the hill. If it were not for Sarina De Cretico's brothers-in-law he would most certainly have boasted to his friends about it. He nudged Giovanni with his elbow and grinned. 'You say you worry about me and Teresa—what happens if you get the widow with child, eh?'

Giovanni smiled back. It was impossible to be cross with Rico for long, he was so irresistibly good-natured. 'No chance of that, she is too clever.'

Rico roared with laughter. He had guessed as much.

THE MEN WORKED a six-day week. Sunday was their day of rest when, to a man, scrubbed up and looking their best, they walked the seven kilometres into Santa Lena to church. Sometimes the young unmarried men went into the village on the Saturday night and ate at the local tavern overlooking the piazza. After they had dined they would gather around the rough-hewn wooden bar and sing along to the piano accordion or take a bottle of chianti into the back room and play cards beside the open fireplace. Then, in the early hours of the morning, they crossed the road to the boarding house where they slept in clean, fresh beds. The married men never went into the village on a Saturday night. The married men always slept at the camp. Contract work paid well and they saved every lire they could, taking their earnings back to their villages and farms to help tide their families through the hard times.

Rico and Giovanni Gianni were the envy of the rest of the workers. They could go home every Sunday, see their family, sleep in their own beds. No matter that they had to set off before dawn on the Monday to return to the work site, it was worth it, the others agreed.

Rico and Giovanni often returned to the village on Saturday night also, but it was not to see their family as the men assumed. In the dead of night Rico would meet Teresa in the stables where her father worked and Giovanni would walk up the hill to the big house and Sarina De Cretico. Before it was light they would return to the small cottage on the outskirts of the village and steal into the back room they had shared throughout their childhood; when the family awoke, no one would be any the wiser. It was accepted that they returned late from the work camp and did not wish to disturb the sleeping household.

The following morning they would chop wood for the kitchen fire or watch their mother and their sisters make polenta for the evening meal and then the whole family, dressed in their best, would walk together to the church, just as they had done for as long as Rico and Giovanni could remember.

There was no reason for Rico to go to the village this Saturday. Without the anticipation of Teresa and her warm, luscious body waiting for him in the stables, there was no real incentive to make the trip which was always tiring after a hard week's work. He would see his family in the morning. Tonight it would be more relaxing to sit around the campfire and drink wine and tell stories.

Giovanni wished he could stay the night at the camp too, but he did not dare. Although he had been living at the camp for over three months now, the widow still demanded he see her every fortnight. Even if she were to demand a weekly visit he would have to oblige, he dared not refuse.

Rico gave him a lascivious wink as he set off. 'Can't leave her alone and keep your poor forsaken brother company, eh?' Before Giovanni could answer, he raised his tin mug of wine in salute. 'Go on, I envy you. Mine will have shrivelled and dropped off by the time Teresa returns.' And Giovanni started down the mountain track alone.

His thoughts were grim as he hugged his thick woollen coat and scarf tightly about him and jogged to keep warm. It was not that the widow had ceased to excite him in bed. Far from it. Even now, as he thought of her body and her abandonment and the tricks she played, he could feel the stirring of desire. But she had trapped him. Like a rabbit in a snare, he was powerless to free himself. And each time he went to her, and their passion was spent, he loathed himself for his fear and weakness.

He jogged faster to distract himself but still he felt like a man going to the gallows.

The blackmail had started nearly four months ago, when Sarina had announced, quite casually, that Mario and Luigi De Cretico were coming to stay with her. Everyone in the village was fearful of the De Cretico brothers, although no one knew precisely why. The De Cretico family had long since moved from Santa Lena to their wealthy homes and businesses in Milano and Bologna. They were rarely seen and they had done no harm to anyone in the village. Indeed, they had contributed generously to the local church and needy families. Perhaps it was simply because the De Cretico family had once been the most powerful in the district and the brothers still owned the tavern and many other properties in the village, not to mention several outlying farms and a large vineyard to the south. Perhaps it was because of the rumours that their city businesses had *Famiglia* connections. Whatever it was, the brothers were treated warily and with the utmost respect.

'They arrive tomorrow,' Sarina had said. Giovanni had simply stared back at her. The De Creticos had not been seen in the village for nearly a year, not since the funeral of their younger brother Marcello.

Sarina had laughed at Giovanni's dumbfounded expression. 'Oh do not be so frightened, my little bull. They will be here for only two weeks.' She always called him her *piccolo toro* and he usually liked it, but that night Giovanni realised the enormity of what he had done. If the De Cretico brothers ever found out that he had been making love to their brother's widow, they would kill him.

Sarina had kissed him as he left. 'Two whole weeks without *mio piccolo toro,*' she had said, and she'd pouted attractively before she closed the door.

Giovanni had not gone back. For a whole month he had not gone back. And when he saw her at church on Sundays, in her widow's black, he avoided her.

Then, one day, she was waiting for him outside. Waiting in the shadow cast by the heavy open church door. She had glided up to him. 'Come to me tonight,' she whispered. He could barely see her face behind the dark veil and he had tried to ignore her. 'Your life is in danger if you do not come to me tonight,' she insisted, then she strolled over to her trap where her servant waited.

And so he had gone to her. Late that night, as he had done so many times before, he stole up to the servants' entrance at the rear of the big house. And, as usual, she was waiting for him, her finger to her lips. Not a word was spoken between them as they crept through the narrow whitewashed corridor with its low wooden doors on either side. Giovanni held his breath—behind those doors were the servants' quarters.

He had always worried that the married couple who had been employed by Marcello would report Sarina's infidelity to the De Cretico brothers. But she dismissed the notion. They were elderly, she said; they retired early and their quarters were far from her bedroom.

Not a word as the lovers crossed the interior courtyard and climbed the wide stone steps to the surrounding balconies. Not a word passed their lips until they were upstairs in her bedroom with its tiny open balcony overlooking the village.

In the safety of her bedroom, Giovanni whispered, 'What danger, what has happened—do they know?'

'Not now,' she had murmured, slowly opening her gown. She was naked beneath and she placed his hand on her breast. As she unfastened his belt she caressed him through the fabric of his trousers. 'Not now. Make love to me. *Mio piccolo toro*, make love to me.'

And then they were on the bed together and she was moaning and thrusting herself back at him. Then riding him on top. Then pulling him ever deeper and deeper into her, ankles around his neck. She was insatiable. Fingernails digging into his naked back until the pain was exquisite. Biting his neck. Whispering obscenities in his ear. Giovanni had been as transported by her abandonment as he always was. There was nothing but the two of them and the blackness of the night and the heat of their passion. Nothing else had mattered. Nothing. Still he had the presence of mind to pull away from her just before he ejaculated. She had taught him that.

She was ready for him as usual, the small hand-cloth beside the bed instantly to the fore. It never ceased to amaze him. But, as she had explained, there must be no sign of semen on the linen when the servant did the laundry. She could surreptitiously wash a small hand-cloth herself; if she were to wash bed linen it would naturally arouse suspicion. It nevertheless amazed him that at the height of her uncontrolled passion she could display such presence of mind.

They'd lain panting for several moments. Then Giovanni had turned to her. 'What has happened? You said my life was in danger.' But she appeared not to have heard him.

'Why have you not come to me, Giovanni?' she asked. 'It's been a whole month.'

'Your brothers-in-law . . .'

'Mario and Luigi left the village a fortnight ago. You know that, everyone does.'

'You said danger,' he had insisted. 'Why could my life be in danger? Do they suspect something?'

Sarina's pretty face had hardened. When she frowned she looked every bit of her thirty-three years. The difference was quite extraordinary. Animated and smiling, with her soft blonde hair and her dimpled cheeks, she could easily pass for a twenty-two-year-old.

'Answer me, Sarina. Do they suspect something?'

She sat up, not bothering to cover her nakedness. 'Not yet.'

'Then why did you say—'

'But they will if you stop coming to me.' He had looked at her, puzzled for a moment. 'If you stop coming to me I will tell them,' she had said simply and her eyes had been hard and ruthless. Unable to speak, Giovanni had stared back at her, his expression one of utter disbelief. 'I will send a message to Mario in Bologne. I will tell him that you raped me.'

GIOVANNI COULD SEE the village in the valley below. The black sky above it was clustered with smoke from the fires which would burn slowly throughout the night. It was late; only a few cottages displayed the lights of their candles or lamps. There was no light evident at the big house but he knew Sarina would be waiting for him, there in the dark.

His life had changed since that night. He had tried to reason with her. He had even tried to pretend that she was joking, although he knew she was not.

'But how can there be any joy in our meeting?' he had finally argued.

'It is not joy I want from you, Giovanni,' she said. 'If you value your life you will come to me.' Sarina did not want to sound hard and ruthless, she knew it was not attractive. She would much prefer to have beguiled him. To have sat on his strong young thighs, her legs linked around his waist, running her tongue along his perfect boy's lips and pretending surprise as she felt him become rigid beneath her. But that would not work, not this time. He was too frightened. Everyone was too frightened of the De Creticos. So she had to be hard. If she remained celibate until the brothers found her the husband they promised, she might never know a man again. 'And you will continue to come to me for as long as I wish,' she said.

From that night on Giovanni's entire existence had become one of self-loathing. He loathed the fact that Sarina continued to excite him. He loathed the fact that he served her like a stallion. He wished he could make himself impotent—then the widow would quickly be rid of him.

But as he crept around the outskirts of the village, passing his family's cottage in the dark, even as his pulse quickened with fear at the thought of discovery, Giovanni could feel the contemptible fire in his groin.

Chapter Two

Sarina had started prowling the house shortly after sundown, impatient for Giovanni. There was no sense going outside to wait in the bitter cold, he would not come for hours yet.

She looked down from the balcony at the courtyard below. In the soft dusk light the paving stones shone deep ochre. The walls and the wide stone steps were terracotta—upon Marcello's instructions, the building materials had been transported from Tuscany—and in the very centre of the courtyard stood the beautiful marble statue. The woman on the pedestal dominated the house. Lifesize: face upturned, arm upstretched, fingers curled as if to capture something from the air—a bird or a butterfly. With her other hand she clasped loose drapes about her milky shoulder, leaving one perfect breast exposed. Marcello had bought the statue for Sarina in Rome. It reminded him of her, he had said.

It was a magnificent statue. It was a magnificent house. Just the house Sarina had wanted when they had married. It stood on the hill above the village looking down at the squat little cottages carved from the rock of the mountains and it symbolised her position of importance.

She hated the house now. Now it mirrored the emptiness of her life. What value beauty when there was no one to share it with?

As darkness descended, Sarina continued to prowl the balconies. She did not care if the servants wondered at her restlessness. Let them. Old fools. So what if they suspected something? Let them tell their tales, she would denounce them as liars and dismiss them. But they would not dare tell. They were too old to find work elsewhere; they would not dare threaten their comfortable existence.

Sarina's was a mock bravado. She trembled with fear at the thought of her brothers-in-law discovering her betrayal. Her blackmail threat to Giovanni had been an empty one. She would never tell Mario and Luigi that he had raped her. They would not believe her. They had always thought her a whore and she knew it. Certainly, if she dared cry rape they would punish Giovanni for having known their dead brother's widow. They might even castrate him. But she was the one they would kill, of that she was certain.

GIOVANNI WAS NOT the only one to whom life was loathsome. Sarina hated her existence. She had hoped that marrying into the wealthy De Cretico family might buy her happiness but she had been wrong.

She could remember being happy once. At twenty-three, when she had married Carlo, her first husband. They had been poor but that had not seemed to matter; they loved each other with a deep abiding passion. She surrendered her virginity to him joyfully, glad that she had not succumbed to any of her other suitors, of whom there had been many. Her body ached for him when he was away working on the railroads, and when they were reunited they did not leave the bed for days, eating and laughing and making endless love amongst the dishevelled linen.

Then the baby had come. A son. Carlo was so proud of her. Their lives were complete. Until the morning nine months after the birth when she found the baby dead in its cradle. There was not a mark on him and there had been no warning sign of sickness. He had simply stopped breathing during the night. Grief and guilt and torment followed but ultimately they still had one another. 'Do not cry, my love. We will make another baby, there is plenty of time. *Non piangere, cara,*' Carlo would say to her over and over.

But there was not plenty of time. Six months later Carlo was dead, one of six men killed in a tunnel collapse. The whole village gathered in the piazza to grieve, but that did not help Sarina. She herself was dead. Cold and dead inside. God had taken her child and her husband from her and to what purpose? Why? She still went to church on Sunday but it meant little to her.

At twenty-five Sarina's life was over and she wondered why she did not kill herself. She supposed she was frightened. To take one's life was a mortal sin after all and, as God was obviously intent upon making her suffer, she did not dare risk the fires of hell and the damnation of her immortal soul.

She did, however, risk taking a lover. Discreetly. After a year of celibacy she decided it was the lesser of the mortal sins. The only time she could lose herself was in the throes of sexual passion and she decided she would risk God's punishment for that. She knew that it was highly unlikely that anyone would marry her. She was no longer a virgin and it was only the widows with money who were granted a second chance.

And then she met Marcello De Cretico.

'AH, SARINA, MY favourite *cameriera.*' She had just arrived at the tavern and Armando, the jovial innkeeper, waved her over. 'Come, meet our landlord,' he cried. 'Sarina is the very best girl I have,' he boasted to the young man at his side, 'and the prettiest too.'

Sarina smiled dutifully as Armando draped a proprietorial arm about her shoulders. She did not allow her irritation to show, but she detested it when he referred to her as a *cameriera*. She was not a serving girl, she was a 'hostess'—that was the arrangement they had made. Armando was showing off.

Armando knew that she was displeased but he'd had enough chianti not to let it bother him—he was the boss after all. He made a show of kissing her hand by way of mollification. Sarina was an asset and he certainly did not want to lose her. 'This is Mr De Cretico, Sarina.'

'Marcello, please.' The man smiled and Sarina thought he looked very young.

'You fetch us another bottle of chianti, there's a good girl.' Armando ignored the flash of rebuke in Sarina's eyes as she took off her coat and hung it on one of the pegs beside the open fire. The innkeeper was having a fine time.

When Marcello had first arrived Armando had worried that a visit from one of the De Creticos might mean a rise in the rent. The family must have heard of the excellent business he had been doing over the past year. But his worries had been unfounded. Marcello was an exceedingly pleasant young man who appeared to want nothing from him.

'This is a very pretty place you have,' he had said as he admired the solid timber bar and the heavy dining-room tables and chairs all made from local pine. 'Very pretty indeed,' he had repeated as he gazed out at the stone courtyard overlooking the piazza.

'Pretty, yes. But she is hard work too. To keep her so pretty costs a lot of money.' Armando always referred to his tavern as a woman. 'Very, very much money she costs.'

Marcello was quick to realise that the man was worried about a rise in rent and equally quick to put his fears to rest. Those had not been Mario's instructions. Thirty-five-year-old Mario was head of the family business and his orders had been precise.

'You are twenty-one now, Marcello. You are of age and it is time you stopped living the good life.' They had been too easy on their little brother, Mario thought; they had spoilt him. The boy seemed to think there was nothing in life but women and wine. 'It is time you took on some business obligations of your own.'

Mario considered Santa Lena a very easy assignment. Simply a case of inspecting the family's real estate. It must all be done under the guise of caring landlords, of course—'Is everything satisfactory? Is there anything you need?' Marcello was to ask—but he was really there to ensure the tenants were not abusing De Cretico property.

'Make yourself known and liked,' he was instructed. 'Mingle with the peasants,' Mario had said. And that was exactly what Marcello was doing.

As soon as the innkeeper's fears were quelled he had played the happy host with gusto and the two of them spent the afternoon in the courtyard eating and drinking, Armando proudly introducing Marcello to the passers-by. It was only when the spring sun had faded and the first chill of evening swept down from the mountains that they had come inside. Just as Sarina had arrived.

Yes, she is certainly pretty, Marcello thought, very pretty indeed. Fair-haired, average height, a slim but well-rounded figure. As Sarina walked away to get the wine he admired her back and her buttocks. Although her high-necked, ankle-length dress was modest enough, it was different from the customary shapeless skirts worn by most of the peasant girls. It was cut to fit her body and Marcello had no difficulty imagining the perfect pear shape of the buttocks beneath.

'You stay and drink and eat some more,' Armando

was saying expansively. 'Soon it will be night and my musician will be here and we will all sing.' Armando's 'musician' was an old man who played a battered piano accordion for free chianti and pasta but he was a big attraction to the customers.

Armando's joviality had started to tire him, and Marcello had been about to leave, but Sarina had changed his mind. There had been something in her smile. Something playful, suggestive.

'I am not sure if I could eat anything more, Armando,' Marcello demurred, 'but perhaps another glass of chianti . . .'

'Ah you have not tasted our *quagli con polenta,* you cannot refuse our *quagli con polenta.*'

Marcello stayed. And he ate the quails. And he was back the next night. And the night after that. He could not resist Sarina and she knew it. So did Armando and he was quick to encourage the flirtation. Anything that pleased Marcello could only be to his advantage.

Marcello tried to bed Sarina for the next six weeks, but his efforts were in vain. Had he not been a De Cretico she might have allowed him to seduce her that very first night but she had other plans. She saw in Marcello her saviour. At first it had been just wishful thinking—she had not seriously considered it possible she could rise so far above her station—but as Marcello's obsession with her grew, she found herself wondering. Sarina De Cretico . . . why not?

After one month of holding her hand and seeing her to her cottage door, being granted one kiss and feeling her body against his, Marcello was in agony. But each time he tried to press his suit further, she was adamant.

'Because I am a widow you think I am not virtuous?' she asked. 'There has been only my husband for me and I remain true to him and to the memory of our marriage.' Sarina said it with utter conviction. In a way she believed it. The several lovers she'd had since Carlo's death had been necessary. They had distracted her, they had assuaged her frustration, but nothing more. They had never replaced her husband. The memory of Carlo and the love she had shared with him remained unsullied.

Marcello believed her. He was bewitched by her, captivated by the unfathomable mystery which seemed to surround her. He had never known a woman like Sarina. She was from peasant stock, like the other village girls, but she did not behave like the others. She did not look like them, she did not talk like them, she did not dress like them. And she was certainly not like the high-class prostitutes he had slept with in Milano and Roma. She seemed to be in a class of her own. Neither peasant nor aristocrat. And it fascinated him.

During the four years of her widowhood Sarina had indeed changed. It had been a conscious decision on her part. If there were ever to be the remotest possibility of her remarrying it would be because a man found her irresistible—she had nothing else to offer.

She started with her dress. Like many of the villagers Sarina made her own clothes and was a deft seamstress. From the wealthy local merchant who owned the general store, she now purchased finer fabrics than the coarsely woven wool favoured by the locals. And she placed an order with the merchant for magazines from Paris detailing the latest fashions. No matter that she could not read; the pictures sufficed. Of course she could not afford the expensive laces and velvets and brocades the models in the pictures were wearing but the basic shape and style of the designs she was more than capable of reproducing.

It was not long before eyebrows were raised at the sight of Sarina, her head held high, her hair swept up with a comb and a velvet bow, parading the streets of Santa Lena in dresses which hugged her back and waist and fitted snugly over her hips before flaring to the ground. And as she walked she held her skirts to one side, just as the models in the pictures did.

Some thought Sarina vain and proud with ideas above her station, some were envious and others impressed; but the male population, each and every one of them, found her attractive.

It was the merchant's wife who paved the way for Sarina's final acceptance. She considered herself the village doyenne of fashion and, in criticising the lack of bustle in Sarina's design, she found herself politely but firmly corrected.

'Bustles are no longer fashionable in Paris,' Sarina answered. 'They have not been fashionable for a year or more.'

Far from being insulted, the merchant's wife was fascinated by Sarina's knowledge of the latest trends. So much so that she commissioned the young woman to design her some garments. It was this endorsement that saw, not only the end of the criticism levelled at Sarina, but the beginning of a lucrative small business, and over the next year or so she acquired several other clients from among the few wealthy families who lived on the hill. They included the mayor's wife and daughter which very much impressed her former critics.

Sarina's self-improvement plans gradually took shape. She started mingling with her wealthier clients, even visiting their homes for fittings. She dressed well, she spoke well and, because of her constant study of the Paris magazines, the villagers even believed she could read. But the whole exercise was expensive. As her obsession with her appearance grew, so did her demand for bonnets and fans and gloves. And although the merchant's wife more often than not agreed to a barter arrangement—a dress for a pair of satin slippers or a blouse for a selection of velvet ribbons—Sarina needed to seek regular employment to keep up with her expenditure.

That was where Armando came in. Sarina, with her saucy smile and elegant appearance, would be a definite asset to the tavern and he needed another serving girl. If she wanted to be called hostess, then so be it. He agreed that she would not be required to clear tables or wash glasses but apart from that her duties would be the same as the other girls'.

Sarina had hoped that she might meet a prospective future husband at the tavern but, two years down the track, it did not seem at all likely. Potential lovers abounded and she succumbed to several (always married men to ensure discretion), but potential husbands were sadly lacking. Until Marcello De Cretico.

'Marry me then, marry me. Become my wife.' Marcello's proposal was a last resort. But even as he said the words in a moment of distraction as she parted from his embrace and was closing her cottage door on him yet again, he wondered why he had not said them earlier. He loved her, he was convinced of it. Of course. Marriage. The perfect solution. 'You are my life, Sarina, I love you. *Sei la mia vita. Ti amo sempre*. Marry me.'

Sarina's heart was pounding. Everything she had hoped for, prayed for, was it possible? She tried to curb her excitement. Marcello was very young, there was his family to consider. Surely they would never allow such a marriage. But try as she might, she could not extinguish an overwhelming surge of exhilaration.

'I love you too, Marcello. And, yes, I would marry you. If it were at all possible I would marry you. But—'

Marcello kissed her deeply and she returned his kiss with equal fervour. As she did, she felt a surge of sexual desire. She longed to make love to him but she could not allow herself to give in. Sarina was fully aware that once the conquest had been made, Marcello's offer of marriage might well be forgotten and she did not dare risk that.

As she had predicted, the family was most certainly opposed to the marriage. Mario and Luigi De Cretico themselves came to Santa Lena as soon as Marcello sent them word of his intentions. There was no invitation extended for Marcello to bring his fiancé to Milan or Bologna in order to meet the family.

Mario had been irritated by Marcello's extended stay in the village. A month should have sufficed to oversee both the Santa Lena properties and the winery, but Marcello had not even been to the vineyard. This affair with a local peasant girl explained the delay and Mario was angry.

'Grow up, Marcello, grow up! You cannot marry the woman, she is a peasant.' He continued before Marcello could interrupt. 'Even with all her fancy airs and graces. Can't you see that? She is a peasant bitch on heat. She is after your money and your position and your name.'

'No, Mario, no she is not,' Marcello insisted. 'She loves me and I love her, I swear it.' Marcello was by now utterly convinced of his deep and abiding love for Sarina.

'You love her, sure. But with your *cazzo*, you fool. You love her with your cock. So take her. Have her. But do not marry her. I will not have you marry her. She will not become a member of this family, *capice*?'

Mario, like most men, had immediately responded to Sarina's sexuality and that made her a harlot as far as he was concerned. There were women you took to bed and women you married and Sarina fell into the former category.

But Marcello was obsessed. 'I am of age, Mario,' he said, when his brother's tirade was finally over, 'and I will marry Sarina with or without the family's approval.'

MARCELLO AND SARINA were married at the Santa Lena church two months later. No member of the De Cretico family attended the wedding, but that was simply their way of voicing their disapproval. They did not disown Marcello or threaten to disinherit him. The De Cretico family always acknowledged their own.

The couple honeymooned in Paris. Then, whilst their magnificent house was being built on the hill, they planned an extended holiday. Rome, Florence, Venice. It was all beyond Sarina's wildest imaginings.

She loved Paris. She could live without love if life could be as exciting as this. She walked down the Champs Elysee, her ruffled taffeta petticoats rustling enticingly. She twirled her striped parasol as she marvelled at the formal gardens of Versailles, and she adjusted her ostrich-feathered bonnet as she gazed up awestruck at the brand-new Eiffel Tower.

The long-awaited sex with Marcello, however, was somewhat of a disappointment. It was neither the prolonged orgy of love-making Sarina had shared with Carlo nor the torrid bouts of coupling she had experienced with her lovers. The fact that Marcello seemed intent upon satisfying only his own desires grew to annoy Sarina. And she did not particularly like his body. It was too slim for her tastes. She liked a man to be sturdy, strong. Like Mario De Cretico.

Although she knew he did not like her, Sarina had sensed Mario's lust and it had excited her. Now, when she and Marcello made love, she fantasised that it was really his brother who was grunting his passion on top of her.

Marcello never questioned whether his new wife was satisfied with their love-making. It would never have occurred to him to do so. All of his sexual experiences had been with high-class prostitutes—his brothers' associates always entertained the De Creticos well when they were doing business. As a result Marcello was accustomed to using a woman's body rather than making love to it.

But it was a price Sarina was prepared to pay. After all, when they returned home she would rule the village. Marcello would be king, she would be his queen and together they would reign. Sarina did not know which excited her more—the travel and the shopping, or the prospect of being the wealthiest and most envied woman in Santa Lena. Yes, a loveless marriage was a price she was more than prepared to pay for her idyllic existence.

But six months after the couple's return to the village, Sarina discovered to her dismay that, far from wishing to reign alongside his beautiful queen, Marcello wanted to become one of the common herd.

Marcello had never known popularity. In the past he had always been 'the young De Cretico'. The De Cretico name demanded respect, but the 'young' had always been dismissive and Marcello knew he had only been accepted into the ruggedly masculine company he and his brothers kept because of Mario and Luigi. Even his brothers' wives and his two older sisters considered him weak.

Now, amongst the villagers and itinerant workers who ate and drank at the tavern, he had discovered a sense of belonging. Marcello was not a stupid man. He realised at the outset that Armando, the innkeeper, saw him as a business asset and that his drinking companions were attracted more by the copious quantities of mulled wine and chianti he bought than they were by his company. But after a while, Armando did appear to genuinely enjoy Marcello's company. With pride he introduced his new friend to all as 'the boss'. 'Come, meet *il padrone*. He is a good man. One of us,' he would boast.

As for the men who enjoyed the alcohol he paid for, it was not long before they realised that Marcello was not merely buying their favour, he was genuinely interested in them. And they returned the compliment in kind. Of course they realised that Sarina wanted no part of them. But then Sarina never had, had she? Even when she had been one of them. And so Marcello was invited into their homes and their farms, and the closer the friendships he forged with the peasants, the greater the rift it created with his wife.

When, a year after their marriage, Marcello agreed to become godfather to a farmer's first son, Sarina was outraged. 'Guiseppe Lorenzelli is one of the poorest farmers in the district,' she complained.

'It is a great honour he bestows upon me,' Marcello insisted as he struggled with the stopper in a bottle. It was late, he had just returned from a night of camaraderie at the tavern and he'd had quite enough to drink, but these days he found himself needing several shots of schnapps to fortify himself against Sarina's nagging. 'Guiseppe is a fine man, he has three daughters and this is his first son. It is a great honour.'

'Guiseppe Lorenzelli is not a fine man at all. He is a lazy drunkard who drinks away the little he earns whilst his wife and daughters wear rags to church.'

'That is enough, Sarina,' Marcello suddenly snapped. 'It is my responsibility to befriend the local people. Mario has instructed me to do so.' He hoped that would keep her quiet, but he was not being altogether truthful.

'It is good that the local people like you and trust you, Marcello,' Mario had said on one of his rare visits. 'But there is no necessity to get drunk with them. You must retain their respect.'

Word had reached Mario of his younger brother's excessive drinking and, exasperating as it was, he resigned himself to it. He loved Marcello but the boy had always been weak and indulgent. He was not likely to change. Perhaps it was for the best, after all, that Marcello had married his local peasant. It was convenient having him preside over the family's Santa Lena properties; his overseeing duties were simple and there was little harm he could come to way up here amongst the farmers and villagers. One aspect of the marriage, however, displeased Mario greatly.

'You have been married nearly a whole year and Sarina is not yet with child. I trust there is nothing wrong.'

'It is certainly not for want of trying, Mario, I can assure you,' Marcello grinned. 'Do not concern yourself. It will happen.'

But a further year later the situation remained the same and Mario grew to detest Sarina. The woman emanated sexuality like a brood mare and yet she was barren. What good was she to the family? He never accused her to her face but Sarina knew he blamed her for his younger brother's fruitless marriage. Of course it could not be Marcello's fault, could it? she thought bitterly. Of course the fertility of a De Cretico could never be questioned. But it had to be Marcello, did it not? She had born a son to Carlo all those years ago.

Sarina had attempted to defend herself. But only once. Mario and Luigi had brought their wives and children with them on this occasion and, although she had met the wives only twice, she could sense their hostility.

She had been playing with the two younger children on the front patio overlooking the valley below when a voice behind her had said, 'Go to your mothers.' As the children ran inside, Sarina turned to see Mario standing by the main doors. She did not know how long he had been there. He walked slowly down the several steps leading to the patio and stood barely an arm's length from her. It was moments before he spoke.

'The children like you,' he said, but it was not meant as a compliment.

'I like children,' she answered.

'Yet you have none of your own.' It was an accusation.

Sarina stood her ground. She felt herself flush, but with anger not fear.

'I said, you have no children of your own.' Now there was menace in his voice.

'I did once,' Sarina replied quietly.

She had told Marcello about her baby a year after they were married, but she knew he had never mentioned it to his brothers. He dismissed her failure to conceive, saying such things took time, the baby would come when it wished to. And he had spoken no more on the matter, refusing to believe his own fertility could be in doubt.

'I had a child to my first husband. A son. He died when he was nine months old.'

Mario knew she was telling the truth. 'You are saying my brother is not man enough?' He stepped closer to her until his breath fanned her cheek, but she did not flinch. Mario hated her more than ever because she was right—his brother was not man enough. He hated her for making him despise Marcello. He hated her because he wanted her. He could have her here, now, on the courtyard paving stones, and he knew that she would cry out her pleasure. 'Is that what you are saying?' he repeated.

Still she was silent, but her eyes held a glint of triumph. Had she read his desire? Mario turned away from her. He would die before he would touch her; it was what the whore wanted, he knew it.

'You will say nothing about your child, do you understand me? The fruitlessness of your marriage will be seen as God's will.' He turned back to her. 'If you say anything to the contrary I will kill you.'

Mario's jibes about his brother's childless marriage had ceased from that day on but his lust and loathing for Sarina remained undiminished.

As for Sarina, she took out her frustration and loneliness on Marcello, nagging him about his drinking and the company he kept. Slowly but surely, she drove him from her until, eventually, she found herself alone each evening with only the company of the servants while Marcello drank with his friends at the tavern.

The local chianti was no longer strong enough for Marcello and he developed a taste for the Bavarian schnapps which Armando purchased from a contact of his across the border. The harsh, rough liquor took its toll and in the early hours of many a morning, Marcello would stagger home in a state of complete inebriation. When he arrived, exhausted, he would invariably sit on the stone steps in the courtyard before climbing up to the bedrooms, and invariably it was there he would pass out and be found by one of the servants at dawn.

IT HAPPENED NOT long after Marcello and Sarina's third anniversary. On a fine day in late spring. It must have occurred just before dawn but the body was not discovered until mid-morning. It would have been found earlier—the road to the village was busy—but there had been a light snowfall during the night. It was only when the rays of the mid-morning sun had melted the fine white shroud of snow that Marcello's body could be seen sprawled face-down in the roadside gully.

He had not fallen far and the wound to his head was superficial, but in his drunken state he had lapsed into unconsciousness and exposure to the elements had killed him. There was no evidence of foul play. His purse and its contents remained intact in the breast pocket of his waistcoat. An ignominious death. Sarina despised him all the more for it. And she became even more bitter. Was she destined to remain a widow forever?

It gave her no heart when the brothers promised to find her a husband. 'Two years' mourning,' Mario told her and it was an order; there was no sympathy in his eyes. 'Two years and then we will find a husband for you. But it must be the right man. A man who can control our interests in Santa Lena. A man to be trusted.'

She knew what that meant. They wanted a lackey and she would be the prize. Sarina De Cretico and the beautiful house on the hill—they would be the incentives for the man the brothers would buy to best serve their interests.

Sarina would receive an allowance, and she could retain the services of Ernesto and Guiseppina Mascani, the elderly couple Marcello had hired, but the other servants would be dismissed.

'You must learn to govern your own household sparingly, like a woman of good breeding,' Mario had instructed her scathingly, 'and in time we will find you a husband.'

Mario detested Sarina more than ever. And more than ever he detested his lust for her. Even in her widowhood she exuded sexuality. He convinced himself that Sarina had killed his young brother with her lustfulness. Unable to satisfy his wife's sexual greed, Marcello had been driven to drink. Well, Mario would not provide a husband who would satisfy her wants. He would search for a man, perhaps much older, a man who did not desire women. Mario was determined not to sate the whore's carnal desires.

And so Sarina was left a lonely prisoner in her beautiful house with her beautiful statue. Occasionally she entertained the mayor and the merchant and their wives but she had long since tired of their toadying. Besides, it was not friends she was in need of. It was a lover.

The boredom of her long lonely nights fed the demons of her sexuality until she could stand it no longer. She plotted and planned who her lover might be. He should be older, married, with a family and responsibilities to ensure discretion. She must choose carefully. Selectively. She would be risking her life. But her body was choosing for her and her body was neither careful nor selective. Her body was responding urgently to the strong, healthy young men of the village. It was youth she wanted. Strong, virile, sturdy youth with hard bodies and fine skin.

In church on Sundays Sarina could not tear her eyes from the young Gianni brothers. Over the years she had often seen the family around the village, but the Gianni boys had been children then. When had they become such fine-looking young men?

Sarina had set her sights on the older of the brothers, Enrico, until she noticed the regular exchange of looks between him and the blacksmith's daughter. They were lovers, there could be no doubting it. She turned her attention to the younger brother, and decided he was her preference anyway. Giovanni, with his finely muscled man's body and his boy's face. He looked so young. Eighteen, perhaps nineteen. So very young. And those eyes. Intense and, as yet, ingenuous—a young man on the brink of discovery. It was the face of a virgin, Sarina decided. Yes, she was sure he was a virgin. Oh, the tricks she could teach him.

It was easy. So easy. Shopping for supplies one Saturday morning, she ran into the boy. 'Giovanni, is it not?' smiling her dimpled smile. 'I have met your father.' Giovanni nodding back self-consciously. He knew who she was, of course, and was flattered that she should speak to him. 'Perhaps you could assist Ernesto. He is getting old and the sack is heavy.'

Ernesto had assured her they were not in need of horse grain—there were two sacks still in the stables at the rear of the house—but she had insisted they purchase another.

And so Giovanni accompanied Sarina and the elderly servant home in order to help unload the sack of grain.

'Thank you, Ernesto, young Giovanni can manage.' She nodded dismissively. 'Unharness and water the horse.' She held the stable door open for the boy and allowed it to swing closed behind them as if by accident.

'Over here, beside the others,' she instructed, admiring in the half-light the strong forearms that balanced the sack with ease upon the fine broad shoulder.

'Thank you,' she said when he had carefully placed it down. Then she put her hand upon the same broad shoulder and felt the firmness of his flesh. She knew that beneath the rough fabric of his shirt the skin would be smooth and silken. 'You have grown, Giovanni. You are a young man now when only yesterday you were a boy.'

Giovanni was surprised. Who would have thought Signora De Cretico would notice him, she noticed no one. As her fingers slowly moved across his shoulder and down his arm until her hand was clasping his, Giovanni held his breath. He was confused. What did the widow want? Surely not . . . But his flesh tingled at her touch.

With her other hand, Sarina played with the soft brown curls that framed his face. Then she caressed his cheek. 'Thank you for your help.' And slowly, very, very slowly, she kissed him upon the mouth. A demure kiss. A mere brush of her lips. 'Come to me tonight and I will reward you.' He opened his mouth. He was not sure whether it was to say something or to kiss her back, but she gently pulled away. 'Midnight,' she whispered. 'By the stable doors.' And she was gone.

As Giovanni stepped out into the sunlight she was standing by the rear doors of the house which led to the servants' quarters. 'Goodbye, Giovanni,' she called, waving to him. 'Thank you for your help.'

AT MIDNIGHT, AS Giovanni crept around the side of the house, his whole body was quivering with anticipation. The expectations aroused by the furtive kisses and fumbling caresses he had exchanged with the village girls were about to be fulfilled. Uninhibited by the restrictions of virginal vows, the widow was going to allow him to take her amongst the hay on the stable floor.

But Giovanni was wrong. Finger to her lips, Sarina led him away from the stables and through the rear door of the house. Past the servants' quarters, across the courtyard and up the stairs to her bedroom.

She undressed him, touching his body, tantalising herself as much as she did him. His body was as magnificent as she had known it would be. The muscles hard and toned beneath the velvet bloom of youthful skin. She ran her fingers over his back and his buttocks and his groin. She licked his chest and his neck and his lips until Giovanni could bear no more and he clutched her breasts and her buttocks and ground his mouth upon hers.

She broke away from him. '*Si*,' she panted. '*Si, si*.'

Then they were upon the bed and Giovanni was only vaguely aware of the sheets beneath him, a silky texture he had never before felt. And then the texture of Sarina as she lowered herself upon him. Then he lost himself, forgetting everything but the feel and the taste and the smell of her.

It did not last long. Not that first time. But Sarina had not expected it to. She kept him with her until it was nearly dawn. They made love again twice and the third time it was Sarina who lost herself. She was like a woman possessed and Giovanni marvelled at his control and the power he had over her.

They barely spoke throughout but, as Sarina ushered him back into the night, she whispered close into his ear, '*Mio piccolo toro*, come to me again tomorrow. At midnight. I will be waiting.'

They met each night for a whole week until Sarina came to her senses and realised that she was courting discovery. Once a week must suffice, she told herself. But the days between each Saturday midnight dragged slowly. And when Giovanni left for the railway work camp and his visits dwindled to only twice a month, she thought she would go mad.

Sarina had become insatiable. She did not love the boy, she knew that. But she loved what he did for her. He freed her. It was only in Giovanni's embrace, at the height of her passion, that she felt alive. The rest of her existence was cold and empty.

SARINA STOPPED PROWLING the balconies. Looking through the open doors of the upstairs salon, she saw the grandfather clock read a quarter before midnight. She would go downstairs and wait for him in case he arrived early.

She knew Giovanni wanted to be free of her. She knew he was fearful of the De Cretico brothers, and he had good reason to be, but she cared nothing for his fear. She needed him desperately, and she would continue to need him until Mario found her a husband.

Sarina pulled her red velvet gown about her as she quietly opened the rear door. This waiting, she cursed, it was beyond endurance.

Nearly half an hour later, shivering with cold despite the heavy velvet gown, Sarina dragged Giovanni inside. 'You are late,' she hissed.

Giovanni looked with some alarm at the doors to the

servants' quarters, but Sarina was already hurrying on ahead of him, through the corridor, across the courtyard. He followed.

Behind them, one of the doors opened and two pairs of eyes watched as they climbed the stairs.

Guiseppina and Ernesto looked at each other and Guiseppina shook her head with more than disapproval. Such indiscretion was dangerous. Her mistress was becoming less and less mindful of the jeopardy in which she was placing them. It would cost them all dear if the signora were to become too careless.

Quietly, Guiseppina closed the door.

Chapter Three

The chalet was by far the largest building Caterina had ever seen. Far larger than the town hall in Ridanna and far taller than the church steeple. Made of timber, the magnificent building stood four storeys high, and that was not counting the attic with its windows jutting out from the steeply sloped slate roof. Each floor was surrounded by wide wooden balconies onto which the shuttered doors of the seventy-two guest rooms opened.

The pine-finished interior was as impressive as the exterior. On the ground level was the bar and lounge with its huge armchairs and heavy rugs. On the first floor, the dining room, its long trestle tables covered in bright red checked tablecloths. On the third floor, the music lounge, complete with piano; and on the fourth the writing room and library with desks, hardback chairs and oak shelves heavily laden with books. And in every communal area was a huge open granite fireplace where giant logs burned day and night.

There were several other timber buildings further down the slope but only one was residential—the keeper's cottage where the chalet manager and his family lived. The staff and servants, like the guests, were accommodated in the chalet itself. Not far from the keeper's cottage was the storage cabin for the ski equipment, where early each morning a queue would form as guests lined up to collect their skis and toboggans. A little further down the slope were the stables and adjoining barn where the sleighs, sledges, harnesses and tackle were housed.

Around the chalet complex the snow-capped Alps reared into the sky, dwarfing all beneath them. But the chalet, with its scarred and weathered timber face, stood undaunted. A haven amongst the elements, a safe house for the cold and weary, it stood as it had for two centuries past and as it would for centuries to come.

Caterina loved the chalet. She worked hard and the hours were long but she was accustomed to that. On her father's farm she was up at dawn to milk the two cows and tend to the house goats and feed the chickens. By the time she returned to help her mother and her younger sister in the kitchen her father and three older brothers had left to work the small property until dusk.

Caterina's day at the chalet also started at dawn. She began by helping with the preparation of breakfast, then throughout the day she cleaned and serviced the guest rooms. Only the experienced girls were allocated duties serving in the dining room or working in the bar but, on occasion, Caterina was sent to wait on rooms when a specific service was requested—cigars here, a newspaper there—and she enjoyed the personal contact with the guests.

'Thank you for your trouble.' The young American exchanged the newspaper for some coins and she slipped them into the pocket of her apron. It was in poor taste to look at one's tip but she could tell that it was substantial.

Although the young Americans had been there for only several days, she had seen them many times as she went about her duties. There were four of them, probably in their early twenties, students on a six-week vacation, she was told. They were very attractive and very confident and very loud. Well, three of them were. The one they called Paul was much quieter, often preferring to look at the view rather than join in the boisterous conversation of his friends. Caterina found the Americans dazzling and sophisticated and was in awe of them.

'Thank you, sir.' She turned to go.

'Just a minute.' He stopped her. 'Do you speak English?'

'Little.' She smiled apologetically. 'Much little.'

'Much little.' His laughter was without scorn. 'That's about as much as I speak Italian. You are Italian, aren't you?'

'Italian, *si*.' In the two weeks that Caterina had been at the chalet she had tried hard to learn as much English as she could but even with the help of her new friend Mary, the Welsh girl who worked in the bar lounge, she found it a very confusing language.

'Stay and talk to me for a while,' the American said.

Even as Paul said it, he wondered why. Unlike his friends, he was not given to flirtation. He had no ulterior motive in asking the maid to stay. No motive except for the fact that she was the most beautiful girl he had ever seen, with her thick auburn hair and her dancing blue eyes.

Caterina stood for a moment, confused. Was there something else the American wished her to fetch?

He gestured to one of the two chairs by the table in the centre of the room. 'Sit down,' he said. 'Talk . . . um . . . *parlez* . . . no, that's French . . . um . . .' He made a chattering gesture with his hand.

She realised what he wanted so she smiled and sat tentatively on the edge of the chair. The servants were ordered not to initiate contact with the guests but, should a guest wish to engage in conversation, then they were to be as polite and helpful as possible. Caterina was not sure whether this included being alone in a male guest's bedroom, however. She had heard several stories of men pressing their attentions upon some of the girls. She had also heard that, should any girl reciprocate, she would be immediately dismissed. The young American seemed harmless enough, though. Besides, the door was open.

'My name is Paul,' he said, pointing to his chest. 'Paul.'

'Caterina,' she answered. *'Io mi chiamo Caterina.'*

'America,' he said, still pointing to his chest.

'Si,' she nodded.

'Boston, Massachusetts,' still pointing. 'You?' Now he pointed at her. 'Caterina?'

'Ridanna,' she answered. *'Una campagna vicino Ridanna'*.

'Ah, Ridanna.' He had a map of the area and he knew that Ridanna was a small village over the border. 'Yes,' he nodded.

Caterina felt frustrated. She wanted the American to know she came from a property near Ridanna, that her father was a farmer. She was proud of her father—his was the largest of all the Panuzzi family farms and there were many.

'Panuzzi,' she said. 'Caterina Panuzzi.'

The American smiled. 'Dunleavy. Paul Dunleavy.'

'No Ridanna,' she insisted. *'Mio padre è contadino.'* What was the English word for *contadino*? Try as she might Caterina could not remember. Mary, the Welsh girl, had told her but then there had been so many words and phrases that Caterina had become confused. 'F . . .' she said. 'F . . .' Suddenly she remembered. 'Former,' she said triumphantly. 'Former.'

'Former?' Paul looked confused.

Caterina bent over in her chair and mimed drawing milk from a cow's udders. 'Former,' she insisted. 'Former.' He still looked confused so she put her hands to each side of her head, forefingers extended. 'Mooo,' she said.

Paul burst out laughing. *'Farmer!* You come from a farm.'

Caterina laughed with him. 'Farmer, *si. Mio padre è* . . . farmer.'

Yes, she looked like a farm girl, Paul thought. Fresh and healthy, with her full, ripe body and those thick auburn curls. But now, as the laughter bubbled from her, Paul was captivated by far more than her beauty. She was so vital, so effervescent, so unaffected.

'A farm near Ridanna,' he said, trying not to stare at her.

'Si. Ridanna. *Dieci chilometri.'*

'Dieci. Ten, yes? The farm is ten kilometres from Ridanna.'

'Si. Farm, Ridanna, ten kilometre.' Caterina was delighted with herself. She was speaking English. And the young American was interested in what she was saying. He had a way of brushing his straight fair hair back from his brow as he concentrated upon their communication that was very attractive. And she liked his kind, grey eyes.

The two of them managed to struggle a little further with their conversation. Turning the pages of an imaginary book and scribbling with an imaginary pen, Paul told her that he was a student.

'Sì, studente.' That was an easy one. But 'mining engineer' was too difficult and, several minutes later, rather than appear stupid, Caterina decided it was time to take her leave. Besides, she might get into trouble if she stayed talking for too long.

'I go,' she said, rising abruptly.

'Of course.' He rose also and accompanied her to the door. 'It was good talking to you.'

'Sì,' she said. 'Good. *Buono.'*

'We must talk again some time.'

She did not understand him but his smile was warm and friendly so she smiled and nodded back.

LATE THE FOLLOWING afternoon the young American was waiting for Caterina as she left the staff quarters.

'Coffee?' he asked. And she agreed.

She agreed the following day. And the day after that. She told herself that it was good for her English, which was improving rapidly, and she bore the brunt of the other girls' teasing with good humour. But, underneath, Caterina was confused. She knew she was falling in love and it frightened her. She should say no when he asked her to drink coffee with him, but she could not. And at night, when she thought of him, she knew she wanted him to touch her. It was a sin, she told herself, she must not think of it.

Paul was also teased by his friends, but in a far more lascivious fashion. One of the young Americans was having an affair with the Welsh girl who worked in the lounge and he teased Paul mercilessly about Caterina.

'You're a fool,' Geoffrey said. 'Why are you wasting your time drinking coffee with her, for God's sake? Hurry up and get her into your bed—we're only here for another month.' At twenty-three Geoffrey was two years older than the others, in the final year of his engineering course, and the self-appointed leader of the group.

'I had not intended trying to get her into my bed at all,' Paul replied stiffly. 'She is pleasing company.'

Geoffrey scoffed at him. 'Oh sure. Sure I believe you. Breasts like hers make very pleasing company.'

Barry and Chris burst out laughing. Geoff always amused them. Besides which, they agreed with him. If they could possibly attract the attention of a girl as beautiful as Caterina, they certainly would not be wasting time having coffee with her.

Paul refused to listen. Finally he snapped at them all. Their remarks were offensive, he told them, and until they ceased their teasing he would avoid their company.

'Take it easy,' Geoffrey placated. 'It was meant in good humour.' Geoffrey had not intended to offend his friend. He was particularly fond and protective of Paul. They both came from Boston and their families knew each other. When Paul had enrolled at Harvard, Geoffrey had immediately taken him under his wing.

The teasing ceased and Paul was thankful. He had found it insulting to Caterina, of course, but he had also found it confronting. He had lied to Geoffrey. He most certainly did want to make love to Caterina. He wanted to make love to her so desperately that he wondered she could be so unaware of his lust.

'Milk?' she would ask, jug poised. And when he nodded, she would add milk to his coffee. 'Sugar? Two?' she would ask and when he nodded again she would carefully measure two teaspoons of sugar into his cup. It was a ritual which charmed him. She was so proud of her English. Laughing delightedly, she would clasp his hand. 'Mine English good, Paolo, yes?' He loved the way she called him Paolo.

'*My* English,' he would automatically correct her as his hand tingled. 'Yes, very good.'

And the laughter would bubble from her again. 'Is you. Is you make mine English good. *My* English.'

Caterina was unaware of Paul's lust only because she was too busy struggling with her own. She clasped his hand on any pretext simply to feel his skin. She delighted in him, she loved him and, mortal sin as it was, she wanted him to make love to her.

'I can show you some English words in books,' Paul said one late afternoon. He had pointed out the words milk and chocolate and coffee on the menu in front of them.

'Yes?' she asked.

'The books are in my room. Would you like that?' He knew that Geoffrey would not be there. He and the others had left to spend the evening in Steinach.

'Yes,' she nodded.

Paul closed the door behind them and picked up a book from one of the bedside tables. He sat on the bed, the open book on his knees, and she sat beside him. He pointed to a word and, as she placed her hand next to his on the page, her wrist rested on his thigh. He said nothing, but covered her hand with his own and he could feel her trembling. When he looked at her she remained staring down at the book, not seeing the page before her. Her eyes were fixed upon their hands and, as he watched her, she turned her wrist so that their palms touched and gently she entwined her fingers with his.

The kiss was soft and tender. Her lips were only slightly parted and they felt like velvet. The book fell from his knees as he drew her to him. Her body was warm and pliable and seemed to meld to his, and he could feel the fullness of her breasts against his chest. The kiss became more urgent, her lips parted a little more and he could feel the moistness of her mouth. Her breathing became heavier and she was quivering. Just as he was. She wanted him, he realised. She wanted him as much as he wanted her. Gently, he placed his hand upon her breast. There was a sharp intake of breath, as if she was going to resist. But she did not. And then they were lying on the bed together. Still kissing. Yet more urgently. And touching and stroking and caressing each other. He started to fumble with his belt, trying to unfasten his trousers without breaking the kiss.

Suddenly Caterina pulled away from him and sat up on the edge of the bed. *'Io sono vergine,'* she said breathlessly. She turned to him and her eyes were wide, not with fear—she was not frightened of him, he knew that. But she was troubled, uncertain.

'Caterina,' he said and he sat beside her on the edge of the bed. 'Caterina, please.' He pushed her hair gently away from her face. 'I will not have you do something you do not wish. We can stop this.'

She looked back at him for what seemed a very long time and the uncertainty left her eyes. 'No stop,' she said. She took his hand in hers and softly kissed his palm. *'Fai l'amore con me,'* she whispered. *'Fai l'amore con me, Paolo.'*

IT WAS A week before anyone knew of the affair between Caterina and Paul. Feigning illness, Paul did not join his friends on the slopes and, each morning, in between her duties, Caterina slipped into his room. Although she dared stay no longer than half an hour, and although their meetings were furtive and hurried, the two fell very much in love.

Geoffrey was suspicious but Paul refused any comment and, surprisingly, it was Caterina who first confided of their love. She simply had to tell someone. Someone who would understand. The priest had not. She had made her trip to Steinach and the village church on Sunday and the priest had been quick to tell her she would be damned forever if she did not cease her abhorrent carnal activities immediately. 'Govern your lust, my child,' he had said. 'It is the devil coming to you in this man.'

Caterina suffered guilt and confusion. She knew she was committing a sin but how could Paolo be the devil? The love he felt for her was as deep and pure as the love she felt for him, she knew it was.

The only person to whom she could turn was Mary. For a week now she had carefully avoided Teresa and the other girls from Santa Lena. But Mary would understand. Mary was not only worldly but she, too, was in love.

Mary was indeed worldly. 'Oh, Catie,' she said. 'Oh Catie, do you think this is wise?' Caterina loved the way Mary called her Catie; it made her sound like a *strani*. A foreigner. Mysterious. Aloof and reserved like the English women who stayed at the chalet.

'Wise? But I love him, Mary, just as you love Geoffrey.'

Catie was so young, Mary thought. Not only in years. Emotionally the girl was very immature. Mary remembered when she too had believed the sincerity of a man's love. It was only four years ago, although now it seemed like a lifetime away. She had been twenty-two when she had become engaged to the German ski instructor she'd met during a holiday in northern Scotland. She had surrendered her virginity to her fiancé and accompanied him to Austria, severing all ties with her family and friends who strongly disapproved.

The ski instructor left her six months later. He had probably never intended to marry her, she realised. Unable to face her family, Mary had remained in Europe. She had hardened since then, but she was not bitter. Mary enjoyed her life. She also enjoyed men and there had been a number of affairs. But she had no illusions—they were holiday romances, just like her present relationship with Geoffrey. She avoided at all costs the major pitfall of pregnancy—the German had taught her that much.

'You must be careful, Catie,' she warned. She knew it would be useless to warn the girl of imminent heartbreak—Caterina was too convinced of Paul's undying affection.

'He is going to remain with me when his friends return to America,' Caterina said. 'He is going to remain with me and he is going to meet my family and then . . .'

Although Mary was silent, Caterina was aware of her disbelief so she said nothing more of Paul's plans. 'When you return to your farm,' he had said, 'I will come with you. I will ask your Papa if I may marry you and he will say yes and then we will go to America. On a big, big ship. *Una grande nave*. A ship as big as the chalet.' In the fragmented Italian she had taught him and in the simple English he knew she would understand, he always spoke to her as if she were a child. 'And we will be happy, Caterina. We will be happy forever.'

'You must be very careful, Catie,' Mary repeated.

Caterina pretended to listen as Mary told her how to avoid pregnancy. Her lover must withdraw at the peak of his passion, Mary said; she must insist upon it. But Caterina was fully aware of the risk she was taking. As she feigned interest in Mary's well-meaning but unattractively clinical advice she knew that, even now, she could well be with child. But pregnancy held no fear for her. Caterina was infected with a sort of madness. She felt gloriously liberated. She exulted in their lovemaking, her body freed of all inhibition. But her freedom went far beyond sexual liberation. So all-consuming was her love that she was prepared to abandon even Church and family. She was convinced that God saw their love for what it was. Pure and unadulterated. Of course God understood. God was love, was he not? And if her family were to disapprove as the priest did—and she was sure they would—then she would live without their blessing, just as she would live without the Church's blessing, until she was married. When she and Paul were wed they would be accepted back into the fold and, until then, she would pray to God and God alone. And if it were God's will she become with child then she and Paul would simply marry sooner.

Paul was overwhelmed by Caterina's love and the

intensity of his own feelings. When he finally admitted his love to his friends and told them of his plans, they were horrified. 'It's insane,' Geoffrey insisted. 'Good God, man, surely you must see that it's insane. Your family will never accept her.'

But Paul refused to listen and his friends could only pray that, in the several remaining weeks of their stay at the chalet, he would either tire of Caterina or at least recognise that theirs was a holiday liaison and nothing more.

Two days before the Americans were due to leave, however, the lovers were as inseparable as ever and Paul was still adamant about his plans. There was little Geoffrey could do but agree to send a telegraphic cable to Paul's family before boarding the ship at Bremerhaven.

'Here is the message,' Paul said, giving him a slip of paper. 'I shall stay at the chalet for six weeks until Caterina's contract has expired. Then I shall meet her family and, hopefully with their blessing, we shall leave for the States.'

'And if they do not wish to give their blessing?' Geoffrey asked.

'It will be unfortunate,' Paul agreed. 'But Caterina is prepared for that.'

Later that evening, Caterina sat with the Americans in the music lounge and drank champagne with them. She was off-duty and the chalet staff and workers were allowed to fraternise if the guests requested it. She was careful not to appear too intimate with Paul but she was aware that the looks they shared were eminently readable and that several of the staff were casting glances in their direction. If their affair were discovered it would mean scandal and instant dismissal but, in her giddy state, that too meant little to Caterina.

'To a certain couple I know,' Geoffrey whispered as he filled Caterina's glass for the second time. 'May they be very happy together.' He clinked his glass against hers and smiled.

'Thank you,' Caterina smiled back. She liked Geoffrey. He was such a good friend to Paul. 'To America,' she whispered as she sipped her champagne.

Geoffrey watched her over the rim of his glass. She was a beautiful girl. She deserved a beautiful life. He felt sorry for her.

They sang along to the piano and drank more champagne. Catarina was not used to alcohol and after three glasses, she felt very light-headed. She noticed the brief look between Paul and Geoffrey and was not surprised when, a moment later, Paul whispered to her, 'Come to the room in five minutes.'

A little while later, as she tapped their signal gently on the door, she felt no shame. It was not degrading to think that the Americans knew what she was doing as they sang along to the piano in the music lounge. Caterina knew no shame and felt no degradation.

After they had made love she lay close to Paul in the narrow bed as he stroked her hair. 'One night more your friends go,' she whispered. He nodded and she lifted herself up onto one elbow. 'You are no . . .' She fumbled for the word. 'No regret?'

'No,' he smiled, 'no regret.'

'Sure?'

'Sure.'

THE FOLLOWING NIGHT Paul had agreed to join his friends for a final night of carousing in Steinach. 'You have to help us with our hangovers,' Geoffrey insisted. 'It's the done thing to sleep it off the next day on the train to Bremerhaven.'

And carouse they did. They ate sausages with mustard and sauerkraut and drank beer in a little tavern overlooking the cobbled square. Then they bought a bottle of schnapps and swigged lustily from it as they wandered through the still, cold, gaslit laneways of the old town. They'd finished the bottle by the time they arrived at the big hotel with its whitewashed face and huge pine door and wooden shuttered windows looking out over the streets.

In the bar, they skolled glass after glass of schnapps as Geoffrey and Barry and Chris kept toasting Paul. Then they entered into a beer-drinking competition with several of the villagers, singing along with their new-found friends and drinking more and more schnapps until Paul's legs felt like jelly and the room was spinning away from him. They must go back to the chalet, he told himself. He pawed Geoffrey's sleeve and tried to say something but his tongue felt several times its normal size. He had never been so drunk. How had this happened? How come the others seemed to be in control? Then Barry fell over and everyone laughed and Paul stopped feeling self-conscious. Everyone was drunk, everyone was having a good time, and he accepted the glass Geoffrey handed him. 'Skoll,' he said and he drained the glass to a rousing cheer and held it out to be refilled.

Geoffrey watched him carefully. Paul had never been able to handle alcohol. He didn't even like the taste of it. Back home he only ever got drunk when it was a mandatory exercise, like after exams to prove he was one of the boys. Paul was a brilliant student with a successful career ahead of him, provided he did not do something stupid, like saddle himself with a peasant wife before he was twenty-two.

Geoffrey pulled his fob watch from his waistcoat pocket. Nearly time to leave for Innsbruck and the connecting train to Bremerhaven. Paul's bags were packed and in the back of the waiting trap. He would wake up the following day and they would be halfway to

Bremerhaven and Geoffrey would convince him it was all for the best. That was why he hadn't sent the telegraph.

Geoffrey had had nothing heavy to drink himself. Nothing but beer. The 'schnapps' he had skolled had been tap water with which he had filled the empty bottle he had swigged from as they wandered the streets.

Geoffrey looked at Barry and Chris. They too were drunk, but he had not plied them with as much liquor as he had Paul and in any event they could handle it better. For secrecy's sake Geoffrey had not told them of his plan but, if they wished to become so inebriated that they missed their connecting train, he did not much care. Barry and Chris were not his responsibility. Paul was.

'Time to go home,' he announced loudly, rising to his feet. 'Sir,' he waved to the innkeeper behind the bar, 'two bottles if you please. One for the road and one for a nightcap at the chalet, yes?' He looked at Paul who nodded and mumbled incoherently. He's close to passing out, Geoffrey thought as he hoisted him onto his feet and started dragging him towards the door.

'A LETTER FOR you, Caterina.'

It was early morning. Caterina had finished her kitchen duties and was in her crisp chambermaid's uniform ready to start on the rooms when the woman at the reception desk called to her.

'Grazie,' she said and took the envelope.

A letter? For her? But she could not read. Who would write her a letter? Her name was on the front. She could read her name, and there it was: *Caterina Panuzzi*. She opened the envelope. Even more bewildering. It was in English.

'Mary. Will you read me this letter?'

Mary was polishing the glasses and setting up the

lounge bar for the busy day ahead. She took the single piece of notepaper Caterina held out to her.

'"Caterina my darling",' she read before glancing down to the name at the bottom of the page. 'It is from Paul,' she said.

Caterina looked puzzled but not troubled and Mary's sense of unease turned to dread as her eyes skimmed the page.

'Come, Caterina, sit down.' It was early and the bar was as yet deserted. She led Caterina to one of the large armchairs by the open fire and, seating herself opposite, she slowly began to translate.

'"Caterina, my darling, I am sorry I did not say goodbye to you. It was wrong of me I know, but I could not face you. I am a . . ."' As Mary struggled to find the word for coward, she glanced at Caterina. The girl still looked puzzled, as if she could not absorb what was being said to her.

'"*Io sono un* . . ."' Mary concentrated on the translation, trying not to think of Caterina's pain. What was the Italian word for coward? There was not one, she was sure. '"*Io sono . . . pauroso*",' she said. 'Afraid', that would have to do. '"My dear it is better this way",' she continued. '"You would be unhappy in America, away from your friends and your family. You are beautiful and you deserve to be happy. I love you and I am sorry. Paul".'

Mary held the piece of notepaper out to Caterina. The girl took it from her and looked at the name on the bottom of the page. 'Paolo?' she whispered. She had never seen his name in writing.

'Paul,' Mary answered. 'He has signed it Paul.'

Caterina's mind was numb. Why had he not signed it Paolo? She rose from the armchair, the letter clutched to her breast.

'Caterina . . .' Mary rose to comfort her but Caterina shrugged off the embrace.

'No, no, I must return to my work. Thank you for reading me the letter.'

Mary watched as Caterina walked from the lounge. No glint of a tear, not a shred of emotion. She watched as the girl thrust the piece of notepaper into the pocket of her apron. Mary felt useless. There was nothing she could do, nothing she could say. It was a cowardly letter but in essence it was right. Caterina was a sweet, simple girl, she would not have been happy in America away from her own kind. The writer of the letter knew that. And Mary knew who had written the letter. She recognised the hand. There had been many notes over the past six weeks. Always signed 'G'.

Mary wondered whether she should tell Caterina that Geoffrey had written the letter. What purpose would that serve? The girl would be tormented; she might even try to follow her lover. If Paul was weak enough to be so influenced by his friends, how would he ever serve as Caterina's protector in a hostile America? She was better off without him. Mary made her decision. If Paul had been abducted against his will, and if he loved Caterina, he would come back for her. In the meantime, it was best to say nothing.

'... AND ROOM 39.'

Caterina took the key thrust to her by the housekeeper and added it to the keyring alongside the other five keys she had been given. The chambermaids were being assigned the vacated rooms to be prepared for the next wave of incoming guests.

Room 39. Paul's room. Caterina had been in a daze for the past two hours since Mary had read her the letter. She kept touching the sheet of paper in her apron pocket. It could not be true, she had told herself. They were only words. Only words Mary had read from a piece of paper.

They were not Paolo's words. Paolo would not say those words.

She opened the door. The two beds on either side of the room were freshly made up. They had not been slept in. She herself had remade those beds the preceding morning. Each day, when the guests left for a morning on the slopes, the maids collected their keys from the concierge and serviced the rooms. Caterina always kissed the pillow when she changed the linen on Paul's bed. Soon her head would be nestled next to his on that very pillow, she would think. But today the key to Room 39 had not been amongst those she had collected from the concierge. Today the housekeeper had given her the key. Could it be true? Had he gone?

She opened the cupboard doors. Nothing. The coats and the suits that smelled of him were no longer there. Nothing but the heavy wooden hangers waiting for the next chalet guest. And the next. And the next.

It was true. He had gone. Caterina lay down on the bunk. Paul's bunk. The narrow bed where they had clung to each other and panted their love. Where they had caressed each other and talked of their plans, of their lives together. Of America. She stared at the ceiling and the tears rolled down her cheeks. Paolo, she thought. Paolo.

For a long time Caterina wept. She wept for her love, and for the girl she had once been and she wept for the girl she would never be again.

Finally there were no more tears. She finished her duties as quickly as she could and that night she went to bed early. She knew she would not sleep, but she needed to rest her body. She must be up before dawn. There was a long walk ahead.

CHAPTER FOUR

Giovanni was excited. Only one more month to go. Just four short weeks and his contract was over. Not that he minded working for the railroads. He enjoyed the physical labour, digging deep into the heart of the mountain. But one day he would be digging for himself. It would be his own mine and there would be gold at the end of the tunnel. That was his dream. And in one month's time he would embark upon the first step toward the realisation of that dream.

It had all started with a newspaper article. One morning two new workers had arrived on the site. They were replacing two men who had been injured the previous week, one in a minor tunnel collapse, the other in a rock slide. Such occurrences were common. One of the new workers had a copy of a newspaper from Milan. It was over a week old but it did not matter, the article he showed them was inspiring. 'THE GOLDEN LAND,' its headlines declared, 'GOLD STRIKES IN AUSTRALIA. PEOPLE RICH OVERNIGHT.'

Neither Rico nor Giovanni could read but the man with the newspaper could. '". . . They flock from all parts of the globe,"' he read. '"Fortunes are made by the bold and the adventurous."' He stumbled over the names. ' "Bendigo, Ballarat . . . Recent strikes in Western Australia . . ."' There was a map of the vast western State of the country with areas and placenames pinpointed. '"The Kimberleys, the Pilbara, and the latest discoveries to the south, Southern Cross, Coolgardie."' And there was a picture of the southern port of Albany which had serviced the goldfields until the building of Fremantle, the man-made port on the western coast. Huge ships. People streaming down gangplanks. '"They come from America, from South Africa, from Europe,"' the article said. '"They flock in their ships to Albany and Fremantle to stake their claims in the golden land."'

'That is where I will go,' the man said, folding the newspaper carefully. 'No more digging for the railroads. I will dig for gold.'

Rico bought the newspaper from the man for a bottle of wine. 'He talks, Gio,' he said to his younger brother, 'but that is all he does. We will not talk, we will go to Australia.'

They had lived their dream from that day on, Rico painting the pictures. 'See it in your head, Gio,' he would say as they crouched over the fire. 'See it in your head. No longer will we have to dig through a mountain so that a train can get to the other side. We'll dig for gold. *Our* gold. Our families will be wealthy. We'll live in big houses, like your widow's, and our children will grow up wanting for nothing. We will be the ones who live in the big house on the hill, eh?'

He said it as a joke but they both knew that the widow was nothing to laugh about. Giovanni had finally confided in his brother. Sarina was becoming more indiscreet, more audacious, as if she cared nothing for the danger that surrounded them. And when his contract with the railroads was over Giovanni knew her demands would be constant. It would be only a matter of time before their affair became public knowledge in the village. Only a matter of time before the De Cretico brothers knew of her betrayal.

Rico wanted to confront the widow but Giovanni had made him promise to keep away. 'Then you must leave Santa Lena,' Rico said. 'You are a fool if you stay, Gio. They will kill you.'

And then the man with the newspaper had arrived. The brothers saw it as a sign. God had delivered them an omen—Australia was to be their destiny.

For weeks now Rico and Giovanni had saved every lire they could. Apart from the money they gave to their mother from their weekly pay packet, and of course the small donation to the church each Sunday, they spent virtually nothing. They stopped drinking wine and gambling with the men at the camp and already they had saved enough to purchase a single boat passage from Genoa to the port of Fremantle in Western Australia.

It was agreed that Giovanni would go on ahead and Rico would join him within six months. 'That will give me time to marry Teresa when she returns from the chalet,' he said.

'What if she does not want to go to Australia?' Giovanni asked, but Rico laughed dismissively.

'Teresa will go to the ends of the earth with me,' he said.

It had been Rico's idea to choose Fremantle over Albany as their port of disembarkation. Fremantle serviced Perth, the capital city of Western Australia, and there would be more likelihood of job opportunities there.

Upon his arrival Giovanni was to find work and send money home to Rico and Teresa. When the brothers were reunited in Fremantle they would continue working until they had sufficient funds and then together they would set off for the eastern goldfields. These were Rico's plans.

One more month to go, Giovanni thought as he

carefully placed the cauldron of coffee to brew on the heated stones. He squatted beside the fire and pulled the tattered newspaper from his pocket. He carried it constantly and several times a day he would pore over the map of Western Australia, accepting with good humour the derision of his workmates. 'Giovanni and his treasure map,' they laughed. 'Giovanni and his gold at the bottom of the world.' But, unperturbed, he would simply smile back at them.

Unlike Rico, Giovanni's voyage to the bottom of the earth was more than a bid for riches. Australia was a whole new world to be explored. It was the other side of the earth, the biggest adventure a man could undertake. Beyond Santa Lena and the mountains there was a vast, brown land. That was what the newspaper called it. Giovanni could not possibly imagine what a vast brown land looked like, but the thought of it was thrilling beyond belief.

Giovanni checked the coffee and stoked the fire. It was late afternoon and soon the others would return from the digging. At the end of each working day one man went on ahead to the camp to build the fire and prepare the coffee. It was a pleasurable duty and they took it in turn. If the fire was not burning steadily and the coffee not well brewed when the others arrived, the man forfeited his next turn.

The air was clear and still, but bitterly cold, the feeling of snow imminent. Yes, he thought, there would be a heavy fall tonight. He fetched his concertina from the tent, sat beside the fire and played. He loved the way the sound rang out through the stillness. He started to sing. 'Torna a Surriento'. His favourite.

As Giovanni sang, he kept looking along the track which led to the work site. He could see no one. They would be another fifteen minutes, he guessed. Yes, the timing of the coffee was right. Then he caught sight of a lone figure in the distance, walking down the mountain track which led to the border.

He stopped singing. The boy must have been walking for a long time, he thought, it was an eight-hour trek to Steinach, which was the closest village over the mountains. He would offer him a cup of coffee, he thought. It would not be well brewed but it would be warm enough.

He stood and beckoned to the boy, who appeared not to see him. Giovanni walked towards the track to intercept him and then he realised it was not a boy at all. It was her. The beautiful girl who had crossed the mountain with Teresa.

'Come and warm yourself by the fire,' he said. 'There is coffee.'

The girl glanced at him vaguely. She looked tired, he thought, tired and cold. 'Have you come from Steinach?' he asked. 'You must be weary.'

She nodded and followed him to the fire where she put down her knapsack and squatted beside him. He stirred the half-brewed coffee and ladled some into a tin mug. 'It is not quite ready yet but it will warm you.'

'Thank you,' she murmured as she clasped her mittened hands around the mug and gazed into the fire. Then she noticed the concertina on the ground and glanced at him briefly. 'It was you singing.'

'Yes.'

'Ah.' Her gaze returned to the fire.

She had not recognised him, he realised. 'We have met,' he said. 'Two months ago, when you crossed the mountain with Teresa.' She looked at him blankly. 'Teresa is promised to my brother Rico,' he prompted. Still her eyes held no recognition. 'We talked, you and I. My name is Giovanni.'

'Ah. Yes,' she said, and her gaze returned to the fire.

She was more than tired, he thought, more than

cold. No longer was there laughter beneath her beauty. Her blue eyes no longer danced. They were lifeless, as if something inside her had died. He wondered what had happened and whether he should ask. He watched as she sipped the coffee.

'I am sorry it has not yet brewed,' he said. 'The second cup will be better.'

'It is good. Thank you.'

Giovanni could not help himself. 'What has happened?' he asked. And when she said nothing he persevered. 'You were happy when you crossed the mountain and now you come back over the mountain and you are sad. What has happened?' She looked directly at him for the first time, but still she seemed not to see him. 'Teresa is not to finish her work at the chalet for a further two months,' he said. Again it was a question but, even as he asked it, he felt guilty. He was prying. Something terrible had happened and the girl did not wish to talk about it.

She looked at him and there was a touch of defiance in her tone. 'I did not like the work,' she replied. 'I am going home.'

'Yes,' he said and he took the mug from her. 'I am sorry.' He started to ladle more coffee but she rose.

'I must go now.' She picked up her knapsack.

'No, don't. Please.' She stopped and looked at him and this time she seemed to see him. 'I am sorry,' he repeated.

'Why? You have been very kind. I am warmer now. Thank you.'

'Please stay. There will be heavy snow tonight. My brother and I have a tent, you will be quite safe, and you can continue your journey in the morning.'

'No. I must go home.'

She lifted her knapsack onto her back and he watched as she started down the track. He wanted to stop her, to entreat her to stay, but he knew it would be useless. He watched until she disappeared into the falling snow and then he once more attended to the coffee.

As he stirred the brew, steam rose in gusts from the pot and the strong comforting smell of coffee filled the air, but he hardly noticed. The image of the girl, sad and beautiful, haunted him.

CATERINA HAD SET out before dawn and cut across country from the chalet. It had been three hours before she had reached the track and, towards the end, her snowshoes had weighed more and more heavily with each step and her legs had felt like lead. The track, although steep in places, had been easier, firm underfoot, and it had been a relief to be free of her snowshoes. She was exhausted.

She had heard the concertina and the young man's beautiful voice long before she had seen the workmen's camp. She had not known where the music was coming from and she had not much cared, but the loveliness of the singer's voice was a comforting distraction.

Soon she must cut across country again, she thought wearily. She knew she would never reach home before sundown but, if she maintained her pace, she should arrive at her uncle's farm, which was much closer, just before dark. Caterina did not intend to go to the farmhouse. She would spend the night in the shelter of her uncle's barn and set off again before dawn; her uncle and his family would never even know she had been there.

She should probably have accepted the young man's offer, she thought. He was kind, he had a gentle face and she knew she would have been safe with him. But the company of people was more than Caterina could bear at the moment. Exhausting as the walk had been, the concentration on sheer physical effort had helped to blanket her mind. Even the young man's questions had been confronting and he did not know her. Caterina dared not think of how she would respond to her family's queries. She would tell them nothing. 'I did not like the work,' she would say. 'I wanted to come home.' Just as she had said to the young man. But of course they would sense something was wrong. And she would not be able to keep her silence forever. Only too soon she would have to tell them.

Caterina knew she was pregnant. For the full month of her affair with Paul her time had not come. But there was more than the physical evidence of her conception. There was the knowledge, deep within, that she carried his seed. Every time they had made love she had taken him into her wholly and unconditionally. In so becoming one, she had virtually willed the conception. To Caterina such uninhibited, joyful invitation had been part and parcel of their love-making and she had thought it had been the same for her lover.

Caterina had no plan. Indeed, there were no options open to her. She must simply throw herself upon her father's mercy and pray for the strength to bear her shame. But whatever the outcome, she would survive. And so would her child. Paolo's child. Caterina refused to believe that the love she had shared with Paolo was wrong. And if she and the child must bear the burden alone, then they would, she would make sure of that.

'ONE WEEK, GIO.' Rico clinked his tin mug of red wine against Giovanni's. 'Just one more week.'

'To the wide brown land,' Giovanni grinned. '*Salute*.'

'To the gold at the bottom of the world. *Salute*.' Rico had bought the bottle of wine to celebrate their last week at the camp, and the last visit Giovanni would pay the widow. Tonight Giovanni was to tell Sarina that when he returned to Santa Lena the following Saturday he must spend time with his family, that it would be at least a week before he could see her again. By the time she realised he had left the village it would be too late.

The brothers were sitting on their bunks in their tent, sleeping bags wrapped around them, the newspaper article spread out on the ground between them. The other men were drinking and gambling in the mess tent.

Giovanni and Rico toasted each other again and again, and when they had finished the bottle they felt heady with wine and excitement and love for each other.

An hour or so later Giovanni was loath to leave. The night was bitterly cold; it had been a long time since he had drunk alcohol and he was feeling the effects of the rough red wine. He wanted to stay in his cosy bunk and talk to his brother.

'Will you come to the village with me?' he asked. 'Company for the journey?'

'No, no,' Rico laughed. 'It is too cold. Go warm yourself in the widow's bed and I will think of Teresa and envy you.'

IT WAS NOT yet eleven o'clock when, from the upstairs salon, Sarina heard the door of the servants' entrance open and close. It could not be the servants. Guiseppina and Ernesto had retired well before ten as they always did. It could not be Giovanni. He never arrived until midnight and, in any event, he did not have a key—she always met him outside. Only she and the servants had a key. Then she remembered. There was one other person who held keys to the house. He always had . . .

She heard footsteps crossing the courtyard and, even before she stepped out onto the balcony, she knew who she would see.

'Mario,' she said. 'Luigi.' The brothers stopped in the centre of the courtyard beside the marble statue. Sarina stood erect in her red velvet gown at the top of the stone steps and tried to quell her rising fear. 'What has brought you to Santa Lena? I was not expecting you.'

Mario nodded for Luigi to remain where he was and slowly walked to the staircase. 'Disturbing news has reached us, Sarina.' Sarina stood her ground, although her heart was thumping wildly. The first step, the second, the third; slowly he mounted the staircase towards her. 'We need to talk, you and I.'

'Disturbing news, Mario?' She tried desperately to steady the tremor in her voice. 'What has happened?'

As he reached the top of the stairs, she backed away slightly. She could tell nothing from his eyes. They were black, impassive. Had he heard about Giovanni? But surely if he had there would be anger in his eyes. What did he want? 'You should have sent word,' she said, trying to smile. 'I would have had Guiseppina prepare a special supper.'

'You have defiled my brother's memory,' Mario said as he slowly circled her. Still his eyes were cold. She would have preferred to see anger there, but there was no emotion. Nothing. Terror struck Sarina. He was going to kill her. He was going to destroy her the way he would a dog that had not done his bidding.

'No, Mario, no. I swear . . .' She started to back away but there was nowhere to go. She felt the corner railing of the staircase dig into her spine.

'You have debased the name of De Cretico.' He did not touch her but his face was only inches from hers. 'You are a whore, Sarina. A *putanna* who gives her body to any man who can pleasure her. Was it worth it? Did the young Gianni satisfy you enough to warrant the degradation of my brother's memory?'

He even knew Giovanni's name. There was no point in denial. All she could do was plead for her life. Sarina started to sob. Painful, racking sobs of desperation.

'Please Mario . . . please . . . you do not know the loneliness . . . You do not know the life I have led in this house. I needed the boy. I needed . . .' She could not go on.

Mario looked at her as she wept pitifully, her body slumped, defeated, and he wondered that he had ever desired her. All these years he had hated her for the lust she had aroused in him, and where was her sexuality now?

Mario felt no sympathy for Sarina but the desire to watch her grovel for her life had gone. He had wanted her death to be tormented. He had wanted her to feel her life ebb away while she begged to be spared. Whether there was actually a spark of pity in him or not, Mario neither knew nor cared, but the relishing of her death was no longer important to him. He would not only make it quick and painless, he would even distract her from its imminence.

'You needed a man,' he said and slowly put an arm around her waist and drew her to him. 'You needed a man in your bed and yet you chose a boy.'

Sarina's sobs slowly subsided. There was something else in his eyes now. She tried desperately to read what was there.

'You always needed a man, Sarina.'

His mouth was very close to hers now and she could feel his body against her. Relief surged through every fibre of her being. He wanted her. That was it. How could a man kill the very thing he wanted? Mario had always desired her, she had sensed it. Even through her fear of him she had sensed it. And she had always wanted him. She remembered her fantasies as Marcello had made love to her. It had been Mario, always Mario. She closed her eyes and, as she felt him take her head in his hands, she opened her lips to receive his kiss.

The crack as her neck broke was audible. For a moment Mario stood bearing the weight of her body in his hands, then, adding just enough momentum, he let her go and watched her tumble in her red velvet gown down the stairs to land in a crumpled heap at the bottom.

He nodded to Luigi who had watched silently throughout. 'Fetch the servants,' he said.

When he met the three of them at the bottom of the stairs Guiseppina was standing to attention like a soldier awaiting orders, avoiding the sight of the body before her. Ernesto was not. Ernesto was staring open-mouthed at Sarina. He had obeyed his wife's instructions. 'The boy will be returning to Santa Lena soon,' she had said. 'I heard them talking. And when he does, the signora will become even more indiscreet and everyone will know. If we do not inform the brothers we will be seen as accomplices and instantly dismissed.'

Ernesto had never been particularly fond of Sarina. She was arrogant and dismissive, but such was the privilege of her class. 'What will they do to her?' he had asked.

'They will punish her, it is their right, but we must look after ourselves, Ernesto.' And, as always, Ernesto had given in. Why was he so shocked now, he wondered. Sarina's eyes stared up at him, surprised, questioning. And her lips were parted as if to receive a kiss. She looked as beautiful in death as she had in life. Perhaps it was her beauty which shocked him. Such beauty should have lived, he thought, lived and been admired. Ernesto wanted no part of it. But Mario was delivering his instructions.

'You saw the accident, the two of you,' he was saying. 'You saw your mistress trip on the uppermost step. You saw her fall down the staircase and when you ran to her aid there was nothing you could do.'

Guiseppina was nodding and Mario turned towards Ernesto. Ernesto felt himself nod back. 'The boy arrives at midnight, you say?'

'Yes,' Guiseppina answered, 'midnight on Saturday. He will come tonight.'

Mario checked the gold watch in his fob pocket. 'When we have taken the boy away, you will report this accident. You will say nothing of the boy.'

Guiseppina nodded again. '*Si, signore.*'

Mario, Luigi and Guiseppina all looked to Ernesto for his affirmation and Ernesto heard himself say, 'You must leave the signal for the boy or he will know there is something wrong.'

'What signal?' It was Luigi who asked. It was Luigi who had communicated with Guiseppina. 'You said nothing of a signal.'

Before Guiseppina could reply, Ernesto said, 'The signora always asked me to light the small lamp by the door to the servants' quarters. I think it was her signal that we had retired and that all was safe.'

Luigi turned to Guiseppina who did not dare look at Ernesto. 'I very often retire before my husband,' she said. 'I did not know of the signal.'

'Light the lamp,' Mario instructed.

The servants were told to wait in their bedroom until, through the shutters, they saw Mario put out the lamp. Ten minutes after that they were to report the accident.

While Mario and Luigi went out into the night to take up their vigil in the shadow of the stables, Guiseppina and Ernesto huddled together in the blackness of their bedroom.

'Why did you lie about the signal?' Guiseppina hissed. 'She never leaves a signal. She waits for him in the dark.'

'I will not be party to another death,' Ernesto

whispered back. 'It was wrong, woman, you should never have spoken out.'

'They will hunt the boy down anyway,' she said sullenly, unaccustomed to criticism from her husband. 'They will hunt him down and kill him.'

'At least we will not have laid the trap. We have given him the chance of escape and you should pray to God that he does. Pray for the salvation of your soul, Guiseppina. It is a bad thing you have done.'

GIOVANNI SAW THE lamp in the distance and he was puzzled. There was never a light left on in the big house when she was expecting him. She always waited in the dark. Sarina was sending him a signal. Had the brothers arrived? Was she warning him? It was certainly not worth the risk of investigation. He turned and doubled back, skirting around the fringes of the village towards his family's cottage.

'WHERE IS THE boy? Why does he not come?' Mario called the servants from their quarters. He and Luigi had been waiting in the snow for almost an hour and Mario was cold and irritable.

'He does not come every Saturday,' Guiseppina said. 'He will not come now, it is too late. He will stay at the camp.'

'Where do I find this camp?'

As Guiseppina told the brothers of the site on the side of the mountain where they were digging the new railway tunnel, she did not look at Ernesto. 'You will find him there,' she said.

IT HAD STOPPED snowing. The air was clear and the moon shone down on the camp, still and quiet in the dead of night. Mario lifted the flap of one of the tents. Four men asleep, two of them snoring heavily.

'Gianni,' he barked. 'Where do I find Gianni?'

One of the men sat up, startled. 'Eh? Eh? What is it, what has happened?' he muttered, groggy with sleep.

The silhouettes of two men stood framed in the moonlight at the mouth of the tent. 'Is one of you Gianni?' a voice demanded.

'Gianni? No. The next tent.' The man pointed to the right and, as the figures disappeared into the night and the tent was once more in darkness, he slumped back into his bunk. It sounded as if one of the Gianni brothers was in trouble. Or maybe it was just a dream. His bunk was warm and sleep was near. Just a dream, he thought, and soon he was snoring again.

'Gianni! Which of you is Gianni?' The sound of his name cut through his sleep and Rico awoke to see the shadowy shapes of two men in the tent.

'I am Gianni,' he said sitting up. 'Is something wrong?'

'Come with us.' The voice was authoritative and automatically Rico rose from his bunk.

'What has happened? How can I help you?'

'Come with us,' Mario repeated.

One of the other two sleeping men woke and propped himself up onto his elbow. 'What is it?' Fernando the Spaniard whined irritably. 'A man is trying to sleep, what is going on?'

'Nothing that concerns you,' Mario said. 'Come.' And Rico felt a hand of steel grasp his arm.

He tried briefly to struggle but another hand grasped his other arm. 'You. Stay here,' Luigi commanded Fernando. And, before he knew it, Rico was dragged out into the bitter cold.

Fernando was wide awake now. He watched as the men dragged Rico outside. Rico was wearing nothing but his long cotton underwear; he would freeze out there. Should he wake Natale? Fernando wondered.

Natale was snoring gently in the other bunk. No. Natale was the undisputed leader at the camp. Older and tougher than the others, he always acted as protector to the younger workers. He would want to interfere. This was not any of their business, Fernando decided. These men were bad men, he could sense it. Let Natale sleep on—he could sleep through anything. If Rico Gianni was in trouble then it was of his own doing and he must bear the consequences. In the dark, Fernando listened to the men's boots crunching in the snow.

Rico was half-carried, half-dragged to the gully beside the track which led to the work site. 'What is it?' he demanded, his teeth chattering from the intense cold. 'What do you want of me?' From the little he could see of the men's faces in the moonlight he did not recognise them. 'I do not know you.'

'But we know you, Gianni. You have defiled our family name.' Luigi released Rico's arm but, before he could struggle, Mario had locked both his elbows so hard behind his back that Rico felt any moment his arms would be ripped from their shoulder sockets. Mario nodded to Luigi who took a short length of steel pipe from his greatcoat pocket.

'She was not worth your life, Gianni,' Mario said. 'You are a young man and she was a whore. Anybody could have had her. We will not take your life.'

Rico's mind was racing. The De Cretico brothers. Of course. He recognised them vaguely now. He had seen them in the village years ago when he was a boy. They thought he was Giovanni.

'She was not even worth your manhood. We will leave you to sire children. But you must pay for defiling the memory of our brother.'

Luigi struck with the steel pipe and Rico screamed as his kneecap shattered.

'You must pay for degrading the name of De Cretico,' Mario continued.

As Luigi raised the pipe again, Rico wanted to scream, 'It was not me!' But he did not. He clenched his teeth and waited for the blow. Again the steel pipe struck and this time Rico did not cry out. He fell to the ground and lay groaning as his shattered knees sank into the snow.

'It will be a long time before you again walk up the hill to the big house,' Mario said.

They carried him to his tent and threw him to the ground. 'Crawl,' Mario said. 'Crawl inside to the warmth or you will die out here in the cold. Either way it matters little to us.'

The brothers left and it was only when Fernando could no longer hear the crunch of their boots that he shook Natale. 'Natale, wake up,' he begged. 'Something has happened.'

'Go away, leave me to sleep.' Natale swatted at the man as he would a fly. But Fernando kept shaking.

'Wake up, wake up.'

Natale was angry. Nobody woke him from his sleep. And certainly not Fernando the Spaniard. Natale sat up and was about to cuff the man when he saw Rico, clawing his way into the tent, his fingers digging into the ground, desperately seeking a purchase as, inch by inch, he dragged himself out of the cold.

'*Gesù Cristo*!' Natale sprang to Rico's aid. He rolled him onto his back and pulled him inside the tent. 'Blankets, Fernando, get blankets,' he ordered. Then he saw the blood seeping through the legs of Rico's rough cotton underwear and he looked at the mess that had been Rico's knees. '*Gesù Cristo*, what have they done to you!'

NATALE SAT WITH Rico and waited for sunrise when a stretcher could be safely carried down the rough mountain track. Throughout the final hours of the night, although he was in great pain, Rico remained conscious and he whispered the truth to Natale.

'If the De Cretico brothers find out it was me they crippled and not Giovanni, they will come after him,' he said. 'You must swear the men to secrecy, Natale. They do not need to know the truth but they must be sworn to secrecy.'

When dawn finally broke, Natale and another of the workers carried Rico down the mountain track to the village. Natale forbade the men to accompany them. It would call attention to the accident, he told them, and Rico did not wish that. The accident had happened at the work site, he stressed, and they were to say nothing more. Each of the men knew something far more sinister had happened but they respected the wishes of Natale and Rico and would keep their silence.

Natale led the way down to the village and to the doors of the Gianni cottage. He was not from Santa Lena but he had been a guest in the Gianni household on many a Sunday after church. Rico was his friend and Natale was ashamed that he had slept while this terrible thing had happened.

It was Vincenza Gianni, Rico's mother, who met them at the door of the cottage. 'Filomena! Ulanda! Giovanni!' she called as she ushered the men inside. 'Come! Come quick!'

The two young girls were the first to answer their mother's cries, their hands still covered with cornmeal from mixing the polenta. When Vincenza lifted the blanket and they saw their brother's wounds they screamed.

'There is no time for that,' Vincenza snapped. 'Heat some water, fetch me clean rags. One of you . . .' She looked at the two men. '. . . One of you fetch the medico.' Natale nodded to the other man. 'The white cottage three houses from the tavern,' she said. The man turned to go. 'The one with two chimneys!' she called after him.

Giovanni appeared at the back door, the axe he had been using to chop firewood still in his hand. 'Rico!' He dropped the axe and ran to his brother's side. Together he and Natale lifted Rico from the stretcher and carried him to the curtained-off section of the living area which housed his parents' bed.

As they eased him gently down, Giovanni was about to say something but Vincenza snapped an order at him also. 'Fetch me scissors, Gio.' Giovanni ran to do her bidding and Vincenza turned to Natale, her eyes burning with anger. 'Who has done this?' she demanded.

Natale looked at Rico. The jarring trip down the rough mountain track had sapped what little strength his friend had left and the pain was acute, but he shook his head slowly.

'It was an accident,' Natale replied.

'An accident! Hah!' Vincenza scoffed. 'This is no accident. A man does not have both his knees smashed like this in an accident!'

Giovanni returned with the scissors and Vincenza started cutting the fabric away from the wounds. 'Gio,' she ordered. 'Go! Go now! Fetch your father and your brothers. It may take four or five days, but you bring them back as quick as you can. They will want revenge.'

Giovanni knelt beside his brother. 'Who did this, Rico? Who did this to you?'

'There will be no revenge.' Rico's voice was weak but insistent.

'Of course there will be revenge.' Vincenza continued to snip away at the cotton. 'The Gianni family must avenge such an act. Your father would . . .'

'There will be no revenge, Mamma!' It was a command and Vincenza stopped, scissors poised. She looked questioningly at her son. Rico? The most headstrong of her boys? The first to wreak vengeance upon any who wronged a Gianni? What was he saying? 'Put down the scissors,' he insisted, 'and go and help my sisters.'

Vincenza was about to refuse. 'Please, Mamma,' he urged. 'I must speak with Gio. I will tell you all later, I promise.'

Giovanni remained kneeling by his brother, a sudden sick feeling in the pit of his stomach.

'They thought that I was you,' Rico said when their mother had left.

'The De Cretico brothers.' It was not a question. 'The De Cretico brothers did this.'

Rico nodded.

Giovanni's face was ashen. Shame overwhelmed him and he bowed his head. He could not look at his brother. '*Perduna mi*,' he whispered. Then he crossed himself. '*Dio mio, perduna mi*.'

Rico was weary and the pain was consuming him. If only he could sleep, he thought. 'There is nothing to forgive, Gio, it has happened.'

Hatred raged beneath Giovanni's shame. 'I will kill them,' he said. 'I will hunt them down and kill them, I swear to you, Rico.'

Rico looked at his younger brother. There was venom in Giovanni's voice and murder in his eyes. Giovanni of all people. Gentle, sensitive Giovanni who would never hurt a soul, who wanted only to sing his songs and play his concertina. This was not the same young man. This young man could kill.

'Listen to me, Gio, listen to me.' Rico summoned up his strength and his voice had the edge of authority to which Giovanni had always responded. 'You will do nothing.' Giovanni shook his head, but Rico continued. 'If you seek revenge you will bring a vendetta upon our family. There will be war between the De Creticos and the Giannis and they are too powerful for us. Would you have your father and your brothers killed?' His words had reached Gio, he could tell. 'You see? You must be sensible.'

Rico ignored the helpless rage he could see in Giovanni's eyes. 'The De Creticos have avenged their brother,' he persisted. 'To them the score has been settled. We will open no more wounds and you will leave the country as soon as possible.'

'No.' Giovanni rose to his feet. 'No, I will not leave and you cannot make me. If the brothers discover their mistake and wish to come for me, then so be it. I will not seek revenge, Rico, I promise, but I will not leave you.'

Rico was too weary and in too much pain to continue. 'Talk to him, Natale. I am tired.'

'We will talk when the medico comes,' Natale said. 'He will give you something for the pain, Rico, something to help you sleep. Rest now.'

When the doctor had been and gone and Rico was finally sleeping, Natale took Giovanni aside. 'We must talk, Gio.'

They sat on the back step of the cottage. It was cold without their coats and scarves but neither of them noticed.

Giovanni stared at the open woodshed and the chopping block where, less than two hours earlier, he had been happily chopping firewood. 'You will not persuade me to do my brother's bidding,' he said stubbornly. 'I will not leave his side.'

'You must. It is his wish.'

But Giovanni was not listening. 'Did you hear the medico? He said Rico may never walk again. And if he does he will be a cripple. Rico, a cripple!' Giovanni wanted to break down and cry but he fought against it. 'I did that to him, Natale. It should have been me. It should be me in there now, on that bed. It should be me.'

'Perhaps,' Natale nodded. 'But it is not. It is Rico.'

Giovanni put his head in his hands. He did not want Natale to see him weeping.

Natale said nothing for a while but, when he sensed that Giovanni was once more in control of himself, he leaned forward and spoke with great urgency.

'Last night as we waited for the dawn, we spoke, Rico and I. It helped take his mind off the pain. Now you must listen, Gio, it will help take your mind off yours.' Giovanni looked up at Natale, his eyes still wet with tears. 'You must use what has happened to make you a man, that is what Rico wants. You are a boy, Gio. You are only two years younger than your brother and yet you are a boy.'

Giovanni looked confused. Natale continued. 'Let us suppose you stay in Santa Lena and let us suppose the De Creticos realise their mistake,' he explained. 'Suppose they come one night and they cripple you too—what does that do to Rico? He has sacrificed himself for nothing.'

Giovanni stared back blankly at the older man.

'It takes two blows to break a man's knees, Giovanni. After the first blow Rico could have told them the truth. But he did not. It was his choice.' Natale could see that the boy was deeply shocked but he continued, brutally. 'He will never tell you this himself and if you ask him he will deny it. He doesn't want you to live with guilt. But you will not be a man if you don't make something of your life to repay your brother.'

Giovanni looked at the ground and nodded dumbly as he once again fought back the tears. Natale embraced him. 'Now weep, Giovanni. Weep. There is no shame in tears.'

LATER THAT DAY the whole of Santa Lena was agog with the news which spread like wildfire throughout the village. Sarina De Cretico was dead. A terrible accident. A senseless death. She had tripped at the top of the staircase; the servants had witnessed it.

The following day, further news set the tongues wagging. There was to be a grand funeral. The De Cretico brothers would be arriving with their families in three days' time, the servants said. They had sent word. And all arrangements were to be made for a ceremony of such pomp and splendour as had never before been seen in the village. Everyone was very excited.

'YOU MUST LEAVE tomorrow, Gio.' Rico was propped up in bed, a tent erected over his legs to keep the weight of the linen from his knees. Already he felt stronger, he said, and he scorned the doctor's prediction. 'Not walk? Rico Gianni? Hah, the medico is a fool. He can barely cure the animals he treats, what would he know?'

It was true the medico was really an animal doctor and, even in the area of veterinary science, his credentials were suspect. But he was educated. He could read and write and whether his potions were magic or medical miracles, he had saved many a life in the village so the peasants credited him with the title medico.

'Not only will I walk, Gio. I will run, I will jump. Maybe not as fast or as high as I once did, but still I will beat you in a wrestling match, you wait and see.'

Giovanni did not know how much of Rico's boasting was for his benefit or whether his brother genuinely believed his own bravado. But he knew he must not question it. 'Yes, Rico, sure,' he said.

Giovanni had given nearly all of their savings to

Vincenza, leaving just enough to get to Genoa. He would find work at the docks there and save again for his passage to Australia. 'Rico must go to a hospital, Mamma,' he had said. 'A big hospital in Milano where they have the best doctors who can mend his legs. As soon as I leave you must arrange it.'

'Tomorrow, Gio,' Rico insisted. 'You are leaving tomorrow, *si*?'

'*Si*.'

'You have the money?'

'Yes, I have the money.'

Rico grinned. 'Find gold, Gio. Get rich. And when you are rich, Teresa and I will come and join you.'

'Yes, Rico.'

They hugged each other and there were tears in Rico's eyes as he held his brother tightly to him. 'Find gold for me, Gio. Find gold for me at the bottom of the world.'

BOOK TWO

The Miners
1900

Chapter Five

Maudie Gaskill stepped out of the Kalgoorlie branch of the National Bank of Australasia into the dry and dusty heat of Maritana Street. She held her hand up to her eyes to shield them from the shock of sunlight. Although it was late afternoon the glare was relentless and the heat oppressive. It was a goldfields midsummer.

She rounded the corner into Hannan Street. It was Friday, payday, and the bank had been busy. Maudie paid her staff every second Friday. The same Friday that the bank paid out the gold sovereigns preferred to banknotes by many of the contract miners. As usual on a late payday afternoon, the main street of Kalgoorlie was bustling with activity. Fashionably gowned women in ornate hats were strolling along the pavements towards the Palace Hotel. Others, in bonnets and worn cotton dresses, were shopping with their children, scrounging in their purses for the last pennies to buy a bargain. Men in wide-brimmed hats, well scrubbed after their eight-hour shift in the mines, were on their way to the pubs for a hard-earned beer and a game of billiards.

Fashionable sulkies drawn by pairs-in-hand shared the street with heavy drays hauled by Clydesdales and men on horseback from out of town. A man in a passing trap doffed his hat to Maudie and the woman beside him gave a graceful wave of her gloved hand. Richard 'Lord' Laverton and his wife, Prudence. Laverton was the General Manager of the Midas Mine and one of Kalgoorlie's elite. He wasn't really a lord at all, but his father was. Lord Lionel Laverton of Hampshire, England, was chairman of the mine's London board of directors. Having given his youngest son an Oxford education and a place in the family firm only to discover that the boy was a wastrel, he had bought Richard an important position in Kalgoorlie, hoping that the rigours of Australia might make a man of him. The people of Kalgoorlie were dutifully impressed and, although the upper echelons were aware that Richard wasn't really a lord in his own right, they were quite prepared to grant him the title. He was General Manager of the Midas, after all. That in itself made him one of the hierachy, and no one could question the fact that he was genuine aristocracy.

To be openly acknowledged in the street by Lord and Lady Laverton was an indication of one's standing in Kalgoorlie society, so when they waved to her from their passing trap, Maudie waved back. It meant little to her personally but it was good for business. As she looked down Hannan Street, many passers-by smiled a greeting, doffed their hats or openly called, 'Afternoon, Maudie', and she nodded to each in return.

Everyone knew Maudie. And not just because she owned one of the most popular pubs in town. Maudie Gaskill was physically imposing, a person who stood out in a crowd. Five feet ten inches in her stockinged feet, she had a build to match and was as strong as a man. Hers was not a handsome face. Having spent all of her life in mining towns, the outback sun had weathered her skin and squinted her eyes and she looked a good ten years older than her twenty-nine years. But Maudie was not ugly. There was humour in her eyes and bravado in her carriage. With her thick brown hair drawn back in its customary bun at the nape of her neck and her black straw bonnet adding extra inches to her height, Maudie was an impressive woman.

She and her mother, Iris, had been two of the first women to arrive at the goldfields. After the death of Iris's husband, Bill, they had stayed on in Coolgardie and run a sly grog shop. Until the discovery of gold by Paddy Hannan and his partners in 1893. Then Iris and Maudie had sold up and joined the Kalgoorlie goldrush. But they did not mine for the precious metal. Alongside the other merchants, they set up their shop: a wooden-fronted billboard announcing their wares and behind it, serving as home and store, a simple corrugated iron hut. Soon, however, word spread that in Iris and Maudie's hut, along with the sugar and tea, the flour and tinned goods, the kerosene and candles, the cheapest and strongest illicit liquor in Kalgoorlie could be purchased, but only on Sundays.

Was that only six years ago? Maudie wondered. She looked down the long, broad boulevard which was Hannan Street and marvelled at the changes. Of course there were some things that never changed. The camel teams still paraded through the centre of the township bearing their loads of precious drinking water and provisions and the endless wood supply for the mines' furnaces. In fact, the camels were the reason for the width of the street, the cameleers needing the space to turn their teams. And, of course, the dust never changed. The red, swirling, outback dust. Even as Maudie watched, a small willy-willy swept its way down the centre of the street. People stepped into shop doorways or turned their backs or simply stopped in their tracks and covered their eyes as the stinging funnel of dust swirled past. Then, seconds later, as quickly as it had ceased, the chatter and bustle of the street resumed and people continued to the relative comfort of the pavement and verandahs and shop awnings as if the willy-willy had never happened.

But it was only yesterday, Maudie thought, that there were no pavements, no verandahs, no shop awnings. Just squat hessian huts and lean-tos and corrugated iron sheds baking amongst the red dust. All goldrush towns grew quickly, but Kalgoorlie's growth seemed to have happened overnight.

Across the street was the impressive Palace Hotel, heralded as one of the grandest in the country. In the airy shade of its wide verandahs well-dressed ladies were sipping tea and affluent-looking gentlemen were drinking cold beer as they watched the passing parade. On the opposite corner was the Australia Hotel, its balconies overlooking the huge intersection of Hannan and Maritana Streets.

Maudie walked several blocks down Hannan Street. Past the confectionist and tobacconist. Past the barber's shop with its hairdresser's chair in the window. Past the drapers and the general stores and the Japanese-run laundry. She looked across the street to the newly completed York Hotel with its silver cupolas and stone arches.

Kalgoorlie was becoming an elegant town, thought Maudie as she pushed open the door to the main bar of the Lucky Horseshoe and breathed a sigh of relief at the movement of air from the two huge ceiling fans. The Lucky Horseshoe was hardly competition for the Palace or the Australia or the York, but it thrived. It was a miners' pub and it catered for the hard-working man. Despite the emblem of the silver horseshoe on its facade it was known to all as Maudie's.

The four o'clock shift was over and the bar was crowded. Noisy. The air was thick with miners' talk.

Business was good. Maudie nodded to the two barmaids and acknowledged the greetings from the men as she passed.

"Lo, Maudie.' At the end of the bar, near the doors which led to the billiard room and lounge and her offices out the back, a thickset man with ginger hair and a red bushy beard stopped her. 'Got time for a chat? There's something I'd like to put to you.'

'Evan. Hello.' Evan Jones was a Welsh miner with a lilting brogue that gave him away every time he opened his mouth. Not only was Evan's beard red, everything about him was red. A reddish-brown. His face, his hands, his clothes. Evan was an independent miner who worked his own small lease for alluvial gold. One could always pick the men who mined their own leases. They were 'dry-blowers'. The big mines, with their access to underground water, could flush the gold from the ore. But the dry-blowers still used the old-fashioned method of bellows, or they would shake the gold-bearing dust through mesh frames or simply shovel it into the air to separate the heavier grains of gold. Inevitably they ended up covered in red dust. Water being precious and bathing a weekly custom at best, the men took on the hue of the land.

Evan Jones was one of Maudie's favourites. Her father had given him his first job as a miner ten years previously in Coolgardie. In fact, Maudie had secretly set her sights on Evan when she had decided she should marry two years earlier. Like most men, however, Evan barely thought of her as a woman at all. She was just Maudie. Straight-talking Maudie. A good mate and a strong ally. So when Evan had returned from one of his regular trips to Fremantle with a brand-new wife, Maudie had heaved an inward sigh and decided that, if she was ever to marry, she would probably have to settle for Harry Brearley after all.

Of course, Evan Jones had no idea that Maudie had ever harboured feelings for him beyond that of mateship, and he was never likely to either—Maudie Gaskill was not one to wear her heart on her sleeve.

She looked at the clock above the bar. A good half-hour before the staff would line up at her office for the payout. 'Of course,' she said. 'Come out the back. A couple of beers, Alice,' she called to the wiry brunette behind the bar.

She led the way into the lounge with its brand-new billiard table of which she was very proud. Maudie's lounge certainly did not compete with the billiard rooms of the Australia and Palace hotels where full-time managers presided over championships and big-time gambling was promoted, but many a friendly wager was lost and won at Maudie's table on a Saturday night.

'Take a seat. What can I do for you, Evan?' She had gestured to one of the comfortable armchairs away from the billiard table where a group of men was laying bets on a game in progress. Then she realised that Evan was waiting for her to sit first. He was such a mixture of a man, she thought. Tough, strong, a man respected by other men and yet, with women, a gentleman. A little lacking in humour perhaps, but as honest as the day was long. A good man.

'How's Kate?' Maudie asked as she sat. 'Must be getting near her time.'

'Three weeks now.' An involuntary smile sprang to Evan's lips and the red beard twitched. 'Do you know when Harry'll be back?' Gentleman that he was, Evan was not given to small talk.

'Within a couple of months I'd say.' Maudie nodded to the barmaid who placed two beers in front of them. 'Thank you, Alice.' She undid the strings at her neck, raised her strong arms above her head, and carefully removed her bonnet, smoothing back the sides of her hair although there was not a strand out of place. 'He says he's raised enough funds for a half share in a lease and now he's looking for a partner.' Coincidentally, a telegraph had arrived from Harry at the post office just several days previously. 'Says he'll be back as soon as he's found someone to match his input.' Maudie downed most of her beer in one draught.

'By April, would you think?'

'Yes, I reckon he might. Why?'

'The lease he'll be wanting to buy, do you think he'd be interested in the Clover?' Maudie stared at him, amazed. 'I said do you think he'd want to buy the Clover?' he repeated.

'You want to sell your mine?'

Evan Jones? Selling out? It was unbelievable. Evan had been mining the Clover for six years, the last three of them on his own. His partner had opted for the security of contract work with one of the big mines so Evan had bought him out, and since then he had been the sole operator. A 'loner', as they were called. The Clover had had its ups and downs. A healthy yield one year, a poor yield the next but, amongst the ranks of the small leases, it was considered to have good potential. And Evan was a good miner who knew his business. The only mystery was why he hadn't taken on a new partner with funds to extend the lease and develop the mine further. But Evan liked his own company, he preferred to be a loner.

'Why?' Maudie asked. 'Why do you want to sell the Clover?'

'Security. I'm signing up with the Midas. Starting April.' He took a hefty swallow of his beer. 'With the new baby I'll be needing security, you see.'

A tousle-haired five-year-old tottered up to Maudie and tugged at her skirts. 'Maudie, I'm hungry.' He reached up and grabbed at her beer.

'Uh, uh,' she said, rescuing the glass.

'Just a sip,' he begged. 'Only a sip.'

'All right,' she relented. 'Just one.' She held the glass while the child took a gulp. He screwed up his face—he didn't really like the taste, he just wanted to be grown up. 'Go and see Dickie in the kitchen and tell him to give you two biscuits. And Jack,' she called after him, 'only two, mind, you're not to spoil your tea.'

Evan watched the boy go. 'Harry must be missing him,' he said.

'Yes,' she replied. 'He idolises the boy, even wanted to take him to Perth.' She downed the rest of her beer. 'God only knows what Harry gets up to when he's out there "raising investment". That's what he calls it you know, "raising investment". Gambling's what I call it. And he wants to take his son along! I ask you! Jack's only five! I wouldn't have it, put my foot down. No good for the boy.'

'Harry's got a real find in you, Maudie, you're a good mother to the child.' Evan took several swigs of his beer and grinned. 'If the man has half a brain he'll marry you quick smart before somebody else snaps you up.'

Evan's attempts at humour were always clumsy, so Maudie changed the subject. She didn't like talking about herself anyway. Good heavens, she thought, it wasn't as if Harry hadn't proposed to her often enough. She'd been the one to set the ground rules. 'Mend your ways, Harry,' she'd said. 'Give up the gambling and make a success of your life, then I'll marry you.'

But she knew she'd give in, and soon, even though she suspected Harry was marrying her for her money. She wanted to be Jack's mother, she loved the boy deeply. And she wanted a child of her own. Yes, she'd marry Harry Brearley and she'd be carrying his child before she turned thirty. That was her plan. If Harry hadn't changed his ways by then, Maudie would set about doing it for him.

'Have you thought about taking on a partner?' she asked.

'Yes, I've thought about it.'

'What about Harry?'

'No.' There was no hesitation in his answer. 'No offence, Maudie. I know he's your intended and he's a good man, but he'd not be the partner for me.'

Maudie was not at all offended, she'd known what the answer would be even as she'd asked the question. Harry was not a 'good' man at all and it was kind of Evan to say that he was. Not that Harry was a *bad* man but, for all his charm, he was definitely lacking in moral fibre.

'No, I'll not be taking on a partner,' Evan continued. 'I've made up my mind and it's the Midas for me. Kate's been living my life for eighteen months now and it's no life for a woman.'

Maudie said nothing. She and her mother had lived the lives of miners' women for years. A humpy in Ballarat to start with, when Maudie was just a child. Then, in '88 when they'd come west to the Yilgarn goldfield, they'd lived in a bough lean-to in Southern Cross until the move to Coolgardie and the hessian hut. They hadn't even had the luxury of corrugated iron until her mother had insisted on setting up a shop.

'Listen to your cough, Bill,' she'd said to her husband. 'Your lungs aren't going to see out the day.' God, her mother had been tough. But so was Bill. 'I'm no shopkeeper,' he'd insisted. 'I work under the ground, woman. It's where I live and it's where I'll die.'

Eventually Iris had stopped nagging. 'So give me some of the money you pour into the mine,' she'd said, 'and I'll do it myself. One day you'll drop dead underground and who's going to look after Maudie and me then?'

It wasn't that her mother hadn't loved him. She'd loved him so much that when he'd died—underground as he'd said he would—she'd refused to take another man. And there had certainly been offers. Although she'd been well past her prime then, there were few women on the goldfields and Iris was a good cook and a hard worker. 'We can do it on our own, Maudie,' she'd said. And they had, until she'd died, two years ago. How Maudie missed her mother.

Evan could sense Maudie's criticism. 'I know, Maudie. I know you and Iris did it. But you two were a breed apart. It's not the life for Kate.'

Maudie couldn't help it. Fleetingly she thought, 'If he'd married me he wouldn't be giving up the Clover; if he'd married me he wouldn't be selling his soul to the Midas.' Then she stopped herself. Stupid thoughts. Besides, she persuaded herself, Evan would probably have bored her. For all his faults, Harry always made her laugh.

'I'm going to work my way up to shift boss within the year,' Evan continued. 'And I'm going to rent a house near the mine. They're nice houses those, Kate'll like that.' He rose from the table. 'I'll get you another beer.'

'No,' she said as she stood. 'No, thank you, it's payout time and I must get on with the wages.'

'So do I wait and give Harry first option to make a bid then?' Evan asked.

'Yes. He'll make a bid, and it'll be the right one. I can guarantee it.' It was a golden opportunity for Harry. And Maudie knew it. She also knew that Evan was making the offer not for Harry but for her. If Harry had a partner and funds to extend the Clover he could become a wealthy man and, as such, he would be an infinitely better marriage prospect. 'I can pay some of the price up front if you wish,' she said. 'Cash.'

'Not necessary.' He extended his hand. 'Your word's enough.' She was a good inch taller than he was and her handshake was as strong as any man's. 'Do you want to come out and have a look at the mine? You've your father's eye. You'll be able to tell she's a good buy.'

Maudie grinned. 'Are you willing to risk it?' Most of the miners would not allow a woman underground—it was considered bad luck. As usual her grin was infectious. The stern face lit up and the slits of her eyes sparkled with mischief. Like everything about Maudie, her grin was impossible to ignore.

Evan laughed, a short bark. 'Put on those trousers you used to wear down your dad's mine and nobody'll know the difference.'

'I'll be there. Monday, noon? Mind if I bring Jack?'

'Monday noon. Yes, of course, bring Jack.'

'CAN I DRIVE, Maudie? Let me drive. Please.'

Maudie passed Jack the reins and, as he leaned forward in the sulky, she tucked one hand firmly into the back of the boy's trousers. 'It's not a race, Jack. Let the Princess go at her own pace,' she said as he tried to urge the horse on, clicking his tongue and flicking the reins.

Jack did as he was told but every now and then, when Maudie was looking out over the short dense scrub and he thought she wouldn't notice, he gave a quick flick of the reins. He was incorrigible, thought Maudie. Just like his father. Incorrigible and wilful and downright irresistible. With his freckles and his unruly mop of curly hair flecked gold by the sun, he was a typical goldfields urchin, a 'dappled' boy. He looked up, caught her eye and smiled his baby-toothed, gappy smile. She couldn't resist smiling back which only encouraged him and he started clicking the horse on again. She took no notice.

They were just out of town, on the dusty track leading north, and the old white horse was trotting slowly and steadily, automatically avoiding the rubble and potholes. Maudie didn't worry about the Princess. The Princess barely needed a rein at all, she responded to Maudie's voice more than anything.

'Good girl, Princess, good girl,' Maudie said. The old mare took no notice of the boy.

The Princess was over twenty now. She'd been an eight-year-old when Bill Gaskill had bought her in Albany, the first purchase the family had made after stepping off the steamship from Melbourne. Maudie could remember vividly the trek from Albany to Southern Cross. The Princess pulling the dray laden with provisions, Maudie and her mother and father walking along beside. Mile after mile, day after day, through the saltbush and the spinifex and the hot, red outback dust. It was impossible to escape the dust, Maudie remembered. She could still taste it. It got in your mouth and your eyes and your hair. The precious water in their tank was reserved for drinking only, so they would try to camp whenever possible near a waterhole or clay-pan in order to wash. But even then the water was muddy with dust.

'Look, Maudie, a camel team!'

Jack was nudging her and pointing up ahead. 'Give me the reins,' she said. 'Walk on, Princess, walk on, girl.' She edged the sulky to the side of the track and eased the horse down to a walk. As the camel team approached, Maudie kept calming the mare. 'Easy girl, walk on, easy.' Like most horses, the Princess did not like camels.

It was a small team. Twelve beasts harnessed in pairs hauled a massive, heavily-laden wood cart, urged on by three turbaned Afghan cameleers walking alongside. They were taking firewood to The Golden Mile, just south of Kalgoorlie. Most of the big mines were centred around the aptly named Golden Mile, where the rich gold-bearing lodes ran deep beneath the earth's surface.

The camels curled their lips, gnashed their teeth and spat as they passed by. 'Whoa, girl, easy girl, good girl.' Maudie eased the Princess to a standstill. The mare was snorting nervously.

Maudie pulled her travelling veil down over her face as the wood cart trundled by and the dust swirled up. She wondered how long it would be before the camel trains were a thing of the past. Soon all the big mines would be bringing in their wood supplies by locomotive-driven steam trains. And as for water—much of which was transported by camels—well, if the government scheme was to prove successful, water would be supplied by pipeline from Mundaring Weir near Perth. They said that the dam was nearly completed, that next year they would start laying the pipes. And they said that the water would reach the goldfields by 1903. But, like many, Maudie would believe it when she saw it.

As far as the Kalgoorlie pipeline was concerned, local opinion was divided. Some thought that O'Connor, the government's chief engineer and designer of the scheme, was a genius. Others thought he was a madman with delusions of grandeur and that the politicians were fools to listen to him. To Maudie, the thought of water being pumped through three hundred and fifty miles of pipeline simply seemed impossible.

'Walk on, Princess.'

Maudie once more allowed young Jack to take over the reins and again she turned her attention to the surrounding countryside. She always loved getting out of the township, away from the bustle of the people and the noise of industry.

All about her was the endless red desert of low spinifex scrub, saltbush and clumps of hardy Australian gum trees which somehow thrived under the seemingly impossible conditions.

Ahead of her lay a shimmering heat haze, through which the uninitiated would swear they could see a vast lake. Behind her, Kalgoorlie was an oasis in the midst of a treacherous landscape, a tribute to man's survival in an unforgiving land. Without shelter or water, a man would quickly perish at the mercy of the elements—many had, their bones bleached white by an unrelenting sun. How the Aboriginal tribes survived in such a wilderness was beyond the comprehension of the white man, but survive they did. In fact, the two local tribes, rarely seen en masse by the townspeople, thrived happily on a land that had yielded up to them its secrets over thousands of years.

Beyond the safety of Kal, the question was purely one of survival and, should a stranger arrive at one of the hardy outlying farms, never a query was made as to where he had come from or where he was going. Even his name was immaterial. The only query of any importance was, 'Need water, mate?'

Maudie looked back at Kal where the clouds of smoke from the mills and the distant stamp of the grinders announced the industry of the Golden Mile. She thought of the ladies in their picture hats sipping tea at the Palace Hotel and the gentlemen parading the streets and tipping their hats at the passing gentry and she smiled. How unimportant it all was. The desert always got things in proportion, she thought as she watched a wedgetail eagle soar several hundred feet up in the sky.

It seemed strange that such a barren-looking place

as the Clover could have a name at all. Just the customary red outback earth with its scrub and eucalypts, its salmon and coral gums and mulga and gimlet trees.

Evan was waiting for them by one of the three windlasses. He'd been working since dawn. He walked over to the trap to help her but she'd already jumped to the ground before he got there so he lifted Jack down.

'Welcome to the Clover,' he said. 'You wore the trousers. Good.'

'I'm certainly not climbing down mine shafts in my skirts,' Maudie answered as she took off her hat and detached her travelling veil. 'I see you have three.' She gestured at the windlasses, the wooden pulley systems erected over each of the shafts.

'Four. There's another over there behind the house.' He pointed to a clump of eucalyptus trees and Maudie noticed 'the house' nestled amongst them. It wasn't a house at all—it was a humpy, a bush shelter made of timber and corrugated iron. Yes, Evan was quite right, she thought. It wasn't the place for a woman to nurse a small baby; he was quite right to sign up with the Midas. She was a little surprised that he hadn't built something more substantial for his wife, but then she remembered that, like her father, Evan lived beneath the earth and poured all of his money into his mine. And he'd been a loner so long he'd probably forgotten how uncomfortable living in a humpy could be.

'When you've had a look at the mine, come up to the house and have a cup of tea with Kate. She rarely has female company.'

Maudie would rather have avoided the social visit, but she knew she couldn't. She'd met Kate only once, and then briefly, and she didn't feel they had much in common. Evan rarely brought his wife into town and when he did it was never to the pub. On the occasion when they'd met in the street Maudie, normally comfortable with her size, had felt huge and raw-boned and somehow awkward beside Evan's beautiful young wife.

They fed the Princess condensed water which Evan kept in stock for his own two horses and Maudie instructed Jack to stay with the sulky.

'I want to come down the mine,' he said.

'Look after the Princess,' she ordered and turned her back before he could argue.

Evan climbed ahead of her down the makeshift ladder to the first level about ten feet below, then slithered on his rump along a rough slope to the next ladder which led to the bottom of the shaft. He thought briefly about helping Maudie, guiding her feet to the safety of each rung, but decided not to. Hell, Maudie was as capable as any man. It was difficult to think of her as anything other than a man at the best of times.

At the bottom of the shaft, twenty feet below the earth's surface, he handed her a 'spider', a wire candleholder which could be hung on the rough crevices of the rock face while a miner worked. He lit a candle for each of them and pointed to one of the two short tunnels leading off the main shaft.

'This is the drive I'm working at the moment,' he said. 'Quite a strong leader, take a look.'

The tunnel was supported by poles of gimlet gum. Maudie crawled several feet inside and held her candle close to the rock face. She remembered, briefly, the wave of panic which had engulfed her the first time she had ever been down a mine.

'Claustrophobia, Maudie,' her father had explained to her. 'Some people never get over it. And some people can't live without it,' Bill Gaskill had added with a grin. 'It's the pulse of the land itself—you can feel it.' And he'd placed the palm of her hand on the rock face. 'Feel it, Maudie, feel its heart beat.' She'd never been frightened under ground again.

In the light of the candle, Maudie recognised the vein of quartz. She also recognised much of the surrounding rock as dolorite, a greenstone formation often containing gold. All the promising signs her father had taught her to recognise.

'Yes, it looks good,' she said as she backed out of the tunnel into the main shaft. 'Very good.'

Evan led the way back up the shaft and, as they walked to the house while Jack ran on ahead, he instructed her. 'If Harry pegs out more ground, tell him not to extend west. Too close to saltbush country. Out of the greenstone belt.'

He pulled aside the hessian curtain which served as a front door and ushered Maudie and Jack in ahead of him. 'Kate,' he called, 'our visitor is here.'

The interior of the hut was as crude as the exterior although Evan had made several improvements since his marriage.

The iron stove in the corner had been added. Prior to that he'd cooked his meals outside over an open fire. And he'd added floor coverings. They were made of used filter cloths discarded by the big mines. After several ore crushings had been pressed through them, the filter cloths became stiff and unusable and they served as flooring in many a miner's home. Evan had even built a bedroom onto the rear of the hut. No longer did he sleep in his swag on the dirt floor. But the rest of the surrounds were as basic as they had been for the past six years. The homemade table and chairs, the hanging chaff bag which served as a larder to keep the foodstuffs away from the endless ants. The cooking utensils of billy cans and cut-down kerosene tins. Maudie recognised them all: it was the way she had lived with her mother and father for years.

There was a display of femininity in the room though. The rough wooden table was covered with a lace cloth and neatly set out was a china teapot and cups. Probably Kate's pride and joy, Maudie thought, touched; Evan would certainly have used tin mugs. And the smell of fresh-baked scones hung in the air.

'Kate?' Evan called. She was nowhere in sight. 'Kate?' He crossed to the hessian curtain which led to the bedroom and pulled it aside. 'Oh my God!' Maudie heard him call. 'Oh my God, the baby!' and she rushed to his side.

The woman was lying on the stretcher bed. Beneath her skirt, her raised knees were spread wide and her arms were above her head, gripping the bedposts as she writhed in pain. Her hair was matted and her face and the thin cotton blouse she wore were drenched in sweat.

Evan knelt by her side and smoothed her hair back from her face. 'Kate? Kate?' He looked up at Maudie, panic-stricken. 'It's three weeks till her time,' he said.

'Oh no it's not.' Maudie knelt by the bed, nudging him aside. 'Jack, go and look after the Princess,' she called over her shoulder. 'Bring me water,' she ordered, 'and clean cloth.' Evan rose, confused, uncertain; he did not want to leave his wife. 'Hurry up, man. Hurry up.'

When he returned she barked further instructions at him. 'Boil water. Sterilise a knife. Bring me thread. And cloth. More cloth. Much more.'

'When did it start?' Maudie asked as she bathed the young woman's face.

'Dawn,' she whispered. 'The first big pain.' Her face contorted with agony as a fresh spasm seized her. 'I . . . was not sure. I did not want . . .' Another spasm. She was panting with the effort of talking. '. . . To worry him.'

'Don't talk any more,' Maudie said. 'Try and breathe

steady, slow.' Over seven hours, she thought. The woman had been in labour for over seven hours. She'd made scones and set out her tea service while the contractions had intensified. Obviously she was tougher than Maudie had given her credit for.

But something was wrong, Maudie could sense it. The labour was heavy, the baby wanted to come. She raised Kate's skirts. The woman had prepared herself and removed her undergarments. She was fully dilated and the baby was coming. But something was stopping it.

Evan returned with more cloth. 'Pull the curtain aside,' Maudie ordered, 'it's too dark in here. And light candles, I need light.

'Breathe easy, breathe easy,' she said gently as she eased her hand inside the woman's vagina. She could feel the baby, but not its head. It was upside down in the womb.

'Don't push,' she said. 'Don't push.' The woman's face was a mask of pain. 'The baby's coming out the wrong way. I'm going to have to turn it.' Kate nodded. 'Scream if you like.'

Maudie pushed her hand deep into the woman's womb. She felt for a leg. There it was. Where was the other?' Kate's jaw was set and she was staring up at the roof of the hut. 'Scream,' Maudie urged. 'Scream—it'll help.'

But she didn't scream. Apart from a regular panting hiss from between her clenched teeth, the woman didn't utter a sound. She's got guts, Maudie thought, she's certainly got guts.

At last. There it was. She'd found the other leg. It was twisted around the umbilical cord.

It took Maudie several minutes to disentangle the leg. Minutes that must have seemed like hours to the woman in agony, but still she did not cry out.

Evan returned with the hot water and the knife and

thread. 'I'm turning the baby,' Maudie said as she saw his ashen face and the fear in his eyes. 'It was coming out the wrong way.'

Evan tried to take his wife's hand but she shook her head and clung to the bedposts with an iron grip, her knuckles white. He knelt beside her, feeling frightened and useless. 'Wipe her brow,' Maudie said. 'It's turning. It's turning, Kate.'

Maudie's eyes were stinging from her own sweat now. She fumbled and pushed and it seemed an age when, all of a sudden, the baby slipped from her grasp and magically she could feel the head in the palm of her hand. Thank God, she thought. 'Push, Kate,' she said withdrawing her hand. 'Push!'

The woman filled her lungs with air and pushed. The baby's head appeared. Again she pushed. And again and again. The head, the shoulders. Her face a mask of pain, she pushed and pushed and suddenly the whole slithering mass of baby appeared in Maudie's lap.

'Good girl, good girl, well done,' Maudie said, smiling with relief. 'Knife.'

As she spanked the baby and busied herself tying and cutting the umbilical cord Maudie didn't notice the bleeding. Neither did Evan. He was too busy mopping his wife's brow and murmuring encouragingly.

'It's a girl,' Maudie said, placing the newborn infant on its mother's breast. But something was wrong. The woman's eyes were rolling back in her head. She was trying desperately not to pass out. Then Maudie saw the blood gushing from between Kate's legs.

The placenta, Maudie thought. There was no placenta. Just blood. Pouring out of the woman onto the bed. Spilling onto the floor.

Maudie thrust the baby at Evan. 'She hasn't contracted,' she said urgently. 'She'll bleed to death if we don't get the placenta out.'

'Oh Jesus, oh sweet Jesus.' Evan watched with horror as the lifeblood poured from his wife.

Once again Maudie plunged her hand into the woman's womb. She groped for the bag. There it was. She pulled out her fist and the bloodied placenta came with it. The bleeding stopped as quickly as it had started and Maudie gently eased Kate's stiffened knees down onto the bed. The woman's eyelids were fluttering, but she fought to remain conscious. She released her grip on the bedposts and signalled for Evan to pass her the baby. He supported the infant while she held it to her breast, feeble, exhausted.

Neither Maudie nor Evan noticed a small figure appear beside the open hessian curtain. But Kate did, and a slight smile played on her lips. When Maudie turned to see what had gained her attention she thought at first the child must be Jack.

'Paolo,' the woman whispered. 'Do not be frightened.'

A small boy of six or seven stood there, his eyes wide with shock at the sight of so much blood. Of course, Maudie remembered, she'd heard that Kate was a widow and had a son by her first marriage.

'It is all right, Paolo,' Caterina whispered. 'You have a sister.'

Just before she slipped into unconsciousness, Caterina wondered whether Evan would mind too much that his firstborn child was a girl.

Chapter Six

When Caterina had arrived in Fremantle in the late summer of 1893 she had been heavily pregnant with Paul's child.

She'd stayed with her uncle and his family, as had been arranged, until after the birth, but she knew that she was tolerated rather than welcomed. She knew that her aunt and uncle did not believe she was a widow, as her father had told them in his telegraph. But then Franco Panuzzi had not expected his younger brother to believe such a story. He had told Caterina as much when he had given her the substantial amount of money the family could ill afford.

'You will pay my brother a weekly sum for your food and lodging,' he had said, 'and for appearances' sake he will believe your widowhood. It is a matter of family honour that he does so. But as soon as you can support yourself and your child, you must cease to be a burden to him.'

Shortly after the birth, Caterina had spent several hours a day trudging around Fremantle in search of work while her aunt cared for baby Paolo. The main thoroughfare of the town, High Street, was active and vital. The town hall with its clock tower stood proudly at the top end and, down the bottom, on Arthurs Head overlooking the sea, stood the Round House, a solid circular stone building, once a prison. The backstreets in between were lined with tiny stone cottages and there was a pub on every corner. There were plenty of jobs to be had around town. In shops and bars and restaurants and the larger hotels where chambermaids and cleaners were constantly required. Caterina had worked hard on her English and could communicate well. It wasn't language or nationality differences that presented a problem. It was the baby that was the complication. Then, just when she was nearing despair, she walked into the Dockside Arms.

Fremantle was a man-made harbour built at the mouth of the Swan River. With no natural headlands to form an inlet, sandbars had been painstakingly dredged to create a land-backed inner harbour, and a long jetty snaked out into the deep water of the Indian Ocean. Steamers unloaded their goods at the jetty and vessels disgorged their hopeful passengers by the hundreds, many of them in search of gold. It was a rough port town with rough hotels and the Dockside Arms was one of them. Down near the wharf, it was run by a burly English couple, Mick and Mavis Forster, from the Midlands.

'Bless you, dear, I can look after the little one. I've six of my own, one still a toddler.' At forty-four, Mavis Forster had sadly acknowledged that her child-bearing years were over and she desperately missed a baby at her breast.

Mick had an eye for a pretty face and a bargain and Caterina represented both. The pretty face was good for custom and the offer of free accommodation meant he could pay her a pittance. Mavis also recognised a bargain—although she sometimes thought pretty girls brought more trouble than they were worth—and a full-time barmaid for the cost of a few shillings a week and the poky little room out the back was an extremely attractive proposition. Besides, she decided, she liked the girl. Behind the china blue eyes and the dimpled smile, the girl had spine, Mavis could tell. And of course there was the baby. As far as Mavis was concerned the baby clinched the deal.

'You could start as soon as you like,' she said in reply to Caterina's query. 'That's so, isn't it, Mick?'

'Sooner the better,' Mick nodded. 'Tomorrow, if you can. Lizzie leaves next week and you'll need to know the ropes by then.'

Caterina enjoyed her work at the Dockside Arms. Mick and Mavis were hard taskmasters but they were fair, and Mavis was wonderful with baby Paolo. So wonderful that Caterina felt an occasional twinge of jealousy—the woman spent more waking hours in the company of her son than she herself did.

Feeding times became precious, and as Caterina watched the tiny mouth, ferocious at her breast, she knew that everything had been worth it. And any hardship yet to come would be worth it too. This was the baby she and Paul had made, high up in the Alps, as they lay together in the narrow bunk, the snow outside blanketing the chalet. This was their son. Paolo.

Initially Doris, the other barmaid, had been wary of Caterina. Here was competition, she thought, wishing that plain Lizzie had not left to get married. Doris had rooms in a boarding house around the corner and conducted a lucrative business on the side. She didn't consider herself a prostitute. She only slept with men she fancied and then on the understanding that they gave her a 'present'.

Doris was a Cockney who admitted to being somewhere in her twenties but was really thirty-five. She had a hard, pinched little face and thin blonde hair which, when pulled tightly up into a chignon, accentuated her beakiness. But her body was neat and pert and when she flirted with the men, the promise in her eyes was attractive. Business was good, so long as there was no competition. Caterina's lush body and her thick auburn curls which refused to be restricted by pins or bonnets posed a definite threat.

Before long, however, it became evident that the Italian girl was not remotely interested in any form of personal relationship with the men, either for business or romantic reasons. Good heavens, Doris thought, the girl did not even dress to attract them. She seemed to own only two skirts which she alternated, and several blouses which she washed and ironed in the back kitchen. Doris was a very conscientious dresser and would never wear the same outfit two days in succession. She also believed in advertising her wares. She corsetted herself so tightly it was a wonder she could breathe and she favoured skirts that accentuated the line of her back, hinting at the pert round bottom beneath. Despite the fact that her blouses were as modest as fashion demanded, the tightness of her stays pushed her neat little breasts into such prominence that it was impossible to ignore them.

Doris noticed that, charming and affable as Caterina was with the men, as soon as they attempted to flirt with her, she ignored them. It was then that Doris, breathing a sigh of relief, decided to take the young Italian girl under her wing.

A strange friendship was forged between the two. Doris, who liked a good laugh, discovered that beneath Caterina's beauty was a well-defined sense of humour. And Caterina delighted in Doris's ability to shock.

'He's a dud, that one over there,' Doris would whisper, pointing to a well-built wharfie in the corner. 'All muscle and no show.' Or, of another regular: 'Big Ben I call him, built like a horse and a regular athlete in bed but he's a mean bugger. Expects to get it for a free dinner.' And Caterina would laugh and call Doris wicked which only encouraged her. But Caterina was grateful for the friendship. Although she pretended to be shocked, she knew that Doris was good-hearted and meant no malice. And Caterina had long since ceased to make judgements. If Doris wished to sleep with the men and accept their presents, where was the harm?

The Dockside Arms had an air of masculine conviviality about it. It was not the roughest of the miners' and workers' pubs. Apart from the occasional drunken brawl, it was usually peaceful and easy-going. The roughest pubs were the ones with the illegal gambling dens upstairs or out the back.

The Dockside Arms was one of several Fremantle pubs known as goldrush pubs. Many of the miners who drank there brought their gold to the city, some because they believed they got a better price, and some because their gold was stolen. Since the big mines had recently come into operation, gold theft was rife and if the theft was of considerable proportion, it was a lot safer for a miner to sell his illicit gold to one of the anonymous shady dealers in Perth who would ask no questions. Other miners came to the city merely for rest and recreation.

Drinking alongside the miners were the wharfies and the itinerant workers and the timbermen from the towns down south. Employed by the railways to cut sleepers for the constantly expanding rail tracks, the timbermen would come up to the city each month to get drunk, have a woman and gamble away most of their wages.

Caterina came to know the regular drinkers. And not just the shift workers who propped up the bar when their day was done. As the months slid by she recognised the timbermen who came to town for a long weekend every now and then. She always remembered their names and she was always good for a long chat when business was slow. Once the men realised that she was unavailable, they enjoyed the feminine company. They all lusted after her but they accepted the fact that they had to go to Doris if they wanted 'a bit of that' and when a newcomer who did not understand the rules overstepped the mark, he was quickly set straight by the regulars.

Caterina tried desperately to save money from the pittance the Forsters paid her. By stinting on her own food and clothing she finally bought a perambulator and Sunday, her precious day, was spent strolling down High Street, windowshopping, with Paolo in his pram. Or she would stand on Old Lighthouse Hill, look upriver to the Fremantle Bridge and the waterways which led to Perth and describe the view to Paolo as he gurgled away happily.

'We will go there one day, Paolo,' she would tell him. 'It is a beautiful city, they say. On a big round lake. And you can sit on a hill just outside and look down on the whole city and the lake and the beautiful trees. We will go there one day.'

But as the years went by, Caterina knew she was deluding herself. Paolo was now three years old; he could walk and talk. She could never give him the life she wanted while she worked at the Dockside Arms. She could find employment which would pay more, certainly, but who would look after the child? The answer was obvious. She must find a husband.

It was then that Caterina started to look at the men who drank at the pub in a different light. She was aware that very few of them were ideal as marriage prospects. But then, neither was she. Indeed, few men would be remotely interested in a woman with a child. But where else was she to meet a prospective husband?

Doris was immensely helpful. Not only because

Caterina's search for a husband posed no threat—a man willing to marry a woman with a small child was not a man looking for an erotic experience in exchange for a generous present—she felt a genuine sympathy for Caterina. In fact she wondered how in God's name the girl had survived for so long without the favours of men.

'We'll find him, don't you worry,' she promised. 'We'll find a good father for Paolo, one with money, you just wait and see.' Doris's only regret in finding the right man was the knowledge that she would lose her friend. She had become very fond of Caterina.

'YOU ARE A miner, Mr Jones, yes?' Caterina had not seen the man before and, when he introduced himself, he was obviously lonely and wanting to talk. His introduction had not been flirtatious, and the bar was not busy, so Caterina was only too happy to oblige.

'Is it that obvious then?' Beneath his bushy beard Evan smiled politely but he couldn't help feeling just a touch offended. He'd scrubbed the red dust from his body till his skin was raw, and bought a brand-new shirt, vest and jacket and he'd rather hoped that he looked like a businessman. His partner had recently informed him that he was leaving the Clover to work for one of the big mines and if Evan was to find a suitable replacement with money to invest, he needed to look successful. Not that he was sure he really wanted to find a new partner—the prospect of working as a loner was attractive.

Evan had told himself that a trip to Fremantle would do him good, but after two days, he was already wishing he was back in his humpy and working his mine. Big towns with crowded streets were lonely places. Strange, that. He never felt lonely when he was twenty feet beneath the ground's surface, just him and his pick and the earth with its promise of gold. Or sitting by his open fire boiling his billy tea after a hard day's work.

He'd stay for just one week, he decided. He'd play the successful businessman, visit several of the goldrush pubs where he may possibly find a prospective partner and then he'd head back to the goldfields.

But here was this young Italian barmaid immediately seeing through his disguise. 'And how did you know I was a miner, might I ask?'

'You come from Kalgoorlie, you tell me,' Caterina answered simply. 'All men from Kalgoorlie are miners, yes?'

'Ah. Well, I suppose they are that, yes.' The directness of the girl was charming.

At thirty-one years of age Evan had from time to time met beautiful women and he had always found them intimidating. But this girl seemed oblivious of her beauty and it was captivating.

'What is your name, Miss . . .?' he asked.

'Caterina,' she said. 'I am called Caterina.'

Caterina's mind flashed back to the Alps. The chalet. Mary. Mary had spoken like that. The same soft lilt. 'You are from Wales?' she asked.

'Yes, I am that. A long time ago. From Cardiff.'

A man signalled for service from the end of the bar and Caterina excused herself, but over the next several hours, when business was slow, she talked to the Welshman. And when he returned the following night, she talked to him again.

'He's keen, Catie,' Doris said approvingly. 'Very keen. You could do worse. But don't you go telling him about Paolo yet. Not until you've got him panting.'

Caterina felt herself blush. It was one thing to talk of finding a husband, but another thing altogether to be confronted with a man upon whom she should set her sights. And he was a nice man, Evan Jones, she could not be dishonest with him.

'SUNDAY TOMORROW. WANT to come out with me?' The Saturday-night rush was on and Evan had to raise his voice above the din. He felt conspicuous but nobody seemed to be taking any notice. 'We could catch the train to Perth and have lunch by the river, what do you think?'

Caterina tried to sound nonchalant as she poured the beers and called back loudly over the hubbub, 'Sundays I am with my son.' She looked briefly at him, noticing the surprise in his eyes. 'I have a little boy. Paolo.'

'Ah.' He nodded, sipped his beer and said no more. Half an hour later, Caterina noticed that he had gone.

'You're a fool,' Doris said after closing time as they wiped down the bar and washed the glasses. 'You're a fool, Catie. I told you not to say anything. It's the last you'll see of him, you take my word.'

But four days later Evan was back. 'I came to say goodbye,' he said. 'I leave for Kalgoorlie tomorrow.'

Caterina wished him a safe journey and it seemed there was nothing more to be said. But Doris wasn't prepared to leave it at that. As Caterina went about her duties and Evan got up to go, Doris sidled up to him and muttered. 'She's a widow, you know.'

'Eh?' He looked at her, taken aback.

'Catie. She's a widow. She needs a good man.'

He nodded and edged his way to the door, obviously unnerved by the confrontation.

Oh well, Doris thought as she watched him go, it had been worth a try. No harm done, he'd been a lost cause anyway. She simply hadn't wanted him to think that Caterina was a loose woman. Not that Doris herself entirely believed the story of Caterina's widowhood—the girl never spoke about her marriage or the father of her child. But she was certainly not a loose woman, of that much Doris was sure.

'DO YOU WANT to come out with me tomorrow?' It was six months later, a busy Saturday night in the late summer of 1897, and Evan was back.

He didn't know why he'd come back. He was no longer looking for a partner, he'd decided to work the Clover on his own. And he wasn't looking for a wife. Certainly not a wife with a young child. Somehow a trip to Fremantle had seemed like a good idea and, while he was there, what was the harm in seeing the girl?

'Tomorrow is Sunday,' she answered. 'Sundays I am with—'

'Yes, your son, I know. I thought we could take him with us. To Perth, what do you think?'

'Yes,' she smiled. 'We would like that.'

'PAOLO, THIS IS Mr Jones.'

'Evan. You can call me Evan.' He was a serious-looking little boy with straight fair hair and large grey eyes. 'How old are you, Paolo?'

The child held up four fingers and Caterina laughed. 'He will be four in two months,' she said as she pushed the boy's hair off his brow. 'He wishes very much to grow up fast.'

They travelled by train to Perth and Caterina marvelled at the beautiful coastline as it passed by. They walked down the broad avenue of St George's Terrace and she exclaimed at the gracious buildings. They had morning tea at the grand Palace Hotel and she gazed in wonder at the heavy oak interiors and the chandeliers.

Evan delighted in her childlike enthusiasm. There was more of the child in her than there was in the boy, he thought. Her enthusiasm was infectious. She was quite right, he decided, Perth was a pretty city, sitting sedately as it did on the banks of the peaceful Swan River. They explored the ornate and elegant town hall—convict-built he'd been told—and they walked up the hill to the army barracks, all the while chatting and clearly relaxed in each other's company. Even the serious little boy seemed to enjoy himself.

After that, Evan stayed on a full two weeks in Fremantle and each evening he went to the Dockside Arms. Several times he took Caterina and Paolo out to lunch during her half-hour break and one Sunday he even hired a sulky. They drove along the coast road, Caterina laughing and clutching her hat to her head as her curls blew free in the hot summer breeze.

Evan knew he must return to Kalgoorlie—he could not afford to spend so much time away from the mine—but he was in turmoil. Caterina enchanted him. Did he dare take a wife? It was something he had never planned. He'd always been a loner in every sense of the word. And the child. How could he take on the responsibility of a child? It had all happened far too quickly. He must get back to the safety of the Clover, he decided. He must have space to think clearly.

His departure was abrupt. 'I am leaving tomorrow, Kate,' he said. It was her lunch break and they had walked down to the main jetty to look at the harbour and the boats. 'Say goodbye to Paul for me.' He always called her 'Kate' and Paolo 'Paul'—he said he had trouble getting his tongue around fancy Italian names. He hoped she didn't mind.

Caterina didn't mind at all. She was very fond of Evan. He was a good man. A kind man. She knew he was falling in love with her and thought that, if he were to ask her to marry him, she might say yes. He would make a good husband and he would be a good father to Paolo.

She didn't listen to Doris, who warned her to be careful. 'He wears the same jacket and vest, Catie. And the same shoes—that's a bad sign. I'm not saying he's not clean, mind—his shirts are always fresh. But you need someone with more money, there are bigger fish in the sea, believe me.'

But Caterina paid no heed. 'Paolo likes him; he would make a good father.' Doris tried to interrupt but Caterina continued. 'If I tell him "yes", Doris, then I will tell him the truth. I will tell him that I do not love him, but that I will work hard to be a good wife.' Finally Doris gave up.

'Goodbye, Evan,' Caterina said, by now used to him disappearing as suddenly as he arrived. 'I will see you when you are next in Fremantle.'

SIX MONTHS LATER, something happened which made Caterina pray that Evan would return. Fremantle was too dangerous a town for a single woman with a small child. She needed a man's protection.

It was a Sunday evening. She had taken Paolo down to the harbour to watch the sunset over the ocean. The night was still and calm and the water rippled silver before them. There was a bank of cloud on the horizon and the sky was vivid with colour. Reds and oranges and pinks fanned out as far as the eye could see.

'Look, Paolo,' she breathed, 'look at our beautiful world.'

The child was staring out over the water, awestruck. He smiled up at her, his eyes wide with excitement, then returned to gaze again at the sky.

'It is magic,' she whispered. And he nodded.

She wanted to walk back to the hotel well before dark but Paolo begged to be allowed to watch the last rays sink below the horizon.

'Until the sun goes to bed, Mamma. Please. Just until the sun goes to bed.'

It was against her better judgement but Caterina allowed herself to be persuaded. As they walked back through the dockside streets, she started to regret it. She had forgotten how quickly the dark descended on these winter nights. It was not good to be out in this area after sundown, particularly not on a Sunday when the pubs were closed and the gambling houses with their plentiful supply of illicit liquor did a roaring trade.

'Hurry up, Paolo. Walk as fast as you can.'

It was a cloudy night, there was little moon, and the light from the streetlamps was gloomy. The walk to the Dockside Arms was uphill and the boy was tiring, so their pace was slow. Slow enough to attract the attention of the men passing by and those leaning in darkened doorways.

Only one more block, Caterina thought. And then she saw the group of men up ahead. She would have to pass them. To avoid them would mean cutting through a back alley and that would be more dangerous. She picked up the protesting child and quickened her pace.

The men were gathered on the pavement outside the Red Dingo. The pub was in darkness, it was not conducting its licensed trade, but she knew there were gambling rooms out the back.

There were twelve or more of them, roughly dressed, some in cloth caps, some bare-headed, and they were jostling each other. She could not hear what was being said, but the voices were angry; a fight was imminent.

As she drew abreast of them, Caterina hugged Paolo to her and walked well out into the street. The men were too intent on each other to notice her. She would soon be safely home, she thought.

'Bloody dago!' a voice shouted and the group suddenly split its ranks and formed a circle. Two men were in the centre, crouched, prepared to fight. Caterina was caught amongst the spectators. She tried to back away but the surrounding men did not notice her as they locked together to watch the fight.

'Get him, Bailey!' someone yelled. 'Get the scab!' And the fight was on.

The two men struggled briefly, locked in each other's embrace, before one gained the advantage. He forced himself free and drove his right fist hard into his opponent's solar plexus. The man fell to the ground moaning and the victor stood waiting for him to rise.

'Come on, Bailey!' the onlookers urged the man on the ground. 'Come on, get the scum!'

Bailey rose and charged, and the two of them once more locked together. But again the first man had the advantage and Bailey was smashed to the ground, blood oozing from his temple.

The mob didn't like it. They booed the victor and jostled each other as they jeered at their would-be champion. 'Come on, Bailey! What are you made of? Show the scab!'

Caterina felt herself stumble. Any moment she was going to drop Paolo. She grasped the man next to her to steady herself. He didn't even notice. 'Get up, Bailey!' he roared. 'Get up!'

The man who was winning scanned the onlookers as he waited for Bailey to rise, wary that a supporter may come to the aid of his adversary. Something seemed to suddenly catch his attention and for a second he remained frozen to the spot.

Struggling to stay on her feet, it was Caterina who saw the knife first. A flash of silver in the dim light of the streetlamps. She watched horrified as the man, Bailey, slowly rose to his feet. 'Dago pig!' he shouted and, knife held high, he hurled himself at his opponent.

As quickly as the mob had formed its circle, the men dispersed. Any moment the police would arrive. In an instant the street was deserted, except for the combatants. Bailey stood panting, knife in hand, and the man he'd called dago lay bleeding in the street, his face cut open.

In the melee, Caterina had fallen. She'd tried to support Paolo as she went down but she felt the child's head crack against the pavement. Then the boot of a fleeing man caught her in the ribs.

She struggled to sit up, a jarring pain in her side. 'Are you hurt, Paolo?' she whispered urgently. 'Are you hurt?' The boy was groggy and there was blood on the side of his face but he was conscious.

'Sssh. Do not cry. Sssh.' Caterina stood up. As she lifted the child to her hip a searing pain cut through her ribs but she took no notice. She ran, as fast as she could, up the hill to the Dockside Arms.

GIOVANNI HAD NOT seen the knife. He was too busy searching the faces in the surrounding circle, looking for the first sign of attack. Then he saw the girl. Or he thought he did. The girl from the mountain. It was her. It had to be her. But in the split second that his attention was caught, he saw her eyes focus on something. He turned. Too late. 'Dago pig!' he heard and the man was upon him.

Giovanni felt the knife rip his face open. There was no pain but the blood flowed instantly and he fell to the pavement.

As the onlookers fled, the man Bailey stood for a moment, disconcerted, unsure whether or not he should flee himself. It was all the time Giovanni needed. He flung himself at his opponent. Bailey was no match for him and Giovanni knew it. He grasped the wrist that held the knife and the man fell, the full weight of Giovanni on top of him.

Bailey still held the knife and, with both hands, he tried to force the blade towards Giovanni's chest, but his strength did not equal the Italian's. Giovanni sat astride him, locked his hands around the man's wrists and slowly twisted the knife until the tip of the blade rested under Bailey's jaw.

'*Vuoi morire*, eh? Eh? You wish to kill yourself? Let me help you.' Slowly Giovanni dug the knife into the flesh. There was a lot of give in the skin beneath the jaw and it was a second or so before blood was drawn.

Bailey was whimpering and trying desperately to release his grip on the knife, but the grip was no longer his—Giovanni's hands were over his own, forcing him to dig the knife into his own throat. A thin trickle of blood started to stream down his neck. It mingled with the blood that dripped upon him from the deep gash in Giovanni's cheek.

'Please. No. Please.' Bailey begged for his life.

'*Basta*? You have had enough?' Giovanni released his grip and the knife fell to the pavement. As he picked it up and rose to his feet he noticed his shirtfront was covered in blood. His face was starting to hurt.

For just a moment, Bailey lay in the street, surprised that his life had been spared. Then he crawled to his feet and staggered off into the dark.

Giovanni walked back to his lodgings, a boarding house only several blocks away. He gripped the gash in his cheek and held his head to one side trying to stem the bleeding. How had this happened? he wondered. He had been in Fremantle barely three weeks. He had caused no trouble, he had looked for none. He'd accepted work on the wharves from a subcontractor and when there had been murmurs about his non-union status the boss had assured him that all was above board.

'They don't like you Italians because you work too hard, that's all it is,' the boss had said. 'You work hard for me and I pay you well, and if they want to complain, let them.'

Giovanni had thought no more about it until that

night, when he'd gone to the Red Dingo to make contact with the timbercutters who gambled there on Sunday nights. That was where the money was, he'd been told. Cutting timber down south paid far more than he could earn on the wharves.

But instead of the timbercutters, he'd run into a group of wharfies waiting for the gambling den to open. One of them asked him what he was doing there. He answered the man in Italian. That was the first thing that angered them. The wharfies didn't like Italians.

'Speak English, you bloody dago.' Then the recognition. 'It's the dago scab,' someone else said. And then it had started. Why? Giovanni wondered. What had he done wrong?

He did not like Fremantle, he decided, as he opened the door of the boarding house and walked down the passage and up the stairs to his room on the first floor. He would go south and cut timber until Rico joined him.

He turned on the light and looked in the small mirror above the washbasin in the corner. It was a bad cut. Deep, from the top of his cheekbone to his jawline. It could have been worse, though. Half an inch higher and he would have lost his eye.

He must stop the bleeding. He took off his bloodied shirt, ran cold water and sponged his face clean with a towel. For half an hour he sat with his head to the side, stemming the blood flow with the cold wet towel.

There were other scars on Giovanni's body—he had been in fights before. The mountain boy had grown up quickly on the docks of Genoa. There was still a boyishness in his looks but now, when the hazel eyes flashed brown in anger, it was a man's anger. The Genoese dockside workers had developed a healthy respect for Giovanni Gianni.

Giovanni did not like fighting, and avoided it when possible. But he did not like bullies. The tyranny of the

De Cretico brothers remained fresh in his mind. It had happened nearly five years ago, but it could have been yesterday. The fire in him burned when he thought of his crippled brother. Never again would he stand by and allow others to threaten him or his own. If they did, he would fight, and if they harmed one of his kin, he would seek vengeance.

The bleeding had stopped. The wound needed stitching. He took several swigs from the bottle of rough whisky on the shelf above his bed, then poured some of the liquor into the wound, grimacing as it burned the raw flesh. He must find a needle and thread.

He tore one of his work shirts, making sure it was a seam which could be easily mended—no sense in wasting good clothing. Then he donned his jacket and walked down the stairs and along the passage to the room at the front, carrying the torn shirt and holding a clean cloth against his cheek. He knocked on the landlady's door.

When Pat Forman, fat and forty and very lonely, saw the handsome young Italian standing there, shirtless, bare-chested beneath his jacket, her heart quickened slightly. She'd made it evident from the moment he'd applied for the room two weeks previously that she'd be happy to halve the rent for a little companionship.

'A widow's life is a lonely lot,' she'd said. She thought that sounded very tasteful. 'And you must be lonely too. A foreigner. Perhaps you'd like me to cook you a meal every now and then.' As a rule she didn't make 'arrangements' with foreigners. Particularly not Italians. Dark, swarthy lot they were—always looked as if they needed a good wash. But this one didn't look Italian at all. With his fine-boned face and his soft brown curls, there was something quite boyish about him. He needed a mother she'd thought as she patted his arm.

Giovanni had recoiled. He did not understand what

she was saying—'No *capisco*, no *capisco*, excuse, *scusi*' he'd said, backing away—but he knew very well what she was offering.

Pat had been disappointed, but it had happened to her before. And now here he was on a Sunday night, shirtless, at her door.

Before she could say anything Giovanni thrust the torn shirt at her. *'L'ago e filo,'* he said. *'L'ago e filo. Per favore.'*

'What's the matter with your face?' she asked, pointing at the cloth he was holding to his cheek.

Giovanni draped the torn shirt over his shoulder, opened his mouth slightly, ignoring the flash of pain as he did, and tapped a finger against a tooth. *'Mi fa male il dente.'*

'Ah, poor boy, come in, I'll give you some cloves to ease the pain.' She stood aside.

'No, no,' Giovanni said and he smiled, hoping that the bleeding would not start again. 'Is okay. *Lago e filo.'* He pointed to the shirt and mimed a sewing action. *'E forbeci.'* He mimed scissors. *'Per favore.'*

'Oh you silly boy, give it to me and I'll mend it for you.' She leaned forward to take the shirt but Giovanni backed away.

'No no!' he insisted forcefully. *'Lago e filo e forbeci. Per favore.'*

'All right. All right.' Pat was offended. She was only trying to be helpful. She disappeared for a moment and returned with a needle and cotton.

'E forbeci,' Giovanni insisted. Again he mimed a cutting action and again he smiled. *'Per favore.'*

Pat hurrumphed, but disappeared and returned with scissors.

'Grazie. Molto grazie. Thank you.' Giovanni nodded and smiled and backed off rapidly, feeling his cheek start to bleed again.

Safely in his room, he once more stemmed the bleeding and then started methodically stitching up the wound.

As he dug the needle into his flesh, he thought about the girl. It was not the first time he had imagined seeing her. On several occasions, in the streets of Genoa, he could have sworn he had seen her. In the distance. He had run towards her only to discover that it was not the girl at all.

Giovanni pulled the cotton through his flesh. Keep thinking, keep thinking, he told himself. Take your mind off the pain. He dug the needle into the other side of the gash. The pain was intense. Keep thinking, keep thinking. And now here he was at the bottom of the world and he could have sworn, yet again, that he had seen the girl. It couldn't possibly have been her, of course. She had become a figment of his imagination, a foolish fixation, and he must put her out of his mind.

He unthreaded the needle, knotted the cotton and, in the mirror watched the edges of the gash in his cheek come together as he slowly tightened the knot. He dabbed the freshly oozing blood from his face with the damp towel and snipped the thread with the scissors. One stitch done. He must be careful to keep them even.

He gritted his teeth, dabbed again at the blood, and started on the second stitch. Twenty minutes later he tied the knot of the ninth and final stitch, images of the girl floating through his pain-filled daze. The girl from the mountain had followed him over the years. He'd seen her image in the streets of Milan and again in the dockside lanes of Genoa. Or he'd thought he had. And now she'd appeared to him again, the image of an angel amongst the snarling faces which had surrounded him in the tangled streets of Fremantle at the bottom of the world. Why did she haunt him?

Giovanni cut the cotton and lay down on the bed,

holding the towel against his face. He felt weak now, tired with the pain. He picked up his concertina and played gently to distract himself. The instrument was a little battered now but the sound it made was as sweet as ever. He felt himself start to relax.

He would not go back to the wharves tomorrow, he decided. He would rest for several days and then he would find a timbercutting job down south. He would leave Fremantle and wait for Rico to send him word as to when he would arrive with his family.

Giovanni smiled through his weariness. How glad he'd been when news had reached him of his brother's marriage, and how he'd laughed, when, six months later, Teresa had given birth to a son.

Soon after he had arrived in Genoa, Giovanni had found out that one of his workmates could read and write, a rarity amongst the dockworkers. For payment of a bottle of wine, this man would write letters for Giovanni and send them to the Santa Lena medico, who would then read them to the Gianni family. Then would come the reply, written by the medico, of course, and Giovanni would sit eagerly by as his workmate read him news of home. He marvelled now that all he had to do was send word to the medico from any telegraph office and his family would know where to reach him.

Giovanni remembered that final letter his friend had written for him. 'Rico,' he had said, 'have the medico send word to me at the telegraph office in Fremantle, Western Australia. I will be there in six months and I will wait for you to join me.' He would go to Australia, Giovanni decided, just as they had planned. And just as they had planned, he and Rico would dig for gold at the bottom of the world and they would become rich.

Chapter Seven

'Giovanni!'

Above the hubbub of voices and the clatter of passengers disembarking Giovanni heard his name but, try as he might, he could not see his brother. Rico, Teresa, their two children, where were they? He stood on the wharf and looked up at the people leaning over the railings of the S.S. *Liguria*. His eyes scanned the faces of those jostling to find a place in the queue to the gangplank.

It was three years since Giovanni had left Italy. Three years before Rico had been able to join him. Teresa was once more with child, the medico's letter informed him. The clerk in the Donnybrook telegraph office read the letter out loud in the doctor's halting English.

Since he had left Fremantle, Giovanni had settled in the southern town of Donnybrook where the timbercutting contracts were plentiful. He had taught himself to speak adequate English and he had a convenient arrangement with the clerk, regularly paying the young man to correspond for him.

After the birth of her baby girl Teresa refused to travel until the child was two years of age, sturdy enough to withstand the rigours of a long sea voyage.

But, in early January of 1900, the letter Giovanni had been waiting for finally arrived. The handwriting was the doctor's but this time the words were Rico's. Giovanni thrilled to the sound of his brother talking to him as the clerk read out the letter in his thin, monotonous voice.

'The *new year*, Gio. The first year of a new century,' his brother said to him. 'What a time to start a new life, yes? And in a new world. Everything we planned, you and I, everything we dreamed of, it will all come true.'

Giovanni returned to Fremantle, rented a room in his old boarding house, and waited impatiently for Rico's arrival. He looked at the telegraph daily, repeating the words he'd memorised and, each time, his brother's voice spoke to him more clearly. This was the brother of his boyhood speaking to him, the same vital, adventurous, irrepressible Rico.

'Gio! Giovanni!'

He turned. Rico had been amongst the first half-dozen passengers down the gangplank, a five-year-old boy perched on his shoulders. Giovanni grinned. Of course, he should have known. Rico would never stand back and wait his turn.

'Rico! Teresa!' He waved and stood back from the crowd, watching as his brother stepped off the gangplank onto the wharf. Behind Rico was Teresa, even taller and more handsome than Giovanni remembered. She had a little girl draped over one hip.

He tried not to look at his brother's legs as Rico walked towards him in an awkward, lurching gait, each stiffened leg kicked out to the side. It was a comical walk, the walk of a clown, the broad shoulders and massive barrel of his chest accentuating the deformity. Giovanni concentrated on Rico's face and kept his smile intact to hide his shock as he embraced his brother. But Rico knew.

'I walk funny, *si*? Now I am a fool. Now they laugh at me.' He kissed his brother on both cheeks, the knees of the child on his shoulders digging into Giovanni's chest. 'But only once they laugh, Gio. Only once if they know what is good for them.'

Rico laughed himself. In his customary loud, bold fashion. But there was no humour in the laugh and there was a glassy warning in his eyes. Giovanni realised in that instant that he had been wrong. His brother had changed.

'Teresa!' Giovanni embraced his sister-in-law. Her black hair had escaped her scarf and she smelled warm and feminine, reminding him that it had been a long time since he had been with a woman.

'Giovanni,' she kissed him affectionately on both cheeks. 'This is my daughter Carmelina. She is beautiful, *si*?' She lifted the two-year-old from her hip and thrust her at Giovanni who had no option but to take the child.

Giovanni was not accustomed to children and he held the infant at arm's length, but the little girl did not seem to mind at all. She clapped her hands at him and smiled fearlessly. It seemed the most natural thing in the world to hold her to him as her tiny arms encirled his neck and her legs fought for a purchase.

Teresa refused to come to his rescue. 'She is a good baby. You see? She loves you.' And she stood back proudly as the child settled itself upon Giovanni's hip.

Rico was obviously irritated by the sequence of introductions. 'Your daughter, eh? What about my son. Hey, Giovanni, say hello to your nephew. This is little Enrico.' He leant over and the face of the five-year-old atop his shoulders was only inches from Giovanni's. 'Enrico, this is your uncle Giovanni.'

Giovanni dutifully kissed the boy. 'Come,' he said, 'the sooner we collect your things the sooner we get through the customs.' He had checked the correct precedure before the vessel had docked and he hurried them through the throng of people. 'I've booked you a room at my boarding house.'

THEY ATE EARLY that night at a cheap restaurant not far from the boarding house. Little Carmelina dozed in the portable cot which Rico himself had made, and Enrico, exhausted, fell asleep over his food. Giovanni, Rico and Teresa ate with gusto despite the unimaginative meal.

'Australians have no love of food,' Giovanni explained. 'There is an Italian who has a shop near the town hall. I've bought some cheese and bread and salami for our supper. We will meet in my room and sing, eh?'

They sang and drank red wine well into the night, Teresa popping next door to regularly check on the sleeping children.

'Ma n'atu sole
Cchiù bello, oi ne' . . .'

The brothers stood together in the centre of the room, Giovanni with his concertina in his hands, Rico with an arm around his shoulder, their voices raised in harmony. Teresa, sitting on the bed, laughed and clapped. 'Bravo,' she cried and spilt her wine.

Around midnight the landlady started knocking on the door but Giovanni took no notice. He would worry about Pat Forman in the morning. Tonight was a night of joy. The Gianni brothers were reunited and they were singing as one, Teresa joining in the choruses.

'O sole mio
Sta nfronte a te!'

It was strange how much shorter Rico seemed. Giovanni stood a good three inches taller. At first he presumed that he himself must have grown during their years apart. He knew his body had filled out but then he noticed that Teresa, too, was an inch taller than her husband. He noticed also that Rico's shoulders and chest, well-muscled as they had always been, were now massive, bull-like. Not merely because they were out of proportion to his wasted legs—his brother's whole body had changed since . . . A warning sounded in Giovanni's head and he closed his mind to the De Cretico brothers. If he didn't, the hatred would consume him.

'It's two o'clock in the morning,' Pat Forman yelled, knocking on the door for the fourth time.

'O sole, 'o sole mio,
Sta nfronte a te,
Sta nfronte a te!'

They completed a final, rousing chorus and Giovanni at last opened the door to the frustrated landlady. 'We finish now, Mrs Forman,' he said. 'We finish, I promise.'

'I want you to leave first thing,' she answered angrily. 'First thing in the morning, you and your family, all of you. Out!'

Giovanni smiled as charmingly as he could. What was wrong with these Australians, he wondered, where was the song in them? 'It is the first time I see my brother for seven years,' he said. 'The first time I meet his children.'

'I don't care. I want you out of here. All of you. Out.' Pat hadn't liked Rico and his family the moment she'd laid eyes on them late that afternoon. They looked too Italian, dark, swarthy. Nothing at all like Giovanni. She'd been so pleased when Giovanni had come back to the boarding house. He spoke English quite well now and was always polite to her when they met in the hall. And at night, when she'd hear him quietly singing along to his concertina, she enjoyed it. She sometimes fantasised that he was serenading her.

Giovanni shrugged and smiled again. 'I am sorry. I am sorry that we keep you awake.' He would speak to her in the morning, when she was not so angry. He knew she had romantic inclinations towards him and he was quite sure he could persuade her to let them stay. If not, who cared. He would find another boarding house. But there would be no more evening singalongs until they had a place of their own, he knew that much—the Australians had no music in their soul. The sooner they went to the goldfields the better it would be for them all.

Teresa retired for the night and the brothers settled down to talk. Giovanni opened the bottle of whisky he had bought specially, poured some into a glass and offered it to Rico, who took a healthy swig. Giovanni waited for the gasp or the cough he presumed would follow, as he was sure Rico would not have drunk whisky before.

But his brother merely cleared his throat and gave a healthy growl of satisfaction. 'Good.' He looked admiringly at the liquid in the glass. 'That's good. Better than grappa and schnapps.'

Another change, Giovanni thought. Rico never drank hard liquor. Wine. Only ever wine. But of course that was years ago. When they were boys. Now they were men. He poured himself a hefty drink and raised his glass. '*Salute*,' he said and downed the whisky in one gulp.

They sat side by side on the narrow bed passing the whisky bottle between them and talking of their family.

'Filomena to be married! She is a baby.'

'She is nearly twenty,' Rico laughed. 'She is a woman, and I tell you, Gio, she looks it.' He weighed his hand in the air. 'Breasts like melons. For three years suitors have been sniffing around her like dogs. I told her if I ever caught her with one, I'd kill the both of them.'

'And Mamma?'

'Mamma is the same. Her hair is white now, but she is the same.'

They discussed their brothers and their friends and the village but, most of all, they discussed their father.

'He is looking old.' Rico shook his head. 'No, that is wrong. Not old. He is as strong as he ever was. He is looking tired. Sad. It is the work, Gio. There is hardly any work. Your money has kept the family fine, you send more than enough, but you know Papa . . . He is a proud man. For his youngest son to support him . . .' Rico shrugged. 'He looks sad.'

Rico stood and stretched. His spine was stiff, it was not comfortable for him to sit without support for his back. 'Things are not good at home. It is the same all over Italy, they say. They told us in Genoa while we were waiting for the boat, that many Italians are leaving the country.'

He pulled the one and only straight-backed chair over to the bed and sat facing Giovanni. 'Enough talk of sadness. We will get rich. So rich that we can bring Mamma and Papa and the whole family to Australia, eh? Mamma can live in a mansion and Papa can dig for gold with us.' He grinned infectiously, his black eyes sparkling, and Giovanni grinned back. They both knew Salvatore Gianni would die before he would leave his beloved homeland and the thought of their Mamma living in a mansion was ludicrous.

'I have already saved enough to take us to the goldfields, Rico. All of us. You, me, Teresa, the children.' Giovanni sprang from the bed and started ferreting under the mattress. 'We'll go to Kalgoorlie—where the big gold is. Look. Look at this.' He produced a bulky brown paper bag and proceeded to pull fists full of notes from it. 'There is enough money here to get us started,' he continued excitedly. 'I've been working two jobs down south ever since you told me you were coming. Look how much I have saved!'

Rico was impressed. 'Good. That is good.'

'Two more weeks in Fremantle, then we leave.'

'And I'll work hard these two weeks and we'll make even more money,' Rico agreed as Giovanni stuffed the paper bag back under the mattress.

'Our own house,' Giovanni said, settling himself back on the bed. 'We'll rent our own house. No landlady. Our own house where we can sing together as loudly as we like.'

Rico nodded then, after a moment's silence, he leaned forward in his chair. 'Now you tell me . . .' he stretched out his hand and, with one finger, gently traced the scar on Giovanni's cheek, 'you tell me how you got this.' A mischievous smile played on his lips. 'You've learnt how to fight at last, eh? The other man—did you kill him?' Giovanni shook his head. Rico's eyes widened in mock alarm. 'Surely he didn't win?'

'He ran away.'

Rico sat back in his chair, eased his stiffened legs out before him and laughed uproariously. When he'd calmed down he grabbed the whisky bottle, took several swigs and passed it to Giovanni. 'So, gentle Gio has become a big tough man, eh? That is good.'

Giovanni felt obliged to take his turn with the bottle although he knew he'd had more than enough. Then, both feeling the effects of the alcohol, they sat in silence.

To Giovanni, the air seemed heavy with things unsaid. He sensed that Rico did not want to talk about the accident. That was the term he had used when they had discussed their plans for the fortnight when Giovanni would serve his notice at the dockyards. 'I still work well,' Rico had said. 'Since the accident I am very strong.' He patted his shoulders and chest. There had been a defiant bravado in his voice and Giovanni had merely nodded and agreed to speak to his foreman in the morning.

Giovanni picked up his concertina and started very gently to play the lullaby their mother used to sing to their baby sisters.

Rico smiled. 'The concertina is looking old. You should buy a new one.'

'The song it plays is still sweet.' Giovanni shrugged. 'Besides, I'm going to buy a piano accordion one day.' Many a time he had saved enough to buy one but his guilt always prevented him. The music would be sour, he told himself, and sent the money to Rico and his family instead.

Rico quietly hummed along to the concertina as he studied his brother. He knew only too well that Giovanni could have bought a dozen piano accordions over the years, just as he could have lived in a fine house as opposed to this hole, had he not stinted himself for the sake of his family. But Rico said nothing. Giovanni had done the right thing—the family must come first, always.

Rico felt a sudden surge of animosity. Was he supposed to feel grateful towards his brother? Giovanni was a good brother, sure, a devoted brother, but Rico had earned such devotion. Many a time during the pain of his recovery he had regretted the fact that he had not cried out to the De Cretico brothers that night. He should have. He should have cried out, 'It was not me! You have the wrong man!' Now he was paying the price for playing the hero. As he looked at Giovanni's fine straight body, he thought, once I too had a body like that. Once I was Rico Gianni, desired by women and envied by men. Suddenly he needed to get out of the room. He needed to get away from Giovanni.

He stood slowly, easing the cramp in his lower back. 'I am tired, Gio.' Giovanni put down the concertina and Rico envied the ease with which he jumped from the bed. 'It is good to be together again,' he said as they embraced. 'I will come to the dockyards at noon.'

Giovanni watched his brother shuffle awkwardly out the door and down the passage. The gait was not so comical now Rico was tired. Without energy it was the shuffle of an old man, defeated. Giovanni wanted to weep.

THE FOLLOWING DAY, however, Rico's facade was back in place and his gait was once more that of a clown. At five to twelve, just before his lunch break, Giovanni looked through the dockyard gates up the hill toward the boarding house which, although out of sight, was only several blocks away, and there was Rico lurching down the street, defying Teresa to keep up with him.

With Carmelina on her hip and little Enrico at her side Teresa's pace was indeed hampered. 'Slow down, Rico,' she kept calling. 'Slow down, it is not a race.'

'Eh, Giovanni!' Rico bellowed when he was half a block away and could see his brother working alongside the other men. 'Eh, Giovanni, we have brought you lunch!' He waved the canvas knapsack stuffed with bread and olives and cheese. *'Mangiare Italiano buono. Non roba Australiana quella.'*

Giovanni was pleased that Rico's buoyant spirits had returned but he looked around self-consciously, wishing that his brother would keep his voice down. The foreman had been dubious about taking on a casual labourer who could speak no English. Strangely enough, Rico's physical disability had meant nothing to the foreman when Giovanni had warned him.

'Who cares if he's a cripple so long as he can work,' Bill Coburn had said. 'And if he works hard like you say he does then he's welcome aboard.' Bill liked the several Italians in his employ, they were all hard workers. But it was a different matter when Giovanni told him his brother could not speak English. 'I don't know,' Bill muttered, 'could be trouble with the others. They don't like it when you dagos don't speak English.'

When Giovanni promised that his brother would keep his mouth shut and they'd work side by side and it was only for a fortnight anyway, Bill said he'd think about it. 'Let me meet the bloke first,' he said. And here was Rico, bellowing at the top of his lungs that he'd brought good Italian food, not Australian rubbish. Giovanni ran to meet him at the gate.

On the dot of noon a whistle blew and all ten of the stevedores downed the sacks of grain they had been carrying from the carts to the dockside. They gathered up their lunches, sat on the sacks and started to eat. They watched as Giovanni greeted Teresa and the children.

'Keep your voice down. *Parla più piano,*' Giovanni muttered to Rico, as he saw Bill Coburn walking towards them.

'*Perché?*'

'They do not like you to speak Italian.'

The smile faded from Rico's lips. What was wrong with speaking Italian? he thought belligerently.

Teresa put Carmelina down and took the canvas knapsack from her husband. 'Look after your sister,' she whispered to Enrico, hoping that the men seated nearby could not hear. She too had no idea why she should not speak Italian, but if those were the rules, she would abide by them.

'This is my brother Rico,' Giovanni said as the foreman joined them. 'Rico, this is Mr Coburn.'

'Morning.' Coburn shook Rico's hand. 'The name's Bill.'

'*Buongiorno,*' Rico replied.

'Come over to the office.' Coburn nodded for both Giovanni and Rico to follow him.

Teresa had taken the paper bag of food from the knapsack and was about to feed the children when one of the men, having fetched a wooden crate, came up beside her and gestured for her to sit down.

Before joining the foreman, Rico turned to his wife, just in time to see the man put his arm around Teresa as he gestured to the crate.

It happened in an instant. So fast that the stevedores, all of whom had been watching Teresa from the moment she arrived, silently and lustfully, were dumbstruck. With a howl of rage, Rico was upon the man. The full impact of his body weight would have forced them both to the ground but the man staggered back against one of the huge wooden carts loaded with sacks of grain and Rico, his hands locked around the man's neck, staggered with him. He steadied himself and tightened his grip.

'Se vai vicino a mia moglie ti ammazzo. I swear I kill you,' he hissed between clenched teeth. The veins in his neck stood out as he channelled every ounce of strength he possessed into his fingers, intent on squeezing the life out of the man.

The other workers were suddenly galvanised into action. Several of them tried to pull Rico away but it was impossible.

'Get a stick for God's sake,' someone yelled. 'Get something to bash him with, the bastard's mad!'

A few men looked around for a weapon while the others kicked at Rico's legs and smashed their fists into his ribs, but nothing would make him release his grip. Like a fighting dog having purchased a hold on its victim, Rico had found his perfect point of traction. His feet were firmly planted, his body weight was against the man and the jaws of his fingers were mercilessly locked. They could batter him to death but, doglike, he would not let go.

The man's eyes were bulging, rasping sounds were coming from his throat. Rico squeezed and squeezed. Tighter and tighter. Then a voice beside him said, 'Rico! *Se tu ammazzi quest' oumo, ti rinnego come fratello.*' In his madness Rico became vaguely aware of Giovanni's face only inches from his. But what was Giovanni saying? What did he mean? Rico glanced sideward.

'Hai svergognato la famiglia.' Giovanni's eyes were cold with contempt. *'Non sei mio fratello.'*

Rico was shocked. 'You disgrace our family,' Giovanni had said. 'You are not my brother.' The voice was like ice. Giovanni despised him, Rico could see it in his eyes. But how could that be? Giovanni idolised him. All of their lives Rico had been a hero to his brother.

'Lascialu stare,' Giovanni ordered. 'I said let him go!'

The madness left Rico as quickly as it had engulfed him and he released his hold. The man fell to his hands and knees gasping and retching, his lungs fighting for air.

Giovanni turned his back on his brother. 'I am sorry,' he said to Bill Coburn. 'I am sorry,' he said to the surrounding men, one of whom was by now clutching a wooden mallet. 'I will take him away.' Still he did not look at Rico. 'Come, Teresa,' he said and waited while Teresa gathered up the children. Finally he turned to his brother. 'Rico.'

Rico recognised the command. His madness had vanished as if it had never been, and he realised that it was a good thing Giovanni had halted his attack—by now he would either have been clubbed to death or facing a murder charge. But he felt no remorse. The man had touched his wife. If they had been alone the man would most certainly be dead, and deservedly so. Rico looked defiantly about him and then followed Giovanni from the dockyard.

When they were out on the street Giovanni stopped. 'Teresa, take the children home. Rico, come with me.'

Teresa looked at her husband. She was grateful to Giovanni but she was accustomed to Rico being in command. Rico nodded, however, so she handed the knapsack to him and started up the hill.

'Where are we going?' Rico asked as they walked along the street towards the Round House.

'We need to talk.'

'Why? Why do we need to talk, little brother?' Rico

felt perfectly calm now. It was a pity he would miss out on a job at the dockyard but he would find work elsewhere. 'A man touches my wife so I teach him a lesson. There is no harm done.' He grinned. 'You did well to stop me from killing him though.'

Giovanni said nothing until they were at Arthurs Head, standing on the grassy knoll beside the Round House overlooking the sea.

He sat on the stone wall and gazed down at the small beach below. It was a still day and the waves lapped the sand lazily. Way out there, beyond the horizon, was Africa, he thought. Across the vast Indian Ocean another whole continent.

Giovanni felt depressed. All these years he had nurtured his desire to explore this vast brown land, to dig for gold. But always the excitement was to be shared with Rico. Since his arrival in Australia three years ago he had done nothing but work towards that aim. And now with whom was he to share all this? A madman. His childhood hero, the brother he had idolised, the man he had most wanted to emulate, was a madman.

Beneath Giovanni's disillusionment rested the terrible burden of his guilt. If the De Creticos had found the right brother that night, all those years ago, Rico would not be like this. Or would he? A germ of doubt was gnawing somewhere in the back of Giovanni's mind. Was it possible that, through his child's eyes, he had never really known the true Rico? Amidst his confusion there was one thing of which Giovanni was sure. He must be responsible for his brother. Rico was the child now and he must be the leader.

'You cannot behave like that, Rico. You must curb your anger.'

'Why?' Rico sat on the stone wall and opened the knapsack. 'The man touched my wife.'

'He meant no harm by it.'

'Hah!' Rico snorted derisively as he lifted out the bread and unwrapped the parcel of food. 'He lusted for her, they all did. I smelled it the moment I walk in the yard.'

'Of course they lusted for her.' Giovanni was exasperated. 'They are men and she is a handsome woman. Are you going to kill every man who lusts for Teresa?'

Rico looked up. In his strong hands he held a large loaf of bread. He was smiling but there was a hint of danger in his query. 'Do you lust for her, Gio?'

Giovanni returned his brother's gaze. 'I admire her,' he said. 'Very much.'

Rico ripped the loaf in two and the loud bark of his laugh was genuine. 'Ah Gio, you have great taste in women. Here.' He handed Giovanni one half of the bread. 'Eat.' He nodded at the food. 'The provolone is good.' He broke the slab of cheese in two then, bread in one hand, cheese in the other, took a large bite of each. He noticed that his brother still looked concerned. He chewed healthily for a minute then gave a repentant frown. 'All right. All right, I did the wrong thing. I am sorry.'

Giovanni nodded but did not appear particularly convinced. 'Eh, Gio, do not look so unhappy.' Rico grinned his irrepressible grin. 'We are alive, and this is a good world to be alive in. Look around, look at that sky, smell the air . . .'

Giovanni concentrated on breaking off a piece of cheese, avoiding his brother's eyes. The cheeky, cocky smile which had always so charmed him no longer did. There was a manic edge to it now, a desperation, as if it were himself Rico was trying to convince.

Realising that his charm had fallen flat, Rico opted for sincerity instead. 'I am sorry, Gio. Truly I am sorry. You are worried about me, eh?' Giovanni's eyes met his and he nodded briefly. 'Do not be. I will be good. From now on I will control my anger, I promise.' He dropped the bread and held out his hand. 'Agreed?'

They shook hands and Giovanni smiled back, although he did not for one moment believe that his brother was capable of curbing his anger. Such anger as had come upon Rico today was not of normal proportions, it was madness and one could not curb madness. 'Sure, Rico,' he said. 'Agreed.'

They ate in silence for a while, each man lost in his thoughts. Rico was convinced he had successfully placated his brother and he was glad. He needed Giovanni, although he would admit that to no one, barely even to himself. He must be careful not to shake Giovanni's confidence in him. He most certainly must not tell his brother about the man he had killed. Such knowledge would worry Gio. Even though the man had deserved to die.

It had happened at the stone quarry two years ago. The quarry was only an hour's walk from Santa Lena and Teresa had decided to surprise him one day by bringing a special lunch out to the work site. There were six men working in pairs and Rico was aware of the glances cast in her direction. It angered him and he led her away from the others as quickly as he could. But after they had lunched together and Teresa had gone, he noticed the two men working the far end of the quarry. He could not hear what they were saying but they were nudging each other lasciviously and one of them mimed breasts with his hands and laughed.

Rico downed his pick and walked over to them, his partner barely glancing up as he left, presuming he was going to relieve himself.

'You're talking about my wife, eh?' he asked the bigger man of the two, the one who had cupped the air with his hands and laughed.

'So?'

'So, if you speak filth about my wife, I will kill you.'

The smaller of the two read the rage in Rico and backed away nervously. He knew the strength of the man. They all did. Rico was the strongest worker on the site. 'We just admire her, Rico,' he said. 'We meant no harm. Truly.'

Rico glared at them both and turned to go but the big man could not resist goading him. 'What is a woman like that doing with a cripple like him?' His voice was deliberately loud.

In an instant, Rico had grabbed the man around the throat and twisted him to the ground. The man had no time to cry out and his partner simply stood by, stunned.

'*Adesso porco morirai.*' Rico lifted the man's head and smashed it down against the rocks with all the strength he could muster. 'Die, pig!' It took only the one blow to crack the man's skull open.

Rico stood and looked about the quarry. It had happened so quickly none of the others had noticed as they went about their work. 'It was an accident,' he hissed. 'He fell. You saw him.' The man's partner stared at Rico, shock and fear in his eyes. 'That is what you will say or I will kill you too.'

Blood gushed from the man's head. It streamed in rivulets amongst the rocks. But his body was not visible to the other workers. 'In two minutes from now you will call out the accident,' Rico ordered.

The partner nodded dumbly and Rico walked back to his own work patch. With his awkward gait it took him the whole two minutes to do so and, no sooner had he gathered up his pick, than the cry rang out.

'*Aiuto!* Gabriel has fallen! *Aiuto!* Help me!'

In the days that followed, there was a lot of conjecture as to whether or not Gabriel's death had been an accident, but none of the workers wished to be involved with the law so the incident was never investigated.

They left Rico alone after that. When Teresa came out to the quarry the men averted their eyes. Rico was glad. Justice had been done.

Rico watched Giovanni flick the row of olive pits off the wall with his finger. One by one. Just as they had done when they were boys. It had been a contest then to see who could flick the pits the furthest. No, he thought, he could never tell Giovanni about the man at the quarry. Once he could have. Once, when he'd been a hero in his brother's eyes and could do no wrong. But Giovanni had changed, Rico thought with regret.

'I must go back to work.' Giovanni stood and gathered up the debris of their meal.

'I will get a job, Gio, just you wait and see. I will get a job tomorrow, I promise.'

TRUE TO HIS PROMISE, Rico found a job the very next day. 'The Red Dingo, Gio. You know the Red Dingo? You have been there?'

'No. But I know of the place.' Since the knife fight several years ago Giovanni had avoided the Red Dingo.

Rico's job was to clear the empty beer barrels from the cellar and unload the fresh deliveries from the dray when they arrived. He had already shown off his strength to his employer.

'I just stand there,' he boasted. 'I pick up a barrel and hand it to two men who roll it on a plank down to the cellars. One of me and two of them, Gio. You see? Half of me is stronger than ever.'

They were sitting in Rico's room. Giovanni had not had too much trouble persuading Pat Forman to let them stay. 'Only two weeks and we go,' he had smiled. 'And we will be quiet, I promise you.'

The truth was that Pat Forman was loath to see Giovanni go. She had long since accepted the fact that he was not interested in romance, but simply to see him each day and exchange pleasantries added that little excitement to her life. Despite the livid scar across his cheek she considered him the handsomest of men and seeing him always set her heart aflutter.

'You are welcome to stay, Mr Gianni,' she had said. 'But any disturbance from your brother and he and his family must leave.'

It was early evening now and the brothers were drinking wine and watching Teresa feed the children. 'A lot of me is still strong, eh Teresa?' Rico winked lecherously at his wife who gave a good-humoured nod in return.

'*Si*,' she said, wiping Carmelina's mouth.

A week later Rico returned from the Red Dingo excited, jubilant. He insisted Giovanni come out with him for a drink. 'Come and drink some beer with me, Gio. You work too hard.'

Giovanni realised his brother wanted to talk to him away from Teresa so they went to the nearest pub.

'Do you know about roulette, Gio?' Rico asked as they sat down with their mugs of beer.

Giovanni shook his head. 'Who is roulette?'

Rico laughed. 'It's not a "who", it's a game. A French game where you can win a lot of money. The boss at the Red Dingo has just imported a wheel from Paris. It cost him a fortune. It's the only roulette wheel in the State—some say maybe the only wheel in the whole country.'

Giovanni continued to look confused.

'The game is played in a big wooden bowl called a wheel,' Rico explained impatiently. 'The wheel is divided into red and black numbers. They spin the wheel and throw in a white ivory ball. You bet on the numbers or on the reds or blacks—there are many ways you can bet—and if the ball lands on your bet you win. Johann showed me the wheel. They have built a special table for it. It's made of jarrah—magnificent.'

Rico had become friends with Johann, the Austrian barman who doubled as croupier on Sunday nights. Johann spoke several languages including Italian and had taken Rico under his wing. 'We must play this roulette,' Rico insisted. 'We might win big money.'

Giovanni looked doubtful. 'Yes, and we might *lose* big money.' He realised now why Rico had wanted to speak to him privately: Teresa would strongly disapprove of their gambling. But the more Rico spoke of the roulette wheel the more Giovanni found himself attracted to the idea.

'Next Sunday is our last night in Fremantle,' Rico insisted when he saw his brother weakening. 'We must have one evening in the big city before we go to the goldfields, Gio. One night to remember, what do you say?'

His excitement was contagious and Giovanni agreed, on the proviso that they set a limit to the stakes. They would gamble no more than their combined fortnight's wages. If the worst happened and they lost the full amount, there was still more than enough in the brown paper bag under Giovanni's mattress to get them to Kalgoorlie and rent a house.

'Six pounds it is,' Rico grinned. 'But we're not going to lose, Gio. We're going to win. And win big. And then we'll *buy* the house in Kalgoorlie. A great big house, eh? *Un palazzo.*' Giovanni laughed, it was impossible not to. Rico winked at him. 'And not a word to Teresa.'

THE UPSTAIRS GAMBLING den at the Red Dingo was the oldest and by far the most famous of the many illicit gambling houses in Fremantle. So long as violence was kept to a minimum, the police were content with their monthly payoff. The sergeant of the watch regularly informed Norman Whaley, the owner, when an obligatory raid was to be staged; then Norman would close the club, line up half a dozen or so stooges and bail them out when they'd been arrested. That way everyone was happy.

From the street, the Red Dingo looked like many of the other impressive hotels. Two storeys high and built of stone, it stood on a corner and was surrounded by wide shady verandahs. Several doors led into the huge bar, the two lounges and the billiards room, and doors on the first floor opened out onto a spacious communal balcony, designed for the enjoyment of the hotel guests accommodated in the upstairs rooms. But, apart from Norm and his wife, there were no guests accommodated in the upstairs rooms. Norm had gutted the place. With the exception of one bedroom maintained for himself, and two backrooms reserved for small-time punters and private card games, upstairs at the Red Dingo was a massive space where, nightly, hundreds of pounds were lost and won.

The conversion had cost Norm a great deal of money—he'd had to reinforce the ceiling and have supporting pillars built—but it had proved worth it. It had been difficult to control the violence when he'd operated the business in separate smaller rooms and, when a man had been killed in a knife fight, the sergeant of the watch had threatened to withdraw police protection. Now, from their vantage points around the perimeter, Norm's six heavies could easily control any outbreak of hostility.

It was a good night, Norm thought, as he wandered amongst the tables and nodded to the regulars. But then Sunday was always a good night. Each of the six tables was busy, three of them with the French game of pontoon, which Australians preferred to call twenty-one, and three of them with the dice game Crown and Anchor. And of course, in the centre of the room, the star attraction, the roulette table. The punters who'd arrived early had seats; others crowded around three, four deep, throwing their chips on the table and calling out to the croupier who placed their bets on the felt-topped table.

Rico and Giovanni had been amongst the first to arrive that evening. They had converted their six pounds and both had sixty chips, each to the value of one shilling, in his pocket, but they had not sat at the table. They wanted to observe the game before they placed their bets and Johann had warned Rico no one must sit without betting. 'It is a rule,' he'd said. 'If someone sits without betting, even for one spin of the wheel, there are fights. The boss will not allow it.'

An hour later, having evaluated the state of play, Rico placed their first bet. 'One to eighteen,' he said to Giovanni. 'The high numbers have come up six times in a row now. It will change soon, it must.'

'Place your bets,' Johann said as he set the wheel in motion and spun the ivory ball in the opposite direction. Rico put his shilling chip onto the table and pushed it into the bracket marked one to eighteen.

The wheel slowed; 'No more bets', and the ivory ball fell into one of the slots.

'Twenty-six, black,' Johann called.

On the next spin of the wheel, Rico placed two chips in the one-to-eighteen bracket. 'Thirty-three, black,' Johann called.

On the next spin, Rico placed five chips on the same bet. 'Nineteen, red,' Johann called.

'You see? The numbers are getting lower,' Rico whispered undeterred and doubled his bet.

Within ten minutes he had lost his money. Giovanni started out placing his bets with a little more caution but finally he too was caught up with roulette fever. There had been ten even numbers in a row, surely the next one had to be odd. He put five chips on. 'Six, black.' Another five chips. 'Eighteen, red.'

Within one hour of having placed their first bet, all their chips had gone. 'This is a game for fools,' Giovanni said. 'I prefer poker. There is some skill to poker.'

'There is a penny poker game in the back room. You want to play?'

'With what?'

'I have money.' Rico felt in his trouser pocket, pulled out four shillings and handed the coins to Giovanni. 'Not much.'

'Enough,' Giovanni grinned. 'Maybe we'll still get rich, eh? Come on.'

'No, you go.' Rico turned his attention again to the roulette table. 'I want to watch a little longer.' Giovanni hesitated. 'Go on,' Rico urged. 'I will join you soon.'

Giovanni shrugged and went in search of the poker game.

Rico hadn't been able to tear his eyes away from the big man seated opposite. The man had bet three times on the red. Not a shilling chip either. A one-pound marker. Each time the red had come up. And each time, when the croupier had placed another one-pound marker on top and started to push the man's winnings to him, the man had said, 'Let it ride'.

No, Rico thought, suddenly understanding, this was no game for fools. There was a way to play this game. You didn't bet *against* the run, you bet *with* it. And the fifty pounds that he'd taken from the brown paper bag beneath Giovanni's mattress was burning a hole in his pocket. He checked that Giovanni was nowhere in sight and went to the cashier's desk.

HARRY BREARLEY WAS having a lucky night. Mind you, he thought, it was about time—he was well and truly due for it. He'd all but wiped himself out last night. This was his last ten pounds and he had to turn it into fifty. He could hardly go back to Maudie Gaskill penniless. She'd never marry him if he did. And Harry desperately wanted to marry Maudie. Not just because of her money, although the fact that she owned one of the busiest pubs in Kal was an attractive addition to his genuine feeling for her. He was fond of her, he admired her and, above all else, he desperately wanted his son to have a mother. The best mother to be found in Kal. And that was Maudie.

Yes, Harry thought as he watched the croupier deftly flick the ivory ball into the spinning wheel, he was desperate.

Not that anyone would know it. If there was one thing that could be said of Harry Brearley, he had style. He was a big man, tending a little to portliness, with thick brown wavy hair turning a premature grey at the sides and a smile that could charm the birds out of the trees, as his Irish mother always said.

Harry had been born in Australia, in a little town south of Perth called Bunbury, but he could easily have been born in Dublin like his parents. He didn't exactly have a brogue but there was a lilt to his voice and everything else about him was Irish. He had the gift of the blarney, another of his mother's phrases. With a voice just a little too loud and gestures just a little too flamboyant, he was rakish and roguish and downright charming.

It was inevitable that, at nineteen, Harry should leave Bunbury and join the goldrush and equally inevitable that he should get a girl pregnant. The surprise was that it was only one of the many girls he'd bedded and that he did the decent thing and married her. He was twenty-four at the time and two years later, when his wife died in the goldfields typhoid epidemic, there were those who worried for little Jack Brearley's welfare.

Harry was a ne'er-do-well, they said; the boy needed a proper father. But Harry proved them wrong. The one redeemable quality in Harry was his unswerving love for his son, and it was that love which had won the heart of Maudie Gaskill.

'Nine, red.' It was the fourth consecutive red call and the croupier looked at Harry as he placed the big man's winnings before him. Harry gave a slight nod.

'Place your bets,' the croupier called and Harry looked at his sixteen pounds sitting on the red square. A number of punters had decided to take their lead from him and there were several one-shilling chips beside his pile. Harry hadn't given his ostentatious 'Let it ride', which he always liked—it was a stylish thing to do—because he hadn't quite been able to trust his voice. He was being a fool, he told himself, he should have taken half the money off the table and hustled up a card game with some mugs he could cheat. Roulette was a loser's game.

He sat back, lit a cigar and looked about the room, ignoring the eager, hungry faces crowded around the table, staring, breathless, at the spinning wheel. He could see Norm Whaley walking towards him. The croupier had obviously signalled that there was a possible big win coming up. Norm always arrived when there was a big win, smiling and congratulating the punter but obviously cursing inside and frantically calculating whether or not he should close the bank, cut his losses and call a halt to the game.

'No more bets,' the croupier called as the wheel started to slow. Norm Whaley arrived at the table as the ball found its slot. 'Seven, red.'

'Having a good night, Harry?' Norm's smile was fixed and he tried not to watch as Johann replaced piles of one-pound markers with tens.

Thirty-two pounds now sat on the red, but Harry

didn't look at them. One more spin, that's all I need, he thought. He nodded to Johann to let it ride and smiled at Norm. 'Yes I am, and a very good evening to you, Norman.'

'Place your bets.'

Harry felt someone jostling for a place beside him. He didn't like being jostled but, before he could turn to see who it was, a hand reached out and placed five ten-pound markers on the red.

All heads turned to look at the man who had placed the bet. All heads except Harry's. Did this mean the end of his run of luck? Jesus Christ, he'd only needed one more spin. Who was this bastard standing beside him? But he smiled at Norm, who'd given up all pretence and was watching the slowing wheel intently.

'No more bets.' The ivory ball took an interminable time to find its slot. 'Fourteen, red.'

An audible gasp from the crowd. Slowly Harry looked up at the man beside him. Eyes black as coal met his. Then, as the croupier started to push the one hundred pound winnings towards him, the man held up his hand.

Johann's eyes met Rico's and Rico nodded, just as he'd seen the big man nod. The big man had said, 'Let it ride', whatever that meant. He looked at the big man and grinned.

You cheeky bastard, Harry thought. Then, before he knew what he'd done, he'd nodded at the croupier to let his sixty-four pounds ride.

Johann looked at Norm. Norm's brow was beaded with sweat. Did he stop the game or not? He raised an eyebrow at Johann and the croupier returned a sign. Five reds in a row. Surely the run would break now, Norm thought. Surely. This was the biggest loss he'd faced yet on the roulette table. One hundred and sixty-four pounds—and probably another five pounds from the smaller punters—sat on the red. Damn it, Norm thought. The wheel was new, it functioned legitimately. He'd recently arranged to have it rigged to spin in favour of the house, but as yet it hadn't been done. He cursed his luck, breathed a worried sigh and nodded reluctantly.

'Place your bets.'

Piles of shillings and several one-pound bets were placed beside Rico's and Harry's wagers, everyone trying to cash in on the run of luck. Harry puffed on his cigar and glanced at Norm. What the hell, he thought, it was worth it for the look on the man's face.

'No more bets.'

Norman Whaley. What a hypocritical bastard, Harry thought. Always there with commiserations for the loser, congratulations for the winner—hoping the punter would come back and lose tomorrow—and never a penny of credit allowed. Of course that was exactly the way Harry would run a gambling house if he ever had the opportunity, but that didn't enter his thoughts. He was enjoying watching Norm Whaley squirm.

Harry didn't look at the wheel, but he heard it slow, and he heard the ball find its slot. Then he heard the words. 'Thirty-two, red.'

A huge cheer went up from the crowd.

'Congratulations, gentlemen.' Norm had pushed his way through to them. 'Well done, Harry.' He shook Harry's hand. 'Sir,' he shook Rico's. 'I don't believe we've met.'

Rico had no idea what was being said to him. He looked to the big man, waiting to take his lead from him. But the man who was still pumping his hand was continuing to talk.

'I'm afraid I must ask you to remove your bets, however. We're running close to breaking the bank and we wouldn't want that now, would we?'

'Of course, Norman. Anything to oblige. I was going

to let it ride, but to appease you, of course.' The big man was scraping up his winnings from the table. Rico followed suit.

'Harry Brearley,' the big man said and he rose and shook Rico's hand.

'Rico Gianni.'

'You must let me buy you a drink.'

Rico realised the big man wanted him to follow, so he did.

Italian, Harry thought. A cripple too. Strong-looking bastard, I wouldn't want to cross him. Still, there must be some way I can get some money out of him. I wonder if he plays poker.

At the bar Harry ordered himself a whisky. 'What can I get you, Mr Gianni? Name your poison.'

Rico looked at him blankly for a moment, then pointed at the barman who was pouring Harry's whisky.

'Whisky it is then. You're a punter after my own heart. I've not seen you at the Red Dingo before, are you new to Fremantle?' Rico continued to stare at him. What's wrong with the man, Harry wondered. Is he some sort of idiot?

'Mio fratello,' Rico said. *'Mio fratello parla inglese.'* And he disappeared into the crowd.

Good God, Harry thought, the man doesn't even speak English. He downed his Scotch and was just about to go and cash in his markers when Rico reappeared with another man. *'Mio fratello,* Giovanni,' he said.

'Harry Brearley. Pleased to meet you, Mr Gianni.'

'How do you do?' Giovanni shook the big man's hand. 'My brother Rico, it is true, he has won two hundred pounds?'

'Well one hundred and fifty to be precise. He put fifty on the red and let it ride.' Harry grinned. 'It was a lucky night for us both. Now what would you like to drink?'

'Do not be angry,' Rico whispered while the big man bought the drinks. 'It paid off, eh? We are rich.'

THAT NIGHT RICO and Giovanni became Harry Brearley's partners and co-owners of the Clover. They shook on the deal.

'No money changes hands until you see the mine,' Harry insisted. 'It's a man of honour you're dealing with, I want you to know that. And then we'll have a proper contract drawn up and I'll introduce you to Kalgoorlie society. Hannan's Club where all the richest businessmen congregate. I can introduce you to Paddy Hannan himself, I swear. How'd you like that?'

Two days later, together with Teresa and the children, the three of them boarded the train to Kalgoorlie.

CHAPTER EIGHT

As Maudie Brearley stepped out of the bank and crossed Maritana Street she registered the odd glance of disapproval. But she could not have cared less as she walked down Hannan Street. She was proud of her condition. She was due in one month and she intended to work until the very last minute.

A big woman at the best of times, Maudie, in her pregnancy, was enormous. And there was a good reason why. It was only the other week that the doctor had lifted his stethoscope from her massive belly and announced, 'I swear I can hear two heartbeats, Maudie. I'd wager a pound to a penny there's twins in there.' From that day on, Maudie had been doubly proud as she walked down the main street defying disapproval. Twins! The doctor had suggested she rest up but she wouldn't hear a word of it. She was as fit as a mallee bull. Why, if nature intended it, she could give birth to a litter of five, she said.

Maudie hoped the birth would come mid-week when business was at its slowest. She would allow herself only two days off and under no circumstances were the babies to come on a payday Friday.

Maudie Brearley was proud of herself. She'd turned thirty-one six months previously and had been well and truly pregnant at the time, just as she'd planned.

She enjoyed being married to Harry even more than

she'd thought she would. Of course he had always been able to make her laugh and he continued to do so. Maudie loved a good laugh. And she'd always enjoyed the love they shared for his mischievous son Jack. But she had anticipated Harry's old habits would die hard and that he would continue to exasperate her.

It appeared, however, that Harry had changed. Ever since he'd come back from Fremantle with his partners and had taken over the Clover, he'd become a responsible, hard-working businessman. Maudie was delighted by this transformation and, as she walked down Hannan Street bearing her swollen belly with pride, she was overwhelmed by a sense of happiness. Not one to view life romantically, Maudie would never have admitted, even to herself, that she had fallen in love with Harry Brearley. She simply recognised that he was now an upright citizen and that he would make a fine father for their children.

Lord Laverton and his wife drove past in their trap as they always did on a payday Friday at this time and, as usual, Richard doffed his hat. But Lady Laverton did not give a wave of her gloved hand. She hadn't waved at Maudie for the past several months, signalling her disapproval of the fact that any woman should so flaunt her condition.

Prudence Laverton could not, however, afford to ignore a person as popular as Maudie, so she gave a brief nod through her travelling veil and held onto her favourite picture hat with its ostrich-feathered plume as a gust of wind threatened to remove it.

It didn't altogether surprise Prudence that Maudie Brearley should behave with such a lack of dignity—the woman owned a hotel, after all. Well, hardly a hotel—a 'pub', when all was said and done. And just recently that braggart of a husband of hers, Harry Brearley, had been appointed to the Town Planning Council. Prudence shook her head. What was happening to the social conscience of Kalgoorlie? She supposed, with a shudder of disapproval, that the two of them would be present at the Municipal Banquet in the New Year, rubbing shoulders with the dignitaries and top-ranking politicians who would be streaming into Kalgoorlie for the great occasion. Rumour had it that Nellie Melba herself was coming to town. Prudence loved the opera, and had seen Melba perform in London. The prospect of meeting her idol was thrilling. But the thought that a diva of Melba's renown should have to mingle with the likes of the Brearleys and the other Kalgoorlie hoi polloi really was too much.

Prudence was content with her position of eminence in Kalgoorlie. As virtual queen of the goldfields, she was aware that she would never have achieved such prominence back in the old country. There she would simply have remained the nobody who had married Lord Lionel's son. But there were, nevertheless, occasions when the lack of finesse in Kalgoorlie irked her. And having to endure the presence of the Brearleys and their like at the Municipal Banquet was just one of those occasions.

Had Prudence known that Harry and his wife would not only be present on the evening but that Harry had recently been elected to the Banquet Planning Committee, she would have been outraged. The members of the committee, all respectable officials and citizens from Kalgoorlie and the sister town of Boulder a couple of miles south, had not elected Lady Laverton to their midst, although she had hinted heavily that she would be willing to accept. The committee decided that for the organisation of such a gala event, energetic innovative people were needed. People like Harry Brearley. Besides, Prudence Davenport was a snob.

The Municipal Banquet promised to be the most lavish social occasion in the history of the town, the grand finale to two days of ceremonies celebrating the opening of the Kalgoorlie pipeline.

The first of the ceremonies would be held three hundred and fifty miles away beside the pumping house at Mundaring Weir on January 22nd, 1903. But the real ceremony, certainly as far as those on the goldfields were concerned, would be two days later when, if all went according to plan, the water pumped from the coastal ranges would reach its final destination—the reservoir at Mount Charlotte on the outskirts of Kalgoorlie.

And the festivities would be topped off by the banquet to end all banquets on the evening of January 24th. It was barely two months away. Until Harry had recently come up with the idea, the committee's principal worry had been the venue. Where could they seat five hundred people to table? Even the grandest of Kalgoorlie's hotels, and there were many, could not accommodate such numbers. But Harry had saved the day.

'The car barn,' he'd announced at the last meeting when the question had been raised yet again. 'We'll turn the car barn into a banquet hall!' The car barn was the vast iron-roofed shed which housed Kalgoorlie's street cars. While jaws gaped at the audacity of the idea, Harry continued to paint the scene for the less imaginative of his colleagues.

'Picture it!' he said. 'Just picture it if you will! The big doors will be open to let the breeze through, decorations will hang from the ceilings. There'll be long tables covered with fine white cloths; with a platform at one end for the speakers . . .'

Gradually the others started to envisage the scene and, after a further twenty-minute spiel from Harry and much discussion, it was put to the vote and finally agreed—the car barn it was. The committee breathed a collective sigh of relief and, a short while later, Harry left the meeting, triumphant.

HARRY BREARLEY LEANED forward in his brand-new trap and flicked the reins. 'Trot on, girl, trot on,' he commanded and the mare picked up her gait. Black Bess was the finest horse in harness, he thought. Finer than Richard Laverton's show pony. Indeed, Richard had had the gall to offer to buy her over a poker game at Hannan's Club only last week.

'I could give you a fine price for that mare of yours, Harry,' he'd said in that silly posh voice of his whilst he fiddled with his ridiculous waxed moustache. Harry preferred to remain clean-shaven himself—even though it was not the fashion of the day, it set him apart.

Laverton was a fool. Harry had always thought so. No wonder his father had fobbed him off to Australia. Unlike most of the residents of Kal, Harry was not remotely impressed by Richard's title. The man was a sissy-boy, he thought. Good God, he even lisped.

'Not a chance, Richard,' he'd laughed. 'Not a chance. Your bid.'

As he bowled through the streets of Kalgoorlie, his planter's hat set at a rakish angle, the chain of his brand-new fob watch dangling from his waistcoat pocket and Black Bess trotting out like a professional harness-racer at the Coolgardie Racetrack, life could not have been better for Harry Brearley.

THE GIANNI BROTHERS were nowhere in sight when Harry arrived at the Clover, just an impressive fresh mound of ore beside the latest windlass. Rico and Giovanni would be underground working their self-determined ten-hour shift. Harry smiled. Luck had been on his side when he'd chosen his partners. God, but they could work! And they wanted nothing to do with the business side of things. They were more than happy for him to keep the books, register the extension of the claim and arrange for the delivery of fresh supplies. They were interested in nothing but digging for gold. It could not have been a better arrangement for Harry, who loathed physical work.

The brothers were not fools, Harry was aware of that. But they were simple. Ignorant. They couldn't read or write and he'd even had to teach them how to sign their names when he'd had the lawyer draw up the contract. 'Sure, you can make your mark,' he'd said, 'a great many miners do. But you're my partners. It's a little more dignified for a partner to have a signature, do you not agree?' Giovanni had translated for Rico and both brothers had been very pleased. Yes, they'd agreed, a signature was much more dignified.

Little as the brothers cared for the paperwork or the general running of the mine, they kept an eagle eye on the yield, the assaying and the payout. They stood in the bank with Harry and watched the teller meticulously as he weighed in their precious gold. And they knew within a pound sterling what the yield would be worth. Later that same day, they would again watch meticulously as Harry counted the money out in three equal shares back at the Clover.

Harry unharnessed and watered Black Bess. When he'd tethered her in the shade he walked over to the humpy which had been converted to an on-site office. He took off his hat and jacket, sat down and started on the figures for November. It had been a good month. A very good month. They could look at once more extending the claim. He waved away the ubiquitous flies, barely noticing them as he opened the supplies ledger. He could have pulled the hessian curtain closed to keep them out but he needed what little breeze the open doorway afforded. Wood supplies. He entered the order he'd placed that very morning. They needed more gimlet gum. Gimlet, the strongest of the local wood, was always used as 'toms' or wall and roof supports for the drives.

Through the open door, he could see clouds of red dust in the distance, near the windlass. He could vaguely discern two figures. The brothers had finished digging for the day and were starting on the exhaustive process of separating the gold from the ore.

'Eh, Harry!' Giovanni yelled, spotting Black Bess. 'You want to come down here and get dirty?'

Harry walked to the doorway and waved back. 'I'd be only too happy to, Gee-Gee, as you very well know. But I'm waiting on a wood delivery.'

Giovanni grinned and walked back into the dust. He 'very well knew' that there was no way Harry would risk getting dirty. It was a running joke between them. Giovanni liked Harry. He even liked the way Harry called him Gee-Gee.

He remembered the first time Harry had used the nickname. He hadn't much liked it then.

'Evan, these are my partners,' Harry had said as he introduced them to the previous owner of the Clover. 'Evan Jones, Rico and Giovanni Gianni.' The alliteration of the name had suddenly hit him as humorous and he'd laughed. 'Giovanni Gianni—we'll have to call you Gee-Gee.'

Giovanni wondered for an instant whether it was a deliberate insult—he'd heard the locals refer to horses as gee-gees. Then he realised that Harry was joking. He glanced at Rico who was smiling and shaking hands with Evan. He hadn't understood a word. It was just as well. If Rico thought for one moment that Harry Brearley was belittling the name of Gianni there would be hell to pay. Giovanni grinned and nodded amiably at Harry. If the man wished to call him Gee-Gee then he'd let him, he decided.

Evan took them over the mine, then down the shaft where he showed them the latest drive and the signs to look for. Like many on the goldfields, he was a little uncomfortable with foreigners, but he felt genuinely sorry for the brothers. They seemed rather naive and he hoped Harry wasn't swindling them.

'I'll leave you to look around for a while,' he said as he started to climb the shaft. 'Come up to the hut in about ten minutes and I'll have some billy tea ready.'

Harry had already climbed back up the shaft—he didn't like being underground any longer than necessary—and he joined Evan as he walked to the hut.

Evan no longer lived in the old humpy. He'd been working at the Midas for a while now and he and Kate had moved to the Golden Mile itself, not far from the mine, into a nice little wood-framed tin house surrounded by verandahs.

'They seem like decent enough fellows,' Evan said warily as he filled the billy can from the waterbag.

'For foreigners, you mean.' Harry leaned back in his chair and put his feet up on the table. He knew the proprietorial action would irritate Evan but he didn't care. Evan had sold the mine to him and there was no way he could back out now. 'Yes, they're good men. They'll make good partners.'

Evan did feel irritated. The brashness of Harry Brearley always irritated him. 'Are they sure they know what they're getting into? One of them doesn't even speak English.'

It was Harry's turn to feel annoyed—he recognised the inference—but he didn't show it. 'I'm having the partnership contract drawn up, all legal and proper. It's a great chance I'm giving them and they know it.' He smiled, a lazy, superior smile. 'Just because they're Italians doesn't make them dumb, you know.' He was aware the remark would further irritate Evan but Harry wanted to annoy him. Evan's criticism rankled. The man was boring. He plodded through life. If he, Harry Brearley, chose to take chances, to soar with the eagles, what right did such a man have to criticise him? He couldn't resist goading Evan further. 'What have you got against Italians, anyway?' he asked. 'You married one.'

Personally Harry couldn't give a damn what a man's race or creed was, so long as he liked to place a bet and have a laugh, but he knew that Evan Jones preferred to conceal his wife's background. He'd even changed his stepson's name to cover her tracks. Paul. He called the boy Paul. Maudie herself had told Harry that the boy had been christened Paolo. And Maudie should know, she'd delivered Kate's daughter.

Evan looked at him sharply, but Harry Brearley was smiling good-humouredly and there had been no malice in his tone. Evan knew that if he took umbrage, Harry would simply accuse him of overreacting. Harry Brearley always covered himself. 'There's sugar in that tin,' Evan said and turned back to the old iron stove.

Evan did not exactly conceal Kate's past, but he did not broadcast it either. It was for her own protection. The hierarchy at the mine could make promotion difficult for a man with an Italian wife, and the higher the promotion Evan could attain, the bigger the money and the better the life he could provide for Kate.

Of course Kate had every right to be proud of her heritage, Evan thought. And, if she wished, every right to boast of it. But she didn't. Her background seemed of little importance to her. She was happy with her new life. He had taught her to read and write; she no longer spoke Italian and her English, although slightly stilted, was perfect. With her auburn hair and her blue eyes and the touch of a Welsh lilt she had picked up from Evan, most who met her thought that she was British. So Evan never actually lied about his wife's ancestry, he merely neglected to mention it. It was more convenient all round that way.

Little more was said between Evan and Harry until,

several minutes later, Rico and Giovanni joined them.

The four men toasted the success of the Clover with their tin mugs of billy tea and when Evan took his leave he shook hands with each of them. 'Good luck, Harry,' he said, then turned to Rico.

Rico grinned as he energetically pumped Evan's hand. '*Grazie*,' he said. '*Mille grazie*.' Rico was clearly excited.

'I don't work Saturdays,' Evan said to Giovanni as he shook his hand. 'I'll come around from time to time and see how you're doing.'

'Thank you,' Giovanni answered. He instinctively liked Evan. 'Thank you, we would value that very much.' Giovanni was as excited as Rico, but he was trying not to let it show too much. He had had his doubts about Harry Brearley, but the Clover appeared every bit as impressive as Harry had boasted.

When Evan had gone, Harry went outside and got a bottle of whisky from under the seat in his trap. The three of them sat in the humpy and discussed their plans, Rico waiting impatiently for Giovanni to translate. They toasted the birth of a beautiful friendship and a perfect partnership and got happily drunk together.

Chapter Nine

Harry had been good to the Giannis. He'd helped them find a house in the northern end of town not far from the mine. A good house by most standards. Certainly by those of the majority of Italian workers who lived in canvas and hessian dwellings in South Boulder nearer the Golden Mile.

The house boasted two bedrooms and a living room, luxury to the many Italian families who slept in one room. Wooden-framed with walls of tin, the exterior was painted ochre so it wouldn't show the dust. The interior walls were of hessian, sized and whitewashed to form a thin but effective partition. The previous tenants had wall-papered the place throughout, little daisies which Teresa liked. A small verandah at the front overlooked the street and, in the back-yard, was an open copper, three clothes lines hanging from post to post and, down the back, a little shack housing the lavatory. Like most Kalgoorlie houses the roof was of galvanised iron which made it hot in the endless summer but, to Teresa's delight, Harry arranged to have a small ceiling fan installed in the living room. It was an unheard-of luxury. Only the hotels boasted ceiling fans. Teresa and Rico shared their bedroom with little Carmelina and a small mattress was set up for Enrico on the floor of Giovanni's bedroom next door.

On the nights when Rico and Teresa were intimate, it was frustrating for Giovanni. He always knew when they were going to make love; he would hear Teresa gently close their bedroom door, normally left open to catch the breeze from the ceiling fan. Then, as he lay in his narrow bed, he would hear through the thin partitioning wall the muffled sounds of their love-making.

So driven was he in his frustration that he started visiting Red Ruby's, one of the whorehouses in Hay Street. There had always been a healthy red-light district in Kalgoorlie. Originally located at the lower end of Hannan Street, a committee of residents had managed to have it shifted away from the main thoroughfare. In a further cleaning-up drive, the Japanese prostitutes, known as chocolate girls, were evicted and forced to ply their trade on the outskirts of town. The girls now working the whorehouses were predominantly French, although when the protests had died down and the brothels were neatly contained in an area the respectable residents could quietly ignore, the odd Japanese prostitute crept back into town and set herself up in business beside her French sisters.

The girl Giovanni took to visiting was Japanese. He had slept with two of the French girls but found them both garrulous. Giovanni did not want to talk to them or to play their games, he wanted merely to use a woman's body. The Japanese girl, Miko, was quick to realise this, and only too happy to oblige.

But Red Ruby's and Miko did not fully satisfy his needs, Giovanni realised. He wanted a woman for whom he could care in return.

Maybe he would find such a woman in Alice, the head barmaid at Maudie's. Alice was thirty-seven, eight years older than Giovanni. Her husband, a miner, had been killed in a cave-in six years previously. They'd only been married five months. 'Buried alive, he was,' Alice told him matter-of-factly. 'Terrible way to go.' She was a tough little woman, attractive in a wiry, capable way and Giovanni had liked her from the outset. When she'd asked him and Rico to the races on Saturday, Rico's eyes had lit up. '*Si*,' he said.

'We work Saturdays,' Giovanni had answered.

'We work our own hours, Gio,' Rico muttered in Italian. 'Your friend Harry Brearley knows we work twice as hard as any miner in Kalgoorlie. If we take a day off and he wants to complain, you send him to me.'

'Sure, Rico, sure. We'll go to the races.' Giovanni didn't attempt to defend Harry. He'd given up trying. Harry himself was always telling them they worked too hard, and he was meticulously honest in sharing the profits. What was it then that Rico so disliked about the man?

The truth was, there was something in Harry's easy charm that reminded Rico of himself before the accident. The world was Harry's oyster, just as Rico had once thought it was his. Life was too easy for Harry Brearley and Rico was envious.

TERESA DECLINED THE invitation to the races. She'd only recently given birth to her third child—to Rico's delight, a son. 'The most important part of me still works pretty good, eh Gio?' he'd boasted as they'd sat in the bar at Maudie's pub celebrating over pints of cold beer. 'We are going to name him after Papa.' He wiped the foam from his thick black beard. Like most of the miners, Rico and Giovanni now wore beards. Giovanni's was light brown, sparser than Rico's and only partially disguised his scar which, in the deep brown of his face, was more prominant than ever.

'To Salvatore,' Giovanni raised his glass. 'Papa will be proud.'

THE FOLLOWING SATURDAY, a fine spring day, was perfect for the races. Not too hot—about seventy in the shade—and there was even a slight breeze. Harry had persuaded Maudie to lend Alice and the brothers her sulky and pair-in-hand. Maudie had agreed, not so much for the Giannis' sake, but because she was pleased to see Alice enjoy her once-a-month Saturday off. Alice was a hard worker and indispensable to Maudie.

The sulky was new and the pair-in-hand a recent acquisition. Princess, the old white mare, was no longer used in harness. She was Jack's horse now. Put out to pasture, she was fat and happy and ridden by no one but seven-year-old Jack Brearley, for whom she would obligingly raise a canter. These days Maudie had her sulky and pair-in-hand and Harry had his trap and Black Bess.

Alice had asked Maudie to join them on the ride to Boulder. But what with the impending arrival of the twins, Maudie would have found the trip, short as it was, very uncomfortable, so she declined. Not that she went to the races often, she left that to Harry. So long as he didn't gamble heavily she was happy to allow him a taste of the old days.

'See you at the track,' Harry called, resplendent in his fine-wool checked suit, his freshly polished fob-watch chain gleaming. He flicked the reins and Black Bess trotted off in style leaving behind a cloud of red dust while Giovanni helped Alice into the sulky.

Giovanni handed Rico the reins and concentrated on Alice. He hadn't noticed before how pretty she was, with her hair up under her pink-ribboned hat and her travelling veil caught at her throat. Her neck was long and slender and the bodice of her gown nipped into a tiny, feminine waist. They hit a pothole in the road and she gripped his arm and laughed. He wanted to put a hand around her little waist and touch her delicate neck.

Alice was happy. She knew she looked pretty and she knew Giovanni found her attractive. That was all she had needed—to get him away from Maudie's where he saw her merely as a barmaid. Alice had had her sights set on Giovanni for a long time now.

The racetracks of Kalgoorlie and Boulder attracted owners and trainers and jockeys and punters from afar. The money was big and the competition was fierce. On the goldfields, where mining and gambling went hand in hand, any form of sport upon which a wager could be placed brought the punters and the players alike. There were simple two-up games, where big money was placed on the fall of two pennies, to stylish billiards championships at the Palace Hotel or professional athletics competitions at the Kalgoorlie sprint track, and the Spring Carnival at the Boulder Racecourse was one of the major sporting events of the year.

Harry had already placed his wager on the opening race when the sulky arrived. He didn't want the others to see how much he was gambling; it wouldn't do if they told Maudie. But he stood with them beside the white picket fence of the saddling yard and pointed out the horses his trainer mates had told him were hot contenders. Every second person at the track seemed to know him. A slap on the back and a 'Got a tip for me, Harry?' from one. Or a tap on the shoulder and a muffled whisper from another which would see Harry slip away to quietly place another sizeable bet. He spent the day mingling about the track but returned regularly to see how Alice and the brothers were doing.

Rico muttered to Giovanni that the man was showing off, but Giovanni thought Harry's concern was generous. Furthermore, his tips were excellent. Harry was having a good day.

It was a good day for everyone, in fact, but for Alice it was the time of her life. She mingled with the ladies in their finery knowing she looked as pretty as any of them. She sat in the grandstand and, when her horse came in, she jumped to her feet and waved her parasol in the air. At times she forgot herself altogether and yelled along with the men, urging her jockey home. Then she'd sit and smile apologetically at Giovanni but it was obvious he didn't mind at all.

In truth, Giovanni liked her lack of pretention. That was the best thing about Alice, he thought, no airs and graces. And suddenly he wanted to kiss her.

He did. That night. Back at Maudie's. In Alice's upstairs room they stood beside the open doors which let in the gentle night breeze. They didn't step out onto the balcony. It would not be good for Alice's reputation if they were seen and Giovanni did not want to compromise her. But he wanted to sleep with her. Desperately. He didn't want to use her body as he did the Japanese girl's at Red Ruby's. He didn't want to fantasise about Sarina De Cretico as he sometimes did with Miko. He wanted to make love to Alice. To kiss her tenderly and feel her respond to him.

Alice would have been quite happy to step out onto the balcony; at this stage she didn't care whether her reputation was tarnished. She only knew that Giovanni wanted to make love to her. And, as he gently pulled her to him, she stood on her tiptoes, put her arms around his neck, opened her mouth to his and fell desperately in love.

Giovanni stayed the whole night and, in the early hours of the morning, they once more made love. Then, before the town was fully awake, he slipped quietly out of the tradesmen's entrance at the back of Maudie's hotel and walked the half mile home.

That was the start of the affair between Alice and Giovanni. From then on, every Saturday night after closing time Giovanni would sneak up the back stairs to

Alice's room. They were careful not to advertise their relationship but word got around and before long everyone knew.

SATURDAY NIGHTS AT Maudie's pub was a regular way to round off the week. Giovanni and Rico would drink and play billiards and talk with the other miners, Harry joining them for an hour or so before he left for Hannan's Club.

'We'll get you signed up at Hannan's one day soon,' he'd say every now and then. 'I'm looking into it, Gee Gee.'

It was Harry's way of fobbing them off and Giovanni knew it, but he was not offended. Harry always treated them as the equal partners they were and he was obviously embarrassed by the fact that there was no possible way he could gain them admission to the club. He was being kind, pretending that he could. It was a well-known fact that Italians were not accepted.

'That's fine, Harry,' Giovanni would say. 'One day, there is no hurry.'

Alice would nudge him when Harry had gone. 'You're a gentleman, Giovanni,' she'd say. 'More than Harry Brearley is, for all of his airs and graces.' And Giovanni would smile and shrug. Who wanted Hannan's anyway? He would only spend the whole evening worrying whether Rico, with his limited knowledge of English, would take offence at some imagined passing remark and cause trouble in the gentlemen's club.

Ever since Rico's attack on the man in the Fremantle dockyard, Giovanni had kept a protective eye on his brother. Many a time he had steered him from volatile situations, most of which had been of his own making, and on the two occasions when he had not managed to intercede in time, he'd had to drag Rico off the person he'd attacked. Each time, the madness was gone as quickly as it had appeared. Afterwards, Rico was at first defensive, then apologetic.

The times when Rico was at his best was when he was working a hard ten-hour shift at the Clover or when he was singing along to the concertina with the family on a Sunday night. Then Giovanni would relax and enjoy his brother's company the way he wanted to.

The Sunday night singalongs had become a favourite part of Giovanni's life. Teresa would cook a fine meal. Huge bowls of home-made ravioli or spaghetti, the ingredients bought from an Italian merchant in Boulder. The same merchant sold rough red wine—only to fellow Italians who would not report him for trading without a liquor licence—and Giovanni, Rico and Teresa would eat and drink and sing for hours, Carmelina clapping her hands in time to the music and seven-year-old Enrico, who knew the words to all the songs, singing along with them. More often than not Harry Brearley and his son Jack would join them; Teresa, who ran the household with a rod of iron, paying no heed to Rico's objections. Like Giovanni, she was grateful to Harry Brearley and enjoyed his company. Besides, young Jack was a fine companion for Enrico. The two boys were of the same age and already good friends.

Maudie never came along. Not only because she would have been uncomfortable in such foreign company but because Sunday was a working day for her, and a busy one at that. Sunday was when she did her stocktaking, Harry told them, and balanced the books. Teresa was a little shocked and more than a little disapproving. Sunday was a day for church and prayer and enjoying one's family.

Over the ensuing year another person joined the ranks of the Sunday singalong. Young Paul Jones, Evan's boy.

True to his word, Evan Jones had regularly turned

up at the Clover on a Saturday to help the Gianni brothers settle in and he invariably brought his young stepson with him.

After a while, Giovanni noticed that the boy paid close attention whenever he and Rico were speaking Italian. Jack Brearley never did. For that matter neither did young Enrico; he was too busy speaking English with Jack—Enrico wanted to be an Australian, just like his friend. But Giovanni noticed that as he and Rico talked, Paul's eyes darted between them. The boy was listening, he could swear it.

One day he decided to put him to the test. *'Capice Italiano,'* he said, turning suddenly to Paul. It wasn't a question but a statement and it took the boy by surprise.

Paul looked guiltily down at the ground for a second, then nodded. 'Yes,' he said.

'Parle Italiano?' This time it was a question.

'Si.'

'Buono. That is good. Speak to me in Italian.' The boy continued to stare at the ground guiltily. 'Why do you look so ashamed?' Giovanni asked, again in Italian. 'It is no sin to speak my language to me.'

The boy looked up at him. 'I don't want to,' he said in English, but Giovanni knew that he was lying. He nodded and the boy ran off to join Jack and Enrico who were fetching water for Black Bess.

'His mother's Italian,' Harry explained when Giovanni questioned him about the incident. 'His real name's Paolo, at least that's what Maudie says.' Giovanni looked puzzled. 'The boy's not Evan's, you know,' Harry went on. 'Kate was a widow when he married her. He keeps her a bit of a secret, don't ask me why. Oh, he does it for all the right reasons, I'm sure,' Harry shrugged. 'To protect Kate and the boy no doubt. There's ill-will towards foreigners in Kalgoorlie. Only from some of the less informed,' he added diplomatically. 'You may have noticed.' Then he winked at Giovanni. 'Perhaps he keeps his wife hidden because she's the most beautiful woman on the goldfields.' He shook his head admiringly. 'No, not just the goldfields. Kate's about the finest looking woman I've ever seen, I swear.'

Giovanni liked Evan and he certainly had no wish to interfere in the man's family affairs, but he wanted to make contact with the boy. And something in their exchange had led him to believe that Paul wanted to make contact with him too. So, the following week when he came to the Clover, Giovanni asked Evan if he would like to bring his family to dine on Sunday.

'You and your wife and your children,' he said as Evan patted his horse and tightened the girth of the saddle, preparing to leave. 'We would like to thank you for all of your help. It is just a family dinner. We eat and we drink and we sing songs.' He sensed that Evan was about to say no. 'Harry and young Jack will be there.'

Evan continued to pat his horse until it relaxed and stopped blowing its belly out, then he tightened the girth one more notch. 'I'd have to ask Kate,' he said. Evan knew that he would be uncomfortable socialising with the Italians, and he knew that Kate would sense his discomfort and so not wish to be there either. But Giovanni was a nice man and Evan didn't know how to say no. He put his foot in the stirrup and slung himself up into the saddle.

'It's a little short notice, perhaps another time.' He put out his hand for Paul; they clasped wrists and in a second the boy was up behind him on the rump of the horse. But, in the instant he'd jumped, Evan had seen the look on Paul's face. 'You'd like to go to Giovanni's tomorrow night?' he asked, and he felt the lad's chin against his shoulderblade as he nodded vigorously.

'Thank you,' Evan said. 'The boy would like to

come. I'll bring him around. At what time?'

'Seven o'clock?'

'Seven o'clock he'll be there.'

Paul grinned at Jack and Enrico who were standing nearby and circled his arms around Evan's waist. Evan touched his heels to his horse and they set off home at a slow canter.

PAUL BECAME A regular fixture at the Gianni family's Sunday gatherings after that, but Evan never brought the rest of his family. He dropped the boy off and picked him up several hours later, and when Paul was presented with a pony of his very own, he rode over alone arriving on the dot of seven each Sunday evening.

Sundays became very important to him. Although his mother never spoke of his father, apart from saying that he was American, she talked a great deal about her childhood in the Alps and she often spoke to Paul in Italian. But always privately, never in company. Not even in front of Evan, and Paul had grown to believe there was something wrong in being half-Italian. Singing along to the concertina with the Giannis, he felt at home, one of them. He idolised Giovanni. But then so did young Enrico and little Carmelina. Giovanni seemed to have a gift with children.

Jack Brearley was the only one who didn't idolise Giovanni, but that was merely because there was no room in the boy's life to idolise anyone other than his father. To Jack, Harry Brearley could do no wrong.

Although he was eighteen months younger than Paul, it was Jack who was the leader among the boys. Spirited and headstrong and thoroughly endearing, it was always Jack who got them into trouble. Jack who smuggled them down one of the old mine shafts at the Clover. Jack who piled them all on top of the Princess and tried to rouse a gallop from the old mare. When

Enrico, who unlike the other two was not a good rider, fell off and broke his little finger, Jack diagnosed the injury. 'Yep, it's broken,' he said, and swore Enrico to secrecy. Fearful of his father's wrath, Enrico bravely bore the pain. The finger grew crooked, but no one was any the wiser.

Although they were the same age, Jack tended to scoff at Enrico, preferring to think of himself as older and wiser like Paul. But secretly he admired Enrico's stoicism and he vowed that the finger was a bond between them. 'That makes us brothers,' he would say as he studied the crooked finger.

AS THE MONTHS went by, Kate noticed the difference in her son and it pleased her. She had worried about the boy's friendless existence. Although he attended the local school and was a good student, he did not seem to mix with the other children. He never came home with tales of mateship. Now when he returned from the Giannis he talked endlessly of the games he'd played with Jack and Enrico. Swearing her to secrecy, he even told her about Enrico's broken finger.

'Mr Gianni mustn't find out you see,' he explained. He was deferential when he spoke of Rico or Teresa, always referring to them as Mr and Mrs Gianni. But, when it came to Giovanni, it was 'Giovanni this' and 'Giovanni that' and at first Kate thought that Giovanni must be another boy he had befriended.

'No, Mamma,' Paul laughed, 'Giovanni and Mr Gianni are partners with Mr Brearley.'

'Oh yes, so they are.' The Gianni brothers, of course her husband had told her about them. Well, she was very grateful to Mr and Mrs Gianni and Giovanni. And, each week, Kate would carefully wrap up a batch of fresh-baked scones or a crusty damper loaf for Paul to take with him.

Evan, too, noticed the difference in the boy and, although he was grateful, he was a little envious of the ease with which Giovanni could relate to the lad. Fatherhood did not come naturally to Evan.

If he'd been a single man, Evan Jones would have chosen to work as a 'loner'. He would have continued to live, quite content, in the old humpy. But it gave him such joy to see Kate so happy in her neat little home that he was content to become a 'company man'.

He was a good stepfather to Paul and he felt a great pride in his daughter, Briony, but sometimes he would sit on the front verandah in the dusk watching Kate play tag or hide-and-seek with the children and wonder how it had come about. All those years alone, just him and his humpy and the Clover. And now this. And then he would hear Kate squeal as loudly as the children. He'd watch her piggybacking Briony, being tagged by Paul, all of them ending up in a tangled heap in the dust. Most other mothers would be scolding their children for playing in the dirt. Not Kate. She was a child herself and her energy was inexhaustible.

Kate had become a creature of the goldfields. She loved the place. Her once milky-white skin was now a deep olive brown and her auburn hair was flecked with gold. Like the hardened, practical women of the area, she was strong. She could not only cook and sew, she could chop wood and build fires and cart water and ride a horse with the best of them. But, for all that, there was a womanliness about Kate that set her apart and, at night, when Evan took her to him and kissed her perfect mouth and felt the fullness of her breasts, he marvelled at the fact that she was his wife.

To Evan, Kate was life itself. His love for her overwhelmed him. He never spoke of it—he didn't know how to say the right words—but he showed it in many ways. He would work through the night to make a piece of furniture for the house or a knick-knack for one of the children. He would return from town with some fine lace or new fabric for curtains or cushion covers. He would insist she accompany him shopping in Boulder so that he could buy her a scarf or a trinket which she didn't want but which she accepted, knowing it was a token of his love.

Kate was fully aware of Evan's love for her. She was deeply fond of him and grateful for the life he had provided for her and her children. In return, she worked hard to be the perfect wife. And when, after nearly two years at the Midas, Evan was promoted to underground boss, she was an undeniable asset. Evan was a shy man at the best of times and Kate was an excellent foil for his social ineptitude.

Shortly after Evan's promotion, Lord Laverton threw a mid-year party and, when he opened his house to the upper echelons of the Midas, it was Kate who effortlessly charmed the host and his guests. The men were attracted by her beauty and the women by her lack of guile. Kate Jones seemed oblivious of the effect she had, they thought, and, collectively, they decided that she was charming and eminently acceptable. Even Prudence, who had taken an instant dislike to her and was preparing phrases like 'an ostentatious beauty' and 'looks that border on the vulgar' to bandy around amongst her friends, finally had to admit that Kate was 'a little lacking in refinement but quite engaging'.

Kate knew she would never have been accepted in such company had she displayed her origins. She wondered what they would all have done had she suddenly started chatting in Italian. The thought of the look on Prudence Laverton's face made her want to laugh out loud. But of course she would never do that to Evan.

There were times when Kate regretted the denial of her ancestry. And then she would remember the struggling years in Fremantle and she would decide it was a small enough price to pay for the love and the brand-new life Evan had given her.

Her husband's desire to anglicise her was not born of intolerance. She knew that he was just being protective of her, that even his own ambition was born of his love for her, and it made her more determined than ever to be the perfect partner for him. Evan Jones was a conservative man and he needed a conservative wife. So Kate never spoke her mother tongue in his presence, not even to her own son. And in public she called her son Paul, although to her he would always be Paolo.

But when they were alone, Kate would speak Italian to him. 'Just you and me,' she would say. 'It is our secret.'

'TO THE NEW Brearleys.' Harry's voice reverberated with pride, emotion and three-quarters of a bottle of the best cognac Kalgoorlie had to offer. 'To my son, James Robert, and my daughter, Victoria Jane.' He raised his brandy balloon and puffed his cigar. Maudie had given birth to twins on Christmas Eve, 1902, just one month before the opening of the Kalgoorlie pipeline. She was back at work two days later (although she kept her duties light and employed a full-time nanny to help with the babies) and, just as she'd planned, she did not miss a payday Friday.

The men gathered around Harry on the spacious verandah of Hannan's businessmen's club raised their own glasses and puffed their own cigars.

'To James and Victoria Brearley,' Lord Laverton responded and even the great Paddy Hannan himself, who to Harry's immense pride had made a point of personally offering his congratulations, joined in the toast.

Patrick 'Paddy' Hannan no longer lived on the goldfields but he had made a brief unannounced visit to inspect the new water scheme. A careful, secretive man, he intended to leave before the swarms of journalists arrived for the official opening the following month.

The man whose gold strike, together with his partners Flanagan and Shea, had led to the creation of Kalgoorlie was not at all 'great' in appearance. In fact, he was a somewhat unprepossessing little man, birdlike and bald. But there was something about him, an alert, charged energy, which engendered respect. And he was, after all, *the* Paddy Hannan.

Harry glowed with pride. He'd made a habit of pretending he knew Paddy Hannan for so long he'd forgotten it was a lie. Well, by God, it was a lie no longer—he'd just shaken hands with the man. To think that there was a time when he would not even have been considered for membership to the club which bore Hannan's name. And here he was, not only socially acceptable but a pillar of the community, a prominent businessman, a council committee member and now, as the proud father of two healthy newborn babies, the very centre of attention amongst the elite members of Hannan's Club. It felt good.

Harry looked out over the clubhouse grounds, the most luxurious on the goldfields. The only grounds which always boasted an expanse of green and an abundance of colour. A full-time gardener was employed and, even when water was at its most precious, the members' fees, their donations and the club's liquor sale profits guaranteed the upkeep of the border of flowering shrubs and the surround of cultivated lawn. The water used was artesian but even so, in the harsh summers when many families left the goldfields altogether, such water was a luxury and the waste of it on the Hannan's Club's grounds was considered by many to be a crime.

The new water scheme would change all that, Harry thought as he studied the row of shrubs beside the club's surrounding fence. Regardless of the wisdom of the Kalgoorlie pipeline—and Harry had heard the odd derogatory comment from several hardened cynics who had their doubts: cynics who believed that three hundred and fifty miles of pipeline was a ridiculous extravagance and that the government should have drilled for water instead—Harry himself was tremendously excited by the prospect. Not merely because of the water supply, but because of the opportunities which were bound to present themselves. The choice would be limitless for a man of vision. And Harry was, without doubt, a man of vision.

The following month would see hundreds of important visitors pour into Kalgoorlie. There would be the scientists and engineers who had created the pipeline; there would be the businessmen and the entrepreneurs—Harry's sort of people; and there would even be the celebrities, such as opera singers, entertainers and sporting personalities. And of course there would be the politicians and speech-makers.

Who knows, Harry thought as he accepted the pats on the back from Richard Laverton and his cronies—'A boy *and* a girl, frightfully clever of you, old man'—who knows, perhaps he'd go into politics. It wasn't inconceivable. With the creation of the Federal Parliament the previous year, a lot of attention had been paid to the eastern goldfields of Western Australia. The miners had been feted as valuable constituents and Sir John Forrest himself, the former State Premier and newly appointed Federal Minister, was to make the official opening speech at the Municipal Banquet. Harry, as a member of the Welcoming Committee, would be seated at one of the several official tables with a number of the visiting dignitaries. Heaven only knew the valuable connections he would be able to make that night.

'You give my very best to Maudie, d'you hear.' Yet another hand was pumping his. 'She's done you proud, Harry, that's for sure.'

It was a pity Maudie wouldn't be with him at the banquet, Harry thought. She was a damned impressive woman and a good ally. To his surprise, Maudie had not been the least bit interested in the banquet. She was excited about the ceremony at the Mount Charlotte reservoir—'a miracle it'll be to see the water come out of that pipe,' she kept saying, 'a downright miracle'. But as far as the banquet was concerned, Harry must take someone else; she was going to stay at home with her babies. James and Victoria were far more important than a hall full of swelled heads, Maudie said, and nothing could budge her.

After pondering the situation for several days, Harry had decided to ask Giovanni. These days, since his fiancée, Alice, had taken to supervising the cut of his clothes and the trim of his beard and moustache, Giovanni looked eminently respectable. Even dashing. Yes, Harry thought, the image of the two of them together could do him no harm.

It was still several weeks till the big night but the fire of Harry's expectations was well and truly kindled. The Kalgoorlie Municipal Banquet would be one of the most exciting events of his life, he knew it. It held the promise of things to come.

LIKE MAUDIE, GIOVANNI was more excited by the spectacle of water gushing into the Mount Charlotte reservoir; but for Alice, like Harry, the evening's festivities held the greater allure. Although she would not be attending the banquet, and she had certainly not expected to, Alice intended to be amongst those lining the pavement for a glimpse of the famous visitors arriving in their finery. And she would dress in her own finery and join the street party which promised to last throughout the night.

Giovanni wished that Harry had asked Alice to the

banquet instead of him and he hinted as much. 'Perhaps it would be more correct if a lady accompanied you, Harry,' he said.

The reply was polite but firm. 'If my wife cannot accompany me then my partner should, Gee-Gee. And if my partner will not, then I shall go alone!'

Harry had realised immediately what Giovanni was hinting at. Good God, the man was naive. Alice was a barmaid and she looked it. Even dressed to the nines she looked it. Harry rather liked Alice, even found her attractive, and she was a damned fine worker, but he thought Giovanni was a fool for marrying her. With his newfound style he could go anywhere—why saddle himself with a liability? Harry did not for one moment think himself a snob, but he was fully aware that one had to be very careful to create the right impression with those who were.

'Sure, Harry. Fine.' He owed Harry a great deal, Giovanni told himself, and accompanying him to the banquet was the least he could do. Besides, he had never been to a grand affair before, it might be interesting.

Unaware of Giovanni's attempt to include her, Alice seemed as excited by the prospect of him going to the banquet as if she were going herself and she insisted he accompany her shopping. She chose a smart new three-piece suit for him in charcoal black and a brand-new white shirt with high starched collar. And, as the evening approached, she insisted he remember every detail in order to recount it to her.

'The food, Giovanni, don't forget the food. And the decorations. And the ladies' hats.' And so the list went on.

EVAN JONES WAS dreading the banquet. He would be seated at Lord and Lady Laverton's table along with a number of the managers from the larger mines and several visiting dignitaries. He'd been underground boss at the Midas for barely six months and he hadn't expected to be invited. But, after due consideration, he thought he knew why. Kate. It had to be Kate. She had so impressed them at their mid-year party that Richard Laverton and his wife must have decided she would be an asset at their banquet table. Evan realised he should be grateful, knew such an occasion would help establish his position at the Midas, but he agonised at the prospect of the social chitchat which lay ahead.

At first Kate was reluctant to go.

'But it's because of you, don't you see?' Evan insisted. 'You're the reason we've been invited, I'm sure of it.' The thought of facing the evening without her was unimaginable.

'Who will look after the children?' she argued.

Then the offer came from the Lavertons that their housekeeper would care for the children and Kate had no further defence. And when Evan insisted on buying her an exquisite new gown with a lace bodice and a bretton hat of the very latest fashion with wide upturned brim and soft blue plume, she couldn't help but feel a flutter of anticipation.

'You must take it back, Evan, it is far too expensive,' she said as she held the dress up in front of her and looked in the bedroom mirror.

Evan ignored her. 'Put it on, Kate.'

Several minutes later, as she held the hat to her head and twirled before the mirror, she laughed like a child. 'Look at me,' she said, fingering the satin lapels of the fitted jacket over the lace bodice. 'Look at me. I am so grand.'

'You are beautiful,' he said. 'Very, very beautiful.'

Chapter Ten

'Forward two three, back two three, forward two three, back two three.' Harry sat in his favourite red velvet armchair and chanted methodically as he watched Giovanni and Maudie waltz around the floor of the upstairs parlour.

Many big women were graceful when they danced, surprisingly light of foot, even nimble. Maudie was not.

'Now the pirouette,' Harry said. '*Turn* two three, *again* two three.' Maudie knew the steps well enough and she didn't trip over or tread on her partner's toes, but she danced by rote, wooden and self-conscious. 'Now the circular waltz. *One* two three, *one* two three.'

The two of them whirled around several times and finally Maudie broke away laughing. 'This is ridiculous, Harry, Giovanni dances far better than I do.'

'Yes, we are all perfectly aware of that, my dear. Giovanni is a natural dancer.' He added mischievously, 'Unlike some,' and Maudie wasn't the least bit offended. 'But it is essential he learn the correct steps. You are comfortable with the Pride of Erin, Gee-Gee?'

Giovanni nodded vigorously. The Pride of Erin was his favourite. But then he liked them all, the Military Two-step, the Glengarry Waltz, the polka . . . Harry had been teaching him to dance for a fortnight now and Giovanni loved it.

'One more time?' Harry asked. 'This afternoon is your last chance to practise.'

Giovanni looked at Maudie who was sitting on the sofa, fanning her skirts to create a breeze. It was a stifling hot day. He shook his head. 'I think no. I think Maudie has had enough dancing.' Personally he could have danced all day.

Maudie smiled gratefully. 'That's very kind of you, Giovanni. Harry'd have me dancing all day if we let him.' But the twinkle in her eyes belied the rancour of her words as she glanced fondly at her husband.

'Nonsense,' Harry retorted. 'Sheer nonsense. I am going to this wretched banquet tonight purely for your sake and for the sake of our children.'

Maudie and Giovanni exchanged an amused look. 'Oh? And how is that exactly?' she challenged.

'The business and political contacts I shall make, my dear. The advancements they could offer I view purely in the light of enhanced financial comfort and community standing for my family.'

Maudie laughed loudly and jumped up from the sofa. 'You're going to the banquet to show off, Harry Brearley, and that's the truth.' She crossed to the door. 'And you're going to love every minute of it. Giovanni, you'll have a cup of tea before you go?'

'Of course he will,' Harry answered for him. 'We have business to discuss, Gee-Gee and I.' As Maudie closed the door behind her, she heard him continue. 'Now you won't forget your promise to shave off that beard, will you?'

Maudie smiled to herself as she walked downstairs. Harry had nagged the poor man for a week before Giovanni had finally agreed—and then only to shut Harry up, she was sure—to the loss of his beard. Despite her innate distrust of foreigners, Maudie had grown very fond of Giovanni. He was a good man, she thought, a kind man. And incredibly handsome. Alice was certainly getting a bargain with that one.

'The moustache, too, don't forget,' Harry was saying as he and Giovanni drew their chairs up to the table by the balcony windows.

'Yes, Harry, a promise is a promise. I shall not forget.'

'By God, we'll make an impression tonight, Gee-Gee, just you wait and see. Those flash city folk think they're coming to a backwater but we'll show them a thing or two. And we'll dance their women off their feet, what's more.'

'That might not be such a good idea,' Giovanni suggested, but Harry wasn't listening. There was something he wanted to say and he wasn't quite sure how to broach the subject.

'The Clover's doing well, Gee-Gee. All thanks to your hard work . . .'

'And Rico's,' Giovanni added.

That was the subject. Rico. Harry wanted Rico out. The man was a timebomb awaiting detonation. He was dangerous. And even when he wasn't posing a threat, he was an embarrassment. 'Yes, of course,' he agreed. 'Rico's a hard worker. A good worker.' Giovanni nodded assuredly and Harry took a deep breath, deciding to get straight to the point. 'But he's not one of us, Gee-Gee. We could go a long way, you and I.'

As Harry Brearley turned and looked out of the window, determined to say his piece, he didn't notice the change in the Italian's customary good-natured demeanour.

Rico's words were flashing through Giovanni's mind. 'He will betray us, Gio,' Rico had said, over and over. 'First me and then you. It is only a matter of time.' Always Giovanni had defended Harry. 'He is our friend, Rico; he has been good to us all. To you and me and

Teresa and the children too. You ask Teresa, she likes Harry, she is grateful.' And Rico would snarl derisively. 'You are fools, both of you. Harry Brearley is good to us only while we are useful to him, you wait and see.'

Now, as Giovanni watched Harry, he wondered if his brother could be right.

'Rico's certainly not afraid of hard work, Gee-Gee,' Harry was saying, 'and that's admirable. He is an asset to any team whose requirements are pure physical strength.'

Harry was being genuine. He was fond of Giovanni and he wanted to share with him the success he sensed was within their grasp. But he also knew that, to attain success, one must at times be ruthless. One must focus on one's assets and dispense with one's liabilities. And Rico Gianni was a massive liability.

'But you have moved on, Gee-Gee.' Now was the time to lay his cards on the table. 'I have plans for us and they cannot include your brother.'

'What are these plans, Harry?' The question was asked calmly. There was no edge to Giovanni's voice and Harry, in his excitement to communicate, failed to notice the set of the Italian's jaw or the fact that his hazel eyes had changed colour.

Rico had been right, Giovanni thought, his anger mounting. For a year now he had put his brother's obsession down to the blind madness which he knew raged within. Now it appeared that it was he, Giovanni, who had been blind. A blind, gullible fool.

'Real estate, my friend.' Harry's eyes burned with a child's greedy excitement. 'The pipeline, don't you see? With the pipeline, the price of land and property will skyrocket.'

Harry stood up and paced the floor, unable to contain his enthusiasm. 'Kalgoorlie will become a city of substance, a city in its own right, not dependent on gold alone. Already it's a centre for the outlying sheep stations and wheat farmers and, with the pipeline, local business will expand, people will flock to buy property. Kal will never die, Gee-Gee. Even if the gold ran out, she would never die. Not like other towns. Coolgardie will; I see a ghost town there some day. But not Kal. Never Kal.'

Harry stopped pacing and pulled his chair up to the table once more. 'I tell you, Gee-Gee, Kal will prosper and we will prosper with her . . .'

'We. You and me. It is you and me who will prosper, yes?'

'You and I, yes.' Harry automatically corrected Giovanni as he always did. 'You and I. We are partners.' Still he did not read the danger signs.

'Rico. He is a partner also.'

It was only then that Harry noticed something was wrong. Never had he seen such a look in Giovanni's eyes. They were the eyes of another man. A man Harry did not know.

He realised it was time to backpedal.

'Of course Rico is a partner, Gee-Gee,' he said, quickly, his smile pure Brearley charm. 'But he's a partner of a different kind. He is . . .'

'You shake his hand the same way you shake mine.'

'Of course I did. We all shook hands. Partners. And it was the right partnership for the right time. But when we sell the mine and move on . . .'

'We will not sell the mine, Harry.' Giovanni stood slowly and, although his voice was not raised, the edge to it was chilling. 'We are partners. You and me and Rico. Three partners.'

'Of course we are.' Harry felt vulnerable sitting so he also stood, keeping his amiable smile in place while he pretended to ignore the Italian's anger. 'It was simply an idea I thought I would put forward to you. If we decide to move on we . . .'

'If we move on, we move on all three of us together.'

'Of course we do, Gee-Gee, of course we do. I merely thought you and I could discuss the possibilities first before approaching Rico.' Giovanni remained impassive, his eyes still searching Harry's, seeking the truth. 'Come along, my friend,' Harry put a comradely arm around the Italian's shoulders. 'You know yourself how irrational your brother can be. I simply considered that a discussion between the two of us would be more productive.'

Giovanni allowed himself to relax, just a little. 'Next time we talk, we talk as three. I will look after Rico.'

'An excellent idea.'

'And we talk soon. On Monday we talk.'

Harry realised it was an ultimatum. 'Why not? Monday then. Tonight the banquet, tomorrow a day of rest and Monday we talk. Excellent.'

The door opened and Maudie arrived with the tea tray. 'I have some of your favourite lemon cake, Giovanni,' she said. 'Just the way you . . .'

'I am sorry. I cannot stay for the tea. I promised Alice.' He crossed abruptly to the door.

Ignoring the query in Maudie's eyes Harry followed him. 'A silly misunderstanding, Gee-Gee. I'm sorry, I voiced myself badly.' He held out his hand. 'To the partners of the Clover. You and me and Rico. What do you say?'

Giovanni nodded. 'To the partners.' And they shook hands firmly.

'Don't you forget now.' Harry grinned and slapped Giovanni on the back. 'That beard goes.'

'A promise is a promise, Harry.' But Giovanni did not smile in return as he closed the door behind him.

'What was that about?' Maudie asked. 'He looked so strange—did you say something to anger him?'

'Ah who knows?' Harry shrugged. 'These Italians

are a volatile bunch, even Giovanni. Maybe there's a touch of his brother in him. No matter, he'll get over it. A storm in a teacup is all it is. Speaking of which,' he looked at his fob watch, 'pour the tea, my dear. I must have an hour with my babies before the procession.'

Maudie smiled as she poured. Harry doted on little Victoria and James. Even when the twins were asleep he would sit beside their bassinets gazing at them adoringly and touching their tiny fingers.

'Just think, Harry, in less than three hours we'll be witness to one of the great wonders of the world.' Having followed the progress of the pipeline to date Maudie no longer had doubts as to its success. 'What a tragedy that O'Connor shouldn't be here to reap the honours.'

It was the talk on everyone's lips and had been for the past eleven months. Ever since Charles Yelverton O'Connor, the designer responsible for the goldfields water scheme, had suicided. Conjecture was rife as to the reason. Stress and overwork, some said. A result of his being hounded by the press, said others. But it was common knowledge that the brilliant man had never doubted the successful outcome of the Kalgoorlie pipeline. So why, on March 10th, 1902, while enjoying his early morning gallop along the sandy shores of the Indian Ocean, had he ridden his horse into the sea and shot himself? No one knew.

As Maudie chatted away, Harry nodded and murmured agreement but his mind was elsewhere.

Giovanni's reaction had shocked him. He obviously did not have the Italian in his pocket as he had presumed. Why was the man behaving like such a fool? Oh, of course a promise was a promise and blood was thicker than water—Harry recognised all of that. But not where Rico Gianni was concerned—the fellow was a madman. Besides, a deal was a deal when all was said and done and Harry would certainly have offered Rico generous compensation. His had been a genuine offer, Harry thought defensively, and Giovanni's reaction had been irrational. The man, through his misguided sense of family honour, was obviously blind to reason.

The more Harry thought about it the more he felt insulted, misunderstood. Yes, his offer had been heartfelt, he told himself, the offer of a friend. The offer of position, fortune, a whole new life. And Giovanni had refused. Well, so be it! One could not be responsible for fools. Especially where money was concerned.

He'd done the right thing by Giovanni—now he must move quickly. It was just as well he had covered himself from the very outset.

GIOVANNI DID NOT go home as he had intended. He needed to be on his own, away from the noise of the family. He needed to think. Anyway, it was only two hours until he must return to Maudie's and meet Alice as he had promised. They were going to join the procession to Mount Charlotte to watch the ceremonial release of the water into the reservoir. He bought a copy of the *Evening Star* and went to the Sheaf, a hotel frequented by Italians.

'Buonosera, Giovanni.'

'Buonosera.'

The group of timbercutters at the far end of the bar beckoned him to join them but he declined, saluting them with his newspaper. He bought a beer and pulled a chair up to a small table in the corner by the window. There were no miners in the bar. Despite the fact that it was the afternoon of the most important celebration in Kalgoorlie's history, it was work as usual at all the big mines. Harry had been the one to insist Rico and Giovanni take the day off. 'You deserve it,' he'd said. 'You work too hard as it is.' Giovanni had half expected to see Rico in the bar but he was glad to discover his brother wasn't there.

In the walk from Maudie's to the Sheaf Giovanni's fury had abated. He was glad. He had lived with such anger during his years on the docks of Genoa and during his first few weeks in Fremantle. He did not like to feel anger.

He sat, pretending to read the newspaper, but churning over and over in his mind every word of his exchange with Harry, wondering whether he had overreacted.

Harry was right, of course: Rico was utterly irrational. It was perfectly understandable that Harry should not wish to discuss business until he had first consulted Giovanni. But all plans included Rico whether Harry liked it or not. They were equal partners, all three.

Giovanni sipped his beer and decided to put aside all thoughts of animosity. If Harry had indeed wanted to buy Rico out, and who could blame him, he was now certainly aware that no such option existed. In any event, such an offer did not amount to betrayal. Yes, Giovanni decided, he had overreacted. Harry had been a good friend and friendship was a thing to be valued. He would apologise to him tonight.

IT WAS A remarkable sight. Never in the history of Kalgoorlie, nor in the history of any other Australian inland town, had there been such a spectacle. And possibly there never would be again. Thousands upon thousands of people—up to twelve thousand, the newspapers later reported—walked through the blistering heat towards the tiny reservoir of Mount Charlotte. Men, women and children. The people of Kalgoorlie and Boulder were joined by the hordes who had arrived by train from the city, and in traps and carriages from other country towns, and on horseback from near and distant farms.

Together they climbed the steep, winding tracks through the searing heat. The elderly who knew they would never live to see such a spectacle again. The very young who simply believed it was a huge party. Mothers carrying babies, fathers piggybacking their sons. All wended their way up the slopes through the one-hundred-and-six-degree heat to witness the miracle. And amongst them were the nation's leaders, the men of vision destined to leave their imprint upon the pages of their country's history.

The crowd gathered around the slopes and, as the leaders disengaged themselves from the masses and one by one appeared before them on the small mound of the reservoir, a mighty cheer went up.

First Sir Willam Lyne, then the Sydney politician George Reid, soon to become Prime Minister, then finally Sir John Forrest, Federal Minister for Defence and the man elected to officially open the scheme. Each was enthusiastically cheered by the massive crowd.

Amongst the thousands were Giovanni and Alice, hands clasped, Rico and Teresa, Rico holding his two-year-old son Salvatore above his head like a tribute. Evan and Kate Jones, Evan bearing little Briony on his shoulders, and Harry and Maudie Brearley, arms linked around each other's waists. They cheered along with the others whilst young Jack Brearley, Enrico Gianni and Paul Jones ran amok thrilling to the noise and the crowd itself.

The masses hushed as Sir John Forrest commenced his address. His voice was loud and clear. 'My mind is filled with humble gratitude for having been permitted to declare this great water scheme open to the public . . .'

When he grasped the large wheel and turned it, not a sound was heard for several seconds. During those seconds, and for the many thousands gathered, time stood still.

Then the water gushed forth and the crowd erupted. Strangers embraced each other. Hundreds and hundreds of hats were heedlessly thrown high to be lost in the crowd. The cheers were never-ending. People wept, people laughed. Jubilation filled the air.

During the trek down the slopes, the exhilaration continued unabated. Many were going to the hotels to drink to the success of the seemingly impossible. There would be parties in the streets. Law and order had no place in tonight's festivities. But law and order would not be needed—people were too happy to make trouble.

Giovanni did not join Rico and a band of others who were going to drink at Maudie's. He had to go home to wash and dress for the banquet.

'He is too grand for us, Arturo.' Rico nudged his friend and minced down the street like a fop, his hobbled legs ridiculous. 'He must look pretty for the men from the city.'

'Oh no, Rico.' Arturo joined in the mockery. 'He would be a fool if he did not look pretty for the *women* of the men from the city.' He made a lewd gesture and the two men laughed. Little Arturo and his wife owned the store in Boulder from which Rico bought his abundant supplies of red wine and the two had become good friends.

Giovanni laughed along with them. The derision was good-natured enough. But nonetheless he refused to join them even for one quick drink. He knew it would take time to shave off his eighteen-month growth of beard and he did not want to break his promise to Harry. Shaving off his beard would be his way of apologising to his friend and dispelling any sense of acrimony that might remain.

TWO HOURS LATER, at the appointed time, Giovanni walked up the back stairs of Maudie's pub to Alice's room. True to her word, Maudie had allowed Alice the night off and Alice had planned her evening meticulously. She and Giovanni would have a drink in the downstairs ladies' lounge and then together they would go to the car barn where they would meet with several of her friends to watch as the dignitaries arrived, one by one. Then, when Giovanni himself entered the banquet hall as an official guest, Alice would glow with pride. Just think! Her fiancé was to mingle with the most important men and the most fashionable women in the country! Then she would join the party in the streets with her friends and wait for Giovanni to come to her room late that night and paint a picture of the banquet for her, every single detail. It would be as if she had been there herself.

Giovanni suspected that it was not the correct etiquette for him to arrive at the banquet after the dignitaries and that Harry would probably be annoyed. But he said nothing and agreed to Alice's plans—he couldn't bring himself to disappoint her.

The din from the crowded downstairs bar was deafening as Giovanni tapped lightly on Alice's door. Men were singing and shouting and spilling out into the street.

Alice appeared, smiling. She had dressed carefully for the occasion. Her very prettiest late afternoon dress with the little yellow daisies and a bolero jacket with slightly puffed sleeves. But she had decided against a hat. That would look too formal. She did not want to appear as if she had delusions, just because her fiancé had been invited to the banquet.

'Giovanni.' The smile froze on Alice's lips. Then slowly it faded.

'Who was it that you expected?' Giovanni smiled at her surprise. 'You look very pretty.' The yellow daisies reminded him of the wallpaper Teresa so liked.

Alice felt as though she had been struck. This was not her Giovanni. She didn't know this man. She knew the suit—she had chosen it herself. Three-piece. Charcoal black. And the fine white shirt with the starched high collar. Gentleman's attire. Giovanni had laughed and said he would look like a clown. But he didn't. The clothes sat upon the body of one born to wear them. Broad-shouldered, straight-backed, Giovanni looked like a nobleman. And the face. She couldn't take her eyes from his face. It was more than handsome. Its mixture of man and boy was beautiful.

A strange sense of despair overwhelmed Alice. Who had she been fooling? she thought. No one but herself, surely. She had known all along that Harry hadn't thought she was good enough for Giovanni but she'd told herself that was just Harry Brearley with his airs and graces. But Harry had been right. Had the others been laughing at her as well? she wondered. She was too old for Giovanni. Too old, too ordinary and too plain.

'What is wrong, Alice?' The fine brow was perplexed and his eyes were anxious. 'What is wrong?' he repeated when she didn't answer.

'You look different,' was all she could manage.

'Ah, the beard.' He laughed and the boyishness of his smile broke her heart. 'You see?' He bent down, took her hand and put it to his cheek. 'You see, I did not even cut myself.'

She felt the texture of his skin beneath her fingers, fine and smooth. And she traced the scar on the side of his face. Even the scar did not disfigure; it enhanced, if anything, making the boy's face that of a man.

'It was a promise to Harry,' she heard him say. 'I made a promise to Harry that I would shave away the beard.'

The beard had been her disguise, she realised. Hers, not his. In his rough miner's clothes with his rough miner's beard she had been able to pursuade herself that he was like the others. But, deep down, she had known he was not. She had seen women look at him. Suddenly Alice's best afternoon dress didn't feel pretty any more.'I will grow it back if you wish.' Why did she look so sad? Giovanni wondered. 'As soon as I am able, I will grow it back for you, Alice.'

'No, Giovanni.' She forced a smile. With or without the beard, it would make no difference. It had all been a dream. 'You look very handsome. Very handsome indeed. Shall we go?' She took his arm and they went downstairs.

As they opened the door to the ladies' lounge the noise from the main bar next door was deafening. But it was no longer the sound of singing and shouting. Voices were raised in anger and there was the shattering of glass.

Behind them, Maudie came thundering down the stairs. 'What's going on?' she yelled. Damn you, Harry, she thought, why aren't you here? Harry was having pre-banquet drinks at Hannan's Club with Richard Laverton and his cronies. She disappeared into the bar.

Then Giovanni heard the familiar roar. Then Maudie screaming, 'Get him out! Get him out!'

'Stay here, Alice.' Giovanni raced through the back door of the bar to see Rico being pushed and dragged to the main doors. The whole bar was intent on getting him out into the street but even with men hanging off him, it was a slow process. Rico, bellowing like an enraged bull, struck out blindly at all in his path.

Giovanni knew it would be impossible for him to fight his way through the crowd to get to his brother. He went back into the lounge and Alice watched, frightened, as he ran through the side door and around to the front of the hotel.

The main doors swung open and Rico staggered out

onto the pavement. He fell, taking four men with him. The men tried to let him go but he wanted to fight all of them at once.

'Don't let him get up,' one of them yelled. 'Sit on him, hold him down!' But it was too late. Rico was on his feet and smashing at anyone who tried to prevent him getting back into the bar.

Giovanni dashed up and managed to grab Rico's arms and pinion them behind his back. Momentarily taken by surprise, Rico paused for a split second. His opponents had been in front of him. Who was this fresh attacker? The arms that held him were strong. In that split second, one of the men from the bar landed a heavy punch in Rico's solar plexus but he appeared not to notice.

With a howl of fury, Rico broke Giovanni's hold and whirled about to face him. 'I kill you!' he screamed, demented. He lunged for his attacker's throat.

A strong hand grabbed his wrist and held him at bay long enough for him to hear the words 'You would kill your brother?' Rico broke the hold and reached out with both his hands for the man's neck. 'Is that what you would do, Rico? You would kill your own brother?'

As his hands found their mark, Rico finally registered Giovanni's face, the eyes, cold and brown, staring at him with disgust.

'Giovanni?' he whispered.

Giovanni continued to stare Rico down while the men backed away toward the bar doors waiting to see what would happen. The dawning of surprise on Rico's face would have been comical, Giovanni thought, had he not been so disgusting. He reeked of cheap rum; saliva ran from the corners of his mouth.

Giovanni reached up and disengaged his brother's hands from about his throat. Rico's arms fell limply to his sides.

'Come. We will go home.' He turned to the watching men. 'I am sorry,' he said. 'For my brother, I am sorry.' And, in that moment, he hated Rico. Why should he have to apologise for the name of Gianni? 'I am sorry, Maudie,' he said when Maudie appeared behind the men. 'For my brother. I am sorry. I will pay for the damage he has done.'

'He's not to come here again, Giovanni,' Maudie said. 'If he tries just once to enter this bar he'll have the law to answer to.'

Giovanni nodded and hooked Rico's arm over his shoulder. He turned, humiliated, and half-carried his brother across the street.

The others stood watching for a moment, then dispersed back to the bar, muttering amongst themselves.

From nowhere, Arturo scuttled up beside Giovanni and took Rico's other arm. Rico was incoherent by now, mumbling drunkenly.

'I am sorry, Giovanni,' Arturo said. 'There was nothing I could do.'

'It is not your fault, Arturo. Help me get him home.' Arturo was a coward but he was quite right, Giovanni thought. In his madness, Rico seemed unable to discern friend from foe, and Arturo was a little man—Rico would have swatted him like a fly.

Teresa was putting Carmelina to bed when they dragged Rico through the front door. Little Salvatore was fast asleep and Enrico had already left to watch the procession of dignitaries with Jack and Paul.

'*Mio Dio*,' she muttered as Giovanni and Arturo dumped Rico into his armchair.

'There was nothing I could do, Teresa,' Arturo said as she pumped water into a basin to bathe the cuts on Rico's hands and face. 'He was drinking rum from the bottle and he thought someone called him a cripple. But they did not. Truly. I heard no one say it.'

'Go home, Arturo,' Giovanni said. 'Go home. Thank you for your help.'

Arturo left, grateful to be gone. Tonight had frightened him. He knew Rico could be aggressive but he had never seen such violence before, such murder in a man. And for no reason.

Giovanni stayed with Teresa while she bathed Rico's wounds. They said little. They both knew there was little that could be said. Then Giovanni rose to go. Poor Alice. He hoped that she had had the sense to join her friends and watch the procession. It would be over by now and the banquet about to start.

'You will be all right?' he asked.

She was kneeling beside Rico, stroking his brow. He seemed peacefully asleep. 'Of course, Gio.' She looked up at him and smiled. 'Never would Rico hurt me, you know that. And never would he hurt the children.' She returned to stroking her husband's brow. 'There is unhappiness in him. Deep inside. You know that too.'

Giovanni felt the familiar surge of guilt, and he wondered whether that was what Teresa intended. But no, she meant nothing. Beautiful, strong, loyal Teresa. Giovanni watched her caress her husband's face. If Rico only knew how lucky he was to have such love from such a woman. But then perhaps he did know. Giovanni felt weary. He didn't want to go to the banquet, but he owed it to Harry. He turned to leave.

'Eh, Gio.' Rico's eyes had sprung open. He took his wife's hand and held it on his knee as he sat up. He no longer looked drunk. 'I would not kill my brother.'

'I know, Rico, I know.'

'Sit, Gio, sit. Talk to me.'

What was there to talk about? Giovanni knew what would follow. Defiance and remorse and then Rico's declaration of love. But he sat nonetheless.

'I did wrong, Gio, I know. But I will not be called a cripple. I am a man. I have my pride.' He was defiant.

'No one called you a cripple, Rico.' Giovanni wondered why he was bothering to contradict his brother, it would lead nowhere.

'Maybe not to my face. But I saw the man. I knew what he was thinking.'

'You cannot fight people for what they are thinking.'

'Yes, yes, I know.' Rico tried to look contrite but didn't really succeed. He changed the subject instead. 'Why do you say such things to me, Gio? "I would kill my brother." Why do you say this? I would kill *for* my brother. I would kill for my family.' He held Teresa's hand to his chest. 'I would kill for my children. I would kill . . .'

'But do you not see, Rico? There is no need to kill.' Giovanni could not quell his exasperation. 'There is no need to kill for any one of us. We are not threatened. You disgrace our family when you do this.'

'Yes. Yes.' Now the remorse. 'I am sorry I disgraced you. I am sorry I disgraced our father and mother. It is the anger, it makes me crazy.'

Giovanni stayed for nearly an hour listening to Rico's excuses and apologies and, finally, the declarations of love. And then he left for the banquet. It would be half over by now, he supposed. Harry would be angry but that couldn't be helped.

Coffee had been served and the speeches were nearing completion when Giovanni arrived at the car barn. He stood in the shadows beside the main doors, hoping no one could see him, and searched the sea of faces for Harry. He had never seen so many people under one roof. How grand it all looked. Lights and decorations hung from the high ceilings. A long bar was at one end of the hall and at the other end, far from the main doors, was a podium from which a florid-looking gentleman was addressing the crowd. The rest of the massive area was lined with row upon row of white-clothed tables at which were seated hundreds of finely dressed men and women. Try as he might, Giovanni could see no one he knew.

But Harry had seen him and in an instant, he was at Giovanni's side. He hurried him to his seat.

'Where have you been?' he whispered urgently. 'It's very rude of you, Gee-Gee. The speeches are almost over.'

'I am sorry, Harry. It was family . . .'

'No matter, no matter.' Harry bustled Giovanni into the seat beside him and flashed an apologetic smile at the attractive middle-aged woman seated opposite.

'Ladies and Gentleman, a final toast,' the florid man on the podium was saying. 'To Charles Yelverton O'Connor and the Goldfields Water Scheme.'

Harry hurriedly poured Giovanni a glass of champagne from one of the many bottles on the table and, together with the hundreds, they stood.

'To Charles Yelverton O'Connor and the Goldfields Water Scheme,' five hundred voices said in unison.

'The beard was a good idea,' Harry muttered. He winked suggestively as they sat. 'You'll win hearts tonight, I tell you.'

Giovanni was relieved that his friend was not angry. Obviously no acrimony lingered from the afternoon's exchange and Harry was not even cross with him for being late. Of course he would probably be cross when he heard about Rico and the trouble at Maudie's but Giovanni would deal with that later.

The podium was being removed and the members of a ten-piece orchestra were setting themselves up at the far end of the hall. 'Well, at least you arrived for the best part,' Harry whispered and Giovanni grinned back. Yes, he was looking forward to the dancing.

There was good reason for Harry Brearley's joviality. For him the evening could have ended before the speeches had even begun. His had been an early conquest.

It had started with the pre-banquet milling. Before the guests had been seated, Harry had already chatted to all three of the federal ministers present, including Sir John Forrest himself. He'd shared a joke with the Mayor of Kalgoorlie—but then he'd shared a joke with Koonan on many an occasion over a brandy at Hannan's—and he'd had conversations with a number of influential city businessmen. But he felt he hadn't yet made his impact. No one had seemed hugely impressed by his ideas or his social position or the fact that he owned the Clover. Then he met Gaston Picot.

He'd heard of Gaston Picot, of course; everyone in Kalgoorlie had. The man was not only a major shareholder in the Midas mine, he owned numerous real estate holdings in Boulder and Kal. Furthermore, he was known throughout the State of Western Australia as a man of fashion, a gourmet and a wine connoisseur.

In his middle forties, Picot resided in Perth and, despite the fact that he cut a dashing and rakish figure, he was by all accounts a happily married family man. He, his French-born wife and their two children, a son and a daughter, lived an opulent life in the district of Cottesloe, eight miles from the city, where their palatial mansion overlooked the Indian Ocean. Several times a year he paid a brief visit to Kalgoorlie. His family never accompanied him, he always stayed at the Palace Hotel and occasionally he frequented Hannan's.

Harry had seen the flamboyant Frenchman at the club on two occasions in the past but, try as he might, he had not been able to gain an introduction.

'Richard!' He pretended not to notice that he'd interrupted a conversation as he shook Laverton's hand effusively. He nodded to Prudence. 'Lady Laverton.'

'Mr Brearley.' Prudence was seething. Gaston Picot had just been complimenting her on her gown.

'Good to see you, Harry, old man,' Laverton lisped. 'You know Gaston Picot, I take it?'

'Oh.' Harry pretended suddenly to notice Picot. 'No, I don't believe I've had the pleasure.'

'Gaston Picot, Harry Brearley,' Laverton said, each 'r' sounding suspiciously like a 'w'. The two men shook hands. 'And Gaston's friend, Madame Renoir.'

'Madame.'

The Frenchwoman offered her hand and when Harry kissed it, she smiled her approval, as did Gaston. Prudence seethed a little more.

Although she must have been in her mid-thirties, Jeanne Renoir was even more beautiful at close quarters. Like most, Harry had only seen her from afar on the rare occasion she visited the Palace Hotel to sip tea on the balcony with a lady friend. She was the widow of a wealthy Frenchman who was said to have been a close friend of Picot's, but rumour had it that she was really Picot's mistress. Pierre Auguste Renoir, the famous impressionist painter, was reputedly her uncle and no one had any cause to disbelieve the fact.

Jeanne Renoir lived with her servants and a lady friend, an Englishwoman, in an elegant house at the lower end of Hannan Street. To the extreme disappointment of the gossip-mongers, she kept very much to herself.

'I believe you own the Clover, Mr Brearley,' Gaston was saying. 'You and your partners.' Harry was deeply impressed. The city businessmen to whom he had spoken earlier had not even heard of the Clover. When they'd discovered the mine wasn't on the Golden Mile they'd lost interest. Harry had found it rather disheartening.

'That's right, I do. She's a grand mine. Doing very well.'

'This is what I hear. *Trés bien.*' Picot's command of the English language was faultless and his accent only slight, but he always injected his conversation with the odd French phrase to enhance his image. Harry recognised the ploy and, far from being intimidated by the man's style, he was encouraged. Harry could compete with any man when it came to style and the ploys he used himself were not dissimilar. In an instant, Harry felt at home with Picot. Despite the man's wealth and power, they were two of a kind.

'I am very interested in your mine, Mr Brearley.'

'I would be more than happy to take you on a guided tour, Mr Picot. At any time.' Harry bowed his head in mock servility. 'I am your servant.'

'Call me Gaston.' Picot stroked his perfectly manicured goatee and the curls of his waxed moustache twitched as he smiled. He too recognised one of a kind. He was reminded of himself ten years ago. But only slightly. Brearley had a lot of catching up to do. Charm alone was not enough; one must be cunning.

An announcement was being made requesting the guests take their seats and, as Laverton and Picot escorted the ladies to their table near the podium, Harry accompanied them.

Surely the man wasn't presuming he could join them, Prudence thought with horror. She had had the seating plan sent to her well in advance and if Richard dared send for another chair and have another place set . . .

'Evan!' Harry exclaimed jovially. At the table a disconcerted Evan Jones was waiting with his wife Kate at his arm, wondering whether or not he should seat her before the arrival of the others.

Evan was uncomfortable in his unfamiliar suit. It

was a hot night and he was sure he was sweating more than most. 'Should we sit, Kate?' he'd whispered.

'No, my dear, wait for the others.' She had smiled encouragingly, aware of his discomfort, but then hadn't been able to resist turning her attention to her surroundings. Kate was having a wonderful time. It was like a fairyland. The lights, the decorations, the people in their finery. She was drinking in every moment, unaware of the looks cast in her direction.

'Harry.' Evan pumped Harry's hand, glad to see a familiar face.

'Hello, Kate,' Harry said and boldly took it upon himself to make the introductions, much to Prudence Laverton's disgust. 'Mr Picot and Madame Renoir, Mr and Mrs Jones.'

Good God, Prudence thought, the man was behaving as if he were the host for the evening.

Harry watched the two women as they nodded to each other. Jeanne Renoir might be beautiful, he thought, but she had more than met her match in Kate.

Harry had seen Evan arrive with his wife. He had seen the swathe they had cut as they walked through the crowd. All eyes had been on Kate Jones. The slender neck with the auburn curls pinned up under the wide-brimmed hat with its blue plume; the breasts, which the modest high-necked bodice could not disguise; the nipped-in waist beneath the little bolero jacket: everything a mixture of innocence and sexuality. As she'd stared, up wide-eyed, at the hanging decorations and whispered, 'Look, Evan, look', she was a child in a wonderland.

Harry tore his attention away. 'Forgive me,' he said, bowing slightly to the assembled company. 'I must search for my table. And indeed for my partner who has not yet arrived. I envy you gentlemen,' he smiled. 'I envy you the company of the most beautiful ladies present this evening.' His gaze shifted from Kate to Jeanne and finally came to rest on Prudence who was an average-looking woman at the very best of times. Fortunately Prudence herself was not aware of the fact. She smiled and nodded graciously, accepting the compliment as her due. She could afford to be cordial, she told herself, now that the man was leaving. And Harry Brearley was very handsome when all was said and done. Perhaps, later in the evening, she might agree to dance with him after all.

'Mr Brearley.' Picot's voice halted Harry as he turned to go.

'Harry, Gaston. Harry. Please.' Harry's roguish grin and the familiar twinkle in his eyes promised an instant and lifelong friendship. The man was cheeky, Picot thought, damn cheeky. Many might find him insulting but Gaston had rather warmed to him.

'Harry,' he corrected. 'Perhaps you would like to join me for an aperitif at the bar before you join your table. Proceedings will not get under way for a good fifteen minutes yet I'm sure.'

'Delighted.'

When the ladies were seated the two men made their excuses and repaired to the bar.

Half an hour later, when he left the bar to join his own table, Harry found that he was seated far from the podium in a rather inferior position near the main doors. But he was not irritated in the least. He was too euphoric to care. He wasn't even annoyed when he discovered that Giovanni had still not arrived. Indeed, given the conversation he had just had with Gaston Picot, Giovanni's absence had proved fortunate.

Now Giovanni had turned up and the more formal aspect of the evening had been concluded, Harry was set for fun.

'This is my partner and very good friend Giovanni Gianni.' He introduced the Italian to the party of guests and then whispered in his ear, 'Dance with Mrs Beresford, Gee-Gee.' He indicated the attractive woman in her forties seated opposite. He had noticed her appraisal of Giovanni when he'd arrived. He had also noticed the way she was watching the musicians. This was a woman who loved to dance.

'Her husband is here,' Giovanni murmured back. 'He may be offended.'

'Rubbish, he's twenty years older than she is and he's got a gammy leg,' Harry hissed out of the side of his wine glass. 'Look at her, her foot's tapping away under that table, she can't wait to be whirled about the floor.'

Beresford, a retired engineer from Perth, smiled gratefully when Giovanni asked his wife to dance. 'Go along, Henrietta,' he said. 'Enjoy yourself.' And he waved at the waiter for another bottle of wine.

'SHALL WE, MY dear?' At the Lavertons' table on the opposite side of the hall, Richard rose and offered his arm to Prudence. He would far rather have asked Kate but it was more than his life was worth. He could already sense his wife's annoyance with the amount of attention he had been paying to the young woman. But what red-blooded male could resist feasting his eyes on such a creature, he thought. Richard couldn't wait for the first progressive waltz when it was customary for the married men to ask women other than their wives to dance. Prudence could hardly complain then.

As Prudence fussed with her evening bag and adjusted her gloves, Evan rose uncomfortably. 'Kate?'

But instead of taking his arm, she put her hand in his and gently shook her head. 'No, no,' she said. 'Let us sit for a moment. It is still very hot.' She took off her evening gloves, as she had seen many of the other women do, and Evan sat down gratefully. He felt guilty;

he knew she was longing to dance and that she was declining because of him. She had gone to a lot of trouble to learn all the steps herself and had painstakingly attempted to teach him. But he was like a bear with two left feet. This was the part of the evening Evan had been dreading the most. Perhaps if he had some more wine. He poured himself another glass to boost his courage.

'A little later then,' he murmured.

'Yes, a little later,' Kate answered. Poor Evan, she thought, he was not enjoying himself.

One by one, the other couples left the table to dance and Prudence, having made the final adjustments to her hat, was ready to join the fray. Behind his wife's back, Richard Laverton smiled at Kate. 'I demand the progressive waltz, my dear,' he said softly, as if it were a promise she was waiting to hear.

Kate smiled back at him and, as he and Prudence swirled away, she leaned close to Evan and lisped in his ear, 'What an ecthiting prothpect.'

Evan gave one of his barking laughs and nearly spilled his wine. 'Stop it, Kate.'

'Why mutht I thtop it?' Kate grinned impishly; she could always make him laugh. 'He ith thuch a thilly man.'

They were overcome with a fit of the giggles and Evan felt himself start to relax. Several minutes later, when the others returned to the table and Laverton opened his mouth to speak, Kate and Evan had to fight to maintain their composure, neither daring to look at the other.

'LADIES AND GENTLEMEN, take your partners for the progressive Pride of Erin waltz.'

It was the moment Richard Laverton had been waiting for. 'May I?' He leapt to his feet with unseemly haste and bowed to Kate.

'I would be delighted, Lord Laverton.' As she left the table on his arm, Kate cast a look back at Evan and there was such mischievousness in the curve of her lip and the gleam in her eye that Evan nearly laughed out loud. He controlled himself and asked Jeanne Renoir to dance instead, relieved that Gaston Picot was offering his arm to Prudence. Since his first onslaught of nerves, Evan had had three more glasses of red wine, to which he was unaccustomed, and had managed to flounder his way through the military two-step and even a fast polka with Kate. He was starting to enjoy himself at last.

'MAY I HAVE this pleasure?'

Giovanni had danced with each of the women at their table, but this was the third time he had asked Henrietta Beresford. She loved the way he said 'this' pleasure. She loved his accent and the way he danced, holding her close. She jumped to her feet, delighted.

Henrietta's husband had long since taken his gammy leg to the bar where he was drunkenly discussing the merits of the Goldfields Water Scheme with several others to whom the wine was of more importance than the conversation. Henrietta was having the time of her life. She felt twenty-five again, and found the handsome young Italian devastatingly attractive.

As Harry offered his arm to one of the other women, he raised an eyebrow and nodded at Giovanni who grinned back, but the suggestive encouragement was lost on him. Giovanni was aware of Henrietta Beresford's lust, but not at all interested in any form of reciprocation. He chose her to partner him simply because she was the best dancer.

The Pride of Erin was his favourite. It was a beautiful dance. He smiled at Henrietta as they completed their circular waltz and she glided on to the man in front. She smiled back regretfully. It was a pity it was a progressive waltz, she thought. She didn't want to dance with every man in the room. She wanted to dance with Giovanni.

Giovanni himself found it all very interesting. One moment he was holding an overweight, middle-aged matron with perfect rhythm in his arms and the next a beautiful young woman with no sense of the music at all. Giovanni loved everything about the dancing. He had never in his life heard a ten-piece orchestra and the music was charging through his entire body. He wanted to dance forever.

He smiled at his partner as they completed the circular waltz and then he turned to the next woman. His arm encircled her and he felt the slim back beneath the satin fabric, her hand in his was small and gloveless. Some women were wearing gloves and some not. He preferred the touch of skin.

'Good evening,' he said to the hat with its soft blue plume. And then the brim of the hat rose and his eyes met those beneath it.

He stopped. The music left him. All sense of rhythm was gone. There was nothing except the face of the woman in his arms. It was the face of the girl from the mountain.

Kate, too, was momentarily frozen. She looked into the eyes that were staring into hers. Where had she seen those eyes before? Where?

There was a mild collision behind them. The line of dancers was progressing and they were in the way.

'I am so sorry,' Kate apologised, embarrassed, then smiled at Giovanni. 'I think we are causing a problem.'

Her voice. It was the same voice. This was no apparition. Giovanni forced himself to dance again. The rhythm came naturally but all he could think of was the circular waltz. Only several more seconds before the circular waltz and then she would move on to the next partner. He couldn't speak, he didn't know what to say.

'I know you,' Kate said.

'My name is Giovanni.' He blurted it out. It sounded clumsy. Only several more steps to go.

Of course. Everything came flooding back. The long, weary trek from the chalet. Her despair. The cold, cold night. The sound of the concertina and the young man singing. The beautiful voice reaching out to her through the still, icy air. The warmth of his fire and the scalding cup of black coffee. And the young man's kind eyes. She remembered thinking 'the young man has a kind face'. She looked up at the face now. It was more than kind. It was beautiful. She wanted to touch it.

'Yes,' she said. 'Of course. Giovanni.' He was staring at her so, but she couldn't take her eyes from his. 'My name is Caterina,' she heard herself saying.

'Caterina.' They started on the circular waltz. 'Caterina,' he said again.

'Yes. And you are Giovanni and you are from Santa Lena. You see? I remember.'

They had finished the circular waltz and she was leaving him.

Giovanni did not see the next woman whose body was against his and whose hand rested upon his shoulder. It took only three waltz steps to deftly change partners with the man in front of him and Caterina was once again in his arms. The surprised indignity on the faces of the man and the woman was comical but it was lost on Caterina and Giovanni.

As they waltzed, Giovanni was once again speechless. All he could think of was the fact that she was here, in his arms. He was touching her skin. The hand in his was her hand. It was real. The body he could feel moving to the rhythm of the music was flesh and blood. No longer an illusion his mind had manufactured in the streets of Genoa or Fremantle. He was holding her to him. His girl from the mountain.

As they started the circular waltz, Kate felt Giovanni draw her closer to him and start to move out of the line of dancers and suddenly she was jolted back to reality. She looked around the crowded floor. Across the circle of dancers she could see Evan. He was watching them, distracted, forgetting to count the rhythm of the dance in his head, and his partner was trying to avoid his feet as he threatened to step on her.

'No. Please. Stay in the line.' He hesitated. 'Please,' she pleaded.

In the final swirl of the waltz Giovanni brought them back into the line and then she was gone. His eyes followed the blue hat as it danced further and further away from him but she did not look back.

Kate wondered why she felt guilty. What had she done? She had met someone from her past, nothing more. A ghost from long ago had momentarily awakened a girl who had ceased to exist. It had come as a shock, that was all.

By the time she reached Evan the unsettling spectre of her past was firmly in perspective. 'I've been watching,' she smiled and whispered. 'You're doing very well.'

'I see you've met Giovanni.' There was nothing condemnatory in Evan's tone but something in his eyes was searching for reassurance.

'Yes,' she answered, surprised. 'How do you know him?' And then she realised. 'Giovanni! Of course!' she exclaimed. 'He is Paul's Giovanni.' The Giovanni of whom her son constantly spoke. Giovanni with his concertina. And his brother, Rico. She had seen him once. Watched him, fascinated, as he and Teresa had kissed unashamedly on the snowy mountainside. She had worked with Teresa at the chalet. And now Teresa and Rico were married and they were here. Here in

Kalgoorlie. And the brothers had bought Evan's mine with Harry Brearley.

Any remaining threat from the past left Kate in an instant. She laughed. All these months she had been sending scones and cakes to the Gianni household with Paul. 'Paul's Giovanni,' she said again. 'How strange life is.' Evan was looking at her questioningly. 'I met him once many years ago. No, twice,' she corrected herself. 'I met him twice. He comes from a village near my father's farm. A village called Santa Lena.'

She smiled, expertly avoiding Evan's feet as they completed the circular waltz, and moved on. Evan felt himself relax. The chill that had overcome him as he'd watched them dance had gone.

Giovanni's eyes followed the blue hat as the waltz progressed. Don't let the music stop, he prayed, don't let the music stop.

'Well, well, here we are again.' It was Henrietta, who had also been praying that the music wouldn't stop. At least not until she was once more in Giovanni's arms. And now that she was, she prayed fervently that it *would* stop. Perhaps then he would ask her for the next waltz.

But the music didn't stop. Henrietta sighed regretfully and moved on and Giovanni watched as the blue hat came nearer. And nearer. Two partners away now. She caught his eye and smiled as she swirled. She was right beside him. Then the music stopped.

She smiled at him once more as her partner started to escort her to her table. He was about to say something but a hand was suddenly and firmly locked into the crook of his arm.

'You dance beautifully, Mr . . . ?' His partner was waiting for him to escort her to her table.

'Gianni,' he said. 'Giovanni Gianni.'

The woman didn't initiate any further conversation and, as she resumed her seat, she wondered how a foreigner, even one that handsome, had come to be invited to the banquet. He must be someone of importance, she concluded and, as he left, she turned to her husband to enquire who he was.

Giovanni did not return to his table. He had noted where Catarina was sitting and as the orchestra struck up the Glengarry waltz he wended his way amongst the milling guests.

'May I have this pleasure?' he asked.

'Giovanni.' It was only then that Giovanni noticed Evan seated beside Caterina. Evan stood. 'I believe you and Kate have met before.'

'Kate?' Giovanni looked from Caterina to Evan, confused.

'Kate Jones,' she said. 'I am Paul's mother.' She took her husband's hand as he stood beside her and Giovanni only vaguely heard what she was saying. Her voice seemed to come from far away. 'I cannot thank you enough for what you have done for Paul. He thinks the world of you.' Kate smiled up at him and the smile was warm, sincere, but it was not the smile of the girl from the mountain. Not the smile of the girl he had just danced with, his Caterina. This was Kate Jones, Evan's wife.

Giovanni heard himself introduced to the rest of the guests at the table. He heard himself respond accordingly; he felt himself shake hands with the men, but it was if he were not there. His mind was saying Caterina, Kate Jones, Caterina, Kate Jones, over and over.

When the introductions were completed Giovanni remained standing, at a loss, and it was Evan who, uncharacteristically, initiated the conversation.

'Giovanni and Kate met each other many years ago,' he explained. Damn it, he thought, he had to say something. Giovanni was staring so at Kate. Surely the others had noticed.

'Oh, really? Where was that, Mr Gianni?' Prudence

asked. It was indeed intriguing to wonder where Kate Jones would have met a foreigner like Giovanni Gianni, Prudence thought. Given his name and his accent she could only presume he was Italian, although he certainly didn't look it. Weren't Italians swarthy?

But Giovanni seemed not to hear her. 'May I have this pleasure?' he asked.

There was a jarring silence which Evan once again broke. 'Go ahead, my dear, you and Giovanni can talk of old times.' He watched them walk onto the dance floor. He watched as they melded into each other's arms and danced as one. And the cold chill returned. They belonged together. Two beautiful people. In love. That was it, he thought. It was not just their beauty; they looked like lovers. Was that it? he wondered. Had they been lovers? Evan was in agony.

'Caterina.' Giovanni could not resist saying her name.

She shook her head. 'I am called Kate,' she said. But, once again, she could not tear her eyes from his. The complacency with which she had layed the ghosts of her past to rest was shattered.

'I know. Evan's wife and Paul's mother.' He paused. 'Paolo's mother.' Suddenly, Giovanni understood. 'You crossed the mountain happy and you come back sad,' he remembered saying to her by the fire in the falling snow.

'Yes. Paolo,' Caterina whispered. And he knew it was an admission.

'He is a fine boy.'

She nodded and there was the glint of a tear in her eyes.

The Glengarry waltz suddenly seemed silly to Giovanni. How foolish to be skipping about a dance floor, he thought.

'Come.' He stopped dancing and took her arm in his. 'It is too hot. We shall walk outside.'

She hesitated only a fraction of a second, then they walked towards the main doors. And through the crowds from across the room, Evan watched them leave.

They walked. Along the broad pavements, beneath the shop awnings. Neither dared stand still. Kate talked, she needed to talk. And she spoke to him in Italian, the first time she had spoken her mother tongue to anyone other than her son in years.

'I have left so much behind, Giovanni.' Her arm was linked in his and he could think of nothing but her touch. 'You bring it all back to me. Is this why I feel the way I do?'

'So what is wrong with the past? You are Italian. You should be proud.' She nodded. Once again the tears were not far away. 'And your son. Paolo too should be proud.'

She continued to stare ahead as a tear coursed down her cheek. Giovanni felt guilty. He had not meant to make her cry. He stopped walking and turned her to him. 'I carry my past with me always, Caterina. The good and the bad. And I carry you with me. Always you are there.'

She looked at him, bewildered, and gently he wiped the tear from her cheek with his finger. 'You are my girl from the mountain and I have seen you in the streets of Genoa. I have seen you in a knife fight in Fremantle.' He smiled and tried to joke her out of her sadness. 'See? This is because of you.' He pointed to the scar on his cheek. 'I should have seen the knife if it were not for the ghost of you.'

Caterina put her hand to his cheek and gently traced the scar. 'It *was* me,' she whispered. 'I was there.'

Giovanni looked at her disbelievingly.

'I was there,' she repeated. 'Paolo was with me. Two men were trying to kill each other and we were caught in the crowd. I did not know it was you.'

Giovanni laughed loudly. 'Ah well, at least one time I was not mad, although I swear I thought you were driving me mad. I would have searched the world for you.'

The smile was fading from his lips, his eyes were once more serious. 'And now I find you it is too late.'

She knew it was not a statement. She knew it was a question. 'Yes, Giovanni,' she said. 'It is too late.'

'I love you, Caterina.'

She knew if she allowed him to kiss her they would both be lost. 'Kate,' she said. 'My name is Kate, and it is time for us to go back.' She turned and took his arm and they were silent as they walked through the dusty streets back to the car barn.

Chapter Eleven

Kal was usually quiet on a Sunday. But not this Sunday. The day after the opening of the Goldfields Water Scheme, the streets were strewn with the evidence of celebration. Hundreds of visitors were still in town, some preparing to leave and some staying to see the sights. Many of the die-hard revellers who had celebrated all night were determined not to give in and, well after dawn, the sounds of carousing could be heard in many parts of the town. In private homes, in pubs, and especially in the red-light district of Hay Street.

To Kate Jones, however, this Sunday was like any other. Sunday was her baking day and, as usual, she would cook an extra batch for her son to take to the Gianni household for their weekly singalong. But this Sunday there would be one small difference. This Sunday Kate herself would accompany Paul. She would stay only briefly, just long enough to embrace Teresa and meet Rico and their children. And she would take Briony with her.

Kate had slept little throughout the night. She had lain on her side, feigning sleep, feeling the solid warmth of Evan's back against hers, hearing the slow steady rhythm of his breathing, and she'd reasoned with herself. Over and over.

When they had returned from the banquet Evan had

confronted her, as much as it was within Evan's power to confront. And even then, it had been the red wine which had lent him the courage to speak his mind.

'I need to know, Kate. What is this man to you?'

She was surprised by the directness of his question. But she did not pretend ignorance. 'Giovanni?'

He nodded and waited for her to answer.

'I met him a long time ago. Briefly.'

Evan's mind had run riot the moment he had seen them leave the car barn. There was a bond between these two. What was it? Had they been lovers? Was Giovanni perhaps the father of her son? Conjecture had tormented Evan.

'Were you . . . ?' He knew Kate would tell him the truth but he wasn't sure if he could bear to hear it. 'Were you intimate with him?' It came out in a rush and sounded awkward.

For the first time, Kate recognised his pain. Had she and Giovanni been that transparent? 'No, my dear. We met twice and we spoke no more than a few words. I did not even know his name at the time.'

Relief flooded through Evan. He knew she was telling the truth. Kate always did. But whether it was the red wine or not, he couldn't leave it alone. 'The man's in love with you.'

Kate smiled. Away from Giovanni it was easy to be confident, sure that she had things in perspective. 'Giovanni is a romantic. He is in love with an idea.' She kissed him. 'Now come along, it is late. Time for bed.'

And then she'd lain awake and reasoned. Or tried to. She had told Evan the truth. She had spoken no more than a few words to Giovanni all those years ago and, it was true, she had not even registered his name at the time. Although now she could remember that he had told her. 'My name is Giovanni,' he had said, just as he did last night. And, on the mountainside, she had been so distracted she had barely registered his face. The young man was kind, that was all she had thought. And now she could think of nothing but his face. What had happened to her?

She finally decided that it was beyond reason and that common sense must prevail. It had been the headiness of the banquet and the reminders of the past, that was all. It was just as she had told Evan, Giovanni was in love with an idea and he had carried her along with him. She was being romantic and foolish. Tomorrow she would visit the Giannis with Paul and Briony and she would laugh with Teresa and meet Teresa's children. It was absurd to think that their families had lived within two miles of each other for over eighteen months and had never met.

It was nearly dawn before Kate fell asleep, hoping she could persuade Evan to come with them tomorrow.

AS DAWN CREPT over the Golden Mile, Giovanni sat looking down at Kate's cottage wondering if she was asleep or if she was thinking of him.

When Kate and Evan had made their departure from the banquet Giovanni too had left. But he hadn't gone home. He couldn't. He'd walked through the streets and out of Kal instead. His mind was a blank. No thoughts, no plans, just the vision of Caterina.

On the very outskirts of town, he realised where his feet were taking him.

It was dark but the moon was full and, when he reached the Midas mine, he climbed the dump and looked out over the Golden Mile. Dotted here and there were the dumps of the other big mines. They were formed of the waste rock, or tailings, from which the gold had been extracted. Having been through a water-and-cyanide treatment the tailings were liquid when added to the dump and quickly solidified to form a hill which grew daily. One day they would be mountains, Giovanni thought. That is if the gold did not run out. And they said that the gold of Kalgoorlie never would.

It was a strange landscape, eerie in the silent moonlit night. Barren. Arid. Here and there the crushing mills where the extraction took place, here and there the huge vats of artesian water used for the cyanide treatments. The bolder of the local children stole in and used the vats as swimming pools during the hot summer nights or on Sundays when the mines were still.

Each mine was represented by its poppet head, standing like a small Eiffel Tower over the main shaft. Twice a day, the poppet heads' pulley systems would lower the cages of men to the honeycombed sphere which lay far below the earth's surface. And, twice a day, they would haul the cages of men back up into the shocking glare of the above-ground world.

Miners were a special breed, Giovanni thought. They loved to be underground. He knew he did. He looked at the poppet heads and wondered what it would be like down the big mines. There were caves as grand as cathedrals, he'd been told.

As the pink of dawn crept into the sky, the air was still and the Golden Mile was silent. It would remain so throughout the day. But come eight o'clock on Monday morning, at the start of the early shift, the air would be dense with steam and dust and the noise would be deafening from the stamping machines in the mills where the ore was being crushed.

Giovanni's eyes searched the outbuildings of the Midas. The offices and the several cottages. Which was Kate's? he wondered. One house was bigger than the rest, surrounded by fences with its own back yard. The mine manager's? No, he had heard that Laverton did not live on the Golden Mile. He had a grand house in town not far from Hannan's Club. Perhaps the accountant's or the engineer's. Evan would not have been allocated a house like that. Of the several other cottages, one had a small and carefully tended plot of garden beside the front verandah. That was where she lived, he was sure of it. Then he noticed, tethered by a small shed at the rear of the cottage, Evan's horse.

He sat and stared at the house for an hour, picturing her, eyes closed, auburn hair strewn across a white pillow, her hand curled beneath her cheek. And it was only when the sun was in the sky and an early morning group of city visitors arrived to look at the Golden Mile before the heat of the day set in that Giovanni finally left his post and walked the two miles home.

'AH, THE CONQUERING hero returns!' Rico was up to his elbows in flour, a tablecloth wrapped around his waist, helping Teresa make the ravioli for the evening feast. 'Look at him, all dressed up. And who did we conquer last night, hey? A fancy woman from the city, was that who, Gio?' Rico was in a fine mood and appeared to have completely forgotten the previous evening's incident. 'You tell your big brother everything.' His grin was lewd.

'Shush, Rico.' Teresa was rolling out a fresh batch of dough and she gestured at the children. Little Salvatore was asleep in his cot in the corner and five-year-old Carmelina was at the end of the table making shapes out of the off-cut dough. 'Anyway,' she added, 'Giovanni is engaged to be married, He has been with Alice. Tell us about the night, Gio, was it grand? Did you dance?'

Alice! Giovanni had completely forgotten. He had promised to go to her after the banquet. Not once had she entered his thoughts.

He changed quickly and left the house with barely a word. Rico and Teresa exchanged looks and Teresa ran to the front door.

'Gio!' she called after him. 'You will be home for supper?'

'Yes,' he called back. 'I will be home.'

Giovanni felt deeply sorry for the hurt he was about to cause Alice but the simple fact was that he could not marry her. He could not marry anyone. He accepted that he could not have Caterina. But in his heart she was his and she always would be. No one could stop him worshipping from afar.

'I AM SORRY, Alice. About last night.'

They were sitting by themselves in the smaller upstairs parlour which Maudie allowed the staff to use as their private sitting room. Alice had suggested they adjourn to the parlour. She hadn't wanted them to talk in her room where they had made love so many times.

'It's all right, Giovanni. I know you had to take Rico home. I watched the procession with my friends.'

'I am sorry I did not come to you after the banquet.'

'I had not expected you to.' It was true. She had somehow known he would not come back. But it hadn't stopped her crying most of the night. In the morning, however, she had been resolved.

Giovanni was surprised. 'But I had said I would. It was wrong of me. I am sorry, Alice. Please forgive me.'

'It is you who must forgive me, Giovanni. I cannot marry you.' It took Alice all the courage she could muster to meet Giovanni's eyes as she said it. But she did. And her tone did not waver.

'I am sorry to be so blunt,' she continued, 'but I thought for a very long time last night and ... No please,' she interrupted as she sensed him about to apologise again. 'It's not because you didn't come back after the banquet. I decided earlier. We're wrong for each other. There are people better suited for you and people better suited for me.' She rose. 'And I decided it was better if we didn't marry. I'm very sorry to be so sudden about this, it's just that I . . .' She had to get out of the room. And quickly. His look was so tender, so concerned, and his lips were parted and all she could think of was the fact that she had kissed that perfect mouth. 'Well, it all happened so quickly you see, I suddenly realised it would be wrong if we married . . .'

His instant acceptance confirmed her fears. He was not disappointed, in fact he was possibly relieved, and he was about to say something. Probably something like, 'I shall always be fond of you, Alice' or 'I shall always be your friend'. Well, this had been her decision she told herself. Hers, not his. And with a strength and dignity she mustered from she knew not where, Alice leant up and kissed him on the cheek.

'I shall always be your friend, Giovanni. I wish you well.'

Safely in her room, Alice blubbered into her handkerchief, but she felt proud. She'd stood by her resolution; she hadn't faltered. The lectures she'd delivered herself in the early hours of the morning had paid off. What had happened to her pride? she'd asked herself. Over the years there'd been men by the score who'd made proposals to her, she was one of the most popular barmaids in Kalgoorlie. And not all the proposals had been indecent either; she must have had at least half a dozen marriage offers, serious ones, over the years.

This was Kalgoorlie, she'd told herself, there was a shortage of women and she was a good catch. And she was only thirty-eight years old, that wasn't altogether over the hill. So she wasn't going to marry a younger man who looked like a god, so what?

Fired with self-derision and armoured with the knowledge that others had probably been laughing at her, Alice had found the strength to confront Giovanni.

For the rest of that day, however, she allowed herself

to cry. She cried for the loss of her one true love. A magic love that only lived in storybooks. And then, first thing Monday morning, she was back in the bar and, on the outside at least, as chirpy as ever. Alice was a survivor.

WHEN GIOVANNI RETURNED home from seeing Alice he offered to help Teresa and Rico with their elaborate preparations for the evening meal but Teresa wouldn't hear of it.

'You have been out all night. You look tired, Gio. Go to bed. Sleep.'

He allowed himself to be persuaded and retired to his room. Not to sleep—he knew he would simply lie there and think of her—but to avoid conversation. He lay on his bunk and stared up at the ceiling seeing Caterina's face as the household noises reached him through the thin partitioning walls. Teresa was scolding Enrico.

'You have been swimming in the vats again, haven't you? Just look at the back of your trousers, they're soaking.'

'How many times do we have to tell you,' Rico joined in. 'It is dangerous. One day you will drown and then you will be sorry.'

'How can I be sorry if I'm drowned, Papa?' Enrico only ever answered his father back if he sensed he was in a good mood. And today was Sunday. Rico was always in a good mood on Sundays. 'Anyway,' he added, when he saw the familiar scowl appear, 'there was no danger. Jack was with me.'

Enrico was, by nature, a cautious boy and would not have swum in the vats at all were it not for Jack. At the best of times one needed to be a good swimmer, which Enrico was not, and if the water level was low, it took a great deal of strength to haul oneself out of the vat. Jack was not only a confident swimmer but a strong boy and

Enrico felt safe with him. Jack would drag him out of the water if need be.

'Jack Brearley. Hah! He will get you into trouble, that one. He is like his father. Not to be trusted, you wait and see.' Rico had no reason at all to dislike young Jack but the boy's natural high spirits reminded him constantly of Harry Brearley and Harry Brearley rankled with Rico.

'Can I help, Mamma?' Enrico cursed his own stupidity. He should not have come home until his clothes were dry, or he should have removed his wet undershorts before putting his trousers back on. Anything rather than risk his father's ill humour. Especially on a Sunday, the one day when he could normally relax and enjoy his father's company.

A rolled-up piece of dough caught Enrico on the side of the face. It was Carmelina, inadvertently saving the day. She squealed and ran behind her father as Enrico picked up the dough and threw it back at her.

'Outside! Outside, the two of you, if you want to play,' Teresa ordered. She, too, was grateful for Carmelina's diversion. These days, the mere mention of Harry Brearley's name was enough to put Rico in one of his moods. She did not know why. She and Giovanni had long given up trying to convince him that he was misjudging the man, and Harry himself, aware of Rico's animosity, had ceased coming to the Sunday singalongs. It was a pity, Teresa thought—she enjoyed Harry's company. 'Go on,' she ordered again as Carmelina picked up another fistful of dough and prepared to do battle. 'Outside. There is work to be done in here.'

Carmelina ran giggling out of the kitchen and Rico smiled fondly after her. Carmelina was Rico's unashamed favourite. She could twist him around her little finger and she knew it. An energetic, good-natured child, with Rico's black hair and black eyes, she was fearless. Just like her father.

As the children played noisily outside, Giovanni finally drifted into an uneasy sleep and it was two hours later when Teresa tapped on his door.

'Arturo and Giulia are here, Giovanni,' she said.

Giovanni roused himself and went out the back to pump a basin full of water and wash his face. The washing hanging from the clothes lines strung across the narrow backyard was flapping as the wind picked up and there was the threat of a late dust storm in the air. Giovanni wondered whether he should take the clothes inside. Whenever a dust storm threatened, the washing was hastily gathered up. If it was left to the mercy of the red dust, the clothes and bed linen would all be stained a dull shade of pink. It would delay him from the company for a while. He was in no mood for singing tonight.

He heard the sound of a trap pulling up out the front. Surely Teresa hadn't invited other guests. With a sigh, Giovanni rose and went back inside.

'Caterina! *Mio Dio*! Caterina!' Teresa was exclaiming in amazement. At the open front door stood Caterina, her daughter on one hip and her son and husband beside her.

'Teresa!'

Barely able to believe it was her, Giovanni watched as the women embraced. Caterina was here, in his house. No one had seen him come in and he stood at the back door, staring at her.

'Caterina! How is this possible? You, here, in Kalgoorlie!' Teresa was laughing and kissing Caterina, then holding her at arm's length, then kissing her again.

'I have been here for years, Teresa. Far longer than you.' Caterina too was laughing, for sheer joy. 'And I have been sending you scones and cakes and you have been teaching my son to sing. Is it not ridiculous?'

Teresa suddenly seemed to see Evan and Paul for the first time. 'Caterina. You mean . . .'

'Kate,' she answered. 'Kate Jones. I am Evan's wife.' The laughter died and Caterina looked a little confused. 'Did Giovanni not tell you?'

The mention of his name shocked Giovanni out of his daze. As he stepped forward, he noticed that Evan was looking at him. And he knew, from the expression on the man's face, that Evan had been looking at him from the moment he had entered the room. Evan had been watching him watch his wife.

'No, I did not tell her.' All eyes turned to Giovanni. He gave an apologetic shrug and a smile which he hoped did not look forced. 'I am sorry, Teresa, I forgot.' He turned to Evan and Caterina, trying not to meet her eyes directly. 'I have been sleeping most of the afternoon. I am afraid that I am not accustomed to late-night banquets.'

Teresa looked quizzically at Giovanni for a moment, then began the introductions. Caterina had met Arturo and Giulia at their shop in Boulder. 'Kate,' she corrected firmly, as Teresa started to introduce her. 'I am called Kate now.' She said it in English and Teresa realised that she was conscious of Evan's discomfort.

'We are being rude,' Teresa announced. 'I am sorry, Evan, we shall speak English for the rest of the evening.' There was something approaching a growl from Rico. 'You too, Rico,' she reprimanded. 'You will speak English too.'

'No, Teresa, no,' Kate said, 'we are not staying for the evening. We came to deliver the gingerbread.' She gestured for Paul to put the parcel wrapped up in white cloth onto the table. 'And I wanted to meet your family. Look, Carmelina.' Carmelina was chatting in a corner with Briony. 'Look at all the gingerbread people.'

The little girls came to the table and watched as Kate unfolded the cloth to reveal biscuits in all shapes and sizes. 'See,' she said. 'A whole gingerbread family.'

Carmelina picked up a biscuit and bit its head off, much to everyone's amusement. Teresa tried to persuade Kate and Evan to stay. 'There is more than enough food,' she insisted when Kate demurred. 'There is food enough for an army. Oh please, Caterina . . . Kate,' she insisted. 'Please!'

Kate desperately wanted to stay. She had successfully avoided Giovanni's eyes—it was not his presence that was deterring her. It was Evan. Despite the fact that everyone was painstakingly speaking English, she could sense his discomfort. She looked at him.

'It's very kind of you, Teresa,' he said. 'We'd very much like to stay.'

Kate wanted to kiss him but she knew it would embarrass him so she gave him a brief hug instead. And, as she did, the child's delight in her eyes was more than enough reward for Evan.

The exchange was not lost on Giovanni. Evan was a shy man, a private man who guarded his thoughts and feelings at all times. But, try as he might, his love for Kate shone like a beacon. Did she love him back? Giovanni wondered as he watched the warmth of her brief embrace and the gratitude in her eyes. Whether she did or not, it was obvious that she was deeply fond of her husband and that she was happy. Although he ached with longing, Giovanni was glad.

IT WAS A night of joy. A night of song and laughter and friendship. And as the air of camaraderie grew, so did Evan's melancholy.

As the wine flowed, the others quickly forgot their promise to speak English and, although Kate clung fondly to his arm and translated for him and Briony, and although Paul sat close to his stepfather and spoke English, Evan could not relax. It was not merely because he felt like a foreigner—it was good to see people enjoy themselves so much—it was because he recognised how at home Kate was. He had deprived her, he thought. All the years she had been with him had she felt as he did now? Had she felt like a foreigner? He had told himself he was protecting her, but all the while he'd been stifling her, cheating her of what was rightfully hers. And all for the sake of being proper. Evan felt utterly miserable.

They sat around the table mopping up huge bowls of ravioli with chunks of white bread as Teresa fed Salvatore who had woken and demanded attention. And then it was time for song. Fresh wine was poured, the concertina placed in Giovanni's hands and the evening began anew.

'Vide 'o mare quant'e bello!' Giovanni started to sing and, one by one, the others joined in. Rico and Teresa, Arturo and Giulia, Enrico and Carmelina. Paul looked at his father, an anxious query in his eyes, and Evan nodded encouragingly.

'Guarda, gua', chistu ciardino,' Paul began and although Evan continued to nod and smile the proud father, his guilt and sadness deepened. Had he been depriving the boy, too, of his heritage?

As always, Giovanni's beautiful voice rang out above the others. His eyes met Kate's and she smiled her recognition. Yes, she remembered. It had been *'Torna a Surriento'* he had been singing that evening on the mountain. She closed her eyes and listened to the words and the haunting melody.

'. . . loving you so much and longing
to bestow a fleeting kiss.
Yet you say: "Farewell I'm leaving" . . .'

When she opened her eyes he was still looking at

her. She knew that he was singing to her and she knew he was saying that he would pose no threat. In that instant Kate felt that she loved him, just as he loved her. It was a strange feeling, but a safe one. She knew neither of them would pursue it and she was at once grateful and regretful. She smiled at him and then turned her attention to Evan who was looking uncomfortable.

'We must sing something in English,' she said as the last strains of the concertina died away. 'Then Evan and Briony can join in.'

'No, Kate,' Evan murmured. 'Briony and I are happy listening. Aren't we, girl?' Briony nodded cheerfully, enjoying Carmelina's company and the noise and festivity of the evening.

'You should sing something in Welsh for us then,' Kate insisted. The wine had gone to her head and she so wanted Evan to enjoy himself. 'Evan sometimes sings with the Welsh miners,' she said. 'He has a fine voice.' Evan was shaking his head. 'Oh please, Evan—'

'I said no, Kate!' It was the sharpest he had ever spoken to her and Kate was startled. She fell instantly silent, knowing she had embarrassed him. She hadn't meant to.

'*"O Sole Mio"*,' Giovanni announced as he played the opening chords. 'Come. Everyone knows *"O Sole Mio"*.' He started to sing and the awkward moment passed.

DURING THE DRIVE home, Kate chattered with childlike enthusiasm, giddy from the unaccustomed red wine and the heady excitement of the evening. It was only when they arrived home and she gently roused young Paul who had fallen asleep, his head resting against her arm, that she realised her husband had spoken barely a word.

'I am sorry, Evan,' she said when they had put the children to bed and were preparing to retire themselves.

'I am sorry that you were uncomfortable and that I embarrassed you.'

'It is I who am sorry, Kate.' When Evan finally spoke, there was anguish in his voice and she wondered why. 'I am sorry that I cheated you of your own kind. They are good people, your people. You should be with them, you should speak your language and sing your songs. I am sorry.'

She held him close to her. 'You are my own kind,' she said. 'You are my people, you and our children.' She would not go to the Giannis' house again, she told herself. It was an easy decision to make. She did not want to be in Giovanni's company anyway. It was too dangerous.

THE FOLLOWING DAY Giovanni worked hard. Thirty feet below the earth's surface, he attacked the rock face blindly, sweat pouring from his body. When Rico took a rest Giovanni worked on, welcoming the physical exertion. His mind was numb as he worked. The harder he worked, the less he thought of her.

So successfully did Giovanni numb his mind that he completely forgot his arrangement to meet Harry. It was to have been the meeting of the partners. But Monday passed. And Tuesday. And Wednesday. The whole week passed and Giovanni did nothing but work and sleep. And on Saturday night he went to Red Ruby's.

Miko was pleased that the Italian had come back. He had always been her favourite client. But she knew better than to comment on his long absence. This one did not like to talk. And Miko herself preferred it that way.

She anticipated a quick, efficient coupling. Whichever way he chose to use her body, this one's ultimate aim had always been the same as hers, to get the whole process over and done with.

This time, however, was different. This time there

was anger in his love-making. He did not abuse her—he was not violent, but she could tell he was angry. And he took a long time. Miko preferred the way it used to be.

As Giovanni felt the Japanese girl's skin against his, the image of Caterina flashed through his mind. As he felt the Japanese girl's breasts, he thought of Caterina's breasts: they would be larger than this girl's. And her buttocks would be rounder. Her thighs longer; the mound between her legs . . . As his hand traced the body beneath him, he angrily tried to force the images from his mind. He did not want to think of Caterina, not here. Not as he degraded himself and this girl. It was Sarina De Cretico he must think of.

But even as he forced Sarina into his mind, Caterina's face would not leave him and that made him even angrier. He was defiling Catarina to think of her in the same instant as Sarina De Cretico. He ground himself fiercely into the Japanese girl, desperate to rid himself of all images, desperate to think of nothing but the satisfaction of his lust. Finally, his body obeyed him and for one moment, as he growled his gratification, his mind went blissfully blank. But, as he rolled off the girl, their bodies bathed in sweat, Caterina was back. He could smell her. He could see her breasts and her buttocks and her thighs. He could feel the warmth of her womb surrounding him.

All the next day Giovanni wondered whether Caterina would come to the house with her son. Teresa had extended the invitation last Sunday and Caterina had said she would send word. Had she? Giovanni did not dare ask Teresa, he knew that she would read his urgency.

When the boy arrived on his own Giovanni felt a strange sense of relief. He knew if he were to look at her across the family table and the bowls of ravioli, he would have defiled her all over again. As he played his concertina and sang his love songs he would have seen her nakedness and smelled her juices and felt her body. Not only would he have defiled her, he would have driven himself to the point of madness. Caterina had made the right decision. They must not see each other.

HARRY BREARLEY WONDERED why Giovanni had not contacted him about Monday's meeting but, whatever the reason, he was grateful. He would only have had to invent an excuse to stall the Italian.

Two weeks later all was in place. Now Harry's only dilemma was how to inform the Gianni brothers that Gaston Picot owned the Clover. The papers were signed and sealed. The money was in the bank. He had deposited the brothers' share into their account. It was all quite legitimate and the Giannis had been remunerated handsomely. In fact, they'd received more than they were legally entitled to under the contract they'd signed. But of course they wouldn't see it that way and Harry didn't want to be the one to tell them.

'IT'S QUITE LEGAL. I've brought the original papers you signed with Mr Brearley.'

It was Saturday and the solicitor had arrived at the Clover just before dusk, as Harry had instructed, when the brothers were cleaning themselves up after their hard day's work.

He spread the papers out on the table in the humpy. 'These are the partnership papers; you see your signatures. There,' he pointed, 'and there.'

Giovanni nodded. He could not believe what the solicitor had been saying. He'd heard the words but he could not believe them. And he'd deliberately refused to translate for Rico. 'Hush, Rico,' he'd said when his brother impatiently demanded to know what was going on. 'Let me listen, I will tell you.'

The solicitor spoke quickly and Giovanni himself was having trouble making sense of what he was saying. Not because of the language barrier, simply because the man was not talking sense. Harry could not have sold the mine. It was impossible. They were partners. Harry could not sell the Clover without all three signatures.

'And you'll see here, it says—' The solicitor was pointing to the contract.

'We cannot read.' Giovanni had had to make the admission a number of times in his life and each time he had felt a sense of shame. Now he didn't. Now anger was starting to burn inside him. A bad anger. The sort of anger he didn't like to feel. 'You tell me what it says.'

Of course, the solicitor reminded himself, Mr Brearley had told him the Italians couldn't read. 'They are very simple men,' he had said. 'I have a feeling they believe they signed a contract of sale but I was quite explicit. I told them the papers they signed were partnership papers only. And, of course,' he'd added, 'you must point out that the remuneration they have received upon the sale of the Clover is well in advance of what they are legally entitled to. I'm sure you'll have no trouble.'

'Very well, Mr Gianni,' the solicitor replied patiently. 'It says that the sole owner of the Clover Mine, Mr Harry Brearley, undersigned,' he pointed to Harry's signature, 'appoints Rico Gianni and Giovanni Gianni,' he pointed once again to the brothers' signatures, 'as his working partners. The agreement being that as long as Mr Brearley retains ownership of the mine, all net profits will be divided equally between each of the three working partners. Should Mr Brearley sell the mine, however, the Messrs Gianni shall each be entitled to the equivalent in cash of one-third of one month's average net profit.'

The solicitor looked up from the contract and removed his spectacles. 'I am happy to inform you that the sum lodged in your account at the National Bank of Australasia is substantially in advance of the sum upon which you agreed. It is more in the order of one-third share each of *six* months' average net profit.' He flicked a spotless white handkerchief from his breast pocket and started to clean his spectacles. 'I think you'll agree,' he smiled, 'Mr Brearley has been more than generous.'

'What does he say, Gio?' Rico demanded belligerently. He had been watching the growing anger in his brother's eyes. 'Tell me. What has Harry Brearley done?'

'Go,' Giovanni ordered the solicitor. 'Go now!'

The solicitor held his spectacles up to the light. The right lens was clean, he started on the left. 'Shortly,' he said, 'shortly. The new owner of the Clover, Mr Gaston Picot, is, I believe—'

'I said go now! Or my brother will kill you.'

The solicitor stopped the meticulous cleaning of his spectacles and stared at Giovanni.

'When I tell my brother what you have said,' Giovanni continued evenly, 'he will not know that you are merely employed to do Harry Brearley's bidding. He will kill you.'

The solicitor looked nervously from Giovanni to the bull-like man beside him. Rico looked menacingly back and the solicitor hastily stuffed his handkerchief into his pocket and looped his spectacles over his ears.

'Yes. Well.' He edged nervously to the door. 'I have no doubt Mr Brearley will contact you.'

'You tell Mr Brearley it is more than his life is worth if he does,' Giovanni warned.

Both brothers followed the solicitor and watched as he backed away down the slope.

'You tell Mr Brearley it is not only Rico Gianni he needs to fear!' Giovanni called after him. 'You tell him if I see him, *I* will kill him!'

Chapter Twelve

It was closing time. Maudie gave Alice the 'no more drinks' nod and did the rounds of the bar saying goodnight to the regulars. They liked the personal touch. It was a measure of one's standing if Maudie chatted to you at closing time on a Saturday night.

'How's the new baby, Alwyn?' Alwyn was a friend of Evan Jones, another Welshman who worked at the Midas.

'She's a little beauty, Maudie,' Alwyn beamed, ever the proud father. He had five now. All daughters.

'Good night, Tom,' Maudie called to a man wending his way unsteadily out the door. 'See you next week.' Tom only ever drank on a Saturday but when he did he put away a week's worth. He never caused any trouble though.

''Night, Maudie.'

An hour later, the bar cleaned, the staff gone and Alice retired for the night, Maudie locked the front doors and switched off the lights of the main bar. It had been a good Saturday, she thought, as she walked through the ladies' lounge and the billiards room, turning off the lights as she went. Loud and boisterous as always on a Saturday night, but not unruly. The way it should be. Maudie didn't like trouble.

She locked the back door and turned on the small

lamp so that Harry could see his way up the stairs when he returned home. He'd stayed later and later at Hannan's over the past fortnight and Maudie hoped he wasn't reverting to his bad habits. They were business meetings, he'd assured her, and explained that he had agreed to sell the Clover to Gaston Picot. 'But what about Giovanni?' she'd asked, concerned. 'What about the brothers?'

'All perfectly above board, my dear.' He showed her the original papers and Maudie, with her trained eye, could see that it was very straightforward. 'A working partnership, that's all,' Harry had said. 'The brothers knew that.' And he told her he was going to give them a very good payout. As a man of honour that was the least he could do.

It was Harry's business, not hers, Maudie thought as she locked the back door and turned on the lamp, but Giovanni would be disappointed and that was a shame.

FROM THE WELL beneath the stairs, Rico watched as Maudie crossed the room. He heard her feet above his head as she climbed each step. Now she was on the landing above. He heard a door opening. Then voices. Two female voices.

'Well, it was a barrel of trouble getting Jack to go to bed, of course.'

'And the twins, have they been good?'

'James woke and cried a little but Victoria slept the whole time.'

The women chatted for a minute or so, then Maudie said, 'Thank you, Betty, you can go to bed now.'

Rico heard the nanny walk along the landing to the little room at the far end. Frustration started to build inside him. It must be nearly midnight. Surely Harry would come home soon.

Rico was pleased with himself. He had been

cunning. He had known during the discussion between Giovanni and the solicitor that Harry Brearley had somehow cheated them. There was no surprise in that, Rico had always known that he would. But with Giovanni's warning, 'Tell him if I see him, I will kill him', he realised that Harry's betrayal must have been total. Giovanni kill a man? Impossible. There was not enough hatred in him to kill.

Rico had waited patiently while Giovanni calmed himself enough to recount the conversation. 'There is nothing we can do, Rico,' Giovanni had said. 'It is all legal.' And he started to explain, curbing his own anger so as not to inflame Rico's.

All the while, Rico had remained strangely calm. He had already made his plan. He had made it the moment he heard his brother's threat. As of this night, Harry Brearley's life was over.

But he must be cunning, he had told himself. He must not appear too complacent or Giovanni would suspect something. He pretended rage and allowed his brother to pacify him. And when they got home the rage broke out anew. Teresa was furious and screamed her own vehemence at Harry. Rico joined in, and then watched as Giovanni signalled Teresa, warning her that they must not incite violence in him. Again Rico allowed himself to be pacified. He drank whisky, far too much of it—they all did. Even Teresa. And when they were inebriated and staggered off early to bed, he made love to Teresa. Loudly, drunkenly. That, also, was part of his plan. It would convince Giovanni that he had no thought of revenge tonight. He was too drunk. But Rico was not drunk. No amount of alcohol could make him drunk tonight.

He had crept out of the house and arrived at Maudie's pub shortly before closing time. The rowdiness of the Saturday night drinkers was at its peak and no one noticed Rico peering through the windows of the main bar. Harry was nowhere to be seen, but the crowd was so dense inside it was impossible to tell whether he was there. Rico was tempted to take the place by storm but he quelled his impatience. There were too many of them, they would stop him killing Harry Brearley. He needed to get Harry alone. Just the two of them. And then he would squeeze the life out of the man.

He stole around to the rear of the pub and slipped through the staff entrance. He could hear the voices of the men placing their wagers on the final billiards game of the evening. Again he resisted the urge to throw open the door to the billiards room. He had been clever and cunning so far, he must not spoil it now.

He looked at the stairs. Harry would have to climb them to go to bed. Rico crept into the well beneath the stairs and settled down to wait.

An hour and a half later, as he watched Maudie lock up on her own, Rico realised that Harry must be out somewhere else. That fancy club he went to, that would be it. Harry would be drinking fine wines and showing off to his fine friends. Probably boasting about how he had fooled the dumb Italians. Those stupid brothers, he'd be saying. Those stupid brothers who could neither read nor write. Those dumb Giannis who had thought they owned a gold mine. The blind fury which Rico had quelled was rekindled afresh. No one made a fool of Rico Gianni and lived. He stepped out from the stairwell and stared at the back door. The man had to come through that door. But the longer he stared, the greater grew his rage. The frustration of waiting was driving Rico mad.

An hour went by. Another hour. Then the thought struck him. Perhaps, all this while, Harry had been sleeping peacefully in his bed upstairs. It was possible. Harry was lazy. It would be just like him to let his wife slave away while he slept. Slowly, step by creaking step, Rico climbed the staircase.

Which door would he try first? He had heard the nanny retire to the room at the far end of the landing. The room at the other end would probably be another smaller bedroom. Either the barmaid's or young Jack Brearley's. He would try one of the middle doors.

Quietly he turned the knob and pushed the door open. The hinges were well oiled, there was no sound. In the gloom, he could see that it was a parlour. He closed the door and proceeded to the next.

As it swung open he could hear the hum of a ceiling fan. Yes, there was someone in this room. A four-poster bed covered with mosquito netting. A form sleeping. Perhaps two forms. It was impossible to tell in the darkness.

Rico crept towards the bed and slowly lifted the fine netting. Behind him, a sound, a cry. He whirled about. In the far corner, more netting, another bed. He crossed to it and dragged aside the mesh. Two large cots, two babies, one of them now wide awake and starting to cry.

'Leave my babies alone!' The voice behind him was harsh. He turned. Maudie stood by the four-poster bed, her arms extended, holding a .455 Webley and Scott revolver in both hands.

'Where is Harry Brearley?' Rico didn't care about the gun. He would take it from her. He would kill her if necessary; she was Harry Brearley's woman, she would have been party to his treachery.

'I said, leave my babies alone!' Maudie's voice was icy. 'Get out! Now! Or I'll shoot you dead, I swear I will.'

The muzzle of the revolver was aimed directly at his head and her hands were steady.

Rico started to walk towards her. 'Where is Harry Brearley? I come to kill him.'

One more step, Maudie thought, just one more step and she would have to shoot him.

Then the two of them heard the downstairs door open. Rico moved with surprising agility. He was out on the landing in a matter of seconds and, seeing Harry in the lamplight below, he bellowed his triumph.

Harry looked up in surprise at the beast hurtling down the stairs towards him; in the same instant, he heard Maudie yell, 'Get out of the way, Harry!' He dived to the floor as the gun exploded. The noise was deafening. Rico tumbled thunderously down the stairs. Harry rolled out of the way as the Italian's unconscious body landed facedown beside him.

'Good God, woman, what have you done?' Harry sat up in a daze as Maudie ran down the stairs and inspected the body.

'He's alive,' she said. 'He's been hit in the shoulder. Help me get him outside before he comes to his senses.'

Doors opened on the landing above. A woman screamed.

'Go back to bed, Betty!' Maudie called out. 'You too, Alice!'

'What's happened?' Betty demanded hysterically.

'I said go back to bed,' Maudie ordered again. 'Do as you're told. Both of you.'

Jack thundered out onto the landing, shocked from his sleep. 'Dad! Maudie!'

'Get Jack out of here!' Maudie yelled and Alice bustled the boy away while Betty, the nanny, backed terrified into her room.

'Now for God's sake, Harry,' Maudie urged, 'help me get him outside.' She rolled the Italian over. He was groaning, already regaining consciousness.

'Jesus Christ! It's Rico Gianni.'

'Of course it's Rico Gianni.' She pushed the back

door wide open and grasped one of Rico's arms. 'Get his other arm. He came to kill you.'

Together they dragged Rico out into the yard. He was muttering in Italian and starting to sit up as Maudie urged Harry back inside. 'Quick!' she said, locking the door and pushing home the security bolt. 'God knows what he'll do. He's a madman.'

Several minutes later they heard Rico's voice. Maniacal. 'Come out, Harry Brearley!' he bellowed. 'Come out and die!'

Several more minutes went by. Had he gone? Maudie wondered. Then a crash as windows shattered.

'Harry!' she hissed. 'The doors to the main bar. The billiards room! Quick!'

There was the sound of more breaking glass as Rico smashed the window clear and climbed inside.

Maudie raced through the ladies' lounge and locked the door to the main bar. In the billiards room, Harry bolted the door only just in time. From the other side, Rico smashed a chair against it. 'Come out and die, Harry Brearley!'

Maudie ran upstairs to tend to the twins, both of whom were now awake and crying, despite Betty's efforts to calm them.

She instructed Alice to stay in Jack's room. 'Just a customer who's had too much to drink,' she said reassuringly to the boy.

'What about the gun?' Jack was now wide awake and wanted to be part of the adventure.

'It went off by accident,' Maudie snapped. 'Do as you're told for once and stay here! Lock him up if you have to,' she whispered to Alice. Then she went downstairs and stood watch with Harry.

For ten minutes, Rico howled his rage. They could hear him, smashing everything he could lay his hands on. Then, suddenly, all was quiet.

After his long night session at Hannan's Club, Harry wasn't thinking too clearly. He was unsure as to what action to take. But Maudie did the thinking for both of them.

'We do nothing until the morning,' she decided. 'If he's unconscious in the bar then let him bleed to death. If he's hiding outside then wait until the daylight when you can see him. First thing in the morning you fetch the police, and you take the gun with you. Now go to bed, Harry,' she said. 'Sleep off some of that alcohol. You may need your wits about you in the morning.'

HARRY WAS SOUND asleep when she woke him several hours later. It was seven o'clock. Cautiously, they opened one of the rear doors to the main bar. Chaos. Bottles and mirrors were smashed, chairs broken and tables overturned. But there was no sign of Rico.

Half an hour later, Maudie watched carefully as Harry stepped out of the back door into the early morning sun. He had the gun in his hand. There was no one in sight. He fetched Black Bess from the stables and harnessed her to the trap. Then he put the gun on the seat beside him, flicked the reins and gave a wave. Maudie, satisfied, closed the back door and returned to her babies.

The trap rounded the rear of the hotel, Black Bess still at a walking pace, and made for Hannan Street. Harry leaned forward to flick the mare's rump and give the familiar command, 'Trot on, Bess'. But, as he did, a figure stepped out of the shadows and sprang onto the step on the driver's side.

Harry felt the trap dip, felt the extra weight of the man right beside him. His heart lurched and he reached for the gun. But a hand got there before him and his revolver was whisked from the seat to land in the dust as Black Bess walked on. Then he felt something hard dig into the back of his ribs. He froze.

'You are going the wrong way, Harry,' a voice said softly in his ear. 'Move over.' Harry did, and the man settled close beside him on the seat. 'Turn the trap around.'

Harry knew the voice. He was about to say something but the gun barrel dug harder into his ribs. 'I said turn the trap!'

When they had travelled several blocks away from Hannan Street and the main thoroughfare of the town, he was instructed to head north, and fifteen minutes later they were at the Clover. It was Sunday and the mine was deserted, no one within sight or sound for miles. Harry shifted nervously in his seat.

'Get down,' Giovanni ordered as he jumped from the trap and held firmly to Black Bess's bridle.

'What's going on, Gee-Gee?' Harry decided to bluff it out. 'Why the melodrama? Good grief, man—'

'You thought this was a gun, yes?' Giovanni raised the short length of steel pipe which he had held to Harry's back. 'I do not own a gun, Harry. And my brother does not own a gun. Yet you shoot him.'

There was no point in bluffing it out. And Harry knew it. The Italian was going to kill him, of that he was sure. 'No, it wasn't me, I didn't shoot him. Maudie did.' There was a flicker in Giovanni's eyes and Harry suddenly saw his way out. 'Good God, man, she was protecting herself and her babies. I wasn't even there when he attacked her.'

Giovanni believed him. Even Harry would not accuse his wife of attempted murder unless it were true. And Maudie herself would not attempt murder without good reason. Not that Rico had lied. By the time he had staggered home he had been so weakened from loss of blood that he had passed out almost immediately. But, before he had, he had muttered, 'I kill you, Harry Brearley.'

'Come along, Gee-Gee.' Harry could read Giovanni's hesitation. 'Your brother's insane, you know that as well as I do . . .'

Giovanni was not hesitating, he was merely changing his mind. He had been prepared to kill Harry Brearley. He was glad now that there was no need. He did not want to wear the guilt of another man's death. But Harry had wronged the Gianni family. Vengeance was called for.

'You thought this was a gun, yes?' he repeated, holding up the steel pipe. He gripped it firmly and tapped it against the palm of his other hand. 'It is not a gun, but it is a powerful weapon. It can do much damage. It can break a man's knees. It can make a man a cripple. Just like Rico.'

Harry started to back away. Despite his moral weakness, Harry Brearley was not a physical coward, but there was such menace in the Italian, such murder in his eyes as he slowly advanced that Harry found himself unable to hold his ground.

'This is wrong, Giovanni,' he stammered. 'This is wrong.'

'You are frightened, Harry Brearley. It is good that you are frightened. You have reason to be. Take off your coat.'

Dumbly, Harry obeyed, his eyes never leaving the steel pipe. He felt sweat beading his brow, and his heart was pounding. Damn it, he thought, he wasn't going to beg for his life. He glanced quickly from side to side, looking for a weapon.

'Good,' Giovanni said as Harry dropped his coat in the dust. 'Now we fight.' And he tossed the steel pipe into the scrub.

Harry's eyes followed the pipe's brief arc through

the air and, as his ears noted the dull thud of its landing, his courage returned. He added up his advantages, studying Giovanni as they slowly circled each other.

Harry was a big man, at least two inches taller than the Italian. His shoulders were broader, his body denser, his reach longer. Yes, he thought, the advantage was certainly his. Giovanni would regret his sense of honour and fair play. He would regret having discarded his weapon.

Harry was so busy making comparisons that he missed the opening move altogether.

Giovanni feinted to the left and before Harry could see where the blow came from, he felt the Italian's right fist slam into his solar plexus. He grunted and staggered backwards, badly winded, but he fought against dropping to his knees. It had been a lucky blow, that's all. He shook his head and gasped the breath back into his lungs.

The next punch landed on his jaw and he felt it crack. Only seconds later came a blow to his temple and he felt the moist trickle of blood seep from above his eye as he tried to marshal his strength. If he could just purchase a hold on Giovanni, he thought. If only the man wasn't so fast.

But Giovanni knew better than to risk getting within Harry's grasp. At least, not until he had weakened the big man.

As the lightning blows landed, Harry's extra bulk proved a liability. It was bulk born of the easy life and no match for Giovanni's fast, honed reflexes. The more Harry tried to dodge, the more the Italian was there before him. Even when he did manage, just the once, to lock Giovanni in an embrace, it was impossible to wrest the man to the ground. He was simply too strong.

Harry, desperate now, backed away into the scrub, blow after blow raining upon him as Giovanni closed in for the kill. His jaw was dislocated; he couldn't see out of his left eye, and his three cracked ribs were aching.

'Enough,' he gasped, shaking his head. 'Enough.' The fight was over. Harry was more than willing to admit defeat and declare Giovanni the winner. He tripped, fell backwards and remained on the ground, his chest heaving, one hand in the air. 'No more. No more. You've won.'

'Stand up.' Giovanni grabbed him by his collar and dragged him to his feet.

Through a veil of blood and sweat and dirt, Harry could see the Italian's eyes. Only inches from his, they burned once again with murder and revenge. Jesus Christ! he thought, the man's as mad as his brother—he's going to kill me. Fear rose in him again.

Giovanni released Harry's collar and prodded him in the solar plexus with his forefinger. 'You are frightened?' he asked in a whisper. Harry stared back at him. 'You want to live?' Harry nodded. 'How much do you want to live, Harry Brearley? Eh?' The voice was harsher now and the finger continued to prod so that Harry gasped involuntarily as the pain stabbed through his ribs. 'This hurts, eh?' Prod. 'Tell me how much you want to live, Harry.' Prod. 'How much?'

Harry backed away further into the scrub. 'Let me go, Giovanni.' He tried to keep his voice steady but he couldn't, he was terrified. 'Let me go.'

'How much, Harry? How much do you want to live?'

Giovanni had finished with Harry Brearley. He wasn't going to kill him; he wasn't even going to bother hitting him again. He had intended to torment him, to make him beg for his life but, as Harry once again tripped and fell backwards to grovel in the dirt, there seemed little point. The man's terror was enough. A constant humiliation, it would live in his memory. Giovanni required no more. He watched Harry for several seconds, snivelling in the red dust, then he turned and walked away.

Everything happened very fast then. The realisation that he was not going to be killed brought a surge of relief flooding through Harry. But an instant later, when Giovanni turned his back, Harry's relief turned to hate. No one humiliated Harry Brearley! Harry was consumed with a murderous rage. Feverishly he looked about for a weapon.

Five yards away in the scrub lay the steel pipe. He crawled to it, picked it up and rose to his feet. Mustering the last of his energy, he charged at Giovanni, screaming like a wounded animal.

Giovanni had heard Harry scrabbling around in the dust behind him, but had thought nothing of it. He hadn't even bothered to turn around. The man was defeated. It was only when he heard the roar and turned to face the charge that Giovanni recognised the danger. Like a wounded bull summoning its last ounce of strength, Harry had covered the several yards at speed. The steel pipe, brandished high and already on its descent, had behind it the desperate power of a killing blow.

As the pipe arced down towards his skull, Giovanni threw himself to one side, instinctively putting his hands up to ward off the blow. The pipe missed his head by a hair's breadth and he landed heavily, jarring his shoulder and grazing his cheek on the parched, stony ground.

Harry staggered, off-balance, and turned to attack again before the Italian could get to his feet. But as he raised the pipe, Giovanni sprang from a crouching position and, both hands clasped, he swung his double fist up and under Harry Brearley's chin like a club.

The big man's head snapped back and he fell heavily to lie deathly still in the dirt.

Giovanni stood rubbing his shoulder. It hurt. He touched his left cheekbone. That hurt too. And there was blood trickling down the side of his face—he must have cut it when he fell.

He wondered if he'd killed Harry. He knelt and examined the battered face. It certainly looked lifeless. Was his neck broken?

As he started to edge his hand under Harry's neck, he felt the carotid artery throbbing beneath his fingers. The pulse was strong. It would take a lot more than a brawl to kill Harry Brearley. Giovanni was relieved. Harry's death would have complicated things.

He fetched the horse and trap and hauled Harry up onto the front seat. It was not yet mid-morning but the sun was fierce. Left unconscious the man would bake to death. He must take him home to Maudie.

MAUDIE HAD BEEN watching anxiously from the front balcony of the hotel for nearly an hour now. It should have taken Harry no more than thirty minutes to return with the police. She hadn't worried at first. It might have required a little extra time to round up Baldy—Sergeant Bob 'Baldy' Hetherington was a slow mover at the best of times. But after a full hour had passed, she had become uneasy. And Jack was getting on her nerves, badgering her about the events of the previous night. She decided to send him on an errand to the farm five miles out of town where she bought her egg supplies.

'But I got two dozen last week,' he argued.

'So? I want you to fetch some more.' She tucked the money into his pocket and handed him the egg bag stuffed with soft rags. 'And make sure you walk the Princess back, please, I don't want them smashed like last time.'

'We never buy eggs two weeks in a row.'

'We do now. Come along, I'll help you saddle up.'

Something strange was definitely going on, Jack thought. She never helped him saddle his horse. He'd been saddling the Princess on his own for a full year now.

'They've probably run out of eggs,' he muttered sulkily as she led the way downstairs. 'They'll think I'm mad coming two weeks in a row.' But Maudie didn't answer as she marched him to the stables.

She looped the egg bag around his neck. 'Now don't forget, wrap each egg separately,' she said as she did every time he rode to the farm. But her instructions were automatic, Jack could tell she was distracted. She was getting rid of him, he knew it.

'Hell, Maudie! Why won't you tell me—'

'Do as you're told,' she ordered. 'And don't swear.' He was about to say something but she didn't draw breath. 'And walk the Princess. All the way, please. There and back.'

'But why—?'

'Go!' she barked. 'Now!' And she watched as he defiantly raised a trot from the old mare and rode out of the open gates.

Maudie went back upstairs and out onto the front balcony of the hotel where she stood watching down Hannan Street. What had happened? Had Rico Gianni been lying in wait for Harry? Somewhere between the hotel and the police station had there been a madman lurking in the shadow of a building, a knife in his hand?

An hour later Maudie's mind was running riot. She told Alice and Betty she was going out and ordered them to keep the doors locked. She donned her bonnet and, as she did up the ribbons at her throat, she cast a final glance through the balcony doors to the main road. Amidst the general mid-morning traffic, Black Bess was trotting down Hannan Street.

Maudie ran out onto the balcony. There were two

men in the trap. But Harry wasn't driving. The one with the reins in his hands was Giovanni. And beside him . . . Well, she knew it was Harry, but she couldn't see his face. He was slumped over, leaning against the Italian. And people in the street were pointing and muttering to each other as the trap drove past.

Maudie ran back into the bedroom, throwing her bonnet aside as she dived for the rifle stored beneath the bed. What have they done, those Gianni brothers, her mind screamed. Have they killed him? Have they killed my Harry?

GIOVANNI TURNED INTO the street beside the pub and drove around to the back of Maudie's. He had intended to leave Black Bess and the trap, with Harry in it, outside the front doors but the looks he was attracting from the passers-by decided him against it. People might demand that the police be called, and this was between him and Harry. And Maudie too, he supposed.

'What have you done to him?'

There she was. On the back steps. Rifle at the ready. Giovanni wasn't surprised. It was a good thing in a way. Better he deliver his message to Maudie than wait for Harry to gain his senses.

'If you've killed him I'll shoot you dead, Giovanni, I swear I will.'

'I have not killed him.'

Harry moaned gently. He had been gradually regaining consciousness during the drive home.

'See for yourself, I have not killed him.' Giovanni pushed Harry away. Not roughly, but the weight of the big man's body toppled him from the trap and he landed heavily on the stony ground.

'Oh, Jesus!' he cried out, instantly jolted into consciousness. He raised himself painfully onto one elbow.

'Harry!' Maudie ran and knelt beside him. 'God

Almighty!' she exclaimed, staring at his bloodied face. 'What happened? What has he done to you?'

'Leave it, Maudie.' Harry's voice was cracked and barely audible as he muttered through broken teeth, trying not to move his dislocated jaw. 'A fight. He won. Get me inside.'

Giovanni had jumped down from the trap. Maudie rose slowly to face him. Just as slowly, she raised the rifle. Giovanni was standing no more than six feet away, Harry on the ground between them, and she raised the rifle until the barrel was pointing directly at the Italian's chest.

'What right do you people have?' Her voice was shaking with outrage. She stood as tall as Giovanni and she faced him as a man would face a man. 'What right? Your brother tries to murder my husband. He smashes my hotel. And you! You, Giovanni, Harry's friend! You drag him back to me half dead. What right do you think you have, you Giannis?'

'We have the right of honour.' Giovanni looked directly at Maudie. 'Your husband is a liar and a thief.'

There was something in Giovanni's eyes that caused Maudie a moment's hesitation.

Harry squirmed himself into a sitting position on the ground between them. 'Don't listen to him, Maudie,' he muttered painfully. 'Crazy dagos.'

Maudie looked down at Harry, confused. But Giovanni took no notice.

'Our family is ruined,' he continued. 'We are ruined because your husband betrayed us. In my country Harry Brearley would be a dead man.' Giovanni felt a resurgence of his anger but he fought to quell it. 'Then would come a vendetta between our families. Our sons would kill each other, there would be much bloodshed.' He shook his head. 'It would be a bad thing. This is Australia. We must not let it happen. But I tell you . . .'

He glanced down briefly at Harry, then back to

Maudie, and his voice was merciless. 'If one of your family ever again wrongs a Gianni that man will be a dead man. I will kill him.' He walked away and Maudie stood motionless watching him.

From down the street, the Princess plodded towards Maudie's and the warm comfort of her stable. Jack saw Giovanni stride out of the yard and was about to call to him when the Italian turned back.

'You Brearleys keep away from us!' he yelled. 'You keep away, you understand?'

Jack forgot about the preservation of the eggs and urged the Princess into a trot.

'From this day the Giannis and the Brearleys are *nemici*!' Giovanni shouted. '*Nemici*, you understand! We are enemies!' He stormed from the yard and took no notice of the old white horse as it trotted up to the gates.

Jack reigned the Princess to a halt. In the dust before him, bloodied and beaten, knelt his father. And Maudie, rifle in hand, stood beside him.

Chapter Thirteen

Giovanni left Maudie's and started to walk home, but several blocks down the street he had a change of heart and headed for the Golden Mile instead. It was a blistering hot February morning and, by the time he reached the outskirts of the town and could see the dumps and the poppet heads in the distance, sweat beaded his brow and his shirt clung to his chest. But he felt good. He had made his decisions.

The slate was clean. He could start anew. Whether his brother would be able to put Harry Brearley's betrayal behind him was another matter, but Giovanni would worry about that when the time came. It would be a while before Rico would be capable of taking any form of action, the injury to his shoulder was so severe. It was not, however, irreparable. He was weak. He had lost a lot of blood, but the bullet had gone clean through.

Giovanni was thankful that he had been spared the role of executioner. Now his main priority was to find a job, and the sooner the better. Until Rico was once more physically fit, it was Giovanni who would be the sole provider for the family.

He could get a job timbercutting, he supposed. But he was a miner, not a timberman. His work lay beneath the ground. Employment with one of the big mines would be the perfect solution. But he was aware that his chances were not good. Very few Italians were employed by the big mines. The language barrier was the common excuse but Giovanni and his friends knew that it was really ethnic discrimination. The underground bosses stuck to their own kind.

Then the thought occurred to him. There was one underground boss who might give him a chance. Evan Jones. Evan was underground boss at the Midas. And not only was Evan a good man, Giovanni had sensed from the very beginning that he had little time for Harry Brearley. Surely he would be sympathetic to the Giannis' plight.

So Giovanni changed direction and headed for the Golden Mile. It was Sunday. He would not wait until Monday morning to line up with the others seeking work. He would visit Evan at his home. He would personally put his case to the man.

As he stood looking out over the Golden Mile, wiping the sweat from his brow, Giovanni thought of Caterina. In his mind, he rehearsed the scene ahead. He would not look at her. He would greet her briefly then he would turn his full attention to Evan. Perhaps Evan would suggest they retire to discuss their business in private. That would help. Perhaps Caterina would be tending to household chores or playing with little Briony and unable to lend her attention to Giovanni's visit. That too would help.

As he approached the house he noticed that Evan's horse was not tethered out the back. Nor was young Paul's pony.

Perhaps there was no one home, Giovanni thought as he knocked on the door. But he knew, before she opened it, that she was there.

'Giovanni!' She stood before him, the air was filled with the smell of baking bread and suddenly her hand was upon his cheek. 'You're hurt!'

He'd forgotten the cut on his cheek. The congealed blood formed a vivid track down the right side of his face.

'What has happened?' she asked, alarm in her eyes, the touch of her fingers soft on his skin.

Nothing could have stopped him. He took her face in his hands and kissed her. One frozen moment of shock, then her lips parted and she returned his kiss. He gathered her in his embrace and, for several moments, the world could have been watching, but neither of them cared.

It was Kate who came to her senses first and pushed herself away from him. It took her a moment to regain her breath. Her eyes were fixed upon the ground, unable to meet his.

'I am sorry,' she murmured finally.

Giovanni could see that she was deeply shocked. He was shocked himself, he certainly hadn't intended such a thing to happen. He tried to ease her discomfort as best he could.

'Why are you sorry? There is no need for you to be sorry,' he insisted. 'It is I who must apologise. Please forgive me. I had no right.' She said nothing but continued to stare at the ground.

'I came to see Evan,' Giovanni explained, trying to sound as though nothing had happened. 'But if he is not at home I can come back later.' He turned to go.

'No.' She put out her hand, but stopped short of touching him. 'No, there is no need.' Then she looked up at him and smiled, and it was a smile that made his heart ache. A smile so warm, so honest, that he had to fight the impulse to touch her again, simply to brush his fingers against her cheek, to stroke her hair. 'Please,' she insisted, 'please, come inside and wait. He will be home soon.'

Giovanni could do nothing but obey. He followed

her into the front room, sat on the chair she indicated and listened to her voice as she called from the kitchen.

'Fresh lemons,' she was saying as she prepared them a cooling drink. 'Mary Kinane, the accountant's wife, grows a beautiful lemon tree and she keeps me supplied.'

Giovanni looked around the little front room. There was love and attention in every detail, from the hand-made curtains and cushion covers to the hardy home-grown flowers carefully arranged in the small glass bowl on the sideboard table.

'Evan planted a lemon tree for me at the Clover,' she said, entering and handing him a large glass, 'but it died. I hope you have a sweet tooth—I put in a lot of sugar.'

He sipped the drink and nodded. 'It is very good.'

'I'll get a damp cloth for your cheek.' And before he could protest she had disappeared again.

She returned several minutes later and handed him a small face towel. 'I have soaked it in salt,' she warned, 'it will sting.'

'Thank you.' He held the warm cloth to his face and was grateful for the momentary distraction as the salt stung into his wound.

She sat in a hardback chair on the opposite side of the room and sipped at her drink as she talked. 'How did you hurt yourself?' she asked.

'I fell.'

'Oh? From a horse?'

'Just a foolish accident.' When she nodded, realising he didn't want to go into detail, he said jokingly to lighten the moment, 'At least one side will match the other now, eh?' And he gestured at the scar which dominated the left side of his face.

'Oh no,' she replied seriously, studying the scar from the knife wound, 'it will not leave a mark like that.' The splendid blue eyes suddenly met his. 'You were lucky that night. He was a coward that man, the sort who could kill.'

Giovanni was taken aback. Why was she speaking of the past as if it was an intimacy they shared? They could not afford to have a past.

He drained his drink. 'Will Evan be much longer? Perhaps I should—'

'No. He will be home any minute. He and Paul have gone to fetch Briony from the Lavertons'.'

'Ah.'

'Little Lucy Laverton is four years old today, and they had a party for her. It started at ten.' She looked at the clock on the sideboard table, it was nearly midday. 'He shouldn't be long.'

She seemed so relaxed. As if nothing had happened. And yet all Giovanni could think of was the texture of her skin and the moistness of her parted lips.

'I am here to ask him about work,' he said, 'at the Midas.' He must keep talking, he told himself. There must be no silence between them.

'Work?' She looked surprised. 'But why would you need work at the Midas? You and Rico have the Clover.'

'Not any longer. Harry sold it.'

'Harry sold the Clover?' Now she looked confused. 'But I thought you were partners.'

'That is what we thought also. There was a misunderstanding.' Her expression was one of such concern that he was distracted. He stared down at his glass as he hurried on. 'So I need a job. As soon as possible. Rico has had an accident and cannot work so I must look after Teresa and the children.'

'So many accidents,' she murmured. And when he looked up to meet her eyes he could stand it no more. If he did not leave he would have to touch her. He rose under the pretext of putting the face cloth and his empty glass on the table.

'Would you like another drink?' she asked, also rising.

'No. No. I think I should leave,' he replied. 'I will see Evan another time. I will call at the Midas tomorrow.'

'Stay, Giovanni. Please.' She indicated his chair. 'Sit and wait.' And, when he hesitated, there was a definite plea in her voice. 'Sit and wait for Evan. Please.'

He did as she asked, knowing that there was something she wanted to say to him, but they sat in silence for several moments before she spoke.

'It would be wise if, from now on, we avoided each other whenever possible, particularly if you are to work with my husband.'

Giovanni stared at the floor, miserably nodding his agreement, and Kate studied him as he examined the floorboards beneath his feet. He looked like a boy, she thought. A beautiful, sad boy. She so wanted to go to him and cradle his head against her breast.

Kate had known from the moment she had responded to Giovanni's kiss that she loved him as completely as he loved her. She could no longer dismiss his love and she could no longer ignore her response to his love. Kate's guilt had disappeared when she returned his kiss. Their love was irrevocable and, although it could never be fulfilled, she felt a great elation in acknowledging its existence.

'But Giovanni ... *caro mio* ...' He raised his head, bewildered by the endearment, and she continued to speak in Italian. 'It would be foolish to torment ourselves by ignoring what is between us. It is better that we declare our love.'

He stared at her, dumbfounded. She smiled that glorious smile again and he could not believe the words he was hearing. 'I love you, Giovanni. It's as if I have always loved you. And I know I always shall.'

'Caterina ...' He didn't dare move and he scarcely

dared breathe her name for fear he would break the spell. 'You love me?' he whispered.

'Yes.' Her smile faded. 'I shall never speak of it again, but I believe it is more honest to admit it. If only to guard against it,' she added with a touch of regret. 'Perhaps I am wrong but—'

'No.' Giovanni felt such joy. She loved him. His girl from the mountain. His dream. His Caterina. 'No. I love you. There is no shame in that.' He wanted to hold her, but she was not his to hold, and he could accept that fact now. Willingly he could accept it. She loved him!

From the opposite sides of the room they gazed at each other. Seated in hardbacked chairs against the walls, neither moving, they drank their fill of each other.

She looked at the man-boy with the gentle hazel eyes and the kind face. The beautiful face. She studied the scar which marred the symmetry of his beauty. She liked the scar—it was something they shared. She had been there that night. If she'd known then that the man was Giovanni . . . If their lives had once again become entwined that night . . .

Kate smiled. No, she told herself. No 'ifs'.

Giovanni watched the smile twitch at the corners of her mouth. He watched the fine feathers of laughter form at the outer corners of her eyes, and he recalled that frosty morning on the mountain how the girl's blue eyes danced, how laughter bubbled beneath the surface of her beauty.

Her face had changed since then. It was no longer that of a girl, with the milky-white skin and the clear, wide eyes of a child. This was a woman. A woman of the goldfields. The skin was tanned and, although she was not yet thirty, life's experience was already etching itself upon her face.

She is more beautiful than ever, Giovanni thought. The blue eyes still danced and there was still laughter beneath her beauty, but there was a strength in her now. The strength of a woman with a will of her own. She was magnificent.

'Caterina. My Caterina,' he breathed.

'Yes, *caro mio*.' She gave herself to him through her eyes. 'I will always be your Caterina.'

They continued to sit in silence. Neither moved, but each was lost in the other's caress. As Giovanni's eyes slowly travelled down her throat, Kate could feel the insistence of his lips upon her neck, then her shoulder, then her breast. Across the distance of the room, she could feel their naked skin pressed together, the weight of his body and the strength of his hands as he pulled her to him. And, when he finally lifted his eyes to meet hers once more, Kate allowed her own gaze to travel down his body.

She looked at his mouth and Giovanni felt their lips meet. He felt the moistness of her tongue. Then the touch of her fingers caressing his shoulders and his chest. Her arms encircling him. The fullness of her breasts, her hands clinging to his back, pulling herself closer and closer to him.

For how long did they give themselves to each other? From their hard chairs on the opposite sides of the little room, how long? A lifetime? A moment? Impossible to tell. Then, outside, the sound of horses. Two horses. One at a canter, one at a trot.

They both heard the horses but still they did not move. 'My name is Kate,' she reminded him gently. 'Always Kate.' He nodded.

The cantering horse was pulled to an abrupt halt outside the front of the house. 'I won!' It was Paul's voice.

'Wait a few years, she'll beat you yet, won't you, Briony girl?' It was Evan's voice as the horse at a trot was reined in alongside.

'We will never speak of this again,' she said.

'I know. And we must never see each other alone,' he added. 'Never.'

'Is it possible to be so sad and so happy at the same time?' she asked.

'Yes.'

They smiled and their eyes drank in the final moment. Then they rose and turned to the front door as the footsteps sounded on the verandah.

The door opened. 'She's the best horsewoman, Kate. She took the reins as though she was born to them.' Evan stood there with Briony, barely three, on his shoulders squealing with delight and nine-year-old Paul, flushed and excited, beside him, and Giovanni felt no pang of jealousy as he watched Kate kiss her husband lightly on the lips.

'How was the party, my darling?' She held her arms up to the little girl who slid from Evan's shoulders into her mother's embrace.

'Giovanni!'

Before Briony could answer her mother's query, Paul had run to Giovanni and hugged him and it was Evan who felt the pang of jealousy.

'Giovanni is here on business, Paul, leave the poor man alone.' Kate slung Briony onto one hip and held out her hand to her son. 'Come along and help me in the kitchen. I'll bring some tea in shortly,' she called over her shoulder.

'Sit down, Giovanni, please.' Evan pulled a chair up to the table by the front window and sat. Giovanni did the same. 'Business, is it? What business could you be wanting to do with me? I hear the Clover's been doing very well.'

Fifteen minutes later, when Kate returned with a pot of tea and freshly baked scones, Evan had heard the full story. Giovanni had told it with as little emotion as he could but his bitterness and hostility were evident.

'I don't suppose I need to enquire where that came from then?' Evan pointed to the cut on the Italian's cheek and, when Giovanni shrugged a reply, he asked, 'How's Harry?'

'Worse.'

'Good. He deserves it. Thank you, my dear.'

Giovanni avoided looking at Kate as she poured the tea, concentrating on the teapot instead.

'I can't say I'm surprised,' the Welshman continued when Kate had returned to the kitchen. 'Harry's always been a slippery one.' Giovanni declined the plate of scones which Evan held out to him. 'Never an out-and-out scoundrel, mind. Never openly robs a man, but as good as, in my book. I'll wager he's convinced himself he's done nothing wrong too.' Noticing the growing anger in Giovanni's eyes, Evan took a bite of his scone and changed the subject. 'Still, no amount of talking is going to get the Clover back for you. I take it you're here to ask for work, is that it?'

Giovanni nodded, appreciating the Welshman's bluntness. 'I am a good worker, you know that I am. And so is my brother. Between us we can do the work of four men. When Rico is recovered you will see—'

'I cannot employ your brother, Giovanni.'

'He has a temper, I know, but I can—'

'Yes, there is his temper to take into consideration,' Evan admitted, 'but that is not why.'

'I can control him, I swear to you I can.'

'I believe you, my friend. In fact, I believe you are the only man who can control your brother. But as far as the Midas is concerned, he is unemployable.' Giovanni waited for an explanation, although he knew the answer. Evan shrugged. 'He cannot speak English.'

When Giovanni shook his head and gave a sigh of exasperation Evan continued, a trifle impatiently. 'Now you listen to me, Giovanni. I know you and all of your friends think that the language regulation is there merely as an excuse not to employ Italians. Or Europeans in general for that matter. But there *is* a reason, believe me. Sure, maybe there are some who exercise the rules for the wrong reasons, but I'm not one of them. If a miner can work well then it's immaterial to me what part of the world he comes from.'

Kate returned with a jug of hot water to top up the teapot and Giovanni forced himself to concentrate on Evan, even though he didn't really believe what the Welshman was saying.

Evan sensed his scepticism. 'You've never worked the big mines, Giovanni. In the big mines a man's ability to communicate is as important as his ability to wield a pick. I tell you, man,' he said, 'down there is a world bigger than you could possibly imagine.'

Kate watched as her husband leaned across the table, intent upon making contact with the Italian. There was an uncharacteristic edge of excitement to his voice and an enthusiasm in his eyes she had never seen before. 'I know that you love working under the ground. Just as I do. And you'll love this world, Giovanni. But it is a far more dangerous world than the Clover. I never truly knew it myself until I started at the Midas. I thought mining was mining. But this is different. You're so far down you could be in the centre of the earth, I tell you. One moment you're working a stope that will barely contain a man, and the next you're in a cavern that could hold the Town Hall itself. Men work in teams. Not just for reasons of efficiency, but for their own safety. And it's for reasons of safety that they must be able to communicate, don't you see? In the big mines, more than ever, a man needs to rely upon his brothers.'

Kate continued to watch her husband, fascinated. She had never heard him speak with such passion. She was touched and at the same time disappointed that he had never discussed these feelings in such a way with her.

Giovanni could sense Kate's response to Evan's rare show of animation and for the first time he felt a surge of jealousy. If the mere mention of a man's passion for the world below the earth's surface could stir her, what could he, Giovanni, do to her? He could lie with her in the red desert dirt in the dead of the night and share with her the diamond-studded sky. Nowhere in the world did the stars shine with such brilliance as in the velvet-black roof of the desert—had the Welshman shared that with her? Had he shared with her a love of the great brown land itself? The soft, powdery texture of the dust when you held it in the palm of your hand, the smell of the saltbush when you crushed it between your fingers, the constant trickle of sweat on the body that tasted like salt if you licked it.

A brief image. Caterina's naked body. The trickle of sweat between her breasts. His tongue licking it away. Giovanni rose and his chair scraped angrily on the bare floor. He knew he was being unfair. Evan was a good man, a man of honour and, no doubt, a good husband. But he was not a passionate man. Caterina was a passionate woman, and she needed a passionate man.

'I understand, and I agree. Rico is not the right man for the Midas.' Giovanni could have argued Rico's case further; he could have told the Welshman that his brother could understand the basics of English, but what was the point? Evan was right, Rico did not belong as part of a team. He could not be trusted.

'I must go,' he said. 'I have taken up enough of your time.' He needed to get out, to get away from the two of them. It was his own passion that was devouring him, he knew that. Surely he should be grateful that Evan was not a passionate man, surely it would be unbearable to contemplate Caterina in the throes of ecstasy . . .

He must leave. He must. 'Thank you for the tea, Kate,' he said.

'It was a pleasure.' Kate was busying herself stacking the cups and saucers. Something was wrong. She could sense it.

Suddenly she was overwhelmed with remorse. What had she done? She had told herself there was no shame in declaring her love. She had told herself she was not being unfaithful, merely honest, when she admitted to Giovanni that she would always love him. But there *was* shame and she *had* been unfaithful. She could still feel their eyes devouring each other. She might just as well have given him her body; perhaps it would have been more honest if she had.

'I'll see you at the mine tomorrow then, Giovanni,' Evan was saying. 'At half past seven—the morning shift starts at eight.'

'I shall be there.' The men shook hands. 'Thank you, Evan.'

Giovanni nodded to Kate and left.

She had done a shocking thing, she told herself as she brushed up the scone crumbs from the table. She had shamed herself, she had brought torment to Giovanni and, above all, she had wronged her husband.

Evan was a little puzzled by the Italian's hasty departure. He'd have thought Giovanni would have welcomed the chance to sit and talk about mining and particularly about the Midas.

'Would you like another cup of tea?' Kate asked.

'No thank you, my dear.'

He watched her carry the tray out to the kitchen. Of course, he realised; it was Kate. Giovanni was in love with her. Kate had insisted the man was a romantic, merely in love with an idea, but she was wrong. He was in love with her. And who could blame him? Evan thought.

Then it occurred to him that Kate, with her woman's intuition, probably knew and was dismissing the man's feelings in deference to him. It was sensitive and thoughtful of her. Evan decided that he would not broach the subject—he would not wish to embarrass her. As for Giovanni . . . Well, Giovanni was not only a man of honour, he was a man with far too much pride to make a nuisance of himself. Evan felt sorry for him.

TWO WEEKS AFTER his fight with Giovanni, Harry still refused to go out. He would not even walk in the street, let alone visit his friends at Hannan's Club.

'Let them see me like this?' he scorned, trying not to move his jaw, which was healing but still painful. 'Never! I'll not have them laughing at me.'

'Oh, for goodness' sake, Harry, look at yourself. You look perfectly all right.' Maudie gestured at the mirror above the mantelpiece as she cut Jack another piece of cake. The boy had just come home from school and the three of them were having tea in the upstairs parlour before Maudie started on the busy evening shift.

Harry walked over and inspected his face in the mirror. Most of the swelling had gone and the black eye had faded completely, but it was the three missing front teeth that really bothered him. He smiled and quickly stopped, horrified yet again by the gaping hole.

'I tell you, I'll not have them laughing at me,' he said as he sat and took a large gulp of the Scotch he'd poured himself.

Maudie felt irritated. She didn't like his drinking mid-afternoon and, damn his missing teeth and his vanity—he could at least help her out in the bar on a busy Friday night.

'But why would they laugh at you, Pa?' Jack asked,

outraged, his mouth full of cake. 'Giovanni tried to kill you, he didn't fight fair ...' Every time Jack thought about Giovanni and the steel pipe he felt overwhelmed with anger.

'Don't speak with your mouth full, Jack,' Maudie reprimanded.

'But hell, that's not fighting fair ...'

'I said don't speak with your mouth full. And don't swear.'

'Like I've told you, Jack,' Harry glanced quickly at Maudie, somehow feeling that she was reprimanding him rather than the boy. 'He only grabbed the pipe at the last minute. It was a fair fight for the most part.'

Maudie's look was sceptical, as usual. She believed the 'steel pipe' about as much as she believed the 'genuine misunderstanding' of the Clover contract.

'You saw the contract yourself, Maudie,' Harry had insisted. 'It was perfectly clear. And I read it out to them word for word, I swear I did!' Harry had sworn to the fact so often that he genuinely believed it.

'I'm going downstairs to help Alice set up.' Maudie rose from the table. 'No more cake,' she said to Jack. 'Will you have the tea things cleared away please, Harry.'

Harry watched her go, depressed. Things were definitely not right between him and Maudie. One moment she'd been prepared to kill for him; the next moment she'd dismissed him. 'Don't say a word, Harry,' she'd said as she bathed his face. 'I am not interested in anything you have to say.' He'd tried to explain again and again but, every time he did, Maudie's mouth set, her eyes glazed over and she seemed to look right through him. God, she was hard, that woman. Intractable. She'd reverted to the tough Maudie of old, the Maudie he'd courted.

Marriage had mellowed her, Harry decided. Until

now. It was all because of those Italians, he thought blackly. He should never have got mixed up with them. The ingratitude! Hell, if it weren't for him those damn Gianni brothers would still be working the Fremantle wharves.

'Can I have another piece, Pa?'

The boy's voice shocked him out of his reverie. Jack's hand was hovering over the forbidden cake. 'Yes, son, of course you can.' He winked roguishly at his son. At least he was still a hero to Jack.

Jack grinned and stuffed his mouth as full as he could, the shared disobedience creating a bond between them. The fruitcake was rich and the boy really didn't want to eat any more, but he hated seeing his father miserable. Jack would have eaten five fruitcakes if it would make Harry happy.

The door opened. 'Harry . . .'

Jack stopped chewing, breathed through his nose and tried to look normal. He hoped Maudie wouldn't ask him anything.

'Gaston Picot is here to see you,' she said.

'Tell him I'm not in.' Harry rose, alarmed. 'Tell him I've gone out.'

'Too late. He knows you're here, he's on his way up.' Maudie glanced at Jack's bulging cheeks and wanted to smile. 'You can't stay locked up forever, Harry.'

A tap at the door. 'May I come in?'

'Please do, Mr Picot.' Maudie stood aside as the Frenchman entered the room.

'Harry. *Mon ami.*'

'Gaston.' Harry smiled tightly, careful not to let his teeth show, and the two men shook hands.

'Have you met Harry's son?' Maudie said. 'Jack, this is Mr Picot.' She couldn't help it, she wanted to burst out laughing. Jack's eyes were as wide as saucers.

'*Enchanté.*' Gaston Picot extended his hand and Jack

shook it as heartily and with as much strength as he could, hoping it would distract the Frenchman. It did. '*Mon Dieu*,' he nodded approvingly to Harry. 'He is a strong young man.'

Maudie decided to save the boy. 'Would you like some tea?' she asked before Picot could return his attention to Jack.

'*Non, merci*.'

'Very well. I'll send Alice up to fetch the tea things. Come along, Jack.'

On the landing she turned to him. 'Now go and spit that out. It'd serve you right if you choked on it.'

She watched him fondly as he galloped down the stairs, grateful to escape. She loved that boy as her own. Always had. Face it, Maudie, she told herself, Jack is the reason you married Harry in the first place. You got what you wanted, there was no sense in being disappointed.

But she couldn't fool herself. She *was* disappointed. Deeply disappointed. Incorrigible as he might be, Harry Brearley had always charmed her, always made her laugh. The eighteen months of their marriage had been the happiest time in Maudie's thirty-one years and, after the birth of the twins, when she was convinced that he had mended his ways, she had finally admitted to herself that she truly did love Harry. Now she wasn't so sure. The blinkers had gone and, with them, the magic. Harry had not mended his ways at all. His charm was turned on when it suited his purpose and when he made her laugh it was because it was to his advantage to do so. Maudie wondered whether she would ever delight in him again the way she used to.

If only he could share the truth with her, she thought. But she believed that Harry had lost all sight of the truth. The more he swore that the Italians had misunderstood the contract, the more Maudie realised that he believed it. And then when he swore Giovanni had attacked him with a steel pipe . . .

'He had a steel pipe?' she'd interrupted, incredulously. 'Giovanni?' And Jack's eyes too mirrored his astonishment.

'Yes! A steel pipe.' He held his hands out. 'This long,' he swore vehemently.

'And he attacked you with it?'

Was there a momentary hesitation then or was Maudie imagining it? She didn't press the issue. What was the point? She didn't want to discredit him in his son's eyes.

Although she didn't believe Harry, as the days passed Maudie couldn't help but be affected by the self-righteous indignation with which he justified himself.

Damn the Giannis, she found herself thinking. Why hadn't they employed a lawyer to negotiate their contract? Then they could have caught Harry out before his blind opportunism had landed him in this mess.

She would never forgive Rico Gianni for the madness of that night. Nor Giovanni for his attack. Whether the steel pipe was factual or not, both brothers had sought violent retribution, and Maudie abhorred violence.

Yes, damn the Giannis, she thought. If the Giannis hadn't come into our lives . . .

'YOU'VE WHAT! GOOD God, man, I sold it to you only a fortnight ago.' Harry stared at Picot in shock.

Picot nodded. 'And I sold it two days later. I see you have lost some teeth.'

Harry was so appalled he forgot to cover his mouth. 'But why? To whom?'

'The Mount Charlotte Mine is extending.' The Frenchman shrugged indifferently. 'There's no money in small leases, there hasn't been for quite some time.' Gaston's accent had diminished considerably now that there was no need to impress. 'I'm surprised Evan Jones didn't sell directly to the Mount Charlotte in the first place, instead of to you and the Italians, but then I have heard that he is not much of a businessman.'

'You sold the Clover two days after you bought it?'

Picot nodded.

'Then you must have made a deal with them before me.'

Picot nodded again. 'They thought I already owned the mine. Gave me double the price I gave you.'

How could the man have done this to him? Harry thought, aghast. And how could he remain so indifferent whilst admitting to such blatant treachery? 'But we're friends,' he protested lamely. 'I trusted you.'

'So? You were friends with the Italian brothers. And they trusted you. Business is business, my friend.' Harry's mouth was still agape and Gaston studied the missing teeth with interest. 'So it is true what they say.' Harry looked blankly back at him. 'That the Italian made a mess of you.'

Hastily Harry brought his hand up to obscure his mouth. 'Who says that?' he muttered. 'Giovanni?'

'No, no, the brothers have said nothing. But people talk. He was seen driving your trap into town. You were in it, smashed to a pulp.'

'An accident.' Harry drained his Scotch. 'An accident, that's all it was. The Italian brought me home.'

'That is exactly what I told them at the Club,' Gaston smiled. 'Now stop looking so betrayed, *mon ami*, and pour me a Scotch; there are things we must talk about.'

Harry found himself automatically obeying and Gaston watched as he fetched the decanter from the corner cabinet. He still felt a certain fondness for Harry

Brearley. Humorous as it was, there was something quite touching about the man's wounded vanity and Gaston, himself extremely vain, sympathised.

'I return to the city in two days. You must come with me,' he said.

'Why?' Harry's tone was churlish as he handed the Frenchman his drink.

'Well, I know of a good dentist for one. He will give you brand-new teeth. Ivory. Better than the ones you have lost. Friends of mine say he is a genius.' The gleaming smile was proof positive of the dentist's talent. Although it was a fact he would never admit, Gaston's teeth were not all his own.

'Besides,' he continued, 'I have a business proposition which I think may interest you. Salute.' And he raised his glass.

Harry continued to glower but it was becoming difficult to remain churlish in the face of the Frenchman's good humour.

'You need to get away from Kalgoorlie,' Gaston continued, 'just for a month or so, while the townspeople find fresh gossip. You will holiday with me and my family, we can discuss our business and all will be forgotten when you return.'

Harry was aware of the honour being bestowed upon him. There was not a person in Kalgoorlie who wouldn't be flattered to receive an invitation to the Picot mansion in Cottesloe. And not only would it give the Kalgoorlie tongues time to find something else to wag about, it would give Maudie time to calm down, time to get back to normal. Harry desperately missed his good-humoured Maudie.

Attractive as the offer was, however, Harry's pride stood firm. The Frenchman had used him, even made a fool of him, and yet he was expected to forgive and forget in return for an invitation to the home of the great

Gaston Picot. Well, not Harry Brearley. Harry Brearley was not so easily bought.

Gaston smiled to himself, fully aware of Harry's dilemma. He threw in his trump card. 'And of course you must bring young Jack with you. He would like a holiday by the sea, *n'est-ce pas*?'

It worked, as Gaston had known it would. He'd heard of the man's devotion to his son.

'The boy would be able to come for only a week,' Harry replied, wavering already. 'Maudie wouldn't have him miss too much school.'

'Of course, of course. We can send him back on the train, that will make him feel very grown up.' Gaston offered his hand. 'It is a deal then?'

Harry accepted the offer as graciously as he could. Not only could he lick his wounds, spend some time alone with Jack and come back with his new teeth to woo Maudie all over again, there was another consideration altogether. One that made the proposition doubly attractive to Harry. It would put time and distance between him and Rico Gianni.

'HE HAS RUN away! The man is a coward! A snivelling coward!' Rico drained his glass of red wine, poured another, then slouched over his steaming bowl of minestrone, shovelling it into his mouth with a spoon, oblivious to the fact that much of it was running down his beard. 'Some bread, Carmelina.'

The family was seated on benches either side of the big wooden table which Rico himself had made. Two-year-old Salvatore, perched on cushions beside Teresa, was trying to feed himself but more soup was landing on the table than in his mouth.

'Slow down, Rico, you will give yourself indigestion,' Teresa said. 'And wipe your chin,' she added, 'you're spilling more soup than Salvatore.' She tried to take the spoon from the little boy but, intent upon feeding himself, he refused to allow her.

Rico ignored the cotton napkin beside his bowl and wiped his beard with the sleeve of his shirt. 'In the soup,' he said to Carmelina as she tore his bread up for him. 'Put it in the soup.' Carmelina meekly obeyed. Normally she answered back to her father, but lately even Carmelina trod warily around Rico.

Giovanni dipped a hunk of bread into his own soup and tried to ignore his brother. For three weeks now Rico had been sitting around the house with his arm in a sling, venting his anger on those about him. Giovanni was grateful for the long, hard hours he worked at the Midas. He would have preferred to have moved out altogether but, until Rico was fit enough to work, every penny earned was necessary for the family's survival.

'He thinks running away will save him? Well, he is wrong.' Rico stirred the bread around vigorously, soup slopping over the sides of the bowl. 'I will be here when he comes back.' He swigged from his fresh glass of wine.

Teresa had given up any pretence of eating. She had not been hungry from the moment they had sat to table. As she mopped up Salvatore's mess with her napkin she could feel her anger mounting, the anger she had been suppressing for days. She had excused Rico long enough. He was in pain, she had told herself for the first week after the shooting. Then the week after that she had told herself it was his boredom and frustration, the hurt to his male pride as he watched Giovanni go to work every day to support his, Rico's, family. But she knew it was more than that, she knew he was allowing his desire for revenge to devour him.

Over and over, she and Giovanni had told Rico that Harry Brearley's treachery had been avenged, that there must be no more violence.

'His woman shoots me in the back and I am not to avenge myself?' he'd raged.

'If a man threatened my babies I would shoot him too,' Teresa retaliated. Although she would never forgive Maudie Brearley her complicity in their betrayal, Teresa had been shocked when she had heard the true facts.

Rico had abandoned his attack upon Maudie, but no amount of reasoning could turn him from his desire for revenge. On and on he raged until their home was poisoned with his hate and Teresa felt she could stand it no longer.

And now Harry had left town.

Enrico had heard the news at school. He and Jack Brearley were in the same class and today Jack hadn't been there.

'I bet you don't know where Jack's gone,' one of his classmates had jeered. Everyone knew about the recent enmity between the two boys.

'I know where I hope he's gone,' Enrico had replied. 'Hell. That's where I hope he's gone. Hell.' 'Hell' was a word he had learned from Jack, a word he got into trouble using at home.

His reaction was pure bravado. Enrico was not a naturally aggressive boy, preferring to remain quietly in the background. Until it came to singing along with Giovanni and his concertina. Giovanni said that Enrico had the voice of an angel but Jack sneered and said that singing was for girls. Which didn't bother Enrico at all—Jack always mocked him. Good-natured mockery. They were brothers after all. The broken finger proved it.

But the fathers had injected their poison into the veins of their sons. No longer were they brothers.

'He's gone with his dad to Perth,' the classmate had boasted. 'And him and his dad are going to stay with Mr Picot and Mr Picot's one of the richest people in the world and Jack's dad's going into business with him. And when Jack's dad gets really rich and your dad and your uncle are still poor it'll serve them right for bashing Mr Brearley up with a steel—'

'I hope they all go to hell,' Enrico had interrupted. 'And I hope you go to hell too.'

Enrico would have been able to forgive Jack just about anything. It was not Jack's fault that his father had brought ruin upon the Gianni family—that was between the grown-ups. And, in his very young heart-of-hearts, Enrico could even believe that his own father had done something terrible, like smash up the Brearleys' pub in the middle of the night. His father sometimes acted crazy, Enrico knew that. But he could never forgive Jack the lies about Giovanni. Giovanni would never attack a man with a steel pipe. Giovanni was a man of peace. And Jack Brearley was a liar, just like his father.

Now Enrico sat staring at his untouched soup, no longer hungry, wishing that he could leave the table.

'And if the coward does not come back,' Rico continued, pushing his emptied soup bowl to one side, 'then I will find him.'

'I'm going for a walk.' Giovanni rose from the table. He'd listened to as much as he possibly could in silence. He knew if he said anything it would start an argument and that was the last thing Teresa wanted. He had sensed her tension. It was palpable as she toyed with her food and stared at the tablecloth.

Now she looked up. 'But the pasta . . .'

'I am not hungry, Teresa. The soup was excellent. Thank you.'

'Giovanni . . .' But Giovanni was already out the door.

'He wants to walk,' Rico growled dismissively. 'Let the man go. I tell you, Teresa, when I am mended I will hunt Harry Brearley down. I will hunt him down and . . .'

Giovanni had been wrong. An argument was exactly what Teresa wanted. More than an argument. Far more. She wanted to scream. She wanted to throw Rico's soup bowl across the room and watch it smash against the yellow daisy wallpaper. She wanted to hit Rico as hard as she could, to feel the palm of her hand sting as it slammed against his cheek. Anything to shut him up. She'd been quiet too long and she could take no more.

'Enrico, Carmelina, put Salvatore to bed please.' She wiped the toddler's face and lifted him from the bench.

Enrico knew something was about to happen. He rose, circled the table and took the child from her. The little boy squirmed and squealed, insisting he be put down so that he could walk on his own.

'But, Mamma,' Carmelina protested, 'the pasta.'

'You can have some pasta when you have put Salvatore to bed.'

Carmelina recognised the steel in her mother's tone and offered no further argument. The two children, Salvatore toddling clumsily between them, walked to the door of their parents' room where the toddler slept.

'Close the door,' Teresa instructed, 'and stay there until I call you.'

Rico drained his glass of wine. It was his fifth but he was not at all drunk. 'What is going on, Teresa?' he asked as he reached for the wine jug. 'Why have you sent the children away?'

'We need to talk.' She said it as evenly as she could although, watching the wine spill from the corner of his mouth as he guzzled from the glass, she wanted to hit him again.

'Mmm? What about?' He didn't appear remotely interested. 'Where's the pasta?'

She wanted to throw the pasta in his face. 'We need

to talk about Harry Brearley,' she said instead. And she watched his face cloud over as she knew it would.

'I will kill him,' Rico muttered, and his fingers tightened around the glass. Any minute it would break. 'Just you wait and see. Very slowly, I will kill him.'

Teresa leaned across the table until her face was barely inches from her husband's and there was a madness in her eyes to equal his. 'If you kill Harry Brearley, I will kill you,' she said.

'Eh?' Rico looked back at her dumbly, the glass poised in mid-air.

'If you kill Harry Brearley then I will take the children and I will leave you. And that will kill you, Rico.'

'What is the matter with you? The man ruins our family and you try to protect him. What is the matter with you, woman?'

'I am not protecting Harry Brearley. When I think of what he did I could kill him myself. But it is not Harry Brearley who is ruining this family. It is you! *You*, Rico!'

'Me!' Rico's face was a picture of comic innocence. 'What have I done?'

The very expression that once beguiled her now irritated her beyond control. 'Giovanni works to support us and you drive him from the house.'

Rico looked exasperated. 'The man went for a walk . . .'

'I would not blame him if he left us all to starve. And as for the rest of your family . . .' Rico was about to interrupt again but Teresa continued. 'Your son lives in fear of you. Even your daughter—'

'My daughter does not fear me.' Rico would not have his relationship with his precious Carmelina questioned. 'She fears nothing.'

Teresa wasn't listening. She barely drew breath. 'But *I* do not fear you, Rico.' She reached out and wiped her hand across his mouth. 'Look at you,' she said disgustedly, 'you dribble your food like Salvatore. You are a pig.'

Rico froze.

'You are a pig, do you hear me?' she repeated, her face distorted now with anger.

Slowly, Rico rose from the table.

Teresa rose also. 'You have the manners of a pig!' Her voice was becoming shrill as her anger found its release. He walked around the table towards her. 'You drink like a pig! You eat like a pig!'

He reached out and she felt his hand clasp the side of her head. She felt his fingers closing on her thick hair, locking into a fist. She grabbed at his wrist but couldn't release his grip.

'I have always eaten like a pig, Teresa.' As the hand held her firm, the eyes drilled into hers. 'Always . . .'

'You cannot frighten me, Rico.' She stopped struggling and stared back at him. 'You will never frighten me.'

'. . . and always you have liked it.' His voice was quiet and he seemed not to have heard her as he continued. 'You have told me before that I eat like a pig,' he said. 'And you have laughed and called me an animal. And you have kissed me and taken the food from my mouth into your own. And we have made love.'

Teresa continued to stare into his eyes. And realised that it was not anger she saw there. It was shock. And hurt. She stood motionless as he ran his hand down the side of her face, resting his thumb for a moment against her lips before continuing on to her throat.

'Do you no longer love me, Teresa?' he whispered. 'Do you no longer love me?' His voice was bewildered, and the look in his eyes was one of utter confusion.

Teresa was lost for words, mesmerised. She had never seen him so vulnerable.

With his fingertips, he stroked her neck and her hair, thoughtfully, studying his own hand as he did so. 'If you no longer loved me because there was another man, then I would have to kill that man, and I would have to kill you too. But if you no longer loved me because your love had died, Teresa, then I would kill myself.' He stopped stroking her and his hand rested lightly upon the base of her throat. 'I would kill myself so that I would never have to see you with another man.'

Teresa took his face in both her hands. 'There is no other man, Rico,' she whispered. She ran her fingers across the massive shoulders, then clasped the hand which rested upon her throat. 'There will never be another man.' And she glided his hand to her breast. 'I love my pig the way he is.' Her open mouth was upon his and she could taste the wine and the soup in his beard. She ground her body against him and felt herself grow moist with desire.

Rico's arm circled her waist and, in one movement, lifted her onto the table. He pushed her legs apart and buried his head between her thighs.

Several plates smashed to the floor and Teresa laughed as he growled and pulled her dress up to her waist. 'No, Rico, stop it. The children.'

She squirmed away, ran to the bedroom and threw open the door. Salvatore was already asleep in his cot but, having heard the sound of breaking crockery, Enrico and Carmelina were standing together staring up at her apprehensively. Teresa was quick to reassure them.

'An accident, that is all,' she said a little breathlessly. 'Now come along and eat your pasta.' She returned to the dining table, grabbing the broom from the corner by the sink, and started to sweep up the broken plates. From the corner of her eye she could see Rico standing beside the door to Giovanni's room, his erection conspicuous beneath his light cotton trousers.

'Carmelina,' she ordered, 'fetch fresh plates. Enrico, serve the pasta.' Teresa swept the debris into a corner of the room away from the children's two small beds which were against one of the walls. 'Papa and I will be with you soon,' she said as she joined Rico. 'You may start to eat without us.'

Together they disappeared into Giovanni's bedroom and it was only seconds later that the children heard the guttural moans and the squeaking bed.

'What are they doing?' Carmelina asked as she carefully put the plates on the table.

'They have stopped fighting,' her brother explained. Enrico had heard the sounds many times before. He did not know what his parents were doing but he knew that, afterwards, his father would be in a good mood. Enrico was always glad when he heard the sounds. 'Everything will be all right,' he smiled. And he served himself an extra spoonful of pasta. Suddenly he was very, very hungry.

Chapter Fourteen

Harry stood on the upper terrace and looked out over the sculptured hedges, the carved stone steps, the marble statues and intricate fountains. He looked beyond the formal gardens, across the gentle hills and sand dunes to the Indian Ocean barely a quarter of a mile away and Rottnest Island on the far horizen. It was a fine autumn day and he had enjoyed a brisk walk to the beach followed by a hearty breakfast, and now, as he sipped the last of the excellent coffee he'd brought onto the terrace with him, he wondered how much longer Gaston would be. The Frenchman had made an early visit into the city and had promised that, upon his return, they would talk business. 'Today is the day, *mon ami,*' he had said. 'The holiday is over. Today we talk business.'

'Would you like more coffee, sir?'

Harry turned to the housekeeper who, as usual, had appeared magically beside him. At the Picot mansion one's every whim was anticipated.

'Yes, thank you.' He handed his cup to her and she just as magically disappeared.

Harry tingled with anticipation. He had been staying at Maison Picot for nearly six weeks now and each time he had broached the business proposition, Gaston had been evasive. 'All in good time, Harry,' he would say expansively, 'all in good time. First you must holiday. Besides,' he would add with a twinkle, 'how can a man discuss business without his teeth?'

To begin with Harry had welcomed the opportunity to relax and regain his strength. He hadn't realised how severely he had been affected by his humiliation at the hands of Giovanni, or how haunted he had been by his fear of the madman Rico. He put the Italians out of his mind and concentrated instead on having fun with Jack.

The boy had never before seen the ocean and his reaction was a joy to behold. He swam daily, throwing himself headlong into the pounding surf and swimming out well beyond the breakers. Harry's initial alarm turned to amazement at the lad's strength and confidence in the water.

'Where did you learn to do that?' he asked.

Jack grinned. 'You can't touch the bottom in the vats, Pa,' he answered. 'If you can't stay afloat there you're a goner.'

Harry laughed. Of course. The vats were out of bounds, Maudie put her foot down firmly about that. He should have known.

With Gaston away daily on business and his wife Gabrielle spending most of her time with their five-year-old daughter, Harry and Jack were left very much to their own devices. They played tennis on Gaston's finely tended, sunken grass tennis court. They played billiards in his jarrah-panelled, parquetry-floored games room. They played hide-and-seek amongst the cypress hedges and rose bushes and statues. And when they walked across the sand dunes to frolic together on Cottesloe Beach, Harry, who loathed the water, even allowed Jack to try and teach him to swim.

Little Simone tried desperately to join them on their daily adventures but Jack didn't have much time for five-year-old girls, which more than suited Gabrielle Picot as she didn't quite approve of either Harry or Jack. Oh, Harry Brearley was certainly handsome, she thought, and she was sure he'd have a way with the ladies, but his manner was just a shade too brash for refined circles. And he should really do something about the manners of his boisterous son.

After a week of fun together, interrupted only by Harry's visits to the dentist, it was time for Jack to return to Kalgoorlie.

'Let him stay for one more week,' Gaston insisted. 'Louis will be home from boarding school for the weekend; the boys must meet.'

Harry didn't need much persuading, although he was fully aware that the meeting between the boys was a flimsy excuse. Jack may have been mature for his age but a boy of barely nine could hardly be of interest to a fourteen-year-old lad.

Harry was right. Louis Picot scarcely deigned to notice young Jack as he chatted on endlessly about his friends at school and the rugby team. Fourteen seemed a ludicrously young age for a person to become a snob, Harry thought.

'Like mother like son,' he whispered encouragingly to Jack, hoping that the boy wasn't feeling hurt or humiliated. But nothing could spoil the grand time Jack was having with his father, least of all the airs and graces of silly Louis Picot.

A week later Jack boarded the train having had the best time of his entire life. And the train trip was an extension of the adventure. He waved goodbye to Harry, sat up straight on the seat of the dog carriage, his feet dangling a good twelve inches from the floor, his packed lunch clasped in his lap, and stared out of the window. He pretended that Maudie wasn't meeting him at the other end. He was travelling the entire breadth of Australia. All on his own.

Harry started to miss him the moment the train pulled out of the station.

'Your coffee, Mr Brearley.'

The housekeeper's voice snapped him back to the present. 'Thank you,' he said, taking the cup from her. 'It is magnificent coffee.' He flashed her his most winning smile. He'd had his new ivory teeth for nearly a fortnight now and his confidence was totally restored. Gaston had been right, the dentist was a genius.

The housekeeper instinctively beamed back—it was difficult not to respond to Mr Brearley's charm. 'Call me if there's anything else you want,' she said.

Harry sipped the steaming brew. He'd never tasted coffee like it.

Yes, he missed Jack. He missed Jack and he missed Maudie too. As soon as he had finalised his business with Gaston he would return to Kalgoorlie. But the time spent at the Picot mansion had been invaluable. Harry Brearley now knew what he wanted.

This was what he wanted. He looked about at the spectacular terraces and sunken gardens, the rose bushes, cultivated lawns and rows of immaculate cypress hedges with not a leaf out of place. 'Topiary is considered an art form in France,' Gabrielle had patronisingly informed him. 'Our man was taught by a topiarist from the gardens of the Palace of Versailles.' Harry had no idea what a topiarist was until Gaston explained.

'Just a man who cuts hedges,' the Frenchman had said, darting a look of annoyance at his wife. Gabrielle was being particularly irritating lately and she had no right to be. She couldn't possibly know of his latest peccadillo; he had been even more discreet than usual.

Harry turned his attention toward the house. That's what Gaston had called it. 'It is just a house, Harry,' he had said with a shrug of indifference. It wasn't just a house at all, it was a mansion. In fact it wasn't even a mansion, Harry thought. Damn it all, the place was a palace. All arches and columns and courtyards.

'Mediterranean style,' Gaston had explained with an airy wave of his hand. 'It is nothing very special. They are everywhere in France. And Italy and Spain.'

Gaston knew Maison Picot was impressive. Even by Mediterranean standards it was impressive, but in Perth—in the whole of Australia for that matter—the like of it had never been seen. Maison Picot was Gaston's pride and joy. It was also a powerful business asset and he was fully aware of the effect it was having on Harry Brearley. That was part of his plan.

Yes, this was what he wanted, Harry thought as he looked about him. He wanted arches and fountains. He wanted hedges, and topiarists to tend them. Well, maybe not hedges, he thought, maybe hedges would look silly in Kalgoorlie. Maybe not even fountains and arches; there wasn't the water in Kalgoorlie for fountains anyway. But he wanted money. He wanted enough money to live like this. To give Maudie a life like this.

'Harry, my dear friend, I am so sorry.' Gaston had arrived. 'The business meeting lasted a full hour longer than I had expected. Anne-Marie,' he called, *'café s'il vous plait.'*

Gaston launched immediately into his proposal—his timing was perfect and he knew it. He knew that Harry was hungry and ready for business, that was the way he had planned it. He had replaced the man's teeth, rebuilt his confidence and watched whilst the magic of affluence cast its spell.

He got straight to the point. His various businesses were allowing him less and less time to travel to and from Kalgoorlie, he said, but he didn't want to sell up his interests there. Kalgoorlie real estate was, in his opinion, a very sound investment. Besides which he had a soft spot for the place.

'I am even contemplating a further purchase,' he said. 'A property in the very centre of Hannan Street. A property which, if all goes according to plan, will bear my name,' he added enigmatically. 'But more of that later.'

He needed an overseer, someone to safeguard his interests in his absence. 'Jeanne Renoir has been keeping an eye on things for me over the past several years, but . . . *merci*, Anne-Marie.' The housekeeper had magically appeared again and was placing a tray on the table. 'No, no, I will pour. Ah, *bon*, pralines,' he said, noticing the bowl of sweets. He seated himself at the table. 'Come, Harry, come and have some coffee.'

Harry sat. 'No more coffee for me thank you, I have already had three cups. It's delicious.'

'A praline then.' Gaston pushed the bowl of sugar-coated almonds in Harry's direction. 'They must have arrived this morning, there have been none for a month or more.' Harry declined. 'They are very good,' Gaston assured him. 'Gabrielle has them sent from France.'

'So she told me,' Harry nodded. And she had, when they'd finished dining awkwardly together in the breakfast room and she'd suggested he take his second cup of coffee onto the terrace whilst Anne-Marie cleared the table. 'Have a praline, Mr Brearley,' she'd said. Why couldn't she call him Harry? He'd feel much more comfortable if she did. 'I have them specially imported. From Paris.'

'Thank you.' And he'd escaped to the terrace where he'd nearly broken one of his brand-new ivory teeth on the wretched thing. Damn it, he swore, they were as hard as rock, and he threw the offending sweet into the nearest hedge.

'No thank you, Gaston,' Harry said firmly. 'No praline. You were saying?'

'Yes.' Gaston stirred his coffee. 'Jeanne has been

looking after things for me . . . you remember Jeanne, you met her at the municipal banquet.'

'Madame Renoir, yes, of course. A very beautiful woman,' he added admiringly.

'Yes, very beautiful,' Gaston agreed, 'but . . . ' there was just the slightest edge of contempt to his voice, 'but, as you say, my friend, a woman. And, much as we admire them, you must admit, women are not naturally equipped for the world of business.'

Harry tried to look as if he agreed, but he didn't really. He'd never met anyone with a better business sense than Maudie.

'I have a feeling that things have been slipping a little,' Gaston said, 'and I need someone there, on hand, to take control for me. Jeanne will remain involved, of course; she will retain my support, but not the control of my business.

'Oh, do not misunderstand me,' he continued reassuringly, 'Jeanne is a very dear friend and I trust her. Completely. But . . . ' He shrugged and smiled and there was no contempt in his voice this time, just a man-to-man complicity. ' . . . As I say, *mon ami* . . . she is a woman.'

Gaston did not trust Jeanne completely. In fact he had had the distinct impression for quite some time now that a sizeable amount of his profits had been ending up in her pocket. He wondered if it was her retribution for his having ended their affair two years ago, but he didn't think so.

He recalled that at the time she had received the news with surprising equanimity. When he had said, 'Gabrielle knows about us and is threatening divorce', Jeanne had simply replied, 'All good things come to an end, *mon cher*.' It was then he realised that, for the entire six years of their affair, he had never seen her ruffled. Neither physically nor emotionally. Jeanne Renoir was immaculate, always. In every way.

'So we will remain business partners, *oui*?' she had said. She'd kissed him, adding seductively, 'And if, every now and then, you wish to celebrate a new business venture, I am here, *oui*?' He hadn't been able to resist. They'd made love then and there on the elegant divan in the elegant drawing room of her elegant house and he'd left Kalgoorlie the next day.

He hadn't taken her up on her offer. He hadn't dared. From that day on, Gaston's trips to Kalgoorlie had lessened both in number and duration. The loss of his wife and children and the adverse publicity which would attend a divorce was simply not worth it. Instead, he settled for a series of discreet peccadillos located conveniently closer to home.

'But you would naturally prefer to be more than an overseer, would you not, Harry?' Gaston drained the last of his coffee. 'I do not envisage Harry Brearley content with collecting rentals,' he smiled. 'So that is where my new purchase comes in. You know the Sheaf Hotel, of course?'

Harry nodded darkly. 'It's where the Italians drink. If that's what you're thinking of buying I want nothing to do with it.'

'I am not thinking of buying the Sheaf, *mon ami*, I already own it.' He smiled at Harry's surprise. 'I have owned it for four years. And no,' he held up his hand reassuringly, 'I do not expect you to be involved in the management of it, I am perfectly happy with my current manager. It is the property adjoining the Sheaf that interests me. Not the business itself—it is currently a draper's store—but the property. Its size and position. I intend to convert it . . .' a theatrical pause whilst Harry waited for him to go on, 'to a restaurant,' he announced.

Harry looked blankly at him. 'A restaurant?'

'Exactly.' Gaston pushed the coffee tray away and

leaned forward over the table. 'When you dine out, where do you choose to go?'

'Hannan's,' Harry answered immediately.

'Of course. A businessmen's club where you eat and drink with your associates. But where would you take a prospective business partner if you wished also to entertain his wife? If you were a young man courting, where would you take your fiancée?' Gaston paused briefly, again for dramatic effect. 'Where do you take your own wife to dine, Harry? Where do you take Mrs Brearley?'

'The Palace Hotel, I suppose. Or the Australia, or the York.'

'Exactly!' Gaston sat back, triumphant. 'Hotels. Not restaurants. The dining rooms of hotels. Elegant hotels, grand hotels, I grant you, but hotels, my friend.'

He rose and started pacing about the terrace. He was genuinely excited by his idea. If spending time in Kalgoorlie did not carry with it the threat of divorce, he would settle there himself for however long it took to realise his dream.

'Restaurant Picot,' he exclaimed. Already, in his mind's eye, Gaston could see the large gilt-edged menus: *Gastronomie de Gaston Picot*, and listed beneath would be his favourite classic dishes. He would employ a leading French chef who would invent new dishes too, ones which would bear his name, *Beouf á la Picot*, or *Fraiches de Gaston*. And the facade and decor of the restaurant would be the most luxurious Kalgoorlie had ever seen. Restaurant Picot would change the social face of the town.

For several years now, it had been evident to Gaston that there was not only wealth on the goldfields, there was a rapidly growing sense of refinement. It was high time Kalgoorlie palates were educated accordingly, he decided. And he, Gaston Picot, was the one to do it.

The interior of the restaurant would be jarrah-panelled, he declared. 'Like my billiards room.' And there would be a large crystal chandelier. 'Like the chandelier upstairs,' he said. 'You have seen the ballroom?'

Harry nodded. He had indeed seen the ballroom. It was the first stop on Gabrielle's guided tour of Maison Picot the day after he'd arrived. The chandelier must have been six feet in diameter and of course it had been imported 'at great expense'.

'So, down to business,' Gaston said, satisfied that he had painted a sufficiently impressive picture of his restaurant. 'I would like you to manage the project for me.' He returned to his chair and studied Harry's reaction. 'You are welcome to invest in the property with me if you wish, but it is no matter if you do not. I have adequate funds available.'

'I should like to invest.' Harry finally found his voice. The prospect was unbelievably exciting. 'After all, I have the money from the Clover sale.' He grinned and the Frenchman grinned back.

'Of course you have, *mon ami.*' Gaston leaned back in his chair and laughed. 'We both have money from the sale of the Clover.' Gaston was delighted that Harry wanted to invest, although he had assumed the man would—it guaranteed a total commitment. And Gaston had a long-term plan. With a little grooming, Harry Brearley would make the ideal partner.

'You have been involved with the local council over the past year or so, have you not?' he asked. Harry nodded. 'Good. The more respectable the profile the better for the co-owner and manager of Restaurant Picot. So now we increase the stakes, *oui*? I presume that you would be happy to accept the office of mayor?'

'Eh?' Things were suddenly moving too fast for Harry.

'The mayoral office, that is what we aim for. I shall

finance the campaign. We should accomplish it in, what do you think? Two? Maybe three years?'

An hour later, they toasted their partnership with Dom Perignon, chilled, vintage '87. Already giddy with exhilaration, the champagne went straight to Harry's head. He could barely believe the turn of events. Not only was he now the official co-owner and manager of Restaurant Picot, he was also the manager of all other Picot interests in Kalgoorlie.

'With the exception of the Sheaf Hotel,' Gaston added, 'and of course my shares in the Midas.' He was thoughtful as he sipped his champagne. 'Although, indirectly, those too will be at your disposal in the near future. Over the next several years, I intend to sell off my Midas shares. And the monies will be invested in real estate, particularly in Restaurant Picot.'

Harry was surprised. Gaston Picot's wealth was legendary. Surely the man didn't need to sell his shares to subsidise his other interests.

'I shall be selling off gradually,' Gaston continued. 'I do not wish to call attention to the fact. So I would appreciate your discretion, Harry.'

'Of course,' Harry quickly agreed. 'But why are you selling?'

'Richard Laverton is a fool. He is riding for a fall. And one day the Midas will suffer as a consequence.'

Harry was fascinated. 'What has he done?'

But Gaston decided that he had said enough. 'Time will tell, *mon ami*.' He leaned across the table and clinked glasses again. 'To the future Mayor of Kalgoorlie.'

Just as Gaston had intended, the toast distracted Harry completely. Mayor of Kalgoorlie, he thought. Imagine! How proud Maudie would be of him. And Jack. And the twins. And as for Hannan's! They'd be queueing up to speak to him at Hannan's.

'You will not forget now,' Gaston was saying, 'three

o'clock tomorrow. Jeanne is expecting you.'

Gaston had told him that he was booked on the mid-morning train to Kalgoorlie and that Jeanne Renoir was expecting him at her house the following afternoon. The Frenchman had obviously taken it for granted that his terms would be agreed upon and Harry was not at all offended. Why in God's name should he be? He was being offered the chance of a lifetime.

'Do not be late,' Gaston instructed. 'Jeanne demands punctuality. But then, do not be early either,' he smiled. 'She is a woman.'

CHAPTER FIFTEEN

Evan Jones had been right when he had spoken of the magic world of the Midas. Certainly Giovanni would have preferred to be back at the Clover. He would have preferred to be master of his own destiny, wielding his own pick and working his own mine. But, for one who loved the world beneath the surface of the earth, the beauty of the Midas was awesome.

Each morning Giovanni assembled with the miners at the main shaft and, as the open cage with its team of men started its descent, he felt a sense of belonging. He stood with the others in the blackness, clutching his candle and his 'crib', or lunch pack, and he succumbed to the sense of peace that pervaded him. It was a welcome feeling. There was no peace for him elsewhere. At home Rico's anger was still breeding tension in Teresa and fear in the children. And it was even worse when Rico and Teresa fought, which they inevitably did. Just as inevitably, they made up and then Giovanni would lie in the room next door, the sounds of their love-making driving him close to madness as the image of Caterina engulfed him.

But hundreds of feet below the crusty red surface, in the very bowels of the earth, Giovanni felt at peace. And when he stepped out of the cage into the carved chamber where the rock face glowed in the eerie light of the oil lamps, he was thrilled by the subterranean world that surrounded him.

There were no oil lamps in the drives that extended from these chambers, or 'plats', which had been excavated at the junction of the shaft and each work level. Deep in the drives, the men mined the rock face with no light to guide them but the feeble flickering from their candles which they wedged in niches or hung from ledges in wire 'spiders'.

Giovanni was a 'trucker', part of a three-man team. They drilled holes in the working face of the rock, then placed explosives in them and retired to safety. After the charges had been detonated, they would wait for ten or fifteen minutes until the fumes had cleared before returning to load the ore into a tipping truck. The truck was then hauled along its tracks back to the plat and the ore tipped into skips which were later loaded aboard the cages and taken above ground. There the ore went through its seemingly endless treatment in the crushing mills and cyanide plants and filter presses.

Giovanni did not much care for the above-ground world of the big mines. At the end of his work shift, when he stepped out of the cage at the poppet head, he felt harshly jolted back to reality. The glare of the day was unbearable, and the ugly, barren landscape confronting. The tangled mess of machinery belched forth a mixture of smoke and dust and the noise from the stampers and crushers and saw mills was deafening. Everywhere amongst the chaos busy colonies of people scuttled like ants. That was the world of the Golden Mile. Some people found it exciting, Giovanni supposed. Not for him. For him the variety and beauty of the ever-changing rock formations in the dim candlelight below ground. For him the camaraderie between the miners and the comfort of their voices in the dark of their cocoon. And when a drive or a cross-cut broke through to a cavern the size of a cathedral, the awestruck silence they shared as they held their candles high.

It had taken Giovanni no time at all to become friends with his workmates, particularly with the senior member of the three-man team, Alwyn Llewellyn, a tall, gangly man of around forty with shoulder-length hair and a handsome beard. Alwyn had been working underground since he was twelve years old. In his native Wales to start with, alongside his father and his uncles and brothers; but when half the male members of his family had been wiped out in a mine explosion in the eighties, he'd emigrated to Australia. 'No more coal for me,' he swore. 'I dig only for gold now.' It was safer to dig for gold, he said. 'No gas, you see.' Alwyn was a likable man and Giovanni warmed to him immediately. But then everyone did. Alwyn was not only an engaging companion, he was a man one could rely upon, an experienced miner, a fond father of five daughters and a fine singer into the bargain.

'If you could learn Italian, Alwyn,' Evan had said as he introduced them, 'and if you could learn Welsh, Giovanni, you'd sing the finest duets a man could hear, the two of you.' As the men shook hands, Evan had introduced the third member of the team. 'And this is Freddie. He's no singer but he'll outwork any man at the Midas.'

Freddie grinned proudly and shook hands with a grip of iron. He was a dark-haired, well-built young man, just turned eighteen, with the eyes of an eager puppy and a beard and moustache that looked oddly out of place on a face so young. He'd only been working at the Midas for six months and Alwyn was obviously his hero.

As the leader of the team, Alwyn was responsible for the blasting of the rock face, but he was happy to teach Giovanni and from the outset had generously shared his skills. 'You drill a larger borehole in the centre of the face, you see,' he had explained. 'The secret is in sequencing the explosions. The centre charge will be fired first and that will create a hole in the middle of the face. That reduces the pressure. When the smaller charges around the hole are blasted in sequence, the face will crumble to the ground rather than shatter out into the drive. Much safer.'

Giovanni was flattered that Alwyn was taking the time to teach him but had felt a little self-conscious that the Welshman wasn't including Freddie.

'Don't you worry,' Alwyn had winked, sensing Giovanni's discomfort, 'Freddie doesn't want to know about explosives, do you, Freddie?'

'Eh?' Freddie straightened up and leaned on his pick. He hadn't heard, he'd been attacking the larger blocks of ore with the relentless energy of a pile driver.

'I said you don't want to know about explosives, do you?' Alwyn repeated patiently.

'Nah.' Freddie returned to his work.

'It's not a job for Freddie,' Alwyn explained and Giovanni had realised then that Freddie was a little simple.

After the working face was blasted, the team would stand aside and wait for the underground boss to conduct his inspection. With a pick, Evan would 'feel the ground', prodding the roof and the walls of the freshly exposed area before proclaiming whether or not it was safe to continue.

It was during these daily exchanges that Giovanni became aware of the friendship that existed between the two Welshmen. When Evan had finished his survey he and Alwyn would stand together in the darkness and listen for several minutes. Alwyn's question was always the same.

'What are they saying, Evan?'

At first, Giovanni didn't understand the question

and he thought it better not to enquire. He noticed that even the exuberant Freddie was standing quietly reverent on the sidelines.

'There's a massive cave ahead of us and above us,' Evan answered one day. 'Do a shallow blast tomorrow. We don't want to risk a rock fall.' Alwyn nodded his agreement. Evan tapped the overhang with his pick to produce a hollow sound. 'And this bad rock'll need to be timbered.' Then he prodded a portion of the freshly exposed wall where the earth was soft. 'This'll need to be dug out and timbered too,' he added. 'I'll send a team in.' At the Midas, the timbering of the drives was subcontracted.

The following morning, sure enough, when the debris had been cleared, they found they had blasted through to a huge cave with ceilings thirty feet high.

'But how did Evan know?' Giovanni asked, marvelling at the spectacle.

'The rocks told him.'

Giovanni peered back at Alwyn. Through the darkness it was difficult to tell whether or not the man was joking but it didn't sound as if he was.

'They talk, you know, the rocks.' Alwyn could sense the Italian's confusion. 'Press your ear against them and you can hear them breathing. Go on, man, do it,' he urged when Giovanni hesitated.

Giovanni pressed his ear to the rock wall. It was a strange experience. The rock was cool against his skin and, in the deathly stillness, it was easy to imagine he could hear something.

'Well?' Alwyn asked. 'Are they breathing or are they not?'

Giovanni straightened up a little self-consciously, still unsure as to whether or not the Welshman was making fun of him. 'I don't know about breathing but . . .'

'But you can hear something, eh?'

'And sometimes they talk,' Freddie interrupted, nodding eagerly. 'Not to me, they never talk to me. But some of the others hear them. Alwyn hears them. Don't you, Alwyn?'

The Welshman nodded. 'But no one hears them the way Evan Jones hears them. The rocks never talk to the rest of us the way they talk to Evan.'

It was crib time so they walked back along the drive to the plat where they would meet up with the other miners. There, they would sit on the benches carved in the rock, heat their billy tea with their candles and share their stories.

'And do you know,' Alwyn continued, 'the man says he doesn't believe it?' He laughed but there was affection in his voice. 'He says that it's fanciful to think that the rocks are talking to him. He says that it's the echoes that tell him what lies ahead. Just the sounds he hears when he taps the rocks, just that and nothing more, he says.' The smile died on Alwyn's lips and, in the gloom, his voice was deadly earnest. 'But he's wrong. It's a whole lot more. And deep down, Evan knows it.' Ahead, they could see the light from the oil lamps in the plat. 'He knows that the rocks are talking to him. And, whether it's fanciful or not to admit it, he knows that he listens to them.'

As they drank their tea, the miners exchanged stories of disasters, probably to impress the newcomer in their midst, and Giovanni realised that Evan had been right. Working in one of the big mines was a far more dangerous proposition than working one's own lease for alluvial gold.

The explosives caused the most number of accidents. Anything could go wrong when one was dealing with explosives, he was told: one could be blown up, smashed to death by rock shards or asphyxiated by fumes. Then, of course, there were the cave-ins—many a man had been buried alive—and the accidents involving the main shaft and the cage. That was what had happened to Freddie's predecessor, they told Giovanni. He'd leaned out of the cage and his arm had been crushed. He'd lived, but he'd lost the arm and could no longer work in the mines. And there was the shocking time when six men had been killed. The brakes had failed at the fifth level and the cage had simply plummeted to the bottom.

'I remember that day,' Alwyn said. 'A Friday. A terrible Friday. It was the afternoon shift. Late in the afternoon. I'd long since finished work and I was at the pub when I heard the sirens. Those sirens make a man's blood run cold. The whole town streamed up to the poppet head. No one knew who'd been in the cage when it crashed. There were twenty men under the ground and no one knew who were the ones who were dead, you see. They had to wait till they hauled them up.

'The faces on the women as they waited, I'll never forget it. Some screamed and some prayed and some just stood there, with their babies in their arms and their children clutching at their skirts. It was a bad day.'

The men were silent as Alwyn finished the story. They all knew of that black Friday six years ago, although none of them had been working at the Midas at the time.

'There was talk that it was the winding-engine driver's fault,' Alwyn continued as he swigged at his billy tea, 'but it was never proved. Thank the Lord.' The men exchanged looks of complicity. It was rare for a death to be labelled anything other than accidental—the miners made sure of that. If human error was proved to be the reason, the mines did not pay compensation.

Six months after the investigation into the deaths, the engine driver had suicided. 'He did the right thing, poor man,' Alwyn said. 'He waited until the case was cleared and each of the widows had received compensation.'

EVAN HAD DELIBERATELY teamed Giovanni with Alwyn Llewellyn. He knew that Alwyn would accept the good-natured Italian at face value and he knew that Alwyn's acceptance would help to dispell any ill-will amongst the others. Despite the fact that a number of Italians worked above ground at the Midas, Giovanni was the first of his countrymen to be employed as a miner and Evan was aware that he might well be courting trouble. To his relief, however, there appeared to be relatively little discontent amongst the ranks. The odd remark came from the quarters which, if there was nothing to grumble about, would invent something anyway. Nevertheless, Evan decided that any such reaction should be nipped in the bud and that an open display of his personal approval might serve as a warning to the dissident minority.

'You must come to dinner on Friday, Giovanni, I insist, and you must bring your concertina.' Before Giovanni could reply, Evan continued. 'Alwyn will be there. You two can learn each other's songs.'

Giovanni, fully aware of the reasons for the invitation, had no option but to accept, although the thought of seeing Caterina was almost more than he could bear. For a month now he had worked hard at the Midas, rarely allowing his thoughts to stray to her. After the work day, he drank a moderate amount of beer at the Sheaf, played billiards in the backroom, and went home to a family dinner. Then he went to bed and the next morning rose early and repeated the entire exercise. Day after day. It was only in his bed, late at night or in the early hours of the morning, that the image of Caterina tormented him. The rest of the time, she was there certainly, but in the recesses of his mind, like a beautiful memory. Giovanni had control of his obsession. Until now.

'HARLECH CYFOD DYFANERI,
Gwel y gelyn, ennyn yni
Y Meirionwyr oll i weiddi
'Cymru fo am byth!''

Giovanni accompanied the men on his concertina. He had picked up the melody easily enough, it was simple march time. But the song was a stirring one. A battle song. 'Men of Harlech' they'd called it. And, although he didn't understand the words, Giovanni admired the three-part harmony and the Welshmen's voices and the power of the song itself.

'Men of Harlech, lie ye dreaming?
See ye not their fulchions gleaming,
While their pennons gaily streaming
Flutter in the breeze?'

Evan Jones, Alwyn Llewellyn and Tony Prendergast, another Welsh miner from the Midas, were delighting in each other's voices and the sound of their mother country. Evan had had several beers during the evening meal, just enough to loosen him up. It was rare for him to sing in the company of anyone other than his Welsh friends and tonight, not only was Giovanni there but Freddie too. Evan had decided that his show of support would be less blatant if he were to invite the three-man team rather than Giovanni alone. Freddie, thrilled beyond measure to be a guest in the boss's house, was having the time of his life, clapping along to the music, a little off the beat.

During the meal, Giovanni had spent the entire time resisting the urge to look at Caterina. And Kate herself, unable to eat, had left the table under every pretext possible to spend as much time as she could in the kitchen. No one appeared to have noticed. No one, that is, except

Giovanni. Evan was concentrating on being a good host and Alwyn, Freddie and Tony were too busy concentrating on the excellent meal.

When Kate had cleared the table, the men sat back and lit up their pipes and no one found her absence amiss as she retired to do the dishes. Then it was Briony's bedtime and Kate had to read her a story. She read three stories, until the little girl was fast asleep. Then she sat on the bed for a further fifteen minutes. Now, as the men finished teaching Giovanni the melody of 'Calan Lan' and launched once again into their three-part harmony, Kate had run out of excuses and had no option but to join them.

She sat in the corner and watched the singers but, try as she might, she could not prevent herself from occasionally stealing a glance at Giovanni. She tried to concentrate on his hands as he played the concertina, tried to pretend her interest was in the music, but every now and then, her eyes flickered to his face. Such a fine face. He was the only one of the men clean-shaven—unusual for a miner. How she longed to touch that face ... Quickly she forced her attention back to the singers.

Giovanni could feel her eyes upon him. He concentrated desperately on the music. A hymn. Haunting. A song of great beauty. Far more difficult to play than the march. He focused on Evan who was conducting him through the melody.

'Nid wyn gof am bwyd moethus
Aur y byd uw berlei man
Gofyd wyf am galon hapus
Galon lwn a galon lan.'

Don't look at her, Giovanni told himself, don't look at her. But even as his eyes followed Evan, he could feel her gaze.

'I seek not of worldly treasure,

Gold nor pearls of any mart.
Give me a heart of joyful measure.
Just a guileless, honest heart.'

He could feel her. Caressing his skin. Her eyes flickering from his hands, as she pretended to heed the music, to his face.

It was because of Caterina that Giovanni had remained clean-shaven. They teased him about it at the mine. A bushy beard was the miner's trademark. But Caterina had touched his face with her hand, and had caressed his face with her eyes that day they had exchanged vows. He did not want to change the face which she had said she loved.

As the men finished their third rendition of '*Calan Lan*', Kate realised with relief that it was Paul's bedtime. 'Come along, Paul, time for bed.' The boy didn't need to be accompanied but she could use it as an excuse to leave the room.

Paul protested. 'But we haven't had a song of Giovanni's yet.' He turned to his stepfather. 'Evan, you promised, remember?'

'Paul's quite right,' Evan agreed. 'I promised him we would teach each other our songs.' He turned to Giovanni. 'I have been selfish. We're so used to singing unaccompanied, you see, it is a treat to have a musician play our songs for us.'

'They are fine songs,' Giovanni said.

'Now one of yours. Sing us one of your songs, Giovanni.' Evan pulled up a chair and sat alongside his wife. 'Let Paul stay up a little late tonight, my dear. There's no school tomorrow.'

'All right, all right,' Kate laughed and surrendered. 'I give up.'

'You must sing with me, Paul,' Giovanni insisted.

The boy looked at his stepfather and Evan nodded. 'Of course. Paul sings with Giovanni's family,' he explained to the others, adding with pride, 'he knows all the Italian lyrics.'

As he spoke, Evan recalled how uneasy he'd felt in the company of foreigners—not so very long ago either. How self-conscious he was—and how over-protective he'd been of his wife's background. He'd been foolish, he now admitted to himself. They should all be singing each other's songs and sharing each other's heritage. Particularly here, in Kalgoorlie. They were brothers under the sun, after all. He wondered whether it was the beer that was bringing on this rush of bonhomie, or whether it was the glow of national pride and brotherly love which 'Calan Lan' always inspired in him.

'What shall we sing, Paul?' Giovanni asked. ' 'Funiculi Funicula?' '

' "*Torna a Surriento*".'

He should have known. It had always been the boy's favourite. Giovanni hesitated for only a fraction of a second and then he played the opening chords.

' '*Vide 'o mare quant' e bello* . . .' '

He did not give himself up to the song. He did not dare. He concentrated on Paul instead, encouraging the boy to sing the lyric.

Kate couldn't help it. Like a magnet, her eyes were drawn to Giovanni. He was smiling at her son. She studied the warmth of his smile . . . the fullness of his mouth . . . the curve of his lip . . . It was only for a few seconds, but her concentration was so total that she wasn't aware of Evan beside her. She didn't register Evan turn towards her; she didn't register his shock. She dragged her eyes away from Giovanni and looked down at her hands, noticing for the first time that her fingers were interwoven and her knuckles white. She regained her composure and looked up, and it was only then that she saw her husband watching her.

She smiled at him. 'It is a beautiful song, isn't it?

And Paul sings it very well; he certainly knows all the words.'

Evan made a show of watching the boy as the song concluded, but he wasn't listening to Paul. He was trying to analyse what he had just seen. The rapture in his wife's eyes as she had looked at Giovanni, surely he had imagined it. He had drunk more than he was accustomed to, and alcohol always went to his head. He wasn't a heavy drinker like most of the other miners. That must be it. He must have imagined it.

For the remainder of the evening, Evan continued to rationalise what he'd seen and, by the time the men finally departed well after midnight, he was more or less convinced that it had been the beer. So why was he left with a vague feeling of presentiment? He needed to go to bed, he told himself. He needed to sleep it off.

Kate had said a general goodnight and retired to the kitchen to wash the coffee mugs. She could hear the men at the front door, congratulating each other on a fine evening. She leaned over the washbasin and put her head in her hands. Guilt overwhelmed her. She knew that as she had looked at Giovanni tonight, she had wanted him. May God forgive her. She had sat beside her husband and wanted another man. She felt sick with remorse. She must never see Giovanni again, she told herself. Never.

As he walked home, Giovanni, too, felt wretched. Evan had helped and befriended him. The man had invited him into his home and the whole night all Giovanni had been able to think of was making love to his wife. It had taken every ounce of self-control Giovanni could muster simply not to look at Caterina. If their eyes had once met, he knew his desire would have been readable to every man in the room. He must never see her again. She must remain the beautiful memory in the recesses of his mind. He must satisfy his lust elsewhere.

When he had reached the southern outskirts of the town, Giovanni did not head north. He turned into Hay Street and headed for Red Ruby's instead.

Harry Brearley reined in Black Bess and checked his fob watch. He was ten minutes early. He sat back in the trap and studied Jeanne's house. It was one of the most elegant houses in Kalgoorlie. Set back from the street, wide, airy verandahs, large windows, with wooden shutters to keep out the harshness of the sun. And a garden. Shrubs and flowers. Hardy shrubs and homely flowers. Geraniums and sweet peas and the like. Nothing pretentious and nothing that could be accused of water wastage. Jeanne was a woman of great taste in every sense of the word.

Harry jumped down from the trap, patted Black Bess and walked about. He didn't really need to stretch his legs but he was too restless to sit and wait.

His double-breasted wool suit was far too warm for the autumn afternoon, but it was in fine check and of the very latest style and he hadn't been able to resist wearing it.

'Harry, you'll bake,' Maudie had laughed.

'Madame Renoir is a very elegant woman, Maudie, and if I'm to work with her I'll need to dress accordingly.'

Maudie smiled to herself. He had returned from Perth with a complete new wardrobe, announcing that this was what they were wearing in London and this in Paris—at least, according to Gaston, and he should know.

Maudie was delighted with the lightweight travelling coat he had bought her and the several hats, particularly the one with the sheerest gossamer veil. And she was delighted by the childish enthusiasm with which he handed out the many presents he'd bought for each member of the family. Soft, cuddly toys for the twins. A double-breasted suit for Jack. His very first.

'Hell, Pa, where am I going to wear that?'

Maudie didn't admonish the boy for swearing. She smiled instead. 'A funeral maybe?'

'One is never too young to develop a sense of style,' Harry said defensively and Maudie, realising that he was a little hurt, came to the rescue.

'We'll have afternoon tea at the Palace on Saturday and he'll wear it then, won't you, Jack?' She winked at the boy and he grinned and nodded good-naturedly. He'd do anything for Harry, even if it meant dressing up like a toff. It was good to have his Pa back. 'And he'll look so handsome that all the girls will stare at him,' Maudie teased. Jack crossed his eyes at her.

But it had been Harry himself who had delighted Maudie more than anything. 'I'm sorry, Maudie,' he'd said. 'And I'm going to make it up to you. You'll be proud of me, I promise.'

Maudie knew, deep down, that Harry would never really change. But she also knew that she loved him. She hoped that this partnership with Gaston Picot would keep him on the straight and narrow path. It certainly sounded as if it would.

'Monsieur Brearley. Do come in please.' Jeanne smiled and stood to one side and, from somewhere in the house behind her, Harry could hear a clock chiming. 'You are exactly on time.'

'Madame Renoir.' He lightly kissed the hand she offered him and she nodded her approval.

'I admire punctuality,' she said. She had seen him arrive early and watched him as he waited. 'And you must call me Jeanne. I may call you Harry, *oui*?'

She was wearing a two-piece afternoon dress in pale grey and pink silk. The high-necked lace bodice accentuated her neat waist, the extended lace cuffs highlighted her neat, perfectly manicured hands. Her abundant light brown hair, secured in a soft chignon, had not a strand out of place. Jeanne Renoir was a neat woman. Which somehow made her even more seductive, Harry thought, as he followed her along the hall, noting the soft sway of her hips and the subtle rustle of her petticoats.

'This is my secretary and companion, Miss Emily Laurie,' Jeanne said as she glided into the main drawing room.

Behind her, Harry quickly averted his eyes from her hips, hoping that he had not been caught out. 'Miss Laurie,' he said.

The Englishwoman rose from the hardback chair in which she'd been sitting. 'Mr Brearley.' She did not proffer her hand as Jeanne had done, but Harry was not offended. He had heard that Jeanne Renoir's companion was English and Englishwomen did not proffer their hands. Besides, her smile was welcoming.

'Do please sit, Harry.' Jeanne gestured to one of the elegant carvers and when the ladies had seated themselves, Jeanne on the divan and Emily once again on her hardback chair, Harry did as he was instructed.

'Tea?' Jeanne asked.

'Lovely. Thank you.'

'A glorious day, is it not?' Emily Laurie made polite conversation as Jeanne lifted a small silver bell on the table beside her. One sharp tinkle and seconds later a maid appeared.

'It certainly is,' Harry agreed.

While Jeanne ordered afternoon tea, Harry studied his surrounds.

'Autumn can be quite the pleasantest time of year in Kalgoorlie, don't you agree?' The Englishwoman was studying Harry as he studied the room. An arrogant man, she decided. Convinced that his looks and his charm were enough. Vulgar too. She had noticed his concentration upon Jeanne's hips as he followed her into the drawing room. Of course Jeanne never minded that sort of thing. Indeed she viewed it as flattering, Emily reflected with irritation. Probably because she was French. But Emily believed in social decorum. There was a time and a place for everything, and lewd glances did not belong in the drawing room over afternoon tea.

Having surveyed the room, Harry had once more turned his attention to Jeanne. It fascinated him to think that she had been Gaston's mistress. Not that Gaston had told him so, of course—they were both gentlemen after all—but the inference had been there. 'She was married to a dear friend of mine, alas now gone,' he'd said. 'We have been very close, Jeanne and I, and I am sure you will like her.' That was all—certainly no admission that they had been lovers—but it was the manner in which he had said it. And here, in Jeanne's house, Gaston's influence was conspicuous. The fine lace curtains, elegant furnishings and Persian scatter rugs may well have been Jeanne Renoir, but the French-polished jarrah-panelled walls and the jarrah parquetry floors—a la Maison Picot—were pure Gaston.

'Of course the autumn evenings can be chilly,' Emily continued. Harry dragged his attention back to the Englishwoman. Her smile was as pleasant as it had been upon his arrival but did he detect the slightest edge to her voice? Well, he couldn't blame her, he had been very rude in not paying more attention to her. It was difficult to pay attention to such a mousy little thing though. Especially when one was in the same room as Jeanne Renoir.

'Indeed they can, Miss Laurie. Very chilly indeed.' Harry turned on the charm. 'It never ceases to amaze me how ignorant people are of our Kalgoorlie weather, do you not find this so?'

'Yes, I do.' Emily was not the least bit taken in by his charm but, as the man was at least observing the social graces, her irritation abated. 'They assume that it is hot and dry for three hundred and sixty-five days of the year. And yet the winter nights can be uncomfortably cold and . . .'

'And the frosts . . .' Harry nodded dutifully, 'such terrible winter frosts.' She really did look like a mouse, he thought, in that dour brown dress with its severe bolero jacket. He longed for Jeanne to enter the conversation so that he could legitimately turn his attention to her once more. He did so love observing beautiful women.

It was nothing more than observation of course. Harry had no thoughts of straying from Maudie. Maudie was no beauty by the accepted standards of the day but she was his Maudie and he loved her. And by God, he thought, last night when he'd held that big woman's body to him, when he'd run his fingers through that thick brown hair which was Maudie's pride . . . by God, last night she'd been beautiful.

Having arranged tea and scones and biscuits and having given the maid some further orders for the afternoon, Jeanne joined in the conversation, which remained frustratingly fixed upon the weather for some unknown reason.

In the middle of a discussion on the occasional cyclones that hit the goldfields, the maid arrived and Harry seized the opportunity. 'Shall we get down to business, Jeanne?'

Emily nodded for the maid to retire and busied herself with the teapot while Jeanne listened to each of Harry's queries. Her answers were simple. The rentals of Gaston's properties were collected weekly by a Mr Donald McAllister and delivered to her house where she and Emily kept the books.

'It is Emily who does the adding up, I am not very good at . . . um . . .?' She looked questioningly in Emily's direction.

'Arithmetic,' Emily answered.

'Oui. Arithmetic.' She smiled charmingly. Everything was very easy, she said. Emily did the banking on Mondays and the bank forwarded monthly statements of the deposits to Gaston.

'I do not know why he needs another partner,' Jeanne said without rancour and then she smiled mischievously, 'except that perhaps he does not trust a woman.'

Emily looked up from her tea. 'He is acquiring more property, Jeanne, it is perfectly understandable.'

'Yes of course.' Jeanne shrugged disinterestedly and changed the subject. She admired the fabric of Harry's suit. 'Such a fine weave,' she exclaimed.

The conversation continued in a vacuous vein and Harry was becoming more and more frustrated. When the maid arrived to clear away the tea things he decided to take matters into his own hands.

'I would like to see the properties, Jeanne. Do you wish to accompany me? My trap is outside.'

Jeanne and Emily exchanged a look and Emily nodded.

'Of course, if you wish,' Jeanne replied and she fetched her pink parasol and her pink silk hat trimmed with ostrich feathers.

At the door, having declined to join them, Emily nodded a pleasant goodbye. 'We will be seeing quite a bit of each other, Mr Brearley. I look forward to a very pleasant working relationship.'

'I, too, Miss Laurie.' He nodded and flashed his gleaming new teeth at the mouse. 'Good afternoon.'

They travelled two blocks down Hannan Street, then Jeanne directed him to the right. 'Are you sure you wish to inspect the properties so early in the day?' she asked.

Harry was a little bewildered. It was nearly five o'clock in the afternoon. 'Why not?' he enquired.

But Jeanne merely shrugged in reply. 'To the left,' she instructed as they reached Hay Street.

As soon as they rounded the corner, she announced, 'We are here.' And Harry reined Black Bess to a standstill. Directly outside Red Ruby's.

'But these are . . . ' He didn't know quite how to put it as he looked, bewildered, up and down Hay Street at the dozen or so brothels on either side of the road.

'Brothels. Yes. Gaston owns three, but he intends to purchase more. "Jeanne," he says to me, "a good whorehouse is where the true gold is in a goldmining town." Gaston believes that one can always rely upon men's desire for pleasure. "To drown their sorrows," he says to me, "or to celebrate. Either way." That is what he says. And of course he is right.'

There was no one in the street—as there rarely was at that time of day—but Jeanne was nevertheless leaning back in the trap so as not to be easily observed.

'I seldom visit the properties, and never in the day, but if you wish to inspect them now I will wait for you,' she said.

'No! No!' Harry flicked the reins urgently. Good God, he thought, what if someone saw him? 'Trot on, Bess, trot on.'

Jeanne clutched her hat, threw back her beautiful head and laughed with delight. 'He did not tell you! I had a feeling that was so.' She glanced saucily at him. 'Oh Harry, *mon cher*, your face. Just look at your face!' And she was still laughing when they pulled up outside her house in Hannan Street.

Chapter Sixteen

Paul Dunleavy walked energetically along Commonwealth Avenue towards Copley Square. He'd recently returned home to Boston from his annual holiday abroad and was feeling not only well rested, but vital, strong and proud of the fact that, at thirty-six years of age, he could ski the top slopes with the vigour of a twenty-year-old. He lifted the collar of his camelhair coat and tucked his lamb's wool scarf more snugly inside. It was a bitter-cold February and the air was biting.

The morning's busy traffic had churned the snow in the streets to a brown sludge but, as Paul rounded the corner, Copley Square was a winter delight. The paths which crisscrossed the tiny central park had been swept clean by a dawn patrol of council workmen but, elsewhere, virgin snow blanketed the ground. The elm trees' winter skeletons were gracefully clothed in white, as were the park benches which had yet to be braved by those willing to defy the elements. At lunch time, encouraged by a glimmer of sun, women with children and men with newspapers and packed sandwiches would vie for the benches.

To the right, stretching the whole length of the square, was Boston's pride and joy, the Public Library, an elegant two-storey building in grey marble. To the left was the old Trinity Church, its saints, ornately carved in sandstone, timelessly watching the daily cavalcade.

Digging his gloved hands deep into his coat pockets, Paul strode briskly across the square and around the corner to the Copley Square Hotel, each breath a puff of white steam in the icy air. It hadn't been as cold as this in Austria, he thought.

Paul's friends, who were also wealthy and who also holidayed abroad every year, always questioned his choice of location. 'You're mad,' Geoffrey would say, 'you can ski here the whole winter long—why in God's name go to the Alps? Why not Capri, or Tahiti? Or at least Acapulco. Get away from the cold.'

But Paul loved the cold. And he loved the European Alps. Particularly the little Austrian village of Steinach close to the Italian border. He'd been going to the remote chalet near Steinach for fifteen years now, ever since his student days, and it had not changed in all that time. Being there made him feel young and each year he returned from his holiday rejuvenated.

Earlier in their marriage, his wife, Elizabeth, who yearned to escape the winter, had once or twice rebelled and holidayed with a female friend in Majorca instead. But when their daughter Meg joined forces with her father, Elizabeth reluctantly gave in to the weight of opposition. These days, she wasn't sure if fourteen-year-old Meg genuinely loved the Alps or whether it was the hero-worship of her father which made her think she did. But, either way, being a good wife and mother, Elizabeth resigned herself to the annual Austrian sojourn.

The doorman at the Copley Square Hotel tipped his hat. 'Morning, Mr Dunleavy, sir.'

'Morning, Albert.'

Paul walked through to the parlour. He had adopted the hotel as a meeting place for the more casual of his business appointments. It gave him a reason to escape the office and was a good half-hour walk away. That was the only problem with consultancy, he thought, it might pay a great deal more than field work but it was, on the whole, a sedentary existence.

As he settled into one of the comfortable armchairs and signalled the waiter for coffee, he looked at his watch. Ten minutes early for his meeting. He was too unsettled to read the newspaper—his mind would only wander as it had for the past week since he'd returned from abroad. Before the end of the year he'd be taking off again. But not for a holiday this time. The journey would be arduous, and the job awaiting him at the other end even more so. Just as well he was feeling fit and strong.

The coffee arrived. He removed his gloves. Damn it, he really didn't want to go. Particularly without Elizabeth and Meg. He'd be gone for a whole year! He would miss them. The older he grew, the more he disliked being away from his family. Still, he had a duty and he must resign himself to it.

Duty. Paul smiled to himself. His father's favourite word. 'You have a duty, Paul. A duty to this family.' Paul could hear him now. 'A duty you should be proud to fulfil.' His father had fulfilled with pride his own duties as the eldest son of one of Boston's oldest families and he was determined to instil in his only son a pride of equal fervour.

Quenton Dunleavy, a staunch Unitarian, had gloried in the fact that his own father had been one of the founding members of the American Unitarian Association. 'Along with the likes of Emerson and Everett,' he would boast. 'And Lowell and Holmes. Your grandfather knew them all and they knew him. Liberal thinkers!' And he'd pound the table with his fist to emphasise the point. 'Liberal thinkers who played their part in the flowering of New England. And your grandfather was one of them!' Quenton Dunleavy was more than a bore, he was a tyrant. And the older he grew the more obsessive his familial pride became.

Despite the brainwashing, Paul finally recognised upon leaving university that his father was anything but the liberal thinker he boasted to be. The man was obdurate, implacable and utterly incapable of moving with the times. It wasn't his fault, Paul supposed, Grandfather Dunleavy had probably been a similar style of tyrant. But years later when Meg was born, Paul determined he would not make the same mistake. He would be a modern father. He would stay young and approachable and understanding, for his daughter's sake.

Paul carefully dropped one sugar cube into his cup and returned the tongs to the sugar bowl. Of course it wasn't always easy, he thought as he stirred his coffee. Meg was already rebelling against her mother, but that was natural. Meg had a fine academic brain. She had more to offer than the average young woman of old Bostonian stock, cultivated by the family to marry young, become a supportive wife, a perfect hostess and, above all, an expert in the social graces. Paul's wife Elizabeth fulfilled each of these prerequisites perfectly. It had been why he'd married her. But it was not necessary for Meg to do the same. Not these days. Good God, he thought with grudging admiration, the girl was even threatening to join the suffragettes. Paul didn't approve of the suffragette movement; he believed it could get a little out of hand, women not truly understanding politics the way men did—but he was proud that Meg wished to voice her political beliefs. It was a sign of strength and intelligence. And at this stage, of course, there was nothing to fear, she was far too young.

She certainly had guts, he thought fondly. Why, only this morning at breakfast she had said she wanted to come with him at the end of the year.

'I'll be nearly fifteen by then, Daddy,' she'd said, as if that made all the difference.

'Australia!' he'd scoffed at first, thinking it was just a childish whim. 'And what exactly do you think you'd do in Australia?'

'I'd join the movement,' she'd answered as they sat in the breakfast room and the maid poured the coffee. 'The Australian suffragette movement leads the world. Second to the New Zealand suffragettes that is,' she added, helping herself to another flapjack. 'I wonder why they're so advanced in the southern hemisphere. Maybe it has something to do with the heat.'

'You're too young—they wouldn't accept you,' Paul smiled, admiring her pluck.

'I may be too young to work in the political arena, Daddy,' she corrected him, 'but I'm certainly not too young to work behind the scenes. And that's what they need. Hard workers!'

Paul's wife, Elizabeth, said nothing. She sat sipping her coffee and watching the father–daughter antics benignly.

Elizabeth knew that Meg was showing off for her father and he was loving it, as usual. There was no rancour in Elizabeth as she watched, she delighted in the love they shared, but there was a tiny nagging fear. She hoped one day that the games they played would not backfire on them. Meg was not a natural rebel, it was a role she'd adopted to impress the father she idolised. If there was a true rebel in the family, it was Elizabeth herself. How she would love to flaunt her upbringing and the constraints of society—how she would love to join the suffragette movement. She thought it was high time women were given a voice. But of course she could never espouse the cause; it would destroy her family if she did. Paul would be incapable of tolerating such an outrage—for all his insistence on being a modern father, Paul was, in his own way, as old-fashioned as Quenton Dunleavy had been. The only reason he encouraged boldness and independence in Meg was because she was the son he wished he'd had. Elizabeth worried just a little. It could be dangerous to imbue the girl with a grit and fervour she did not possess.

'You're not coming to Australia and that's that,' Paul said good-naturedly as he rose from the table. 'You must finish your schooling before you think of aligning yourself to anything at all, let alone the suffragette movement.'

'I believe the schools in Australia are very good,' Meg countered, although she had no idea whether they were or not. 'I could finish my schooling there while I work for the movement.'

Paul looked at his watch. He would be late if he didn't leave immediately.

'I think we're all forgetting one little thing.' Elizabeth gently dabbed her lips with her linen napkin. 'I doubt very much whether there would be a suffragette movement in Kalgoorlie.' The others stared blankly at her for a second. 'You may clear, Edith,' she said to the maid and she laughed as she rose from the table. 'It has such a bizarre ring to it, does it not? Kalgoorlie. A pretty word. I like it.' She kissed her husband on the cheek. 'You must not be late, my dear.'

Meg felt irritated. Her mother was trivialising the conversation. And as always, Paul felt a wealth of affection and admiration for his wife. What a witty woman she was and her timing, as usual, was impeccable. 'Goodbye, Elizabeth,' he smiled, 'I'll not be late.'

'Paul!' A newspaper landed on the table beside Paul's coffee cup, closely followed by a bulky, beribboned folder. 'Sorry I'm a little late, old boy.' Godfrey Brigstock plopped into the armchair beside him. 'Slept in.' Godfrey had arrived from London the preceding day. 'Devilishly tiring all that travelling.' He signalled the waiter for coffee.

Godfrey and Paul had met in South Africa ten years

previously. Both of them had been young married men at the time and highly qualified mining engineers, Godfrey a graduate of Oxford University and Paul a graduate of Harvard. Both had been extremely ambitious but Paul's ambitions had been a little more purist than Godfrey's. Paul wanted to be the most respected in his field. Godfrey wanted to be the richest.

'Consultancy, that's where the money is,' he'd said to Paul. 'Ten times less work, ten times more money. It's where I'm aiming, old man, and you're mad if you don't too. We could become partners.'

They hadn't become partners, Paul had continued to work in the field for a good five years before following Godfrey into consultancy. These days their respective firms worked in partnership and the rewards were lucrative.

'You must be quite looking forward to this,' Godfrey said as he undid the ribbon around the folder.

'What? Going to Australia?'

'That's true—pity it has to be Australia. But the work, old boy. You always did love field work. Being on site, mingling with the workers, what? Well, you'll be doing all that and getting paid consultancy fees into the bargain. Best of everything, wouldn't you say?'

'Sure. Halfway around the world. No family.' Paul grimaced. 'And all that heat.'

'Chin up, I'm told they have snow on Mount Kosciusco.' Godfrey laughed loudly. 'And I'm told Mount Kosciusco's one hell of a long way from Kalgoorlie.'

He opened the folder and spread the contents out on the table. 'Here you are, old boy. The full story of the Midas. From the sublime to the ridiculous. Minutes of shareholders' meetings and stock reports,' he pushed a pile of papers to one side and picked up a handful of press clippings, 'to all the gory details as related by Fleet Street's finest.'

Dumping the clippings on top of the reports, he opened the folded newspaper. 'Brought you a copy of *The Times* too. Look at the headlines the day I left London. They won't leave the story alone, I tell you. It's been two damn years since the whole ugly mess but they dredged it up again five weeks ago.'

'"LAVERTON FAMILY TRAGEDY",' Paul read. '"A mother's grief takes its toll".'

'Lady Charlotte had a stroke,' Godfrey continued, 'and they're blaming her death on the strain of this whole business. The press are being frightfully sympathetic but of course they're jumping for glee. The wretched Fleet Street hounds are getting twice their money's worth.'

Beneath the headlines was a picture captioned 'Lord Lionel is consoled by his favourite daughter-in-law, Prudence'. Paul looked at the picture. He'd never met Prudence Laverton, but he'd certainly met old Lionel. Lord Lionel and his cronies had called upon Paul's expertise several times in the past. Simple feasibility reports as a rule—sample evaluations and cost-effective studies. This time, however, their request was a little more complicated. This time they needed him to salvage their gold mine in far-flung Kalgoorlie.

Paul looked at the granite face glaring at him from the front page. What a monster, he thought, and felt a sudden affection for his own father. The tyranny of Quenton Dunleavy paled by comparison. He looked at the favourite daughter-in-law who was 'consoling' Lord Lionel. It was the face of a rather plain woman with a haunted look in her eyes. Good luck to you, Prudence, Paul thought. You'll need it.

He bundled all the papers together and called for more coffee. 'I shan't look at them now,' he said, 'I've plenty of time to become acquainted with the Midas. Now, tell me, how's the family?'

PRUDENCE LAVERTON HAD finally achieved the social standing to which she had always aspired. She attended the first day's play of the Test match between Australia and England at Lord's; she was always offered the best house seats at Drury Lane Theatre on opening nights and she maintained a regular box during the Covent Garden opera season. And all because she was, indeed, Lord Lionel's favourite daughter-in-law, a role which opened far more doors than that of the youngest son's wife. But it was a hollow victory. The wives of the other three sons detested her, as did both of the Laverton daughters. It was jealousy, she knew—they were all of them jealous that the old man openly preferred her, desperate as they were to curry favour with him before he died. They'd have a long wait. Although he was in his late seventies, Lord Laverton was as strong as an ox.

Prudence couldn't even take pleasure in the old man's alleged affection. He still terrified her and she wasn't sure whether she hadn't preferred it when he simply failed to notice her. Besides, it wasn't really affection at all, Prudence realised; it was gratitude for the way she had behaved that day and for the days and months that had followed as they were hounded, more mercilessly than ever, by the press.

'By God, she's a true Laverton woman, this one,' Lionel had boasted to the rest of the family. 'You'd do well to take a leaf out of her book, I'll tell you.'

During the three-month sea voyage to England, Prudence Laverton had had no idea she was pregnant. She thought she was just seasick. So frightfully seasick that even her monthly cycle, which normally arrived with clocklike precision, had been disrupted. Things would return to normal, she told herself, once they were at the family estate in Hampshire. A holiday in the English countryside was exactly what she needed.

But then, to her horror, she had discovered that they

had not returned to England for a holiday at all.

'You didn't even tell your wife!' Lord Lionel had roared. 'Good God, man, what's the matter with you? It's times like these a man's wife must be seen standing beside him. Family support, that's what it's all about.' Lord Lionel had always despised his youngest son. Weak. No backbone. It was why he'd sent him off to Australia in the first place. Perhaps the outback would make a man of him. He'd obviously been wrong. 'The trial's in two months for God's sake,' he snarled, 'so you better start setting her straight on a few of the facts right now!'

'What trial?' Prudence had asked after her father-in-law had stormed off. 'You said we were coming home to see the family.' Then Richard, with the aid of half a decanter of brandy, had painstakingly narrated the whole sordid story.

He was to stand trial for misrepresenting the mine's yield. The monthly reports he'd been sending to the London board of directors had been false. 'I've not only been selling off my own Midas shares at inflated prices,' he said, 'I've had a go-between in London who's been raising investment on the false reports I've been sending him of new finds.'

He didn't attempt to hold anything back. 'I got in so deep there didn't seem to be a way out,' he said calmly. It was a relief to tell her the truth at last. 'It's been going on for over five years. They're calling it fraud on a massive scale. It'll mean prison, I'm afraid.'

As Prudence listened, everything started to fall into place. Richard had been drinking heavily for a long time now. And then there was that evening when she'd come home from the church committee meeting to find Gaston Picot there.

'You're a fool, Richard,' she'd heard the Frenchman say.

Richard hadn't seemed in the least offended, he'd simply ignored the insult. 'You'll sell them off gradually, won't you?' he'd said. Gaston had agreed and it was then that Prudence had made them aware of her presence. She hadn't wanted them to think she was eavesdropping.

'Why did he call you a fool?' she'd asked when the Frenchman had taken his leave.

'He's selling off his Midas shares to build this fancy restaurant of his and he thinks I'm a fool because I won't invest in the damn thing. I ask you! The man's selling rock-solid shares in a gold mine to set up a place where people may or may not choose to dine! Who's the fool?'

It was she who'd been the fool, Prudence decided, not to have realised that something was shockingly wrong. And, as the weeks passed and the trial grew closer, she wondered what on earth was expected of her. The women must stand strong beside their men, Lord Lionel had said. But the press had latched onto the story with such a vengeance that she was too terrified to face them. When Richard ventured out in public, she locked herself and young Lucy up in the bedroom. And, when she finally found out that she was four months pregnant, she'd used her pregnancy as an excuse to retire altogether, even from the family gatherings, which she found loathsome.

Prudence wasn't the only one shocked by the ferocity of Fleet Street's attack. Lord Lionel himself had been horrified. Not that he'd expected to get off scot-free—he'd known the family name would be bandied about. But he'd expected something along the lines of YOUNGEST SCION SHAMES HOUSE OF LAVERTON and had decided that they would blame the whole episode on Richard's youth. Well, not exactly his youth—he was nearly forty, after all. But the youngest member of a family was often considered the weakest and it seemed as good a defence as any.

When the headlines screamed the question CORRUPTION IN THE PEERAGE? and the press hinted heavily that Lord Lionel had been in league with his son, the old man was apoplectic with rage. 'Laverton the Younger is manager of the one of the wealthiest gold mines in Australia,' the newspaper reports stated. 'Laverton the Elder is chairman of its London board of directors. Just who should be standing trial for the falsified gold yield reports?' It was a personal attack upon him, Lord Lionel decided—someone was out for his blood—and in the meantime, the house of Laverton was being dragged through the mud. It was intolerable. And all because of that young worm of a son of his, a son who didn't deserve to bear the family name.

It was barely a fortnight before the opening day of the trial when Lord Lionel made his decision, then wondered why he hadn't made it earlier. He called Richard into his study where they sat behind locked doors for a good hour or more. The following day, he informed his wife Charlotte, Prudence and little Lucy that they were going to London for the weekend. They would stay at their townhouse in Mayfair.

Surprisingly enough, at the last minute, Prudence refused to budge. 'I'm going to stay with Richard,' she said as she stood on the front steps with Charlotte and Lucy watching the chauffeur pack the luggage in the boot of the car.

Richard had been awake half the night and twice he'd vomited, but he'd refused to admit that he was not well. 'Something I've eaten is disagreeing with me, that's all,' he'd assured her. 'Go back to sleep, Prudence.'

Her father-in-law was about to insist, Prudence knew it, but for once she would not give in. Something had happened in that study last night and she was going to get to the bottom of it. 'He's not well,' she said. 'Lucy may go with you but I shall stay here. Take my portmanteau back inside, George,' she said as the chauffeur started to load her suitcase into the boot.

'Do you know why he's not well?' Under the shaggy leonine brow her father-in-law's eyes were penetrating. 'Did he tell you of our meeting last night?'

Prudence didn't know what gave her the strength but she returned his gaze and didn't answer.

'Do you know what's going on?' he insisted.

She had her suspicions, but she didn't dare voice them until she had spoken to Richard. 'I know enough,' she answered enigmatically, hoping it would make him leave her alone. It did.

Prudence hugged Lucy goodbye, kissed Charlotte on the cheek and waved to the car as it slowly drove down the tree-lined avenue to the main gates. Then she went inside.

She found Richard in his father's study sitting behind the huge mahogany desk staring out the bay windows.

'The inner sanctum,' she smiled. 'Whatever would your father say?' He didn't reply. She decided to get straight to the point. 'What went on in here last night, Richard? Is your father going to disinherit you?' Still he didn't answer. 'I'm your wife. I have a right to know.'

He shook his head wearily. 'No, Prudence, he didn't talk of disinheriting me. You have nothing to fear.'

She relaxed. Thank God for that. 'You look pale, dear. Come for a walk with me, it's a fine day.'

'No, no. You go. I want to sit for a while.'

'Please, Richard . . .'

'Go for your walk, Prudence.' It was an order, not a request, and she was a little taken aback, unaccustomed to Richard issuing orders like his father. 'I'm sorry, my dear, I didn't mean to snap,' he added. 'Walk down to the stream and I'll join you there shortly.' He returned his gaze to the bay windows as if she were no longer in the room.

'Very well,' she answered, a trifle piqued.

She fetched her shawl from upstairs and went out onto the front steps. It was indeed a fine day. But she didn't want to walk to the stream on her own. She decided to wait for Richard, and strolled over to the vine-covered arbour, just fifty yards or so from the house, to wait for him. The climbing roses were beautiful this time of year, she thought as she picked one from the trellis and threaded it through the top buttonhole of her blouse.

She looked back at the house. It was the style of home she had always longed to call her own—twin-gabled, of Georgian design, and nestled in seventy acres of England's glorious green countryside. When all this ghastliness was over, she decided, she would be happy here, far, far away from the endless red earth and loathsome heat of Kalgoorlie.

A sound cracked the air and, for a moment, she wasn't sure what it was. Then she realised it was a gunshot. And, in that instant, she knew what had happened. She ran to the house, her shawl dropping from her shoulders.

The servants were gathered in the hall. A hysterical maid was being comforted by the housekeeper.

'Don't come in, Ma'am, you don't need to see,' the butler assured her, but she ignored him and she walked straight into Lord Lionel's study.

He was still sitting in his father's chair, but he was no longer staring through the bay windows. He was sprawled face-down on the desk. He'd shot himself through the temple with his father's Webley .455 calibre revolver and his head rested in a messy pool of blood on the fastidiously polished mahogany tabletop.

Richard had left a note which said all the right things. He had taken the only course of action open to a man of honour, he declared, and went on to exonerate his father from any knowledge of his activities in Kalgoorlie and to beg forgiveness of the family whose name he had sullied. He'd even thought to include Prudence. He thanked his wife for her love and support during the years of their marriage.

The months which followed became a blank to Prudence. She heard herself say to the press, 'My husband was a fine man who couldn't live with the shame he'd brought upon his family'. She heard her father-in-law say, 'There's a Laverton woman to be proud of', and realised that he thought she had known of Richard's intention. But of course she hadn't. She'd had no idea.

Prudence's stoic behaviour in the aftermath was due to the fact that she was in a state of shock.

The realisation that Lord Lionel had forced his son to suicide was horrifying, but his assumption of her complicity so sickened Prudence that her life became unbearable.

When she gave birth to her son and successfully overruled Lord Lionel's objections by christening the baby Richard, it was a hollow triumph. She should have taken the loathsome old man's grandson away from him, she told herself. She should leave the family fold and raise her children on her own. But she knew she never would. So she accepted Lord Lionel's favouritism and watched the unveiled dislike on the faces of her sisters-in-law as he embraced her and called her 'a true Laverton'.

Chapter Seventeen

Gaston Picot had been right. It had taken just under three years to get Harry elected to the mayoral office. But there had been one slight change in plan.

'*Deputy* Mayor, Harry,' he'd said during his brief visit for the gala opening of Restaurant Picot in the middle of 1905. 'We will have you elected *Deputy* Mayor.' He continued before Harry could interrupt. 'It is better we elect a mere puppet to the position of Mayor.' Harry was disappointed and wanted to argue the point but Gaston was adamant. 'Believe me, *mon ami*, you will wield far more power if the full focus of attention is not upon you.' And Harry had agreed, albeit reluctantly, to the Frenchman's plan.

Yet again, Gaston had been proved right. There were no questions asked when the town planning committee agreed to the acquisition, by one Donald McAllister, of a further two properties in the brothel district of lower Hay Street. Neither were there questions asked when the purchaser's application for rezoning was speedily addressed. Town planning and property zoning were but two of the many offices comprising the busy portfolio of the newly appointed Deputy Mayor, Harry Brearley.

Harry had adjusted very quickly to the business conducted in Gaston Picot's Hay Street properties. Gaston had known that he would; that Jeanne and Emily would have all the right answers to soothe Harry's moral indignation.

'But they are merely real estate holdings,' Jeanne had answered as he had assisted her from the trap outside her Hannan Street house that day. And when Harry had continued to expostulate—she had insisted he come inside, have a glass of brandy and discuss the matter. 'You must talk with Emily,' she said. 'Emily has a wonderful understanding of business.'

Still in a state of shock, Harry had agreed. Emily! he thought in disbelief. Emily the mouse running a string of brothels!

'They are real estate holdings, Harry,' Jeanne purred, 'nothing more.' She poured a healthy measure into his brandy balloon. 'Monsieur Picot is a landlord, that is all.' Her smile was so innocent, so serene, that Harry was momentarily lost for words. 'You explain, Emily,' she said, 'you do it so much better than I.'

'Jeanne is quite right.' Although Emily's voice was brisk and businesslike, her arguments were as eminently seductive as Jeanne's. 'Mr McAllister collects the rentals, we keep the records and deposit the cash sums, and the bank forwards to Mr Picot the statements of his accounts. It is all quite simple. The business conducted at the premises owned by Mr Picot is entirely incidental. And nothing at all to do with us.'

After an hour or so, lulled by several brandies and the propriety of the two women, Harry did feel that he had overreacted a little. By the time he was confronted, several weeks later, with cash figures and the proof of Gaston's full involvement in the lucrative brothels, Harry was further lulled by his own percentage of the takings. The women were indeed right, he told himself, it was nobody's business as to what was being conducted behind the closed doors of the buildings in lower Hay

Street. Besides, the only name recorded on paper was that of Donald McAllister. Harry himself was in no danger of being connected with the brothels.

Several months later, Gaston informed him by telegraph that the drapery adjoining the Sheaf Hotel had been acquired and that arrangements for the building of Restaurant Picot were well under way. Furthermore, steps were being taken to devise a solid council election campaign: 'Harry Brearley, the people's choice'. By this time, Harry had decided that any moral doubts he may have had about brothels (which were, after all, legal on the goldfields) were utterly inconsequential. He was a partner in Gaston Picot's Kalgoorlie enterprises and he owed the Frenchman his loyalty and commitment.

Following a quick inspection—late at night with his hat on, his collar up and McAllister doing all the talking—Harry decided that the brothels were not working to capacity. They could be making a far greater profit if they employed more girls—at least three more at Red Ruby's alone. And if extra girls were employed then of course the rentals could be increased.

The percentage of the daily takings must also be increased, he announced—according to Emily there had been no increase for two years. Each of the three madams was to be notified of the new arrangements.

'They won't like it,' McAllister grumbled as he swigged his mug of tea and slouched over Jeanne's kitchen table.

Jeanne and Emily never conducted business with McAllister anywhere else but in the kitchen. He entered by the rear door and left by the rear door, and always at night. It wasn't just to protect their reputations. Neither of them liked the humourless Scot with his rasping Glaswegian accent, his ill-fitting clothes and his big clumsy boots. 'He'd quite ruin the finish on the drawing-room floors with those boots,' Emily confided to Harry. But the women needed McAllister. He was big and strong and, although he liked to grumble, he did as he was told.

'The madams won't like it at all,' he repeated. 'Particularly Ada at Red Ruby's—she thinks she owns the place.'

'Well, she doesn't. And the amounts will be small,' Harry said dismissively. 'With the profits they'll be making from the additional girls, the madams will barely notice.' He rose from the table. 'Then in a year we'll review the situation and, depending upon profit margins, we will once again increase both rentals and percentages.' Harry was enjoying himself. It was a pity there were not others to see him playing the businessman—it was a role which suited him.

McAllister shrugged and shuffled to his feet. It made no difference to him anyway. He was paid a healthy regular amount by Gaston Picot to act as front man, so who was he to argue?

When McAllister had gone, Harry gently chided Jeanne about her expenses and suggested they be cut back a little. Jeanne pouted prettily and said she wasn't sure how she would manage but she would do her best. Emily signalled her approval immediately.

'Quite right,' she agreed. 'You waste money ridiculously, Jeanne, and you know it.' It had been a constant bone of contention between the women. Emily worried continuously that Picot would find out he was being robbed and call a halt to their arrangement. Emily would be forty-five soon—not a good time in a woman's life to be left high and dry—and she did not intend to be deprived of her meal ticket if she could possibly help it.

Emily Laurie had been the madam at the brothel in Fremantle where Gaston Picot had first met Jeanne Renoir—although of course she had not been Jeanne Renoir then—and Emily had watched as, like many before him, Gaston became besotted with the young prostitute. So much so that he refused to share her with anyone.

He had property in Kalgoorlie, he told her. He could set her up in a grand house and visit her there regularly. 'But I would be bored, *mon cher*,' she said. 'What would I do in *Kalgoorlie*?' She made it sound like a disease. Gaston offered to make her a receptionist at one of his hotels but she displayed no enthusiasm at all. 'What do I know about hotels?' she had shrugged with disinterest.

It was then that Picot had decided to open a brothel in Kalgoorlie—a string of brothels, if that was what she wanted. She could be his manager, he told her. 'Discreetly, of course,' he added. 'From a distance.' No other man was to come near her; those were his rules.

She'd kissed him and said that she was very tempted, very tempted indeed . . . But she would be so lonely in a place like . . . *Kalgoorlie* without female company. And Emily was like a mother to her . . . Gaston had no alternative. Emily became part of the bargain.

It was an arrangement which proved eminently practical in the long run. Not only was Emily a talented businesswoman but, with her impeccable English manners and appearance, she was the perfect smokescreen of respectability. Furthermore, she was a clever and creative ally. The story of Jeanne's widowhood and the friendship which had existed between her deceased husband and Gaston was just one of Emily's many inventions.

Years later when, pressured by his wife, Gaston ended the affair with Jeanne, Emily assumed he would also terminate their comfortable arrangement. She was deeply thankful when he did not and watched, with horror, as Jeanne proceeded to unashamedly rob her benefactor.

'Expenses,' Jeanne would gaily declare, extracting

half a dozen pound notes from one of the bundles delivered by Donald McAllister. She refused to listen to Emily's protestations and there was nothing Emily could do but invent a list of expenditures that might sound vaguely plausible.

The end was in sight, Emily was sure, and she worried. While Jeanne was Gaston's mistress her extravagances were quite permissible. Indeed, the man loved to pamper her. But he was no longer receiving payment in kind.

'Why should he spend good money when he's getting nothing in return?' she argued time and time again. But Jeanne wouldn't listen.

There was nothing Emily could do but wait for the end. If she and Jeanne were to be thrown out of their grand house and deprived of their income, they would face the consequences together. Although she never spoke of it, Emily's love for Jeanne was far more than maternal.

And then came the arrival of the charming, arrogant and ambitious Harry Brearley. Surely this spelled the end, Emily thought. But it didn't. Harry had succumbed to Jeanne's allure, Emily realised, as all men did, but he didn't appear to want to sleep with her, and he obviously was not going to report her misdemeanours to Gaston. Emily swiftly revised her opinion of Harry Brearley and assisted him in every way she could. She became his ally and he trusted her implicitly.

Now, secure in his position as Deputy Mayor and co-owner of Restaurant Picot, Harry barely concerned himself with the brothels.

He was too busy basking in his glory. Restaurant Picot was flourishing as the social centre of Kalgoorlie's elite and, although he had appointed a manager, Harry was invariably to be found there of an evening. Not only did he enjoy playing the host, he simply loved being in the place. It was magnificent.

Gaston's love for jarrah was reflected throughout the splendid building. The floors and the grand staircase and railings showed off to perfection the rich red hue of the timber. In the front of the restaurant were wooden booths with plush leather seats which looked onto the pageant of Hannan Street through large plate-glass windows. The booths were popular during the weekend luncheon hours when men brought their wives or their sweethearts to dine and be seen by the passing parade. The rest of the ground floor, dominated by the grand central staircase, constituted a spacious lounge and bar—table service only—while upstairs was the essential Restaurant Picot with French windows opening onto a balcony overlooking the street.

Restaurant Picot was a masterpiece, just as Gaston had envisaged, complete with huge gilt-edged menus, silver cutlery and fine linen napkins. The only missing element was the giant chandelier. In its stead, on each table, was a flickering candle in a delicate, silver candlestick.

'Upstairs will be elite,' Gaston had declared. '*Haute cuisine.* Upstairs will be for the lovers of fine food and wine. Downstairs . . .' His shrug was patronising. 'Downstairs will be fashionable, a place to mingle, a place to be seen. But the food will be more . . . general.' His tone implied 'for the hoi polloi': Gaston did not yet trust the palates of Kalgoorlie. 'Besides,' he added, 'we will accommodate more tables that way.'

In the early dusk, Harry would stand on the upstairs balcony saluting the passers-by with his cigar and enjoying the soft background music which emanated from the brand-new Berliner gramophone in the corner. The gramophone was the most sophisticated of musical inventions, Gaston said, vastly superior to the Edison phonograph, and he'd had it specially imported from Germany. The first of its kind in Kalgoorlie, it was Gaston's and Harry's pride and joy.

As the evening progressed, Harry would greet the diners on their arrival and pass briefly amongst the tables to enquire whether all was satisfactory. He enjoyed playing the host. Particularly when the guests included those who, not so long ago, wouldn't have given him the time of day. And this evening was no exception.

'Perfectly delicious, Harry, thank you.' Beatrice Bromley, wife of Dr Garfield Bromley, prominent physician, hated calling the man Harry but she couldn't afford not to. Everyone who dined upstairs at Restaurant Picot called him Harry; she couldn't have people thinking she wasn't on a first-name basis. 'The creme caramel was superb. As always.'

'Thank you, Beatrice.' She winced. She did every time. 'I'll tell Jean-Marc; he'll be delighted. Garfield?' Harry turned to Bromley who had pushed the dessert he'd barely touched to one side and was leaning back in his chair. 'Is everything satisfactory?'

'Yes. Excellent, old man, excellent,' Bromley answered in his plummy tone which denoted superiority, 'just not very hungry that's all.' He fiddled with one end of his waxed antennae-like moustache and gave a vague wave of his hand. 'I say, could you get that fellow to bring me your best French brandy?'

'Shall we wait for the coffee, dear?' Beatrice asked tightly.

'No, no. Now's fine, now's fine.'

'Of course, we have an excellent cognac. I'll send the waiter over immediately.' As he left, Harry heard Beatrice hiss, 'You should have waited for the coffee.' But Bromley was always more interested in the liquor than he was in the food. Harry could never understand why the man was the most sought-after physician on the goldfields. People obviously didn't know he was a drunk.

As Harry caught the waiter's eye and gestured to the Bromleys' table, he heard a disturbance through the open French windows behind him, raucous men's voices from the street below.

Damn, he thought, the waiters hadn't closed the windows. Harry had instructed them always to close the balcony windows early on a Friday. Friday was payday for the timbercutters who frequented the hotel next door. Payday and the end of the work week. Friday was a rowdy night at the Sheaf.

Harry quickly crossed to the windows, noticing that one or two of the diners were already distracted by the din. He signalled a waiter to turn up the gramophone and, as he stepped out onto the balcony, the string quartet swelled in volume.

Harry closed the windows behind him and looked down into the street below. Half a dozen men had staggered out of the Sheaf and one voice was raised above the general drunken din. It was a voice Harry knew. Rico Gianni. He stepped back out of the light, not wishing to draw attention to himself. But it was too late. Rico had sensed the figure on the balcony and looked up. He yelled something out in Italian and his voice was ugly.

'Look, my friends!' he was shouting. 'Look at who is watching us from his castle. Mr Deputy Mayor himself!' The others tried to quieten him, but he refused to listen. 'Tell him to come down and join the common people,' he jeered.

As his friends dragged him away, Rico yelled up at Harry. In English this time. 'You are a thief, Harry Brearley! You are a thief and a coward and one day you will pay for it.'

'Come on, Rico,' one of the men urged. 'Leave him

alone, it's not worth it.' Every couple of months Sergeant Baldy Hetherington was forced to lock Rico up for the night. Drunken behaviour, inciting an affray, using indecent language in a public place, and always relating to the Brearleys. 'It is still early. We will go back to your house and drink some wine,' the man insisted. 'Come on.' And the others started to drag the protesting Rico down the street.

'*Bastardo*!' Rico kept screaming up at Harry, but he allowed himself to be led away.

Harry slipped back inside the restaurant, angry more than shaken by yet another episode. If there was any way he could have the entire Gianni family run out of town he would. But Giovanni Gianni was a respected citizen, and although Rico was generally avoided, there were many who sympathised with Teresa and the constant fight she must have in protecting her young family from her husband's madness.

Teresa had not expected Rico home this early tonight. She did not like the raucous group of timbercutters he had brought back with him, but it was safer for him to bring his work friends home to drink. He was less likely to get into trouble that way.

Teresa looked at her son and shrugged her shoulders. She knew Enrico hated it when his father came home half drunk. She worried about the boy. Carmelina still knew how to charm her father, and six-year-old Salvatore was Rico's pride and joy . . . but Enrico, who had always been a sensitive boy, was withdrawing more and more from the brutality of his father. And the more he withdrew the more Rico challenged him.

'Stand up for yourself, boy,' he barked constantly. 'You are thirteen years old. Soon you will be a man; you must learn to fight.' This followed the time Enrico had come home with a swelling eye and a bloodied face.

'Just a boy at school,' he had explained, knowing

that if his father found out it was Jack Brearley, there would be hell to pay. Enrico wanted no repercussions from the fight—it had been a fair one. Although it was out of character for him, he had entered the fray as readily as Jack—the two of them had been spoiling for a fight for a very long time. But Jack Brearley was undoubtedly the stronger and more aggressive of the two and Enrico had been sorely beaten.

As a result of his beating, Rico had insisted his son learn to fight. Enrico detested the whole exercise—not so much the lessons themselves but the hostility they brought out in his father.

'What's the matter with you?' Rico would yell, exasperated when the boy failed to respond. 'Where is your rage? Fight me! Come on fight me!' When Enrico's efforts continued to be half-hearted, he would throw up his hands. 'You are just like your uncle. Soft. Giovanni would walk away, too, before he would face his enemies. Well, go to him, see if I care.' And Rico would walk off in disgust.

The truth was, Rico was jealous of the boy's relationship with his uncle. Since Giovanni had left the family home, Enrico had been slipping away to spend more and more time with his idol. And recently, when Giovanni had bought a piano accordion, he had given Enrico the old concertina.

'Shut up that noise,' Rico would bellow on the occasions when, in his drunkenness, the music became a symbol of the distance between him and his son. And then Teresa would turn her full venom upon him.

'If he stops that noise I will leave this house!' she would yell back at him. And later, when they had made love, she would try to talk sense to him. 'Why do you fight the music, Rico? You love the concertina, you love to sing along. And the boy is a fine musician, Giovanni always said he was.' Even as she sensed the tension,

Teresa continued boldly. 'You must let him spend time with Giovanni, he is a sensitive boy.' And, for a while, there would be a grudging sense of peace until the next drunken rage.

Knowing the effect Rico was having on his son, Giovanni had tried to discourage Enrico's constant visits. If they exacerbated his father's anger they served no purpose. But eventually it was Teresa herself who encouraged the relationship.

'It is better that the boy sees you, Giovanni,' she had said during one of his visits to the family home.

Giovanni had deliberately called on a Friday night when Rico was out drinking so that he could insist she accept some money from him. 'For the children, Teresa. Please take it. What else can I spend it on?' She had reluctantly agreed.

'He is the firstborn,' she continued. 'Rico is trying to mould him as himself. It is wrong. When Enrico is grown perhaps he will be able to see the pain in his father. If not,' she shrugged, 'at least he will be able to defend himself. He needs you, Giovanni.'

So the visits had become more and more regular. And Giovanni enjoyed the company of the boy. Enrico never spoke of his unhappiness at home and Giovanni never encouraged it. Instead, he asked the boy to teach him to read and write, a request which filled Enrico with pride. And they played music together and sang and sat in silence watching the sunset and then Giovanni would say, 'It is time to go home, Enrico,' and the boy would reluctantly leave.

'ENRICO, BRUNO'S GLASS is empty,' Rico shouted drunkenly. 'More pasta, hurry up, boy . . .' His brush with Harry Brearley had enraged Rico and as usual, he decided to take his ill-humour out on his eldest son. Any interruption from Teresa merely angered him the more.

'Shut your mouth, woman. The boy wants to behave like a girl, let him be treated like a girl. He can wait on the men like a good daughter should.' The other men took no notice as they played their cards and held their glasses out to be filled.

When one of the glasses smashed to the floor, Enrico was roared at, as if it was his fault, and ordered to clean up the mess. He stood looking at the glass for several moments while the men returned to their cards. Then he picked up his concertina and walked to the front door.

'Where are you going, boy?' Rico growled. 'I told you to clean up that mess.'

'Clean it up yourself,' he answered. There was a deadly silence and all eyes were turned on Rico, waiting for his reaction. Rico was momentarily lost for words. Never had his son answered back to him.

Enrico glanced briefly at his mother. 'I'm going out,' he said and he didn't look at his father as he gently closed the door behind him.

It was barely dusk when Enrico arrived at the boarding house where his uncle lived, but Giovanni was already on his way out.

'Can I come with you?'

'No, Enrico, I am sorry.'

The boy nodded, but he looked so forlorn standing there, his concertina in one hand, the other hand in his shorts pocket, eyes downcast, studying his worn boots as he scuffed them in the dust of the front verandah.

'Is there something wrong?' Giovanni asked.

'No.'

'Has there been a bad fight at home?'

'No.' The accompanying shrug said, 'No worse than usual', but Giovanni sensed something had happened.

'Well, I suppose my friend won't mind if I am a little late. I see you have brought the concertina—would you like to play for me?'

Enrico looked up. 'Can I play you my song?' he asked hopefully. 'I finished it yesterday.'

They sat on the steps of the front verandah and Enrico played. It was a pretty song of his own composition; he'd been working on it for weeks. As he played, Giovanni watched the boy's tension fade away until there was nothing but his concentration upon every note. Music was Enrico's salvation, Giovanni thought. His father would never be able to take that from him.

'It is a fine song,' Giovanni said as the boy concluded. 'You are a true musician, Enrico.'

The boy smiled happily. Giovanni would never say that if he didn't mean it. 'It's a love song,' he said. 'I am going to write words for it.'

Giovanni laughed. 'Well, you're a better man than I am.' Learning to read and write was still a painful process for Giovanni. 'And is there someone you write this song for?' he asked with a suggestive wink. 'A girl at school maybe?'

'No,' Enrico answered in all seriousness. 'Not yet.' He had indeed been noticing the girls at school. 'But I like love songs. I like the way you sing them.'

Giovanni rose and spanked the dust from the seat of his good trousers. 'I must go now.' He knew the boy was loath to leave. 'It is Saturday tomorrow. Will you give me a writing lesson in the afternoon?' The boy nodded eagerly.

'It is time to go home, Enrico.'

Enrico watched as Giovanni walked down the street. He wished they could have sat and played and sung together for hours. What would happen when he went home? he wondered. Perhaps his father would beat him. It had never happened before. For all Rico's violence he had never laid a hand upon his children. But then Enrico had never defied his father before.

He didn't want to go home. He couldn't face that

yet. So he followed Giovanni instead, stealthily, from a distance. When they turned into Hay Street and he saw Giovanni enter Red Ruby's, Enrico felt a sense of shock. He knew what Red Ruby's was. The boys at school told fascinatingly lewd stories about the brothels and what went on inside them.

He sat on the kerbside a block away from Red Ruby's fantasising about what was going on behind the bright red shutters through which the soft rose light glowed. He mustn't think less of Giovanni, he told himself when the initial shock had worn off. Giovanni was not a married man, there was not a woman in his life. And men needed women. Enrico had known for a long time now what his mother and father were doing when the bed squeaked and he heard their moans and grunts through the thin partitioning wall. It stirred him. He wondered what it was like, being with a woman.

As he watched from the kerbside, he saw other men arrive. Not only at Red Ruby's but at the many other brothels that lined the street on either side. He didn't hear the light footsteps behind him. So absorbed was he that he didn't notice her until she spoke.

'What are you doing, young man?'

Startled, Enrico looked up. Although it was a bright moonlit night, he couldn't see her face clearly. But her voice was young and humorous and her accent fascinating.

'What are you doing sitting in the gutter?' He could tell she was smiling.

'Um . . . I was just . . .' He started to get up. He could feel himself blushing.

'No no,' she insisted. 'Do not stand, it is not necessary.'

He watched, astonished, as she bent and gathered up her skirts, raising them to her waist and displaying the layers of petticoats underneath. Then carefully holding her skirts in her lap, she sat beside him in the gutter.

'I must not spoil my dress,' she said. 'It is pretty, is it not?'

He stared back. He could see her now, in the moonlight. A lace shawl covered her head and he wasn't sure what colour her hair was, but soft curls framed a face that was one of the prettiest he had ever seen.

'You like it?' she insisted. 'My dress?'

He realised that he had been staring at her, jaw agape. 'Yes . . . um . . .'

'You did not answer my other question.' Her smile was mischievous. 'What are you doing sitting in the gutter staring at the houses?'

'Um . . .' Enrico was flustered, the guilty images still in his mind. Didn't she know what those houses were?

Solange laughed and decided to save the boy from further embarrassment. 'My name is Solange Bouchet. What is yours?'

'Enrico Gianni.'

'How old are you?'

'Fifteen.' He lied without hesitation. 'How old are you?'

'Nineteen,' she said. She didn't believe the boy for one minute. Perhaps he was fourteen, certainly no more. But such a beautiful boy, she thought, with his serious dark brown eyes.

'Where do you come from?' Enrico asked. He couldn't stop staring at her. 'The way you speak . . .'

'I am from France,' she said. 'A little town called Houilles not far from Paris.' He waited for her to go on. Lost for words, he simply wanted to hear her talk. 'The people in Houilles are miners also, but they do not mine for gold. In Houilles they mine for coal.' She wrinkled her nose comically. 'Coal is not so romantic, so I come to Kalgoorlie instead.' Still he said nothing.

Oh well, Solange thought, if he was not going to be amusing she would go. She was already late for work, Ada would be cross. But then she was always late for work and Ada was always cross. Never for long though. The youngest girl working at Red Ruby's, Solange was Ada's favourite.

She noticed the concertina. 'You play music?' she asked.

'Yes.' Still he stared.

'Ah,' she said, gathering her skirts and preparing to go. 'That is nice.'

'I compose music too,' he said desperately. She mustn't go. She mustn't. 'Would you like me to play you a song?'

She leaned forward and hugged her knees. 'Yes,' she said. 'I would like that very much.'

He played her his song as beautifully as he could, concentrating on every single, faultless note and, as the last note died away, his smile was jubilant.

'Do you like it?' he asked. He knew he had played it perfectly.

'Yes.' The boy was delightful. 'I like it very much.' She leaned forward and kissed him on the cheek. Then she was up in an instant, fluffing out her skirts. 'I must go,' she said.

Enrico scrambled to his feet. 'I could play you another song. I know many.'

'Yes, you must play for me again, but some other time. Now I must go.'

'Where are you going?' he asked eagerly. 'Can I come with you?'

'Come with me? Where?' Her laugh was like music to him. 'To Red Ruby's?'

Solange saw the shock in his eyes and felt a shadow of regret. She had assumed he knew. That's why she had flirted with him. Now, for some reason she could not explain, she did not want him to think badly of her.

'Oh, you silly boy,' she said, giving her skirts an extra flounce, 'I go to visit my cousin, she works there.' Still he looked so serious. 'She is a chambermaid, nothing more.' She blew him a kiss and walked away. 'Good night,' she called over her shoulder.

Enrico watched her walk across the street. He wanted to call after her but he couldn't think of anything to say. So he played his concertina instead. He stood and played his love song once more as he watched her walk briskly towards the rose-coloured lights.

Hearing the music, Solange slowed her pace. She did not look back, but by the time she had reached the doors to Red Ruby's she was dawdling. Such a beautiful tune, she thought, marvelling that the boy had composed it; he was no more than a child. She paused for a moment, then reluctantly opened the door and slipped inside. Ada would be very cross by now.

Enrico continued to play his song over and over, imagining that perhaps she could hear it from behind the red shutters. The song had a name now. 'Solange's Song'. And tonight he would write the words to it.

Chapter Eighteen

The entire town of Kal was celebrating as the *Kalgoorlie Miner* headlines announced the incredible rescue of Modesto Varischetti. The Italian miner had been trapped for ten days at the bottom of the Westralia mine, just north of nearby Coolgardie.

'They'll never get him out,' people had said for the first five days.

'He's buried alive—just sitting there in his tomb,' many a miner commented. 'Terrible way to go.'

'My oath,' others agreed. 'Better to cop it quick. A cave-in, or an explosion even.'

Varischetti had been working a rise—a stope above the lowest level of the mine—when one of the heavy storms that occasionally struck the area had caused a flash flood. As the main shaft and the lower levels took in water, miners were quickly brought to the surface but, in his airpocket halfway between the flooded ninth and tenth levels, Varischetti had worked on, oblivious.

When news of his entombment had reached the surface, a special train with equipment and experienced divers was rushed from Perth and a desperate rescue bid attempted. But few held out hope.

'Divers work in the sea,' was the laconic view of the average miner. 'How's a diver going to find his way down shafts and along drives and up into rises?'

'Their air hoses'll be cut and there'll be more deaths,' was the pessimistic answer. 'It's not worth the risk.'

Then a Kalgoorlie miner with diving experience, a Welshman called Frank Hughes, volunteered to join the rescue team and local opinion changed.

'If anyone can get him up, Hughes can,' the Kalgoorlie miners said.

And when, on the sixth day, Hughes reached Varischetti and his message was read out by the underground manager to the crowd gathered on the surface—'Happy. Shook hands with man. All right'—the Kalgoorlie miners congratulated each other. One of their own was a hero.

Four days later, when Varischetti was brought out, weakened by his ten days in hell but very much alive, the *Kalgoorlie Miner* heralded the news and the men could speak of nothing else.

'I always said Frank could do it,' Tony Prendergast boasted that morning as the men reported for work at the Midas.

'They're calling him Diver Hughes now,' Alwyn said, and Evan nodded as he ticked the various teams off his work list. It was a fine day to be Welsh.

But it wasn't only the Welshmen who were proud. It was a fine day to be a Kalgoorlie miner and they all claimed Diver Hughes for their own.

'What's it got to do with him being Welsh?' young Freddie countered. 'He's a Kalgoorlie man—that's what counts.' Then the men started taking sides and an argument ensued. But it was good-natured—a rescue like Varischetti's made everyone proud.

Evan listened to the friendly bickering and tried to join in but he couldn't feel a part of it.

Evan was deeply unhappy. For a long time he hadn't realised what was causing his unhappiness. At first he hadn't even realised that he *was* unhappy. He'd only known that things were somehow different; something in Kate had changed, and it disturbed him. What was it, he'd wondered. She was as considerate and affectionate as ever, as responsive in their love-making and as good a wife and mother as she had always been. But there was something brittle in her gaiety, something forced, and there were times when he thought he saw the shadow of unhappiness in her eyes.

'Is something wrong, Kate?' he would ask. And Kate, perhaps realising she had been caught unawares, would smile, kiss him reassuringly and say, 'Of course not, my dear, I am just a little tired that is all'. But something was not right.

Since his promotion to underground boss, Evan had taken a keen interest in the welfare of his fellow miners. He saw it as a necessary extension of his position. Indeed, it had been mainly due to his efforts that the Midas had been one of the first of the big mines to introduce the shilling fund. Each miner consented to a weekly deduction of one shilling from his pay packet and was thus entitled to free medical and hospital treatment. It was a good scheme and Evan's involvement with its instigation quickly attracted the attention of the trade union activists. The union was young and weak, they told him, unlike the miners' unions in New South Wales and Victoria. It needed men like him, they said. Would he join them? Evan had agreed.

With the distraction of constant meetings and union responsibilities, there was less and less time for Evan to dwell on the change in Kate and he had all but forgotten his concern until one Sunday night when Paul pressed the issue of a visit to the Gianni household.

'Please, Mamma,' he had begged. 'Come with me—just this once.'

'No, Paul. How many times have I told you, it is not right that Teresa should have extra guests. She feeds enough people as it is.' The words came out automatically. Kate had said the same thing so many times in the past that Paul had long since stopped asking her to come with him to the Giannis' for the Sunday singalong.

'But this will be the last time—'

'I said no.' Kate was surprised that the boy should badger her so, but she thought little of it as she stood at the kitchen bench washing the dishes in the big bowl and passing each one to Paul to dry.

'But, Mamma, you must!' the boy insisted. 'Giovanni is leaving.'

She couldn't help it. The dish remained poised above the sink. 'Giovanni is leaving?'

'Yes.' He put out his hand to take the dish but she held it, suds dripping over the bowl, staring ahead blindly. 'It will be the last time, Mamma, you must come.'

'Where is he going?'

Behind her, through the open door that led from the kitchen to the living room, Evan watched her face in the little mirror above the kitchen bench.

He had been only half aware of the conversation as he sat at the dining table with his notes spread out before him. It was the way her tone changed when she said, 'Giovanni is leaving' that caused him to look up. And it was then he saw the terrible truth in her eyes.

He heard Paul say, 'He is moving out of the Gianni house', and the instant passed. The boy chattered on as Kate handed him the dish and continued washing up.

Evan had stopped listening. He stared down at his notes but he didn't see them. How could he have been so blind! He had known it, deep inside, ever since he had seen that look of rapture in his wife's eyes as she had watched Giovanni singing. How long ago had that been? He had known of Giovanni's love for his wife for far longer than that—possibly from the moment they first met, when they had danced together at the banquet. He could still see them. The perfect couple, waltzing to the Pride of Erin. He had forgiven Giovanni for falling in love with his wife—what man could fail to love a creature like Kate—but the knowledge that she returned his love was more than Evan could bear.

He rose and walked to the front door, unaware that behind him a folder of papers had fallen from the table and scattered upon the floor.

Kate, hearing him leave, turned and called after him. 'Are you going out, my dear I am just about to make some tea', but he couldn't trust himself to answer.

He walked for hours that night and when he came home she was sleeping. She half-woke as he slid quietly into their bed.

'Evan, where have you been?' she murmured.

'Sssh, my dearest, go back to sleep,' he whispered. She snuggled against his back as she always did and he lay awake wondering if, in her dreams, it was Giovanni's body she felt next to hers. From that night on, Evan's life had become a misery.

He knew she was faithful to him. He knew, also, that Giovanni was not pressing his suit. In some ways it would be better if the man did, Evan agonised. If a love like theirs belonged together, why didn't he fight for her?

Over the months that followed, he tested Giovanni. 'Come home with me,' he would say with forced jollity. 'Come and sing with me and Alwyn.' Giovanni always refused.

He tested Kate. 'Let's visit the Giannis,' he would say. 'Teresa is a close friend of yours, you don't see her often enough.' But even though Giovanni had shifted from the family home, Kate would not risk a visit. Every now and then she would arrange to meet Teresa and go shopping but that was the extent of her communication with the Gianni family.

Finally, driven to distraction, Evan even tried to offer her release from their marriage. The prospect of life without Kate was unbearable to him but, so too was the thought that their life together was making her unhappy.

'If you wanted to be free, Kate,' he said late one night as they prepared for bed, 'I would only wish you well.' He had been planning his speech for months but it had taken every ounce of his strength to finally say the words.

She was startled. 'Why should I want to be free, Evan?' Her expression was one of utter surprise.

He couldn't bring himself to say it out loud. 'You are in love with another man'—that's what he should have said. He should have told her to go to him, but he couldn't.

'I sometimes feel that you are not happy,' he said instead. 'And your happiness is my greatest concern, you know that.'

'Oh my dear.' Tears sprang to Kate's eyes. She couldn't help it. She knew she should laugh and tell him he was being silly, but, as she looked at the pain in her husband's eyes, she knew that she couldn't. He knows, she thought. Dear God, he knows! The tears streamed down her cheeks. 'All I wish is to be a good wife to you, Evan. If I make you unhappy, please forgive me.'

'There is nothing to forgive, Kate. But if you wished to leave me . . .'

'I will never leave you.' Anger gave her control over her tears. Anger with herself. She did not deserve him. She sniffed loudly and bent to grope beneath her pillow for the handkerchief she kept there. 'If you were to throw me out of the house, you would still be my husband, Evan. My husband and Briony's father.' She blew her nose loudly. 'You will always be my husband and father to both of my children. I do not wish to change that and I never shall.'

She had finished blowing her nose and was looking defiantly at him. Evan didn't know what to say. He wished he could voice his fears. Were they to ignore the fact that she loved another man? Could they live with that terrible knowledge? But he was silent. He couldn't say the words.

WHILE THE CAGE lowered its human cargo into the darkness and the teams alighted at each level, the talk of Varischetti continued. And when, at level ten, one thousand feet below the surface, Alwyn, Giovanni and Freddie lit their candles, they were still talking about the miraculous rescue.

It was only when they were deep in the drive, when all sound and light was swallowed by darkness and each man was no more than a flickering silhouette to his workmate, that the talk ceased.

The above-ground world always ceased at the work face. It was not only Evan who was thankful for that fact. Giovanni, too, breathed a sigh of relief. It was below ground, at the work face, that he also finally felt a sense of peace.

The morning's work progressed smoothly. They drilled the face, placed the charges in formation and Alwyn detonated them sequentially, as the men listened to the muffled explosions from a safe distance. Then Alwyn, Giovanni and Freddie waited in the plat for the fumes to clear and for Evan to conduct his inspection.

The cage clanged in the main shaft behind them. Evan had arrived, for his first inspection of the day.

He greeted Alwyn in Welsh as he always did; Freddie lit a candle for him and the four of them walked along the drive, the two Welshmen leading the way.

Evan knew there was something wrong as soon as they arrived at the work face. The others hung their candles from rock ledges and prepared to observe the customary silence—it would be several minutes before Alwyn's query, 'What are they saying, Evan?' But this morning Evan didn't wait for the question. Evan Jones knew only too well what the rocks were saying.

'Run!' He wheeled around to face the others. 'Get out of here. Quick! Run!'

Freddie obeyed every order the instant it was issued, and was already running for his life towards the plat. Giovanni, jolted from his momentary shock, followed blindly. But, as he did, he heard the ominous rumble behind him and had to look back.

Earth was showering from above and smaller rocks were tumbling into the drive. Giovanni knew the signs—precursors to a cave-in. He saw one of the rocks strike Alwyn who was running behind him. The Welshman was thrown to the ground and lay there unconscious. Giovanni grabbed him by the shoulders and dragged him back along the drive. Where was Evan? he thought, panicking. Where the hell was Evan?

A crack like thunder split the air. Through the shower of dust and earth, for a second, Giovanni saw him, a motionless shadow in the last flickering light of the remaining candle.

'Run, Evan, run!' Giovanni heard himself scream. The figure started to run towards him. Then there was a massive roar, the candle went out, and the world came crashing in upon them.

Giovanni threw himself to the ground, covering Alwyn's head with his body and shielding his own head with his hands while the forces unleashed their might.

The noise was horrendous. In the coal-blackness, the gods and demons of the underworld wreaked vengeance upon the intruders, roaring and screaming their outrage.

It seemed an eternity before the noise finally died away and Giovanni dared lift his head. The rubble and earth fell from his body as he slowly raised himself to his knees, scarcely believing that he was still alive. A fit of coughing overtook him as the dust bit into his lungs. Beside him, he felt Alwyn stir, then heard him groan in pain. Where was Evan?

'Evan!' he called. 'Evan, where are you?'

'Run, Giovanni.' The voice was not far away. Only several yards deeper into the drive. Giovanni crawled forward.

'I said run, man,' the voice urged. 'That was only the beginning.'

Giovanni was close to the voice now, but he could crawl no further. There was a wall of rock before him. He felt about in the blackness. A hand. He clutched at it. 'Evan! Are you hurt?'

But, even as he said it, his other hand had traced Evan's head, shoulders and chest, before hitting the wall of rock, and Giovanni knew that the Welshman was buried from the waist down.

'Did the others get away?' the voice asked.

'Freddie did. Alwyn is hurt—I don't know how bad.'

'Get him out. The whole drive will go any minute.'

'Can you move?' Giovanni demanded.

'I'm buried, man. Get out I tell you.'

Giovanni started to claw desperately at the rocks.

'Dear God in heaven, man, did you not hear me?' The voice which snarled at him was surprisingly strong. 'I'm trapped, I can't move. Now get Alwyn out of here.'

Giovanni felt himself start to panic. Evan was alive. How could he leave?

'You must get him out, Giovanni.' The voice was quieter now, but just as resolute. 'Alwyn has five daughters.' There was a moment while neither man spoke. Then, 'God go with you,' Evan said.

'I'll come back, Evan.'

'Fine. Fine. But you get him above ground first.'

Giovanni crawled back along the drive until he reached Alwyn. The man was groaning, but unable to move. Giovanni dragged him out of the rubble and several yards further down the drive to where he could stand and hoist him onto his shoulders. As he did, Evan's voice reached him from out of the blackness.

'Giovanni!'

Giovanni turned and looked back down the drive, into the pitch black.

'Look after my wife for me,' Evan's voice called to him. 'Look after my Kate.'

'I'm coming back.'

'She is yours, Giovanni. She has always been yours.'

Giovanni paused for only a moment. 'I'm coming back, Evan,' he called into the blackness. 'I'm coming back.'

EVAN COULD HEAR the Italian stumbling through the darkness towards the plat. He concentrated on the sound until he could no longer hear it. Then he stared up at the roof of the drive and filled his head with the silence. He could see the rock formations above him, he was sure of it. And it wasn't silence he was listening to at all. The rocks were talking to him, he could swear it. What were they saying? Was it 'freedom'?

He'd fallen on his back and felt strangely comfortable lying there. He didn't attempt to move his head or his arms—it was excruciatingly painful if he did. But, oddly enough, he couldn't feel the lower part of his body which was trapped under the rockfall. His legs were numb, as if they no longer existed.

He wondered why he hadn't run faster, sooner, escaped the cave-in. He wondered why he'd stayed those extra seconds.

'Freedom,' the rocks said, over and over. Perhaps that was why.

He breathed deeply, amazed that it didn't cause him pain, and listened to the rocks. But they were no longer talking to him. He could hear a perfect sound. A perfect voice, joined by other perfect voices. It was a glorious choir he could hear. The rocks were singing to him. And they were singing 'Calan Lan'.

GIOVANNI COULD SEE the lights as he stumbled towards the plat. He could see the cage and young Freddie sitting beside it, whimpering like a lost, forlorn puppy.

'Freddie!' The authoritative voice brought the youth immediately to attention and he sprang to his feet. Someone was going to tell him what to do. Freddie knew no fear if someone simply told him what to do. Giovanni appeared at the entrance of the drive. 'Help me get him into the cage.'

Strong as an ox, Freddie lifted Alwyn from Giovanni's shoulders and Giovanni gratefully sagged against the wall of the plat. Every bone, every muscle was aching.

It was then that they heard it. A baritone. Strong and clear.

'Nid wyn gof am bwyd moethus
Aur y byd uw berlei man
Gofyd wyf am galon hapus
Galon lwn a galon lan . . .'

There was a low rumble and the plat itself seemed to shudder. But the voice sang on.

'I seek not of worldly treasure,
Gold nor pearls of any mart.
Give me a heart of joyful measure.
Just a guileless, honest heart . . . '

AS EVAN SANG, he gloried in his voice. 'Calan Lan' was the finest hymn ever written on God's earth and never had he sung it so well. He wished his choirmaster at

Aberystwyth could hear him now. 'Sing up, boy!' he could hear the old man say. ''Tis a fine voice, don't be afraid to let it be heard. Sing up!' So Evan sang with all his might. He felt no pain. He felt nothing but the power of his voice as he sang with the rocks. He could see them clearly now, the rocks, his choir. And they were the rocks of the Welsh hillside and the tunnel was filled with light.

FROM THE CAGE in the plat, Giovanni and Freddie stood silently listening.

'Only guileless hearts keep singing,
Singing day and—'

Then a mighty bellow roared from the very centre of the earth, followed by the crashing of huge boulders, and dust billowed like smoke from the entrance of the drive. And the voice was silenced.

As the cage ascended, Giovanni and Freddie watched the walls of the plat slowly start to crumble. Then, there was nothing but the inky black of the main shaft and the inferno's roar still ringing in their ears.

Chapter Nineteen

At the poppet head there was no sound. A hundred people or more were gathered but there was no sound, no movement. The siren had stopped screaming and all eyes were directed at the entrance to the main shaft. Silent, motionless, they waited for the cage to appear.

Tears still streaked the faces of the women who'd watched and waited for their men. Who was dead? Who was alive? Each time the cage appeared, a woman would run to her man, or she would fall to her knees and thank God while the others stood, breathless, some clutching their children to them.

When most of the teams were above ground, the men compared notes. Some had heard noises, some had felt tremors. There had been a minor cave-in on level nine and one man had a broken arm. Level ten was the disaster area, they agreed, as they waited for the final cage.

With them was Freddie's mother and Eileen Llewellyn, Alwyn's wife, her arm around her eldest daughter. And next to her stood Kate Jones.

When the cage finally surfaced, there were three men in it. The first was easily recognisable. Freddie saw his mother, forgot all else and ran to her. But the other two? As one man wearily hoisted the other upon his shoulders and stepped out of the cage, it was impossible to tell who they were. Covered in dust, they were the colour of the earth.

Willing hands assisted the unconscious man and, as he was gently lowered to the ground, Kate heard the intake of breath from Eileen Llewellyn beside her. Then, the man who had been carrying Alwyn looked up and Kate felt her own intake of breath. The man had no beard.

Giovanni looked out at the crowd and his eyes immediately found Kate's. Slowly, he walked towards her.

She didn't move, but her eyes didn't leave his. She knew that Evan was dead and she knew that God might damn her but she couldn't help it. Giovanni is alive! her mind screamed. Giovanni is alive!

He stood before her and no words were spoken. It was only when he gently shook his head that she finally averted her eyes. 'I know,' she whispered. 'I know.'

'I will take you home.' She did not move. 'Come, Caterina.' Gently, he took her by the arm but she pulled away from him.

'I must tell the children.' She turned and walked away from the poppet head. The crowd watched her go. News of the tragedy had spread quickly and people had arrived at the mine to offer help and comfort, but it was obvious Kate did not want either just then.

Giovanni walked beside her, at a loss as to what to do. She was not weeping, she did not want his support. How could he comfort her in her grief?

'He died bravely and honourably, Caterina. He had thoughts only for the safety of others.'

Still she kept walking and still there was no sign of a tear. She was in torment, Giovanni knew it. If only she would stop, if only she would sob on his shoulder, share the burden of her grief with him.

'He made his peace with God, I know he did,' he continued desperately. 'He sang, Caterina. Such a beautiful sound. Evan was not afraid to die, I swear it.'

She stared resolutely ahead and quickened her pace.

'His last words were of you.'

Finally she stopped. 'What did he say?'

'He asked me to look after you.'

Kate closed her eyes for a moment as the full measure of her guilt overwhelmed her. The shame of her joy when she'd seen Giovanni step from the cage. Of course Evan was not afraid to die, her mind screamed. He wanted to die, what reason did he have to live?

'Come, Caterina, let me take you home.' He took her arm once again, but she pulled away from him more sharply than before and there was anger in her voice.

'Leave me, Giovanni! Leave me alone!'

Don't you understand, Giovanni, she wanted to shout, Evan knew! He'd known for years! That's why he wanted to die!

'I must tell the children,' she said. And Giovanni watched, helpless, as she walked stiffly away from the mine.

ON THE EVENING following Evan's memorial service several days later, Giovanni was sitting on the verandah of the small, dingy boarding house where he lived. He was thinking of Caterina as he sang softly to himself.

'Non ti scudare di me,
La vita mia legata 'e' te . . .'

Many had attended the service for Evan. Giovanni had watched from the back of the church as Caterina sat motionless in the front pew, Paul and Briony on either side.

Afterwards, she was surrounded by friends and well-wishers and, as she appeared to be avoiding his eyes, he left without formally offering his condolences.

Now, he wanted desperately to go to her. They belonged together. They both knew it. And Evan had known it too. 'She is yours, Giovanni,' Evan had said. 'She has always been yours.'

'Io tamo sempre piu,
Nel sonno mio rimani tu . . .'

And he had always been hers, Giovanni thought as he sang. Always. Since that very first morning on the mountain, she had owned him, heart and soul.

The street was deserted, people were in the town centre or in their homes with their families. He did not see her standing in the deepening dusk, watching him.

She had been panting when she'd arrived at his house. It was a good twenty minutes from the Golden Mile, and she'd run most of the way.

She'd heard the piano accordion from several houses away. As she caught her breath and stole towards the little verandah, she heard him quietly singing. An old Italian song—one she knew well.

'Don't ever forget me,
My life is entwined with yours . . .'

She stood mesmerised, watching him sing to the dusty verandah floorboards. On her way to him, she had felt guilt. But now, with the music calling to her, there was no longer guilt. There was no sin in their love, she knew it. His voice and the music told her so.

'I love you more and more,
In my thoughts you will always remain . . .'

As the last notes of the song died away, Giovanni looked around and saw her.

She watched him come to her. They said nothing as they embraced. Then he kissed her and he felt her lips move against his as she whispered, 'I love you, Giovanni, I love you,' over and over. And he took her into the small dingy room in the small dingy boarding house, but neither of them noticed. It could have been a palace.

ENRICO GIANNI HAD written the words to his love song the very same night he had met Solange. He had weathered the storm of his father's rage and retired to his room with 'Solange's Song'.

The following day after school, he had waited on the opposite side of the road a block away from Red Ruby's. But she hadn't come. He'd waited the next day. And the next. Then it was Saturday.

He had waited all day, and in the late afternoon had been mustering the courage to cross the road and knock on the door when he saw her rounding the corner in the distance. She was wearing a simple brown day dress and a straw hat with a yellow bow on the front and she was carrying a bunch of wildflowers, vivid red and green kangaroo paws.

Enrico couldn't take his eyes off her. She was as pretty by day as she had been by night. He could see now that her curls, beneath the pert straw hat, were the colour of honey and, to his delight, she was no taller than he was.

As she approached him, Solange became aware of the fact that the boy in the street was staring at her. She gave him a saucy smile, then realised who it was. The boy with the concertina.

'*Bonjour*, Enrico.'

He was thrilled that she remembered. 'I've been waiting for you,' he said, drinking in her green eyes.

'Here,' she said, handing him a kangaroo paw, 'for you. They are beautiful, yes? But they have no smell.' She kept walking and Enrico was forced to walk with her. 'The boronia is not so beautiful but it has a fragrance beyond compare. I could find no boronia.'

'I wrote the words to my song.'

'Ah *bon, bon*.' He wished she would stop walking. They would be at Red Ruby's any second now. 'It is so strange, is it not? For such an ugly little flower like the boronia to have such a beautiful perfume.'

'I have been waiting for you every afternoon this week,' he said. Thank goodness she was there at last.

Solange felt irritated. She didn't like being spied on. 'I visit my cousin only on a Saturday or a Sunday,' she said primly. 'And I think it is not a good thing at all for a young boy to be lounging around outside a place like Red Ruby's.'

Enrico registered the rebuke and tried desperately to undo the damage. 'I wanted to play you my song. With the words. To see if you liked it.'

Solange's irritation dissolved immediately. The boy was so earnest, it was impossible not to warm to him. 'But you do not have your concertina.'

'I could go and get it.'

'No, no,' she smiled. 'I must visit my cousin.'

'Tomorrow then. We could meet somewhere.' She seemed uncertain. 'The rotunda,' he added hastily, 'we could listen to the brass band and then we could go for a walk and I could play you my song.'

She laughed. 'Very well. The rotunda. At three o'clock. Goodbye, Enrico.'

They met once a week after that, on either a Saturday or a Sunday. They would go for a walk and gather wildflowers, or they would take a picnic lunch into the bush and Enrico would play her his latest song. He couldn't stop writing songs now; they poured out of him. And every once in a while they would go to the rotunda and listen to the brass band.

Sometimes Solange would look at Enrico and think fondly that her young brother in Houilles would be close to his age now. It was good to have such a friend, she thought. Outside of the brothel, she had no friends. Few of the prostitutes did. They kept to themselves. It was better that way.

FLAGS WERE FLYING in the streets of Boulder and lines of

bunting stretched across Burt Street, the main thoroughfare. The Municipal Brass Band played 'Land of Hope and Glory' and hundreds of sightseers lined the pavements as the Governor's party and guests of honour arrived for the official opening of the Boulder Town Hall.

The weather was not in keeping with the celebrations. It was a bleak, damp winter afternoon in June, but Paul Dunleavy was thankful as he watched the ceremony with the Kalgoorlie mayoral contingent and other select guests of honour. Paul had arrived on the goldfields in February and he'd thought the summer would never end.

The official party was received by a guard of honour from the Goldfields Infantry Regiment and, as His Excellency the Governor Sir Frederick Belford opened the front door of the hall with a souvenir gold key, the crowds applauded vociferously.

Inside the hall, Paul sat next to Kalgoorlie's Deputy Mayor Harry Brearley and his wife Maudie and studied the architecture. It was simple but of a pleasing design, he decided, casting his eye over the high wooden-panelled ceilings and the heavy carved dress-circle balcony.

'Impressive, isn't it?' Maudie whispered, her mind numbed by the endless official speeches.

Paul smiled. 'More impressive than Mr Gribble,' he whispered back as the Boulder Town Clerk concluded his speech. Paul liked Maudie. He wasn't so sure about her husband, 'Flash Harry', although he'd agreed that the Midas Christmas party was to be held at Restaurant Picot. It was a whole six months away—he wondered how he'd allowed himself to be persuaded. But then, Harry Brearley was a difficult man to say no to.

Paul had met Harry at Hannan's Businessmen's Club several months after his arrival and had accepted the Australian's offer to dine with him and his wife at Restaurant Picot. After a superb meal of international standard, which had greatly surprised Paul, Harry had cross-examined him about the Midas.

'Rumour has it the Midas is going to be closed down,' Harry had said, leaning back in his chair and lighting up his Havana. He'd registered Dunleavy's surprise at the service and cuisine and was proud of himself. He'd shown the American they had style here in Kalgoorlie. 'Is it true?'

It was certainly true that Paul's initial impulse upon inspecting the mine had been to advise Lord Lionel Laverton and the London board of directors to cut their losses and close down the Midas, but he was hardly going to admit that to Harry. He was taken aback by the man's presumption in questioning him so. Despite his conviviality, his tailored clothes and social flair, Harry Brearlely was crass, Paul decided.

'No,' he answered simply, 'no, the Midas will not be closed down.' He hoped that the brevity of his answer would terminate the conversation.

'But the mine manager's been dismissed,' Harry insisted, 'and workers are being laid off, left, right and centre.'

Paul had indeed dismissed the mine manager, along with a number of employees in key positions. The manager had been the second appointed since the Laverton debacle and he and his predecessor had both been utterly incompetent. Not criminally so, but they had been incapable of repairing the damage wrought by Richard Laverton.

'We will appoint a new manager in due course,' he replied, wishing the man would shut up.

'And the miners . . . dozens of men laid off I'm told.'

'Harry!' Maudie had recognised Paul's reticence. 'Stop pestering Mr Dunleavy,' she said good-naturedly.

Paul appreciated Maudie's motives but the forthright way she expressed herself didn't really help matters. He was, after all, Harry's dinner guest. 'It's perfectly all right, Mrs Brearley, I assure you. We will, of course, be re-employing miners when further assessments have been carried out.' He nodded gratefully to the waiter who offered to refill his coffee cup.

Paul had quickly realised that his impulse to recommend the closure of the Midas had stemmed from his desire to return home—he had taken an instant dislike to outback Australia. But such an action would be cowardly. It was his duty to rescue the Midas, and to restore it to its past glory. It wasn't as if there was a lack of gold to be mined, the problem was merely finding a cost-effective way of going about it. The fact that the underground manager, employed since the disaster of the previous year, had been dishonest hadn't helped. Gold stealing was rife amongst the miners. He'd dismissed at least fifty per cent of them and set about finding a trustworthy underground boss.

It had been Alwyn Llewellyn, the longest-serving employee at the Midas, who had recommended Giovanni Gianni.

'An Italian?' Paul had queried.

'Yes, but he's educated, he can read and write. He's a damn good miner and he's as honest as the day is long. Furthermore, he saved my life. He's a man you can rely on, Mr Dunleavy, sir.'

The injuries Alwyn had sustained in the tunnel collapse prevented him from ever again working underground. His femur had been broken and he still suffered severe bouts of pain in his left hip. In recognition of his services, however, he had been guaranteed full aboveground employment upon his recovery. Paul Dunleavy had immediately evaluated him as an honest man amongst the ranks and had looked to him for inside information.

'Tell me more about this Gianni,' Paul had said. 'His private life?'

'He married recently.'

'Good. Good.' Paul liked employing married men in positions of authority. He found them more stable.

'And he supports two children by his wife's previous marriage.' Alwyn desperately wanted his friend to get the job—Giovanni needed the money, he knew it. 'She was a widow,' he added hastily.

'Ah, I see . . . Two children. Good. Good.' A man with family obligations, Paul liked that too. 'Very well,' he'd said. 'I shall interview Mr Gianni.'

As the waiter finished filling his coffee cup, Paul decided that brevity was perhaps not the way to put an end to Harry's unwanted interrogation. Whenever there was a pause, the man fired another question. He must pretend to offer information without being specific. 'Why, only the other day I employed a highly recommended underground manager,' he nodded a thank you to the waiter, 'and following our further assessments, we will appoint experts at every level. I assure you, Mr Brearley, the Midas will flourish once more, have no doubt of it.'

'Harry. Please. Call me Harry.'

'Harry. Of course.' Paul breathed a sigh of relief. The questions were over. 'And you must call me Paul,' he added reluctantly. He would rather not have encouraged familiarity, but as Flash Harry was his host, he had no option.

'So who have you appointed as underground manager, Paul?'

Dear God, would the man never stop? As yet, no announcements had been made and Paul was damned if he was going to pass on any inside information to Harry Brearley.

Maudie laughed loudly. 'Harry,' she said, 'you're incorrigible.'

In her own way, Paul decided, Maudie was as crass as her husband. But there was something open, honest and eminently likeable about her. 'As a matter of fact,' he said, trying to evade the question, 'I'm looking forward to meeting the families of the men I appoint.' He directed his conversation toward Maudie hoping that, by engaging her, he would distract Harry. 'It is a method very much employed in America, to involve the families of company staff. To form a bond, to improve morale. A mid-year picnic is the custom, or a Christmas party for all the families.'

Harry was finally distracted. 'That's it!' he exclaimed. 'A mid-year party for the Midas families. Right here at Restaurant Picot. You could book out the whole place!'

Paul had to admire the man's eye for the main chance. 'It's a little early for that, Harry,' he smiled. 'We haven't even appointed the principal players yet.'

'A Christmas party then.' Like a dog with a bone, there was no way Harry was going to let go. 'You'll need Restaurant Picot for a Christmas party, my friend.' Harry had so admired Gaston's form of address that he'd adopted it himself. It was a pity he couldn't actually use '*mon ami*', but that would have been a little too pretentious. 'It gets damned hot in Kal at Christmas. But here,' he waved aloft at the huge ceiling fans, 'here you'll be as cool as a cucumber.'

Christmas in Kalgoorlie. Paul shuddered at the thought, a brief image of snowmen in Copley Square flashing through his mind. How he'd hoped to be home for Christmas. But of course it would be impossible. It would take a full year to sort out the problems at the Midas.

'Fine, Harry. A Christmas party at Restaurant Picot would be just fine.'

'ALWYN LLEWELLYN SPEAKS very highly of you, Giovanni.'

'He is a good friend.'

Paul Dunleavy recognised the simplicity and sincerity of the man. The eyes were direct and honest, as were the answers to his questions. The records before him stated that Giovanni Gianni was born in 1872, but he appeared younger than his thirty-six years. Probably because he was clean-shaven, Paul thought. But the scar looked as if it were the result of a knife wound.

'You've been involved in the odd fight or two I take it?'

'Only when I have had to.' It didn't occur to Giovanni to lie.

Paul respected him for it. 'You've recently married, Alwyn tells me.'

'Yes, sir, Mr Dunleavy.' The mere mention of his wife brought an involuntary smile to the Italian's lips, his face glowed with a boyish happiness. 'In February.'

Caterina had refused to marry Giovanni until one year after Evan's death and, during that year, no one had known of their affair. Regularly, on Sundays, Giovanni had visited Caterina and the children but he always left before nightfall. And regularly, in the veil of night, Caterina had visited him. They'd make love in the dingy little palace of his room and he'd sing to her and they'd talk and laugh and hold each other close. Then, before dawn, she'd quietly steal home.

When they had married, the townspeople were happy for them. Giovanni had been so good to the family since Evan's death. Why, the boy already thought of him as a father. Young Paul Jones was calling himself Paolo Gianni these days. It was a good thing for all concerned, they had decided. Kalgoorlie was no place for a widow with two children. Kate needed a husband.

'And you have two children?' Dunleavy continued.

'Yes, sir.'

'Excellent. I like employing family men, men with responsibilities.'

Giovanni nodded, his eyes never leaving Dunleavy's. He knew the American was appraising him but he wasn't sure what was expected of him. He'd anticipated questions about mining procedure, the duties of an underground boss, not enquiries about his personal life.

When Alwyn had first mentioned the job, Giovanni had had some trepidations as to his abilities. 'The rocks don't speak to me, Alwyn,' he'd said, 'I can't hear the rocks.'

Alwyn had smiled. 'We none of us know if we can truly hear them, Giovanni.' Then, realising the Italian's concern was genuine, he'd added, 'But if the rocks are going to talk to anyone it will be to a man with music in him. That's why they talked to Evan, I swear.'

Giovanni decided to answer the questions as briefly and simply as possible. Mr Dunleavy was a clever man, educated, accustomed to command. He recognised also that, like most men in a position of authority, Mr Dunleavy enjoyed exercising his power.

The interview did not last long. They shook hands and Paul said, 'I look forward to meeting your family one day, Giovanni.'

'Thank you, Mr Dunleavy, sir.'

IT WAS A fine September morning, a Sunday, when the children were out playing with their friends and Caterina and Giovanni had stolen back into the bedroom to make love, that she told him.

Curled, naked, her head against his shoulder, one thigh draped over his, she whispered, 'I am going to have a baby.'

Before that morning Giovanni had thought that nothing could make his life richer, fuller. He'd been wrong. His smile was one of pure joy as he smoothed her hair back and kissed her. Then he noticed the concern in her eyes. 'What could be more wonderful?' he asked.

'Babies cost money, Giovanni, and there is the children's schooling.'

Although Giovanni had been employed as underground boss for nearly four months, their expenses had been substantial, particularly their move to a three-bedroomed house. 'Paolo will need his own room to study when he goes to the School of Mines,' Giovanni had said proudly. 'Just think, Caterina, we will have a scholar in the family.'

Now he laughed at her concern. 'Why do you think of money when we are having a baby, you foolish woman?' He continued to laugh as he rolled her around on the bed until, infected by his exhilaration, she laughed with him. They were still laughing as they made love.

Later in the day, over lunch, they informed the children. Eight-year-old Briony was sceptical—'Will it be a sister?'—but Paolo was happy, simply because his mother and Giovanni were happy.

'Can I tell Enrico?' he asked. Despite an eighteen-month age difference and a healthy rivalry for Giovanni's affection, the two boys were firm friends.

Giovanni looked at Caterina who nodded. 'Yes, you may tell Enrico,' she said and Paolo bolted from the table. 'After you have washed the dishes.'

But he was already out the door. 'It's Briony's turn,' he yelled over his shoulder.

SIXTEEN-YEAR-OLD Paolo was happier than he had ever been. For the first time in his life he felt a sense of identity. It was all because of Giovanni. He loved the way Giovanni called his mother Caterina—everyone else still called her Kate—and he loved the way Giovanni spoke of Italy. Now Paul Jones was Paolo Gianni and he was proud of his newfound identity. It gave him a sense of belonging, a completeness he had never experienced before.

Paolo headed directly for the rotunda where a brass band always played on a Sunday afternoon and where Enrico was invariably to be found.

A popular weekend gathering place, the rotunda was Kalgoorlie's pride and joy. Picturesque and ornate, it sat in a small square park off Hannan Street in the very centre of town, the greenery of the park defying the surrounding countryside.

Today Enrico was not in his customary position, tapping his foot and marking time with the band. Paolo looked about for him. A group of youths, several of whom he recognised, were milling in the far corner of the park and he walked towards them.

'Bastardo!' It was Enrico's voice. A scream of rage. Paolo could hardly believe it.

In the centre of the group, a fight had broken out. Paolo elbowed his way through the surrounding boys who were shouting their encouragement.

Jack Brearley and Enrico Gianni were wrestling and it was Enrico who had the advantage. His attack had come as a complete surprise and now he straddled Jack, his hands around the other boy's throat. *'Bastardo!'* he yelled as he smashed Jack's head back hard against the ground. *'Bastardo!'* And again Jack's head was smashed against the ground as Enrico desperately tried to throttle the life out of him.

For a moment, Paolo stood amazed. He had never seen such rage in his friend. He stepped forward to pull Enrico away but, as he did, the tide of battle turned. Neither Enrico's element of surprise nor his rage were a match for Jack's superior strength and weight. The Australian smashed his fist hard into the Italian boy's ribs. Then again. And again. Enrico's grip weakened and the two of them rolled together in the dirt, Jack punching and kicking as hard as he could until, seconds later, he was the one on top. Now it was his hands around Enrico's throat. He held him down with ease, one hand only, as he scooped up a fistful of dust.

'Have you had enough? Do you give in?' he panted as he trickled the dust over Enrico's face. The boy spluttered and twisted his head from side to side. 'Go on,' Jack sneered, 'say it. Say "I give in".'

Enrico was choking now, the dust in his mouth, his nose, his eyes, but he snarled as he twisted under Jack's weight. Never would he give in. Never.

'Let him go.' Paolo gripped Jack's collar and tried to drag him off Enrico, but there was no budging him.

'Not until he says he gives in.' Jack didn't even look up at the person who was intervening as he gathered another fistful of dirt. 'Say you give in, dago.'

Paolo stood to one side. 'You're a coward, Jack. You're a bully and a coward.' Jack didn't release his grip on Enrico, but he did look up. 'You've beaten him before,' Paul continued, 'where's the competition? Why don't you try me instead? It'd be a fairer fight.' Paolo had never been in a fight in his life and he didn't relish the prospect now, but he stood prepared.

Slowly Jack got to his feet. Paolo was a good two inches taller than he was, although their weight was about the same. He knew he could beat the older boy, but he didn't want to. He'd always liked Paul, always respected him. Paul was clever.

'I'm not a bully and I'm not a coward. He picked the fight.' Jack looked at Enrico who had rolled over onto his knees, coughing and spitting. 'It's up to him to finish it.'

'He'll never give in and you know it.' Paul had always liked Jack too. He didn't any more. 'That's what makes you a bully.'

Jack shrugged. 'All right. I'll leave him alone. But

you keep him away from me, Paul, or he'll cop it again. By hell he will.'

'My name's Paolo.'

'Yeah,' Jack sneered. 'You're a dago just like him. Why don't you go back to your own country?' He swaggered off, several of the other boys swaggering with him, patting him on the back. But he didn't like losing Paul's friendship and respect. He didn't really feel he'd won at all.

'Let's get out of here.' Paolo half dragged Enrico into the back street behind the park. People were looking and any second Sergeant Baldy Hetherington might arrive. They sat on the kerb, Enrico still spitting the last of the dust from his mouth.

'Here.' Paolo handed him his handkerchief. Enrico didn't look at him as he wiped his face and he didn't offer any explanation. 'What was it all about?' Paolo asked finally.

'Nothing.'

'But Jack said you started it.'

'I did.'

'Why?'

'Thanks.' Enrico handed him back the handkerchief and stood up.

'Enrico—'

'I don't want to talk about it.' He started to walk away, then turned. 'Thanks for standing up for me.'

Paolo watched his friend cross the park. What had happened?

ENRICO DIDN'T SLEEP much that night. The ugly scene with Jack kept playing over and over in his mind and he kept hearing the words that had made him sick with anger.

'Where's your girl?' Jack had jeered. 'Found something better to do on a Sunday afternoon, has she?' His tone was suggestive and the boys with him sniggered.

'What girl?'

'Your girl from Red Ruby's. The Frenchie.'

'She's not from Red Ruby's,' he answered defensively. 'She visits her cousin who's a chambermaid there.'

'The hell she does.' When Jack laughed, Enrico felt his anger swell and, even before the words were uttered, he knew he wanted to smash the lascivious smirk from the Australian's face. 'She lives there, you dumb dago. She's a whore.'

And, as the other boys joined in the laughter, Enrico heard himself scream '*Bastardo!*' He felt the explosion of his rage as he hurled himself at Jack.

Now, as he lay in his bunk, reliving the scene, Enrico no longer felt sick with anger, he felt sick with the knowledge that Jack was right. And with the realisation that, deep down, he had always known. From the very start, from that first time he'd played her his song as they sat in the gutter, he'd known. But he had refused to recognise the truth.

Enrico rose early the following morning, breakfasted with the family and, as usual, left for school carrying the lunch his mother had packed. In the evening the family dined together and retired early as they always did during the week. And, whilst the rest of the household was sleeping, Enrico stole the money from his mother's housekeeping jar.

It was after eleven o'clock when he arrived at Red Ruby's and it was raining. Not heavily, but relentlessly, the drizzle converting the red dust to mud. Enrico was soaked but he didn't hesitate at the shuttered doors; he pushed them open and stepped quickly inside.

The large lounge area was dim but not gloomy. The lighting brackets on the walls gave off a rosy glow that was warm and cosy. There was a bar at the far end of the room. A heavy-set man sat on a stool beside it and a girl was pouring drinks. Several other girls were lounging around and two men and women were seated in sofas and armchairs, chatting intimately. Enrico hadn't known what to expect but it all looked very orderly and companionable. Perhaps he'd been expecting something a little more bawdy. Then he noticed that the women were wearing very little beneath their open smocks and gowns and he quickly averted his eyes.

There was a desk beside the front doors and a middle-aged woman had risen from her seat behind it. She was smartly dressed, wore steel-rimmed spectacles and had the no-nonsense face of a schoolteacher.

'Can I help you, young man?' She had the voice of a schoolteacher too, and Enrico suddenly felt a little nervous. But he answered boldly.

'I want to see Solange.'

Ada frowned. For a long time now, from her front corner apartment, she had watched the comings and goings of Solange and the boy during weekend afternoons. Ada prided herself on running the most efficient and well-ordered brothel in Kalgoorlie and she wanted to know who her girls associated with and where they went. She didn't disapprove of Solange's association with the boy, but it was her rule that personal relationships were always to be conducted outside the brothel.

'Mr McAllister.' She beckoned to the heavy-set man beside the bar who rose and joined them. 'If Solange is available she may have a quick word with her young friend.' Ada knew only too well that Solange was available. Her last client had left a quarter of an hour ago. She would have douched and powdered by now in preparation for the next.

McAllister begrudgingly clumped away to fetch Solange. He didn't like Ada ordering him around but, always, there was something so prim and polite in her manner that he found himself automatically obeying.

'Take your muddy boots off, boy.'

Enrico had been prepared to put his money on the table and demand time with Solange. That was how they did business in brothels, wasn't it? You paid your money and you bought a girl. But the manner of the schoolmistress was intimidating. Enrico did as he was told.

'Enrico.' Solange was surprised to see him, certainly, but she didn't appear at all mortified. Somehow Enrico had expected her to be mortified. She didn't even bother to close the front of her lace-trimmed smock which openly displayed the satin corset and knee-length knickers beneath. Enrico could plainly see the full swell of her breasts above the light-boned corset. 'What are you doing here?' she asked.

'I came to see you.' He wondered whether now was the time to ask 'How much?' and to put his money on the desk for the madam to see that he could pay.

'Personal meetings take place outside, Solange,' Ada said sternly, 'you're fully aware of that.'

'Yes, I am aware of course and I am sorry, Ada, truly I am. But I did not know that he was going to come here.' She gave the madam her most disarming smile. Solange was one of the few who could get around Ada. 'And I can hardly take him outside now, can I? It is raining. Has something happened, Enrico?'

'Oh, for goodness' sake, girl,' Ada muttered, 'you can't stand around discussing your personal affairs. The boy's soaking wet. Take him away and get him dried off.' Solange beamed another smile. 'No more than half an hour, mind. Leave the boots here,' Ada added as Enrico bent to pick them up.

Solange led him through the door beside the bar at the far end of the lounge and into one of the rows of little shuttered bedrooms.

'This is my room,' she said, closing the door behind

them. 'It is prettier than the others. I bought the lamp-shade and the counterpane myself.'

He stood silently staring at her. At her breasts and her bare legs. How could she chatter on as if nothing had happened?

Solange sighed. Was he going to make a scene? Always they had such fun together, she and Enrico, why must he be so serious now? She sat on the bed, her smock fully open, but she didn't appear to notice. 'Why did you come here, Enrico? You get me into trouble by coming here.' Still he stared at her; she could feel his eyes as they roamed over her breasts and her calves and ankles. Solange didn't mind. She liked to be looked at and admired and she had known for a long time that Enrico was in love with her. She'd enjoyed it, reacted to it, flirted with him. She'd found it amusing, even touching. She was genuinely fond of the boy. He was her friend. And now he was going to spoil it all.

'Oh come, Enrico, why so serious? You knew. Why pretend that you did not? We played the game of my cousin the chambermaid, but you knew.' She suddenly felt a touch of uncertainty. 'You did, didn't you?'

'Yes, I suppose I did.'

'Then don't judge me, you silly boy.' Although she said it with humour, she meant it. 'I don't judge others, you don't judge me.'

Enrico felt a flash of resentment. He didn't like being called a 'silly boy'. 'I didn't come here to judge you,' he said and he took the money out of the top pocket of his rain-soaked shirt. 'I came here to buy what you're selling.' He threw the small wad of damp notes onto the bed beside her. 'Is it enough?'

She looked up at him. He wasn't angry, she realised, he was hurt. 'How old are you?'

'Seventeen.'

He was certainly not seventeen, but she knew better

than to laugh or question him. Fifteen? Sixteen? What did it matter, she told herself. He was a young man—he was ready. Solange herself had lost her virginity when she was fourteen.

'Your first time?'

He nodded, and for some strange reason, muttered it in Italian. *'Io sono vergine.'*

The instant Solange laughed, the atomosphere was broken. It was the laughter she had shared with him so many times. Girlish, impudent, infectious. 'I should hope so,' she said.

She stood and unbuttoned his shirt. 'Get out of these wet clothes,' she ordered. 'Here,' she said, handing him a towel as he fumbled impatiently with his trousers, 'dry yourself, or it will be like making love to a fish.'

Enrico had never been naked in front of a woman before but he didn't have time to feel awkward or embarrassed. Suddenly she was naked too. Gloriously, beautifully naked. 'We have only fifteen minutes,' she said. She put her arms around his neck and kissed him and the moment he felt her breasts and her thighs against him, Enrico was on fire. He clasped her shoulders and her back and her hair and her buttocks. He fumbled for her breasts and her buttocks; he couldn't get enough of her. They stumbled backwards onto the bed, Enrico landing on top, and Solange laughed. 'But of course young men like you do not need much time,' she said.

He didn't. Even as she reached down to guide him, he was inside her, thrusting, groaning, delirious. And, expertly, she met his every thrust. It was only a matter of seconds before his world exploded and he lay panting on top of her, dazed by the experience.

Solange laughed as she pushed him off her. 'You do not need lessons, Enrico,' she said, 'but next time we do it, we will do it more slowly.'

'Next time.' She had said 'Next time'. Enrico grinned up at the ceiling, euphoric.

'Now hurry and get dressed or Ada will be very angry with me.' She jumped up from the bed.

'I love you, Solange.'

'Of course you do, you silly boy.' This time he didn't mind the 'silly boy' at all. 'And here,' she picked up his damp shirt and pushed the little wad of notes back into the upper pocket, 'you keep your money. This was not business.'

'Solange . . .' He sat up and reached for her but she eluded him.

'No, no,' she said, thrusting his trousers at him. 'Quick, you must go.' She helped him as he fumbled about with his clothes and then, pushing him to the door, said, 'I will meet you on Saturday and we will have a picnic.' She grinned mischievously and the way she said 'picnic' held a cheeky promise. Enrico tried to kiss her but she pushed him away.

'Don't forget your boots,' she hissed and thrust them into his arms just before she closed the door.

Chapter Twenty

It was a goldfields December. As hot and dry and dusty as the February Paul had arrived. It had only been ten months ago, but it felt like a lifetime. He missed his beloved Boston, and longed for the charm and wit of his wife and the rebellious chatter of his daughter. But Paul was proud of the success he'd achieved at the Midas. The mine was already back on its feet and in six months it would be flourishing as it had in its heyday. Then he could go home, proud of the fact that he had done his duty. But he quailed at the thought of the long, relentless summer ahead.

It was the middle of the day and Paul stood in the downstairs lounge of Restaurant Picot, welcoming the arrival of the Midas staff and their families, grateful to Harry Brearley for the choice of venue. The man had been quite right, Restaurant Picot must surely be the coolest place in Kalgoorlie, he thought as he felt the welcome breeze from the giant ceiling fans.

'Henry!' Henry Vandenberg was the recently appointed mine manager, hand-picked by Paul himself. A humourless Dutchman who ruled with a rod of iron, he had worked with Paul in South Africa. Paul didn't like the man much but had to admit that he was the best in the business.

Paul greeted Vandenberg's wife and family and

made the correct noises about how much the three children had grown since he'd met them as babies. Then he encouraged them to move on and mingle with the others as he turned to greet the next arrivals.

Alwyn Llewellyn and his wife, Eileen, with their five daughters, each one dressed to the nines. Alwyn introduced his family with pride then politely withdrew, not wishing to monopolise too much of Mr Dunleavy's time.

'What do you say, my friend, a triumph already and the party has not even begun. What do you think of the decorations?' Harry Brearley was at Paul's side, puffing on his interminable cigar, thumbs tucked in his waistcoat pockets, surveying the scene like a king his realm. Maudie was busy organising the endless stream of waiters with trays of drinks and hors d'oeuvres for the adults and treats and lemonade for the children.

'Very impressive, Harry, very impressive. You've done a fine job.' The decorations were indeed Harry's triumph, particularly the massive Christmas tree in the far corner of the lounge, woven with a sea of coloured lights which flickered on and off. It seemed incongruous to Paul, a fir tree in this godforsaken place, and he wondered where Harry had got it from but he didn't bother asking. 'Spare no expense,' he'd said to Harry, and Harry hadn't.

'There's more to come,' Harry boasted. 'Just you wait till you see the luncheon, the chef has done himself proud.' The adults were to dine upstairs in the restaurant proper and the children were to picnic downstairs and be entertained by clowns and a magician.

'Australian crayfish,' Harry continued. 'Packed in ice, delivered fresh from Esperance this morning. Took all night to get them here.' He plucked the cigar from his mouth and rocked on his heels, relishing the announcement. Harry had put on a little weight lately and grown a huge handlebar moustache. He knew he looked good—prosperous. 'I'll wager you've never tasted anything like Australian crayfish.'

A brief vision of the fresh lobsters from Maine which were his passion flashed through Paul's mind. 'I'm sure I haven't Harry, I'm sure I haven't.' Mercifully Paul was rescued from Harry's further bragging by the arrival of Tony Prendergast and young Freddie.

Freddie was thrilled at his inclusion. He had not expected an invitation at all. But, as it turned out, any man who had worked an honest living at the Midas for three or more years was invited to the Christmas party. Freddie had worked at the Midas for just on five years and, as Alwyn said, no man had worked harder or more honestly than young Freddie.

Harry waited impatiently for Prendergast and Freddie to leave. He had been enjoying his conversation with Paul, he hadn't even mentioned the string quartet yet. That was his big surprise and he couldn't wait to boast about it. He looked out at the street and the other guests arriving, a number of them in automobiles.

Harry himself had been amongst the first in Kalgoorlie to acquire a motorised vehicle and he was very proud of his twenty-five horsepower Talbot Tourer.

'We must move with the times, Maudie,' he'd said when she'd complained that automobiles would frighten the horses. 'This is the age of the motor vehicle.' And he was right, of course, as, more and more, the clip-clop of horses' hooves was drowned out by the honk of horns and the sputter of car engines.

Maudie, however, remained unconvinced. 'No good will come of them,' she said, 'they're not natural.' And every time a motor car back-fired and the horses shied, so did Maudie.

Harry's beam of satisfaction suddenly faded. Giovanni Gianni, his wife Kate and her children Briony and Paolo had just rounded the corner, on foot of course.

They did not own a vehicle of any kind, not even a horse and buggy.

Harry didn't excuse himself, he turned tail and walked upstairs to the restaurant. He would not make a scene. He had known only too well that Giovanni had been invited. He had done his utmost to prevent it but Paul Dunleavy had been adamant. 'In that case we must find another venue, Harry,' he had said, and that had been that. But Harry was not about to welcome any member of the Gianni family into his midst.

Harry's hasty departure had not gone unnoticed. Giovanni had seen him standing beside Paul Dunleavy and had anticipated trouble. Giovanni did not want trouble. He'd had his misgivings about the Christmas party from the outset and had said as much to Caterina.

'Harry Brearley's restaurant,' he had said. 'I will not go.'

'Giovanni, of course you must go,' she'd insisted. 'You owe it to Mr Dunleavy. He has done you a great honour, you said so yourself. An Italian underground boss! No Australian would have given you such an opportunity.'

She was right, of course; besides, Giovanni could not afford to insult Mr Dunleavy—it might cost him his job. The welfare of his family must come first.

Now, as he crossed the street with his wife and children, he was grateful to see Harry deliberately avoid him. Good. Harry Brearley did not want trouble either.

Giovanni smiled at Caterina. She would be the most beautiful woman at the party, he thought with pride. She was wearing the blue hat with the satin plume. The one she had worn to the banquet all those years ago. He could remember how he had watched the blue hat draw nearer and nearer during the Pride of Erin waltz. How he'd prayed that the music wouldn't stop before the hat reached him and his girl from the mountains was in his arms. And now she was his wife. And she was to have his baby. Giovanni was bursting with pride.

'You will be the most beautiful woman present,' he whispered.

A small willy-willy swept down Hannan Street. As they stepped from the pavement, it whirled about them and Kate grasped at her hat. The unruly auburn curls she had so painstakingly pinned up escaped in an instant. 'I will be the untidiest woman present,' she laughed as they walked up the front steps to the Restaurant Picot.

'Giovanni.' Paul Dunleavy broke off his conversation with Tony Prendergast and Freddie and extended his hand to the Italian. 'And your family. At long last I meet your family.' Paul glimpsed a beautiful face beneath the blue hat as the woman smiled at her husband.

'Yes, sir. Caterina, this is Mr Dunleavy. Mr Dunleavy, my wife—' Giovanni had been about to say 'Kate', but Dunleavy interrupted.

'Caterina . . .' The eyes that had looked up to meet his were eyes so blue that they danced. Her mouth was full and sensual, rich auburn curls framed her face, and Paul recognised her in an instant.

Caterina was momentarily disconcerted. She knew this man. From where? 'I am called Kate,' she corrected politely but firmly. 'Caterina is a family name.' This might well be the powerful Mr Dunleavy, she thought, but only Giovanni called her Caterina. She smiled to soften the words and hoped she did not sound rude, but Mr Dunleavy appeared not to have heard. His eyes, strangely familiar, remained transfixed upon her. He reminded her of someone. Who? And suddenly she remembered. Paul. Her Paul from the chalet. His name had been Dunleavy—how could she have forgotten?

There was a moment's awkward pause as they

stared at each other. Giovanni was confused, tongue-tied, knowing something was happening between his wife and Mr Dunleavy. It was Tony Prendergast who came to the rescue and continued the introductions.

'This is Kate's son, Paul,' he said.

'Paolo, sir. How do you do?' Paolo's correction was automatic as he shook the hand extended to him.

'And this is Briony.' It was Giovanni who finished the introductions and the girl bobbed a curtsy as her mother had taught her. But Paul Dunleavy had not released the boy's hand. Now it was Paolo upon whom his gaze was focused.

The eyes that looked back at him could have been his own, Paul realised. Clear, grey, questioning eyes. He was looking at himself as a boy.

'Paolo was it?' he said. He knew he was holding onto the boy's hand too long, but he was loath to relinquish it. Paolo. He'd loved the way she'd called him Paolo, he remembered now, particularly as they lay in each other's arms, warm and sated, watching the snow through the chalet windows gently blanket the mountainside.

'Yes, sir, Paolo Gianni.'

'Well,' Paul turned to Giovanni, forcing his mind back to the present, 'this is a fine family you have, Giovanni.' He beamed his most avuncular smile at the girl he'd ignored. 'And Briony must be the prettiest young lady in Kalgoorlie, she obviously takes after her mother.' He risked a smile at Kate. She'd recognised him, he knew it. He would try and see her alone later. 'Please, enjoy yourselves.' He gestured expansively to the waiters with their trays of food and drinks, then turned to greet the new arrivals.

'Look after Briony,' Kate instructed as Paolo left to join a group of the younger guests. She accepted a glass of champagne from the tray a waiter offered them.

Giovanni said nothing, but watched her closely as he sipped from his own glass. There was a query in his eyes and she knew he was waiting for the answer.

'I knew him,' she said, 'a long time ago.' She looked at Paul Dunleavy as he played host. He wore his power and wealth with ease. He had been born to it, she realised. He had always been born to it; she had simply been an adventure. He was very recognisable to her now. Age had thickened his body and his fine patrician face had coarsened a little with time but he was the same man, even in the way he swept his now greying fringe from his brow. She smiled to herself. How easily she had forgotten him. He darted a glance in her direction and she looked away. 'A very long time ago,' she said.

'Paolo . . .?' Giovanni asked. He already knew the answer.

'Yes.'

'Did you love him?'

'I thought I did.' As she put one arm around his waist, he automatically returned the embrace and he could feel the softness of her skin under the fabric; she was nearly five months pregnant and no longer wore corsets beneath her gowns. Giovanni wished they could go home and make love. Gently, lying sideways as they now did during her pregnancy.

'He was the first,' she continued. She could feel Giovanni's thigh against hers and, beneath her fingertips, she could feel his hip bone. If she were to run her fingers lightly down that beautiful groove between his hip bone and his groin . . . She wished they could go home. 'He was the first,' she shrugged, 'so I thought I loved him.' She moved her thigh very gently against his and he slid his hand up from her waist until it was almost upon her breast. They smiled teasingly at each other. 'I was very young,' she whispered, 'how was I to know?' His hand closed upon her breast and he leaned down under the blue hat to kiss her, but she ducked quickly out of the embrace, spilling her champagne. 'Giovanni!' she hissed, but her eyes sparkled with desire as she darted self-conscious looks at the guests milling about.

'Nobody would notice if we went home,' he murmured.

'Yes they would.'

'But we have a responsibility,' Giovanni said seriously. 'We must discuss what has happened, whether we tell Paolo or—'

'There is plenty of time to discuss what has happened,' she smiled. 'Paolo has lived without the knowledge of his father for sixteen years, a day or two more won't hurt. Now come along.' She put her arm firmly into his. 'We are going to mingle and we are going to say all the right things to all the right people.' She led him into the fray.

IT WAS TOWARDS the end of the luncheon that Paul Dunleavy approached her. He had been seated at the far end of the restaurant, at a table near the balcony, with Harry and Maudie Brearley and Henry Vandenberg and his wife. Kate and Giovanni had been seated at the far wall, on the other side of the main staircase. Harry had made sure of that.

'Mrs Gianni,' he said quietly. She turned to see him standing beside her chair. 'May I have a word with you?' Kate looked at Giovanni who nodded. She thought it rude of Dunleavy not to have referred to her husband.

'Of course,' she said and she accompanied him downstairs to one of the deserted front booths, away from the excited cries of the children being entertained by the magician at the rear of the lounge.

She was pregnant, he realised. Not hugely, but noticeably. He didn't comment upon it. It was unusual for a noticeably pregnant woman to be seen in society—but then, this was Kalgoorlie.

'Caterina . . .'

'Kate.'

'Yes, of course. Kate.' He was disconcerted. He remembered the vividness of her blue eyes. He remembered, as if it were yesterday, how they had looked at him so trustingly. *'Io sono vergine,'* she had said. How could he have forgotten? Now, these same blue eyes disconcerted him. He didn't know where to begin.

'I wanted to come back and find you,' he said. It was a lie. He hadn't. He had married Elizabeth only months after his return from Steinach that winter. Everyone had approved. Elizabeth was old family too. A true Bostonian.

She nodded and smiled and he sensed that she didn't believe him, but also that she didn't care and that it didn't matter. He was even more disconcerted. He cleared his throat. 'Paolo . . .' he began.

'Paolo is your son.'

Paul wasn't sure whether he admired her for such a blatant admission or whether he found it tasteless. There were ways of conducting such a conversation, surely.

'Yes.' He fought against clearing his throat again. 'Does Giovanni know?'

Kate felt intensely irritated. Not only by his intimation of a secret shared, but by the manner in which he referred to her husband. She understood the protocol within the hierarchy of the Midas, she had learned it through her years with Evan. Paul Dunleavy was 'Mr Dunleavy, sir' and Giovanni was merely 'Giovanni', she understood that. But she found the condescension in Paul's tone offensive.

'I have no secrets from my husband,' she replied stiffly.

Paul realised that he had offended her in some way

but he didn't know how. Damn it, why was the woman being so proud? The situation was awkward enough as it was.

'What exactly does Paolo know of his natural father?' He thought he had voiced the question delicately. Surely the boy didn't know he was a bastard?

Kate relaxed a little. She wondered why she was being so defensive. Paul Dunleavy was a proper man and he was finding the situation very confronting. But what did he want of her? An oath of silence? Did he fear that she would broadcast the news of his bastard son? Was he afraid that she would blackmail him? She wished he would get to the point.

'I have not lied to Paolo,' Kate said. 'I told him when he was very little that his father was an American. No more, no less.'

'I see.' He seemed about to say something, then thought better of it.

'What is it you want . . .?' She couldn't bring herself to call him Paul and she was certainly not going to say 'Mr Dunleavy'.

Blunt as her question was, there was no animosity in her voice and Paul found himself answering with equal bluntness. 'I would like to know my son.'

Kate was taken aback—it was not what she had expected. She studied him for a moment. 'I will speak with Paolo,' she said finally. 'If he wishes to meet with you I will have no objection.'

Paul rose from the table, relieved that the interview was over. 'Thank you, Caterina,' he said.

'Kate.'

'SHOULD I DO it?' Caterina asked Giovanni that night. 'Should I tell Paolo?'

To Giovanni the answer was simple. 'Yes. It is a good thing for the boy to know his natural father.'

Paolo's reaction proved to be just as simple. So the American who happened to be his father was none other than the powerful Mr Dunleavy. Paolo was impressed, but it meant no more than that to him. He couldn't really think of Mr Dunleavy as his father—as far as Paolo was concerned Giovanni was his father. But the boy was proud that the American showed an interest in him.

So each weekend, on a Saturday afternoon, Mr Dunleavy paid a visit and they would talk together. Usually away from the house. Kate would offer tea but invariably Mr Dunleavy would say, 'Let's have a walk, Paolo, what do you say? I need the exercise.' And the boy came to recognise that Mr Dunleavy was not comfortable in the presence of his mother and Giovanni.

Paolo fascinated Paul Dunleavy. The boy didn't belong in Kalgoorlie. He was a brilliant student, just as Paul himself had been. And, just as Paul had done, he wanted to study mining engineering. He intended to enrol in the Kalgoorlie School of Mines.

There was nothing wrong with the Kalgoorlie School of Mines, Paul thought, it was a recognised place of learning. But it was not Harvard. And when the boy had graduated, what then? He would be stuck for the rest of his life in Kalgoorlie. Looking after his peasant family, marrying a peasant daughter of one of their peasant friends. No, the boy did not belong in Kalgoorlie at all. He didn't even look the part. His was a patrician face, his whole bearing was one of breeding. There was Dunleavy blood in him.

As the months went by, Paul filled the boy's head with stories of his travels. Then he fired the boy with excitement at what lay ahead for a successful man in his chosen field. 'A first-rate mining engineer has the world at his feet, Paolo.' He wanted to say 'son' but he dared not. Paul was aware of the bond between the boy and Giovanni, he knew he must tread warily. He talked of the vast mines in South Africa and North America, all the while watching the growing excitement in the boy's eyes. Paolo wanted to travel, he was hungry to adventure and see the world. And so he would.

As the summer passed and the goldfield's brief suggestion of autumn slid into winter, Paul became obsessed. Soon he would be returning to Boston, to the home where the boy belonged. The boy was his son. His only son and heir. The boy belonged to him.

'IT'S A VERY generous offer, Paul.'

Kate had become comfortable enough with their first-name basis, Paul noticed, but Giovanni had not.

'Yes, it is very generous,' Giovanni agreed. 'Have you spoken to Paolo?'

'No, no, no,' Paul waved a magnanimous hand as if outraged by the suggestion. 'I couldn't possibly fill the boy's head with such dreams if his own parents were against the idea. But I know that he is very keen to travel, and Harvard will most certainly accept him, be assured of that.' He smiled and added, 'I happen to be on the board of directors.'

'Why would you wish to do this?'

It was the question Paul Dunleavy had been expecting. Kate's eyes were searching his, measuring his every word, and he knew he must answer carefully. He had the feeling that Kate didn't particularly like him, although he didn't know why, and she certainly didn't trust him. Giovanni was the simple one, Paul had come to realise. A good man who expected goodness in others. There was a shrewdness in Kate and she was the one he must convince.

He leaned forward in his chair in the little front parlour of the Giannis' house where they were taking afternoon tea, and spoke with the earnestness of truth.

'He is a fine student, Kate. You know that. With his

academic abilities there is no limit to the heights he could achieve. And the Kalgoorlie School of Mines, excellent as it is, could never offer the connections he would make at Harvard. One must not underestimate the power of the old school tie.'

'That doesn't really answer my question.'

Paul refused to be disconcerted. 'I am deeply fond of Paolo, as I'm sure you're aware.' He addressed himself to Giovanni as well as Kate now. 'But I have no wish to interfere with his family life. It would mean only four years at the university and then he could have his choice of positions right here in Kalgoorlie.' He grinned at Giovanni. 'Why, he could even qualify for my job. How would you like your son as a boss, Giovanni?'

Giovanni smiled politely back. He saw no reason to distrust Mr Dunleavy. It seemed a fine opportunity for Paolo if he wished to accept the offer.

Paul relaxed. 'And of course it would allow you the financial freedom to concentrate upon your new arrival.' He glanced at the cradle in the corner where the three-month-old baby girl lay peacefully asleep. 'That is surely worthy of consideration.'

'It is worthy of no consideration at all.' Paul was taken aback by the edge in the Italian's voice. 'There will be money enough to educate Paolo, you need have no fear of that.'

'Well of course, Giovanni, of course.' Paul cursed himself. Damn it, that had been a mistake. 'I'm merely offering—'

'It is a generous offer, as we have agreed,' Giovanni cut him short, 'but it is Paolo's decision. He is of an age when he can choose his own future. I will fetch the boy.' He left abruptly and Paul was nonplussed. He had expected to win the Italian over with ease. Kate was the one whose arguments he'd feared. But he had a further weapon to use if necessary, and now was the time.

'Life's opportunities, Kate, one must always seize them when they arise, God knows they may never materialise again.' He smiled and leaned back affably in his chair. 'Giovanni, for instance. It's a rare thing for an Italian to achieve the status of underground boss. There is an element of dislike for foreigners here in Kalgoorlie. Of course I personally disapprove of such discrimination—the best man for the job is what I say, and Giovanni is certainly that—but I would hate to see my successor revert to the discriminatory pattern which seems to be the rule.'

'You would go that far?' Her voice was cold.

'Oh no, Kate, no. Good God, you misunderstand me.' Excellent, he thought, she had read his veiled warning and he was glad that he'd been saved a more explicit threat. 'Of course I shall ensure that Mr Vandenburg honours Giovanni's contract. I'm merely pointing out how advantages must be grasped when they are offered.'

The blue eyes drilled into his. 'Why? Why do you want to do this for Paolo? You have still not answered my question.'

'I want to see the boy realise his potential, Kate, no more than that. I want to offer him the opportunity to do so.'

'Very well.' She didn't believe him for a minute and he knew it. 'As Giovanni says, it must be Paolo's decision.'

'Fine, fine.' Paul relaxed. He knew what the boy's decision would be.

In eighteen months' time, when he was eighteen, Paolo would come to Boston. It was a pity he had to wait so long, Paul thought, but Kate would most certainly be suspicious if he urged the boy to join him before his eligibility for Harvard. In the meantime, he would write regularly to Paolo, and keep the fire of excitement raging in the boy.

Kate believed in the power of her influence over her son, Paul realised. She believed that, after his schooling, he would return to the family fold. She was wrong. Once Paul had him in Boston, the die would be cast. His son and heir would never return to Kalgoorlie. Paul Dunleavy would see to that.

BOOK THREE

The Soldiers
1914

Chapter Twenty-One

'It's a matter of days I tell you.' Lord Lionel Laverton took a final sip of his tea, placed the Royal Doulton cup and saucer back on the lace-clothed table and blotted his heavy handlebar moustache with a damask napkin.

'Call for another brew, my dear,' he muttered to Prudence and without drawing breath continued loudly, 'it's been going on for forty years or more, ever since the Germans took Alsace-Lorraine from the French. "The weak were made to be devoured by the strong", that's what Bismarck said then and, by Jove, it's what that megalomaniac of a Kaiser is saying right now. It will only be a matter of days before it comes to a head.'

Godfrey Brigstock and Paul Dunleavy were taking afternoon tea at the Ritz Hotel in London with Laverton and his daughter-in-law. When the three men had concluded their business meeting in the boardroom of Lord Lionel's offices in Piccadilly, Godfrey had suggested they adjourn to his club, but Lord Lionel wouldn't hear of it.

'I am to meet Prudence for tea,' he'd said. 'You must join us.'

No one refused Lord Lionel and so Godfrey Brigstock found himself sipping Darjeeling in the intricate elegance of the Ritz tea lounge when he'd far rather have been swigging on a large gin and bitters in the comfortably masculine surrounds of his club.

Lord Lionel was fully aware of Godfrey's irritation and didn't care one whit. Lord Lionel himself regularly enjoyed a good cognac and cigar in the comfort of his Mayfair club and in the company of his fellow members, all men of the old school, but never before seven of an evening. Four o'clock in the afternoon was far too early for a respectable man to be seen drinking alcohol in public. Furthermore, he wouldn't be caught dead in Brigstock's Knightsbridge club which catered to dandies and poseurs. In Lord Lionel's opinion, Godfrey Brigstock was not only a dipsomaniac, he was a fop.

'Mind you, Kaiser Bill's all talk,' Lord Lionel continued, 'he's been blustering for years. Why, he all but threatened war on Britain when he proposed a German protectorate in the Transvaal. Well Britain won't turn a blind eye much longer, I tell you.'

Paul Dunleavy well recalled the South African crisis, he'd been working in Rhodesia at the time, but he didn't join in the conversation. No one did when the old man was ranting. Paul watched the others instead, fully aware of Godfrey's discomfort—he was certainly an alcoholic—and Prudence's boredom. Lionel Laverton was a monster, he thought, but one had to respect the old boy. He was in his mid-eighties and yet his mind was as sharp as a tack. He was a little deaf and his hair was white but he walked briskly, without the aid of a stick, and seemed in fine fettle for a man of his years.

'Now, with Austria all out to attack Serbia, Germany extending her control over the Turkish army, and Russia seeking a Balkan alliance, all hell's about to break loose.' The old man was really warming up. 'They're talking war every one of them, but that's all they're doing. Talking. Britain won't talk I tell you. She won't desert France, whatever the wretched Kaiser threatens. There'll be no "mailed fist" from this side of the Channel.' He smashed his own fist so hard on the table that the Royal

Doulton rattled alarmingly and people seated nearby cast glances in his direction, but there was no stopping him now. 'The Kaiser won't know what hit him, mark my words. It'll be war I tell you. Global war!'

Paul stopped himself saying that America would certainly not involve herself in a European war, so it could hardly be global. It was never a good idea to disagree with the old man.

Paul was becoming bored with the talk of war. It was a pity the turmoil in Europe was going to involve Britain, he'd so enjoyed his stay in London, as he always did. The sooner he got back to Boston the better, he thought.

'There, there, Daddy, don't upset yourself.' It was Prudence, patting her father-in-law's hand. She couldn't really care less whether the old man upset himself but she wished he wouldn't do it in public, everyone in the lounge was staring.

'Yes, you're quite right, my dear, quite right.' Lord Lionel had had his say and was content to let Prudence think she'd calmed him. 'No point in getting all worked up over the inevitable, is there?' He rose abruptly from the table. 'Come along. Time we were leaving.'

Prudence could see the waiter approaching with the tea. The old man had forgotten that he'd asked her to order a fresh pot; his short-term memory was becoming more and more erratic lately.

'The tea, Daddy,' she reminded him.

'Ah yes. Don't feel like it now. Come along, m'dear.' And to her utter humiliation, they left without paying the bill. Prudence didn't quite have the nerve to remind him the tea had been at his invitation. One reminder of a memory loss was acceptable, two irritated him. But was it a memory loss? she wondered. Sometimes it was hard to tell.

'Put it on my bill,' Paul said when, seconds later,

Godfrey fled for a cab to Knightsbridge, 'and bring me an afternoon paper.' He drank three more cups of Darjeeling and read the *Daily Telegraph.*

'PAA-EEP-ER! PAPER!' THE newsboy chanted on the corner of Regent Street and Piccadilly. 'Archduke murdered, read all about it!'

Paul shoved a shilling in the boy's hand and didn't wait for the change. It was lunch time on the 28th of June, 1914, and the afternoon tabloids had just hit the stands. He looked at the headlines as he walked down Piccadilly. ARCHDUKE FRANZ FERDINAND AND WIFE SOFIA SHOT DEAD AT SARAJEVO.

'My God,' he said out loud.

Archduke Franz Ferdinand, heir to Francis Joseph, was murdered by Slav nationalists with the aid of a Serbian secret society known as the Black Hand. And it had happened that very morning. At eleven o'clock. Ten o'clock Greenwich Mean Time. Less than three days after their tea at the Ritz. The old man had been right.

WHEN THE AUSTRALIAN newspapers announced the murder of Franz Ferdinand, conjecture of a war in Europe was rife. Many were disinterested and said it could hardly affect Australia. Others said that if Britain entered the war, the Commonwealth countries would be called upon as allies. 'Why should Britain declare war?' was the reply. 'What does Britain care about Serbia?'

But, a month later, when Germany issued an ultimatum to France giving her eighteen hours to declare her neutrality in a Russo-German war, it was obvious to all that Britain's involvement would be total. And, on the 2nd of August, when Belgium refused Germany free passage for her troops, the die was cast.

Two days later Germany invaded Belgium and, on

that same day, the 4th of August, at 10.00 pm Greenwich Mean Time, Britain was at war.

In Kalgoorlie, wagers were placed as to when Australia would enter the fray. It was only a matter of time, they said. Excitement was in the air. Many on the goldfields wanted to go to war. The world price of gold was down, the big mines were in trouble and miners were being laid off by the dozen. A war was just what they needed. A man could sign up. He could join the army and see the world.

THERE WAS CHAOS at Kalgoorlie railway station as the special Perth-bound train prepared to leave. Hundreds of people crowded the platform. Somewhere in the street a military band played. There was always a military band playing these days. The lads were going to war. Mothers hugged sons, wives clung to husbands and lovers exchanged hungry kisses. Hampers of food and bottles of beer were thrust at the departing heroes by people they'd never met. The whole town, it seemed, had turned up to wish the boys of the 11th Battalion godspeed.

The recruiting office in Kalgoorlie had been besieged by volunteers from the moment it had opened its doors. Not just the boys from Boulder and Kal but from towns much further afield. Workers from the construction camps of the Transcontinental Railway had downed tools and caught the first westward-bound train when they'd heard that recruiting had started in Kal. Amongst them were the three husky Brereton brothers, Tom and Ben and Bill.

Many lied about their ages in a desperate bid to be accepted by the army. Some succeeded, some didn't. Rico and Teresa's thirteen-year-old son, Salvatore Gianni, was laughed at—'Come back for the next war,' the officer told him—but forty-year-old Tony Prendergast was not. Like all the men of the goldfields, he was a fine physical specimen and, like many, quick of wit—'The sun withers the skin out here, man,' he'd answered immediately when the officer from Perth said he looked older than his thirty-four years.

At the railway station, Tony Prendergast promised young Freddie's mother he'd look after her boy—Freddie was twenty-eight now but, simple as ever, he was still 'young Freddie' to all.

Jack Brearley and Enrico Gianni were typical of the stream of volunteers who queued outside the recruiting office. Nineteen years of age, fit, eager to join the army and excited at the prospect of fighting a war on the other side of the world.

'GIANNI, IS IT?' the recruiting officer asked.

'Yes, sir. Rick Gianni.'

'Born here?'

'Yes, sir,' Enrico lied. 'My Dad's Italian.' Enrico 'Rick' Gianni had decided that he was as Australian as the next man and he was going to fight alongside other Australians in the 11th Infantry Battalion of the 1st Australian Division.

At the railway station, Jack Brearley was too delirious with excitement to worry about the two girls who'd come to see him off. He'd been sleeping with both of them and neither knew of the other's existence. Who cared? He was going to fight a war.

Solange was not there to see Enrico off. She had returned to France six weeks earlier. 'You'd be much safer in Kal,' he'd argued, but she wouldn't listen. 'Who cares for safety?' she'd shrugged. 'If there is to be a war I must be with my family.' They'd made love, and she'd kissed him tenderly and told him that she would always love him.

Enrico pined when Solange left. Not a day went by when he didn't think of her. But, on the railway platform, as he hugged his mother and Giovanni and Kate—his father was not present, Rico thought his son a fool to fight for a country which was not his by birth—Enrico too was imbued with the excitement of it all.

The train journey to Perth was extraordinary. A party all the way. At every station they passed, cheering crowds of well-wishers were gathered and, at every stop the train made, the boys were plied with yet more beer and wine and whisky and food.

They were in fine spirits when they tumbled out of the train at Bellevue Station and, during the march to Blackboy Hill Training Camp just outside Perth, there was much ribaldry directed at the uniformed officers. But it was good-humoured and the officers accepted it. They knew that a certain amount of larrikinism was to be expected from the boys from the bush.

Blackboy Hill Camp was a camp in name only and the men arrived to nothing but gum trees and scrub. Orders were issued to draw tents for shelters and, when they'd pitched camp, details were allotted.

It was Tony Prendergast who scored the cook's detail and he elected young Freddie as his assistant but, when the steaming cauldrons were lifted from the fire, the contents were found to be inedible.

'What the bloody hell's this?' Jack Brearley demanded as, squatted on the ground outside their tents, dixies in hand, a gathering of twenty or so men dug their bread into the brown gruel.

'Stew, boyo, what do you think it is?'

Rick Gianni was seated beside Tony Prendergast. 'Never hire a Welshman to do an Italian's job,' he muttered and pretended to choke on the food.

The surrounding Aussie bushmen and miners and shearers and railway workers took up the joke. 'Cripes, it's enough to make a man spew,' Tom Brereton said, feigning a noisy vomit.

'I've been bloody poisoned,' his brother Bill moaned, holding his stomach and rolling on the ground.

'You've killed us, mate.' Ben Brereton clutched his throat and gagged. 'You've bloody killed us!' Soon, every man present was groaning and retching and choking.

'I like it,' young Freddie said, but nobody heard him above the din so he just kept eating.

'Hey, Lieutenant,' Jack Brearley stood and called to the adjutant who was checking the supply tent fifty yards away, 'I'm going into town for some decent tucker,' and he swaggered off in the direction of Perth, the Brereton brothers immediately joining him. The other men, including Tony Prendergast, fell in behind and Freddie, who wasn't really hungry any more but who didn't want to be left out of the fun, joined up the rear.

The lieutenant didn't stop them. These were early days, there was plenty of time for discipline. He'd have to watch young Jack Brearley, he thought, you didn't want a troublemaker in your midst, but they were a hardy bunch these outback boys. They'd make good soldiers.

It wasn't long before training at Blackboy Hill started in earnest. Drafts arrived from all over the State and the men were formed up into the eight companies which were to constitute the 11th Battalion. Of the twelve infantry battalions in the 1st Australian Division, the 11th was the battalion from the western State and, as far as possible, each of the eight companies within it was composed of men from the same portion of the State. The boys from the goldfields and surrounding areas were therefore destined to remain together through the thick and the thin of it all, which suited them just fine.

An undeclared truce existed between Jack Brearley and Rick Gianni. They made sure they were not allotted the same tent or allocated fatigues and duties together, but friction inevitably occurred. Particularly as, in their own way, they were both popular with the men. Jack invariably led the way into town and the pub, closely followed by his mates the Brereton brothers. But, around the campfire, it was Rick who won the votes. With his battered old concertina he led the singalongs, just as his uncle Giovanni had done each childhood Sunday he could remember. But, unlike Giovanni, the songs Rick played were not Italian. Rick Gianni had quickly taught himself each of the men's choices and played every one of them upon request, sometimes over and over if they happened to be a common favourite. 'Bound for Botany Bay' was a popular one and 'Click go the Shears Boys' for the shearers. But there was always the Scot who wanted 'Ain Folk' or the Irishman who demanded 'Rose of Tralee'. Rick knew them all. The general favourite though, was the parody of the popular song 'I'd Love to Live in Loveland'.

'I'd love to live in Blackboy for a week or two,
And work all day and get no pay,
And live on Irish stew.'

Men from the other companies would gradually gather around the goldfields contingent and the rousing chorus would be sung again and again.

Jack kept his peace, but he didn't much like the singalongs, he didn't like being witness to Rick Gianni's popularity. As the weeks went by, more and more often he inveigled the Brereton brothers to join him on a walk to town and a session at the pub rather than a singalong with the others. The brothers joined him because they were not musical and Jack was a good bloke and, furthermore, no Brereton ever knocked back the prospect of a hearty drinking session.

Late one Saturday night when they returned to camp, the brothers were happily drunk as usual, but Jack had got into the rum and was feeling aggressive. It annoyed him to see Rick Gianni still holding court. The beer the boys had laid on for the Saturday singalong had long since disappeared but still there were ten or so die-hards demanding Rick play them just one more song.

'I don't know any more,' he insisted. 'I've played them all a dozen times, I don't know any more. Honest.'

'Play us one of yours then.' It was Tony Prendergast. 'Sing us one of your songs, Rick.'

'Yeah. Sing them a dago song, Enrico.' All eyes turned to the shadowy figure of Jack Brearley standing just beyond the glow of the campfire, the Brereton brothers behind him. It was Jack's tone which had caught the men's attention, not his words. 'Dago', 'wog', 'mick', they were all terms used in the camp, but they were used with affection, just as 'you silly bugger' and 'you clever bastard' were. It was Aussie humour. But there was nothing humorous in Jack's tone and the men knew it.

'What are you calling him Rick for anyway, Tony, his name's Enrico and you know it.' Jack swayed slightly as he stepped forward into the light of the campfire. He was very drunk. 'He's a bloody dago and he doesn't belong here.'

Tony was a good ten years older than most of the men, twenty years older than many and, although they called him 'the old man' or 'the old bugger', he was well respected.

'Rick belongs here as much as you do, Jack. He's here for the same reason we all are.' Tony rose to his feet.

'He's a dago and he should go back to his own bloody country.' Jack turned to the Brereton brothers for support. 'His bloody name's Enrico, he's a bloody dago.'

Tom and Ben and Bill looked at each other, a little confused.

'So what?' Bill asked. The brothers were full of beer

and camaraderie and couldn't understand Jack's aggression.

'What's the matter with you, mate?' Ben asked.

'Hey, Rick,' Tom, the older of the brothers, called, 'sing us a dago song, I'm bloody sick of "Click go the Shears".'

The men around the dying campfire cheered and urged Rick on. He picked up the old concertina.

'O sole mio . . .'

The brothers squatted by the fire with the other men and all attention was turned to Rick.

Tony took Jack aside. 'You're drunk, Jack,' he said. 'Go to bed and sleep it off. But sleep off more than the rum, boyo.' He could smell the cheap dark rum a mile off. 'Sleep off your family feuds—they don't belong here.' Tony didn't know, and didn't care to know, the background between the Brearleys and the Giannis, but their hatred for one another was common knowledge in Kalgoorlie.

The rum was turning to bile, Jack could feel it. He didn't know why he'd got onto the bloody stuff, he didn't even like the taste. He should have stuck to beer, but he'd wanted to get drunk. He wished Tony would stop lecturing him. Jesus Christ, his own father didn't lecture him like this.

'I'm serious, man,' Tony continued, 'personal hatreds won't win you any friends in the army, you can bet on that.'

'Sure, Tony, sure.' Jack started to back off. If he was going to be sick there was no way he was going to do it in public. 'I'll sleep it off. Night.'

Tony knew Jack was trying to escape him. The boy was going green around the gills, and was probably going to be sick. At least then he'd feel better in the morning. Not that he'd learn of course. Headstrong boys like Jack rarely did. But he wasn't a bad lad at heart and he had qualities which could serve him well in the army. He was a leader, and fearless. All he had to do was grow up.

'Night, Jack,' he said.

After Jack had vomited in the bushes behind his tent, he lay in his sleeping bag and cursed his own stupidity. He'd humiliated himself in front of his mates. Why had he made such a fool of himself? He didn't hate dagos at all. It was Enrico Gianni he hated. And his madman father, Rico, who'd smashed up Maudie's pub that terrifying night. And that bastard uncle of his, Giovanni.

Jack could remember the hot February afternoon as clearly as if it were yesterday. It was over ten years ago now, not very long before his ninth birthday, when he'd sat astride the old Princess and watched his father, face bloodied, squirm in the dust. He could remember sitting motionless on the old white mare and watching the Italian stride from the yard. He could still hear his parting words. 'From this day the Giannis and the Brearleys are *nemici*. *Nemici*, you understand! We are enemies!'

Of course he hated Enrico Gianni, it was beholden upon him to hate anyone bearing the name Gianni.

Jack fell into a drunken sleep, hatred seething in him, his own humiliation forgotten as that of his father's burned vividly in his brain.

CAMP LIFE BECAME more regimented as uniforms began to arrive piecemeal. The men had originally been issued with rifles, boots and puttees only and had paraded in a variety of civilian garb. They looked a motley lot, mostly in flannels and dungarees, some in stiff white shirts. But, as the uniforms arrived, the men started to take pride in their appearance. Much as they still hated route marches and battalion drill, and much as they remained larrikins who scorned army convention, they were becoming soldiers.

Then the restlessness crept in. They were more than ready to go to war. Where were their orders? They were straining at the leash—at this rate the war would be over before the 11th Battalion had had a taste of it.

Towards the end of October, rumours abounded. Their orders would come through any moment now, they told each other. Why, when they'd marched through the streets of Perth, the people of the city had given them rousing ovations at every corner; surely that meant their departure was imminent. But still no word.

Then, at four o'clock on the morning of the 31st of October, the men were paraded and informed that their embarkation orders had finally been received. They were to pack their kitbags and prepare for transportation to the port of Fremantle.

The huge convoy of thirty-eight ships carrying approximately thirty-five thousand Australian and New Zealand troops finally formed up in the ocean off Fremantle. The majority of the 11th Battalion was aboard the SS *Ascanius* and, on the 2nd of November, the convoy slowly began to steam its way towards Colombo.

From Colombo to Aden, from Aden to Suez and then, at the end of the month, the disappointed discovery that their destination was not England, as most had assumed, but Egypt.

'CRIPES, HOW DO you reckon they did it?' Tom Brereton, awe-struck, leaned on his pick and gazed up at the pyramid. It was their first day's work and they were setting up a training camp at Mena at the foot of the great pyramid of Cheops.

'One of the wonders of the world, Tom,' Jack grinned. 'One of the great wonders of the world.'

Setting up camp was no mean task. There were huge stones to be broken up and moved, but even such arduous labour could not dampen the men's spirits.

Many of them had never been outside their home State and the awesome pyramid was symbolic of their great adventure. It was a constant reminder that they were indeed on the other side of the world.

Training proved to be just as arduous. Marching in the loose desert sand was exhausting. But regular leave was granted and, only a mile away were the tramcars to Cairo where the lads had a grand time bartering at the bazaars and drinking arak in the bars and, many of them, against orders, sleeping with the girls in the excitingly sordid area of Wazir.

Dear Maudie and Pa, Jack wrote. *Tell Jim and Vicky that I bought them some presents in Cairo the other day. They're just trinkets, I can't fit much in my kit bag, but you won't see the like of them in Kal.*

The trip over was bonzer although we lost our joey in Alexandria. Tom Brereton (he's my main cobber) smuggled him aboard at Fremantle as a mascot. The locals had never seen a kangaroo before so I suppose one of them stole him. I hope he didn't end up in an Egyptian cookpot.

One of the men died on the trip, just two weeks out to sea. Pneumonia. Poor bloke, how's that for luck? He didn't even get a shot at the other side.

Can't wait for the action. Have a beaut Christmas. Hoo roo, Jack.

Christmas Day saw the first Australian mail the troops had received since leaving Fremantle and, shortly afterwards, on New Year's Eve, British commanding officers visited the camp to inspect the 1st Australian Division.

'Thank God!' Sir George Reid declared in his inspiring speech. 'Your mission is as pure and noble as any soldiers undertook to rid the world of would-be tyrants . . . If any stains come on your bright new flags they must and will be stains of honour won by valour.' And the boys from the goldfields, in Company C of the

11th Battalion—one of the four battalions of the 3rd Brigade—were as proud as any man present.

Still, there were two more frustrating months before orders were given to strike camp and then a further two months spent, mostly aboard ship, at Mudros Harbour on the island of Lemnos. Their days on board were taken up by arduous disembarkation training—scrambling down rope ladders carrying full gear, piling in and out of small boats—until news came of their final destination, sixty miles away. Gallipoli.

ON APRIL 17TH orders for the attack on Gallipoli were issued. The objective of the 3rd Brigade was to seize a series of high ridges running from Gaba Tepe to Chunuk Bair and to secure them, so allowing the rest of the Australian and New Zealand Army Corps to advance to the high ground at Mal Tepe. Mal Tepe overlooked the Narrows which the troops could then free for the British Navy to proceed to the Sea of Marmara and on to Constantinople.

The Commanding Officers of each of the four battalions had previously been taken by warship to inspect the coast and view the objective.

The 3rd Brigade was under the command of Colonel Sinclair-MacLagan, a Scot by birth and a respected soldier who had served in India and South Africa. Sinclair-MacLagan was fully aware of the immense task before them. 'That post is too big for a brigade,' he commented to his fellow officers. And later, to General Bridges: 'If we find the Turks holding these ridges in any strength, I honestly don't think you'll ever see the 3rd Brigade again.'

But in the letter read out to the troops, Colonel Sinclair-MacLagan urged, 'You have been selected by the Divisional Commander as the covering force, a high honour which we must all do our best to justify. We must be successful at any cost . . .' He continued, however, with an ominous warning. 'We are, after all, only a very small piece on the board. Some pieces have often to be sacrificed to win the game and, after all, it is to win the game that we are here.' But, by now, the troops were too feverish with anticipation to think of anything but the impending battle.

The landing was to take place at night and A and C Companies of the 11th Battalion were to form the first line. No rifles were to be fired and no shot to be loaded until daylight. The men were to be landed in small boats which would be towed as close as possible to the shore by steam pinnaces. The troops would then row ashore and make for land as best they could, the warships *Majestic*, *Triumph* and *Bacchante* shelling the Turkish positions to cover their landing.

The men of A and C Companies loaded their transport ship, HMS *London*, and, on the 23rd of April, Colonel Lyon-Johnston addressed the 11th Battalion. 'The position of honour has been assigned to us in being thus chosen as vanguard for one of the most daring enterprises in history. Boys, the General informs me that it will take several battleships and destroyers to carry our brigade to Gallipoli; a barge will be sufficient to take us home again!'

Grim as his humour was, loud cheers greeted the colonel's address.

The following night, the crew of the *London* treated the 11th Battalion to an issue of rum as they rested before the attack. Sailors and troops exchanged knives and mementos. Some men spent the night yarning, others slept. And many wrote letters to their families and sweethearts back home.

Dear Mamma . . .

Enrico Gianni wrote his letter in English. He had never learnt to write in his mother tongue; but it made little difference anyway: both Teresa and Rico were illiterate. He addressed the letter to his mother, however, as a mark of respect, knowing Carmelina or Salvatore would read it out to the family. He chose his words carefully.

After all these months we are about to engage in battle and many of the men are excited by the prospect—they want a bit of a scrap, they say. For me, I am not so sure, but it is certainly why we are here and I shall do my best.

If I should not return, I want you and Papa to know that I love you and I am grateful to you both for the life you have given me.

My love to Carmelina and Salvatore,

Your son, Enrico.

To his uncle Giovanni, Enrico was not so circumspect.

I hope you have kept up the reading and writing lessons since I left—I'll bet Kate has made sure of it — as you are the only person I feel I can talk to from my heart.

Tomorrow we attack and, after the months of waiting, I suppose we are eager for the event. The odds are not in our favour, however, and I see fear in the faces of many. I am fearful myself. I do not want to die. But we all know why we are here, to take the risk and to pay the price, if such payment is necessary.

The concertina is with me still. It has been a friend to me and a friend to all. Particularly the men from Kal. During training we would sit around the campfire each night and sing the old songs and this is why I needed to write to you. To thank you for everything you have given me. Above all the music. The music in a man's soul makes him a brother to all men—this is what you have given me, Giovanni. I have written a song about it and I will enclose the words with this letter. It's called 'Kal' and it's about people, just simple people, but I have a good tune in my head. When I come home I'll sing it to you. But, if I shouldn't, please make up a fine tune for me.

My love to Kate and the family,
Your friend, Enrico.

THE LANDING BEGAN shortly after three in the morning of the 25th of April, 1915.

Out to sea, the destroyers waited silent and motionless, watching as the battleships advanced towards the shore with their small boats in tow, churning the dark waters.

Just before dawn, the tows were cast off and in raced the pinnaces to take them up. Then the race for shore was on, the men crouching in the small boats, waiting for the moment when they would be cast adrift to row for their lives.

The destroyers now entered the action. They were ordered through the slow-moving battleships, to approach as close to the shore as possible and provide covering fire.

The sea was a turmoil of activity and the air throbbed with the noise of engines. But there was not a movement, not a sound, from the land.

The dawn light had not yet tinted the sky when the pinnaces prepared to cast off their tows and, in the dark and confusion, they had lost direction. They were roughly one thousand yards too far to the north, but by now it was too late.

Two hundred and fifty yards to shore and still no sound from the land. Two hundred yards . . .

'Prepare to cast off!' was the command aboard the pinnaces. One hundred and fifty yards. Still no sound from the land. One hundred yards . . .

Then it started. The hellfire from the shore. A flame from the funnel of one of the pinnaces shot high into the air lighting up the confusion of men and boats in the churning black waters. The light died as quickly as it had flared and, from the inky wall of the shore, rifle bullets cracked and machine-gun fire cleaved the air. The tows were cast off. The men of A and C Companies were on their own.

'It's up to us now, lads!' Tony Prendergast yelled, grabbing his oar.

Freddie, in front of him, grabbed his and started to row with the strength of a bull. On the other side of the boat the Brereton brothers set to with all their might.

Packed like sardines in the centre, the men leant what help they could with the weight of their bodies and their eighty-pound packs, leaning forward and aft as the rowers heaved on their oars.

'A bit bloody early for birdsong, don't you reckon?' Tom Brereton grunted as the bullets whistled all about them. The men laughed.

Not fifty yards away, Jack Brearley focused on Rick Gianni's head in front of him as they strained on their oars in unison. 'Pull, two, three, four!' he yelled over the constant crack of the gunfire. 'Pull, two, three, four!' The men took up the chant.

It was ironic he was sharing the same boat as Enrico Gianni, Jack thought. He'd far rather have been rowing alongside Tom Brereton. He smiled grimly; it was hardly the time to quibble.

The first of the boats reached the shore. Bowed under their heavy equipment, the men struggled through the shallows for the beach. Most were mowed down before their boots hit dry sand.

Fifty yards. Thirty yards. The boats kept coming. Men were being hit now before they were able to scramble out into the shallows and shrapnel screamed all about them. The one comforting sound was that of the shells whistling overhead as the warships fired on the enemy.

'Give it to them, boys!' Tom Brereton screamed, but he didn't turn around to look, he just kept rowing as hard as he could. They all did.

The first glimmer of dawn revealed the chaos. The beach was strewn with the bodies of men who had made it to shore but no further. Some were struggling up the beach to the higher sand and safety. Boats were overturned and bodies floated in the water. Others lay drifting in the shallows.

Suddenly Freddie slumped forward, shot through the head. A man in the centre of the boat grabbed the oar, jostled into his position and started to heave the body over the side.

Tony stopped rowing. He grabbed young Freddie's arm. 'No,' he ordered. 'No, man, let him be.'

The boat was changing direction. Tom stopped rowing. 'Let him go, Tony,' he yelled. 'We're sitting ducks. Let him go, mate, or we'll all cop it.'

Knowing Tom was right Tony helped push Freddie's body overboard and as he heaved on his oar once again, each time he chanted over and over to himself, 'What will I tell Freddie's mother? What will I tell Freddie's mother?'

Now the sun was on the horizon and, in the clear dawn light, the Turks could pick their targets with ease.

Concentrated machine-gun fire caught four men in Jack's boat simultaneously. In the struggle for control, the boat capsized and the men started swimming to shore. They were easy prey.

'Stay with the boat!' Jack yelled. 'Stay with the boat!' but no one seemed to hear. As Rick Gianni started to swim, Jack grabbed his arm. 'Stay with the boat,' he yelled again.

The two of them swam around the stern, keeping the boat between them and the shore, and watched as, one by one, their comrades were picked off in the water. Easy, slow-moving targets.

The boat was drifting into the shallows and they stayed with it until they felt their boots touch the sand.

When they were less than waist-deep, Jack yelled 'Run!' And they ran, he and Rick Gianni. They ran for all they were worth as the machine-gun fire whipped the sand about their ankles and the noises of hell screamed in their ears.

Chapter Twenty-Two

'The Aussies are copping it at Gallipoli,' Paolo announced to the family as he entered the breakfast room. Early each morning he collected the newspaper delivered to the Dunleavy doorstep and he'd been avidly following the progress of the war.

Paul Dunleavy helped himself to one of the boiled eggs in the steaming bowl the maid had just placed on the table. He knew what was coming next.

'I want to go home, sir.'

Paul stemmed his irritation as best he could. 'We've had this out before, Paolo,' he said, placing the egg in his silver eggcup and carefully tapping the top with his teaspoon. 'You know only too well that I deeply respect your desire to fight alongside your countrymen.' He didn't; why anyone should fight a war when they didn't have to was beyond his comprehension. 'But we agreed that you would finish your final year at Harvard before you make any such decision.' Hopefully the wretched war would be over by then.

'But that was before Gallipoli,' Paolo insisted. 'Look, sir.' He spread the newspaper out on the table, overturning the small silver salt salver in his excitement. 'Oh,' he said, startled, gathering up the grains in his fingers, 'I'm sorry, Elizabeth, I didn't mean . . .'

'It's perfectly all right, Paolo,' Elizabeth smiled.

Unperturbed, she nodded to the maid who had just arrived with Paul's fresh rack of toast. 'Some more salt thank you, Edith.'

'Where's Gallipoli?' Meg asked. She'd recently become a little jealous of her father's protege, who lately seemed to pose a threat to the place she held in her daddy's affections. Which was a pity because, from the very outset, she'd found Paolo Gianni fascinating. Meg had never met an Australian before, let alone one who insisted he was half-Italian.

'There's a map here.' Paolo turned the page of the newspaper, threatening yet more damage to the breakfast table, but Paul interrupted.

'Look it up in the big atlas, Meg. You may go into my study. You too, Paolo; it will do you good to acquaint yourself with the precise location . . .' Paolo was about to protest. 'We will discuss the personal aspects of the matter this evening.'

Recognising the suggestion as a command, Paolo left the table with Meg.

'Never fear,' Paul said when they'd gone, more to himself than to his wife, 'I'll persuade him otherwise.'

Elizabeth nodded, resigned. She was sure he would. Her husband was a very persuasive man. He had certainly managed to talk the boy around the previous year, when the Australians had first entered the war and Paolo had wanted to return home and join the army.

'One man more or less will hardly alter the course of the war,' had been Paul's caustic opening remark, but he'd quickly changed tactics when he'd recognised that the boy was in earnest. 'You'll have an engineering degree in only eighteen months, Paolo, don't throw it away . . .'

The boy was no fool, and eventually he had seen the sense of the argument. Elizabeth had no doubt that her husband would once again convince him. 'Wait until the end of the year,' she could hear Paul say, 'just until the end of the year. And, if the war is still in progress you may join the army with my blessing.' That's what he'd say, but of course the boy would join the army over Paul's dead body. Indeed she now realised, if Paul had his way, the boy would never leave Boston.

'He is my natural son, Elizabeth,' Paul had told his wife the night he'd returned home from Kalgoorlie. Elizabeth had simply stared back at her husband in a state of shock. As Paul explained his intention to bring the boy to Boston in two years to study at Harvard, she continued to stare blankly at him.

'He's a brilliant student,' Paul was saying enthusiastically, 'and he will come to live with us when he's eighteen.'

The man's insane, Elizabeth thought. She had always been aware of her husband's intense desire for a son. Indeed she had felt guilty for years after the complications of Meg's birth had left her unable to bear more children.

'Of course, he will be known simply as my protege, but he is my blood. He belongs here and he will remain here.'

Elizabeth was barely hearing her husband as Paul continued with his plans. Was he honestly proposing that he bring his bastard son to live openly with them? He wasn't even asking her permission, Elizabeth realised, the subject wasn't even being opened for dicussion.

'And the boy?' she asked, barely trusting herself to speak. 'The boy is happy to be bought?'

Paul was so carried away he didn't register the coldness in her voice. 'He doesn't know and he mustn't until I have won his trust. He simply thinks I am furthering his education and he remains loyal to his peasant mother and her husband. But that will change with time.'

'Am I to have no say in this whatsoever?' Elizabeth

had found her voice and Paul finally recognised the anger in her tone. 'Do you have any idea of the effect this could have on your daughter?' she continued. 'The repercussions it could have on your entire family?'

They argued well into the night but Paul was adamant and Elizabeth was finally forced to agree to his plans. She made her conditions quite clear, however.

'No one must know this boy is your son. Will you promise me, Paul? He must never be recognised as a Dunleavy. Will you swear to that?'

'Of course, my dear.' Paul embraced her. 'The boy will be known as my protege, I swear it.' She felt warm and soft in his arms. The embrace had been a distraction, his promise ambiguously worded—the boy could be his protege *and* his son—but the touch of her reminded Paul how long he had been away. 'Now surely it's time for bed, Elizabeth.'

Elizabeth was a sensual woman, and she had missed her husband. But even as she felt her desire grow, she could not rid herself of her fearful misgivings. In the bedroom, as she undressed, aware of his eyes lingering on her body in the half-light, she forced the subject out of her mind. It was a whole two years away, she told herself. The boy might even change his mind over the next two years. Away from Paul's influence, he might even decide to stay in Kalgoorlie.

But he didn't. Paul's weekly letters kept the flame of excitement burning in the boy and, three months after his eighteenth birthday, young Paolo Gianni was standing on the Boston Railway platform meeting his half-sister and her mother.

'How do you do, Paolo.' As Elizabeth shook the young man's hand, she couldn't help but register his resemblance to her husband. Why, she could have been looking at the young Paul Dunleavy, she thought with a sense of shock. The young man who had swept her off her feet. 'This is our daughter Meg,' she said, strangely taken aback.

Paolo was surprised at the strength of Meg's handshake. He wasn't accustomed to shaking hands with girls at all, and certainly not with one who shook hands like a bloke. But she was very attractive, with a strong-boned aristocratic face like her mother's and the clear grey eyes of her father. And of himself too, Paolo realised, momentarily startled. He wondered if he and Meg looked alike. Paul Dunleavy's letters, however, had been quite explicit. No one, Meg included, was to know of their true relationship.

The sea voyage to America and the day Paolo had spent, awestruck, wandering the streets of New York before boarding the New England train should have prepared him for Boston. But nothing had prepared him for the elegance of the Dunleavy home and lifestyle. They had a housekeeper and a maid and a butler. Paolo had never known anyone who had servants. And the house itself was huge. Four storeys.

The servants' quarters were in the basement, with separate access downstairs from the street, and the main entrance was up several steps to a large landing. Two magnificent wooden doors opened into a marble-floored hallway. A drawing room was to the right, a large front lounge to the left, and behind the central wooden staircase with heavy curved railings which led to the upstairs studies and bedrooms was the formal dining room and family breakfast room. Paolo's and Meg's bedrooms were up yet another floor, in the attic with its decorative slate roof and copper cupola. To Paolo's delight, he even had his own study. From his table by the little attic window, he could look out over the broad tree-lined boulevard at the other grand houses of Commonwealth Avenue.

Paul Dunleavy delighted in the boy's open admiration. 'The Back Bay area all about here is reclaimed,' he said. 'You're standing on land which was once part of the Charles River. Extraordinary, isn't it?' He'd bought the house ten years ago, he explained, although he still owned the original family home in Beacon Hill. 'I'll take you there one day and show you where my father lived. And his father before him.'

Paul would dearly have loved to have said 'your grandfather and your great-grandfather', but he knew he must bide his time and not overwhelm the boy.

There was so much for Paolo to marvel at, each day seemed a new adventure. The bite of the Boston air, the heavy jackets with fur-lined hoods and, above all, the snow. The pictures he'd seen in books and the stories his mother had told him of her childhood in the Alps hadn't prepared him for the wonder of snow.

The first night it snowed he stood outside on the pavement for hours watching the falling flakes, reflecting yellow in the light of the street lamps, settle gently on the ground and on the houses and in the bare, forked arms of the elm trees.

Meg, sent to bring him inside, was bemused by his fascination. 'I've never met anyone who's never seen snow,' she said.

'Listen. Listen to the sound.'

'There isn't any sound.'

'That's it. That's what I mean. The snow covers the sounds. It's a different sort of silence.' He stood listening for several moments. In the Australian outback, he had always loved the stillness of the night. But now, recalling the endless sounds of insects and frogs and nocturnal birds, he realised that there was no such thing as stillness. Not in the outback. 'It's a very peaceful silence,' he added.

How could silence not be peaceful? Meg wondered. As yet, she wasn't quite sure what to make of Paolo Gianni. She certainly liked him, and there was no denying his good looks, but she wasn't sure whether he was smarter than she was or whether it was the other way around. He was six months older, but so naive at times that she felt herself to be quite his superior, eminently more sophisticated and worldly. And then he would make some serious observation, and she would feel immature, 'a giddy girl', as her mother used to say.

'Wait until tomorrow,' she said, 'I'll show you just how peaceful snow can be.'

And she did. They pelted each other with snowballs until they were laughing so much they had to declare a truce; then she introduced him to the joys of tobogganing and building a snowman.

THE MONTHS PASSED, then a year, and Paul Dunleavy became increasingly delighted by the rapport between his daughter and Paolo. 'Already they're brother and sister,' he said to his wife one night as he stoked the large open fire in the front lounge.

But Elizabeth was apprehensive. 'So long as their affections remain that way inclined.'

Paul prodded the glowing logs, returned the poker to its shiny copper stand beside the grate and waited for her to continue, but she didn't. She merely sat in her alcove seat at the bay windows and concentrated on her petit point.

'What do you mean by that?' he snapped, irritated. He hated women when they were enigmatic.

'Just what I say, dear,' Elizabeth replied calmly. 'I would hate to see their affections take a different path.'

Now Paul felt angry. 'Good God, woman, what do you take my son for?'

'Ssssh!' She looked up sharply from her tapestry, her eyes darting a warning to the door.

'She can't hear, she's upstairs studying,' Paul said,

but he lowered his voice nonetheless. 'The boy knows she's his half-sister, do you think for one minute he'd . . .'

'No. No, I don't, but Meg is eighteen years old . . .'

Paul didn't hear a word as he sailed on. 'Besides, he's deeply committed to his studies. He topped his first year, just like I said he would. The boy simply doesn't have time for—'

'It's not Paolo I'm talking about,' Elizabeth interrupted angrily. 'It's Meg.'

It infuriated Elizabeth that Paul found Meg's studies insignificant in comparison to Paolo's. Meg had just started her first year of Arts at Cambridge and her father, having successfully opened the doors of academia for her, professed pride in his daughter's scholarly aspirations, but Elizabeth knew otherwise. Paul was too wrapped up in his 'protege' to take much interest in the child who had once been the very centre of his existence.

'It's your daughter I'm talking about,' she repeated and her tone was sharp. 'Your daughter. Meg.' It was rare for Elizabeth to speak crossly and Paul's attention was finally arrested.

'But Meg's just a child.'

Dear God in heaven, Elizabeth thought, was the man blind? But she softened her tone. 'She is a woman, my dear, barely two years younger than I was when we married.'

'And you think she's set her sights on Paolo?' There was absolute horror in Paul's voice.

'No, no, of course I don't,' Elizabeth was quick to reassure him, 'but any moment now there will be suitors at the door. She is at an age where young men notice her and she notices them.'

'Well, you make sure she doesn't notice Paolo.' Elizabeth returned a small sigh of exasperation. 'I mean it, Elizabeth,' he said in earnest. 'You're the diplomat in this family—you talk to her. If you really think there's any danger then you tell her she's to leave Paolo alone. Tell her he has his studies to attend to; put it however you like.'

'All right, all right,' Elizabeth said as he paced, agitated, about the lounge, 'don't get overexcited.'

'Everything's going according to plan, he's fitting in perfectly,' Paul continued, oblivious. 'Not only does the boy love college, he's made valuable friends there and he's becoming more American by the minute. Why, he even follows the blasted Boston Red Sox! I'll not have him disturbed in any way.'

Elizabeth knew there was little point in discussing the subject any further. Her husband was obsessed. Utterly obsessed. She returned to her petit point.

'You'll speak to her?' he insisted.

'I'll speak to her.'

Elizabeth's response was chilly. A talk with Meg would do little except widen the already existing rift between mother and daughter. She wouldn't tell Meg it was her father's request that she spend less time with Paolo. There was no sense in alienating the girl from both her parents.

Elizabeth was an eminently sensible woman, just like her mother, Mehitable. 'Girls always rebel against their mothers, dear.' That's what Mehitable told her time and again. 'They rebel against their mothers and hero-worship their fathers. But don't you worry your head, they always come back to their mothers in the end.'

As Paul rang for their bedtime hot chocolate, Elizabeth could only pray that Mehitable was right.

'THE BOY LOVES college,' Paul Dunleavey had said and he was right. If anything, his words were an understatement. Paolo loved Harvard with a passion. Sometimes he would leave home early and walk across Harvard Bridge, dawdling and enjoying the views up and down the Charles River Basin. Other mornings, he would opt for public transport and, as the streetcar rattled around the curved tracks of Harvard Square, he would thrill to the thought that he, Paolo Gianni from the goldfields of Kalgoorlie, was a student at the oldest college in America.

He was exhilarated, too, by the mental challenge. His brain seemed on fire with the stimulation of learning. Harvard was changing Paolo. No longer the withdrawn, contemplative young man, he was becoming more eager, more competitive and, in Paul Dunleavy's eyes, more American.

The greatest evidence of this was undoubtedly Paolo's devotion to the Boston Red Sox, an allegiance which had initially disturbed Paul who strongly disapproved of baseball. Much as Paul Dunleavy liked to think of himself as modern, he could not help but agree with his friends who insisted that the sport infecting the youth of America was the devil's game. The players looked for all the world as if they were attired for gladiatorial combat in their dingy knickerbockers, heavy boots and vulgar peaked caps. Paul would vastly have preferred to see his son follow the dignified ritual and white-flannelled grace of cricket, the sport of gentlemen.

Paul was further frustrated by the knowledge that, along with several fellow students, his son frequented the saloon bar at the Copley Square Hotel. Not that there was anything wrong with the Copley Square Hotel, it was an eminently respectable establishment and Paul still used the place for the odd business meeting. But it was common knowledge that the saloon bar of the Copley Square Hotel was a gathering place for the followers of the Boston Red Sox, and even the team members themselves when it was a home game. God alone knew the class of people with whom Paolo might be associating.

'Whom do you see at the Copley Square Hotel, Paolo?' Paul tried to sound as casual as possible. 'Just as a matter of interest, you understand.'

'It depends whether the Red Sox are playing at home, sir,' Paolo answered. 'I've seen Tris Speaker a couple of times and last home match when the Red Sox played the Detroit Tigers I saw Ty Cobb. Hugh Duffy's retired now but he sometimes—'

Paul smiled at the boy's literal interpretation of the question, his lack of guile was certainly charming. 'No, no, son, I meant who are the friends that you meet there?'

It had taken well over a year for Paul to muster the courage to call the boy 'son' and, when he had, he'd watched Paolo's reaction carefully. There had been none. No doubt the boy presumed it was just a term of address, but it wasn't. Each time Paul said 'son' he felt a rush of paternal pride. Just as he did when Paolo called him 'sir'. Not that the boy recognised any personal connotation in that either. It had been quite obvious from the outset that Paolo referred to any older man as 'sir'.

'No thank you, sir,' he'd replied, the very first day he'd arrived, when the butler had asked him if he would like some refreshment.

Paul had been quick to point out that the butler's name was Geoffrey. Then he'd added that 'sir' was the form of address Paolo should reserve for Paul, as his benefactor. He didn't mention that, for his entire life, he had called his own father 'sir'. And each time from that day on, when the boy said 'sir', Paul felt a fatherly pride. He had a son, a son who called him 'sir'.

When Paul's gentle interrogation revealed that Paolo's fellow baseball devotees at the Copley Square Hotel saloon bar were none other than David Redmond—a distant cousin of Elizabeth's—and Stephen Sanderson—whose mother was one of the Saunders girls, Paul was sure—the situation took on a whole new perspective.

'And both boys go to Harvard, you say? Excellent contacts, son, well done.' Two fine old Bostonian families, Paul thought; yes, that was excellent, excellent.

Paolo was irritated by the comment but he didn't let it show. He liked David and Stephen only because they shared his passion for baseball. Personally he was a little weary of Stephen's preoccupation with social position and David's preoccupation with girls. It was Ira Rubenstein who remained Paolo's closest friend, but he knew better than to mention that to Paul Dunleavy.

Ira had been the first friend Paolo had made at Harvard. They hadn't actually met at Harvard at all, but in the Boston Public Library, poring over their respective books at their respective wooden tables beneath the massive domed ceilings of the reading room. Paolo had noticed Ira on campus, and decided to introduce himself. He stood, pulled back his chair, wincing as the wooden legs squealed alarmingly on the marble-slabbed floor, and walked over to Ira's table.

'Hello,' he said. 'I'm Paolo Gianni, I've seen you on campus.'

'I'm Ira Rubenstein.'

They shook hands and Paolo sat. 'You're always on your own,' he said.

'I'm a Jew.'

'So?' Paolo didn't understand.

'They don't like Jews at Harvard.' Ira shrugged as though he didn't care. 'No matter, I'm at Harvard to study, not to win popularity contests.'

From that day on, the two boys became close friends. They had a lot in common. They were both living away from home—Ira's parents were in New York which, he admitted wryly, was a little closer than Kalgoorlie—and they both came from poor families. Ira was a scholarship student.

'I guess even the anti-Semites at Harvard can't ignore the truly brilliant Jews,' he grinned. 'And you?'

'I have a wealthy benefactor who thinks I'm brilliant—same thing I reckon.'

Ira was very impressed. 'I didn't think things like that happened any more.'

Paolo and Ira quickly discovered they shared a mutual passion for learning. They stimulated each other's intellect and, despite utterly dissimilar personalities, genuinely liked each other.

Ira was a dour-looking young man. Dark, pensive and given to heavy cynicism, which Paolo reasoned was mainly for self-protection, he nevertheless found people deeply interesting and his shrewd observations always came as a surprise from one who appeared so melancholic and introverted. His Russian parents had fled European persecution to arrive in New York in 1894 and Ira had been born one month later. His mother had been as sick as a dog during the ocean crossing, he said, and swore that as a result he couldn't even catch a Manhattan ferry. 'So many things happen in the womb, Paolo. Amazing.' And Paolo didn't know whether he was joking or not. With Ira it was often hard to tell.

Mostly they met at the library, or walked along the river or through the parks. Ira didn't care to keep company with anyone, even Paolo, on campus.

'It would mean I'd have to associate with those other friends of yours,' he explained, 'and they don't like me.' When Paolo started to protest, he smiled that gloomy smile of his. 'I don't like them either, believe me; I far prefer to be on my own. And we can always meet and talk elsewhere.'

Paolo asked Ira home to the Dunleavy house in

Commonwealth Avenue but he refused. 'I'd rather not,' he said, but he wouldn't explain why.

When, after he'd been attending Harvard for several months, Paul Dunleavy asked Paolo if he'd acquired any special friends, the boy was quick to answer. 'Yes, sir,' he said, 'one really good mate. Ira Rubenstein. He's a funny bloke though. Private. Sort of—'

'He's a Jew.'

It wasn't a question and the tone was accusatory. Paolo was taken aback.

'Yes, sir.'

Paul realised the boy was shocked by his brusqueness. Not that he'd meant anything by it of course. He had nothing against Jews himself, but it simply wasn't to Paolo's advantage to befriend a Jew at Harvard. What gain could there be in such a friendship?

'Don't misunderstand me, Paolo,' he said, his voice mellow, his smile benign, 'I have absolutely nothing against the Jewish community, but you must be aware that, besides your degree, there are other advantages to be gained from Harvard, not least among them the cultivation of valuable friends.'

He went on about the importance of making connections with old Bostonian families, meeting sons of influential men who could advance a young man's career, but Paolo had stopped listening. He was studying Paul Dunleavy closely, suddenly aware that he was seeing the man clearly for the first time.

Why did he feel such disillusionment? Paolo wondered. This was a world he had never known, a world where people behaved in a fashion foreign to him; he had no right to criticise. But he couldn't help it. He had recognised, and with a strong sense of disappointment, that there were flaws in the benefactor he had so unquestioningly admired.

Ira Rubenstein's name was never mentioned again

and, a year later, when Paul displayed his open approval of the other friendships his son had forged, Paolo simply neglected to mention that Ira Rubenstein remained his closest friend.

WHEN PAOLO PASSED his second year at Harvard, once again with flying colours, a lavish family dinner was held in his honour at the stylish new Copley Plaza Hotel. Built barely two years previously, the Copley Plaza was the gathering place for Boston's urbane society.

'Invite your friends,' Paul insisted, and Paolo couldn't help but wonder what would happen if he were to ask Ira—but of course Ira wouldn't come even if he did. To appease the family, Paolo asked Stephen Sanderson and David Redmond instead. He also invited Mary-Jane Stewart, the pretty young arts student who was in love with him.

The current object of David Redmond's desire, a saucy redhead called Amy, was also in attendance and Meg found herself seated beside Stephen Sanderson, squirming in the knowledge that he obviously presumed he was her date. Her father did little to discourage the young man's misconception.

'Stephen Sanderson's mother is one of the Saunders girls, Elizabeth,' he'd said to his wife as they'd dressed for dinner. 'It would be an excellent match.'

Elizabeth felt for her daughter as she watched Meg's discomfort—the Sanderson boy certainly was pompous for one so young—but then, she thought, one couldn't always marry for love. Meg could do a great deal worse.

Between tightly polite responses to Stephen's monologue, Meg was casting surreptitious glances at Mary-Jane and Paolo, both of whom were in conversation with her father. She wondered whether they were sleeping together. Yes, of course they were, she decided. Mary-Jane's manner to her host had all the deference of youth to middle-age but, when she turned her attention to Paolo, she couldn't disguise the glow in her eyes. She was a woman in love. Fascinated, Meg looked for similar signs in Paolo but couldn't see any. If he was in love then he was cleverly concealing the fact. But then it was often difficult to tell what was going on in Paolo's mind, Meg thought; that was what made him so very attractive.

She turned her attention to David and Amy. No guesswork needed there, they were definitely sleeping together. Meg thought their behaviour most unseemly, it was quite obvious they were holding hands under the table. Did they have to be so blatant? But, despite her disapproval, she was fascinated. The lust between them was palpable.

More and more these days Meg found herself wondering what it would be like. When she felt her breasts she wondered what it would be like if the hand caressing them was a man's hand. She had even touched herself intimately between her legs and wondered what it would be like to feel a man inside her. Then, quickly, guiltily, she had stopped.

A month previously, late at night, after the freshmen's ball, Meg had received her first sexual kiss. She hadn't particularly liked the young man but he was a Harvard sporting hero and when he'd asked her to walk along the embankment she couldn't resist being seen leaving the ballroom on his arm. She'd expected to be kissed, of course. She knew she looked beautiful in her pink silk gown. And the full-length, fur-trimmed evening coat she had gathered about her for the chilly walk to the embankment made her feel very sophisticated and fashionable. A recent birthday gift from her mother, the coat was the most expensive and chic item of apparel Meg had ever owned.

A romantic moment overlooking the Charles River was exactly what Meg anticipated so, when he took her in his arms, she tilted her head back, closed her eyes and waited for the gentle meeting of lips she had experienced several times before with Peter, the very nice boy who always contrived to sit beside her during lectures.

She was a little surprised by the degree of pressure on her mouth. And she hadn't expected to be held quite so close. The whole length of his body was pressed against hers and his hand, in the small of her back, was suspiciously close to her buttocks. However, she didn't want to be considered a prude, so she suffered the brutality of his embrace.

But when her lips were forced apart and she felt his tongue thrust its way into her mouth, she started to pull away. There was no escape. He backed her against the embankment wall, one hand locked behind her head, holding her mouth against his. Then she felt his tongue circle hers, the tip of it flicking over her teeth, forcing itself along the soft inside of her lip. His tongue was everywhere. She was repulsed—it was detestable. With his other hand, he roughly pulled open her beautiful coat, exposing her silk-gowned body to his as he forced himself even closer. Then his hand was on her breast and, with horror, she felt the hardness of him pressing against her. She struggled with all her might, grunting with the effort, as she fought to be free of the sickening tongue and the loathsome erection.

The struggle only lasted a matter of seconds, although it felt longer to Meg.

'Jesus Christ,' he exclaimed, finally allowing her to push him away, 'what's the matter with you?'

She didn't answer but started walking back along the embankment as quickly as she could.

'Good God, Meg, it was only a kiss.' He caught up with her but she didn't look at him. During the entire walk back to the ballroom she didn't look at him once.

Daily, ever since that night, Meg had thought of the

kiss. And the more she thought of it, the less repulsive it became. She explored her mouth, pushing her tongue along the soft inside of her lips, flicking the tip of it along her teeth and hard palate. The textures. The warmth and wetness. That's what he would have felt, she thought. With his tongue. Perhaps if he'd been a little more gentle. Perhaps if it had been a different boy, someone she genuinely liked. Peter perhaps. No, Peter would never kiss like that.

Meg looked across the table at David and Amy. They would kiss like that, she was sure of it. She felt a mixture of revulsion and envy.

The sorbet dishes were being cleared in preparation for the main course and Stephen had finally stopped talking long enough to tell the waiter which of the three wines he would prefer with his duck, when Meg dropped her napkin. She simply had to see if David and Amy were holding hands.

They were. Beneath the damask table cloth, fingers entwined, their hands rested together upon David's knee.

But there was something else far more shocking going on under the table. On Paolo's black-trousered thigh rested the delicate hand of Mary-Jane and the fingers were moving almost imperceptibly. She was feeling his flesh through the fine wool fabric of his evening suit.

Meg rescued her napkin and sat bolt upright, hoping that her face was not flushed. When she had recovered her composure she glanced at Mary-Jane. Sweet, innocent Mary-Jane—who would have thought it possible? She glanced at Paolo, but his face was unreadable as he examined the claret bottle the waiter was proffering. His thigh was being intimately caressed by the woman with whom he was obviously having a passionate affair and yet his face registered nothing. Meg was shocked but excited. She sipped her wine and, under the pretext of savouring the flavour, ran the tip of her tongue over her teeth and inside her lips. As she did, she wondered what Paolo's tongue would feel like inside her mouth and she knew that, were Paolo to kiss her in such a way, she would not find it at all repulsive.

From that night on, Meg's feelings for Paolo became confused. She was jealous of the respect accorded him by her father. 'A gifted scholar' was the term Paul Dunleavy applied to his protege. It hurt Meg that there was not the same display of pride or interest in her and as the months passed, her feelings towards Paolo became increasingly ambivalent. His company provoked a jealousy and anger which seemed to grow in direct proportion to the adolescent fantasies he aroused in her.

Paolo, in the meantime, was completely unaware of any difference in Meg's attitude towards him. He was deeply fond of his half-sister, admiring her good humour and her high spirits. But his concentration on his studies and the diversion of Mary-Jane Stewart left Paolo little time to note the change in Meg's disposition. Indeed, Mary-Jane Stewart left him little enough time even for his studies.

Mary-Jane Stewart, with the face of an angel, had a voracious sexual appetite and Paolo had been shocked when he had lost his virginity to her in the back seat of her father's imported Daimler. He wasn't in love with her but he was obsessed with her body. And of course her ready availability to a young man who had just discovered the joys of sex was impossible to refuse. She swore she loved him, but Paolo had his doubts, particularly when he noticed her studying the handsome young men on campus the way a hungry person might contemplate an attractive dinner menu.

When his end-of-term examination results revealed how adversely his work had been affected by Mary-Jane and their activities, Paolo realised he must address the situation. But Mary-Jane did it for him. Unhappy at the prospect of seeing him once a week only as he had suggested, her attention wandered to the third-year dental student who captained the A-grade football team.

Paolo was not unduly heartbroken. By now his attention was very much taken up by the daily reports of the war and the part the Australians were playing in it.

'I WANT TO go home, sir,' he said and he meant it. When he read of the relentless massacre of Australian forces in Gallipoli, Paolo felt guilty about his life of luxury in Boston. He must go home and join the army; he must fight alongside his countrymen.

As Elizabeth had predicted, her husband talked him around, but it took all of Paul Dunleavy's persuasive power and manipulation to simply convince the lad to finish his course.

'Until the end of the year, Paolo, that is all. That is all I ask in return for the financial investment I have made in you . . .'

Of course, young Paolo had to give in to such emotional blackmail, Elizabeth thought, but he was so adamant about returning to Australia in December that she sincerely doubted her husband would be able to dissuade him when the time came. Much as she liked Paolo, Elizabeth was glad. Paul's obsession with the boy was unhealthy and disruptive. Elizabeth wanted her family back the way it used to be.

Paul Dunleavy had no doubts whatsoever that his son would remain in Boston. The boy was acting out of a sense of loyalty and responsibility in professing his desire to go home. They were admirable qualities, but when all was said and done, Paolo Gianni didn't even admit to being wholly Australian. America was his home! He was a highly principled young man, and could not be bought in cold, hard cash, but he could most certainly be bought by America.

Paul held all the aces and he knew it. He'd been right to bide his time. The boy loved America and the way of life to which he'd become accustomed. The city of Boston had seduced him, Paul thought. Whether he was aware of it or not, young Paolo was a true Bostonian at heart. And well on the road to becoming a true Dunleavy.

Chapter Twenty-Three

'Hitchie's here,' Rick Gianni announced to the weary men from C Company who sat slouched against the walls of the dugout having just been relieved after forty-eight hours in the line. 'It's all right, Private,' he nodded to the young lad who hovered by the entrance, 'let him in, he's one of us.'

The lad was newly arrived from Egypt, one of the reinforcements, insufficiently trained and very, very young. Were we that young? Rick wondered. Before the lifetime of the past three months, were we that young?

The lad stood aside and watched suspiciously as the bearded man with the dark, tanned face and the piercing eyes entered. The man carried a Turkish bandolier and a Mauser rifle and looked for all the world like a spy.

'Hitchie!' The eyes of the battle-weary men lit up in an instant. Corporal HV Hitch was the 11th Battalion postmaster who lived in a small dugout behind battalion headquarters from which he dispensed the all-too-infrequent mail. He was not only popular as the sole link the men had with their homeland, he was also well respected as one of the army's most efficient snipers. His disguise as a local was at times too successful, however, and, legendary as his success was in dispatching Turkish snipers, he was all too often arrested by his own troops as a spy and had to be identified and bailed out by a mate from the 11th.

Rick Gianni was doubly glad to see Hitchie, today of all days. Last night's raid had been a devastating one for the men of C Company, although the mission itself had been highly successful. A vital line of Turkish trenches had been captured and, even now, relief troops were consolidating the victory. Soldiers of the 11th Battalion were not only fighting off the Turks who were attempting to return, they were barricading the communication saps which led back to the Turkish position. But it was the men of C Company who had led the attack and suffered the heaviest losses and, right now, mail from home was just what they needed.

'Gianni ... Brereton ... Salter ... Brearley ... Hayes ...' As Hitchie read out the names, the fresh-faced young private who had remained positioned by the entrance with his bayonet at the ready, convinced that these battle-fatigued men couldn't recognise a Turkish spy when they saw one, finally relaxed.

The letters were handed around to the dozen or so soldiers in the dugout and, when there was no response to a name, Hitchie pocketed the letter and said, 'I'll try the beach', but the men knew that many of the names would not be on the beach, where the medical tents, canteen and supplies had been set up.

There were two envelopes for Rick Gianni. One was addressed to 'Enrico' and the hand was awkward. His uncle, Giovanni. The other was in a bold hand. 'Rick Gianni' it said. His sister, Carmelina. It was the first letter he had received from her. She would be writing on behalf of his parents and he hoped that she hadn't told them of his change of name. Rico Gianni would not take kindly to his son calling himself Rick.

He opened Giovanni's envelope first.

Dear Enrico, I have made up a tune for 'Kal', I hope you

will like it. It is a fine song and I look forward to hearing you sing it when you come home from the war. Which I hope will be very soon . . .'

Rick smiled at the simplicity of the letter. He glanced around the dugout at the others. Now seasoned soldiers, they were young men who had grown old in battle. None of them would be coming home from the war 'soon', he thought. Well, not alive anyway.

He noticed that Jack Brearley, who was squatting in the corner of the dugout, had opened his letter but was staring unseeingly at the pages. Jack had been in the forward party of the centre column, right beside the men when it had happened. Rick wondered whether he should say something. No, there was no need. Jack Brearley was tough.

He returned to his letter.

Everyone at home sends their love. Your mother and father are well. And Salvatore. And Carmelina who says she is going to write to you. If you could only see her, Enrico. She has grown into a beauty, your little sister. A black-haired beauty with all the fire of her father. The looks she gets as she walks down Hannan Street make Rico so mad he would kill every man in Kal if he could.

Rick smiled. It was good to read of the people he loved, to escape the trenches just for a moment. To forget the horrors he had been through in this godforsaken place and return to the Kalgoorlie goldfields.

Following the landing at Gallipoli, British Commander-in-Chief Sir Ian Hamilton's instructions had been simple. The troops were to dig in. 'You have got through the difficult business,' was his encouraging signal from the *Queen Elizabeth*. 'Now you have to dig, dig, dig until you are safe.' So dig they did. The great holes torn out of the chalky soil by the shells from their own battleships formed a good basis for many of the dugouts which would eventually reach a depth of thirty feet or more.

Three days after the landing, on the night of the 28th of April, the front-line troops were relieved. Whilst the battle raged on for the men of the 3rd Brigade, those of A and C Companies of the 11th Battalion who had led the attack, were instructed to rest for twenty-four hours on the beach where the stores were being unloaded and the wounded relayed back to the ships. Then, two days later on April 30th, the 11th Battalion was paraded. The tally showed 378 either killed, missing or wounded, 617 still in action.

Again, the orders from Sir Ian Hamilton were simple. The Australian and New Zealand Army Corps were to continue their advance. They must attack and overtake each of the Turkish positions. The fact that the Turks' elevated positions afforded them a vastly superior field of fire seemed immaterial to Sir Ian, and the fight to gain the higher ground became not only desperate but suicidal.

The men knew it. As they scrambled up out of the trenches and over the parapets they did so with the knowledge that they were going to die. Waiting for the signal to advance, many said goodbye to each other; many left farewell notes pinned with their daggers to the sides of the trenches, some even left their wedding rings. Then each man charged into the hail of gunfire to meet his death in his chosen way.

Some dodged and ducked as if they were on a football field. Evading the enemy and staying alive even a few minutes longer was a triumph in itself. Others roared their defiance as they ran. Being the first to fall was *their* triumph: the early fallen took the bullets for the men behind. And some simply blanked their minds, followed their bayonets and ran to their death in silence.

Through sheer determination, many made it to the

enemy lines. And once there, having survived that fearful distance, they threw themselves into the trenches and fought like tigers, each man seemingly with the strength of ten. They could see what they were fighting now. They were confronted with the flesh of their enemy and, after the helpless exposure of No-Man's-Land, there was a hideous relief in the thrust and twist of their bayonets.

Sometimes they won. Sometimes they lost. And when, with a sense of bewilderment, a man found himself alive after such a battle, he thought of his comrades who'd fallen beside him and prepared himself for the fact that tomorrow it would probably be him.

The wholesale slaughter continued until a brief respite was called on the 24th of May. A formal truce had been organised between the Turkish and British headquarters in order to bury the dead and a line was fixed midway between the two fronts. For nine hours from 7.30 am the Turks were to bury the dead on their side and the Australians and New Zealanders on theirs.

'Jesus Christ!' Jack exclaimed to Tom as they surveyed the scene. 'I thought Jacko the Turk was winning.'

The reaction was the same from all the Aussies. They had presumed they were the only ones being decimated but the hundreds of Turkish dead far outnumbered the Australians and New Zealanders.

'G'day, Jacko. I'm Ben, this is me brother Bill.' The Brereton boys were shaking hands with a couple of young Turkish soldiers.

Rick looked around and noticed that many others were doing the same. Before long, the men of both armies were grinning and lighting each other's cigarettes and swapping souvenirs, displaying a camaraderie born of relief that, for a few hours at least, there would be no killing.

Then followed the gruesome business of collecting

the dead. The stench was horrific and the sticky, green-backed flies which plagued the men in the trenches were clustered inches deep over the rotting corpses.

'Give me a hand, Tom.' It was Jack Brearley who found Tony Prendergast. He'd been searching for him among the dead. Three days previously Jack had been beside Tony when he fell. At the time, amidst the cacophony of battle—the whistle of shells, the blast of dynamite and the constant crack of machine-gun fire—one explosion was no different from another. Some a little closer, that was all. But suddenly the Welshman running beside him had been flung four feet into the air and Jack had presumed he'd been blown to pieces. Dodging and weaving and yelling like a banshee, Jack had run on and lived through the charge.

Now, as he bent to pick up his friend, he noticed that Tony's right leg was several yards away from his body and that there was a tourniquet tied to the stump of his thigh. Jesus, Jack thought, how long had the poor bastard been conscious?

He heaved the body over his shoulders in a fireman's lift and, as he did, he heard a sound. The faintest, dry, husky whisper. 'S'trewth,' Jack said to Tom Brereton, 'he's alive.'

There were a number of men in Tony's condition. Men who, by all accounts, should have been dead. They were laid out on the beach to await medical attention and transferral to the ships but little hope was held for their chances. Most died as they lay there on the sand.

The doctor shook his head. 'Don't reckon your cobber's going to make it, mate, I'd say my goodbyes now if I were you.' And he moved on to the next casualty.

Jack stayed for as long as he could, bathing Tony's face and keeping the flies away but, by the time he had to report for duty, the Welshman showed no sign of regaining consciousness. Jack took the doctor's advice and said his goodbyes.

As sapping and tunnelling was the most effective method of gaining ground with minimum casualties, the men of Company C of the 11th Battalion, coming as they did from the goldfields of Western Australia, were inevitably detailed as tunnellers. Their digging and mining experience made them experts. The 'saps' were deep, narrow trenches directed towards the enemy line. The Turkish army occupying the higher position, the Australian and New Zealand Army Corps, now affectionately known as the ANZACs, had literally to burrow forward in order to keep the distance of open attack to a minimum. The saps had various operational uses. A number of them might be linked to form a new front-line trench or, from the sap heads, tunnels might be dug and explosives placed under enemy lines. These 'mines' not only inflicted damage, they created diversons during which the ANZACs stormed the Turkish trenches.

The men of the original 11th Battalion were by now under severe strain. Their numbers had been halved and their reinforcements were ill-prepared. Many of the recruits, newly arrived from Egypt, were picked off by sniper fire whilst training on the beach and never saw battle at all. Three months after the landing, the battalion found it necessary to shorten the hours of duty. Forty-eight hours in the line, the same in support and reserve.

'Cripes, the brass is getting soft,' Tom Brereton remarked. 'It's a bloody holiday.' But, despite the responsive laughter, the men of the original 11th were exhausted. Physically, mentally and emotionally.

Immediately following the forty-eight hour limit, orders came through that the battalion was to storm and capture the line of Turkish trenches directly in front of 'Tasmania Post', as a section of the Allied trenches was nick-named, and that C Company was to lead the attack.

'Some holiday, you stupid geezer.' Jack punched Tom's arm. 'They must have been bloody listening.'

'Crikey, mate, it's an honour, can't you see that?' Tom rubbed his corked bicep. 'It's a bloody honour. I can't wait, I tell you. I just can't wait.'

The cocky bravado of Tom and Jack invariably helped raise morale and soon the men of C Company were joining in their good-humoured larrikinism. It was the Aussie way of getting through the day. There wasn't much point in doing otherwise, most thought. No sense in dwelling on things you couldn't change.

The operational plan was basic. From each of the four sap heads, tunnels were to be dug and explosives placed beside the Turkish line. On the night of the 31st of July, when the signal was given, the Engineer Company was to detonate the explosives, and the men of C Company were to storm the Turkish trenches.

As the moon rose in the night sky, they waited. In the sap heads, the four columns of men, bayonets fixed, hearts pumping and bodies poised, waited for the signal. There it was. Behind them. The red flare glowing on the parapet of the Allied trenches. A second or so later, there was an explosion. Then another. A few more seconds. They waited for two more explosions, but they didn't come. The two centre mines had hung fire. No more time to waste. The order to advance was given and the four columns stormed over the parapets and charged across the intervening ground towards the enemy.

Jack Brearley was amongst the forerunners. A dozen or so men were in front of him and beside him were the Brereton brothers. Screaming like banshees, all three of them, as loud and as long as their lungs would allow. They always did. It was infectious. And Jack screamed along with them.

The landscape and the mass of charging men were suddenly illuminated as the Turks fired flares into the air in order to see and target their enemy's approach. The light was unreal. Vivid, cartoonlike, it etched and highlighted the madness of battle.

Closer and closer to the Turkish line. They were there now, ready to throw themselves upon Jacko Turk. In the light of the Verey flares they could see the enemy clearly. The Turks were in disarray. Some were fleeing, some falling to the flashing bayonets of the men of C Company who'd got there first. Jack and the Brereton brothers screamed even louder. Then the world exploded.

Jack staggered as the force threw him to one side. Tom fell to the ground. But it was Ben and Bill Brereton who suffered the full impact of the blast. The explosives were right beneath them.

As if in slow motion, Tom Brereton watched his brothers fall headlong into the trenches. He lay powerless on the ground as he watched them, in the garish light of the flares, being buried alive. Even as he hauled himself to his knees, dirt and debris continued to fall all around him, but he had no mind for the surrounding chaos as he clawed at the freshly created grave.

'Tom!' Above the din he heard Jack's voice and turned in time to see the glint of the Turk's dagger. He threw himself to one side, the dagger slicing through his upper arm, and then the weight of the man's body was upon him as Jack's bayonet found its mark. Tom heaved the body aside and once again started clawing at the rubble.

'Leave it, Tom! Leave it!' Jack was yelling and trying to pull him away.

'Our own bomb, for Christ's sake!' There was hysteria in his voice as he dug frantically. 'We blew them up with our own bloody bomb!'

'It wouldn't do any good, even if you could get them out!' Jack shouted. 'They copped the full blast; they've had it, mate!' The hysteria in Tom Brereton died as quickly as it had manifested itself. 'They've had it,' Jack repeated.

Tom nodded, picking up his rifle and bayonet. The Turks had fled the section of the trench which had been directly hit by the explosives but there were whole pockets of resistance where the battle raged on. Jack followed Tom as he charged into the fray.

THE DAY'S FIRST light revealed the full success of the attack. Only one portion of the enemy line remained in Turkish hands. Relief forces were called in to build a barricade across the trench and further barricades across communication saps leading back to Turkish positions. The relief forces continued to repel any Turks attempting to return and the victorious men of C Company had been retired to safety behind the lines.

Tom Brereton leaned against the dugout wall, his left arm hanging limply by his side. Blood dripped from his fingers and his face was deathly white. Any minute he was going to faint.

Jack stuffed the letter he'd barely read into his top pocket and crossed to his friend. 'We need to get you to the iodine king, mate.' He tried to sound as hearty as he could although he felt sick himself at the memory of the Brereton brothers and their moment of death. No time to think about that now.

'Look at it.' Tom thrust the envelope he clutched in his right hand at Jack. 'Just look at it, will you? "The Brereton Boys", that's what it says. Bloody stupid. That's Dad. He thinks we're all going to make it through this war, the stupid bastard. It's a miracle the three of us got this far.' He swayed and would have fallen had Jack not caught him in time.

'Give us a hand, will you?' Jack turned to the nearest man for help. Rick Gianni was immediately by his side. 'We have to take him to the beach.'

'Sure. I'll get a stretcher.'

'No.' As Rick turned to go, Tom's voice stopped him. 'No stretcher.'

He wouldn't let them carry him although he was so weak he could barely walk.

'Lean on me,' Jack insisted, hitching Brereton's uninjured arm over his shoulder and holding him firmly around the waist.

Tom staggered as he tried to pick up his kit.

'It's all right, mate,' Rick grabbed the rifle and backpack, 'I've got your kit, don't worry.'

Three times during the trek to the beach he nearly fell and eventually Rick and Jack took a shoulder each and virtually carried him. He didn't seem to feel any pain from his injury, although Rick was covered in the blood which flowed anew from the exertion.

'Hell of a thing to happen, eh?' Tom talked continuously as they went. 'Copping it from your own bomb.' He gave a derisive snort, as if the whole incident were some shockingly tasteless joke. 'I mean, being smudged is one thing, but being smudged by your own bloody bomb! Hell of a thing to happen.' He looked at the letter, now a crumpled blood-stained mess, still clutched in his hand. 'The Brereton boys! The Bloody Brereton boys! Hell of a thing to happen.'

He was delirious by the time they got him to the medical tent.

'He'll make it,' the medical officer said on examination. 'The wound is superficial but he's lost a lot of blood. You should have got him here earlier.'

The officer's tone was censorious and for a moment Rick thought Jack was going to hit the man.

'Come on, Jack,' he said, 'let's get out of here. I've

saved my rum ration, I reckon we've earned it.'

Jack followed him automatically and, as they sat on the beach together, Rick handed him the little tin flask of rum from the top pocket of his tunic. The night before a battle, the men were given a rum ration and, not being much of a drinker, Rick invariably kept his.

They sat on the beach together staring out to sea. A Gianni and a Brearley sharing a drink. Rick wondered vaguely what their fathers would say. Rico and Harry would surely disown their sons if they could see them now.

He glanced at Jack and realised that Tom Brereton was not the only one suffering the effects of shock. The little tin flask which Jack had placed beside him had tipped over and rum was spilling out onto the sand. But Jack hadn't noticed. He was staring blankly ahead. His jaw was clenched, his breathing was shallow and fast and a muscle twitched in the side of his neck. Delayed shock. Rick knew all the signs. He'd seen them and suffered them himself. Many times. They all had. Distraction was the answer.

'I got a couple of letters from home,' he said taking them from his pocket. Better not mention that one of them was from Giovanni, he thought. 'My sister, Carmelina,' he said, opening the letter he'd not yet read. 'You remember Carmelina.'

The banal chatter distracted Jack and he turned, irritated by the voice. Bloody Enrico Gianni, he thought. Pity it wasn't him who'd copped it instead of the Brereton brothers. The bastard was only good for playing his bloody concertina anyway.

He returned his gaze to the ocean, but he didn't see the waves lapping the shore, or the clear blue horizon. He saw Bill Brereton's body exploding in front of him. In the gaudy light of the flares, he saw the recognition of death in Ben's eyes as he was hurled into the trench to be buried alive.

'Who was your letter from?' The voice again. Jack didn't answer. 'I saw you got a letter,' the voice insisted. 'Who was it from? Anyone I know?'

Jack turned, and the images disappeared as he saw Rick Gianni nodding, encouraging.

'Your letter. Who was it from?'

It was then Jack realised that he'd been hyperventilating. He stared down at the sand and noticed that the rum had spilled from the flask. 'A girl,' he said. 'No one important. Just a girl.' Jack felt his breathing subside.

The images would return tonight of course. The death of the Brereton brothers would join the list of hideous images which would haunt his sleeping hours for the rest of his life. There was surely not one ANZAC who did not wake with his own image of the horrors of battle. But Jack's shock reaction was abating and he was grateful to Rick Gianni's distraction for that.

He picked up the little tin flask and wiped the sand from it. 'I'm sorry about your rum,' he said as he handed it back. 'I'll give you my next ration.'

Rick shrugged. 'I don't really drink much, it doesn't matter—'

'I'm no bludger and I owe you.' There was a grudging thanks in his voice. 'I'll give you my next ration.'

'Rightio.'

Chapter Twenty-Four

The Cremorne Gardens stood at the top end of Hannan Street not far from the railway station. In an effort to justify the name, the surrounding ten-foot-high tin fence had been scenically painted with trees and bushes and flowers. In reality, however, the Cremorne Gardens was anything but a garden. On the other side of the tin fence, the ground was gravelled and there was not a tree or flower to be seen, just rows and rows of hessian deck chairs under the open sky. All facing the magic, silver screen.

Carmelina Gianni loved the Cremorne Gardens. Every Friday, she and her girlfriends would be the first to queue for tickets. They would sit anchored to their deck chairs, eyes glued to the screen, transfixed by the smouldering intensity of Wallace Reid or the exotic sexuality of Theda Bara and, for a precious two hours, they would escape the humdrum life of Kal.

When Louis Picot invited Carmelina to the Cremorne Gardens, it was a dream come true. Not only was he the wealthy son of the famous Gaston Picot and the new manager of Kalgoorlie's most glamorous restaurant, Louis could have stepped right off the screen himself. His were Hollywood looks. From the dark, curly locks which framed his face to the passionate eyes and pencil moustache.

Louis himself had taken great pains to acquire the image he presented. He had always admired his father's professional Frenchman act and, indeed, Gaston's advice to him had always been, 'Be interesting, Louis . . . be different . . . stand out in a crowd'. So Louis had adopted the Latin lover image. It was quite the fashion of the day and served him well. There were few enough young men left since the outbreak of war, let alone ones who looked like matinee idols. He regretted the fact that he didn't have a foreign accent but his parentage and his name were glamorously European and that sufficed.

Louis and Carmelina met at Smedley's Haberdashery where, for the past six months, Carmelina had been employed to sell the ladies' goods—the gloves, ribbons, buttons and threads—and, at the end of the day, to tidy the displays and sweep the floors. It was a happy arrangement. Smedley found having a beautiful young girl about the shop good for business, and Carmelina was delighted to be out of school, which she had always detested, and earning her own living.

'Such a sweet girl,' Albert Smedley remarked when he noticed how taken Louis Picot appeared to be with his young assistant. 'Remarkable to think she has only recently celebrated her seventeenth birthday.'

Louis's eyes were cold. Was there an element of censure in Smedley's tone? Impossible—the man could not afford to lose his prize customer. 'Which makes her even more attractive surely,' he smiled. 'The bloom of youth is irresistible, is it not?'

'It most certainly is, Mr Picot.' Smedley reverted to servility; he had made the gesture after all, that was enough. 'She is indeed a very beautiful young woman.' He carefully wrapped the silk cravat Louis had purchased and pretended not to hear him ask Carmelina to dine at Restaurant Picot.

Carmelina knew that to dine at the restaurant was out of the question—word would inevitably reach her father. 'I'm afraid I already have a dinner engagement, Mr Picot. Just a family gathering,' she added hastily in case he should think she had a beau.

'Ah well, no matter.' Louis checked his image in the mirror behind the counter and slightly adjusted his trilby. It was probably just as well she wasn't available, he told himself. He hadn't realised that this luscious-bodied temptress was only seventeen. Of course, that made her all the more desirable, but if the girl's family was around, it simply wasn't worth the trouble. 'Thank you, Albert,' he said as he accepted the package from Smedley.

'Thank *you*, Mr Picot.' Albert Smedley bobbed a sort of curtsy.

'However . . .' She was at the door in a flash and all Louis could think of was how beautiful her breasts looked under the white, starched blouse. 'However,' she repeated breathlessly, 'there is a new picture opening at the Cremorne Gardens and I have made an arrangement to go with some friends and . . . um . . .' Her voice petered out as he looked at her with his smouldering eyes. Eyes just like Wallace Reid's in *The Affairs of Anatole*, Carmelina thought, her heart pounding with excitement.

Louis was undone. In an instant, caution was thrown to the wind. The girl was not only beautiful, she was a virgin; he was sure of it. Ripe and ready and panting to explore her own sexuality.

'Then perhaps, if your friends could forgo the pleasure of your company,' he said, smiling his Latin lover smile, 'you might allow me the pleasure?' Her brown eyes, wide as saucers, were staring disbelievingly up at him. 'Would you accompany me to the Cremorne Gardens, Miss . . .?'

'Gianni. Yes . . .' Carmelina couldn't believe it was happening. 'Yes, that would be nice.'

'Where do you live? I shall pick you up in my car.'

'No, no, there's no need, I'll meet you at the picture theatre.'

He'd known of course that she would say that. God forbid he should meet her family. 'Very well. Shall we say eight o'clock?'

A MACK SENNETT film was showing that night but neither of them were really watching. Not even Carmelina, despite the fact that Mabel Normand was one of her favourites. Prior to the interval, all Carmelina could think of was the envious looks her friends cast in her direction. And after the interval, all she could think of was the fact that Louis Picot was holding her right hand in both of his. But he wasn't really holding it at all. He was making love to it. The fingers of his left hand were interlaced with hers and, as he placed their hands upon his knee, she could feel the warmth of his body. With his right hand, he stroked her wrist, her forearm, the back of her hand. And she felt the caress of his fingertips through her whole body.

As for Louis, he had not an inkling of the film they were watching. Neither the title, nor the stars, nor the story. He could feel her quivering. Virgins always excited him. Virgins on the brink of discovery, wanting to know, wanting to experience and be taught. And the tuition was such a delicate exercise. One had to be so careful.

At twenty-six, Louis Picot was a debauched young man. A product of his upbringing, he saw no wrong in his behaviour. He had been taught that one's activities behind closed doors were immaterial so long as, in society, one behaved like a gentleman.

Shortly before his seventeenth birthday, Louis had

lost his virginity to the madam of a high-class brothel.

His father had been proud of his reported performance. 'Madame Clarisse says that you performed like a man, Louis. *Bon. Tres bon.* It is beholden upon a man to be a good lover.'

Over the following year, proud of his son's good looks and sophistication, Gaston took the boy on many an evening foray, gambling, drinking, womanising. He boasted to his friends that Louis was only seventeen and yet already a man of the world.

'Discretion is the key to social success, Louis,' Gaston advised. 'One can move in all circles if one is discreet. From the crudest of whorehouses to the most patrician of homes—why to royalty itself—one can make love to harlots one night and the wives of aristocrats the next . . . so long as one is discreet.'

Gaston explained all of his business dealings to Louis shortly after the boy turned eighteen, including the string of lucrative brothels in Kalgoorlie. After all, Louis would own them one day. Far from being shocked, Louis was deeply impressed. His father's business profile was so respectable.

It was a lesson which Louis took to heart but, as the years progressed, even the worldly Gaston Picot might have been a little shocked had he known the extent of his son's depravity.

Louis knew he must move with caution. The girl wanted to be taken, certainly, but despite the quickened pulse he could feel beneath his fingertips and the quivering which he knew was coursing through her entire body, he must feed her fantasy until she was ready. If his sexual advances were too overt she would be frightened off.

'Shall we walk a little?' he said when the film was over.

Carmelina nodded, aware of her friends peering

over the tops of their deck chairs down the front, whispering and nudging each other. She hoped desperately that they would keep her secret and that word would not reach her father, but she was bursting with pride as she walked out of the Cremorne Gardens on Louis Picot's arm. She felt like a Hollywood princess and it was worth risking her father's ire for that. It was worth risking anything for that.

They walked past the Mount Charlotte Mine. The night was soft and dark, the barest of crescent moons in the sky. He stopped and, without a word, drew her to him. She said nothing, but she felt herself tremble.

Their bodies were very close and his hands were caressing her hair, and her shoulders, and the small of her back. His mouth was gently kissing the side of her neck. Up towards her ear. Her chin. Her mouth. When their lips finally touched, it was not experience that opened her mouth to his, it was something she had never felt before. An urgency. And her breath came in short gasps as she pressed every inch of her body against his, her mouth now open and hungry.

Louis was pleased—she was more ready than he'd thought. It appeared he didn't need to wait at all. 'Shall we go to my room at the Palace?' he whispered.

It was the shock Carmelina needed. The spell was broken. She had been mindless to everything but the touch of his mouth and his hands and the closeness of his body.

'No,' she said breathlessly. 'No, I must go home, my father will kill me if I'm late.'

Louis was fully aware that he could have had her, right then and there on the ground, but he didn't want it that way. It would be over too quickly and the pleasure would be wasted. Besides, the night was dark and he wanted to see her body; to watch her moan and writhe and beg for more as he played the master.

'I must see you again.' He tucked her arm caringly into his and they walked back towards the Cremorne Gardens.

'Yes.' Carmelina was still fighting for control. She had shocked herself. It was passion she'd felt, she knew that. But where had it come from? She'd felt like an animal. Like a bitch on heat. 'Will you be coming to Smedley's Haberdashery again soon?' She must try and sound normal.

'Oh my dear,' he smiled, 'how many gloves, cravats and stick pins does one need?' That sounded too flippant, he decided, it would be wiser to play the young Lothario. This one was worth more than a single experience. This one was very young and very passionate and could be trained. 'Besides,' he added gently, 'I would prefer us to be alone. I don't care to share you with others.'

Carmelina was once more in control of herself. Her heart still beat wildly, but now it was for sheer romance. Everything he said was straight out of a Hollywood picture.

Louis stopped as an idea occurred to him. 'How would you like to work at Restaurant Picot?' he asked abruptly. In the stunned silence which followed, he added, 'It would be a very respectable position. You would greet the guests and help them on and off with their shawls and cloaks and hats.'

He was struck with the brilliance of his idea. A pretty young girl as cloakroom attendant would be far more effective than the current uniformed bell-hop. But of course that was why his father had recently appointed him manager of Restaurant Picot. 'Innovative ideas, Louis,' Gaston had said, 'that is what what we need. Innovative *young* ideas. Harry Brearley has become too complacent, too middle-aged. Naturally,' he'd added, 'you must not tell him I said that. Let him parade around—as he will wish to of course—but you, my son, will be the driving force behind Restaurant Picot.'

'We will buy a beautiful black evening dress for you,' Louis went on, genuinely enthusiastic, 'and you will look like a film star when you greet the guests.'

'Oh.' Carmelina could barely breathe for excitement.

'I AM GOING to say yes, Papa. Whether you like it or not.'

Young Salvatore grabbed another hunk of bread and watched his sister do battle. She certainly had guts, he had to give her that. But, as always, she was the one most likely to get around their father's defences.

This time, however, Rico would have none of it. 'It's Harry Brearley's place,' he said. As far as Rico was concerned, that was the end of the matter.

'No, Papa, it's not!'

Carmelina had told Louis that Harry Brearley would be the reason her father would object and Louis had come up with all the right answers, many of them bordering on the truth. 'But your father must tell no one,' he'd warned.

'That is why Mr Picot has taken over,' she continued. 'His father is getting rid of Harry Brearley but no one is supposed to know yet. Not even Harry himself. Mr Picot's father says that Harry Brearley is finished in Kal.'

Rico looked at Teresa across the breakfast table. 'That is something I would like to see,' he said.

'I can tell you everything that is going on there, Papa.' Carmelina could see that the idea intrigued her father so she went in for the kill. Defiant, proud, she played the scene just the way one of her Hollywood heroines would have played it.

'It is a very respectable position I am being offered, greeting the guests as they arrive at Restaurant Picot. I will be looked up to and admired.' Now the emotional plea. 'Oh Papa, I don't want to spend the rest of my life sweeping up the floor of Smedley's Haberdashery.'

It was all that was needed. Of course Rico gave in, as Teresa knew he would. Laughable as she found Carmelina's performance, she rather envied her daughter's ability to manipulate. Was it just the moving pictures which had taught her, Teresa wondered, or was it born in her?

'What do you think, Teresa?' Rico's voice interrupted her thoughts.

'Of course she should accept—it's a very good job.' Teresa didn't know why they were bothering to discuss it. 'And I'm sure it will pay more than Mr Smedley does.' She began to clear the table. 'Giovanni has had a letter from Enrico. He is bringing it around to read to us tomorrow.'

Carmelina rose and started scraping the dishes. She could have kissed her mother. First thing Monday morning, when Louis arrived at the haberdashery, they would tell Mr Smedley, together, that she was leaving. Louis had said that she could start work at Restaurant Picot as soon as possible. 'Just as soon as we buy you the prettiest black dress in Kal,' he'd added.

'Will you write to him, Carmelina?' her mother was saying. 'Write to him from all of us.'

Carmelina was confused for a second. Of course, Enrico. 'Yes, Mamma, I'll write to him,' she promised.

Rico watched his wife carry the pile of dishes to the sink. Teresa was looking tired, he thought. And old. The fire had left her and she looked all of her forty-three years. And yet their lives had never been easier. The children were no trouble or expense. Carmelina donated half her salary to the household and, although Salvatore was still at school, he earned his own pocket money delivering newspapers. As for Rico himself, he received a far better salary as a miner than he ever had as a timbercutter.

When the vast percentage of miners had joined the army and left to fight the war, the big mines had been desperate. They needed men. Rico had approached the Midas for a job and Giovanni had been only too happy to help, knowing that, with young Enrico off to war, times would be hard for the family.

Rico loved working once more below ground. He felt reborn, stronger and fitter than ever, and it saddened him to see his beloved Teresa tired and worn when she should have been enjoying these comfortable middle years of their life together. He knew why she was weary, her heart was aching. Daily she pined for Enrico. Every minute of her waking hours she thought of him. And he, her own husband, could only watch, powerless, unable to help her.

Rico cursed his eldest son. He was a fool. Only fools fought another country's war. They were all fools. But Enrico was the biggest fool of the lot. Not only was Enrico fighting another country's war, he believed he was fighting alongside his fellow countrymen, his fellow 'Aussies'. That was the most foolish notion of the lot. Enrico was not an Aussie, the Australians were not his countrymen and they never would be. The good old Aussies themselves would never allow him to be one of them, couldn't he see that? Didn't he hear what they called him? Wog. Dago. Didn't he see the looks on their faces in the street?

Of course the people of Kal wouldn't dare offend Rico Gianni these days. But the feeling was the same. It always would be. And that fool of a son of his couldn't see it. There he was, fighting alongside his good old Aussie mates, risking his life and breaking his mother's heart in the process. Well damn him, Rico thought. Damn him, he deserved to get blown to pieces.

'So Giovanni is bringing a letter from Enrico with

him tomorrow?' Thinking about his son put an edge to Rico's voice.

Teresa recognised it. Oh please, Rico, she prayed, don't start again, please. 'He will bring his piano accordion too,' she tried to sound cheerful, 'and we will sing, all of us, just like the old times.'

'The boy writes to his uncle and not his Mamma and Papa, that's a good son for you.'

'Giovanni can read, Rico,' God give me patience, she thought, 'and we cannot. Besides . . .'

'Carmelina and Salvatore can.'

'Besides he has written to us just recently. Now it is Giovanni's turn.' He looked as if he was about to interrupt again so she raised her voice and continued. 'And who's to say there is not a letter in the post to us right now!'

Leave it, Rico, she begged silently, leave it. She knew he only berated Enrico because he blamed the boy for her unhappiness. But his condemnation didn't help as, each day, Teresa waited for the news of her son's death.

Rico finally shut up. He could see the tension building in her. It was all Enrico's fault. The fool of a boy. He scowled down at the table.

Relieved by the silence, Teresa started to wash the dishes. She should be feeling happy, she thought. Giovanni was coming around tomorrow with a letter from Enrico. She pushed aside the horrible thought that, by the time the mail reached Australian shores, many more soldiers would be lying dead on Turkish soil. It was foolish to think like that. She must keep her spirits up. Tomorrow they would sing songs and read aloud Enrico's letter.

AT FIRST HARRY had reacted badly to Gaston's suggestion.

'He wants to make that dandy of a son of his the

manager of Restaurant Picot!' he complained to Maudie the night after Gaston's telephone call. 'And he's actually pretending he's doing me a favour! "Have a well-earned rest, *mon ami*," he says, "you've earned it." What does he take me for, a fool? That boy has been in Kal for two months, "to learn a little of the restaurant trade" I was told, and now he knows it all, and he and his father want to kick me out.'

Maudie chose not to enter into the conversation. The outcome of the disagreement would make very little difference to Harry's lifestyle anyway. He spent his evenings at Restaurant Picot gambling with his friends. If he now needed to change his venue, what difference would it make? Surely it was immaterial whether he gambled at Restaurant Picot or at Hannan's Club.

Maudie had given up nagging Harry about his gambling. If he wanted to throw his money away, then he could, she'd decided. It had been unrealistic and foolish of her to ever presume she could make him change his ways.

But no amount of self-chastisement could alter the fact that Maudie was once again disappointed in Harry—he seemed hell bent on presenting her with a lifetime of disappointments—and she kept her own money well and truly locked away. Just as well she was a self-sufficient woman with a healthy business, she thought, Harry was not a good provider.

He was still a good father to the twins, however, and for that Maudie was thankful. The twins worshipped him, just as little Jack Brearley had done.

Jack. God how she missed him. Of course he was probably giving the army as many headaches as he'd given her—he was trouble, that boy, she thought, with a wistful smile.

Maudie never let herself think of Jack dying. Even as she read the horrific newspaper accounts of the casualties at Gallipoli, she told herself that it wouldn't happen to Jack. The boy would come home, she told herself. He was the sort that did.

'What good will Louis Picot do for the restaurant anyway?' Harry was still ranting on. 'He's a poseur. All he cares about is the cut of his hair and the clothes on his back.'

Maudie didn't point out that, for the whole of Harry's life, he had been consumed by self-image and was a slave to fashion. He was probably envious of Louis Picot, she thought. These days, because of his weight, Harry opted for bulky comfort rather than slenderness of cut, although he still insisted upon the very finest of fabrics. Yes, that was it, she thought, he was envious of young Picot.

It was true that Louis Picot's sartorial elegance irked Harry who, in the main, successfully avoided full-length mirrors and anything else that would tell him the truth. Until recently, he had enjoyed cutting a fine figure as he circulated amongst the diners. He was still a splendid-looking fellow, he told himself. His face was still handsome; he still had a fine head of hair and he certainly felt as young and debonair as ever.

But these days, when young Louis Picot walked into the restaurant, Harry would watch the heads turn and he would catch sight of his own reflection in a window or mirror and realise that he was a bloated middle-aged man with a florid nose, puffy eyes and rather large ears. It was always a shock and he hated it.

The mere thought that this arrogant young peacock was going to usurp his position was intolerable and, for days, Harry fumed. Whether the boy was Gaston's son or not, what right did the Frenchman have to make such a decision? Harry had shares in the restaurant, after all; surely he had some say as to who should manage the place.

But, after the initial assurance that Harry should take a rest, Gaston had studiously avoided him. And now he had left for Europe. Or so Gabrielle had informed Harry when he'd telephoned Maison Picot. Not that Harry had believed her. Picot would be a damn fool to go to Europe now there was a war on. There was little Harry could do but wait for Gaston to contact him.

He'd be waiting a long time, however.

Gaston Picot had finished with Harry Brearley. His own son now had the maturity and experience to take over Restaurant Picot, the legitimacy of the brothels had long been established and, as far as Gaston was concerned, neither Harry nor his position as Deputy Mayor were of any further use. Indeed, it had only been Gaston's money and influence that had kept Harry in office over the last several years, the people were no longer interested in him and the next elections would certainly not see him reinstated. If, after that, Harry were to become too much of a nuisance, the Frenchman held the final ace. Harry had used his shares in Restaurant Picot as collateral to raise money and pay off his gambling debts. It would be simple for Gaston, through his contacts, to have the loan called in. That would certainly finish flashy Harry Brearley.

LOUIS SEDUCED CARMELINA two weeks after she commenced work at Restaurant Picot. He could have accomplished the seduction much earlier, probably on the first night, but he so enjoyed tantalising her that the wait became exquisite.

For days, in dark corners when no one was watching, Louis had kissed and caressed her and whispered such passionate endearments that, by the time they were actually alone in his room at the Palace Hotel, Carmelina couldn't wait for him to undress her. Any modesty she might once have felt at the prospect of appearing naked in front of a man had vanished. Her passion had been teased beyond endurance, and she now needed to feel his caresses upon her bare skin and to feel his flesh against hers.

Louis was as gentle as possible when he entered her. In total control, he nursed her through the initial pain. 'My darling,' he whispered over and over again, 'you're beautiful. You're beautiful, my darling.' And, when he sensed that she was beyond the pain and there was nothing left but pure pleasure, he brought her to the brink of fulfilment, then withdrew. Again and again he teased her until she was begging him, clutching him, trying to draw him deep inside her. But he wouldn't allow it. Not until he sensed that she could not be tantalised once more without climaxing.

'No,' she begged as he withdrew. 'No.'

'One more time, my darling.' It had been dangerously close then, he thought. 'Just one more time.' Then one more time after that. And yet again. 'Just one more time, my darling, one more time.'

Louis was enjoying himself now. This was the way he liked it. He was the master and she the slave, begging for pleasure. Or pain. It made little difference to Louis so long as he was the one in total control.

It was only when she was close to passing out, when she was hyperventilating and her eyelids were fluttering, that he delivered her from her torment. By then, the ecstasy of her orgasm was born of sheer relief and she cried out as she clung to him, her body heaving.

Louis finally allowed himself to ejaculate but, as usual, his climax was the least important aspect of the exercise. A necessary release of energy, that was all. It was Carmelina's responses which had truly excited him. And this was only the beginning. There was so much for her to learn, so much for her to discover, and Louis's pleasure lay in her discovery. He would teach her. He would help her to explore herself and then he would watch as she surrendered to the sexuality which raged within.

Carmelina was the new jewel in Louis's crown and already he had plans for the next step.

'". . . THE ATTEMPT TO capture the Dardanelles, and eventually Constantinople, has been acknowledged by the High Command as a complete failure",' Carmelina read out loud. '"Tomorrow, Monday, the 20th of December, will mark the completion of the evacuation of Australian troops from the bloody shores of the Gallipoli peninsula."'

Teresa and Salvatore sat beside her listening in rapt attention as she continued, whilst at the head of the table sat Rico, feigning disinterest.

'"The now legendary valour of the ANZACs has cost Australia dearly. Over 8,000 dead and over 19,000 wounded on this barren finger of land . . ."'

There was silence as she put down the newspaper.

'At least they are away from that dreadful place,' Teresa said. She crossed herself and silently prayed that Enrico was amongst the soldiers evacuated.

'I must go now, Mamma.' Carmelina rose and carefully smoothed down the skirts of her new dress which she'd taken care not to crease as she sat at the table reading.

'But Caterina and Giovanni will be here soon,' Teresa said, taken aback. 'And Briony and little Rosalina.'

'Where do you go?' Rico demanded suspiciously. 'Where do you go in your new dress?'

Rico was scowling but Carmelina interrupted before he could say anything. 'You like my pretty new dress, Papa?' She twirled about flirtatiously. 'That's why I'm wearing it. To show it to Maria.'

'But why do you go to Maria's today?' Teresa argued. 'Today your uncle is coming, and your cousins. Why do you go to Maria's this Sunday?'

Carmelina stopped twirling and picked up her purse. 'Because I promised.'

'You stay here,' Rico commanded. 'You stay here and entertain your cousins.'

'But Sunday is the only day I have off, Papa,' Carmelina protested. 'It's the only day I have to see my friends.'

'You stay here and help your Mamma.'

Teresa shrugged. She didn't need help and she was not going to enter the argument. What was the point? Rico would give in to Carmelina anyway, he always did.

'But that's not fair, Papa.' Carmelina was on the verge of tears. 'I work so hard at Restaurant Picot, you know I do.'

That was it, Teresa thought, that was the argument which always won him around. Carmelina never actually mentioned the substantial weekly contributions she made to the household finances but it was an argument that couldn't really be refuted. Even Rico had to admit that the girl earned the right to do as she wished on her day off.

'Sunday is my special day.' She was wheedling now, she knew he was weakening. 'Please, Papa.' Her hand was around his shoulders, any minute she would sit on his lap and nuzzle up to him as she used to do when she was a little girl.

'Go on,' he said gruffly. 'Off with you. And don't be late.'

'I won't.' She kissed the top of his head. 'Bye, Papa, bye, Mamma, bye, Salvatore.' And she was gone, leaving Salvatore shaking his head in admiration.

IT WAS A pleasant Sunday. It always was when Caterina

and Giovanni and their two daughters came to visit. If, somehow, a little bittersweet for Teresa. When she looked at Caterina, as beautiful as ever, Teresa could not help but feel a deep envy. It was easy for Caterina to remain beautiful, she told herself—Caterina's firstborn son was not at war. There were no visions in Caterina's mind of a bloodied Paolo dying an agonising death on foreign soil.

Again and again she would shake her envy from her. Dear Caterina was so caring. And Giovanni loved to read aloud the letters Enrico sent him. The boy was closer to Giovanni than he was to his own father.

Teresa knew that Giovanni censored the letters as he read them but even so they revealed an intimacy Enrico could never have shared with his father. It was good, Teresa thought. Enrico was a sensitive boy and he needed a man to whom he could reveal his innermost thoughts. But she cursed her own illiteracy. If only her son could write to her like that.

There were no letters to read aloud this Sunday so they rejoiced in the fact that the troops had been evacuated from Gallipoli. Before eating, Teresa, Caterina and Giovanni sat and discussed the newspaper reports whilst Rico smoked a pipe and refused to join in.

Outside, in the gathering dusk, Salvatore sat and watched his cousins play hopscotch on the dusty pavement. 'Nah, that's a girl's game,' he insisted from the comfort of the front verandah when Briony asked him to play. Secretly, he would have rather liked to join in, it might have led to some chance contact with Briony. When he'd tackled her in the football game they'd played last visit, he'd actually felt her breasts, unintentionally of course, and he couldn't wait to repeat the experience. But it would be more than his life was worth if any of his mates saw him playing hopscotch with girls.

Briony was nine months older than Salvatore—she

would be sixteen early next year—and she too would have preferred not to play hopscotch, it was a game for babies, but she'd promised Rosalina. She threw the taw into the first square. 'Just the one game, Rosie,' she said.

'Do you want to play football instead?' Salvatore asked hopefully.

'No,' she replied with a touch of regret. 'This is a new dress, Mum'd be mad.'

Salvatore had noticed the new dress. It suited her. She looked very pretty. But then Briony always looked pretty, even in her old dungarees. She had a body verging on womanhood. Budding and healthy. Her eyes were as blue as the sky on a summer's day and her hair was as red as the outback earth itself. But it wasn't just because she was pretty that Salvatore liked her. Briony wasn't like other girls. She didn't giggle and tease and she didn't play devious games like his sister. Briony always said exactly what she thought. She was more like a boy in that regard. Briony was bold and Salvatore respected her for that.

It was only over the past several months that Salvatore had really come to know Briony. Only since Carmelina had been working at the restaurant. Before that, when the two Gianni families gathered, Carmelina and Briony would huddle together to talk, ignoring Salvatore for the most part. But that had changed now that Carmelina was away all the time, working at the restaurant or with her girlfriends on Sundays.

'I was born out in the scrub. In a humpy. And my mother nearly died.' That's what Briony had told him when they'd sat on the verandah after their football game and swigged water from the old hessian water bag which hung from a nail by the door. He'd been impressed.

Salvatore watched the game of hopscotch impatiently. He wished they'd hurry up so he and Briony could sit and talk before they were called in for dinner.

Briony was thinking the same thing. 'That's it, Rosie, you've won.' She made it a habit to let her little sister win every third game. 'Go inside and wash your hands, it'll be dinner soon.'

Rosalina did as she was told and Briony joined Salvatore on the porch. 'Where's Carmelina?' she asked.

'At Maria's.'

'Oh.'

'I thought there was going to be a fight to start with,' Salvatore continued. ' "Stay here and entertain your cousins", that's what he said. But she got around him. She always gets around Papa. I don't know how she does it, but she does.'

There was a moment's pause whilst Briony gazed up at the sky. It would be night soon. A clear night, and the stars would be very, very bright. She loved such nights. 'Rosalina's your cousin,' she said.

'Yes, I know,' Salvatore replied, mystified.

'I'm not.' When he looked blankly back at her, she added, 'Giovanni is not my father, I'm not your cousin.'

Of course, he realised, she was right. It had never occurred to him before.

'I'm not related to you at all, Salvatore.'

He stared back at her, but her gaze had returned to the sky. 'The stars are going to be very, very bright tonight,' she said, then got up and walked inside.

After dinner, Giovanni played his piano accordion and they all sang. Just like old times, they agreed. Except that Giovanni himself did not sing. 'My voice is weary,' he said, 'it would not sound good,' and he encouraged the others to sing instead.

Giovanni, too, had aged, Teresa thought. He was as handsome as ever, perhaps even more so, his youthful beauty now hardy and weathered—why was it, she wondered, that life's experience sat so well upon the face of a man and not upon that of a woman?—but he had certainly aged.

Rico got drunk. Harmlessly so, but drunk nonetheless. Filled with brotherly love, he toasted Giovanni. 'To the finest brother a man could have.' He toasted Teresa. 'To the only woman I have ever loved.' He toasted the family. 'To the Giannis, a name to bear with pride.' And the only time he became even mildly aggressive was when he berated Carmelina for not being present. 'A night such as this, the girl should be with her family,' he muttered. 'With her own blood.' And he raised his glass once more. 'To the Giannis!'

CARMELINA'S SENSES WERE screaming. Every inch of her body had been explored, it seemed, and yet still she was left wanting. Her flesh trembled where tongues had teased and fingers had touched. She'd been played upon intimately and expertly and now she begged him to give her the final release.

'Please, Louis, please,' she moaned, her body writhing on the pink satin sheets, her face turned to him imploringly.

He sat, fully clothed, beside the door, watching in the soft rose-coloured light as the two whores knelt over her. One of them looked at him, a question in her eyes. He shook his head imperceptibly.

'Soon, my darling, soon,' he said. 'You're so beautiful.'

Through the haze of her pleasure, she could see him watching her. He was touching himself. He wanted her, she thought. He was deeply aroused and soon it would be just the two of them, making love. Carmelina would do anything for Louis, anything that excited him and made him love her.

At first it had been the forbidden thrill of making

love in a brothel. 'At Red Ruby's,' he'd whispered, 'I hear they have satin sheets and rose-coloured lights, it is a pleasure palace.' He'd kissed her and assured her that no one would find out. 'It would excite me,' he'd said and the mere mention of his excitement had aroused Carmelina.

Then it had been a whore to caress her whilst he watched. If it pleased him, she thought, where was the harm? And, just recently, it had become two whores to play upon her body until she abandoned her senses. And if that was what Louis wanted, if that was what made him love her, then Carmelina was more than willing to abandon herself.

'Please, Louis, please,' she implored and, finally, he nodded to the whores who quickly gathered their robes and left as quietly as they'd arrived.

He crossed to her and lowered his trousers. He didn't bother to fully undress. It wasn't necessary, she would climax as soon as he entered her.

'My darling,' he murmured, pretending a haste he didn't feel as she groaned her ecstasy.

Louis would rather have remained watching. There were many more carnal pleasures Carmelina had yet to be taught, many more thresholds yet to be overcome. And Louis would derive his own pleasure from watching her learn. But, for now, she required that he serve her. He was a patient man, he could bide his time and the waiting would be well worth his while, Louis knew it.

CHAPTER TWENTY-FIVE

'When do you leave?'

'The day after Boxing Day.'

'So soon?'

It was Christmas Eve, late afternoon, and Paolo had come to say goodbye. He and Ira were sitting, huddled beside the oil heater, in the parlour of the boarding house where Ira Rubenstein rented his cheap room.

Both young men had successfully passed their final examinations in May and were now qualified mining engineers. Ira, however, having returned to New York to spend the summer vacation with his parents, was now back at Harvard to complete his masters degree.

Upon graduation Paolo had agreed, with a reluctance he concealed, not wishing to appear ungrateful, to work for six months at the offices of Dunleavy and Company, Mining Consultants.

'We'll call it an apprenticeship, shall we?' Paul Dunleavy had joked. 'An apprenticeship that starts you at the top—not many graduates get a chance at that, eh?' And Paolo had to admit that he would be a fool to refuse such an opportunity.

To Paul Dunleavy the offer had meant only one thing. Dunleavy and Son, Mining Consultants. After six months in a position of power and with such a proposal put to him, the boy could hardly yearn for the tin sheds of the Golden Mile and a life in the field with the simple miners of Kalgoorlie. At Christmas, when the six-month 'apprenticeship' had whetted the boy's appetite, Paul would announce his plans.

Ira had decided to stay in Boston for Christmas. It was too disruptive to go home, he'd maintained, and too expensive.

'It's paid off,' he said.

Paolo looked a query.

'Staying in Boston. I've lined up a part-time job at the library, starting early in the New Year. I'll be able to study and save money at the same time.'

'You're going to be a success, Ira, there's no doubt about that,' Paolo said, toasting his friend with his coffee mug.

'Bon voyage and bon chance,' Ira replied, raising his own mug. 'I shall miss you.'

'And I you.'

They clinked mugs, sipped their coffee and Ira shook his head, as usual. 'Needs a little assistance,' he said, pulling the familiar hip flask from his pocket.

Paolo smiled and accepted the generous tot of rum which Ira poured into his mug. 'I can't stay long,' he apologised. 'I promised I'd spend Christmas Eve with the Dunleavys.'

Paul Dunleavy had been a little critical when Paolo had announced he was going out to see his university friends—the only lie was the plural, Paolo had reasoned. 'Christmas Eve is not a time for gallivanting about, Paolo, it is a time to be shared with those closest to you,' he had said. 'I shall expect you home for a family dinner.'

Paolo had felt annoyed. If the festive season was a time to be shared with those closest to him, then he should be at home in Kal. That's what he'd wanted to say. But he didn't. He never mentioned his family or Kal these days, sensing that it irritated Dunleavy, who had become rather overpossessive. For a long time now, to avoid friction, Paolo had even taken to collecting his mail directly from the maid before she left it on the hall table. That way it was not evident how regularly he was in contact with those at home.

Having agreed to spend Christmas in Boston, Paolo had secretly booked his passage to Australia on the 29th of December. He would depart for New York on the 27th and, grateful as he was to Paul Dunleavy, no amount of emotional blackmail would make him change his mind. Paolo was going home to Caterina and Giovanni and his sisters.

During his years in America, Paolo Gianni's commitment to his studies had helped him avoid undue homesickness but, now that he had completed his degree, Boston had lost its hold over him. Beautiful as the city was, he found himself longing to escape its formality. He yearned for the untidiness of the Australian outback, the scruffiness of the red landscape and the careless drawl of the people. Ice and snow had lost their fascination, Paolo wanted the ferocity of the Kalgoorlie sun.

'You're really serious about joining the army?' Ira asked as he topped up their coffees and added more rum. 'You're going to war?'

'Yes.' Paolo had recently received a letter from Rick, who told him the troops were pulling out of Gallipoli.

'. . . We are leaving so many men on these shores, Paolo,' Rick had written, 'men who have fought for their country with such fervour and men I am proud to have owned as friends . . .'

Now, more than ever, Paolo was determined to join the army.

'You think I'm a fool don't you?'

'Of course I do, a war could kill you.' Ira shrugged. 'Why court trouble?'

Paolo laughed. 'That's a very Jewish outlook,' he said.

'So? It's how we survive.'

They drank two more mugs of rum-laced coffee before Paolo insisted it was time he left. 'You must come to Kal one day, Ira.'

'Perhaps I will,' Ira agreed. 'An engineering degree makes the world a much smaller place. Who knows when or where we may meet again.' And, when they'd embraced, he added, 'You take care with your war, Paolo.'

Paul Dunleavy was a little irritated when Paolo returned half an hour later than he'd promised, with rum on his breath too. Then Paul chastised himself. He was only annoyed because he was excited. Tonight was the night he would make his announcement. He had deliberately chosen Christmas Eve, which had always been a very special night in his family. But he must be patient. He had everything planned so perfectly, he must not rush it.

'I REMEMBER CHRISTMAS Eves just like this when I was a child,' Paul said. He was comfortably nestled in his favourite armchair, the one which had been his father's, his legs stretched out towards the open fire, his tumbler of Scotch on the coffee table beside him. 'My parents and I would sit around the fire, just like this.'

Meg exchanged a smile with Paolo. She adored her father but as they both knew, he always waxed lyrical about the family on Christmas Eve.

'My mother would play the pianola,' Paul continued, 'and my father would sing. A fine, bold voice, do you remember, Elizabeth?'

Elizabeth, in her customary seat at the bay windows, looked up from her petit point and nodded. 'Yes, a bold voice.' Bold, certainly, she thought. Quenton Dunleavy had bawled his favourite hymns with such fervour, and never once baulked when he hit a wrong note, that Elizabeth's mother-in-law would wince as she valiantly accompanied him on the pianola.

'You will play some Christmas carols for us after dinner, won't you, my dear?' Paul asked. He was proud of his wife's musical virtuosity, it was a sign of good breeding. A number of years ago he had purchased for her a grand piano which stood in pride of place in the drawing room.

'Of course I will.'

'Excellent.' He rose to pour himself another Scotch. 'And we shall all sing along. Would you like another, Paolo?' he asked, offering the whisky decanter.

'No thank you, sir.'

'Best not to mix, eh, son? I'm sorry I have no rum.' His smile was good-natured and there was no censure in his tone. Paolo smiled back. The one whisky he'd had was mingling unpleasantly with the rum and he was feeling a little queasy.

Elizabeth declined another dry sherry but Meg held out her glass and Paul topped it to the brim. He was feeling very mellow after his third Scotch. But Christmas Eve was a time to be mellow, and this Christmas Eve more so than any other.

As he sat and talked of his father and his grandfather, Paul felt an immense pride in the tradition of the Dunleavy family. 'I remember my father sitting in this very armchair—of course we weren't in this house then,' he added, 'we were in the old family home at Beacon Hill—and I can remember him telling me of his own childhood.'

Again Meg smiled at Paolo. Her father was waxing even more lyrical than usual. But then this was his fourth whisky, he usually only had two.

'Every Christmas Eve my grandfather would take my father skating on Jamaica Pond and on the way home they would follow the carol singers—at a discreet distance of course—and they would sing together. As father and son, you understand,' he corrected hastily, 'not with the group.' He shook his head with affectionate admiration. 'Such a bond,' he sighed. 'Such a bond between father and son.'

Loath as he was to admit it, there had never been quite such a bond between Paul and his father, and Paul had never really been able to understand why. He'd always felt he'd been a bit of a disappointment to Quenton.

Now he looked at Paolo. The men of whom he was speaking were none other than Paolo's own grandfather and great-grandfather—did the boy comprehend that? Probably not; he and Paolo had not once spoken of Paolo's inclusion in the family since he had been in Boston. Well, all that was about to change. From this night onwards, Paolo Gianni would have a family to proud of and he, Paul Dunleavy, would have a son with whom he could forge a bond, just like the bond between his father and grandfather.

'I remember my father telling me once that he and his father—'

'They're here, Daddy.' Meg jumped up and Paul scowled at the interruption. 'They're here. Listen.'

Outside, through the falling snow, they could hear the strains of 'Good King Wenceslas' approaching.

'Ah.' Paul rose, annoyance forgotten, and collected his scarf and overcoat from the hall stand. The singing of Christmas carols was very much a part of the traditional festivities. As much a part as tomorrow's early morning church service, the distribution of presents around the tree, and the formal Christmas dinner. Tradition, that's what it was all about. And Paul stood with his family on the front porch, applauding the carol singers gathered on the snowy pavement of Commonwealth Avenue.

'Can we follow them, Daddy?' Meg asked five minutes later when Paul had distributed a silver coin to each of the singers and the group had crossed the street. She knew Paolo didn't want to go back inside, not just yet anyway. 'Only for a little while, please?'

Paul looked a question at Elizabeth.

'Cook will wish to serve dinner in half an hour,' Elizabeth warned.

'Fifteen minutes. We'll be back in fifteen minutes. Come along, Paolo.' Meg pulled the hood of her jacket over her head, grabbed his hand and they crossed the street through the lightly falling snow.

From the opposite pavement, as they watched the front door close, Meg exhaled a comic sigh of relief. 'Daddy's worse than ever this Christmas Eve. God only knows why—the whisky I suppose.'

'It's not doing me any good either, the whisky.' Paolo tilted his head back so that the snow fell upon his face.

'But you only had one.'

'And three large measures of rum a few hours ago.' In his slightly bilious state, Paolo had found the Dunleavy lounge room claustrophobic. The sting of the night air was doing him good.

'Serves you right then.'

He didn't answer but stood, eyes closed, head back, enjoying the snow's caress upon his face and the voices of the carol singers as they moved on down the street.

'You'll miss this, won't you?' Meg asked after a moment or two. He had told her that he had booked his passage to Australia. 'But I don't want you to say anything yet, Meg,' he'd warned her. 'I want to tell your father myself, in my own time.'

Meg had mixed feelings about his imminent departure. It would be good to have her father to herself again, but she would miss Paolo. He was the only man with whom she shared a genuine friendship. More importantly, he was the only man to whom she felt she could surrender her virginity, a sacrifice which, at the age of twenty-two, was becoming an obsession.

'Men are to marry virgins and women are to marry "men of the world",' her emancipated girlfriends complained, all in agreement that it hardly constituted equality. 'Every woman should have a lover before she marries,' they said loudly and outrageously. The only trouble was, thought Meg, who would that lover be? Stephen Sanderson, who with her parents' encouragement had courted her for over a year, had bored her utterly and although many of the boys she met at college attracted her, their overt masculinity and experience frightened her, and she didn't dare allow them more than a chaste kiss, although she would die before she would admit that to her girlfriends.

Paolo was the only one. Paolo from the other side of the world who, even after his years in Boston, was still different, still intriguing. She'd been wondering, for months now, if she dared make an overture towards him.

Meg looked at Paolo, his upturned face thoroughly wet from the snow, unmelted flakes still sitting on his lips and lashes. He looked so eminently seducible, she thought. But how did one go about seduction? She wouldn't know where to begin. Why didn't he make the first move? Damn it to hell, Meg cursed, was she really destined to lose her virginity in the proper manner? The husband, the wedding night, the bridal bed? What was the point of being a modern woman?

'I said you'll miss all this, won't you?' she repeated. Paolo obviously hadn't heard her, he was in a world of his own.

'What was that?' He opened his eyes, blinking away the snowflakes.

'You'll miss it. Boston and the cold and the snow.'

He glanced briefly at her before gazing down Commonwealth Avenue at the carol singers, now several houses along the street. 'I'm not sure whether I'll miss it,' he said, 'but I'll certainly remember it. For as long as I live.'

She wasn't quite sure what to make of his tone, it was so serious. But then she often didn't know what to make of Paolo.

'Let's go inside,' she said, 'before you catch your death of cold.'

After an excellent dinner, the four of them gathered for Christmas carols in the drawing room, Elizabeth settling herself carefully at the piano stool and playing the opening chords of 'God Rest Ye Merry Gentlemen'. But, several carols later, it was evident that Paul Dunleavy's heart was not truly in it. He kept glancing towards the grandfather clock at the far end of the room.

'I feel like a little male companionship,' he said at the end of 'Oh Come All Ye Faithful'. 'Let's go to my study, Paolo, we'll have a cigar.' He could curb his impatience no longer.

Paolo was nonplussed. 'I don't smoke, sir.'

'I know, I know. High time you learned.' One of the grandest moments in Paul's life had been the first time Quenton had offered him a cigar. 'Have Edith bring some coffee and cognac up to my study, would you, dear?'

What on earth was going on? Meg wondered. Her father, normally an abstemious man, had had too much to drink and was obviously excited about something. And cigars? Her father didn't even like cigars, he only smoked them when he was celebrating a business coup or wanted to impress somebody.

Elizabeth rose from the piano stool. 'Play something for me, dear,' she said. 'One of the nocturnes, you play them so prettily.'

'Of course.' Her mother was uneasy, Meg could sense it. She sat, arranged her skirts about her, and painstakingly played a Chopin nocturne. Meg's musical abilities were average and she did not enjoy performing for her mother who was an excellent pianist with a fine natural ear. But even as she watched her fingers and concentrated on each note, her mind was filled with questions.

Finally, she excused herself. 'I need to go to the bathroom, Mother, I shan't be long.' Her mother nodded distractedly. She hadn't really been listening to the music at all, Meg thought as she slipped quietly from the room.

Meg was right. Elizabeth felt distinctly ill at ease. It had started with her husband's announcement as they were dressing to go downstairs for pre-dinner drinks.

'This is going to be a momentous Christmas Eve, Elizabeth.'

'Oh yes, dear, in what way?' She hadn't taken much notice at first. Christmas Eves were always momentous for Paul.

'I have plans. Plans which will affect the future of this family.' He'd refused to tell her more, but had promised, mysteriously, that all would be revealed by the end of the evening. Still, she hadn't worried too much; Paul enjoyed creating dramatic suspense. He was probably going to announce a business merger or a property investment.

But, as the evening unfolded, he had drunk far more than he usually did and his manner had been so distracted that Elizabeth had started to feel a little uneasy. And when, after dinner, he'd demanded that Paolo join him in the study, her unease had turned to alarm as she recalled his mysterious announcement in the bedroom.

Something was going on, Elizabeth realised, and she didn't like the feel of it at all.

PAOLO WAITED UNTIL the maid had left the room. 'I'm sorry, sir, I don't understand,' he said as Edith pulled the study door closed behind her.

Out on the landing, before she could turn the doorknob, a hand appeared on top of Edith's. She glanced up, startled, to see Meg, a finger to her lips.

Edith smiled conspiratorially, she and Meg had been partners in crime on a number of occasions. If Miss Dunleavy wished to eavesdrop on her father, then it was nobody's business but her own, Edith thought. She nodded obligingly and trotted back downstairs to the kitchen.

Meg held the door an inch or so ajar and peered through the gap. Her father was seated behind his desk and Paolo, with his back to her, was seated in the armchair opposite. 'Adoption, boy,' Meg heard her father say a little impatiently. 'Legal adoption—what could be more simple?' Again there was a pause. Paolo seemed to be as confused as she was, Meg thought.

This was certainly not the response Paul Dunleavy had expected. Paolo remained staring at him, as if the words he was hearing were incomprehensible. Then he realised. The magnitude of his offer was overwhelming; of course, that was it. 'Yes, Paolo,' he said expansively. 'You are to be my son and heir. Everything I have will be yours. My name, my home, my property.'

Meg gripped the doorknob, her knuckles white. 'You will give this family sons,' she heard her father say. 'Sons to continue the Dunleavy bloodline . . .'

Paul sucked heavily on his cigar. The rich taste of tobacco, the heavy claret he'd drunk during dinner, the headiness of his words, all mingled fittingly. '. . . One of the finest bloodlines in the history of this country.' He pushed his chair back loudly and picked up his brandy balloon. He felt drunk with pride, this was the most momentous night of his life. 'I tell you, Paolo,' he started to circle the desk, 'I tell you . . .'

In the second before Meg pulled the door shut, her father seemed to look directly into her eyes. The latch clicked loudly. They must have heard. Heart pumping, she crossed the landing and stole quickly down the stairs.

'. . . you will be a son I will acknowledge with such pride.' Paul had neither seen nor heard Meg as he stood beside Paolo and raised his brandy balloon in salute.

But Paolo had heard the latch. He turned briefly, thinking someone had entered the room but, when he registered no one there, he returned his gaze to his coffee cup. He could not believe the words he was hearing and he could not meet Paul Dunleavy's eyes. They held the fire of fanaticism; the man was behaving like one possessed. He was drunk of course, but he was nevertheless in deadly earnest. Had this always been Dunleavy's intention? Paolo cursed his own naivety. How could he have placed himself in such debt to a man who had simply wanted to buy a son?

Never once had Paolo thought of Paul Dunleavy as his father. Strangely enough, he had felt more distanced from the man here in Boston than he had during their meetings all those years ago in Kalgoorlie. There had been a bond of sorts then, between the outback boy and the worldly American who had fed his dreams of travel and adventure. But of course that would all have been part of his plan. Paolo cursed himself again. How could he have been so stupid?

Having drunk deeply from his brandy balloon, the fumes of the cognac adding fresh fuel to his exhilaration, Paul was waiting for a response. He sat heavily on the corner of the desk, his legs a little unsteady. 'So, Paolo, what do you say? My legally adopted son and heir. What do you say to that?'

'Well, sir . . .' Paolo picked up his coffee cup and drained the contents in an effort to buy time and to eradicate the foul taste of the cigar he'd been forced to light up earlier. It now sat burning in an ashtray on the desk, a wisp of its smoke constantly and magnetically finding its way into his left eye.

'I think . . .' Of course! That was it! He had the answer! He put down the coffee cup and looked up, his eyes finally meeting Paul's. 'I think it would not be possible to adopt me, sir.'

Dunleavy was momentarily halted. Through the haze of cigar and cognac fumes he wasn't quite sure whether he'd heard correctly. 'Why would that be?'

'Legally I am already your son, sir. I do believe it would be impossible to formally adopt your natural son.' Paolo wasn't absolutely certain he was right, but it was a pretty fair assumption, and it might rescue him from this awkward situation. One fact of which he was sure, Paul Dunleavy would never acknowledge a bastard son. 'So you see, the only way you could recognise me as your son would be to admit to . . . well, sir, to my illegitimacy.'

Damn it, Paul thought, the boy was right. It was something which, during all the years of his planning, Paul had never taken into consideration. Of course, he should have checked with the authorities, but the boy was bound to be right.

So what? Damn propriety, Paul thought with reckless abandon. He would do as Paolo suggested; he would claim the boy as his own son. A sense of freedom overwhelmed him. The boy was true Dunleavy blood when all was said and done, and he would let the world know it!

It was an audacious idea and one which Paul would

not have entertained sober. Allow a bastard to bear the Dunleavy name? Why, his father would turn in his grave. And how could he expect Elizabeth to acknowledge another woman's bastard son as rightful heir to the Dunleavy name and fortune? Why, she might well leave him if he suggested it. But, in his drunkenness, Paul was so fired with the notion of a son that, even as such objections raised themselves, he instantly dismissed them.

'Then that is what we will do, Paolo,' he announced, triumphant. 'We will admit to your illegitimacy and I will recognise you as my son. Now come, let's drink to it.' He thrust Paolo's brandy balloon into his hand. 'And then we'll smoke our cigars together. Father and son.'

Paolo stared back, at a loss for words.

MEG HAD RETURNED to the drawing room for only a moment. 'I don't feel very well, Mother,' she said. 'I'm going to bed.'

'Of course, dear.' Elizabeth was relieved. Still wondering what was going on between the men in the study, she couldn't help but think that perhaps it was for the best that Meg retire. 'I'll have Edith bring you a hot water bottle.'

'No.' Meg sensed her mother's relief. 'I don't want a hot water bottle. Thank you.' Her mother obviously wanted her out of the way so that they could talk about their plans. Well, of course, her mother was part of it, her mother had never cared about her, in fact the whole idea was probably her mother's. 'Good night.'

Automatically, Meg washed her face, cleaned her teeth, brushed her hair, put on her nightdress. But all she could hear were her father's words.

'. . . My son and heir . . . everything I have will be yours . . . my name, my home, my property . . .'

She lay in her bed staring blankly at the night sky through her attic window.

'... You will give this family sons ... sons to continue the Dunleavy bloodline ...'

But *she* was the Dunleavy bloodline. What about *her* sons? The sons from her womb would be Dunleavy flesh and blood, did that mean nothing to her father? Perhaps if she were to demand that the man she married change his name. Yes, that's what she'd do. Then her children would be born Dunleavys in name as well as blood. Anything. She would do anything for her father.

Until Paolo Gianni had arrived, Meg had been the centre of her father's existence, she had been his son, his daughter, the very pride of his life. Gradually anger overtook her pain. Anger at Paolo Gianni. How dare a stranger attempt to usurp her position. How dare Paolo Gianni attempt to steal her father's love.

She dozed fitfully and she wasn't sure what woke her, but when she heard a door opening, she knew it was Paolo. His bedroom was not far from hers, several doors along the landing and, as she thought of him, her anger returned.

PAOLO WAS TIRED. The emotional fencing match with Dunleavy had been exhausting. 'It's a great honour, sir, and I'm deeply flattered ...' he'd started to say.

'Flattery be damned, son, this is about love. Family love. The love between a father and a son.' Paul picked up the decanter and poured himself a liberal measure of cognac.

'Perhaps we could discuss it a little more fully in the morning, sir.' The man was well and truly drunk now. Paolo could only hope that, come morning, the magnitude of admitting to a bastard son would discourage Dunleavy from the course upon which he appeared set.

'Yes, yes, you're right, boy, of course. "The wine's in, the wit's out" as my father was wont to say. No point in further discussion . . .' He plonked himself heavily in the armchair alongside Paolo's. 'But come, let's share a drink.'

Paolo picked up his untouched cognac. 'I'm deeply grateful for all you've done for me, sir,' he said diplomatically.

'Ah,' Dunleavy waved his cigar in the air. 'It's no more than any man would do for his own flesh and blood.'

They clinked their glasses and sipped their cognac and Paolo even forced himself to smoke a little of the abominable cigar whilst Dunleavy once more expounded upon his father, his grandfather and the bond between all Dunleavy men.

Over an hour passed before Paolo was able to make his escape. 'If you don't mind, sir,' he said as Dunleavy rose to refill their glasses, 'I'd like to retire. It's been a night of surprises,' he added quickly, warding off objection. 'There's a lot I'd like to think about.'

'Of course, son, of course.' Paul was disappointed, but he could see that the boy was overwhelmed. It was only natural. 'We'll discuss everything over breakfast,' he said, clumsily embracing Paolo.

Paolo went downstairs and out into the cold night air to clear his head, the study had been dense with cigar smoke. He walked to the embankment and looked out over the Charles River, his mind a blank. Apart from the shock of Dunleavy's announcement, there was really very little to think about. In the sober light of day, faced with the prospect of a bastard son, Paul Dunleavy would retract his offer, Paolo was sure of it.

An hour later, when he crept in the front door and up the stairs, the lights were out and the household was sleeping.

By now Paolo was worn out. Let tomorrow bring what it may, he thought, as he undressed and tried to clean the taste of cigars from his mouth, there was nothing that could be done tonight. He lay down and was asleep in a matter of minutes.

He didn't hear her come into his room and he didn't hear her gentle whisper.

'Are you awake, Paolo?' In the dim light from the open doorway, Meg could see him. Lying on his side, his back to her. Was he awake? She couldn't tell. 'I wanted to say goodbye,' she whispered, very quietly. Still no answer. She pulled the door closed behind her. They were in darkness now.

She undid the sash at her waist and let her dressing gown drop to the floor. Naked, she crossed to the bed and pulled back the covers.

Anger and hurt had lent Meg all the courage she needed; seduction was easy if revenge was the motive. But, as she lay silently beside him and felt the warmth of his body so close to hers, she couldn't help herself. She was aroused. If, in seeking revenge she could satisfy her curiosity and assuage her desire, then all the better, she thought.

Paolo was dreaming. Fingers were touching the naked skin of his back. Gently, very gently, they were tracing the curve of his spine. It was pleasant and he murmured in his sleep.

In his dream, there was a body beside him, easing closer, an arm encircling him, the fingers now caressing his chest. He willed himself not to wake up, it was a wonderful dream. Now he could feel a woman's breasts against his back and the fingers were moving downwards, towards his groin.

He fought to stay asleep but the dream was becoming too real. Then the fingers stopped, confused by the knot tied in the cord of his pyjama pants, and Paolo was wide awake. This was no dream. He rolled over to face her, his hand brushing a naked thigh.

'Sssh, Paolo, sssh.' Her breasts were against his chest now and her mouth close to his.

'Meg! Jesus Christ!' He threw aside the covers, jumped out of bed and turned on the light. 'Jesus Christ! Meg!'

She didn't attempt to pull back the covers but lay looking up at him, her naked body fully exposed. 'This might be our only chance, Paolo,' she smiled seductively. 'Wouldn't you like to make love to me?'

'Jesus Christ!' Paolo looked around wildly. Her dressing gown was lying on the floor. He picked it up and threw it over her. 'Get out of here, for God's sake!'

She stood, ignoring the gown, and took his hands in hers. 'Make love to me Paolo.' She placed his hands on her breasts.

'My God!' He pulled away from her as though he'd been burned and once more grabbed her gown. Thrusting it about her shoulders, he pulled her towards the door. 'Get out of here, Meg. Get out of here.'

As he opened the door and pushed her onto the landing, she started to scream.

'Shut up, they'll hear you,' he hissed. What on earth was happening? he thought frantically. 'Go to bed,' he urged. But she only screamed louder. And louder. Paolo was getting desperate. 'For God's sake, Meg, calm down,' he cried, trying to drag her along the landing to her room. But by now the screams were no longer theatrical. The girl was becoming hysterical.

Downstairs, doors opened. Concerned voices called out.

'Meg? Meg, are you all right?' Elizabeth, worried.

'What the hell's going on?' Paul Dunleavy, still slurred with alcohol.

Footsteps on the stairs. Elizabeth the first to appear, horrified. Paul, close behind, agog at the sight of his naked daughter. Geoffrey, the butler, following at a discreet distance, eyes averted, standing by for instructions.

Meg continued to scream hysterically, the dressing gown slipping from her shoulders as quickly as Paolo fought to keep it there.

'Thank you, Geoffrey,' Paul dismissed the butler, 'we have no need of you. Tell everyone to go back to bed.' Damn it, he thought, the servants would already be gossiping below stairs.

Elizabeth took control. 'Come along now, Meg. Come along now,' she forced her daughter's arms into the sleeves of the gown, 'dress yourself.'

Elizabeth's natural authority over her daughter asserted itself and the screams died down to sobs as Meg allowed her mother to take over.

'What's happened?' Paul demanded. 'What's going on here?'

'He tried to rape me,' Meg threw herself at her father and clung to him desperately. 'He tried to rape me, Daddy,' she sobbed.

In the shocked silence that followed, broken only by Meg's distraught weeping, Paul attempted to put a fatherly arm about her, but he was painfully conscious of the fact that Meg's gown was open and her breasts visible. 'Don't be silly, Meg.' He signalled Elizabeth to come to the rescue. 'That's impossible.'

His tone was so dismissive that Elizabeth was shocked. He was drunk, she realised that—when they'd gone to bed nearly two hours previously, he'd been as drunk as she had ever seen him. Indeed, if she'd not insisted they retire, he'd have stayed up for the rest of the night toasting his triumph. 'I have a son, Elizabeth,' he'd kept saying, 'I have a son.'

Elizabeth had realised then that her fears had been justified. Father and son had spent a night of camaraderie celebrating their relationship. Well, first thing in the morning, Elizabeth vowed, when the man could draw a sober breath, she would remind her husband of his earlier promise. 'The boy is never to be recognised as a member of this family . . . Will you swear it, Paul?'

Now, watching her husband trying to extricate himself from Meg's embrace, Elizabeth felt deeply angered. He'd spent a night getting drunk with his bastard son and yet, confronted by his daughter who was genuinely distraught, he showed a complete lack of concern.

Elizabeth took Meg in her arms. She knew that Paolo had not molested her daughter, but she would not have her husband simply dismiss the claim. 'Why is it impossible?' she demanded. 'Sssh, my darling, ssh. Why is it impossible? Look at him, he's half-naked.'

Paolo stood, bewildered, speechless. He always slept half-naked. Until he had come to Boston, he had slept entirely naked. In Kalgoorlie he had never even owned pyjamas.

'Come along, Meg,' Elizabeth insisted. 'Come along to your room and tell me what happened.'

But Meg would not be led away. She broke from her mother's embrace, screaming, 'He tried to rape me, Daddy, I swear it, he tried to rape me!'

Paul's embarrassment was turning to anger now. 'Do as your mother says and go to bed, girl, you don't know what you're saying.'

Meg was once again becoming hysterical. 'He tried to rape me. He did. He did, Daddy. Why won't you believe me?'

'Stop it, Meg!' Paul's own voice was raised now, he took her by the shoulders and shook her. 'I said stop it! Calm down!'

But the more he shook her the more hysterical Meg's screams became. 'He raped me! He raped me! He raped me!'

'I said stop it!' Paul struck her hard across her left

cheek. There was a sharp intake of breath and the screaming stopped as she stared back at him in shock. 'He did not rape you. He's your brother!'

In the total silence which followed, Meg looked slowly from her father to her mother and, finally, to Paolo. Something was wrong, she thought. No one was contradicting her father.

'You're going to adopt him,' she whispered, 'that's what you said. You're going to adopt Paolo as your son and heir, I heard you say it.' Elizabeth turned to her husband, confused. Surely Meg had it wrong, surely he couldn't have said that. But Paul could not meet his wife's eyes.

'He is already my son and heir,' he said. 'There is no necessity for adoption. He is my blood and will be recognised as such.'

Elizabeth's confusion turned to shock. Her husband was going to recognise a bastard? Clearly he was prepared not only to break his daughter's heart, but to humiliate his wife as well.

'Forgive me, sir, but I will not.' Paolo had registered the look of utter horror on Elizabeth's face and finally found his voice. 'I will not be recognised as your son.' Turning to Elizabeth, he said, 'I'm sorry, Elizabeth, I had no idea this was what he wanted.' She looked at him sceptically. 'That may sound naive, but it's true.' Then he turned to Meg. 'I'm sorry, Meg. I'm truly sorry for having hurt you.'

'Rubbish, son, she'll get over it.' Paul's voice was hearty, jovial. The boy didn't mean what he was saying, he was merely affected by the women's emotional overreaction. 'A touch of jealousy, that's what it is. Perfectly natural.' They all stared at him but, in his intoxication, Paul didn't register the antagonism. 'Now let's go to bed, it's been a long night, we'll discuss it in the morning.' And he turned to go.

'No, sir, I shall be leaving first thing in the morning.'

Paul wasn't sure if he'd heard correctly. Slowly, he turned back. The boy's eyes met his directly. It was clear he was serious. Paul tried to paint the smile back on his face. 'Oh come, come, Paolo, don't let the women's reactions affect you. They'll get used to it.'

He looked at his wife. 'Elizabeth, tell the boy he's a welcome member of the family.'

But Elizabeth said nothing. Her arm protectively about her daughter's shoulders, she stared unwaveringly at her husband. So Paul would sell them both for a son.

Paul read the accusation in her eyes, but his attention returned to Paolo, a note of desperation creeping into his voice. 'You're my son, Paolo, nothing else matters. Damn it, this is your family. This is your home. You belong here.'

'No sir. This is not my family and this is not my home. I do not belong here.' Paolo walked along the landing to his bedroom.

'Now just a minute, boy, you listen to me.' Dunleavy strode after him and Paolo turned at the bedroom door to face the man. Dunleavy's face was distorted now. Rage and frustration made him ugly. 'Do you realise how much money I've spent on you?' he snarled. 'Do you have any idea? God damn you, boy, you owe me!'

'Yes, sir, I do. And I shall repay you. However long it takes. Every cent.' Paolo closed the door behind him. Any minute Dunleavy would start throwing punches.

In his bedroom, Paolo dressed, packed his suitcase and sat on his bed waiting for the dawn. Apart from his beloved books, the ones he'd acquired in his weekly foraging through second-hand bookshops with Ira, he took only the barest of essentials.

When the first glimmer of morning shone through his attic window, he stole quietly out onto the landing.

'Meg!' She was huddled in a blanket on the stairs,

waiting for him. 'How long have you been there?'

She shrugged, she didn't know how long she'd been sitting in the cold. 'I wanted to make sure I didn't miss you,' she said. 'I'm sorry, Paolo.' Her eyes were puffy from crying.

'Oh, Meg.' He sat beside her.

'I'm sorry.' She couldn't help it, she started to cry again. 'I'm really, really sorry,' she whispered through her tears.

'Sssh, it's all right.' He put his arms around her. 'Stop crying, it's all right.'

'I feel so ashamed.'

'There's nothing to be ashamed of. Sssh.'

'Do you forgive me?'

'Of course I forgive you.' He stroked her hair until the crying was reduced to sniffles. 'Come on now, go back to bed, I have to leave before your father wakes up.'

'Are you leaving because of me?'

'No.' He rose and hauled her to her feet. 'I have my own family and my own home, you know that.'

'Will you be my brother, Paolo?'

'Of course I'll be your brother,' he grinned. 'I'll always be your brother.'

They hugged each other warmly. 'It's good to have a brother,' she whispered. 'Happy Christmas, Paolo.' She watched as he crept down the stairs.

Things would never be the same again, Meg realised. But something positive had come out of the hideous events of the night. She'd grown up.

'Your father loves you very much, Meg,' her mother had said after she'd taken her to her room and tucked her into bed like a child. 'You must forgive him.'

It was then that Meg had seen the shock and pain in her mother's face. But her mother never showed emotion. It frightened Meg. 'What's going to happen?' she asked, her voice a whisper.

'Nothing.' As she sat on the side of the bed, Elizabeth fought back the tears of hurt which she knew she must not shed until she was alone. Neither her husband nor her daughter must see her cry. 'There is nothing on this earth that can destroy this family, my darling,' she smiled. 'Never forget, we are Dunleavys.' She kissed Meg's forehead. 'Now get some sleep. And try to be kind to your father in the morning.'

Meg had impulsively hugged her mother and they'd clung to each other for a moment or two before Elizabeth had silently left.

Life would go on as usual, Meg realised. But things would never be the same again. She'd grown up.

TWO DAYS LATER Ira Rubenstein insisted upon accompanying Paolo to the railway station.

'You've done enough for me as it is,' Paolo said as they left the boarding house.

'Rubbish, it's been a most companionable Christmas. Besides, there's nothing better than a railway platform farewell.'

Ira bought a newspaper for Paolo to read on the train. 'Well, well, well,' he said, glancing at the sports pages, 'your Les Darcy's done it again.'

'What?'

'World middleweight champion, Eddie McGoorty, a clear knockout. Look.' He handed Paolo the newspaper.

'Knockout Win for Australia's Golden Boy of Boxing at Sydney Stadium', Paolo read. 'Nice news to go home to,' he said. Then he read further. 'United States authorities have not recognised the match as a "title" match, it is therefore unclear in boxing circles as to whether or not Darcy is the World Middleweight Champion.' He smiled. 'We Aussies can't take a trick can we?'

'All aboard!' The guard blew his whistle.

Paolo tucked the newspaper under his arm and

boarded the train. 'Thanks, Ira. For everything,' he said as he leaned out the window. 'You're a good mate. I mean that.'

'Will you take a word of advice from a good mate, Paolo?'

'Yep, sure.'

'Don't join the army. You don't have to fight in a war to be a hero.'

Steam billowed out over the platform and Paolo saluted with his newspaper as the train chugged out of the station.

Chapter Twenty-Six

It was early in the misty morning of the 5th of April, 1916, that the SS *Corsican*, with her cargo of 28 officers and 942 enlisted men of the 11th Battalion, arrived at the French port of Marseille.

Only 330 men, less than one-third of the original 11th, had survived the massacre of Gallipoli, and in January, with the arrival of reinforcements, it had been decided to create three new Australian divisions. All original battalions were to be halved in order to take advantage of the seasoned troops' experience. In the case of the 11th, the odd-numbered sections were to remain with the battalion while the even-numbered sections were sheared off to form the core of the 51st Battalion. To their great satisfaction, the boys of the goldfields of Western Australia were destined to remain with the 11th Battalion.

'Only right, I reckon,' Snowy Wilson, a miner from Boulder, remarked. 'You get used to a name.'

The first sign of Marseille was the beam of the lighthouse blinking through the morning fog. Then, gradually, the shadow of the shoreline came into view.

'Crikey, look at that,' Jack Brearley breathed to no one in particular, but Tom Brereton and Rick Gianni standing beside him nodded in silent agreement, equally awestruck.

They were not the only ones. There was a general sense of wonder from the men gathered on deck as the rugged mass of the Ile D'If with its majestic chateau loomed before them. Then, beyond the island, materialising like magic from out of the mist, was the great harbour of Marseille. Ships crowded the massive wharves, guns threatened from all sides and, stretching as far as the eye could see, was a vast city of spires and chimneys. A city so vast it was beyond the imagination of the boys from the goldfields.

'Crikey,' Jack whispered again.

The troops were confined to the ship for most of the day until the order came, in the late afternoon, to march the half mile to the railway station.

'Vive l'Australie! Vivent les Australiens!' Their reception was overwelming. Elderly men, matrons and young girls crowded the pavements as the soldiers marched through the cobbled streets of Marseille; then, at dusk, as the train steamed out of the city, crowds of citizens continued to wave and wish them well.

Through the low, tree-covered hills of the outlying countryside the train steamed across bridges and viaducts until, in the middle of the night, a halt was called at the small town of Orange. There, for the first time in France, the bugle call of 'Welcome to the Cookhouse Door Boys' sounded and the men tumbled from the train for a meal and hot tea provided from the quartermaster's stores.

Then they were back on board and once more on the move. For over two hundred miles they travelled beside the River Rhône, through countryside alive with the fertility of spring. Orchards in blossom, hillsides covered with endless vineyards and fields which flourished under the care of the women and children who tended them. All along the route it was the women and children who worked the farms and railway crossings—Frenchmen of military age were serving at the front.

Mâcon, Lyons, Avillon, past Châlons where a halt was called and a good meal served again to the troops. A number of the diggers decided to go into town.

'*Bonjour. Je suis Australien. Je m'appelle* Jack.' It was the only French Jack had so far managed to learn and his accent was appalling. But he was so earnest that it worked and an hour later he, Tom and Rick returned to the train with extra provisions acquired by trading the sugar and chocolate saved from their Red Cross parcels. The extra provisions were in the form of a bottle of whisky and two bottles of red wine.

The men had not been told of their destination but Rick, having earlier traded his rum ration with Snowy Wilson for a map of France, had been assiduously following their route.

'We might be close enough to Paris to see it from the train soon,' he said after they had passed Dijon.

Word spread and the men crowded to the windows. A loud cheer went up as they caught a far-off glimpse of the Eiffel Tower but, disappointingly, that was all they managed to see.

'Cripes, what's that?' Snowy exclaimed a little while later as they passed a great palace surrounded by acres of formal gardens.

'It's the Palace of Versailles,' Rick said. 'Seventeenth century. Built by Louis XIV.'

'The gardens are famous for their topiary,' Jack said and he smiled smugly at Rick's look of surprise.

'What the bloody hell's tope—?' Snowy floundered for the word.

'Topiary,' Jack replied with an air of vast knowledge. 'It's the art of hedge cutting.' An image of the gardens of Maison Picot in Perth flashed through his mind. 'It's an art form, Harry,' Gabrielle Picot's disdainful tone as she patronised his father.

'You're pulling my leg,' Snowy said, craning to get

a last look at the Versailles gardens as the train sped on.

'Nope.'

Rick was strangely quiet after they'd passed Versailles and Jack thought that perhaps, like Tom, he'd drunk too much, although it'd be out of character for him. Tom of course was a different matter. Tom had already drunk half the bottle of whisky they'd traded and was staring morosely out the window. Since the death of his brothers, Tom's drinking was no longer raucous and good-humoured. It was hostile and aggressive. Poor old Tom, Jack thought, he was a bitter man in the drink.

'What's the matter, Rick?' For a long time, Jack had tried to maintain the family enmity—out of a sense of duty more than anything. He would not be a traitor to his father, he told himself, and whenever Rick Gianni attempted to exchange pleasantries, he would snap back or walk away. But, in the face of battle, it had become more and more senseless to continue the feud of their fathers. If they ever made it back to Kal, the enmity would be there, waiting for them, Jack knew it. But they were on the same side here, fighting a common foe.

Finally, it had been the very nature of Rick himself that had won through. He was a gentle man, a man who didn't belong on a battlefield, but he did his job as well as any other soldier and Jack couldn't help but respect him for that.

'What's the matter?' he asked again. Rick was still staring down at his map, his mind a million miles away. 'You feeling crook?'

Rick had been praying for the train to stop. Any minute now, surely, he'd been thinking. They were well due for a tucker break. And as they passed out of the picturesque countryside and into the industrial landscape where the military traffic was heavier, the train was slowing down. 'We must be near Houilles,' he replied, as much to himself as to Jack. 'Versailles is just south of Paris and we're travelling northwest and Houilles is about five miles northwest of Paris. We must be quite close.'

'What's at Houilles?' Jack asked, mystified.

'Solange.'

'What are you going to do?' Jack asked. 'Jump?'

Such a notion hadn't entered Rick's mind, he'd just been daydreaming, hoping that the train would stop so that he could simply stand on the ground and imagine that he was near the town where Solange had spent her childhood, the town where perhaps, even now, Solange was living with her family. He looked wistfully out the window. Jump? It was tempting.

'Go on,' Jack grinned. 'I dare you.'

Rick grinned back. 'You're a troublemaker, Brearley.'

In order to cause as little disruption as possible, small townships were chosen as stopping points to feed the troops and the next stop was a tiny village just north of Saint Germains.

'Well?' Jack had finished his meal and walked over to Rick whose pannikin sat virtually untouched on the ground beside him. 'How close do you reckon we are?'

'What?' Rick looked up, distracted.

'Houilles. How far away do you reckon it is?'

'About four or five miles I suppose.' It was exactly what Rick had been thinking.

Jack squatted on the ground beside him. 'Well, I'm game if you are.' A blank silence. 'Face it, mate, you'll never do it on your own. I'll come with you.'

'Why?'

'For fun,' Jack shrugged.

'Absent without leave? There'd be trouble.'

'What do you think they'd do to us? Firing squad?

Send us home in disgrace? Well, that wouldn't be too bad, would it?'

Rick continued to look at him, bemused; he could never really tell when Jack was joking.

'Come on, mate, we've earned some fun,' Jack urged. Then, in his posh English officer voice, 'Good God, Sergeant Gianni, we're officers now, it's high time we granted ourselves a little well-earned rest and recreation, what?'

Rick couldn't help but smile. 'I'll do it,' he said suddenly, 'but I'll do it on my own. No sense in both of us copping it.'

'Copping what?' Jack was excited now, this was an adventure. 'We wandered off to have a look at the countryside and we got lost and when we got back the train had gone. Simple.'

'What do we do then?'

'We report to the nearest military headquarters and say we're sorry.'

IT TOOK THEM less than two hours to reach Houilles. They walked half the distance and the other half they travelled in the back of a dray. Whilst the horse clopped along the country road, the driver, a wiry talkative Frenchwoman, chattered to Rick in Italian. Her husband's mother was Italian, she said, although her husband had been born in France.

Jack sat silently in the back of the dray, frustrated at not being able to join in the conversation or practise his atrocious French, but enjoying the countryside nonetheless.

They were barely ten minutes' walk from Houilles, she told them as they got out of the dray. Maybe, at the front, they would meet her husband, he was a soldier too. In the valley of the River Somme, she said, that's where the fighting was, and she wished them well.

The family Bouchet was well known in the village of Houilles and by late afternoon they had found the house. A modest little stone cottage on the outskirts of town.

'I'll wait for you in the pub,' Jack said. He'd taken careful note of the tavern during their walk through the village. 'Don't be too long, we'll need to find a room for the night.'

THE WOMAN WHO opened the door was plump, fair-haired with a pleasant face. She had once been very pretty.

'Bonjour, Madame,' Rick said.

'Bonjour, Monsieur.'

'Madame Bouchet?' he queried.

'Oui.'

'Je suis Australien. Je m'appelle Rick.' As usual, Jack's introduction worked.

'Ah. *Australien.*' She beamed.

'I am a friend of your daughter,' he explained. The woman stared blankly at him. 'From Kalgoorlie.'

'Oh. Kalgoorlie.' She beamed again.

'Is Solange here?'

'Oui, oui. Solange est ici. Entrez. Entrez. Je vais la chercher.' The woman hustled him inside, calling as she did, *'Maurice! Il y a quelqu'un pour Solange . . . il est d'Australie!'*

As she ushered Rick into the small front parlour, a nuggety middle-aged man materialised by her side. Black-browed and solemn, his hair was wet and his face shiny. A man well scrubbed after a hard day's physical work.

'C'est le père de Solange,' Madame Bouchet said. Then, to her husband, *'Il vient de Kalgoorlie.'*

'Rick Gianni, sir, how do you do.'

They shook hands and, although the man's face

remained expressionless, his clasp was firm and welcoming and there was a touch of reverence to his tone as he said 'Kalgoorlie'.

Kalgoorlie had always impressed Maurice Bouchet. Anywhere as rich in gold as Kalgoorlie impressed Maurice and he no longer recalled his initial anger when Solange had left the family home. Now he was proud that his daughter had had the courage to adventure so far and return so wealthy. Other men's daughters remained with their mothers and fed the chickens.

The men sat whilst Madame Bouchet ran off to fetch her daughter. '*Solange, Solange, il y a quelqu'un qui veut te voir. Il est de Kalgoorlie,*' they could hear her calling.

For several minutes they sat in silence, Rick self-conscious under the relentless scrutiny of Maurice Bouchet.

Then Solange was at the parlour door. Rick jumped to his feet. She was beautiful. More beautiful than ever, in her peasant dress and apron. His Solange. But she seemed tentative, nervous. Rick was confused. He understood her reserve in the presence of her parents, but where was her pleasure in seeing him?

'Hello, Enrico.'

Her mother insisted they all sit and talk. She would get coffee, she told them. '*Oui*, coffee. Sugar,' she said to Rick, as proud of the English words Solange had taught her as she was of her hospitality. Coffee and sugar were rare to come by these days, but Marie Bouchet would gladly offer up her precious reserves for a friend all the way from Kalgoorlie.

They talked a little about the war whilst she was gone. His son, too, was in the army, Maurice told Rick, Solange translating. Young Georges had left for the front only six months previously.

'He is too young,' Solange added.

The discourse was stilted, awkward. She was evading his eyes, Rick thought.

When Madame Bouchet returned with the coffee, the conversation changed. *'Solange nous a beaucoup parler de Kalgoorlie,'* she said.

'Kalgoorlie, *oui,*' Maurice nodded. He, too, wanted to talk about Kalgoorlie. *'A Kalgoorlie les gens sont très riches. Solange est revenu riche aussi. Elle nous a dit qu'il y avait de l'or dans les rues.'*

'Gold, *oui,*' his wife said proudly.

'My parents are proud of the money I saved when I was working at the shop in Kalgoorlie,' Solange hastily explained.

'Shop, *oui.*' Again her mother smiled proudly. 'Gold.'

'I brought some gold home with me, sometimes the customers at the shop would pay me in gold.' It was true, her clients at Red Ruby's had often paid her in small nuggets. Solange's eyes were pleading with Rick. Don't tell them, she was saying, don't tell them.

So that was why she was nervous. Rick could have laughed with relief. He sipped his coffee as fast as he could, the sooner they finished the coffee, the sooner he could suggest they go for a walk. 'Yes,' he smiled, 'it was a fine shop. Kalgoorlie is a rich town and there is much gold.'

Solange smiled gratefully and translated for her parents.

'Et cet argent va lui permettre de faire un bon mariage,' Marie Bouchet added with pride. Her husband glared at her, offended, the insinuation being that the match he had made with Jean-Pierre, the son of his friend, was not good enough. But Marie continued chatting on, regardless. *'Le fiancé de Solange est propriétaire d'une grande ferme.'*

Amidst the indiscernable gabble of French, Rick had heard the word 'fiancé'. He turned to Solange. Her face was ashen and he suddenly knew the reason for her fear. 'You are to be married,' he said.

'Yes,' she whispered, her heart racing, fearful of what he would do. She had not answered the endless letters he had written, assuming that in time he would forget her. But his love was as strong as ever, she had known it the moment she had entered the room. The exquisite delight in his eyes as he'd jumped to his feet. Was there anger in him now? Would he expose her? Many men would. Solange was terrified. Her father would disown her. Her fiancé would refuse to marry her.

'Do you love him?' Rick asked.

'He is a good man.'

'*Oui*,' her mother had understood. 'A good man. Rich.'

Rick wanted to get out of the room. Away from Solange. He couldn't bear the plea in her eyes. She felt nothing for him, he realised, nothing but the fear of exposure.

'Congratulations.' He tried to smile. Then he drained his coffee and rose. 'I must go. Thank you for the coffee, Madame Bouchet . . . *merci*.'

'*Mais il faut rester avec nous. Il est tard. Passez la nuit chez nous?*'

'She wants you to stay the night,' Solange translated.

'Thank you but no,' he shook his head. 'I must be leaving.'

'*Voulez-vous un autre tasse? Parlons de Kalgoorlie.*' Marie Bouchet loved having visitors.

'No, no, thank you. It will be dark soon and I have a friend waiting.'

They all accompanied him to the front door. 'Would you like me to walk with you?' Solange asked.

'No,' he answered brusquely. 'I know the way.'

'Goodbye, Enrico.' She offered her cheek for him to kiss but he shook her hand instead.

'Goodbye, Solange. I wish you every happiness.'

They stood at the front door of the little cottage, all three of them, and waved him farewell.

'WHAT HAPPENED?' JACK asked, when Rick joined him at the inn. Obviously the news was not good—the man's anguish was palpable.

'She's going to be married.'

'Oh.'

'I think I'll have a drink. What's that?' Rick gestured to the half-empty bottle on the table.

'The local wine. It's not half-bad, I'll get you a glass.' There was nothing more to be said and Jack knew it but, as he wandered over to the wooden bar in the corner, he felt a touch of envy. For all the women he had slept with, he had never once been in love. He wondered what it would be like.

'They've got a couple of rooms here,' he said, handing Rick the glass, 'but there's only one left so we'll have to toss for the bed.' He grinned. 'Or we could share it—so long as Tom and Snowy don't find out.'

But Rick hadn't heard him. He was busy downing the glass of red wine. Tonight, for the first time in his life, he was going to get drunk. It was what heartbroken young lovers were supposed to do, wasn't it?

'WHATEVER HAPPENED TO the Princess?' Rick asked. It was only an hour later but the unaccustomed wine had gone straight to his head and he was enjoying the conversation. Although he and Jack Brearley had formed a friendship of sorts they had never once spoken of the past. The only time they mentioned Kal was when letters arrived from home. Now they were speaking of their childhood, and it was good.

'The Princess?' Jack smiled at the memory of the old white mare. 'She was thirty-one when she died. Only five years ago it was. She'd been a bit crook and Dad kept saying he was going to put her down but Maudie wouldn't let him. Not that she was in pain,' he added quickly, 'Maudie wouldn't have that. But she was an old horse, her time was up. Then, one morning, Maudie went into the stables and there was the Princess, lying on her side, unconscious, breathing heavy, and it really cut Maudie up, seeing her like that.'

Jack poured another glass of wine from the fresh bottle, their third so far, and shook his head in admiration. 'I'd never seen Maudie cry before, but I'll swear there was a tear in her eye that morning when she came in to get the rifle. I offered to do it for her. Dad did too of course, but she wouldn't have it. She made Dad and me wait outside while she went into the stables. We listened for the shot, but it didn't come.'

'Well, go on, what happened?' Rick urged as Jack swigged from his glass.

'When we went inside, Maudie was sitting in the hay with the Princess's head in lap. The old mare was dead, but Maudie seemed really happy. She said that when she'd come into the stables and raised the gun, the horse had lifted its head and looked at her. She couldn't shoot it like that, of course, so she sat down and put its head in her lap and the old mare just closed her eyes and gave a bit of sigh and died. Maudie reckoned that the Princess had picked her own time to die and she'd just been waiting to say goodbye.'

'Good way to go,' Rick said, staring vacantly down at his empty glass.

'Too right.' Jack poured him another. 'Hey, remember the time you fell off the Princess and busted your finger?'

''Course I do.' Rick held up the crooked finger. 'How could I forget?'

They both heard the words then. 'That makes us brothers,' Jack had said. And the oath they'd sworn as children had been as solemn as an oath could be.

'It's bollocks, isn't it?' Jack said a moment or so later. 'This fight between your dad and mine, it's just a load of bollocks.'

'Yep,' Rick nodded. The world was starting to swim a little.

'Stupid old bastards. When we get back to Kal we'll sort them out, eh?'

'Too right we will.'

They downed their wine and it wasn't long before Rick was nodding off to sleep. Jack half carried him up the narrow stairs and dumped him on the bed.

Typical Gianni, the man couldn't handle his drink, Jack thought as he happily passed out on the floor.

Chapter Twenty-Seven

Paolo was worried. Giovanni was not well. It wasn't just the deepened grooves in his cheeks and the silver-grey in his hair. That was simply the passage of time. Or so Paolo had initially thought. It was four years, after all, and people aged in four years. Why, little Rosalina was at school now, and Briony, no longer a rough-and-tumble tomboy, had blossomed beautifully into womanhood. Giovanni had simply grown older.

But on the first night, after supper when they had gathered around to sing to the piano accordion, Giovanni's voice could not be heard above the others.

'Why are you not singing, Giovanni?' Paolo had asked.

'My voice is not what it was,' Giovanni smiled, evading a direct answer, 'and it's best to let people remember you at your finest, do you not agree?'

That was when Paolo first became suspicious. Nothing stopped Giovanni from singing. Something must be wrong.

Several days later, when he awoke in the very early hours of the morning, Paolo went to the kitchen to fetch a glass of water and heard a muffled sound from the back verandah. He opened the flyscreen door and saw Giovanni sitting on the verandah steps, coughing. A deep rasping cough, and he held a rag to his mouth to muffle the sound. It was then that Paolo knew.

'You're ill,' he said.

When the coughing spasm was under control, Giovanni looked up and nodded. 'Miners' complaint,' he said, his voice husky.

'How long?' Paolo sat beside his stepfather.

'A year or so,' Giovanni shrugged, 'maybe two. It's worse early in the morning, when I've been sleeping.'

'Or when you sing?' Paolo understood now.

'Yes, if I sing the big notes,' Giovanni grinned. 'And what is the point of singing if you don't sing the big notes, eh?'

'Why do you keep it a secret, Giovanni?'

'The girls would worry.'

'And Mamma?'

'Oh, your Mamma knows. From the very beginning she has known, you can never hide anything from your Mamma.' He nodded, unperturbed. 'It is good that she knows, there are never secrets between Caterina and me. At first she wanted me to stop working underground,' he smiled, 'but she knows I cannot do that.'

'Why not?' Paolo asked. 'You've proved your loyalty to the Midas. They'd give you a job above ground.' Giovanni looked away, he didn't want to continue the discussion. 'They would, Giovanni,' Paolo urged. 'You know they would.'

'And what would I do?' Giovanni rose and, hands on hips, stretched his back. His chest was aching, it always did after a coughing fit. 'I am no good at facts and figures. I can barely write a letter.'

'But there are many—'

'And I would never earn the wage that I earn underground.' Giovanni knew that Paolo meant well but, as far as he was concerned, the conversation was over. 'You will say nothing to the girls of this.'

'Of course.'

'And you will speak to no one else, Paolo. Men are laid off when it is known they have miners' complaint.'

Paolo knew only too well of the fears associated with miners' lung disease. At Harvard he had read and learned far more about the problem than Giovanni himself would know. For years miners' premature deaths from lung disease had been diagnosed as pneumonia. More recently, it had been proved that the deaths were a direct result of constant dust inhalation and, if the rock being drilled contained silica, then a miner's years were definitely numbered.

The common fear amongst the miners was not lung disease, however, it was the fear of being made redundant should their illness be discovered. The South African mines had recently implemented compulsory medical testing in an attempt to fight the spread of lung disease and there had been vague talk of a similar system evolving in Kalgoorlie. But the unions were set against the idea—no miner wished to be made redundant, especially not a family man.

'I understand, Giovanni,' Paolo agreed. 'I'll speak to no one . . .'

'Good. Now go back to bed, there's time for sleep, it's barely dawn.'

'. . . except Mamma. Is it all right if I speak to Mamma?'

Giovanni laughed. Not too loudly, he didn't want to risk another coughing fit. 'So long as the two of you do not join together and nag me.' He embraced his stepson. 'It is good for your mamma to have you home.' Then he took Paolo's face in his hands. 'She is very proud of the fine young man you have become. And I am very proud of you too.' Giovanni kissed Paolo on both cheeks. 'Now go back to bed.'

It was barely two hours later when Paolo sought out Caterina. She'd waved goodbye to Giovanni as he left for his early morning shift, carrying his crib which she'd carefully packed with his favourite Italian sausage, bread and cheese. She'd fed Briony and little Rosalina and then farewelled them from the front door as they set off for school. And now she was tackling the weekly washing in the large tin tub on the back verandah.

'You slept in,' she said as the flywire door slapped shut behind him and he stood at her side.

Paolo nodded. He hadn't slept in at all. When he'd left Giovanni, he'd gone to his room and sat on the side of his bed deep in thought. He'd heard his stepfather leave and he'd heard the family breakfast noises and the girls' customary dash for school, and it was only then that he'd gone in search of his mother.

'I know about Giovanni, Mamma.'

Caterina barely paused as she scrubbed fiercely at the collar of one of her husband's work shirts with a wooden scrubbing brush. 'I didn't think it would take you long to guess.' She stopped scrubbing and started to squeeze the shirt dry.

'I'll do that.' Paolo took it from her, squeezing the excess soapy water into the bucket which always stood by the old wash table on the back verandah. Leftover bathing and washing water was saved to nurture the little front garden.

'At night I put eucalyptus oil on his pillow to help ease the congestion,' she stooped and took another shirt from the basket at her feet, 'and in the mornings he goes outside to cough so that the girls will not hear.' Caterina shrugged as she started once more to scrub. 'But Briony knows. She asked me only the other day and I had to tell her. Giovanni doesn't want her to know, but she is a bright girl, she can see for herself.'

'So we're all to pretend that there's nothing wrong?' Paolo asked.

She nodded. 'That is the way Giovanni wants it.'

'Is there no chance of convincing him to get a job above ground, Mamma? It would be possible.'

'No. I've tried Paolo, believe me. But he is a miner, he says, he will live and die a miner. I have no right to demand he do otherwise.'

There was mischief in her eyes as she lifted the wet shirt from the tub. 'I could, you know. I believe my Giovanni would do anything for me. But he'd be unhappy. It would break his spirit to work in a clerk's office or behind a shop counter.' She handed Paolo the wet shirt and selected another from the basket. 'Giovanni is a true miner, Paolo, he loves his world below the ground.' She smiled. 'He loves his world above the ground too, he's proud of the fact that he provides well for us.'

His mother looked happy, Paolo thought, content. And yet it was unlikely her husband would live for more than a few years, particularly if he insisted on working below ground; did she not know that?

'Dear Giovanni,' Caterina said softly, 'he wants no more than to see us all happy, singing along to his accordion . . .' She paused briefly. '. . . It's a pity he no longer sings in company, he worries that it might bring on a coughing fit and that people might guess. But, oh Paolo,' her blue eyes shone and her smile was radiant, 'when we're alone, my Giovanni sings to me. So gently . . . such love songs . . .'

Yes, he realised, she knew. They both knew, she and Giovanni, that their time was limited.

How beautiful she is, Paolo thought. Unlike the others in Kal, his mother had not changed, his mother was as splendid as ever—in his eyes anyway—and Paolo's pride in her was as fierce as his love for her. He was glad now that he'd made his decision. As he'd sat on his bed listening to the household's morning bustle, he had not wanted to make such a decision, but his sense of duty had told him that he must. Now he was glad.

'I am not going to join the army, Mamma,' he said. 'I will apply to one of the big mines here in Kal. Not the Midas. That could present difficulties if Giovanni's illness is discovered, but one of the other big mines, the Lake View, the Boulder, the Perseverance . . .'

Caterina looked up from her washtub.

'I may have to do a year's field work underground,' he continued, 'but after that I could have my pick of positions. Why, I could be General Manager—I have the qualifications. And then, Mamma, the money I'll make! I'll look after the family, I promise.'

'You had your heart so set on going to war, Paolo. It was your duty, you said. Your duty to your birthland.' Caterina was studying him intently. 'What about the letter you had from Enrico in Gallipoli? Enrico is not even Australian and yet he is fighting for this country—that's what you said to me.'

'Mamma, what's the matter with you?' Paolo was bewildered. 'You begged me to think about it. You told me not to do anything and not to tell anyone until I was absolutely sure of my decision. You begged me! Well I haven't done anything and I haven't told anyone, and I'm sure of my decision.'

'Oh Paolo, my darling.' Caterina dried her wet hands on her apron and pushed her unruly curls back from her face. 'I'm happy this is your decision, I don't want to see my son go to war; dear God in heaven, what mother would? But if you've changed your mind because you feel obligated, then I won't allow it. It's your life, Paolo, just as Giovanni's is his, and you must live it the way you wish.'

'How old was I when you married Evan, Mamma? Five? Six?'

'Nearly six,' Caterina nodded, surprised by the non sequitur.

'I didn't want you to marry him. I suppose I was

jealous, it had always been just you and me. But you said we needed a man to look after us. And I said, I could look after us, do you remember?'

Caterina smiled. 'Of course I do.' That solemn little boy, she thought, with his big grey eyes. So earnest.

'I know it was a foolish thing to say. I knew it then. But do you remember what you told me?'

'Yes. I said, "One day you can look after us, Paolo, one day when you are grown-up".'

'I'm grown-up now, Mamma.'

'Yes, I know.'

'And I want to look after you. . . . One day you will need me to look after you.'

She looked away. Was she crying? he wondered. Had he upset her? He didn't want to, but she must confront the future. She was a woman with two daughters.

Caterina was not crying. She could have shed a tear, for pure joy, but she dared not—Paolo in his seriousness would misunderstand. 'With all your education,' she said, picking up another shirt from the basket, 'you would choose to stay in Kalgoorlie?'

'Mamma, Kalgoorlie is one of the most exciting mining cities in the world. The goldfields here are young and rich, their potential is endless . . .'

'All right, Paolo, all right,' she turned to him, laughing. 'You've convinced me. You wish to stay with us.' She stopped laughing but there was still a smile in her eyes. 'And you're right, one day I will need you. But until that day, there will be no sadness in this house.' She kissed him and returned to her washtub.

'I'M GLAD YOU'RE staying,' Briony said. Late that afternoon, when she'd come home from school, Paolo had told her of his talk with Caterina and there was a strong sense of sibling camaraderie as they swore their oath of secrecy. 'Even though I lose my room,' she added, 'I'm glad you're staying.

'Don't worry,' Paolo assured her, 'when I have a good job I'm going to rent my own place.' She looked surprised and he gave her a cheeky wink in return. 'A bloke needs his privacy too, you know.'

They were on the front verandah, Briony sitting on the wooden swinging seat which Giovanni had made for his girls as a Christmas present. Despite the fact that no amount of oil could disguise its squeak, they loved it.

'Do you like being back?' she asked after a moment's pause.

'In Kal? Yes, I love it.' He sat on the verandah railing, his back against the corner post, and looked down the road. It was going to be a perfect autumn evening. The afternoon was still and thick with heat, but the searing bite of summer had passed. Children, home from school, played in the dusty street whilst parents watched, gathering the faintest breeze from front verandahs. Sounds from houses, a baby's cry, the odd bark of an excited dog in a backyard. The cosy blanket of the afternoon and the familiarity of the sounds engulfed Paolo. 'I love this place.'

Briony pushed her heels against the wooden verandah and the seat gave a protesting squeak as it started to swing. 'Only because you got out.'

'That's not true, Briony. I always loved Kal. I only left to further my education.'

'And to see the world,' she corrected him. 'That's what you told me, years ago, when I was a little girl.'

'And I meant it,' he replied. 'I *did* see the world.'

'You saw Harvard.' Briony's tone was sceptical. 'And if you hadn't had an offer to "further your education", I don't reckon you would have gone at all.'

He wasn't sure which was most annoying, the squeaking of the seat or her detached appraisal of him.

But then Briony had always been ruthlessly honest, even as a child. It had been her most disarming quality, that and her sense of humour.

His obvious annoyance didn't bother her at all as she sat crosslegged, swaying to and fro. 'Don't get snaky, Paolo, I just think you're a creature of Kalgoorlie, that's all.'

'And what exactly is a "creature of Kalgoorlie"?' he asked, still scowling. 'I wasn't even born here.'

'And I was,' she laughed. 'In a humpy, in the outback. Stop looking so serious, it wasn't an insult.' The seat slowed down and gave its final squeak of protest. 'Kalgoorlie can get in anyone's blood. You don't have to be born here.' In the silence that followed, Briony herself became serious. 'Kal is a place you never want to leave or a place you can't wait to get out of.'

Her words were heartfelt. 'And you want to get out?' Paolo asked. She nodded. 'It's a place you always want to come back to, Briony.'

'Maybe.' She swung the seat until it squealed again. 'But I won't know that till I get out, will I?'

'HUGHES VISITS THE FRONT' the headlines proclaimed. 'While in France, Prime Minister Hughes visited the Australian troops and was briefed by General Sir Douglas Haig . . .'

It was a Sunday and the whole clan was gathered at Rico and Teresa's house. They always discussed the news from the front and it was Briony's turn to read from the paper as they sat around the family table.

Paolo was amused to see Salvatore, yet again, dive for a place on the bench beside Briony. 'Young Salvatore's besotted with you,' he'd told his sister when the clan had first gathered to welcome him home.

'Don't be silly, Paolo,' she'd answered dismissively, 'he's a baby.'

'Do you want to play football, Briony?' Salvatore asked when they had finished with the newspaper and the adults were discussing the politics of the day.

'No, I don't.' Briony refused to acknowledge the I-told-you-so look in Paolo's eye. 'Do you want me to help?' she asked as Caterina and Teresa rose from the table to prepare the meal.

'No, no, you children go outside and leave us some space,' Teresa answered. 'Caterina and I like to talk while we work.'

Rosalina jumped up immediately, but Salvatore hung back waiting for Briony.

'I won't be late.' Carmelina was up from the table in a flash. She had been waiting impatiently, as usual. 'Bye, Papa.' She kissed the top of Rico's head. 'Bye, Mamma, bye everyone.' And she was out the door.

Paolo watched her as he sat at the table with the men, Giovanni opening a bottle of red wine, Rico lighting his pipe. Carmelina always left before the meal on a Sunday. 'It is the only time she has with her friends,' Teresa had apologetically explained. 'She works so hard at the restaurant.'

Carmelina had changed more than any of them, Paolo thought and he marvelled that the family couldn't see it. What friends did she visit with such desperate anticipation? Certainly not her girlfriends. Who could the man be? Paolo wondered. And, if he was an honourable man, why the secrecy?

He had tried, as gently as possible, to broach the subject with Carmelina. 'Why are you leaving? Stay and talk with me.' It had been the second Sunday the family had gathered and, once again, she had left as soon as she could. He'd followed her quickly out onto the verandah. 'I haven't seen you for so long and we haven't exchanged a word alone since I've been home.'

'You don't need to talk to me, Paolo, you have the whole family.' Her smile was brittle and he knew she wanted to get away.

'But I'll have the whole family for the rest of the evening,' he'd urged, 'sit and talk to me. Just for a little while.'

'I can't.' She was already edging towards the verandah steps. 'You heard Mamma, Sunday is my only day off, the only day I have to see my friends.'

'What friends, Carmelina?' He knew he was treading on dangerous ground. 'What friends could be more important than your family?'

There was no pretence left in her eyes now, no attempt at a smile, brittle or otherwise. He was making her late and Louis was waiting. 'Leave me alone.'

'Carmelina, please. We are family, I care about you.' He had tried to take her arm. 'And whilst your brother is not here . . .'

'I said leave me alone!' She had wrenched her arm away and her voice had been as loud as she dared with the family sitting inside. 'I am eighteen and what I do is none of your business.' Carmelina hated him then—she hated them all. Italian peasants. 'And if Enrico were here it would be none of his business either,' she had said as she ran down the steps and into the street.

Paolo had wondered, for quite some time after that, what he should do. He dared not tell Rico. And Giovanni was a sick man, he needed no added burden. So, guiltily, Paolo kept Carmelina's secret. Perhaps, after all, she was right. She was of age, she was a woman, and this was Australia, not a peasant community where the brothers were beholden to avenge their sisters' honour.

Paolo persuaded himself that perhaps everything would turn out for the best. Perhaps the man with whom she was in love was honourable and Carmelina was simply keeping her affair a secret for fear of her father's reaction. Perhaps it was only a matter of time before her beau would declare himself. If so, Paolo wished him luck. He would need to be a bold man to approach Rico.

'Caterina tells me you have another letter from Enrico,' Teresa said as she set the table. 'You will read it out to us after we've eaten?'

'Of course,' Paolo answered, meeting his mother's eyes as she smiled an apology behind Teresa's back.

When Paolo had received Enrico's letter only several days previously, Caterina had made him promise to bring it to the family gathering on Sunday.

'But you saw what happened when I read out parts of the letter he sent me from Gallipoli, Mamma,' Paolo had protested. 'It only gets Rico going again.'

Indeed, there had been very few portions of the letter Paolo had dared to read out. Before he had even started, Rico had embarked upon his 'fool of a boy, fighting for a country which is not his own' crusade.

'I know, I know,' Caterina had agreed, 'and Rico will do it again, he does every time. But take the letter, Paolo. For Teresa's sake.' When he still appeared reluctant, she added. 'Make it up as you go along. Teresa won't know and it will make her happy.'

Women were so devious, Paolo had thought as he put the letter in his pocket, even his mother whom he so much admired.

'Yes, of course I'll read it to you,' he said to Teresa. 'After we've eaten and before we sing. I promise.'

CARMELINA CRIED OUT as the pain knifed through her. But it would ease soon. Soon she would be able to bear it without crying out.

In the rose-coloured room at Red Ruby's, Carmelina rarely achieved her own pleasure any more. But it didn't matter. It was his pleasure that mattered. And afterwards, when he'd defiled her, he would hold her close and kiss her gently and tell her how much he loved her.

He no longer brought the whores in to make love to her whilst he watched. 'Just you and me, my darling,' he'd whispered that first time and she'd been glad. He'd caressed her until she was insane with desire. 'Every part of you is mine, Carmelina,' he'd murmured, 'will you pleasure me with every part of you?' She moaned her acquiesence, there was nothing she would not do for him. And then he'd defiled her in a way she could never have imagined.

Afterwards, as she lay shocked and degraded, he made love to her with his tongue and his hands. 'You're mine, Carmelina,' he whispered, 'I own you, every part of you, I love you, I love you . . .' And, unbelievably, her body had responded. She'd cried out in ecstasy even as her humiliation was still fresh in her mind. It was true. He owned her.

It was a little different these days. Sometimes he gave her her pleasure, but more often he did not, and Carmelina's satisfaction now lay in the vows of love which followed her degradation. Louis's pleasure was all she lived for now.

Louis himself had not expected the affair to last this long; he'd expected to be bored after six months. But how could he tire of one prepared to surrender to his every whim? Her devotion was total and his power absolute. The prospects which lay ahead were limitless and irresistible. It would be a long time before Louis Picot would tire of young Carmelina Gianni.

'". . . WE'RE BILLETED IN Sailly, in an area known as the Armentières sector. It's named after the town of Armentières on the River Lys".' Paolo read Enrico's letter out loud to the assembled family, his eyes scanning ahead for the sections he knew he must avoid.

'"I'll send this letter to Kal as I know you'll be home by now. You lucky geezer".' Paolo looked up to catch Rico frowning. Rico didn't like his son's use of soldiers' slang, be it Aussie or Tommy vernacular.

'"Are you still thinking of joining up? Don't be a fool, mate, stay at home—"'

'Ah now at last he wakes up,' Rico growled derisively.

'Be quiet, Rico,' Teresa snapped without even looking at him. 'Go on, go on,' she urged.

'". . . although I must say the countryside around Sailles is peaceful and pretty. Hard to believe there's a war raging all about us. We're only a couple of miles from the front line and mid-way between the towns of Ypres and Loos, both of which have seen some heavy fighting.

'"They're holding us in reserve and they drill us hard—the Frogs are fond of cobbled streets, a right bastard for marching on—but we have it fairly easy on the whole. The calm before the storm.

'"The villagers are a beaut bunch and we've become mates with some of them. We even sat up all night last week waiting for a cow to calve. In the middle of a war, just think, a bunch of us squatting about the old stove, taking turns to stroke the cow's head and all of us murmuring encouragement like a mob of midwives. When she had twins there was a whopping great celebration. The villagers broke out the plink plonk—white wine—and everybody got right royally stonkered. Well, not me, I'm still not mad about the stuff, but my mate had a bugger of a hangover".' Paolo had thought quickly and replaced the word 'Jack' with 'my mate'. '"He tells me the local vino's pretty rough stuff".'

Paolo skipped ahead. He certainly couldn't read aloud the next paragraph.

'Yes, Jack Brearley,' Rick had written, to Paolo's utter amazement. 'Bet you're surprised. We've become good mates, it's too stupid to be anything else over here. I know you'll be glad to hear it, Paolo, you always were the peacemaker, and you were right. Jack's as wild as ever but he's a good mate. We even left the train for a couple of days on the trip north, I thought we'd get into terrible strife, but Jack wasn't worried. When we reported to the nearest military headquarters and told them we'd got lost, the Tommy officer gave us a whopping dressing down, went on about the lack of discipline in the Aussie ranks and the fact that we're noncommissioned officers now (sergeants, how about that!) and we should have more regard for our rank. On and on he went, but there was nothing he could do. You should hear Jack's toffee-nosed Tommy imitation. Has all the blokes in stitches.

'We're a bit of a duo act actually. Jack does the joke-telling and I play the concertina . . .'

'Go on,' Teresa was urging once more. 'Go on, what does he say?'

' ". . . I play the concertina",' Paolo continued, catching his mother's sympathetic glance.

'I drive Jack mad with the old concertina.' He couldn't read that. 'Jack says he's spent his whole childhood listening to the bloody thing but the other blokes love it.'

' ". . . the other blokes love it",' Paolo read out. ' "I'm surprised I can even get a sound out of the old thing now. It's held together with string and glue and sticking plaster. But it manages a tune and the men sing as if their hearts would break".'

Paolo glanced up at Giovanni as he read the next part. ' "I told Giovanni, in a letter I wrote to him from

Gallipoli, that the music he gave me is my salvation, and it's true, Paolo. Mine, and many others. I've seen a song raise men's spirits the way nothing else could. I've seen men on the brink of madness join in a song with their mates and, for that moment at least, the horror's forgotten.

'"That's all for now".' Paolo again skipped the next bit. 'It's good to be able to talk openly to someone,' Rick had written. 'I owe Jack my life, Paolo. At Gallipoli, he saved my life, and there's no one in Kal I can tell, apart from you. Not even Giovanni, and I speak to Giovanni from my heart.

'Jack and I have agreed that, when we come home, we'll end this family feud. Why fight a war in Kal when the whole world is doing it? Kal is a place to be safe. Kal is home.'

'"... Look after yourself",' Paolo read, '"and congratulations on Harvard and all that. You'll be a real toff by the time I see you. Your good mate ..."' Paolo changed the 'Rick' to Enrico. He looked up to see Teresa with tears streaming down her face.

Chapter Twenty-Eight

'Good God, did we really send men to fight in that?' It was after the conclusion of the third battle of Ypres, referred to as Passchendaele, that General Kiggell, Haig's Chief of General Staff, made his first journey to within a few miles of the front. Many reports said that he wept.

General Douglas Haig, British Commander in Chief of the Allied Forces, was directly responsible for the disastrous choice of terrain which resulted in a battleground that was no more than a boggy marshland.

The British generals were warned that the ground on which they planned to launch their attack had been reclaimed from the sea. Centuries of labour had been employed in building and preserving the intricate drainage system of dykes and culverts and the farmers themselves were under penalty to keep their dykes clear and well maintained. Any bombardment, the generals were told, and the land would revert to marshland. Haig refused to listen.

The first two weeks of shelling proved the accuracy of the warnings. The troops were forced to lay down tracks in order to advance. If a man strayed from those tracks he could find himself up to his armpits in mud. In the first battle alone, half the British tanks were lost in the quagmire and the remaining tanks were of little use. Trenches were impossible to maintain under the relentless enemy barrage and many troops were buried alive in the mud.

Haig was advised of the appalling conditions and the prospect of failure but such opinions were unwelcome and he ignored them. The battle was to continue as planned.

'PLAY US A song, Rick,' Snowy said and the other half-dozen men, crouched in the ditch beside the derelict wagon, urged him on.

'Give a bloke a break,' Jack loudly complained, 'we've had enough music for one day. The Germans have played us a whole bloody concerto—how about a bit of peace and quiet?'

Tom Brereton howled him down and the others joined in as they always did. The concertina had become a running gag between Jack Brearley and Rick Gianni and the men enjoyed it.

The gunfire had indeed been severe all day and, as night drew on and the shelling became more sporadic, the relief from the constant noise was intense. Not that they were ever entirely free of shelling. Every now and then a growl would sound overhead and, somewhere amongst the grey wasteland, a geyser of mud and water would explode into the air.

It was the end of October and the men of the 11th Battalion were on their third tour of the line. The Westralian diggers had seen it all and there wasn't a man amongst them who didn't awake in the muddy trench after his several intermittent hours of cold, wet, lice-ridden sleep to wonder at the fact that he was still alive. Snowy, Tom, Jack and Rick made a joke of it. 'Still here, mate?' was their good morning greeting to one another.

The 11th Battalion headquarters were in dugouts at Zonnebeke but the troops of the 3rd Brigade, on the line near Decline Copse, were existing under terrible conditions. Having relieved the 2nd Brigade, the 3rd was acting as protection and decoy for the right flank of the 4th Canadian Division which was making an attack on Passchendaele, and the gunfire had been so heavy for so long that there was not one area of ground untouched. In the welter of mud and broken trenches it was up to the troops to find shelter for the night as best they could and, all over the battleground, pockets of men huddled in holes in the ground.

In the ditch by the wagon, the group dragged out their waterproof sheets from their packs, settled themselves down in the mud and lit their cigarettes whilst Rick pulled the old concertina from his kitbag.

'"Piccadilly",' Charlie Blanchard insisted. Charlie was a Cockney and he always wanted the old vaudeville songs. 'Give us "Piccadilly" first.' The Aussies didn't howl him down the way they used to do. By now, the Diggers knew the Tommy songs as well as they knew their own and, in No-Man's-Land, any song was a good song.

They sang in desperation at first, to drown out the sound of gunfire and erase the memory of the day's hideous battle. Then cries of 'Good on you, mate' sounded from other ditches and craters and broken trenches and, here and there, a man stood and waved. More and more voices joined in. Wherever the sound of the concertina could be heard, men sang and, gradually, down the line, the song swelled to become a rousing chorus of defiance. '". . . dear old London's broad highway!"' They shouted the finale.

Requests were yelled from afar. '"The Road to Gundagai!"'

'"My Old Man!"' And everyone's favourite, '"The Rose of No-Man's Land!"'

'There's a rose that grows,

In No-Man's-Land . . .'

Jack studied Rick, playing valiantly on and on, never missing a beat. Even when a shell exploded nearby and they were showered with mud, Rick played on.

'. . . It's the one red rose,
The soldier knows.
It's the work of the Master's hand . . .'

Today of all days, they needed Rick Gianni, Jack thought. Today had been a day from hell.

''Neath the world's great curse
Stands the Red Cross nurse.
She's the Rose of No-Man's-Land!'

Whilst men from all over the battlefield roared the final words Jack looked around at his mates. He and Rick and Mad Tom Brereton—they called him Mad Tom these days to his face, Tom seemed to like it—and Snowy Wilson and the others. How the hell had they lasted this long? Jack wondered. How the hell had they lasted this long?

There had been a purpose to start with, or at least they'd told themselves there was. Reach the front line, man the trenches and advance when the order came through. Pretty simple really.

Through the communication saps and over the parapet they'd gone, with the hundreds of others. Through and over the endless maze of trenches, amongst the shell holes and barbed wire, ignoring the bodies that lay strewn in their wake. There had been many a fight for the ridge ahead and both sides had suffered heavy losses. No time to think about that now. The Germans were retreating. Orders were to advance.

The front line. They'd made it. The trench was full of bodies, Germans as well as Allies. So Fritz had got this far, they thought. Some men were not yet dead. Stretcher bearers would come under cover of darkness for those who could last that long.

Ahead of them was No-Man's-Land. And the orders to advance once more at dawn.

They'd advanced, all right, Jack thought as he looked at the others—they were singing 'It's a Long Way to Tipperary' now—but, here in No-Man's-Land, there were few left to tell the tale. This was a gunner's war, an artillery duel between the Allied and German batteries, and heaven help the poor infantryman caught in the middle. If they could only meet Fritz face to face, in man-to-man combat, at least they would feel they were serving a purpose.

Finally, the men stopped singing. As the blackness of night crept in about them, broken every now and then by German flares and a fresh burst of gunfire, they fed themselves from their kitbag rations. Then they curled up in the mud and tried to give their weary bodies whatever minutes' or hours' sleep their nerves would allow.

'I'll take first watch,' Charlie Blanchard offered. Nightly watch was maintained not so much for fear of attack, as for fear of the dreaded mustard gas. The minute the familiar shower of popping gas shells sounded, the alarm went out and the men had only seconds to don their gas masks before the yellow-green haze wreaked its deadly havoc.

Jack's mind drifted off and the visions appeared, as they always did. Old ones were joined by the fresh unspeakable horrors of the day and he couldn't rid himself of the man's face. The man drowning in the mud that very afternoon. As they'd frantically dug to free Snowy, the mortally wounded man had been barely five yards away. Buried from the shoulders down, he'd been blown to pieces. God knew how much of him was left beneath the mud. But he was conscious and struggling feebly. The more he struggled the quicker he sank and, by the time they'd dug Snowy out, the man had gone. But Jack had seen the final look in his eyes and now, in fitful sleep, the man was back. His mouth opened he was about to say something.

Jack awoke, startled, the sweat of alarm mingling with the drizzle of rain. A noise nearby. 'What was that?' He sat up.

'Rats, mate.' It was Snowy. 'Rats, that's all. Go back to sleep. You too, Charlie, I'll take over the watch.'

'Right you are then,' and Charlie curled up in his waterproof sheet.

Tough little Snowy Wilson was having trouble sleeping. Each time he closed his eyes, panic rose in him. He could feel himself drowning as the trench closed in about him. Jack was pulling on one arm and Tom on the other whilst Rick dug frantically at the mud. But it was no use, Snowy was being sucked down into his grave. He kicked with his feet and felt the bodies of the men buried beneath him. His foot found a purchase and he started to climb. The limbs of dead men were the steps of the ladder he climbed to safety as his mates pulled him from the slime. Tough little Snowy Wilson was having trouble sleeping.

Tom Brereton was not. Mad Tom always managed to sleep. But there was no respite in it and he usually awoke more tormented than before. In his sleep, an endless array of torn flesh and limbless bodies paraded behind his eyelids and every dead man bore the face of one of his brothers. Now Ben, now Bill; they seemed to take it in turn. Even the faceless bodies, those with a stump where a head used to be, were the headless bodies of his brothers.

Rick Gianni had managed, more successfully than the others, to exorcise his nightly demons. As the images started to appear, he concentrated on the music in his brain. Always the same tune, the very first one he'd written. He'd been just a boy. 'Solange's Song' he'd called it. And then he would conjure up her face. Not as he'd last seen it, with nothing but the fear of discovery in her eyes. But loving. Impudent and laughing. During every tormented night, the memory of Solange was Rick Gianni's saviour.

The image of the drowning man would not allow Jack sleep so he and Snowy talked quietly together.

'Not a good possie, this,' Jack said, referring to the ditch in which they were huddled. It was beside one of the few existing roads across the battlefield and roads were regularly shelled to prevent the supplies getting through to the Allied front line.

'We'll be out at dawn, mate. They'll signal the advance.' Snowy lit up another cigarette. 'We've got to press forward and get under the barrage. We're sitting ducks out here.'

'Reckon we can make it to the ridge?'

'I reckon.'

Dawn's first light revealed the carnarge. Behind the men there stretched miles of wet, grey wasteland strewn with bodies and debris. A low mist rolled across the boggy marshland and, here and there, lay evil pools of yellowish liquid, remnants of the hideous mustard gas.

Far ahead, the German lines looked green and untouched. Virgin country, in stark contrast to the Allied lines and No-Man's-Land. Strange to think that the hideous slime in which they lay was the victor's ground and that the Germans were in retreat.

They could see the ridge ahead and, as the signal sounded, men rose like ghosts from the mud. Were there really that many of them left, after all? Jack wondered as he ran with the others.

The noise from the heavy German bombardment was horrendous. Shells roared overhead like freight trains to explode in a shower of mud and men. Still they ran, staggering, falling in the mud, and rising again, those who could. As he ran, Jack's mind was strangely lucid. Snowy was right, he thought, they were spot in the middle of the heavy guns' target range. If they could just get forward. If they could live that long. Usually the cacophany of artillery became one nightmare roar, but something told Jack's mind that there was less sputter of machine-gun fire. Amongst the growl of shells and the squeal of field guns, where was the constant rat-tat-tat of machine-guns? Was it true then? Had the Germans retreated? Was the ridge theirs for the taking?

Closer and closer to the ridge. Soon they'd be under the heavy barrage. Then a wall of mud engulfed them and Jack was thrown to the ground, Rick beside him. 'You right?' he yelled, but Rick was already struggling to his feet. So were Charlie Blanchard and Snowy. The shell had missed them. Mad Tom Brereton, the strongest and fastest runner of them all, was twenty yards ahead, screaming like a banshee.

On they ran. And on. They'd left the shells behind now. But the fierce splutter of machine-gun bullets suddenly surrounded them and Charlie Blanchard's chest ripped open. Three other men beside him fell. Jack saw them, to his right. On he ran. The ridge was in front of them now. The ground was slightly firmer underfoot. Bayonets at the ready, they charged.

Tom disappeared in front of them. Over the ridge and he was gone. But, through the inferno's noise, they could hear his screams. Then they, too, were over the ridge, Jack and Rick and Snowy. And there was Tom, bayonet plunging. Thrust, twist, withdraw. Thrust, twist, withdraw.

But they were dead men. Mad Tom Brereton was fighting dead men. Beyond the ridge were shell craters filled with bodies. The craters of their own shells, Jack realised. And the bodies were those of both sides; the Allies who had led the previous charge and the Germans who had been too late in their retreat.

Tom, in his madness, at least had wits enough to bayonet the enemy uniform. 'Bastard!' he was screaming. Thrust, twist, withdraw. 'Bastard!'

'Leave it, mate,' Jack yelled, while the others dived for cover. There was machine-gun fire nearby.

'Bastard!' Thrust, twist, withdraw.

'I said leave it!' Jack grabbed Tom's arm. 'Leave it!' Tom whirled on him, madness in his eyes, bayonet at the ready. Then recognition dawned. 'They're dead, mate,' Jack said.

They huddled in a crater amongst the bodies and looked back at the butchery of No-Man's-Land. The mists had lifted and a cold wind blew across the battlefield. Troops who had nearly made it were being mown down by machine-gun fire from further along the ridge.

'It's up ahead,' Snowy said, 'not far.'

They all knew what they had to do but, as usual, Jack took command, leading the way as they dodged amongst the rubble and craters and mutilated bodies.

In a large bunker, a number of enemy troops were manning the gun. Behind the blockade of sandbags and barbed wire, it was impossible for Jack to see how many. But they were effective. The blokes coming in this end of the line didn't stand a chance. He wondered if there were more guns further along the ridge covering the Germans' retreat.

Jack, Rick, Tom and Snowy huddled for a moment in the whistling wind.

'Now!' Jack yelled, and together they charged.

There were four enemy troops in the bunker. One German fell dead on the sandbags, a bullet through the head. Snowy Wilson was a crack shot. The soldier manning the machine-gun whirled about, bullets spurting in all directions. Mad Tom's arm was ripped apart but, even as he fell screaming 'bastard!', his bayonet found its mark and a German soldier fell dead beneath him.

Jack hurled himself at the soldier manning the gun, driving his bayonet into the man's side. Twist, withdraw, and a club to the head with the rifle butt. Another soldier was upon him but Snowy's bayonet had caught the German in the shoulder. A shot to the head from Jack and the man was finished.

Snowy and Jack collapsed amongst the bodies, Mad Tom writhing beside them, clutching his mangled arm and muttering 'bastards' between clenched teeth.

Before they could regain their breath, two men had wriggled over the sandbags and into the bunker.

'Good on you, boys.' It was Captain Bob Bains, a popular officer, and with him was Tiny Nelson. They were from the original C Company and Jack knew them both. 'We'd never have made it if you hadn't drawn their fire. Bloody good work.'

But Jack had suddenly noticed that Rick wasn't there. Where the hell was he?

He peered over the top of the bunker. Twenty yards away, Rick Gianni lay face-down on the ground. His pack, shot to pieces, hung in the coils of barbed wire beside him.

'Rick!' Jack started to climb from the bunker, but fresh machine-gun fire sounded from behind them.

'Get down, man!' Bob Bains yelled. 'Get down!'

They had broken their cover in charging the bunker and the retreated enemy troops, from the safety of their new position a quarter of a mile away, were concentrating their attention on the pocket of men who had gained the ridge.

But Jack didn't listen. 'Rick!' He yelled his friend's name as he scrambled out of the bunker and charged across the twenty yards of ground, bullets cracking the air all about him.

'Jesus,' Snowy muttered, peering cautiously from the bunker, 'the man's mad.'

Then, as Jack hauled Rick up into a fireman's lift and turned to run for safety, Snowy threw caution to the wind. He stood and screamed with all his might. 'Run, mate! Run! Run!' Tiny Nelson and Bob Bains also stood. 'Run, Jack! Run!' All three were yelling now.

The twenty-yard sprint back to the bunker seemed a lifetime to Jack, with the weight of Rick's body on his shoulders. Any minute he expected to feel the bullets tear into his flesh. Fifteen yards to go. Ten yards. Five. Any minute now. But miraculously, he escaped the gunfire which screamed about him.

Eager hands grabbed at Rick as Jack tumbled the body from his shoulders and dived headlong into the bunker. There was a hard thump and a burning pain as a bullet hit him in the calf.

'Good on you, mate. Good on you.'

Jack didn't even feel the others thumping him on the back as he settled Rick against the walls of the bunker. His face was only inches from his friend's and he could feel the breath fanning his cheek. 'Hold on, Rick,' he muttered. 'Hold on, mate.'

The others too turned their attention to Rick as they tried to stem his bleeding.

'He's copped it in the back, mate,' Snowy said. 'He won't make it.'

'How do you know?' Jack snapped. 'You're not a bloody doctor.'

'Don't get maggoty. I'm just saying he's copped it in the back. I don't reckon . . .'

'Shut up, Snowy.'

'All right, all right.'

While the others tended Tom's wounds, Jack took a cloth from his pack and wiped the mud from his friend's face. 'Hold on, Rick,' he said, 'they'll bring the stretchers in when it's dark. They always manage to somehow, don't they? Just hold on till then, mate. They'll get you back.'

Snowy Wilson was a tough little man. The job in a war was to stay alive and not let yourself get rattled. That was the way Snowy viewed things, and nothing rattled him much. Except getting buried alive in the mud—he wouldn't forget that in a hurry. Jack Brearley was tough too, but Jack was rattled, he could tell. He supposed it was understandable, Rick and Jack were best mates. Perhaps he'd better try and say the right thing.

'Yeah, maybe he'll make it,' he said helpfully, 'if they haven't hit a vital organ that is . . . '

'I said shut up, Snowy.'

By now, Tom Brereton had lapsed into unconsciousness, broken every now and then by a moan of pain. But Rick Gianni hadn't uttered a sound. He was still breathing, though, that was the main thing. 'You'll make it, mate,' Jack kept saying. 'Just hold on until nightfall—they'll come and get you then.'

It was Captain Bob himself who dressed Jack's leg. 'Only a flesh wound, son, you'll live,' he said reassuringly. 'It was a courageous thing you did.' He nodded at Rick. 'A bloody fine thing. You'll get a medal for that, I'll see that you do.'

'That's not why I did it, sir,' Jack snapped.

''Course not, son.' The lad was rattled, Bob could tell. Pity his mate wasn't going to make it.

Dodging amongst the cover, Bob Bains, Tiny Nelson and Snowy did a 'recce' further along the line. There was jubilation amongst the troops who had survived the charge. The ridge was in Allied hands.

The men returned to the bunker. 'You've done your job, boys,' Captain Bob congratulated them. 'Dig in till nightful and we'll look after the wounded then. Stay with the lads, Snowy.' And he and Tiny Nelson left.

Over the next several hours, Rick seemed to drift in and out of consciousness. He made no sound, but his eyelids flickered and once or twice they opened and he looked at Jack, although he appeared not to recognise him. 'Hang on, mate,' Jack said each time, 'not long to go.'

The boom of heavy artillery was more distant now and less constant. Without the immediate threat of danger, it was peaceful in a way. The cold wind picked up and whistled along the ridge and even that was a sort of comfort—anything other than gunfire. Snowy fell asleep.

It was late afternoon when Jack heard the concertina. Was he going mad? he wondered. There was no particular tune, just sounds. Mournful sounds coming to him on the wind.

He stood on one leg, pain shooting through his wounded calf, and looked around. Then he saw it. The concertina was twisted up in barbed wire alongside the other contents of Rick's pack, his waterproof sheet and his gas mask. Even as Jack watched, the sheet took off and sailed across the battlefield like an avenging wraith. But the concertina remained hanging on the wire. Each time a fresh gust blew, it wailed.

Jack sat down once more beside his friend. Rick's eyelids were fluttering. Could he hear it? 'Jesus, mate, you won't leave it alone, will you? Even out here I cop your bloody concertina.'

Rick's eyes opened. Yes, Jack thought, he could hear it. Rick Gianni was listening to something, of that Jack was certain.

Rick could hear the concertina. But not the mournful wail borne on the wind of the battlefield. He could hear 'Solange's Song'. He closed his eyes; soon he'd see her face. He heard a voice. 'Hang on, mate, not long now.' He could swear it was Jack Brearley.

There was the sound of popping shells in the air and

Snowy Wilson was instantly awake. 'Gas!' he yelled, grabbing at his pack.

Jack ripped his own mask from his pack and put it on Rick. Rick's eyes opened once more. Yes, it had been Jack's voice he'd heard. He opened his mouth. 'Thanks, Jack.' Whether he said the words or just thought them, he couldn't be sure.

What a nice thing for a mate to do, Rick thought. The sound of Jack Brearley's voice mingled with the music and the image of Solange, and he was quite at peace as he died.

'You're a fool,' Snowy hissed, donning his gas mask and grabbing Tom's from his pack. 'He won't need that and his mask's out there blown to buggery.'

'These blokes use them too you know.' Jack was feverishly opening one of the dead German's packs, valuable seconds wasted as he fumbled about.

'Jesus, mate, hurry!' Snowy urged, fastening Tom's mask. 'Hurry!'

There it was. He'd found the German's gas mask. But, even as he ripped it over his head, the dense cloud of mustard gas surrounded them.

Jack tried to hold his breath but, in the split-second before he pulled the mask down over his face, the hideous vapour attacked.

He fell, writhing, to the ground. His throat was being torn out, iron hands clutched at his chest—any moment he would choke. Inside his gas mask, he gasped for air. His eyes were burning, the pain was intense. Was he dying? If he was, God in Heaven make it quick! Through his agony, he could hear the concertina. That damn concertina was playing his lament. Was Rick dead? Was he dead himself? Was this where it ended?

There was an echo, Snowy's voice coming to him from out of a deep, deep tunnel. 'Jesus, mate, did you cop it?' Then all Jack could hear was the wail of the concertina as he sank into merciful oblivion.

MIDDLESEX WAR HOSPITAL had been a women's lunatic asylum, the new patients were informed by the old, and there were jokes about the bars on the windows and the fact that it was hell to break out for a night on the town. Not that anyone ever did; there were few who could leave their beds. After the fierce fighting at Passchendaele, only the severely wounded remained for any length of time at the Middlesex War Hospital; the rest were farmed out to convalescence hospitals to make way for the never-ending stream of severe cases.

Mad Tom Brereton was moved on fairly quickly. He'd been close to death but they'd saved him and, although he'd lost his right arm, he would be returned to Australia once he'd undergone a lengthy convalescence.

Jack Brearley was a different case. His heart had been affected by mustard gas and he was to be transported to the 1AA Hospital at Harefield Park in Essex for special treatment.

Jack had little memory of the field hospital at Poperinghe or the train which had carried the wounded on stretchers to the coast.

He had little memory of the flimsy wood and canvas hospital at Etaples Base.

He had little memory of anything but pain.

He was blind, without the power of speech and in such agony that his conscious moments were spent praying for death.

The drops they applied regularly to his eyes burned like liquid fire, and whatever it was they tried to make him drink from the feeding bottle was impossible to swallow. The mere act of breathing was difficult, as each single intake of air seared painfully through his lungs.

There followed further train travel to Calais and a

murderous Channel crossing to Dover while the steamship bucked and rolled and brought on such a bout of seasickness that Jack thought his heart was being torn from his body.

It was only as he lay on his stretcher in the huge iron shed, amongst the rows and rows of wounded awaiting the trip to Middlesex, that the will to live returned. Perhaps it was the knowledge that he had left the ghastly battlefields of France. Perhaps it was the return of his sight, although his eyes were shaded and he could see little more than cloudy shapes. But most likely it was the voices of the English nurses as they wandered amongst the men tending to their comfort and offering encouragement to the downhearted.

How Jack loved those nurses. They were angels, each and every one of them, and they made him aware that life was worth a fight.

After his transfer from Middlesex to Harefield Park, Jack took up the fight in earnest. Harefield Park was an Australian war hospital and it was the voices of the Aussie nurses and doctors that finally inspired him. He determined to get well and strong just as soon as he possibly could. He wanted to go home where he belonged. He wanted to go home to Kal.

Shortly before Christmas, Jack was moved to the convalescent wards at Hurdcott, near Salisbury, but it was to be almost nine months before he was considered strong enough to return to Australia.

By the time Jack Brearley stepped off the ship at Fremantle, the war was well and truly over.

Chapter Twenty-Nine

The streets of Kalgoorlie were festooned with flags and it was bedlam at the railway station as the trains pulled in—the goldfields boys were home from the war.

Brass bands played, there were parades in the streets and jubilation abounded. But the lads who'd returned were vastly outnumbered by those who had not, and the seemingly endless parade of injured—the limbless, the blind, the shell-shocked—was a sobering reminder that a generation of young men had been virtually wiped out.

Other injured diggers were amongst the welcoming hordes, diggers who had been wounded earlier in the war, treated, and sent home to their families. Amongst them was Tony Prendergast.

'Tony!' With his one arm, Mad Tom Brereton embraced the Welshman. 'We thought you'd kicked the bucket! The medico on the beach told Jack you wouldn't make it. Jesus, mate, you copped it bad.'

'So did you, by the look of it,' Tony said and actually raised a smile, a rare thing for him these days.

'G'day, cobber.' Snowy tried to steady the Welshman as he shook his hand. Mad Tom had nearly knocked the poor bloke off his crutches. Christ, but Tony looked crook.

'So how's Jack then? Did he make it?'

'Dunno,' Snowy said, shaking his head. 'Mustard

gas. He was pretty bad when they carted him off. Rick Gianni copped it.'

'Yes, I heard.' Like all of Kalgoorlie, Tony read the casualty lists which the newspapers published regularly. 'Heard you three got awarded DCMs too.'

'Yep.' Mad Tom nodded proudly and jabbed at the medal pinned to his chest. 'And bloody old Jack got the VC. Captain Bob saw to that, just like he said he would, didn't he, Snow?'

Snowy nodded. 'Hell of a price to pay though—they say you're never the same after mustard gas.' He slapped Tony on the back. 'Come on, it's time for a beer.'

They walked to Maudie's pub at a snail's pace, Tony slow on his crutches, Snowy worrying all the while that the Welshman would fall. Tony was obviously not used to walking far, he could barely stand for any length of time. Struth, he looks awful, Snowy kept thinking. Skinny and gaunt-faced. But the eyes were the worst. The eyes were hollow, devoid of hope.

Tony Prendergast was the worst type of war casualty. He'd lost far more than his leg; he'd lost his spirit and his will to live. It was strange, because he'd certainly had it on the battlefield.

Tony could remember vividly the days and nights amongst the bodies in No-Man's-Land, fighting to stay conscious, tightening and easing the tourniquet on his thigh, losing the battle with the blowflies and watching the maggots feed on his flesh. He'd heard men say that the maggots ate the gangrene. The maggots were his friends, he told himself; that way he could watch them at work and not be sick.

The only thing that had kept him going was the thought of his three children. If he gave in now, he kept telling himself, he'd never see them grow up. He fed himself from the packet of nuts and raisins in his kitbag, the last of his Red Cross parcel, rationing himself to a handful a day and sipping carefully from his water bottle. Never once did he think of giving in; he willed himself to stay alive.

Even during his hospitalisation, when his life had hung in the balance and every day was racked with pain, Tony had never given up the fight. And, when he came home to Kal, he'd fooled himself for a while that things would be all right.

Giovanni Gianni had pulled strings to get him a job as a filing clerk in the accounting office at the Midas. 'A man there owes me a favour,' Giovanni had said and Tony was grateful, knowing that it was out of character for the Italian to call in favours. But when Giovanni had been taken ill and had left the Midas, the man in the accounting office forgot the favour and Tony was out of a job.

He'd swallowed his pride and applied for whatever menial work he could get. He was a man with one leg and three children—pride was a luxury he could not afford. He begged favours of friends and borrowed money where he could. But when the favours and friends ran out, the hopelessness set in.

He would look at his wife, still an attractive woman. If he hadn't come home from the war, he'd think to himself, Megan could have found herself another man. It was then that Tony wished he'd lost his battle for life out there on the heights of Gallipoli.

It showed in his eyes, and it broke his wife's heart. Didn't he know that she loved him? Times were hard, yes, but they would manage on his war pension and she could take in washing. Daily, Megan Prendergast tried to raise her husband's spirits but he sank deeper and deeper into despondency, until she too was reduced to despair.

Tony Prendergast was the worst type of war casualty.

WHEN THE HYSTERIA of welcome had died down and the homecoming heroes sought to pick up the pieces of their lives, a rude shock awaited them. Many found that they were not needed, that jobs were few and far between.

It was something they had not anticipated. The women had been the workforce in their absence, or so they'd been told, manning the factories and the farms. And the women would be only too happy to return to their homes when the men came back from the war. But the workforce in Kalgoorlie had not been drawn from the female ranks. A woman miner was unheard of. The jobs had gone to the migrants.

'A bloke goes off to war and comes home to find a foreigner's got his job,' Snowy complained loudly. Most of the others were saying the same thing.

Even Mad Tom Brereton, who refused to accept his amputee status as any form of handicap, joined in the whinge. He'd decided to settle in Kal. There was more money in the mines than there was in the railways.

'Give a digger a go, mate,' he said to the underground boss at the Midas. 'Chuck out the foreigners and give the diggers back their jobs.'

Big Pete Grainger was a little taken aback. A miner with one arm? He wasn't sure what to say.

'But you're a timbercutter.' He hedged. 'You worked for the railways, that's what you said.'

'Too right,' Tom answered, 'and they finished the Transcontinental two years back, didn't they? There's bugger-all work for a bloke there.'

Pete Grainger decided that the man was mad. 'But you've had no experience,' he argued lamely.

'What experience does a miner need?' Tom's tone was getting belligerent.

Two arms for a start, Pete thought and decided to bite the bullet. 'Mate,' he said gently, 'you've only got one arm.'

'So what? I can swing a pick and pull a cart. I'm just not too good with a shovel, that's all.'

'Sorry,' Pete said in the end, 'there are no jobs left.'

''Course not, the bloody Italians have got them, that's why. It's a bloody disgrace!'

As Tom walked off muttering, Pete wondered what his reaction would have been had he been confronted with the previous underground boss. A bloke with a name like Giovanni Gianni would not have gone down too well with Tom Brereton.

Dissatisfaction and ill-will grew as more Aussie troops returned home to no work, and their anger focused upon the Italians, who seemed to hold most of the jobs. Italians were hard working, everyone knew that, but it wasn't natural for a man to work harder than he needed to. It was even rumoured that the Italians paid the underground bosses for extra shifts, and that was downright robbery. Those shifts could have gone to a digger!

There were brawls in pubs and, in the street, Aussies now openly hurled abuse at Italians. The old antipathy was fed with fresh fuel and the wounds reopened. Kalgoorlie was seething.

One evening, after downing a few beers at Maudie's pub, Snowy and Mad Tom were heading home to their boarding house and, as they passed the Sheaf Hotel, Tom insisted on one last drink before it closed.

Snowy shook his head. 'You don't know Kal, mate, that's a dago pub.'

'Good,' there was a glint in Mad Tom's eyes, 'let's stir 'em up.'

Before Snowy could stop him, Tom was through the doors and Snowy felt obliged to follow. The place was crowded with men, mostly Italians, scrambling for last drinks before the pub closed. Tom ordered a beer at the bar, then demanded loudly, of no one in particular,

'Which one of you blokes won a medal in the war?'

Gradually the hubbub died down.

'Shut up, mate,' Snowy muttered, 'there's too many of them.' Snowy didn't mind a good pub brawl but, here tonight, they were vastly outnumbered and the dagos looked like a surly bunch.

It was true. The Italians, fed up with abuse, were ready to retaliate.

'Well, I won a medal,' Tom said, 'and so did he.' He waved his beer in Snowy's direction. 'We fought for this bloody country and you blokes have stolen our jobs.'

'My son, he fought for this country.' The voice came from a seat in the corner. A big burly man, black hair flecked with grey. 'My son, he died for this "bloody" country, and he won a medal too.'

Tom was momentarily halted, but the burly Italian wasn't. He rose, his black eyes burning with anger. 'You two want to fight about that?'

The Italian was a good six inches shorter than he appeared when seated and Tom realised, with surprise, that the bloke was a cripple.

'Jesus, it's Rico Gianni,' Snowy muttered to Tom. Every local for miles knew the madman Gianni.

'Gianni? Rick's dad?' Tom grinned, his anger gone in an instant. 'I fought with your son, Mr Gianni. He was a good bloke, Rick.'

'Rick!' The Italian spat out the name as if it was poison. 'Rick! His name was Enrico!' He started pushing through the men who stepped aside to make way for his lumbering gait.

'I work in the mines,' he said when he stood before Snowy and Tom. 'You want to fight me for that?' Tom was taken aback. Fight him? The man was a cripple, and he had to be fifty. 'Come on and fight,' Rico goaded. 'You have only one arm so I take you both on.'

'Let's go, Tom,' Snowy said, starting for the door.

'But I haven't finished my beer.'

'I said, let's go.' Snowy grabbed his arm and marched purposefully out of the pub.

'Why did we leave?' Tom asked out in the street.

'I didn't want a fight, that's why.'

'But I wouldn't have hit him, he's a loony cripple.'

'He's a cripple, yeah, and he's a loony, all right, and they say he can break a man's neck with his bare hands.' Tom Brereton might be mad, Snowy thought, but Rico Gianni was insane, and there was a difference. 'Let's go home,' he said.

THESE DAYS RICO spent every night drinking at the Sheaf.

Teresa had stopped nagging him; she didn't seem to care what he did any more. But then Teresa didn't seem to care about anything any more. Except the church. She was always at that damn church—either there or at Giovanni's. She'd talk to Giovanni and Caterina but not to her own husband! Of course, Giovanni was dying, so that could explain why—she was probably preparing his soul for the hereafter. She had become obsessed with religion since the death of her son.

Everything had gone wrong in Rico's world. It had started with the news of Enrico's death. He'd accepted that—he'd more or less expected it—but when the citation had arrived announcing the awarding of the Distinguished Conduct Medal to one 'Rick' Gianni, it had been the final insult.

'The fool of a boy doesn't even die with his own name!' he'd roared. Teresa had simply stared at him, the grief in her eyes turning to hate. 'It is not enough that he dies for a country not his own, he dies bearing a name not his own!'

Teresa had barely spoken to him since. Rico had even tried to apologise. It had been his grief speaking, he'd told her, the grief they should be sharing over the death of their son. But she wouldn't listen. She went to church instead. And, once again, Rico blamed his son. If the fool of a boy hadn't joined the Australian army, if he hadn't gone to war . . .

Everything was wrong. His wife didn't speak to him. His daughter, his precious Carmelina, didn't speak to either of them. And now his brother was dying. No wonder Rico spent his nights at the pub.

THEY HAD STOPPED lying about Giovanni's illness a year ago. There was no longer any point. 'I must leave the Midas, Caterina,' he'd said. 'They know I'm ill, I can no longer hide it.'

'I'm glad,' she'd answered. 'It will be good to have you home where I can look after you.' And it was.

The months before Giovanni became incapacitated were amongst the happiest times they had spent together. They both knew he was dying, they didn't need the doctor's 'a year, maybe a little more'. They didn't speak of it, but they made every moment count. And, when his illness became so pronounced that they could no longer make love, they lay on the bed and made love with their voices and the mere touch of their hands.

Giovanni was fully prepared for his death, and so were those around him.

'I'll look after Mamma, Giovanni.'

'I know you will, Paolo. You're a good son and a fine man. We are all very proud of you.'

After a year of field work, Paolo had become the youngest mine manager to be appointed in Kal.

'And I will look after Briony and Rosalina too.'

Briony had set her sights upon Perth University and Paolo was proud that he had been her inspiration. 'It may not be Harvard, Paolo,' she'd said with a touch of defiance. 'But I'll be a success like you one day.'

'Are you too proud to accept my assistance?' he'd challenged.

'Of course not,' she'd laughed. 'You're rich, you can afford it, and you're my brother.'

Giovanni studied his stepson, so solemn, so responsible. 'It is good that you look after your mother and your sisters, Paolo,' he said, 'but look after yourself as well.' He smiled. 'I was once a very serious young man like you; it was your mother who gave me the gift of laughter. Find a good woman, Paolo. Find a woman who can teach you the frivolity of life.'

'WHY DOES RICO not come to see me?' Giovanni asked Teresa one day as she sat in the bedside chair. His lungs wheezed as he breathed and his voice rasped so, it was painful to listen. He had been confined to his bed for a month or so now.

'I think he is frightened of death, Giovanni.'

Teresa wasn't. Teresa would welcome her own death if it weren't for her son. Young Salvatore was all that was left in her world. She no longer loved her husband and even her daughter was no reason to live. The girl was secretive, sullen and wilful and Teresa could do nothing but pray for her soul.

'I think he has always been frightened of death.'

'Poor Rico,' Giovanni murmured. 'If things had been different . . .' His words tailed off, breathing was difficult, but Teresa knew what he was thinking.

'Don't you dare carry guilt to your grave, Giovanni.'

But he did feel guilty, he couldn't help it, as he thought of that night on the mountainside all those years ago. 'The madness in Rico,' he said, shifting his position in the bed a little, 'if it weren't for the accident—'

'If it weren't for the accident he would still be mad. You listen to me, Giovanni, for I should know.' Teresa leaned forward and there was a zealous light in her eyes, as though at that moment she was a messenger from God. 'When we were courting, there was many a time Rico would have killed a man who so much as looked at me if I had not stopped him. The De Cretico brothers may have broken his knees but they did not send him mad. There has been madness in Rico for all of his life.' She sat back in her chair once again. She had spoken God's words. 'So you go with a clear conscience.'

'She's a tiger,' Giovanni whispered to Caterina when Teresa had gone. 'Ferocious. You should have seen the light in her eyes.' Caterina laughed. 'She is, I tell you,' he insisted, encouraging her laughter. 'A tiger! I pity poor Rico when she turns her religion on him.'

They laughed together until it brought on a coughing fit. He sat up in the bed and she held the bowl for him and when it was over she lay beside him.

'Well, she's a tiger who is right,' Caterina said.

Giovanni dozed all that afternoon and slept fitfully during the night. The next day he was weaker, each coughing bout leaving him frail and exhausted, and the next day weaker still.

Caterina stayed with him. She lay next to him, stroking his hand as he dozed on and off, and she herself dozed for a while to awake to the faintest sound of a song. He was humming, very quietly, and she recognised the tune. *'Torna a Surriento'*.

She leaned up on one elbow and pushed the damp hair from his brow. He opened his eyes.

'My girl from the mountain.' His breathing was heavy and laboured, his voice the huskiest whisper.

'Yes,' she smiled, 'it's me. I'm here.'

Giovanni held her hand as he closed his eyes. He could see the young girl in her brother's trousers, excitedly climbing the mountain. 'You look like a boy,' he'd said. Then he saw her eyes, saddened and distant, over the rim of the tin coffee mug as she crouched in the snow by the fire. 'My name is Giovanni,' he'd said. He heard the Pride of Erin waltz and saw the blue hat. He watched it. Nearer and nearer it came. The face beneath looked up, the blue eyes met his and he heard himself say, once again, 'My name is Giovanni'. Images of Caterina swirled through his mind and Giovanni smiled as he fell asleep.

Caterina didn't know what time he died, but she awoke at dawn to feel his skin cool against hers. The same gentle smile was on his lips as she kissed him. And, at last, she allowed herself to cry.

'Giovanni,' she whispered. 'Giovanni, *mio amore.*' She curled up against him, her head in the crook of his arm, and lay there silently, pretending that they were sleeping.

'Mamma.' Rosalina was at the door.

'You and Briony get yourselves breakfast, darling,' she called back, keeping her voice steady. 'Tell Briony to pack your school lunch for you, there's a good girl. I won't be out for quite a while.'

She stayed with him until noon. Finally, she stopped pretending they were sleeping and said her last goodbye. '*Mio amore,*' she whispered and kissed him one more time. Then she went out into the kitchen where Briony was waiting.

Chapter Thirty

Jack Brearley came home to a hero's welcome. As he stepped off the train, photographers and journalists were there to greet him. The newspapers heralded the return of Jack Brearley, recipient of the Victoria Cross, the highest military honour accorded a soldier in battle.

The mayor wanted to hold a banquet in his honour; the keys of the city were his. But Jack would have none of it.

'There you go, Jimmy.'

The very afternoon of his homecoming, he sat with the twins in the upstairs lounge at Maudie's and handed his young brother James the medal. A simple iron cross, with a simple inscription. *For Valour*.

'Crikey,' seventeen-year-old James's eyes were on stalks. 'The VC,' he breathed, and his sister Vicky, sitting on the floor beside him, was equally wide-eyed.

'They say it's made from the metal of a cannon seized by the British at the Battle of Sebastapol,' Jack told them. He didn't want to spoil Jimmy's excitement at the gift, but the medal meant nothing to Jack. He could barely remember the bunker and the bullets. He didn't feel he deserved all the fuss.

He recalled the presentation ceremony in the Red Room at Buckingham Palace. King George V himself had pinned the medal on his chest. There had been other recipients of the Victoria Cross, nearly all of them dead. The medals were posthumously awarded, the citations read out acknowledging noble and heroic acts, but all Jack could think was, 'They're dead—do they care?' And Rick Gianni was dead too.

Jack heard the words of his citation. '. . . and further, Sergeant Jack Brearley did, in the face of intense machine-gun fire, leave his own position of safety in order to save the life of a fellow soldier . . .'

But he hadn't, had he? Jack thought. He hadn't saved Rick's life. Perhaps if Rick Gianni had lived, Jack might have felt he'd earned a medal. Perhaps. But it all seemed rather pointless somehow.

RICO'S REACTION TO the newspaper headlines which Carmelina read out at the breakfast table was, predictably, violent. 'Jack Brearley a hero! Hah!' he scoffed. 'No Brearley is a hero. They are cowards, the lot of them.'

'He risked his life to save Enrico,' Teresa snapped back as she washed the breakfast dishes. She usually ignored him these days or took herself off to church when he started on one of his tirades, but she was not going to let this one go. 'He risked his life to save our son!'

'But he didn't, did he?' Rico goaded. 'He didn't save our son.'

'He tried.' Teresa looked down at the suds in the washing-up bowl, wondering why she was bothering to answer him back. It never worked. She gritted her teeth. 'He risked his life to save Enrico,' she said again.

'You think so?' Rico was ready to do battle, any mention of the name Brearley fired him up. 'Jack Brearley was always a braggart and a fool. If Enrico had not followed him, the boy would be alive today . . .'

Teresa stopped washing the dishes. She took off her

apron, dried her hands on a tea towel and collected her scarf from its peg by the door. She checked that she had a coin in the pocket of her skirt for the poorbox as she walked out the door.

'That's right,' he roared after her, 'walk away! Go to your church!'

Carmelina drained the last of her coffee, rose from the table and left the room. Seconds later, she returned with her jacket and purse.

'Where are you going?' Rico demanded.

'To work.'

'You don't start until lunch time.'

These days Carmelina worked the daytime shift at Restaurant Picot. She liked it that way; it left her evenings free for Louis. No longer were their meetings restricted to Sundays only—now, several nights a week, she would wait for him in the room at Red Ruby's.

Carmelina took no notice of her father. Like her mother, she walked out without a word and Rico remained at the table alone, with no one to talk to until his afternoon shift at the mine.

He wished Salvatore was here; he could sometimes talk to his son. But eighteen-year-old Salvatore, now a miner himself, left for the early shift at seven each morning.

Rico contemplated getting himself another cup of coffee but he couldn't be bothered. He was bored, he wanted to go to work. For the past year, he'd been working double shifts and that was the way he liked it—worth every penny of the bribe money it cost him—he enjoyed physical labour and the mine was a much happier place than home. Recently, however, most underground bosses had disallowed double shifts and were giving the jobs to the diggers.

What had he done, Rico thought, to deserve such misery? Why had the two women most precious in his life turned against him? He'd been forced to accept the fact that his wife no longer loved him and he blamed religion for that. But his Carmelina, his precious Carmelina, why did she hate him? What had he done to deserve the loss of his daughter?

CARMELINA DID NOT hate her father. Nor did she hate her mother. She neither hated nor loved anything in her life, except Louis Picot. She was totally dependent upon him now. Upon Louis and the laudanum he supplied her.

The drug had started as a sexual enhancement. 'Just a sip my darling, just for fun,' he'd said the first time as he offered the spoon. 'For me,' he'd added on noting her hesitation. He thought the laudanum might be amusing for a change. And of course she'd obeyed.

Louis himself had taken some laudanum and their love-making that night had been sensual and erotic. Like it used to be, Carmelina thought, her senses lost in carnal delight. She felt no pain; he didn't defile her—in her opiate state, she felt nothing but pleasure.

Laudanum was her friend from that night on. Even when he brutalised her, the drug freed her from pain and she floated in a cloud.

He gave her a bottle upon her request. 'If it pleases you, my darling,' he said, although Louis himself had little time for addicts.

Carmelina relied upon the drug to relieve the stresses at home. Her father screaming, her mother remote, closed off, it was easy to lie on her bed in her room and drift away to another world.

Louis Picot was becoming bored with Carmelina. The pain he administered seemed to have little effect. She no longer cried out, which detracted from his pleasure; there were no fresh fields to discover, no surprises he could inflict upon her. Whatever he did, she accepted quietly in her drug-induced state. He would need to get rid of her soon, he decided. Besides, he was too busy for Carmelina, his mind was on other things.

Since his father's stroke six months previously, Louis had set about establishing his newfound authority. He had dismissed the efficient, long-serving managers of the hotels and replaced them with subservient men who would know their place. He had been about to dismiss Harry Brearley too but decided that, perhaps, there was a little further use to be gained from the man.

'I am prepared to preserve the public image of your involvement with the restaurant, Harry,' Louis had said with magnanimity. 'It will serve as excellent cover whilst you commit yourself to the brothels. Their management needs to be taken strictly in hand now that those intolerable women are no longer there.'

Harry had been shocked to hear that Louis had ruthlessly dismissed Jeanne Renoir and Emily, giving them a week to get out of Kal.

'If you're not gone by next Friday, Jeanne,' Louis had said quite calmly, 'I'll expose you as a whore to the entire town.' Jeanne had been shocked to the core—this was the little boy she had once bounced on her knee. 'Your reputation, my dear,' he'd announced, 'is entirely in your own hands.'

'She's a parasite,' Louis had said when Harry had challenged him. 'A parasite who's been feeding off my father for years. Well, she's of no use to him now. The poor old bastard can't even control his bladder—what use is a whore?'

However, when Louis had boasted of his actions to his stricken father, he'd noticed a glint in the old man's eyes. It was a glint of anger, Louis could have sworn it. 'Jeanne's old now, Papa,' he'd said defensively, 'she's old and she has wrinkles—you'd want nothing to do with her, I swear.' The glint was still there. 'Besides, she's been robbing you for years.' But his father would have known that, Louis realised; no one put anything past Gaston Picot. Surely the glint of anger was not directed at him, he thought. No, it was just a reflection of light through the bedroom window. The old man was catatonic, he could comprehend nothing. But the eyes continued to glare accusingly and Louis felt uncomfortable as he recalled the doctor's words. 'You never can tell with stroke victims,' he'd said, 'perhaps they do understand, we can't be sure.' So Louis stopped visiting Maison Picot.

Now, with the soldiers home from the war, business was hectic for Louis Picot. The restaurant was thriving and the brothels had never been busier. But they needed to expand, to recruit more girls, and Harry Brearley was utterly useless. It would be left to Louis to take over the brothels, just as he had the restaurant. There was so much to be done.

While Carmelina floated on laudanum during the nights at Red Ruby's, Louis's mind was on other things.

JACK BREARLEY WAS appalled by the chaos in Kal. There were brawls in the streets and drunken diggers lounged outside pubs yelling abuse at any Italian who happened to pass by. They taunted anyone who even looked Italian. Greek merchants hung signs in their windows. 'We are Greeks, not Italians'. This was peacetime, Jack thought, the war was over. Why so much hate?

'There always has been,' Maudie said as she sat at the kitchen table darning a hole in one of Jimmy's socks. 'They're just letting it out now, that's all.'

'Back in an hour or so, Maudie,' Harry came in, downing a glass of whisky, 'bit of business to attend to.'

He had just received a telephone call from Louis Picot, nagging him again about the need for more whores, and Harry was annoyed. He wished he could tell young Picot to go to hell, but he didn't dare. Since Gaston's stroke, his son Louis was now a powerful man.

Harry was no longer interested in the brothels—they were too much hard work and they were tawdry when all was said and done. He belonged at Hannan's or Restaurant Picot amongst his own style of people.

Damn it, Harry thought, he'd go and see Ada at Red Ruby's and leave the whole business to her. He really wasn't up to those trips to Fremantle any more, and those shady dealings with prostitutes in grubby backrooms. It had been different when Jeanne and Emily were about, they had lent a dignity and style to the whole sordid business.

'Shan't be long,' Harry said, no longer able to put off the inevitable. He dumped his glass in the sink and left. It was four o'clock in the afternoon, Jack thought, and already his father was into the whisky. Maudie no longer noticed, but Jack did.

Jack had been home barely a week and he was horrified at the change in his father. Harry Brearley, once his childhood idol, was now a hopeless alcoholic. Even his wife had given up on him. Tough, honest, no-nonsense Maudie looked tired, and a touch defeated. Well Jack was determined that things would change. If he couldn't help his father, he'd get that light shining in Maudie's eyes again. She had been a mum to Jack all his life. The best mum a bloke could have.

'They've never liked foreigners on the goldfields, Jack.' When Harry had gone, Maudie continued the conversation as if he'd not been there and she hadn't once looked up from her darning. 'You know that.'

'You always taught me that if a man was honest it didn't matter where he came from.'

'Ah yes, but I've never been too comfortable with foreigners, all the same. They're a funny bunch, speaking a different language, and you never quite know what they're thinking.'

Old habits died hard, Jack thought. There was a touch of bigotry even in good old Maudie. A bloke had to go away to war to realise that men were pretty much the same. He recalled the truce at Gallipoli and the Turkish soldiers they'd exchanged cigarettes with. Young blokes they'd been, just like himself, with the fear of dying in their eyes.

Jack didn't bother contradicting Maudie, what was the point? He grabbed his hat as he headed for the door. 'I'm going out to hire us a barman,' he said.

Maudie looked up from the sock. 'Make sure he's a digger. They need the work.'

'You bet I will.'

'Good on you, Jack.' She smiled and her eyes crinkled up the way they used to.

The smile remained in Maudie's eyes for a full minute or so after Jack had gone. God, but it was good to have the boy back. He was going to manage the pub, they'd talked it all through. Business was booming with the soldiers' return and Maudie was at the point of exhaustion. Alice was still with her, but then Alice, like Maudie, was no spring chicken. They were both too old for such hectic work.

'Alice can serve in the ladies' lounge,' Jack had said. 'And you can sit in your office and run the business. How'd you like that?'

Maudie would like nothing better. She loved facts and figures and balancing the books. She loved paydays and the visit to the bank every second Friday. Maudie loved running a business.

'We might get you a secretary,' Jack suggested.

'No fear,' she said. 'You just leave me with the books and get on with the hard work.'

It had taken a fair amount of persuasion before Maudie had agreed to the hire of another barman. She wasn't accustomed to throwing money around, she said.

'We need two behind the bar, Maudie, you know that,' Jack had insisted. 'You and Alice are worked off your feet. I'll need somebody with me if we're to give good service.'

They both knew what he was saying, but neither wanted to mention it. Harry had grandly suggested he forgo his 'duties' at Restaurant Picot and take over the bar with Jack.

'We'll make a fortune,' Harry had said. 'We'll stick your VC up behind the bar. In a gilt frame, on red velvet. People'll come for miles to be served a beer by the winner of the Victoria Cross,' and he'd slapped Jack on the back. 'We'll make a fortune, you'll see.'

Jack had tried to laugh it off, but he knew his father wasn't joking. Harry working the bar was out of the question, and Maudie and Jack both knew it. He would only get staggering drunk and make a fool of himself.

'Pa'll be better off at the restaurant,' Jack had gently suggested.

'Hire the barman,' Maudie said.

Jack's first stop was the boarding house where Snowy Wilson and Mad Tom Brereton had rooms. Snowy and Tom had paid him a visit the second night he'd been back and the reunion had been riotous.

They'd got very drunk in Maudie's bar but Maudie hadn't minded. They were soldiers returned from the war and they needed to let it all out. But she worried about Jack—he didn't look very strong. Oh well, she told herself, they were men now; if they wanted to make themselves sick with grog it was up to them.

'You look as if you could do with a bit more weight, mate,' Mad Tom had said first up, digging Jack uncomfortably in the ribs.

'You too, cobber.' Jack prodded Tom's stump in return.

'So where's your VC then?' Snowy asked.

'Upstairs,' Jack answered evasively. But, before Snowy could demand a look at it, Mad Tom was thumping his own chest with pride. Despite the fact that he was in 'civvies', Tom always wore his medal pinned to his shirt.

'You're not the only one to get a medal, cop that,' he said proudly. 'Snowy and Rick and me, we all got one.'

They talked of Rick and their other mates.

'Have you seen Tony Prendergast?' Snowy asked.

'S'truth, I thought he was dead.' But Jack's grin of delight faded as his mates shook their heads.

'Might as well be,' Snowy said dourly.

Not long after that, they'd got drunk and sung loudly. All the old songs Rick used to play. Maudie let them drink on long after closing and it was one in the morning when they had called a halt.

For the following two days, Jack had been as sick as a dog. He couldn't drink like that any more, he told himself, his body couldn't take it. Well, he'd been warned, hadn't he? 'Look after yourself, Jack,' the doctor had said. 'No strenuous exercise, no heavy living. You take care of that heart, it's still pretty weak.'

'NO THANKS, MATE, I'm staying clear of the grog,' Jack said when Snowy offered him a beer. Mad Tom wasn't there, he was at the post office, sorting mail. It was a good job, five days a week. Just as well, Jack thought—he could hardly justify a one-armed barman to Maudie. 'You're full-time back at the mines aren't you, Snow? You don't need work?'

'No, mate, morning shifts, regular as clockwork.' It had taken Snowy four months to get work but he'd stuck at it, reporting daily to the mines, and now he was under contract.

'Where do I find Tony then? I want to give him a job.'

'Tony Prendergast?'

Jack nodded.

'What job?' Snowy asked.

'Barman at Maudie's.'

Snowy shook his head. 'He couldn't handle it, mate.'

'But you said he needed a hand.'

'Let's pay him a visit.' Snowy downed his beer. 'You'll see what I mean.'

'WANT TO OFFER you a job, mate.' Jack sipped his tea and avoided the incredulous stare from Snowy.

Ten minutes' walk out of town, on the road to Boulder, the little canvas and tin shack where Tony lived with his wife and three children had once been a miner's humpy. But it was spotlessly clean and, as they sat on packing cases, Megan Prendergast served them tea as formally as if the tin mugs were imported china. The light of hope in her eyes was painful to see as she heard Jack's words.

Crikey mate, Snowy cringed inside, don't offer the bloke a barman's job, can't you see he can barely stand?

'What job would that be then?' Hope was not reflected in Tony's eyes; he'd been knocked down too many times.

'Maudie needs a secretary.'

Snowy coughed into his tea. 'Sorry,' he gasped, 'went down the wrong way.'

'Yeah, she needs some help with the books,' Jack explained. 'The pub's pretty busy with the diggers home, and I'm taking over as manager.'

'More tea, Jack?' Megan had the pot poised over his

mug. What a pretty woman she was, beneath the care-worn fatigue.

'Yeah, beauty, thanks, Megan. Not bad, eh, Tony?' Jack winked at the Welshman. 'Jack Brearley, pub manager, and I'm going to extend the place too. Get rid of the stables out the back, we don't need them any more.'

It was the first Snowy had heard of it. Jack, too, for that matter, but it seemed like a damn good idea. 'We'll have a back bar, and a games room just like the big posh places—'

'Maudie's a pretty good businesswoman,' Tony interrupted, 'everyone knows that. She's never needed a secretary before.'

'Ah, but with the extensions she will. We've talked it all over, her and me.' Well, they would as soon as he got home, Jack thought. 'And we'll need someone there in charge all the time to oversee the blokes doing the building.'

The more Jack thought about it, the better the whole idea seemed. Even as he spoke, his mind was working overtime. They'd need a hefty loan and Maudie'd have to go into bat with the bank manager but that'd be sure to bring the light of battle back into her eyes. Maudie liked nothing better than a fight with the blokes at the bank. 'What do you say, Tony?'

Megan Prendergast seemed to be holding her breath.

'No,' the Welshman shook his head. 'It wouldn't work.'

'Why not?'

'It's a bit of a walk to your pub. I couldn't do that every day.'

'My dad's got an automobile, I can pick you up and take you home.' Tony was still shaking his head. 'Come on, mate,' Jack urged enthusiastically, he was raring to go now. 'Be a sport, it'll give me an excuse to drive it.'

Megan carefully put the teapot back on the rickety old table, afraid she might drop it. She wanted to scream at her husband, to shake him out of his torpor, but she dared not utter a word.

'Come on, mate, what do you say?'

The seconds seemed to tick by before Tony finally nodded. 'Well, I suppose we could try it for a while and see if it worked. I wouldn't want to let you down.'

'You'd be doing us a favour, mate.'

On the walk back to town, Snowy pumped Jack's hand. 'You're a beauty, Jack.'

JACK BREARLEY HAD not forgotten the promise he and Rick Gianni had made to each other in the little town of Houilles that night.

The fight between their families was just a load of bollocks, they'd agreed. 'When we get back to Kal we'll sort them out eh?' Jack had said. 'Too right we will,' Rick had agreed before he'd passed out.

'The Giannis?' Harry muttered darkly when Jack tried to broach the subject. 'Don't talk to me about the Giannis. I should never have done them the favour I did.' His son tried to interrupt but Harry was in no mood to listen as he splashed another healthy measure of whisky into his glass. 'Those stupid dagos couldn't even speak the language, for God's sake, and then when they decided they didn't like the contract they'd signed, they blamed *me*!' Harry's voice rose in moral indignation. 'They even tried to kill me! Both of them!' he said, downing his whisky.

Jack realised that it wasn't just the alcohol talking. Over the years, Harry Brearley had convinced himself that he was, and always had been, entirely in the right.

If contact was difficult with his father, Jack was sure that it would be impossible with Rico Gianni. He decided, instead, to pay a visit to the home of Caterina and Giovanni and, one Sunday, as he was about to knock on the front door, an automobile pulled up in the street behind him.

'Jack!' a voice called. 'Jack Brearley!'

The young man who stepped out of the brand-new Ford Tourer was tall, elegant and stylishly dressed. A toff, Jack thought. Who the heck was he? Jack didn't know any toffs.

The man bounded across the pavement and up the little path to the verandah. 'Hello, Jack, it's good to see you.'

'Crikey! Paolo!' The two men shook hands warmly. 'The blokes told me you were one of the big nobs these days,' Jack said, 'but I didn't know you were this big.' He gestured towards the shiny automobile and then ran his eyes up and down Paolo's fine linen suit, taking in his planter's hat in matching beige. He whistled, a mixture of mock and genuine admiration. 'You look like you should be in the pictures, Paolo, honest you do. I've never seen anything like it.'

Paolo shrugged, a little self-effacingly. 'Got to look the part, you know. The blokes at the mine expect it.'

Jack grinned. 'It's Sunday.'

Paolo found himself smiling too. You couldn't put one over on Jack. 'Yeah, I kind of got used to it, I suppose,' he admitted. It was true, he liked the trappings of success. He wondered if he should feel guilty.

But Jack let him off the hook. 'I reckon you deserve it, mate, good on you.'

Paolo relaxed. 'I'm glad you made it home, Jack.'

'Me too.'

They were both thinking about Rick and each of them knew it. 'He wrote to me,' Paolo said.

'I know. He loved getting your letters. He let me read them—hope you don't mind. Letters were pretty important to us over there.'

'I should have written to you myself,' Paolo said apologetically. 'The family feud,' he shrugged, 'it affected us all.'

'That's why I'm here,' Jack replied. 'We said we'd sort it all out if we ever got home, me and Rick.'

'You won't have any trouble with my mother.' Paolo wondered if Jack knew. 'Giovanni died about five months back, just before you got home.'

'Yes, I heard. I'd like to have seen him.'

'Let's go inside.'

The cosy smell of fresh-baked bread greeted them as they opened the door. Sunday, as always, was Caterina's baking day.

Since Giovanni's death, the rituals of Caterina's life had become more important than ever. As she stood at the washing basin on the back verandah, she imagined it was his work shirts she was scrubbing and the evening meals she prepared were always his favourites. And on Sundays when she baked, the very smell of the dough brought a smile to her lips. How Giovanni loved Sundays.

At night the bed remained a lonely place and she longed for the warmth of his body but, during the days, Giovanni was always with her.

'Jack Brearley! Welcome home.' There was a warmth in her voice which Jack had not expected. The beautiful Caterina Gianni, he thought, she must be in her mid-forties now and yet she was still desirable.

'Rosalina is at a school friend's birthday party,' Caterina said, 'she'll be sorry she missed seeing the famous Jack Brearley.'

'Hello, Jack.' Briony shook his hand firmly and Jack was a little nonplussed, unaccustomed as he was to shaking hands with girls.

'Briony, you've grown up.' He cursed himself for stating the obvious but he was rather disconcerted by the boldness of the girl. She didn't have her mother's beauty, he thought, but she was striking nonetheless with her flaming red hair, and the challenge in her blue eyes demanded attention.

So this was Jack Brearley, Briony thought. She'd seen him around town when she was a child and she'd heard rumour of his exploits as a daredevil and a womaniser but of course he was a Brearley and she'd been forbidden to make his acquaintance. 'Yes, I've grown up.' There was a touch of friendly mockery in her smile. 'Welcome home.'

Whilst Briony made coffee and Caterina continued with her baking, the talk was mostly inconsequential.

'I hear you're becoming a big nob yourself, Jack,' Paolo smiled. 'Rumour has it you're extending the pub.'

'Yep, the plans are being drawn up and we'll be building before Christmas,' Jack said proudly. 'It won't be the Palace or the York, but that's not what we want anyway. It'll stay a pub for the workers like it's always been, but Maudie's pub'll be the best workers' pub that Kal's ever had.'

It was only when Caterina's fresh batch of scones was safely in the oven and Briony had served the coffee that Jack turned the conversation to the reason for his visit.

'I was very sorry to hear about Giovanni,' he said.

'Thank you,' Caterina answered, 'it was miners' complaint. He was fully prepared.'

Jack nodded. 'Rick talked about him a lot.' He sensed a reaction from Paolo and glanced sideways to see him mouthing the name 'Enrico' as he picked up his coffee cup. 'Giovanni was very special to Enrico,' he said. 'He played that old concertina of his every single day and he never stopped talking about Giovanni.'

'Yes,' Caterina agreed. 'He loved him very much. Giovanni was a father to Enrico.'

'I wish I'd been home in time to say goodbye. I would like to have made my peace with him.'

'Giovanni had no argument with you, Jack. He didn't hold you responsible for the sins of your father.' The condemnation of Harry Brearley was clear in her tone. It wasn't going to be easy after all, Jack thought, and he chose his words with care.

'I wanted to make more than my own peace, Caterina,' he said. 'It all happened such a long time ago and I wanted to bury any ill-will between the Giannis and the Brearleys. Enrico and I promised each other we'd end the family feud if we ever got home to Kal. We'd even hoped that my father and Rico—'

'Never.' Her words were a sharp warning as she interrupted him. 'Never must you try and arrange a meeting between those two. Rico would kill your father if he had half a chance. If provoked, he would even kill you, Jack. His desire for revenge has not faded with the years.'

She rose from the table. 'I must tend to my scones. Take my advice, Jack, stay away from Rico and his family.' Her voice softened, 'But I know Teresa would want me to thank you for trying to save Enrico's life. She is truly grateful.'

'We were best mates,' he said.

'That is good.' She smiled. 'That is very good. Now why don't you boys take your coffee onto the verandah and Briony will bring you hot scones. Then you must sweep the floors,' she instructed her daughter with an apologetic aside to Jack. 'The family is coming here for dinner tonight. We meet most Sundays.'

Paolo and Jack did as they were told. It was a fine spring day and they sat on the railings and talked. When Briony arrived with a plate of scones, they were so heavily in discussion that neither of them noticed her.

'It's been nine months since the war ended, Paolo,'

Jack was saying, 'and the diggers are all home now. It's tough, I know, but they're finding jobs, and yet the hatred remains. It's festering between the Aussies and Italians. There's more hatred here than there was amongst the soldiers fighting on opposite sides. Why?'

Jack had always admired Paolo. Paolo was the academic one, the one with brains—they'd all known that. And now, not only had Paolo been educated abroad, he'd remained true to his identity. An Australian proud of his Italian antecedents. Surely Paolo would have the answer.

But he didn't. 'I don't know, Jack,' he said in all honesty, 'I don't think anyone knows, but—'

'I do.' Briony put the forgotten scones down on the verandah and plonked herself into the swinging seat. 'I know why there's hatred in this town.' The men looked at her, momentarily silenced. 'It's Kal, that's what it is. Kal breeds violence. It always has.'

Jack was surprised at the intrusion but Paolo encouraged Briony to join in their conversation. He was proud of his high-spirited sister and always humoured her, even when he thought her opinions naive.

'That's a rather sweeping statement,' he said good-naturedly. 'Why do you think Kal breeds violence?'

'Because it was created from greed.' Briony warmed to her topic. 'People came here for gold. They were greedy for gold, and then they stayed to fight. That's what Kal's all about. It's about greed and about gold.'

'Well of course it's about gold,' Paolo said a little impatiently. 'That's the town's industry, its livelihood.'

Jack joined in the argument. She'd fired him up and he'd forgotten that she was a young girl who had annoyingly interrupted their conversation. 'Kal's about more than gold. Far more. We've grown since the goldrush days. We're a city surviving in the outback. I was born in Kal, but I'm not here for the gold. I'm not a miner.

I'm here because I love the place, it's unique, and one day people will come from all over the world—'

'Of course they will. They already have.' Once Briony got going it was difficult for anyone to get a word in, and the fact that both men were arguing with her only encouraged her more. 'And why? For the gold, that's why. Because they're greedy, that's why. And greed creates violence.'

Paolo gave in, to shut her up more than anything. 'All right, all right, every town has its good and bad. Let's leave it at that.'

'You're wrong, Briony,' Jack said, ignoring Paolo's attempt to halt the discussion. 'There are people who come to Kal not for the gold at all. They come because it's Kal, a place like no other. A goldrush town that will never die.' He could have been his father speaking, Jack suddenly realised.

How many times as a child, he wondered, had he heard his father talk of his visions for Kal. It saddened Jack to think of the empty shell the man had become. But Harry Brearley's dreams had not fallen on deaf ears. Jack, too, had visions for Kal.

'So how do you explain the violence?' Briony brought the argument around full circle and Jack was stumped for an answer.

'Human nature, Briony,' Paolo said. 'It's as simple as that.'

'That's not fair.' Briony looked annoyed.

'What's not fair,' Paolo laughed, 'human nature?'

'You're patronising me.'

'Rubbish, I never patronise you. I get annoyed with you, but I never patronise you.' Paolo's smile faded. 'I do think it's human nature. It's sad but true, I think. Perhaps one day the Aussies and the Italians will be friends. And then, who knows, they may band together and turn on somebody else.' Paolo picked the plate of scones up from the verandah. 'It's human nature, Briony, it's not just Kal.' He thought of Ira Rubenstein. 'They hate the Jews at Harvard,' he added.

'Well, human nature's sure at work right here in Kal,' Jack said as Briony gave up the argument and pushed the swinging seat until it squeaked. 'There'll be full-blown riots any day now. The town's going mad.'

Paolo offered him the plate of scones but Jack shook his head. 'No thanks, mate, they're covered in ants.'

Chapter Thirty-One

Carmelina moaned as his hands found her breasts. They fondled with urgency but there was no pain. He was not twisting her nipples until she wanted to scream. And his mouth on hers was forceful but his teeth were not biting her lips and drawing blood. Louis must have taken some laudanum too, she thought. It was going to be one of their nights of true love-making. And, as she drifted in her world of delight, Carmelina gave herself to him, wholly, with such pleasure, as she had in the past.

It was only when he was climaxing that she realised something was strange.

'Oh, you're good, so good,' he grunted, 'so good, so good.'

Louis never grunted when he climaxed, and he never spoke to her. Never once had Louis said a word in his final moment of pleasure.

He collapsed, his energy spent, and rolled off her, gasping for breath.

Carmelina came out of her cloud and looked at the face beside hers. It wasn't Louis she saw. A stranger lay beside her.

It was a dream, she thought. She was having a dream. 'Who are you?' she murmured to the young man in her dream as he rose and started to dress.

'Louis sent me. Do I pay you or the madam?'

'Louis?' The cloud was lifting and all of a sudden Carmelina knew this wasn't a dream.

'Louis Picot,' he said, buttoning his trousers. The girl kept staring at him. 'You're Carmelina, aren't you?'

'Yes, I'm Carmelina.'

Her voice was distant and her eyes were clouded. Was she ill? the young man wondered uneasily. 'Shall I pay at the door?'

'Yes, pay at the door.' Again the voice was distant, a monotone, and as he sat to pull on his boots, she started to moan. An animal sound, like a creature in pain. The young man fled.

From behind her desk, Ada counted his money. 'Everything satisfactory?' she asked.

'Yes.' The young man had never been with a whore before. It had been Louis Picot's idea.

At Restaurant Picot the previous night, the young man had been drunk and bemoaning his predicament. He'd gone off to the war and his sweetheart hadn't waited, he complained, and it had been so long now since he'd been with a woman . . .

'Try Red Ruby's,' Louis had advised. 'Early tomorrow evening, before the place gets busy. A girl called Carmelina.'

It had seemed like a good idea at the time, but the girl's moans had unsettled the young man and now he couldn't wait to get out of the place. 'Quite satisfactory,' he said to the madam.

ADA HADN'T AT all approved of Louis undermining her authority. She interviewed and vetted every girl who worked under her roof, she told him, and if Carmelina wished to turn professional, which Ada didn't believe for one minute, then it was only proper the girl should observe the customary procedure.

'It's all right, Ada,' Louis had said, attempting to mollify her as she glared at him through steel-rimmed glasses, lips tightly set in disapproval. 'Carmelina is perfectly ready. I think she's looking forward to a little variation; she's a very sensual young woman.' He gave his most charming smile. 'And if she doesn't enjoy the experience she can always leave. The decision is hers.' Ada's lips remained set. 'I'll send over a client tomorrow, early,' Louis said, ignoring her, 'and we'll see how she goes.'

Ada knew better than to argue, but she was piqued. This was no way to do business. The girls at Red Ruby's were professionals, hard workers who gave good value and earned good money. This was just another game between Louis and his mistress and Ada found it deeply offensive.

She had been forced to accept the loss of a room when the lovers used the brothel for their assignations. She had kept her mouth shut when Louis demanded one or two of her girls for their added pleasure. But she hadn't liked it.

If Louis had paid like a client, Ada wouldn't have minded. She had margins to maintain, a reputation to uphold and, boss or not, Louis Picot was eating into the profits. Now it appeared, for the titillation of his mistress, he was offering her clients the services of an amateur. It wouldn't do, Ada thought, it simply wouldn't do at all.

It was not Louis's intention to titillate Carmelina, nor did he think she would make a good whore. More was the pity, it would solve everything if she did. It was simply the most expedient way to rid himself of her.

Louis had always believed in signalling his intentions. Loudly, clearly, to ensure no misunderstanding. But, whenever possible, he made it a habit to avoid personal confrontation.

When the young man had gone, Ada waited for half an hour for Carmelina to appear. Clients were already arriving, the girls were chatting and drinking with them; it was going to be a busy Saturday night.

It was just as she'd suspected, Ada thought, the girl was not interested in business. She had not douched herself and reported for duty. After her 'adventure', the girl had simply left through the back door, scarf over her head, as she always did, and disappeared into the night. Ada signalled the maid to clean the room.

The scream, only seconds later, was blood-curdling. McAllister, seated as always at the bar, sprang to attention and disappeared through the door to the rooms out the back. The screams turned into hysterical sobbing as Ada ordered her girls to stay with the clients. 'It's nothing, I assure you,' she said. 'The maid is prone to fits, that's all.' The girls looked bewildered—it was the first they'd heard of any such thing—but they did as they were told and poured the men fresh drinks.

Ada went through the door to the back. The maid was on her knees in the passageway, weeping loudly. 'Be quiet!' she ordered, 'the clients can hear you!' The sobs subsided to a whimper and Ada joined McAllister in the red-shuttered room.

Carmelina was lying on the bed, her eyes staring up at the ceiling. She had cut her throat with the jagged edge of a broken hand-mirror and the walls were sprayed with her blood. In the rose-coloured light through the shutters, the whole of the room seemed red with her blood.

Ada and McAllister stood for a moment, surveying the scene, before Ada sprang into action. 'Call the police,' she ordered McAllister. 'Make sure you speak to Baldy Hetherington, nobody else.' Then to the maid, 'Lock this door and say nothing to the others.' The maid pulled herself to her feet. 'Control yourself, girl, and go about your duties,' Ada commanded before returning to the lounge to reassure the whores and the clients. There'd been a little accident, she told them, nothing to worry about.

This was the worst possible thing for business, Ada thought. They needed to tidy it up as soon as possible.

'A SIMPLE SUICIDE, Bob,' she said half an hour later when Inspector Hetherington was making his report. 'A lover's tiff, I have no doubt.' She kept her voice to a whisper so that his two offsiders shouldn't hear as she added, 'The girl was Louis Picot's mistress; they occasionally used one of my rooms.'

Ada held all the aces and she knew it. Louis Picot was a powerful man and Baldy Hetherington, nearing retirement, wanted no trouble. He'd keep his report simple for all concerned. For himself and for Louis and for Ada too. Enough money and favours had gone Baldy's way over the years to put him in Ada's debt.

'We'll take the body to the morgue,' he said.

'Out the back way?'

He nodded. 'And I'll inform the girl's family.' Ada was relieved. Business would not be disrupted after all.

IT WAS NINE o'clock in the evening and Rico was just about to leave for the Sheaf Hotel when there was a knock at the door. It was Inspector Hetherington.

'Mrs Gianni . . . Rico,' he said, 'I won't beat about the bush. I've got some bad news for you.'

Teresa's hand went to her throat. 'Salvatore,' she breathed, fearing the worst.

'No, it's your daughter Carmelina.' Baldy had his eye on Rico Gianni. He'd brought two burly officers with him for backup and he hoped there'd be no trouble. 'I'm afraid . . . she's dead. Suicide.' He looked at the madman, wondering what Rico was going to do. But there was silence.

Rico had heard the words. 'Your daughter is dead.' That's all he'd heard. Someone had killed his daughter. Someone had killed his Carmelina.

Baldy watched as Teresa crossed herself and whispered, 'Suicide.'

'Yes,' Baldy said. 'Tragic thing.' Rico was standing motionless. 'I'm sorry.'

Rico was thinking, who? Who killed my Carmelina?

'But why?' Teresa was shaking her head, dumbfounded with shock. 'Why?'

Baldy gave what he hoped was a caring shrug.

'Where?' Teresa asked. 'Where was she when she . . .' Teresa couldn't bring herself to repeat the word, even saying it seemed like a mortal sin.

'At Red Ruby's,' Baldy answered after a moment's pause. This was the news which would inflame the Italian, he thought, his daughter dead in a whorehouse.

'Red Ruby's? The brothel?' Teresa's voice was incredulous.

Still Rico said nothing. The man looked as if he hadn't heard a word.

But Rico had heard every syllable. His daughter was dead in a whorehouse. And, in his head, a voice was saying 'someone has defiled my Carmelina'.

'I'm afraid so,' Baldy heard himself saying. Rico's silence was worrying. 'Her body's at the morgue, the doctor's making out his report. If you'd like to come down and see her . . .'

'Yes, soon,' Teresa said numbly. 'Soon.'

Baldy started out the door, but decided on a warning before he left. 'I know this has come as a terrible shock, but I want no trouble, Rico, you understand?'

Inside Rico's head was a simple plan. Someone

had killed his Carmelina, someone must die. But who? Maybe the whole town, Rico didn't care, he'd kill whoever was necessary. But he realised that a reply was expected of him. He must put Baldy's mind at rest.

'Trouble?' he asked. 'You will get no trouble from me, Inspector. My daughter was a bad girl. A whore. She was found in a brothel.' He looked at his wife, but she was frozen in horror. Then back to Baldy. 'I wipe my hands of her. My daughter deserved to die. You will get no trouble from me.'

Teresa saw the murder in her husband. She knew he was playing a game. The moment the policemen left she begged him, 'Rico, no! Don't seek revenge! She killed herself, you heard him say it. There is nothing you can do! Nothing!'

'Someone defiled my Carmelina,' he hissed. His eyes were black with rage and Teresa, desperate, grabbed at his arm as he walked to the door.

'No! No killing, Rico!' He threw her aside and she fell to the floor. 'She killed herself,' Teresa screamed. 'You heard him! There is no one upon whom you can seek your revenge.'

'A man defiled my daughter! That man is dead!' He stormed out of the house.

Teresa scrambled to her feet and ran after him. 'But what man, Rico? What man will you kill?'

'Every man in that whorehouse!' he roared.

ADA HERSELF HAD removed the blood-stained sheets, the maid had refused to re-enter the room. McAllister was scrubbing the walls and Ada inspecting the damage. 'The mattress and pillows are ruined,' she said. 'You'll have to take them out the back and burn them. Do it in the morning when the girls are sleeping.'

It was only minutes later, when she'd returned to

her desk, that the doors of the brothel smashed open and the crippled madman stood there.

'Which of you killed my daughter?' he roared.

Even in her fear and alarm, Ada cursed herself. How could she have been so stupid? She'd known that Carmelina was the daughter of the crazy Rico Gianni. She should have insisted that Baldy post guards at the door.

There were only three men in the lounge, chatting to the girls; and three others in the rooms out the back. It was still early for a Saturday night; the pubs had not yet closed.

Rico dived for the nearest man. 'Was it you?' he screamed, grabbing him by the throat and hurling him across the room. The man's body crashed into the bar, bottles and glasses smashing to the floor around him. 'Was it you?' He grabbed another.

The girls were screaming. They backed up against the wall while the man he'd attacked struggled, winded, to his feet.

'Did you kill my daughter?' Rico was throttling the second man.

Ada raced out from behind her desk. 'Nobody killed your daughter!' she yelled. 'Your daughter killed herself!'

McAllister appeared from out the back, behind him a half-naked girl and a fat man rapidly pulling on his trousers.

'Someone defiled my Carmelina!' The fingers were like a vice around the man's neck and the breath was rattling in his throat. Rico threw him aside like a rag doll and turned to grab the next. But the terrified man had joined the girls against the wall. Only McAllister appeared prepared to take on the madman. He grabbed a bottle from behind the bar.

'Which of you defiled my daughter?' Rico screamed.

'Louis Picot!' The words were out before Ada could stop herself. She knew she was digging her own grave the moment she said it, but she couldn't stand by and let this maniac wreak havoc. 'Louis Picot was your daughter's lover. He's been her lover for years.'

Everyone froze for several seconds, seconds which seemed like a lifetime. McAllister by the bar, the bottle in his hand, the girls huddled against the wall, the fat man clutching his trousers. And, in the centre of the room, standing over the man who lay gasping for breath, Rico Gianni.

Louis Picot! Rico could see him—rich, handsome, debonair, silken-voiced. 'You must work hard for Mr Picot,' he'd always instructed Carmelina. 'Mr Picot, he pays you good money.' It was always said with great respect.

Then, a moment later, Rico was gone, the doors crashing loudly behind him. Ada's mind raced. What should she do? If she called Restaurant Picot to warn him, Louis would know it was she who had given Gianni his name. She might as well suicide herself. She called Baldy Hetherington instead.

But Inspector Hetherington was not at the station. 'He's been called out to a bit of trouble in the centre of town,' the charge-room officer told her. 'Shall I give him a message?'

Ada thought quickly and simply said, 'Tell him Rico Gianni is looking for Louis Picot.' That would do, she thought, as she hung up the receiver. If Baldy got there in time, then Louis was saved. If not . . . well, neither she nor Baldy could be held responsible for the attack of a madman.

THERE HAD BEEN trouble threatening in the centre of town, but Baldy and his men had it under control. A couple of young Aussie blokes, drunk, had been thrown out of Maudie's for fighting. Maudie and Jack ran a tight ship and they wouldn't have brawls in their bar. The boys had staggered a few blocks north and thrown a rock through a merchant's window.

'Go home, dago!' the boys had yelled. They hadn't taken into consideration that the merchant's shop was opposite the Sheaf Hotel.

Several Italians came out onto the pavement and a street brawl started, the yells of 'Dago bastards' attracting the attention of a few other Aussies who joined in the fight. By the time Baldy Hetherington and his men got there it took them a good five minutes to quell the brawl. Order was restored and four men arrested, including the lads who'd started the fracas. But, as the crowd disbanded, fuses were short and men were still muttering, frustrated, longing to fight.

Amongst them was young Salvatore Gianni. As he and his friend Alfio were crossing the street to help the merchant board up his window, Teresa arrived, breathless. She'd run all the way from the house. Tears streaked her face as she ran and she ignored the curious glances of the people she passed in the street.

'Salvatore,' she panted. 'You must stop your father. He's gone to Red Ruby's, he says he's going to kill them.'

'Kill who?' Salvatore rested a calming hand on Teresa's shoulder. 'Calm down, Mamma.'

'The men who defiled his daughter. He says he will kill every man at Red Ruby's.'

'Carmelina?' Salvatore supported his mother as she slumped onto him, about to fall. 'What has happened to Carmelina?'

'She killed herself.' Teresa started to sob, deep racking sobs which tore at her chest. 'They found her at the whorehouse. And Rico has gone there to kill.'

Salvatore's face was flushed as a sickening anger

rose in him. His sister, dead in a whorehouse? His reaction was exactly that of his father. A man had defiled his sister. Someone had killed Carmelina. He muttered to the merchant, 'Look after my mother, take her into the shop.'

'Go after him, Salvatore!' Teresa cried as the merchant half-carried her inside. 'Go after him! Stop him from killing!'

Salvatore stood for a moment on the pavement. His eyes reflected the madness of his father as he stepped off the kerb and strode down the centre of Hannan Street.

'Where are you going?' Alfio called to him.

'To find the man who raped my sister.'

Salvatore's calm reply chilled him, and Alfio knew he could do nothing to stop his friend. He raced into the Sheaf Hotel. 'Somebody help me!' he shouted. 'Salvatore is going to kill a man.' The Italians crowded around him and he blurted out what he knew. 'Somebody raped his sister . . . she was found dead in a brothel.'

Within seconds, the news fuelled the anger that simmered amongst the Italians. An Australian had raped and killed the virgin daughter of one of their own. It had to be an Australian—no Italian would do such a thing. Men streamed from the hotel, brandishing bottles and broken glasses. Alfio himself was caught up in the frenzy. He'd intended to stop his friend. But the others were right, he found himself thinking. The Aussies had gone too far. This was war. He too grabbed a bottle and joined the throng.

RICO HAD TURNED into Hannan Street and, far ahead, he could see Restaurant Picot. There was a crowd pouring out of the Sheaf Hotel next door to the restaurant and men were marching towards him down the centre of the street. He could hear their distant massed voices, but he paid no heed. All he could see was the restaurant which bore the name Picot.

'Louis Picot, come out and die!' he roared into the air and he kept roaring as he lumbered towards the restaurant. 'Louis Picot is a dead man!' he chanted. 'Louis Picot is a dead man!'

At Maudie's, several men, including Snowy and Mad Tom, had taken their beers out onto the pavement to escape the heat of the bar. They were confronted by Rico Gianni on the opposite side of the street and his threat was clearly audible. 'Louis Picot is a dead man!'

Snowy raced inside. 'Rico Gianni's on the warpath,' he announced urgently. 'He's belting up the street yelling that Louis Picot is a dead man.'

Many of the men in the bar brought their beers out onto the pavement to watch the action. They had no intention of stopping Gianni—that was up to the coppers. Besides, no one liked Louis Picot. But it wouldn't hurt to wander up to the restaurant and watch the sport, they thought.

Further up the street, however, they spotted the band of Italians, obviously angry and marching their way. Word passed back to the other men in the bar. Were the Italians out for a battle? Well, if they were, the Aussies were ready and would meet them head-on. Men armed themselves with bottles and stepped into the street.

From behind the bar, Jack yelled, 'Leave it alone, Snow!' but his friend wouldn't heed the warning. Like the others, Snowy had been busting for a fight. Jack watched him and Mad Tom join the march. Bloody fools, he thought, the whole town's gone crazy.

Jack would have none of it. He stayed behind the bar serving beers to the few remaining drinkers—several elderly men who'd decided they were better off keeping well away from any trouble. The men sat by the windows observing it all and giving a commentary on the proceedings while Jack hoped it wouldn't be too long before the coppers arrived.

A little while later, Jack overheard the old blokes talking about Rico. 'He's probably killed Louis Picot by now,' one of them said. 'That's what he was yelling he was going to do, and you can't stop that crazy bastard.'

'Yeah,' another agreed. 'I'll bet you a quid Rico kills Louis. He was headed for the restaurant.' And the old blokes started laying their bets.

The restaurant, Jack suddenly realised. His father was at the restaurant. And if Rico Gianni was bent on murder, the first man he would kill would be Harry Brearley. Poor drunken Harry would be no match for the mad Italian. 'Take over for me, Sid,' Jack called to the barman as he ran out into the street.

Rico had taken no notice of his countrymen storming down the centre of Hannan Street. He'd stuck to the pavement, still roaring Louis Picot's name as the throng of twenty or so passed him by.

Salvatore had seen his father and tried to fight his way back through the Italians. But he was no longer their leader and the rape of his sister no longer their cause—they'd forgotten their purpose and he was dragged along with them as they surged ahead. They could see the Aussies down the street and were bent on war.

By the time Salvatore had struggled back through the throng, Rico had reached the restaurant. 'Louis Picot is a dead man!' he yelled as he walked up the steps to the main doors.

Chapter Thirty-Two

It was busy in Restaurant Picot. Downstairs, the booths were full, the barmen were serving as fast as they could and the drinkers' lounge was a flurry of waiters.

Upstairs, in the salubrious surrounds of the restaurant proper, no sign of haste was evident. That wasn't the style of Restaurant Picot; elegance, as always, was the order of the day. At candlelit, linen-clothed tables, diners chatted quietly while dinner-suited waiters poured their wine and, in a corner of the dining room, a chef carved sides of beef on a silver-topped, heated trolley. In the centre of the dining room, on a marble pedestal, was a huge floral display of dried banksias, wattles, Kangaroo Paws and boronia.

Harry Brearley and Louis Picot walked leisurely among the tables, greeting a diner here and there, ensuring that all was in order. Nowhere was there a hint of the bustle of industry which always prevailed in the kitchen.

When a pair of drunken louts had smashed a shop window on the opposite side of the street and the sounds of a brawl had ensued, Louis had ordered Harry Brearley to ring the police. He would not suffer the noise of the common herd disrupting his diners. It was insufferable. Those bloody Italians! He reminded himself to dismiss the manager of the Sheaf in the morning; if the man couldn't control the pub, then Louis would find someone who could.

When the police had broken up the brawl and made their arrests, the crowd dispersed and Louis breathed a sigh of relief. But, now, barely fifteen minutes later, the sound of angry voices once again rose from the pavement and Louis looked down from the balcony to see men storming out of the Sheaf.

He stepped back inside, closing the French windows as he did, annoyed because it was a hot night and they needed what little breeze the open windows afforded.

'Keep them shut,' he ordered Harry Brearley, 'and turn up the gramophone.' Johann Strauss's 'Tales from the Vienna Woods' swelled as Louis went downstairs to once more call the police. Baldy Hetherington would barely be back at the station by now, he thought irritably. The police should never have left. The town was a madhouse tonight. It was hot, it was Saturday, the pubs were full, and violence was rife in the streets of Kal.

Harry was not about to miss out on the spectacle. He stepped onto the balcony, closing the windows behind him, and looked down the street to where the Aussies and the Italians were about to clash. He was too engrossed in the impending fight to see the familiar figure below, lurching up the steps to the entrance.

The telephone was at the front desk beside the main staircase and, as Louis picked up the receiver, Rico appeared at the open doors.

'Louis Picot is a dead man!' he bellowed, his voice echoing throughout the restaurant.

Louis dropped the receiver, his mouth dry with fear. There was nowhere for him to run. His way was barred—a maddened bull filled the doorway.

'Come out and die, Louis Picot!'

Louis realised that Rico hadn't seen him, huddled by the desk.

'Louis Picot is a dead man!' the lunatic chanted as he stormed towards the bar at the back. 'Louis Picot is a dead man!'

People screamed and ran for the doors as Rico cut a swathe through the lounge.

Galvanised into action, Louis dived for the doors only to be blocked by the diners and staff who were also rushing for safety. He fought to get through. Too late. Lurching about, throwing tables and chairs aside in search of his victim, Rico had turned and seen him.

Louis raced for the staircase. There was a gun in his office at the top of the stairs.

UPSTAIRS, THE DINERS were restless. The Strauss waltz still played on the gramophone, but the uproar below was clearly audible. Everyone remained seated, however, considering it bad form to show any interest in a street brawl.

Out on the balcony, Harry Brearley had also heard the madman's roar. He'd recognised the voice. Harry was no fit opponent for anyone these days, let alone Rico Gianni, and he knew it. Fear clutched at his chest. But Rico was after Louis Picot. Perhaps, Harry thought, if he stayed on the balcony . . .

When Louis Picot appeared at the top of the stairs, wide-eyed with terror, the diners could no longer ignore the commotion. Waiters hovered, unsure what to do. Several men rose from their tables, protectively edging their wives towards the staircase railings. Others, unwilling to show their consternation, refused to budge but sat warily watching.

Louis threw open the doors to his office. There was no time to lock himself inside, he could hear the Italian behind him. The gun, he needed the gun! He pulled open the top drawer of his desk and grabbed the Belgian .25 calibre automatic.

At the sight of Rico bellowing for Louis Picot, the diners panicked. As Rico lunged forward, they scrambled for the staircase, knocking each other over in the rush.

Suddenly a shot rang out and Rico staggered backwards into the dining room, glasses and crockery smashing as tables overturned. He crashed into the marble pedestal and fell to the floor amongst the debris.

Over the final chords of 'Tales from the Vienna Woods', men yelled and women screamed. There was a stampede on the staircase, as diners, chefs, waiters, kitchen staff, all fled for their lives. A woman fainted and fell down the stairs. Others trampled over her in their panic whilst her terrified husband tried to lift her to her feet.

'Grab an arm each,' a welcome voice said. It was Salvatore attempting to climb the stairs in pursuit of his father but held back by the crowd. The two men carried the woman out onto the street.

On the balcony, quaking with fear, Harry was the first to notice the fire. The dried flowers had been ignited by fallen candles and were burning rapidly. Harry had contemplated jumping from the balcony rail, but had been too frightened—he'd break both his legs, he was sure. But, anyway, it was safe now to go inside, Rico Gianni was dead.

ALL LOUIS PICOT could feel was the cold sweat of relief. He'd shot the Italian dead. He'd hit him in the chest, he knew he had, but shakily he raised the gun again, just to make sure.

The growl that came from Rico's throat was like that of a wounded lion. He'd felt no pain, just a thump in the chest; he'd been winded, that was all. He launched himself at Louis.

Louis fired wildly. One of the last of the men scrambling for safety was shot in the side and two others helped drag him down the stairs.

Rico felt another thump, in his shoulder this time, but it meant nothing as he grabbed Louis around the throat and lifted him from his feet. 'Die, Picot!' he screamed.

SEVERAL BLOCKS DOWN Hannan Street, the riot was in full swing. Close to forty men had met head-on and fists were smashing into flesh and bone. Men grunted and wrestled in the dust, legs kicking, fingers clawing, and many were bloodied from broken bottles. Two men lay unconscious on the road, but, as yet, no one was dead. They'd forgotten why they were fighting. The Italians were no longer avenging the rape of a virgin daughter, the Aussies were no longer fighting for their jobs; they were venting their mutual antagonism, the years of hostility and conflict, in the heat of the Kalgoorlie night.

Jack Brearley crossed the street and ran along the pavement to avoid the fracas. He was past the riot and a block from the restaurant when the shots rang out.

At first they all thought it was the coppers shooting into the air to get their attention.

Men stopped to see where the gunshots came from and it was Snowy who yelled out, 'Fire!' Several more punches were thrown but it wasn't long before the riot disbanded and the men started towards the restaurant where the fire's glow could be seen through the windows.

RICO HAD RELEASED his grip. Why kill Louis quickly? he thought. The man should die slowly, in fear and agony. He let Louis's body drop to the floor and watched as he crawled towards the stairway, gasping and whimpering like a puppy.

The blaze was growing now as the tablecloths ignited. The silver-topped trolley in the corner had overturned and methylated spirits was slowly leaking from the heaters. Soon the place would become an inferno.

Out on the balcony, Harry Brearley had wet himself. The Italian wasn't dead! Harry looked over the balcony. He had to jump, he told himself, but he was frozen to the spot with terror. He cried out to the people below but there was pandemonium in the street as the rioters joined the hysterical crowd from the restaurant and no one heard him.

Suddenly he saw Jack dodging amongst the crowd. Again Harry cried out but Jack neither saw nor heard him.

'Have you seen my father?' Jack was asking. 'Have you seen Harry Brearley?'

A man was tending to his wife who'd fainted. 'He was upstairs the last I saw,' the man said and, as Jack raced for the doors, he was joined by Salvatore.

Relief surged through Harry as he saw Jack and a young man enter the restaurant. Jack would save him, he thought, as he peered through the windows at the fire which now raged inside. Hurry, Jack, he prayed, hurry!

THE HEAT IN the restaurant was intense, but Rico didn't notice it. He grabbed Louis's shoulder and turned him around, forcing him back against the railing. Once again, he held him around the throat. But not too tight this time; he didn't want Louis to die too quickly. Make it slow, make him beg, make it hurt. He lifted Louis's body a little, off his knees, and bent his head back over the railing.

'You killed my Carmelina,' he said. 'Which way would you like me to break your neck?'

'I love Carmelina, I swear it!' Louis blubbered, his arms flailing uselessly out to the sides, trying to grab at the Italian's wrists. 'I want to marry your daughter. I love her, I swear!' Rico's shirt was saturated with blood. Louis knew he'd hit him in the chest, so how was the man still alive?

'So you leave her dead in a whorehouse. That is the way you show your love? Shall I break your neck this way . . . ' He twisted Louis's head to the left.

Carmelina dead in the whorehouse? But he'd had nothing to do with it, Louis thought—someone else had killed the girl. 'It wasn't me,' he begged, 'it wasn't me, I had nothing to do with it, I swear!'

'Or shall I break it this way?' Rico twisted Louis' head to the right. 'You tell me, Louis Picot. You tell me which way I should break your neck.'

As Louis's head was forced to the right, he saw a shape through the fire, a frightened face at the windows. 'Harry!' he said, with all the voice he could muster. 'It was Harry Brearley.'

Rico paused for a moment. He'd intended to play with the man for several minutes before breaking his neck.

'Harry Brearley . . .' Louis gasped. This was his chance. Everyone knew of Rico's hate for Harry Brearley. 'Harry Brearley owns the brothel. He made your daugher a whore. It was Harry—'

Louis Picot had cheated himself of several minutes of life. Rico broke his neck in a second.

The fire was raging now. Any minute, Harry thought, petrified as he saw Rico toss aside Louis's lifeless body, any minute Jack would appear.

Yes, there he was! Jack, with the young man at his side, had appeared at the top of the stairs, behind Rico. But Rico had turned towards the windows and, through the flames, his eyes had met Harry's. And Harry knew he was dead.

In that very instant the methylated spirits ignited. A

wall of flame divided the men and they could no longer see each other.

Harry finally found the strength to jump. There was still a chance, he thought, and he grasped the balcony rail.

Behind Rico, a voice yelled, 'Papa!' but Rico didn't hear it as he charged through the wall of flame. No fire would stop him now. Harry Brearley was about to die and Rico Gianni screamed his name.

Salvatore started towards the flames but Jack Brearley held him back. 'Get downstairs!' he yelled. 'The whole place is going up!' and he dragged Salvatore down the staircase as the fire raged behind them.

In the street, people looked up in horror as the balcony windows shattered. A figure was astride the railing, apparently about to jump, when a ball of fire that was a man smashed through the windows.

'Die, Harry Brearley!' The madman's scream hung in the air and sheets of flame burst from the window as Rico flung himself upon Harry. Locked in a fiery embrace, they crashed through the railings and plummeted to the pavement below.

As Jack and Salvatore ran out of the restaurant, men were extinguishing the flames which licked at the bodies of Rico and Harry. Others were fleeing the scene, shielding their wives' eyes from the gruesome sight.

Someone rolled Rico off Harry and the two men lay side by side, their dead eyes staring into the smoky night sky.

'Papa!' Salvatore ran to his father's side.

Jack stood on the steps and looked down at the bodies. Harry Brearley, his father, his one-time hero. A weak and greedy man, his dead face was now a mask of fear. And, beside him, the twisted face of Rico Gianni bore the hatred and triumph of a lifetime's vendetta. They were the faces of Kal, Jack thought, and an unreasoning anger rose in him at the sheer senselessness of it all.

He looked at the men gathered in the street. The same faces were all around him. Faces of greed, of fear and violence, bloodied, bruised and battle-scarred. What was wrong with them? he thought, the war was over! And, suddenly, he screamed it.

'*The war is over*!'

His voice rang out above the approaching clang of the fire trucks' bells and the subdued mutterings of the crowd. People turned their attention from the bodies on the ground to the figure standing on the steps.

'It's Jack Brearley,' several muttered and the crowd grew silent. Jack Brearley was Kalgoorlie's hero.

'The war is over!' he screamed again. 'What is wrong with this town? What is wrong with you people? We should be brothers! Look at them!' He pointed to the corpses of Harry and Rico. 'Didn't we leave enough bodies over there?'

The crowd parted to make way for Jack as he strode down the steps to stand on the pavement beside his father. Behind him, smoke billowed through the doors of the restaurant. The fire had reached downstairs, but no one heeded it.

'This man is my father, Harry Brearley,' Jack yelled. 'He robbed this man, Rico Gianni, and Rico Gianni swore revenge. For nearly twenty years they've hated each other and now they've paid the price. Dear God, can't we leave it here?' He pointed at Rico. 'I fought with this man's son. We watched others die around us. Thousands of them!' He looked about at the men. 'You watched them too, Snowy. And you, Tom.'

Jack walked amongst the crowd, pointing at the faces of diggers he knew. 'And you. And you. And you. Those men died for this country—so that we could live in peace! And this is how we repay them? By killing each other? Aussies and Italians cutting each other up with broken bottles in a country that's not at war?'

The fire trucks had arrived now and firemen were unreeling hoses. Behind Jack, the fire roared and smoke belched out into the street but his rage rose above it all.

'I've seen men kill. I've seen Turks, Australians, Englishmen, Frenchmen, Germans, all of them killing each other.' There was no stopping him now, as his fury grew to fever pitch. 'And they didn't want to! Can't you understand that? They didn't want to kill each other! They did it because they had to. Because their countries were at war. Jesus Christ! What is it you men are fighting for? Does anybody know?'

Amidst the chaos, the crowd of men stood silent. Jack's chest was heaving now and he felt a stab of pain, but still he couldn't stop.

'You have your families and your friends and your freedom. You live in God's own country, in a town that's rich with gold. And what do you do? You create your own war! Shame on the lot of you!' He wanted to strike every face he could see, to beat sense into every man there. 'You make a mockery of the men who fought for your freedom. You make their deaths useless. You've forgotten them! This whole town's forgotten them!' The pain was stronger and breathing was suddenly difficult, but his fury was unabated. 'You've forgotten them all, haven't you, the boys who died over there? Shame!' he yelled again with all the strength he could muster. 'Shame on the whole bloody lot of you!'

He gasped for the breath to go on, but there wasn't any left. Inside his chest, iron fingers were closing into a fist.

Jack clutched at his heart as he fell to his knees. Damn you! he thought. Damn the lot of you! And he fell unconscious in the dust beside his father.

The men clustered around Jack amidst the smoke and confusion and the fury of the fire.

'He's alive,' Snowy said, kneeling beside him. 'Someone get the doctor.'

Mad Tom took off at the rate of knots whilst several diggers lifted Jack gently from the pavement. Amongst them was Salvatore.

Snowy couldn't help it. The bloke was an Italian, he thought. What right did he have to carry Jack?

Salvatore had registered the glance. 'I'm Salvatore Gianni,' he said.

Rick's brother, Snowy thought. Right. Fair enough. He nodded to Salvatore. And they carried Jack to Maudie's.

Chapter Thirty-Three

It was nearly three months after the terrible night of the fire that Briony visited Jack. Maudie showed the girl upstairs to the balcony where he was sitting in a rocking chair looking out over Hannan Street. It was late afternoon and the balcony was shaded from the heat of the January sun.

'Maudie won't let me out during the middle of the day,' Jack complained. 'Says the heat's too tiring, It's a bloody bore. She even bought me this rocking chair. The woman's turning me into an old man.'

'I doubt it,' Briony smiled. 'You look well.'

'You're lying. I look bloody awful.'

He did look gaunt. Thin and weak, she thought, but as roguish as ever. 'I don't tell lies, Jack. You look well for a bloke who nearly died. Very well, in fact.'

'Fair enough,' he conceded. 'Getting better by the minute too. I'll be back at work by the time the renovations are finished. They're looking good—did Maudie show you around?'

'Tony did. Yes, they're very impressive.'

Jack gestured to a chair and Briony sat down. 'Paolo tells me you're leaving for Perth soon,' he said. 'To go to the university.'

'In two days. I came to say goodbye.' Briony looked

over the balcony at the passing parade of Hannan Street. 'I probably won't be back.'

'That sounds dramatic,' Jack smiled. 'What about your mum? And Paolo and Rosalina? You'll want to see your family.'

'Well, of course I'll come back and see them now and then,' she replied with an edge of irritation—she wanted Jack to take her seriously. 'But you know what I mean. I'll never come back to Kal. Not to live.'

'I'll bet you you do.' He was grinning now and Briony felt well and truly irritated. 'It's in your blood. You and I were born here, we're creatures of the place. You'll be back, Briony—I'll bet on it.'

She shook her head. 'Maybe you, not me. My father was Welsh and my mother was Italian . . .'

'Exactly. And you were born in a humpy on the goldfields—a perfect product of Kal.'

He was still grinning and Briony felt more annoyed than ever. He was patronising her, like Paolo sometimes did. 'All the more reason to leave,' she said, changing her tactics. 'I can't wait to get out of the place.'

'Fair enough.' Jack waited patiently for her to latch onto another argument. He knew she would.

'You have to admit, it's no place for a woman,' she said finally. She had him there, she thought.

'Try telling that to Maudie,' Jack answered, not letting her get away with a trick.

'That was the old days,' she said defensively. 'When it was all a battle. It's different now.'

'No, it's not.' Jack was suddenly serious. 'It's still a battle and it always will be, this town. You were right that day when we talked, you and me and Paolo. Kal's a greedy town, and it's violent. But Paolo was right too. It's human nature. And somehow Kal brings out the worst in us. But it can bring out the best too, Briony, and that's what we should fight for. The men *and* the women.' He smiled when he said it, but he was no longer making fun of her. Jack admired Briony.

She was instantly mollified. Jack was her hero and she wanted his respect. There was a moment's silence.

'Salvatore told me what you said to the men that night. He remembers every word.'

Jack himself could remember very little, but he nodded. 'I meant what I said.'

'Salvatore reckons that you've changed this town—he says the men are still talking about that night.'

Jack laughed. 'Nothing will ever change this town.' He looked out over the street. 'Oh, it'll grow. It'll be a city thriving in the wilderness, just like Dad said. But it'll never change. You've got to take the good with the bad in Kal. But it's unique, Briony, you've got to admit that. And that's what'll bring you back.'

TWO DAYS LATER, Briony looked out of the train window at the vast expanse of red dust and scrub. For several minutes, she watched the pipeline, until it disappeared into the sand. But it was still there. Whether you could see it or not, you knew it was still there.

The train clacked rhythmically, mile after mile, and she thought of the pipeline, seemingly endless and indestructible. She thought of Kal behind her, where life was grinding remorselessly on. Kal was like the pipeline, she thought, unchanging, unrelenting. Even when you couldn't see it, you knew it was there. You knew it would always be there.

She thought of Jack. 'You and I were born here,' he'd said, 'we're creatures of the place.'

She heard his voice. 'You'll be back, Briony. I'll bet on it.' She looked out across the endless red desert and wondered whether he was right.

that, whatever should [illegible] than a [illegible] [illegible] the [illegible] which [illegible] of [illegible] was [illegible] [illegible] of the [illegible] [illegible] usually [illegible] [illegible] the [illegible] [illegible] when you came to [illegible] the [illegible] every word.

Jack himself could [illegible] [illegible]

[illegible] that you [illegible] [illegible] [illegible] [illegible] the [illegible] [illegible] [illegible] [illegible] the [illegible]

[illegible] of the [illegible] [illegible] [illegible] [illegible] the [illegible] [illegible] [illegible] still [illegible]

[illegible] the [illegible] of the [illegible] [illegible] [illegible] [illegible] [illegible] [illegible]

[illegible]

BONUS CHAPTER SAMPLER

JUDY NUNN

Beneath the Southern Cross

'A night of debauchery it was . . .' Thomas Kendall stood with his grandsons beside the massive sandstone walls of Fort Macquarie. He smiled as he looked out across Sydney Cove. 'That night they brought the women convicts ashore . . .'

In 1788, Thomas Kendall, a naïve nineteen-year-old sentenced to transportation for burglary, finds himself bound for Sydney Town and a new life in the wild and lawless land beneath the Southern Cross.

Thomas fathers a dynasty that will last more than two hundred years. His descendants play their part in the forging of a nation, but greed and prejudice see an irreparable rift in the family which will echo through the generations.

It is only at the dawn of the new Millennium – as an ancient journal lays bear a terrible secret – that the family can finally reclaim its honour . . .

Beneath the Southern Cross **is as much a story of a city as it is a family chronicle. Bringing history to life, Judy Nunn traces the fortunes of Kendall's descendants through good times and bad, wars and social revolutions to the present day, vividly drawing the events, characters and issues that have made the city of Sydney and the nation of Australia what they are today.**

Port Jackson I believe to be, without exception, the finest and most extensive harbour in the universe and at the same time the most secure, being safe from all the winds that blow. It is divided into a great number of coves, to which His Excellency has given different names. That on which the town is to be built is called Sydney Cove. It is one of the smallest in the harbour, but the most convenient, as ships of the greatest burden can with ease go into it, and heave out close to the shore. Trincomale, acknowledged to be one of the best harbours in the world, is by no means to be compared to it. In a word, Port Jackson would afford sufficient and safe anchorage for all the navies of Europe.

From the records of Surgeon General
John White, 1788

PROLOGUE

It was a moonless night, the night it happened. Which felt strange to young Thomas Kendall. The most successful forays for a warrener usually took place when the moon was full. Then the warrener could hunt out the burrows with ease, net the openings, send in the ferrets and set the lurcher on the rabbits, the dog, too, needing the light of the moon to pursue its quarry through the bracken.

But tonight Thomas and his father were not hunting rabbits. They were not wearing their warreners' smocks. And their lurcher, faithful old Jed, had been left at home.

'It be a bigger prize we hunt tonight, Thomas,' Jonathan Kendall had told his son, 'and you must say naught to your mother.'

Since the age of ten, Thomas had hunted with his father. He had learned how to press his ear to the earth and listen for the sounds of activity beneath the surface. He had learned to handle a shovel, to dig deep and fast, three feet in a matter of seconds, to get to the rabbit before the ferret moved off with it. And he had learned to huddle and gut his catch with swiftness and precision—the butcher was always pleased with the Kendall delivery. 'A pleasure to see,' he'd say, 'rabbits hulked proper—no mess, good and neat.'

Now, nine years on, young Thomas Kendall was a warrener as skilful as any on the Norfolk Brecklands. But this moonless night was different. As he crept along the banks of the Little Ouse River on the outskirts of the village of Thetford with his father and Bill 'Ferret' Bailey, young Thomas knew that a crime was about to be committed.

Beneath his ragged overcoat, tucked in the crook of his arm, was a large cloth bag. 'Hide it, lad, hide it,' his father had said as he handed it to him, and Thomas had noted both Ferret and his father stuffing similar bags inside their coats. 'Keep your eyes and ears open and your wits about you.'

They turned away from the riverbanks and cut through a grove of birch trees. Was it poaching they were up to, Thomas wondered. But they hadn't told him to bring his staff, he would need his staff if they were to go poaching.

He was distracted by a badger. Apparently oblivious to the presence of the men, it trotted along beside them, head down, hindquarters swaying flirtatiously side to side like an overweight coquette. Thomas liked badgers. After several moments, however, the badger paused to listen, body motionless, nose twitching, aware of danger present. They left the animal behind and Thomas's attention once more returned to the men. In the instant they broke out of the grove, he realised their intent.

The road to Norwich was to their left. In the darkness ahead was Burrell and Sons Works, and to their right, surrounded by lavish trees and gardens, was the home of the Widow Pettigrew. A brief thrill of shock ran through Thomas. So that was it! They were about to go thieving.

He said nothing as they straddled the low stone wall. He said nothing as they approached the house, keeping well under cover amongst the elms and oaks, maples and sycamores, but his mind was racing. This was a mad thing his father was contemplating. Was the widow at home tucked up in her bed? Were the servants in their quarters at the rear? There was no light visible, but that meant nothing. To rob this house was the action of a madman.

Thomas had few misgivings about the robbery itself, the widow could certainly afford to be relieved of some of her possessions, and if these were his father's instructions, Thomas was duty-bound to obey. But for the first time in his life he found himself questioning the wisdom of his father's actions.

'Saturday is the servants' night off,' Jonathan whispered, as if divining his son's thoughts, 'and the widow goes out to dine with friends in the village.'

'I've watched her,' Ferret added. 'She leaves at dusk and doesn't return till nigh on midnight.'

They were around the side of the house where a large window-frame with small thick panes of glass was set into the knapped flintstone walls. Thomas watched with admiration as Ferret drew a cold chisel from his coat pocket and levered the window open with comparative ease. It was a skill born of long practice. Ferret was an expert, Thomas realised. Then, one by one, they clambered over the sill.

Inside the widow's house they crouched in the darkness while Jonathan struck the flint of his tinderbox and ignited three tallow candles. As the light filled the room each man stood, candle in hand, and looked about in silence.

On the mantel stood an ornate porcelain vase, several fine china ornaments and a pair of silver candlesticks. In a glass cabinet were a silver salver, a cutlery service and a set of goblets. A carved wooden chest in the corner was opened and revealed sets of linen and lace—sheets, towels, tablecloths and napkins.

'I told you so.' Ferret was the first to speak. He grinned greedily, his yellow teeth gleaming triumphant in the gloom. 'A haul fit for a king.' He crossed excitedly to the fireplace. 'Jonathan, look!'

On the table by the open hearth stood an ivory snuff box, a hand-carved humidor, a brass pipe-rack and a pewter jug with matching tankard. All preserved in memory of the widow's late husband who had died barely six months previously. Widow Pettigrew still wore black and, in church on Sundays, her mourning veil.

'She's even kept his coat,' Ferret cackled as he dropped his own threadbare garment and donned the heavy wool greatcoat which was draped over the armchair. 'A big man, old Pettigrew,' he added, the coat hanging off his scrawny frame.

'We'd best get to work.' Jonathan Kendall was already stuffing the silver candlesticks into his cloth bag. 'Thomas lad, you go upstairs. The widow's bedroom. It will be to the left.' Thomas hesitated. 'Ferret's kept watch these past three Saturdays,' Jonathan explained, 'he says that the upstairs light in the room on the left is the last to be snuffed at night.'

Thomas turned to do his father's bidding.

'Satin and lace and fine leather gloves fetch a good price,' Jonathan instructed. 'And feather bedding. And mind you check the dressing table,' he added, 'for that's where she'll be keeping her jewels and trinkets.'

Holding his candle aloft, Thomas stepped out into the main hall and up the stairway, each wooden step creaking alarmingly. Turning left at the top, he crept to the door at the end of the corridor and gently turned the knob.

As the door swung slowly inward, Thomas heard a noise. A noise he recognised. It was the noise he himself made when he was with Bertha in the little back room at the alehouse, passion mounting, nearing his release.

The light of the candle illuminated the room and he saw them. The naked man, buttocks pounding. Grunting. The woman pinioned beneath, invisible but for her bare parted legs high in the air and her hands clutching at the man's back.

The scene froze for one shocked instant. Then the grunting stopped. The man turned. The woman screamed. And Thomas dropped his candle and ran.

In the darkness he groped for the bannister railings and all but fell down the stairs. He heard the man in pursuit, saw the glow of candlelight ahead, thrust open the door to the lounge room and gasped, 'Run! Run!'

But Ferret and Jonathan had heard the commotion. Ferret was already halfway out the window and Jonathan, realising there was no time for all three of them to get out, grabbed his son. Together they pressed themselves against the wall by the door to the hall so when, with a howl of fury, the naked man appeared in the open doorway, he failed to see them in the half darkness.

'Now!' Jonathan yelled as the man entered the room, giving an angry growl at the sight of Ferret halfway out the window. Father and son dived into the hall and made for the main doors. 'Run, lad! Run!'

My God! Jonathan registered in the second he turned back to check that his son was close behind him. My God, but it's young Captain Pettigrew!

Fletcher Pettigrew also turned, momentarily indecisive as to whether to pursue the felons running for the main doors or the man escaping out through the window. Then he noticed that the man at the window was wearing his coat. With another furious roar he launched himself at Ferret.

Upstairs, in her bedroom, Mathilda Pettigrew clasped the fine linen bedsheets about her naked body and whimpered. She was not fearful for the safety of her lover. Fletcher Pettigrew was renowned for his skills in combat; the fact that he was naked and wore neither blade nor pistol was immaterial, fisticuffs would suffice. But did this mean that her secret was to be made public? Was the whole village about to know that she had been intimate with her dead husband's brother? That she had indeed been intimate with her husband's young brother for a full year before Ezekiel Pettigrew's tedious, lingering illness finally took him to his long-overdue grave?

They had been so careful, she and Fletcher. After Ezekiel's death, Mathilda had regularly visited her lover on Saturday nights when the servants were dismissed. She had dined publicly with friends, then gone to his rooms afterwards. And occasionally he had come to the house. On foot. After dark. Always entering through the servants' entrance at the rear. No-one had been any the wiser. And now, because of a common, grubby thief, her dreadful secret was sure to become public knowledge.

Mathilda Pettigrew had no cause for concern, however. When, three days later, Jonathan and Thomas Kendall, along with Bill Bailey, were arrested and held in Thetford Gaol to await sentence, the virtuous reputation of the Widow Pettigrew was of little concern to them. A crime such as theirs would demand one sentence and one sentence only. The gallows.

Their incarceration in the poky little gaolhouse on Market Street was not prolonged. Soon after their arrest the town of Thetford came alive, as it did these two special weeks of every year, for the Lent assizes.

People flocked from miles around. The local gentry returned to take up residence in their townhouses. Business was good. The hotels were full, copious amounts of ale and liquor were consumed, and numerous entertainments were held, the crowds delighting to the bawdy vaudeville and rustic classics performed at the theatre in White Hart Street. And throughout the festivities there was the constant excitement of men and women being sentenced to death, transportation or incarceration.

'General gaol delivery' poured into Thetford—waggons of prisoners transported from Norwich Castle Gaol for sentencing at the Lent assizes. Twenty-three in all this year.

Amongst the twelve prisoners charged with capital offences that

March of 1783 were Jonathan Kendall, his son Thomas and William Bailey.

Jonathan pleaded his son's case vociferously. 'The lad is only nineteen years of age, Your Honour,' he begged. 'He has never committed a crime. Indeed he knew nothing of our intention until the very night of the felony, I swear. The boy was simply obeying me, his father.' Jonathan's final plea was desperate and emotional. 'For the love of God, Your Honour, let him free!'

But his words fell on deaf ears and all three men were convicted and sentenced to the death penalty. A public hanging at Melford Common beside the road from London to Norwich.

'Where your bodies will remain for a time,' Judge Baron Eyre decreed, 'dangling from the hangman's rope, to serve as a lesson to passing travellers. And may the Lord have mercy on your souls.'

Chapter One

'A night of debauchery it was.'

Thomas Kendall stood with his grandsons beside the massive sandstone walls of Fort Macquarie. He smiled as he looked out across Sydney Cove at the hustle and the bustle of pedestrians and soldiers and horse-drawn vehicles in the dusty streets of the busy town. It hadn't always been like that. Thomas could still see it as it had been all those years ago. Barren and unforgiving.

'Debauchery the likes of which will never be seen again, I swear, that night they brought the women convicts ashore.'

At sixty-five, Thomas preferred to view the old days with a sense of humour. It was more comfortable than dwelling on the grim realities of the past.

After languishing for a month in Thetford Gaol, young Thomas Kendall had escaped the hangman's noose only days before the execution of his father and Ferret Bailey. On the grounds of his youth, Judge Eyre had granted the lad a last-minute reprieve, and Thomas's sentence had been commuted to transportation, for a period of seven years.

He was transferred to Norwich to await his transportation, and there, for three long years, Thomas had withstood the brutality, squalor and depravity of Norwich Castle Gaol. Far from breaking his spirit, however, it had moulded him. From a simple, unquestioning lad into a resilient and resourceful young man, strong in mind and body. A man whom others learned to respect.

'The ships were hove to in the cove and the longboats collected the women and pulled in ashore yonder.' The old man pointed towards the Tank Stream on the western side of the bay. 'The livestock had been landed first, mind; cattle being more important than convict women. They'd landed the livestock a good ten days or so before, right here on this very point. They called it Cattle Point then. Course the fort wasn't here. Or the town. Nothing was here. Just scrawny trees that seemed to grow, God knew how, out of barren rock. And tents of course. By the time they brought the women convicts ashore there was a whole township of tents.

'Dressed in their finery, those women were,' Thomas continued, painting the picture for his grandsons, particularly young James who was enthralled. Unlike his cousin, William, James had never heard his grandfather's stories before. 'Leastways, they were pretending it was finery. Makeshift ribbons and bows they had in their hair. Primped and preened and saucy as could be. Excited too, every one of them, at the prospect of feeling solid land beneath their feet. We men had been living ashore for a week or more, see, clearing the land and setting up camp. But the women were hungry for the feel of the earth. Even the earth of that wretched God-forsaken wilderness, for it was a wilderness all right. Barren and hostile and downright fearsome.'

Thomas could still smell the fear of those early days, the fear of the unknown. He could remember the repugnance each and every one of the men had felt for the alien life that buzzed and crawled and slithered about them. The flies and spiders and snakes. And the birds. The demon birds. Some that screeched like banshees, others that cackled with the laughter of the devil himself, all of them chilling a man's blood each dusk and dawn.

Nowadays, of course, the cockatoos and kookaburras were considered amongst the more charming elements of the colony. William and James would laugh, Thomas realised, if he told them that insects and birds had been perceived as objects of terror by the hardened criminals of the first fleet. His grandsons were not to know that fear born of the unknown was the worst kind of fear to a lonely man in a foreign land.

'The soldiers and the sailors were accustomed to fearsome foreign parts,' he explained, 'but we who'd come, albeit in chains, from the civilised mother country found this to be a dreadful place.'

Seventeen-year-old William nudged his younger cousin. He'd told James about the old man's stories and James, wide-eyed with fascination, wasn't disappointed. James had met his grandfather on only one previous occasion, that he could remember anyway, and then it was in the company of his mother who refused to allow any discussion of her father-in-law's convict past.

The old man smiled again. It was easy, from his position of prosperity and comfort, to smile back down the years. For Thomas this was no longer a dreadful place. He looked at the boats in the bay. He could see one of his very own barges ferrying its load of passengers and provisions across the harbour to the village on the northern point. He looked at the thriving township; the five-storey-high Waterloo warehouse, the marketplace where the cries of the cockney seafood vendors rose above the bustle of human activity; he looked at George Street on the far side of the cove, the commercial centre of Sydney Town with its magnificent, wide-verandahed post office, its shops and taverns and cottages; at the traffic of the dusty streets, the men on horseback, the women in gigs and phaetons, the working horses and drays. And, amongst the endless procession, a gang of convicts being led to work at the stone quarries. Despondent, despairing. New arrivals, Thomas thought, and he wished them well.

He glanced out at the peak of the western point where the lighthouse stood. The latest allotment of land he had purchased was not far from the lighthouse. Soon he would be able to see his new cottage from here, high up there on the peak, overlooking the harbour and the whole of Sydney Town. Thomas felt proud. He had helped build this place, and this place, in return, had been good to him. Thomas loved Sydney Town with a fierce and personal pride.

'Those who had religion swore that God had visited his wrath upon us sinners that night.' Thomas turned to his grandsons, both of whom were waiting breathlessly for him to continue. 'For no sooner had the women's feet touched the soil of Sydney Cove than an almighty storm broke out. There was a crack like Satan's whip, an angry flash of gold, and in an instant the giant tree which stood in the very centre of the camp was split in two. It killed five sheep and a pig, which was a terrible thing in those days, livestock being highly valuable for future breeding.'

James nodded encouragingly. He wasn't really interested in the value of livestock. 'What about the people? Were any of the people killed?'

'Not by the storm they weren't. But there were many who met with floggings as a result of that night, and the floggings nigh on killed them. It's a wonder that some didn't meet the hangman's noose. No-one heeded the law, you see. There was brawling and riots and fornication throughout the camp; and whilst most were satisfying their lust, there were those who used the debauchery of the night as a cover for theft. And theft in those days,' Thomas added seriously, 'was punishable by hanging.'

'What about the soldiers?' James asked breathlessly. 'Didn't the soldiers try and stop it?'

'The soldiers were as lustful as the convicts,' Thomas declared. 'The soldiers were in the women's tents and the women were in the soldiers' tents and the sailors had all gone back to the ships to get drunk. The captains were relieved that the women were no longer their responsibility, see, for they had to pay a heavy penalty if a convict went missing. So they allowed the men grog and, above the thunder and the lightning, we could hear those sailors, drunk as lords, singing and carousing all through the night. Oh I tell you lads, everyone was a sinner that night.'

'What were you doing, Grandpa?'

William had tried to catch his cousin's eye, tried to warn him not to ask that question. The old man might have raved on for hours about rape and fornication, which was exactly what the boys wanted, had he not been asked about his own involvement. Too late.

'Me?' The mischievous smile faded and Thomas seemed a little saddened himself to be halted midstream. 'Ah, not for me the unbridled lust.'

James glanced at his cousin and William gave a wry shrug.

'How old are you, James?' Thomas asked, noting the brief exchange. 'I see you so little I lose track of your age.'

'Thirteen.'

'Well, it'll not be too long before you're a man. The day will come when you'll know women and lustful feelings.'

James flushed with the secret knowledge that he couldn't take his eyes from women's breasts, even his own mother's at times.

Thomas noticed the reaction and was sensitive enough not to make some ribald remark. James was a shy boy, he could tell, a lonely boy, and he was suffering the agonising guilt of pubescence. Well of course that mother of his wouldn't help. Surely Richard could be more of a confidant to his son though, Thomas thought critically. But then, Richard too was under the blasted woman's thumb.

'Don't misunderstand me, lad, I was a lustful young man myself in those days, as lustful as any that stormy night. The desire between men and women is as natural as breathing, young James, and nothing to be ashamed of, but the abandonment of that night meant nothing to me for, you see, I had my Anne.'

It had been in the third year of his incarceration in Norwich Castle Gaol that young Thomas Kendall had met Anne Simpson. Like him, Anne had escaped the death penalty due to her youth: she too had been nineteen years old when convicted of theft. But unlike Thomas, Anne had been no novice.

'Just the first time I got caught is all,' she openly admitted. 'Dear God in heaven, if they knew but a quarter of the thieving I've done, I'd have met the hangman long ago.'

She was a bold girl with a gypsy's face. Sensuous. Features too overgenerous to be beautiful, but wild hair and a mouth that beckoned. Thomas was smitten.

Both sexes were housed at the gaol and, discipline being a mixture of brutality and laxity, fornication was not uncommon. In fact, over the years many a child had been born as a result of couplings within the prison confines.

The cells having been built against the old walls of the roofless and dilapidated castle keep, it was not long before Thomas found a weak spot in the wall to the women's quarters. It didn't take him long to dislodge enough stone and dirt to wriggle his way through—as others had done before him—and, once there, his copulation with Anne was fast, fierce and lustful.

Mindless of the women around them, some urging them on, some fondling each other, some hissing obscenities and masturbating, Thomas and Anne fed on each other's passion. They soared above the prison walls, free of the squalor and confinement and, when they were spent, they kissed and laughed and made ribald comments to the others who were by then grumbling with envy and discontent.

When the news of imminent transportation finally spread throughout the gaol, Thomas and Anne prayed that they would be amongst those sent to a life in the colony of New South Wales.

Feeling amongst the other prisoners was uncertain. America having won its independence, the transportation was to be to the newly discovered south land. Half the world away. Surely it was better to serve out one's time in the old country, many said. The south land was a heathen place, hardly a land of opportunity like America.

But Thomas felt differently. 'They call it New South Wales, Anne,' he said. 'Just think, a whole new country! A whole new life!'

The union of Thomas Kendall and Anne Simpson had developed far beyond mere lustful congress. Together they nurtured each other's hopes and shared each other's strengths and, in the barren, dank gloom which was Norwich Castle Gaol, a genuine love had grown between them.

When they found that they were not only to be transported to New South Wales but aboard the very same ship as well, it was truly as if the gods had smiled upon them. And when Anne announced that she was with child, it seemed all the good fortune in the world had been laid at their feet.

'Ah, my Anne,' the old man murmured, unaware that his grandsons were waiting, spellbound, for the next instalment of the orgy. 'How it felt to hold her once more.' He could see her now, at the bow of the longboat, their child in her arms, the child he'd felt in her swollen belly but had never seen. He could feel Anne's lips against his and the softness of the baby's cheek against the stubble of his own. 'I'd not seen her since they'd transferred her from the *Friendship* to the *Charlotte* in Cape Town,' he said as he registered the boys' attention. 'Three long months it had been.'

Thomas had worried about Anne's condition and the hardship of the voyage, but she would have none of it. 'It's only a baby, Thomas, women bring babies into the world every day of the week.'

But it was hard. Thomas knew that it was hard. When the ship bucketed and rolled and the child in Anne's belly kicked, he would watch her try to hold down the victuals that would feed her unborn baby. He would help her press her hand to her mouth and watch as she tried to swallow her vomit.

When the fleet reached Cape Town and changes were made to accommodate the livestock boarded at this, their last port before Botany Bay, Anne and several other women were transferred to the *Charlotte*. Anne was near her time and Thomas, fearing for her safety, was all for demanding he be transferred with her, or they be offloaded to await the birth of the child. Again, Anne would not hear of it.

'You have earned the trust of the officers and the crew, Thomas,' she said. 'I have seen it. We can use this to our advantage in the colony; you must not cause trouble now.

'Listen,' she had insisted as he'd tried to argue, 'when my time comes I will be better attended by the women aboard the *Charlotte*.' Then she had kissed him. 'I'll see you in Botany Bay, my love, with a baby in my arms.'

But he didn't see her in Botany Bay. He didn't see her until Wednesday the 6th of February 1788, when the female convicts were finally landed on the shores of Port Jackson. It was then that Thomas saw his Anne, and, as she'd promised, she held their baby daughter in her arms.

The old man stood silent as he recalled their reunion that night they'd brought the women ashore. His coupling with Anne in the corner of the tent had been quiet, intense, oblivious to the raging storm and the threshing bodies about them. One week later, he and Anne, along with several other couples, had been the first convicts to be married by the Reverend Richard Johnson. As they had made their mark in the Register of Marriages, being able neither to read nor write, Thomas had whispered, 'This is just the beginning, girl, just the beginning.' The old man's eyes filled with tears as he recalled his joy that day.

James and William exchanged a glance but remained silent, respectful of the old man's reverie; they knew how much Grandpa Thomas missed his wife.

James had never met his grandmother, although she had died only four years ago, but William remembered Anne clearly. Having been brought up on their father Matthew's market gardens on the Surry Hills, a walkable distance from Thomas's house in the centre of town, William and his younger sister Hannah had seen a great deal of their grandparents. William remembered Anne as an unconventional old woman who, despite her physical frailty, was never shy of speaking her mind. He and Hannah had been very fond of Grandma Anne.

It was time to change the conversation, William decided. He didn't like to see his grandfather saddened by painful memories.

'May we go to Rushcutters Bay, Grandpa Thomas?' he asked. 'May we go and see Wolawara?'

Thomas knew why William was changing the subject and he appreciated the boy's good intentions. Of course the lad didn't realise that to think of Anne was never painful. The precious bittersweetness of her memory was a joy to Thomas always. He would treasure the taste and the touch and the smell of his wife until he drew his very last breath.

'Very well.' Thomas made a quick decision, knowing it would wreak havoc with his son and daughter-in-law. 'We shall go and see Wolawara.' It was time to extend young James's education. God alone knew when that wretched mother of his would once again allow the boy the company of his grandfather.

'I must warn you, James,' he said solemnly as they walked across the Government Domain towards Farm Cove, 'that Wolawara and his family are my friends. They are not oddities for you to boast of to your friends at school.'

'Yes, Grandpa Thomas.'

James couldn't believe his luck. He was going to meet Wolawara. Even his cousins, William and Hannah, didn't know the true story of Grandpa Thomas and Wolawara. The relationship between the two men was shrouded in mystery.

Several weeks previously, on a visit to James's family home in Parramatta, William and Hannah had boasted that Grandfather Thomas was best friends with an Aborigine.

'You must not listen to such nonsense,' James's mother had said when his cousins had departed. 'Your grandfather may have some passing acquaintance with the black servant of one of his friends or, knowing your grandfather, even one of the beggars in the streets of Sydney Town, but he is not "friends" with a native. No-one is "friends" with a native.'

Mary, aware of the presence of her husband Richard, knew she must soften her tone, but mentally she cursed the old man. Everything about her father-in-law grated with Mary. His common rural accent, his scruffy ill-kempt beard, his baggy breeches and shirtsleeves.

Thomas had no regard for personal appearances and was quite happy to wander about jacketless, which Mary considered disgraceful. He was a wealthy, successful man, he had a social position to uphold. But far more than his manner of speech and dress, it was the old man's pride in his ignoble past which Mary most abhorred.

'Grandfather Thomas is lonely, my dear,' she said as gently as she could, 'particularly since Grandmother Anne passed away, and he romanticises the past as if it were something of which to be proud.' She couldn't help it, the bite of disapproval returned to her tone. 'Believe me, it is not, James. It is a shameful thing.'

'Don't turn the boy against his grandfather, Mary.' Richard's remonstration was mild but it was there. He rarely questioned his wife, leaving the governing of the household and the upbringing of their two children in her capable hands. He agreed that it was only right, for the sake of the children, to distance themselves from his father's past; he had even agreed, ten years previously, to her suggestion that they change the spelling of their name to Kendle so it could not be traced to the shameful records of those who had arrived in the colony in chains. But Richard would not have his wife malign his father of whom he was not only fond, but to whom he was deeply grateful for the assistance given him upon his marriage. Indeed, without the family business and the lands at Parramatta which Thomas had transferred to his son's name, it was doubtful Mary's family would have agreed to the marriage at all. 'My father is a good man,' Richard insisted, 'and we owe him a great deal.'

'I am not turning the boy against his grandfather,' Mary replied a little tightly, 'and I am fully aware of the debt we owe, Thomas.'

There the discussion ended and, as usual, Mary had the last word.

But several weeks later Richard surprised her by insisting that James and his older sister, Phoebe, accompany her on a shopping expedition to Sydney Town.

'They are to meet their grandfather,' Richard announced. 'I must insist upon it, Mary.' He sensed that she was about to argue the case. 'They barely know him, it is not right.'

Mary wondered momentarily whether she should do battle, but reluctantly decided against it. Damn the old man, she thought.

If Mary Kendle could have had her way, her children would remain forever in Parramatta, and all ties with the Kendall side of the family would be severed. It was nothing personal, but for the good of her children's future they must be brought up as exclusives, of free British stock. Not only was their paternal grandfather an ex-convict, he believed in equality. Thomas Kendall maintained that prisoners who had served their sentences, and emancipists such as himself who through good conduct had been prematurely granted pardon, should be openly and immediately accepted into respectable society. Worse still, he believed in equality for the ticket-of-leavers, those convicts who had been granted a certificate from the Governor entitling them to seek their own employment and living quarters. The fact that applicants for a ticket of leave required a long record of exemplary behaviour, character references, letters of surety, meant little to the exclusivists. Ticket-of-leavers were still convicts. They were still serving their sentences, and it was a crime against society that they should be entitled to mingle freely.

To many in the colony, the views of Thomas Kendall and his ilk were outrageous and dangerous, and although Mary swore she bore Thomas himself no ill will, she was protective of her children and thoroughly convinced that no good could come of their connection with their grandfather.

Mary would allow her husband to have his way. Just this once. Her acquiescence would please him and maintain the peace, and a visit to the old man could do little harm, so long as the children were not left alone in his company. But she determined that such visits were not to become a habit.

'I shall not be accompanying you, my dear,' Richard announced to her further annoyance. 'The purchase of dresses and bonnets does not interest me as it does you and Phoebe. Besides,' he added, flashing her his most winning smile, 'I would be of little use, my taste is lamentable.'

Always elegantly attired, Richard's dress sense was faultless, and he knew it, just as he knew that his charm, as usual, would have the desired effect.

Mary laughed. 'You are shamelessly obvious, Richard.'

'Of course I am my dear. I am afraid I really am too busy to accompany you however,' he apologised, 'and I see Father and Matthew regularly on business trips to town. You don't mind *too* much do you?'

'I suppose I have no option.'

'And you will enjoy Emily's company,' he added, 'you always do.'

Richard had never quite been able to comprehend Mary's comfortable relationship with his brother's wife, they were such opposites. Not that Richard himself disliked Emily, far from it. Indeed, he found her an extremely attractive woman, in an untidy way—most men did. With little regard for convention or fashion, Emily prattled disarmingly, apparently unaware of her sensuality. In the early years of Matthew's marriage, Richard had even felt a little envious of his older brother. The foolishness of youth, he now thought, as he looked at his wife with comfortable affection. He had made a far finer match than his brother: Mary came from impeccable stock and was an exemplary wife and mother.

He winked at his daughter Phoebe. 'You and Hannah can play fine young ladies and have cakes at the teahouse in George Street.'

Fifteen-year-old Phoebe, pretty, fragile, her father's pride and joy, smiled excitedly. She liked her cousin. Despite the fact that Hannah was six months her junior, Phoebe deeply admired and envied her. There was a wild streak in Hannah.

And who exactly will be looking after my son, Mary wondered. The old man? She looked steadily back at her husband, once more considering battle, but Richard continued, apparently oblivious, 'And James will have William for company.' Before his wife could contest the arrangement, he added with a note of finality, 'The lad needs male companionship, my dear. Father and Matthew will entertain the boys whilst you do your shopping.' For once, it was Richard who had the last word.

The family gathering in Thomas's front parlour went smoothly enough. Matthew had not yet arrived, but to Mary's relief, the old man's conversation was perfectly harmless. They chatted about the weather and commented on the stirring sounds of the drums and fife which could be heard from the nearby garrison.

By the time she and Emily, together with their daughters, were preparing to take their leave, however, Mary was feeling distinctly agitated. Matthew had still not arrived.

'Matthew was to look after James and William,' she said rather pointedly to her sister-in-law.

'Oh good heavens no,' Emily declared, 'it's crop planting. He's far too busy. As a matter of fact, I had quite a time of it persuading him to allow William the day with his cousin. Poor Matthew needs all the hands he can get at the moment, particularly as he refuses to accept the government's offer of convict labour.'

'Why?' Mary was momentarily distracted from her dilemma. 'If the government sees fit to support the market gardeners, why in heaven's name should Matthew refuse cheap labour?'

'He is of the opinion that convict labour should be employed solely by the government,' Emily replied. She pointed a gloved finger forcefully at the ceiling, in imitation of Matthew in full tirade. '"It is up to the free settlers to provide work for the ticket-of-leavers and those who have served their sentences."' She punched the air with her fist. '"They are in need of employment to set themselves up in their new lives, and it is our bounden duty to assist them."' Emily smiled about at the assembled company, proud of her performance and of her husband.

'He's a good man, Matthew,' Thomas nodded approvingly.

It was the sort of conversation Mary did not wish to encourage in the presence of her children. 'But James and William . . .' she said, 'who will look after them?'

'I'm seventeen, Aunt Mary,' William laughed. 'I'm perfectly capable of showing James the sights.'

It was then that Thomas chimed in. 'I shall look after the lads, Mary,' he said with all the joviality of a favourite father-in-law. 'We shall go for a walk, just the three of us.'

The look of horror on Mary's face gave Thomas a rush of perverse pleasure. He despised the beliefs of Mary and her fellow exclusivists. In a new colonial society, the evils of class distinction should have been left behind in the old country. The fact that social injustice and racial intolerance abounded in a new land where equality should have free reign upset him deeply.

His smile was as benign as he could make it, which further irked Mary. 'We shall have a grand day, shan't we, lads?'

'Oh please may I come with you, Grandpa Thomas?' It was fifteen-year-old Hannah, the old man's unashamed favourite. Thomas glanced hopefully at Emily who shook her head and laughed.

'No, my darling, you may not.'

Emily had told Hannah as much before they'd left for Thomas's house. 'I don't want to go shopping with Aunt Mary,' the girl had said, 'she fusses so.' Emily had stated emphatically that Hannah was to accompany them, but she had known that her daughter would try again. Hannah was incorrigible.

'You can see Grandpa Thomas any time you wish, Hannah, you must let the boys have a day with him on their own. They can talk men's talk.' Emily winked at Thomas. 'Whatever that is.'

Mary turned her horrified gaze to her sister-in-law, but Emily was utterly oblivious to it. 'Now come along, Mary, the sooner we complete our shopping the sooner we can have tea and cakes and I am eager to hear all the gossip.' It was true the bond between the women was Mary's chatter, mostly slanderous, about the Parramatta landed gentry and her husband's wealthy business associates. Mary had the freedom of knowing that the stories would never get back to Richard's influential friends, and Emily the novelty of hearing people spoken of in a way no farming person on the Surry Hills would ever speak of their neighbour.

There was little Mary could do, but at the door she hissed to the old man, 'You are not to fill James's head with your nonsense, Thomas; he has led a sheltered life.'

It was then that Thomas had decided to tell the boys whatever stories they wanted to hear. The bawdier, the gorier, the better.

'You lads go on ahead,' he said as they walked through the Botanic Garden, 'I shall keep my own pace. And take your jacket off, James, 'tis far too hot to be wearing a jacket.'

He watched as the boy hesitated then took off his smart checked jacket and carefully folded it over his arm. Mary obviously didn't like her son being seen in public in his vest and shirtsleeves. He looked so vulnerable, Thomas thought, beside his older cousin. William, bareheaded, sleeves rolled up to his elbows, forearms well muscled and brown from toil in the sun, already had the body of a strong man. Like his father, Matthew. Both boys reminded Thomas of his sons, but James painfully so. James, awkward in his smart felt hat with its checked ribbon band matching his jacket, could have been Richard at the same age. Richard had always been painfully self-conscious, even as a boy.

Much as Thomas wanted to blame his daughter-in-law for the hurt his son had done him, he knew that Richard was equally at fault. Richard was too easily dictated to, by both society and his wife—which were much the same thing, Thomas thought grimly. To him, Mary typified the ignorance and bigotry of the British middle class.

Richard Kendall's denial of his family name had been one of the cruellest blows Thomas had ever been dealt. Crueller than his banishment from his mother country, for he had paid for his crime and embraced his new life. But to what crime did he owe his son's denial?

'Kendle sounds the same, Father,' Richard had said, 'so we are not really *changing* the name as such, merely the spelling. You cannot expect us to emblazon a convict name in gilt lettering on the sides of our coaches, it is simply not good business.' Richard misinterpreted his father's silence as misunderstanding. 'The coach service from Sydney Town to Parramatta is becoming famous,' he continued. 'Surely you must admit we need a name which can be respected.'

Nothing more was said on the subject, but it broke Thomas's heart.

Anne tried to soften the blow. 'Richard loves you dearly, Thomas; he intends no hurt.' And when Thomas refused to be mollified, she continued in her characteristically direct fashion. 'As his mother I should perhaps not say it, but Richard is a weak man. He always has been. He does not have your strength, my love, neither yours nor Matthew's. It is why I have always approved of his marriage; it is why I insisted you sign over the coach business and some of the Parramatta lands to him.' By now she had Thomas's undivided attention; in fact, his jaw was agape.

'Much as you may dislike Mary and much as we may both disagree with her views,' Anne continued, 'she is a strong young woman and Richard needs such strength. He's a superficial man with little depth of character, and I do not believe for one moment that he would survive with a weak wife.'

Thomas had finally found his voice. 'You always told me he was sensitive.'

'Yes, that is what I told you.' She had given him one of her impish smiles and kissed him. 'So do not let the weakness of his actions break your heart, my love, for that is all they are, the actions of a weak man. Forgive him.'

Try as he might, however, Thomas had not been able to find it in himself to forgive Richard, and from that day on he had seen his son through different eyes.

The old man and his grandsons left the mudflats of Woolloomooloo Bay behind them and started to climb the Darlinghurst Hill. The windmills which lined the Darlinghurst Ridge were picturesque, contributing to the description of Sydney as a town of windmills. Some of wood, some of stone, some operated manually, some mechanically, the windmills endlessly churned out the flour for a colony chronically short of adequate supplies.

As they walked, Thomas wondered whether young James was weak like his father. If so, how long would it take before self-consciousness became affectation, before social decree outweighed matters of principle? Not long, Thomas thought, living under the same roof as that woman. Well, today young James Kendle would learn a thing or two, the old man would make thoroughly sure of that.

Upon reaching Rushcutters Bay, Thomas led his grandsons beside the small stream which ran down to the harbour until it was lost in the swamp of rushes beside the bay. It was here, towards the eastern end of the cove, that Wolawara and his family lived in their hut amongst the reeds and spinneys.

They were at the edge of the clearing, twenty yards or so from the hut, when they were distracted by a rustling noise in a clump of nearby bushes. As they turned to investigate, a man leapt out at them with such swiftness and aggression that James gave an involuntary cry of alarm. Instinct told him to run, but Thomas and William were standing their ground, so the boy stifled his fear and edged closer to his grandfather instead.

The man rolled his eyes and, in the blackness of his face, the whites of his pupils shone with a madness that terrified James. Twice he sprang towards them, emitting a growl from the back of his throat like an animal intimidating its prey.

Thomas appeared unmoved and William, after a nervous glance at his grandfather, continued to stand his ground. James's feet were rooted to the spot; he doubted whether he could have run if he'd tried.

The man changed his tactics. Slowly he started to prance about them, knees bent, arms extended, palms upward, in a clumsy, uncoordinated dance. He was mumbling now, although the words were incoherent. And his manner was no longer aggressive, his eyes no longer mad. In his ragged shirt and breeches, and stinking of rum, he was in fact a pitiful figure.

'Massa, gim me rum. Rum merry good.'

The fear in James subsided. So this was Wolawara, he thought with a surge of disappointment. His mother had been right after all. Grandfather Thomas's native friend was no more than a drunken beggar.

'Good day, Yenerah,' Thomas said, although he made no move to give the man money.

The Aborigine did not heed the greeting, continuing to importune with his parody of a dance. 'Rum make me drunk like a gemmen. Rum merry good.'

'*Wuruwuru*!' The voice, with an angry edge, was one of authority, and the drunken man turned to face the figure which had appeared at the door of the hut. They all did. An imposing Aboriginal man in a red soldier's coat stood before them. In his middle sixties, grey-bearded and stern, he was not a big man, either in height or build, but there was a command about him which was impressive.

'*Wuruwuru*!' he repeated. '*Dadadadadadadada*!'

The drunken man stared back for a second, then turned his gaze to the ground. He scuffed his bare feet in the dirt for a moment or so. '*Yanu, yanu*,' he muttered, before shuffling pathetically off into the bushes.

There was silence as they all watched him go.

'Stay here,' Thomas muttered to the boys, then he walked up to the hut and offered his hand to the man in the red coat.

'Wolawara, *gamaradu*,' he said. The two men shook hands.

'*Ngandu*, Thomas,' Wolawara said, '*Ngandu*,' and there was an infinite sadness in his voice.

'No harm is done,' Thomas replied. '*Gamarada, gay, gay*.'

James watched, awestruck. 'Grandpa Thomas is speaking his language,' he whispered to William. Never before had James heard a white man talk to a native in anything other than New South Wales pidgin English. 'I've never seen anyone do that before.'

'And you never will again,' William replied quietly with obvious pride. 'It is the native tongue of the Gadigal people, a clan of the Dharug, Grandpa told me so.'

Ignoring the boys, the two men squatted on the ground beside the hut.

'We must stay here until we are asked to join them,' William instructed. 'And you are to tell no-one that Grandpa Thomas speaks their tongue, James. No-one. Only Hannah and I know, and now that he has let you into the secret, you must never breathe a word.'

James nodded, still staring, eyes like saucers, at his grandfather squatting in the dirt with Wolawara.

Thomas had been dismayed to witness the degradation of his old friend's son. Yenerah was Wolawara's only remaining boy, his other two having died of the smallpox many years previously.

It must be breaking the man's heart, Thomas thought; but recognising Wolawara's shame, he did not pursue the subject.

'I have not come to you for some time, Wolawara, but when I dream you are there.'

'When I dream you are there, Thomas.'

The men conversed in a mixture of pidgin and Dharug. These days it was rare for even Wolawara himself to converse purely in the native tongue of the Gadigal people. The language was dying out and, to his shame, much as he encouraged them, his own grandchildren spoke little Dharug.

'Wiriwa, she is well?' Thomas asked.

Wolawara nodded. 'Wiriwa, come!' he called to his wife. 'Thomas our friend is here.'

Wiriwa appeared at the door of the hut. She was dressed in a white cotton garment and carried an infant on one hip, her latest grandchild. She had known Thomas was there and had been waiting for her husband's call.

'*Gumal*, Wiriwa,' Thomas said. He smiled his greeting but did not rise.

Wiriwa smiled in return and nodded shyly before sitting on the ground at the opposite side of the entrance to the hut. She remained silently rocking her sleeping grandchild in her arms, pleased that she had been called into the presence of the men.

Thomas leaned forward and fingered the tattered lapel of Wolawara's coat. 'You have a jacket of fire,' he said. It was a personal observation and they both knew it. Wolawara had always loved the colours of fire. In Thomas's mind an image flashed briefly. The image of an excited young Aborigine with his new headband of yellow and red. '*Guwiyang*,' the young man was saying. '*Guwiyang*.'

Wolawara, pleased by the comment and proud of his new attire, explained that his daughter, who now served a military man's family, had brought home several articles of the soldier's old uniforms.

'And from his wife, dresses. Dresses white like the summer clouds for Wiriwa,' he added.

Wiriwa touched the lace yoke of her dress, which in actuality was a nightgown, and smiled back.

Emboldened by the fact that his grandmother and baby brother had been called to the company of the men, a ten-year-old boy had crept to the door of the hut. He had intended waiting until he too was called, but he had noticed William and James standing patiently at the edge of the clearing and couldn't resist.

Turumbah knew better than to run to the boys and make their acquaintance. His grandfather's rules regarding the meeting of menfolk were strict. But Turumbah also knew that he was his grandfather's favourite and that, if he pretended a patience he didn't have, his grandfather would eventually give in. He sidled out the door.

William and James watched as the boy crept up behind Wolawara. He was dressed in baggy trousers cut off above the knee and held up at the waist by twine from which hung several implements. He stood just behind his grandfather and gave them both a cheeky grin, but William nudged James, warning him not to react.

Fully aware of his grandson's presence, Wolawara continued his discussion with Thomas.

'Wiriwa holds my new grandson,' he boasted proudly and Wiriwa nodded once more, acknowledging the child as if he were her own. 'Four grandsons I now have. And three granddaughters.'

Thomas's eyes flickered to Turumbah who was shuffling in the sand behind his grandfather. The two men exchanged a smile.

'Two of my grandsons are now grown to manhood,' Wolawara continued. 'The fourth, I am not sure where he might be. Shall I call for him, Thomas?'

Thomas appeared to deliberate for a moment before agreeing. 'Yes. Call for him, Wolawara.'

Wolawara turned and pretended surprise as he bumped into the bare knees of his grandson.

'Ah, Turumbah. You remember our friend Thomas?' Turumbah nodded, but his eyes kept darting towards William and James. Particularly young James whose hat was becoming more fascinating by the second.

'Five years it has been,' Thomas said. 'You were a boy when last we met, Turumbah, now you are nearly a man.'

The boy shuffled about impatiently. When would the formalities be over? When could he play? He wanted to talk to the boy with the hat.

'These are your grandsons.' Wolawara indicated William and James. 'One I have not met.' It was the first time Wolawara had acknowledged the presence of the boys standing immobile at the edge of the clearing. 'They have fine manners,' he said approvingly, then glanced up at Turumbah. Turumbah, however, appeared not to have heard the admonishment, he was too busy grinning at the boys.

'May I greet your grandsons?' Wolawara asked.

'They would be honoured,' Thomas replied, and beckoned the boys to come forward.

After formal greetings were made in pidgin English and after much shaking of hands, it was finally time for Turumbah's introduction.

'Turumbah, this is Grandson William, and this is Grandson James,' Thomas said.

'Gran'sun William, Gran'sun James,' Turumbah repeated. There was more shaking of hands, and the boys were told they could go and play. Turumbah let out a whoop of excitement and started to skip about, until a sharp word of command from Wiriwa stopped him in his tracks.

All heads turned to her, it was the first time she had spoken. Her eyes met Wolawara's. She held his glance for a second or two until he nodded, then she returned her attention to the baby who had awoken at the sound of her voice.

'You are not to swim, Turumbah,' Wolawara commanded. The boy was about to argue back, but his grandfather continued, 'You have been sick, your grandmother says you are not to swim.' It was obvious that, for all her apparent compliance, it was Wiriwa's word that was law when it came to the health of the children.

Turumbah did not appear too upset. Instead, he grabbed James by the hand and dragged him in the opposite direction of the water. 'Gran'sun James come. Come, Gran'sun James.'

James was unaccustomed to such boisterous familiarity, but there was something so cheeky and likeable about Turumbah that it seemed pointless to resist. William followed after them with a regretful glance over his shoulder. He had hoped that he might be invited to join the men, but they were once more in deep conversation and took no note of the boys' departure.

'It was the ...' Wolawara was saying, searching for the word, '... the croup. Deep in his chest. Another white man's sickness.'

Talk of Turumbah's recent illness led Wolawara to discuss the plight of his people. He lowered his voice so that even Wiriwa might not hear but, intuitively, she knew what her husband was saying. Wolawara told Thomas that he should not have stayed so long, that he should have left Eora many years ago, as so many of his clan had. He should have fled inland to escape the white man's drink and disease.

Eora was the Dharug name for the coastal area which was the home of the Gadigal people, and, like many, Wolawara had found it hard to leave the waterways of his ancestors. 'We belong to the sea and to the rivers,' he had said when talk of leaving had first started. 'We are water people. It is wrong to take our families into the arid land.' And his stubbornness, he admitted now, had resulted in the deaths of two sons and a daughter. As for Yenerah, his last remaining son ...

The admission was difficult and Wolawara's gaze remained fixed on the ground. 'With your own eyes you have seen him, Thomas. He is possessed. Once a fine young man, now he begs in the streets for the rum to feed his demons.'

Wolawara raised his head and, behind the guilt in his eyes, was an angry resolve. 'This is not the fate which will befall my grandchildren. While there is strength enough left in this old man, it is Wolawara who must save them.'

Thomas paused for a moment before asking, 'What will you do?' He glanced briefly at Wiriwa who was listening intently for the answer.

'We will leave Eora.'

It was obvious from the fleeting shock visible in Wiriwa's eyes that Wolawara had not discussed his decision with her.

Thomas looked from one to the other. Wolawara and Wiriwa are old, he thought. Like me, they are old. Now was not the time for them to leave the home of their ancestors.

He said nothing. But, as Wolawara continued to talk, the seed of a plan germinated in the mind of Thomas Kendall.

'I've never seen anyone swim like that.'

James and William were lost in admiration as they stood watching young Turumbah's naked body cut through the water like a dolphin. One minute the boy had been submerged, the next he had leapt to the surface, emitted a squeal and disappeared again, only to reappear seconds later, twisting and rolling and diving like a creature delighting in its natural element.

When he had finished showing off, Turumbah swam closer to the point on which the boys stood and beckoned them to join him.

'Come massa! Come along! Come!'

For William the temptation was too great. The afternoon was hot, there was no-one about, so he took off his shirt.

'William!' James was horrified.

'No-one can see. Come on, James.'

Stripped to his undergarments, William flopped clumsily off the rocks. He could swim enough to keep himself afloat but he didn't venture too far from the point. Turumbah joined him and a splashing match ensued.

James wandered back along the point to the reedy shallows. Today had been a succession of shocks to him. From the fearful black man and his threatening dance, to Grandfather Thomas speaking in the native tongue and, finally, to the unashamed nakedness of Turumbah. That had been the biggest shock of all.

When Turumbah, signalling silence, had led James and William in a circle behind the hut to the water's edge and proceeded to strip to his bare skin in front of them, James's shock had left him speechless. No-one should be seen naked. For as long as he could remember, his mother had told him that nakedness was a sin. 'Cover yourself, James,' she would say when, as a very small boy, he emerged from the tin bathing tub, 'cover yourself.'

Shocking as today might have been, however, it was exciting

and unpredictable, a day like no other, and James wanted to be a part of it. He found a flat, dry rock, sat down and carefully took off his shoes and stockings. With equal care, he took off his vest, folded it with his jacket and placed his new felt hat on top. Then he pulled his trouser legs up to the knees and waded out into the shallows, enjoying the water, cool against his calves and the sand, coarse beneath his feet.

A shadow glided amongst the reeds ahead, then stopped. Too curious to be alarmed, James waded stealthily towards it. Just when he was convinced it was nothing, merely a play of light, the shadow reappeared right in front of him. About a foot in length and breadth, its sides appeared to gracefully curl, and once more it glided ahead of him, only to disappear in a brief flurry of sand.

James was fascinated. For a full ten minutes he followed the small stingray through the shallows until the creature retreated to the deeper water.

When he finally returned to the rock where he'd left his clothes, he found William and Turumbah dressed and sunning themselves as they waited for him.

'I saw a fish! A fish with a long tail!' James called excitedly. 'I followed it everywhere!'

'*Daringyan.*' Turumbah called back. 'Catch him towsan this place.' It was only then that James noticed, perched atop the Aboriginal boy's head, and at a rakish angle, his new felt hat.

James's dismay must have been evident, and he felt himself flush as William laughed loudly. 'Give it back to him, Turumbah, I told you he would be angry.'

Regretfully, the boy took off the hat. He examined it briefly to make sure it was unmarked—it was only a little damp inside—before handing it back with a mischievous smile.

James put the hat on and concentrated on the buttons of his vest, keeping his face averted. His shocked reaction had been instinctive. He didn't really mind Turumbah wearing his hat. He wished that William hadn't laughed.

As James knelt to put on his shoes and stockings, Turumbah stopped him. The boy repeated a word several times, a word which the other two didn't understand. '*Badangi, badangi,*' he said, then beckoned impatiently. 'Come, Gran'sun James, come along.'

They followed him, Turumbah unfastening a knifelike implement made from shell which dangled from the twine about his waist. It was time to shuck oysters from the healthy crop which grew along the rocks of the foreshore.

An hour later, when the boys returned to the hut—Turumbah ensuring that his hair and clothes were dry and that their approach was from the opposite direction to the bay—James's hands were scratched and bleeding and one trouser leg was torn. The big toe of his right foot was painful where he'd stubbed it on the rocks, and he knew that inside his shoe blood was oozing onto his stocking.

But James didn't care. He wiped his hands on the once pristine white handkerchief and returned it to his vest pocket. He savoured the sea-salt taste of the oysters on his tongue. The day had been the most exciting and memorable of his young life.

Thomas noticed James's dishevelled appearance but said nothing.

Wolawara rose to farewell them, and the two men shook hands.

'I beg of you, my friend,' Thomas said, taking both of Wolawara's hands in his, 'do nothing until I next come to you. I will return within seven days. Until then, please do not leave Eora.'

Wolawara nodded his consent and Thomas and his grandsons turned to go. But Turumbah would not leave it at that. He made a great show of shaking hands as vigorously as he could with William and James. Particularly James.

'You like Turumbah, Gran'sun James? Turumbah *budjerry* fellow.'

Before he knew what he was doing, James had taken off his new felt hat. He couldn't help himself. Holding it in both hands, he offered it to Turumbah.

The boy stared at the hat and the outstretched hands, bewildered.

'Take it, Turumbah,' James said. 'It's yours, a gift.'

No second bidding was necessary. In a moment the hat was on Turumbah's head, and when Thomas and his grandsons finally set off, the boy was still leaping about excitedly, dancing, waving and pointing to his new possession.

Thomas studied his younger grandson as they walked away from the clearing. There would be hell to pay when his mother found out he'd lost his new hat.

James felt his grandfather's eyes upon him. He looked up and smiled reassuringly. He had no regrets. He didn't quite know why he had done what he'd done, but he would weather the storm.

Thomas was pleased. More than pleased. It was a breakthrough. James was not yet entirely under the influence of his mother. It was time for him to learn some truths.

'Let's walk to the Common,' he said, 'and sit and talk. There is a story I wish to tell you both.'

He would tell them the story of Wolawara. But he would not tell them of his plan. Not yet. The boys would find out soon enough, for it would alienate him from his younger son forever. Now was the time for his grandsons to know the truth so they may judge his actions accordingly.

Much as Thomas railed against the exclusivists and their class system, the truly unpardonable sin in his eyes was the lamentable predicament of the native, who had been stripped of all he'd owned, including dignity. His numbers had been decimated by white man's diseases and he had been left to beg in the streets, his women to exchange their bodies for food. It was not the way Governor Phillip had wished it. It was not the way the King of England himself had instructed the colony be governed.

Thomas and his grandsons reached the vastness of Sydney Common where cattle and goats grazed and where, on misty mornings, groups of gentlemen regularly held swan-shooting parties. When they had settled themselves on a grassy hillock in the late afternoon sunshine, Thomas told them his story.

Other titles by Judy Nunn

Khaki Town

It's March 1942. Australia is on the brink of being invaded by the Imperial Japanese Forces. And overnight the small Queensland city of Townsville is transformed into the transport hub for 70,000 American and Australian soldiers destined for combat in the South Pacific.

But the Australian troops begrudge the confident, well-fed 'Yanks' who have taken over their town and their women. There's growing conflict, too, within the American ranks, because black GIs are enjoying the absence of segregation. And the white GIs don't like it . . .

Khaki Town was inspired by a true wartime story that remained a well-kept secret for over seventy years.

Sanctuary

On a barren island off the coast of Western Australia, a rickety wooden dinghy runs aground. Aboard are nine people who have no idea where they are. Strangers before the violent storm that tore their vessel apart. While they remain undiscovered on the deserted island, they dare to dream of a new life . . . But forty kilometres away on the mainland lies the tiny fishing port of Shoalhaven. Here everyone knows everyone, and everyone has their place. In Shoalhaven things never change. Until now . . .

Other titles by Judy Nunn

Araluen

On a blistering hot day in 1850, brothers George and Richard Ross take their first steps on Australian soil after three long months at sea. All they have is each other.

A decade on, and they are the owners of a successful vineyard, Araluen, nestled in a beautiful valley near Adelaide. Now a successful businessman, George has laid down the roots of a Ross dynasty, born of the New World. But building a family empire – whatever the cost – can have a shattering effect on the generations to come . . .

Pacific

Australian actress Samantha Lindsay is thrilled when she scores her first Hollywood movie role, playing a character loosely based on World War II heroine Mamma Tack.

But on location in Vanuatu, uncanny parallels between history and fiction emerge and Sam begins a quest for the truth. Just who was the real Mamma Tack?

Territory

Territory is the story of the Top End and the people who dare to dwell there. Of Spitfire pilot Terence Galloway and his English bride, Henrietta, home from the war, only to be faced with the desperate defence of Darwin against the Imperial Japanese Air Force. From the blazing inferno that was Darwin on 19 February 1942 to the devastation of Cyclone Tracy, from the red desert to the tropical shore, *Territory* is a mile-a-minute read.

Other titles by Judy Nunn

Heritage

In the 1940s refugees from more than seventy nations gathered in Australia to forge a new identity – and to help realise one man's dream: the mighty Snowy Mountains Hydro-Electric Scheme. From the ruins of Berlin to the birth of Israel, from the Italian Alps to the Australian high country, *Heritage* is a passionate tale of rebirth, struggle, sacrifice and redemption.

Floodtide

Floodtide traces the fortunes of four men and four families over four memorable decades in the mighty 'Iron Ore State' of Western Australia. The prosperous 1950s when childhood is idyllic in the small city of Perth . . . The turbulent 60s when youth is caught up in the Vietnam War . . . The avaricious 70s when WA's mineral boom sees a new breed of entrepreneurs . . . The corrupt 80s, when greedy politicians and powerful businessmen bring the state to its knees . . .

Maralinga

Maralinga, 1956. A British airbase in the middle of nowhere, a top-secret atomic testing ground . . . *Maralinga* is the story of Lieutenant Daniel Gardiner, who accepts a posting to the wilds of South Australia on a promise of rapid promotion, and of adventurous young English journalist Elizabeth Hoffmann, who travels halfway around the world in search of the truth.

Other titles by Judy Nunn

Tiger Men

Van Diemen's Land was an island of stark contrasts: a harsh penal colony, an English idyll for its gentry, and an island so rich in natural resources it was a profiteer's paradise . . . *Tiger Men* is a sweeping saga of three families who lived through Tasmania's golden era and the birth of Federation and then watched with pride as their sons marched off to fight for King and Country.

Elianne

A captivating story of wealth, power, privilege and betrayal, set on a grand sugar cane plantation in Queensland. In 1881 'Big Jim' Durham ruthlessly creates for Elianne Desmaràis, his young French wife, the finest of the great sugar mills of the Southern Queensland cane fields, and names it in her honour. The massive estate becomes a self-sufficient fortress and home to hundreds of workers, but 'Elianne' and the Durham Family have dark and distant secrets; secrets that surface in the wildest of times, the 1960s . . .

Spirits of the Ghan

It is 2001 and as the world charges into the new Millennium, a century-old dream is about to be realised in the Red Centre of Australia: the completion of the mighty Ghan railway, a long-lived vision to create the 'backbone of the continent', a line that will finally link Adelaide with the Top End.

But construction of the final leg between Alice Springs and Darwin will not be without its complications, for much of the desert it will cross is Aboriginal land . . .